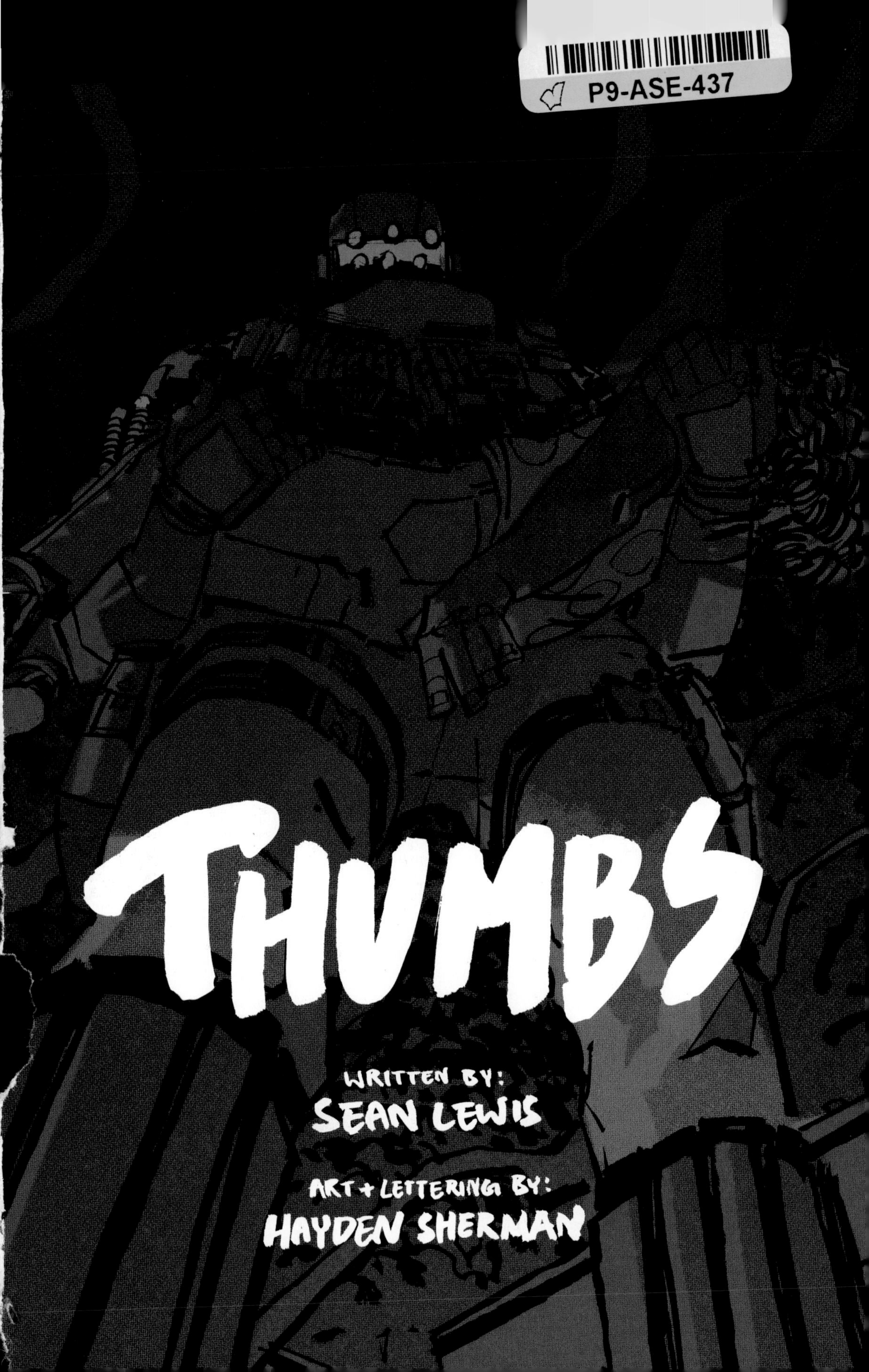
THUMBS
WRITTEN BY:
SEAN LEWIS
ART + LETTERING BY:
HAYDEN SHERMAN

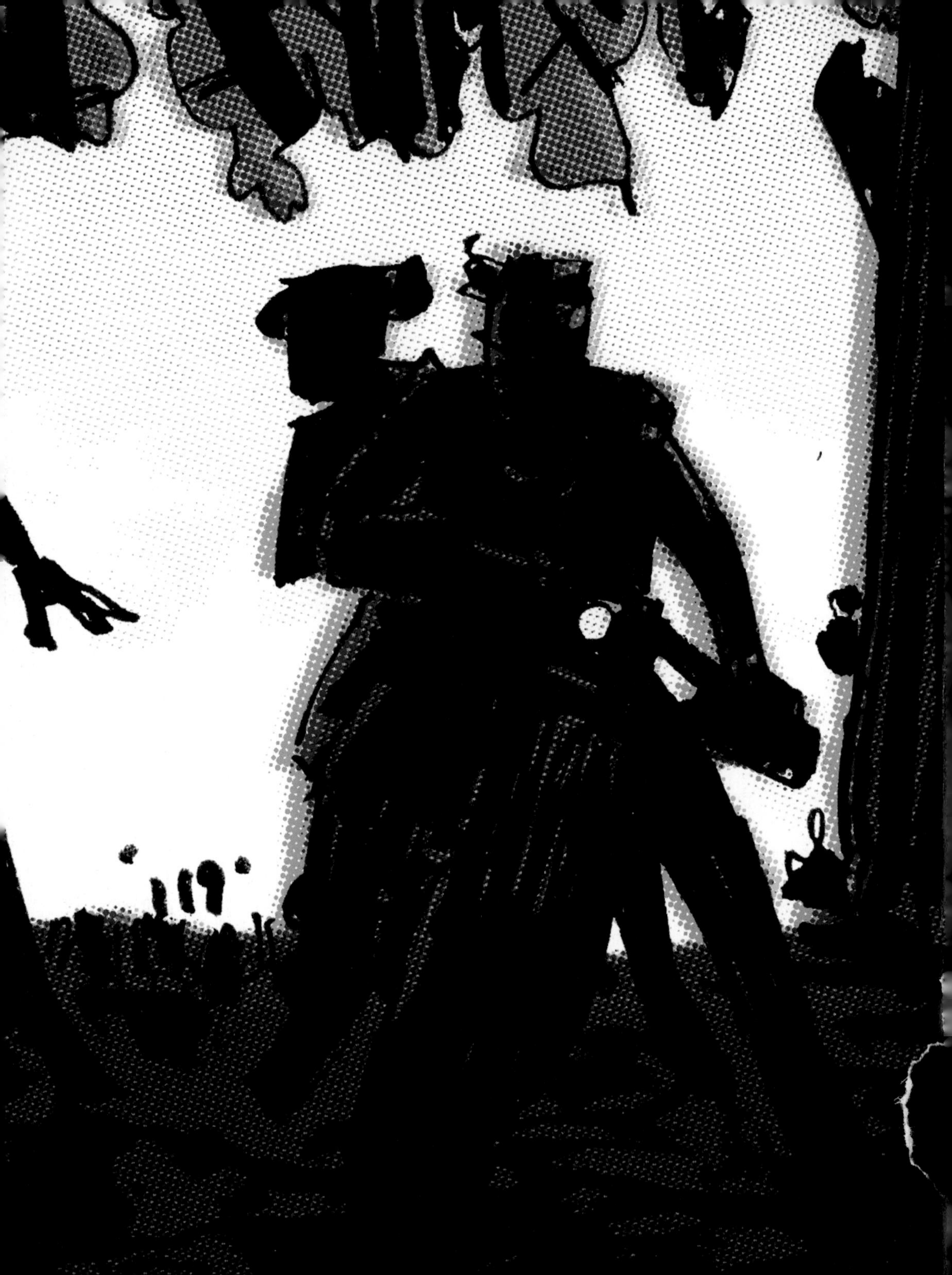

IMAGE COMICS, INC.

Robert Kirkman: Chief Operating Officer
Erik Larsen: Chief Financial Officer
Todd McFarlane: President
Marc Silvestri: Chief Executive Officer
Jim Valentino: Vice President

Eric Stephenson: Publisher / Chief Creative Officer
Jeff Boison: Director of Publishing Planning & Book Trade Sales
Chris Ross: Director of Digital Services
Jeff Stang: Director of Direct Market Sales
Kat Salazar: Director of PR & Marketing
Drew Gill: Cover Editor
Heather Doornink: Production Director
Nicole Lapalme: Controller

I don't hate technology.

I have an iPhone. I am typing this on a MacBook. My son and I will Skype with his grandma later. I don't hate technology. I wouldn't even have this book in your hands if there weren't technology. It's an amazing tool.

But I like humans more.

Strike that. I love humans.

I love how we can accomplish things that seem impossible.

I love how we continue to learn throughout our lives.

I love how we can care for strangers in need...

and, of course, I'm confused how we can turn our backs on those closest to us... How we can choose narcissism... How we can group each other, define one another, dismiss each other...

THUMBS is about a kid who just wants to win his video games. He's a stand-in for us. He wants to enjoy his life. He wants some status. He wants to be on the right side, even before he knows who the right side is... He is us.

And he comes into contact with zealots on both sides, extremists, fascists... things that crush humanity, not embolden it. Tech is a tool. It's not an answer. The people you see every day are an answer.

On a side note, Hayden's work in this series is beyond phenomenal. He's starting to become that generational guy and it's a real pleasure to work with him. And I love the book. I can honestly say it goes places you wouldn't expect. It dares to be sincere.

Like humans... it's gonna challenge you with its heart.

So, thanks for picking it up. We made it for you.

Sean Lewis

This book was a joy to make. It was a chance to experiment and grow and meet new people along the way. I'm so proud of what we made here. Thank you for taking a look at THUMBS, for flipping through it, reading it, or doing whatever you intend to do with it. From here on out, it's all yours to do with what you please. I hope you'll enjoy it.

Thank you also to the incredible people I'm lucky to have on my side. My partner, who I couldn't go a day without. My parents, whose encouragement has never failed. My siblings, who are a bunch of loveable wonderful doofuses who give life light. My friends, each of whom I consider as strong as iron. And of course, Sean. He dreams up these worlds for us to inhabit and I wouldn't have it any other way.

Hayden Sherman

PART ONE

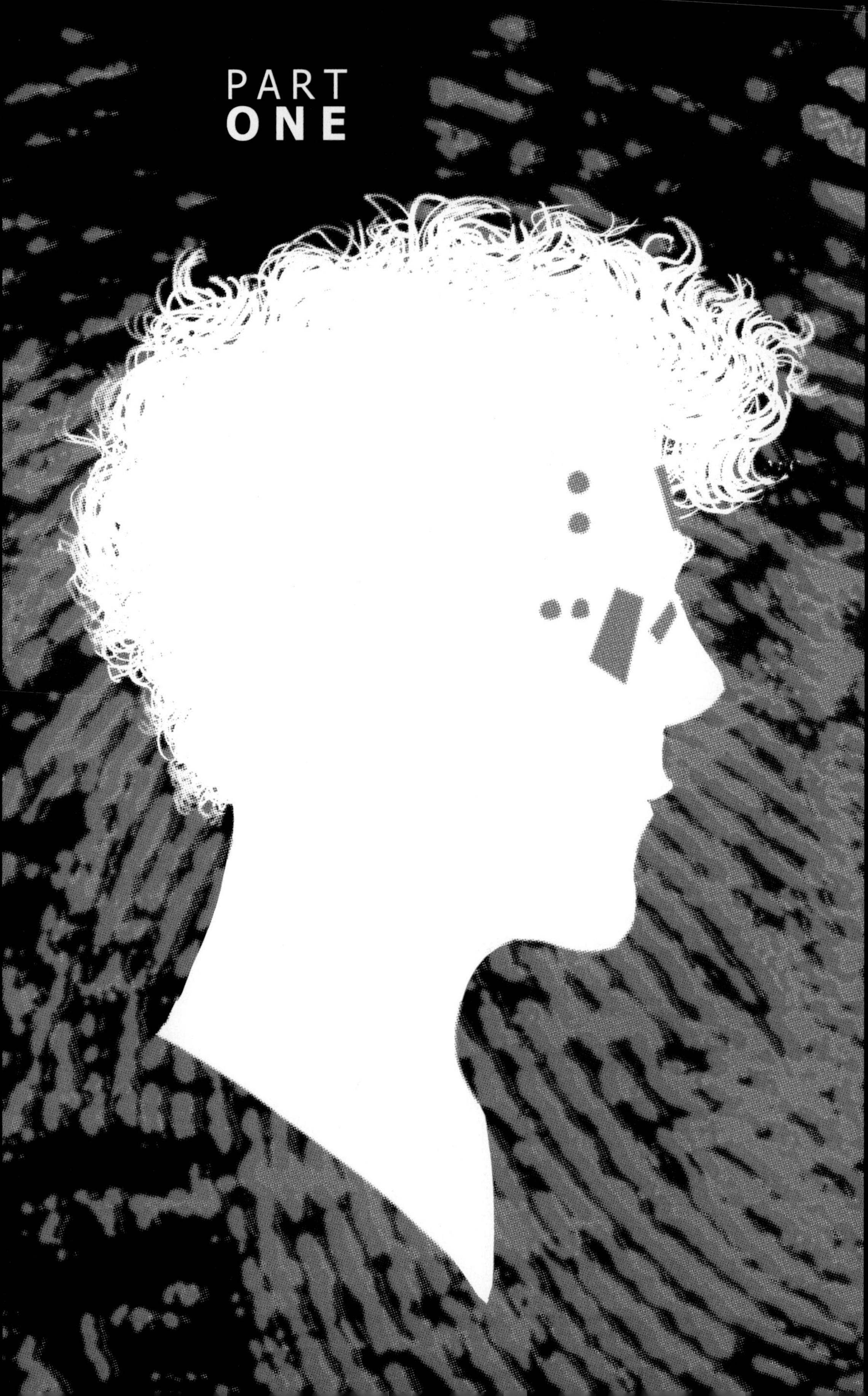

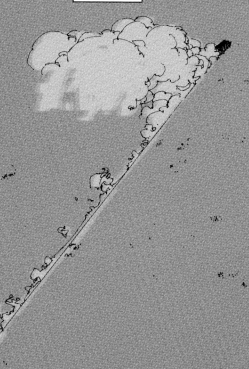

"HE LOOKS *BAD,* CARLOS, PICK UP THE *GODDAMN PACE.*"

WHEN YOU DIE YOU DON'T GO ANYWHERE.

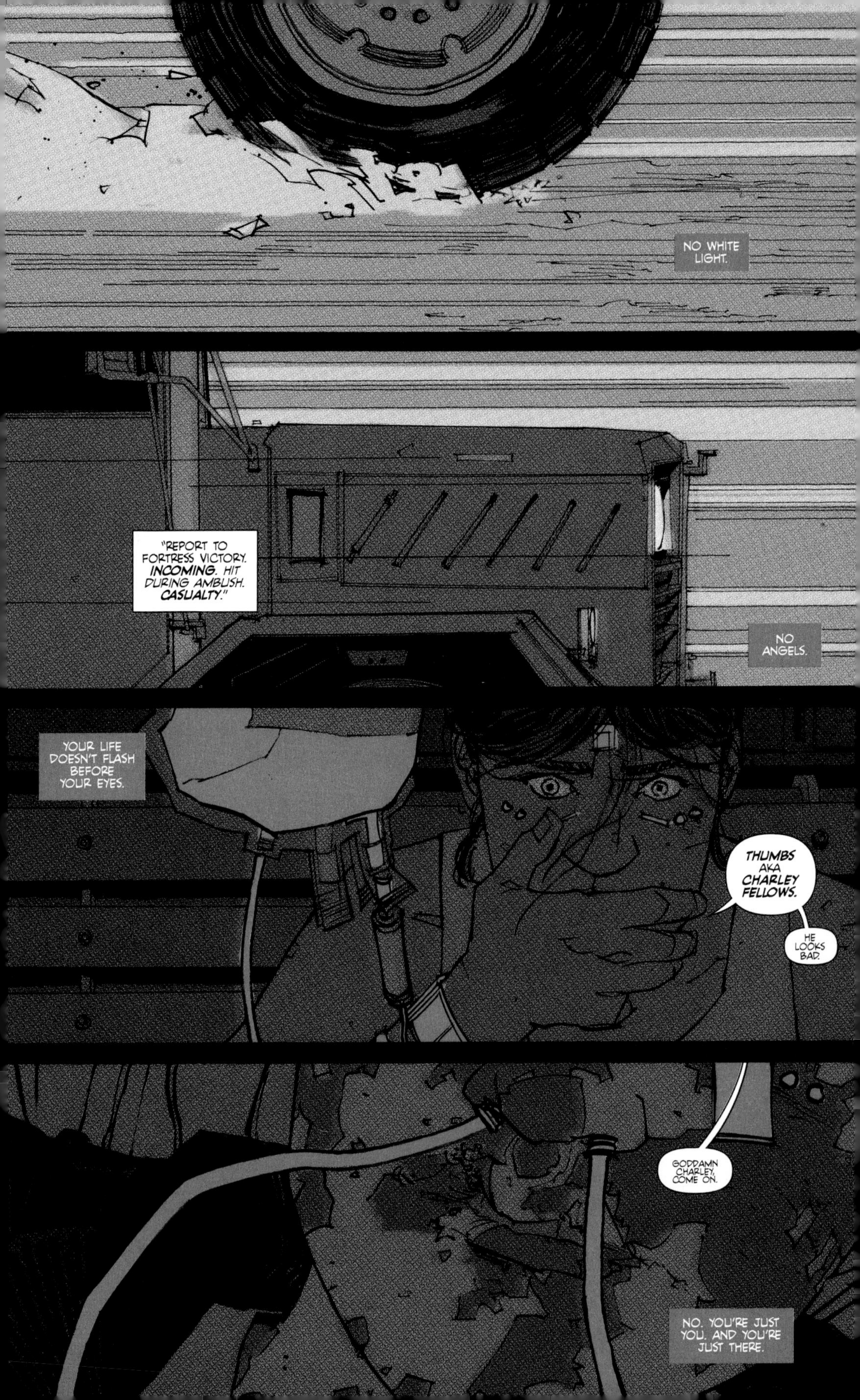
NO WHITE LIGHT.
"REPORT TO FORTRESS VICTORY. INCOMING. HIT DURING AMBUSH. CASUALTY."
NO ANGELS.
YOUR LIFE DOESN'T FLASH BEFORE YOUR EYES.
THUMBS AKA CHARLEY FELLOWS.
HE LOOKS BAD.
GODDAMN CHARLEY, COME ON.
NO. YOU'RE JUST YOU. AND YOU'RE JUST THERE.

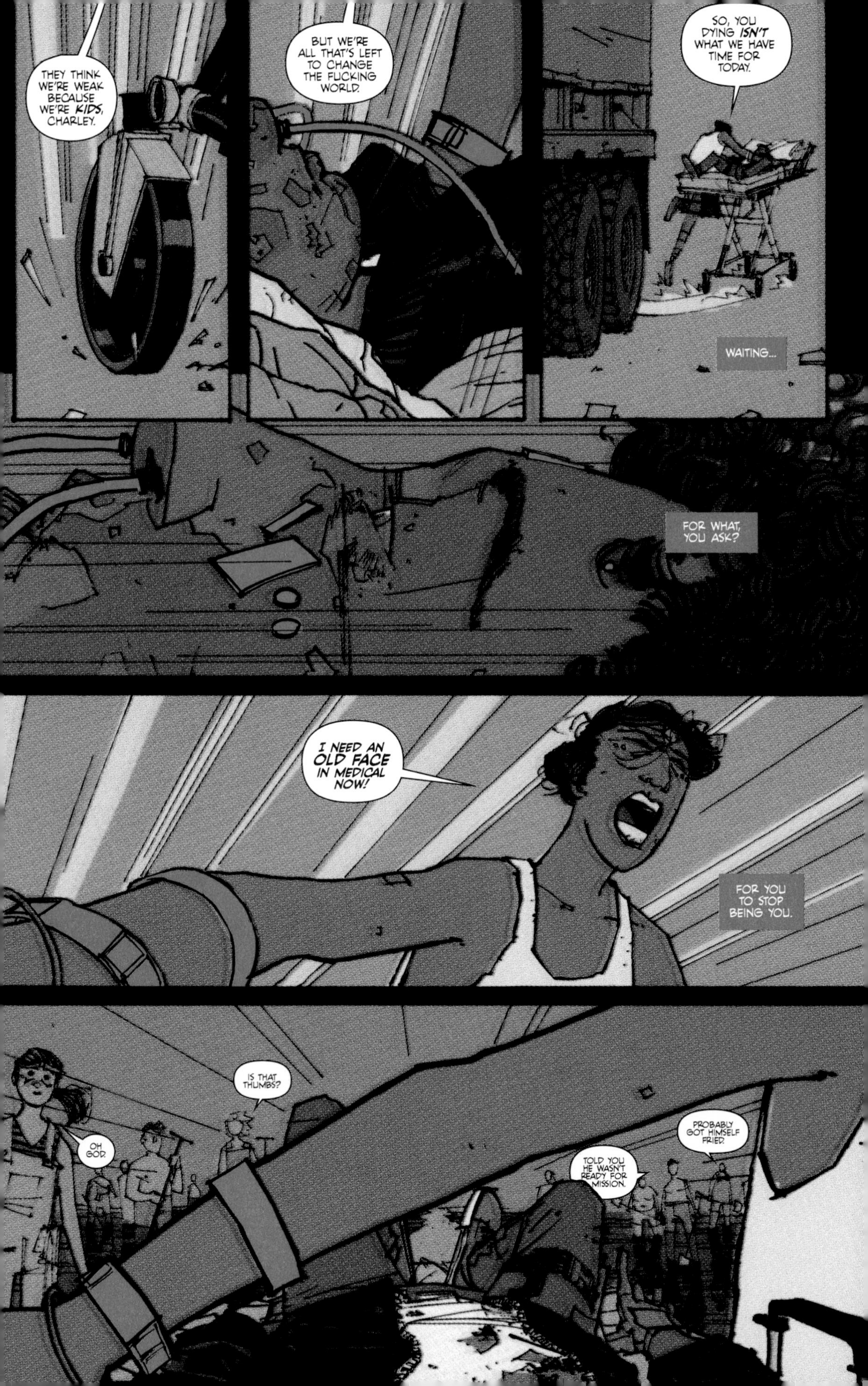
THEY THINK WE'RE WEAK BECAUSE WE'RE KIDS, CHARLEY.
BUT WE'RE ALL THAT'S LEFT TO CHANGE THE FUCKING WORLD.
SO, YOU DYING ISN'T WHAT WE HAVE TIME FOR TODAY.
WAITING...
FOR WHAT, YOU ASK?
I NEED AN OLD FACE IN MEDICAL NOW!
FOR YOU TO STOP BEING YOU.
IS THAT THUMBS?
OH GOD.
TOLD YOU HE WASN'T READY FOR MISSION.
PROBABLY GOT HIMSELF FRIED.

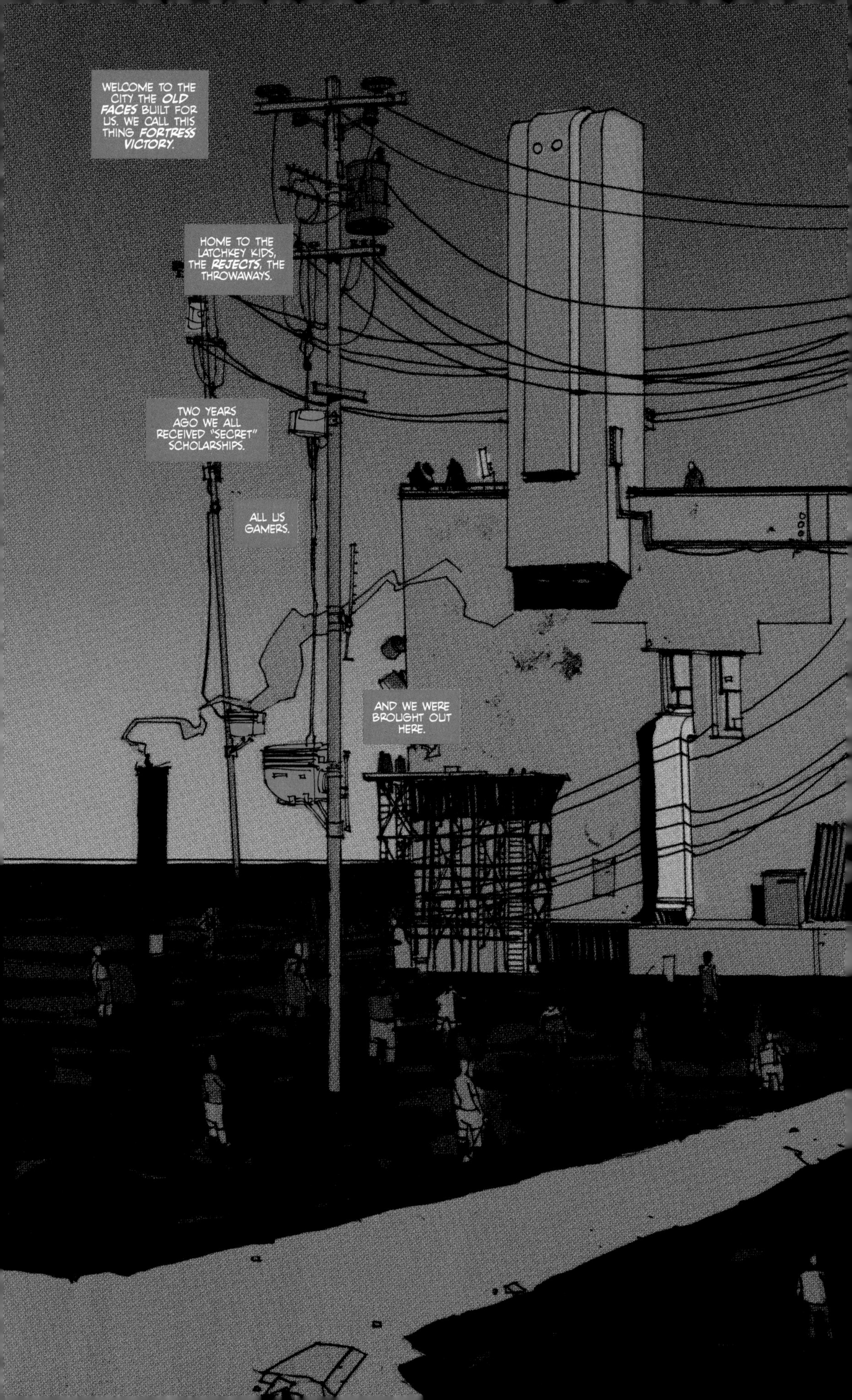
WELCOME TO THE CITY THE ***OLD FACES*** BUILT FOR US. WE CALL THIS THING ***FORTRESS VICTORY.***
HOME TO THE LATCHKEY KIDS, THE ***REJECTS***, THE THROWAWAYS.
TWO YEARS AGO WE ALL RECEIVED "SECRET" SCHOLARSHIPS.
ALL US GAMERS.
AND WE WERE BROUGHT OUT HERE.

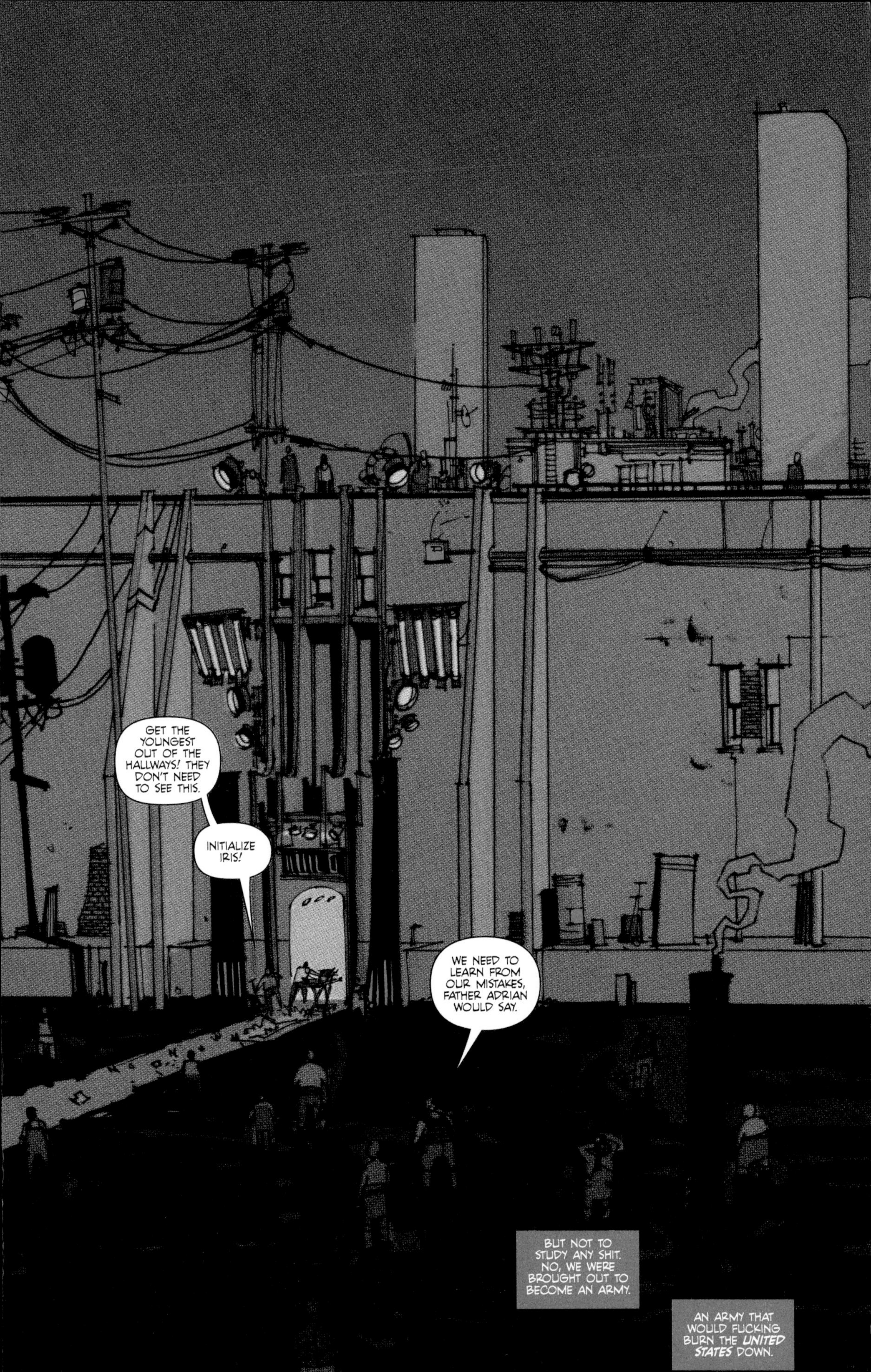
GET THE YOUNGEST OUT OF THE HALLWAYS! THEY DON'T NEED TO SEE THIS.
INITIALIZE IRIS!
WE NEED TO LEARN FROM OUR MISTAKES, FATHER ADRIAN WOULD SAY.
BUT NOT TO STUDY ANY SHIT. NO, WE WERE BROUGHT OUT TO BECOME AN ARMY.
AN ARMY THAT WOULD FUCKING BURN THE UNITED STATES DOWN.

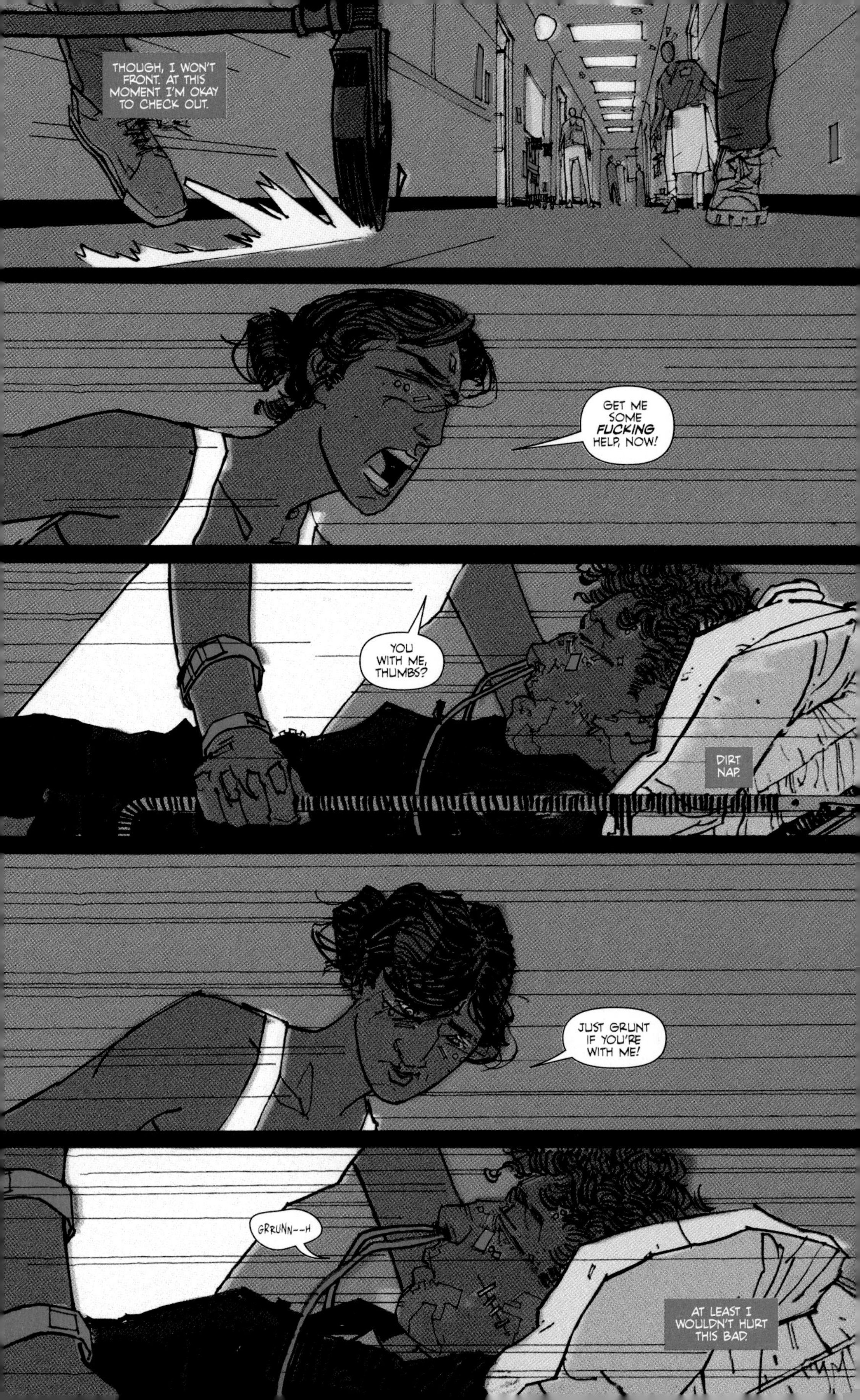
THOUGH, I WON'T FRONT. AT THIS MOMENT I'M OKAY TO CHECK OUT.
GET ME SOME *FUCKING* HELP, NOW!
YOU WITH ME, THUMBS?
DIRT NAP.
JUST GRUNT IF YOU'RE WITH ME!
GRRUNN--H
AT LEAST I WOULDN'T HURT THIS BAD.

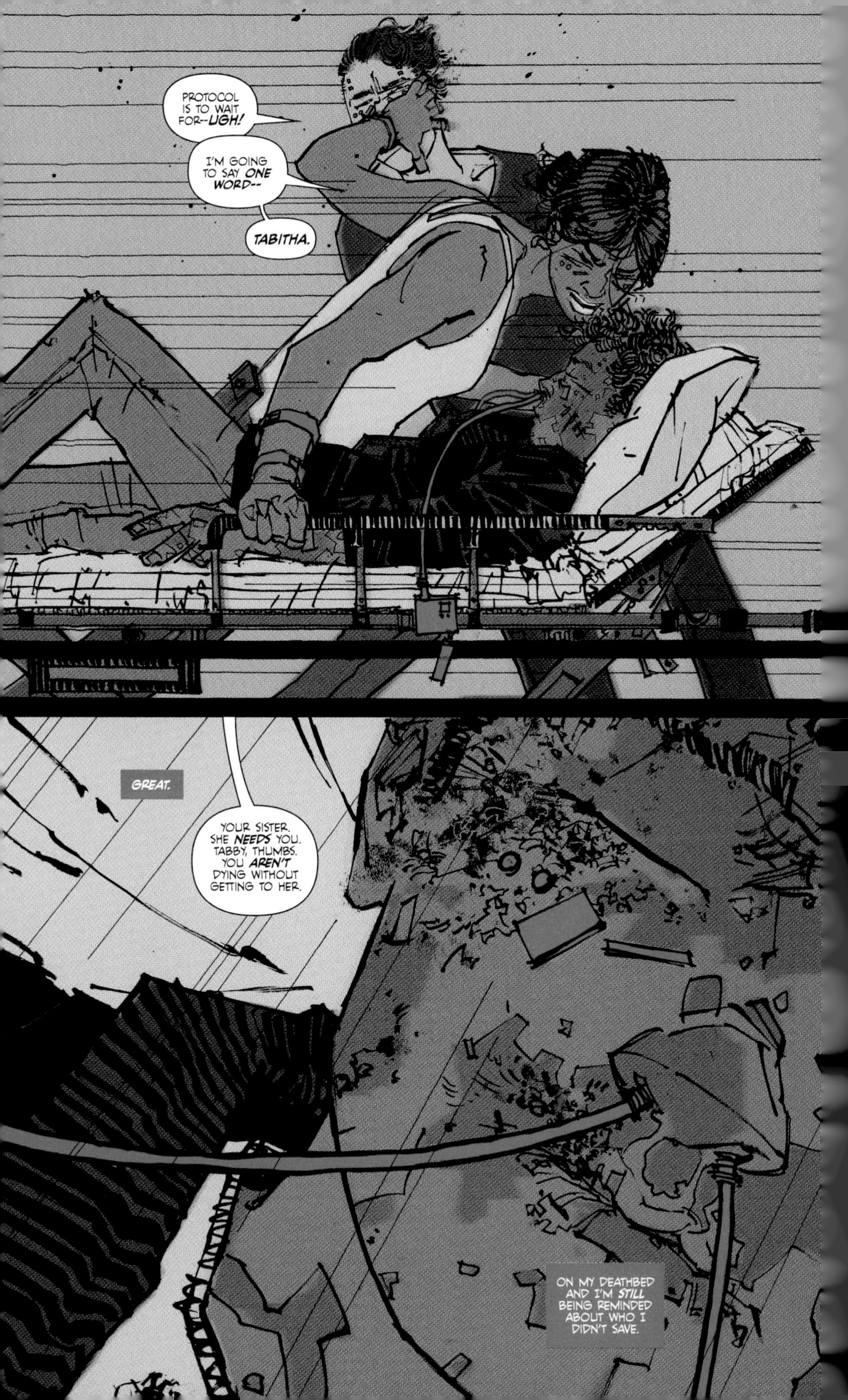
PROTOCOL IS TO WAIT FOR--UGH!
I'M GOING TO SAY ONE WORD--
TABITHA.
GREAT.
YOUR SISTER. SHE NEEDS YOU. TABBY, THUMBS. YOU AREN'T DYING WITHOUT GETTING TO HER.
ON MY DEATHBED AND I'M STILL BEING REMINDED ABOUT WHO I DIDN'T SAVE.

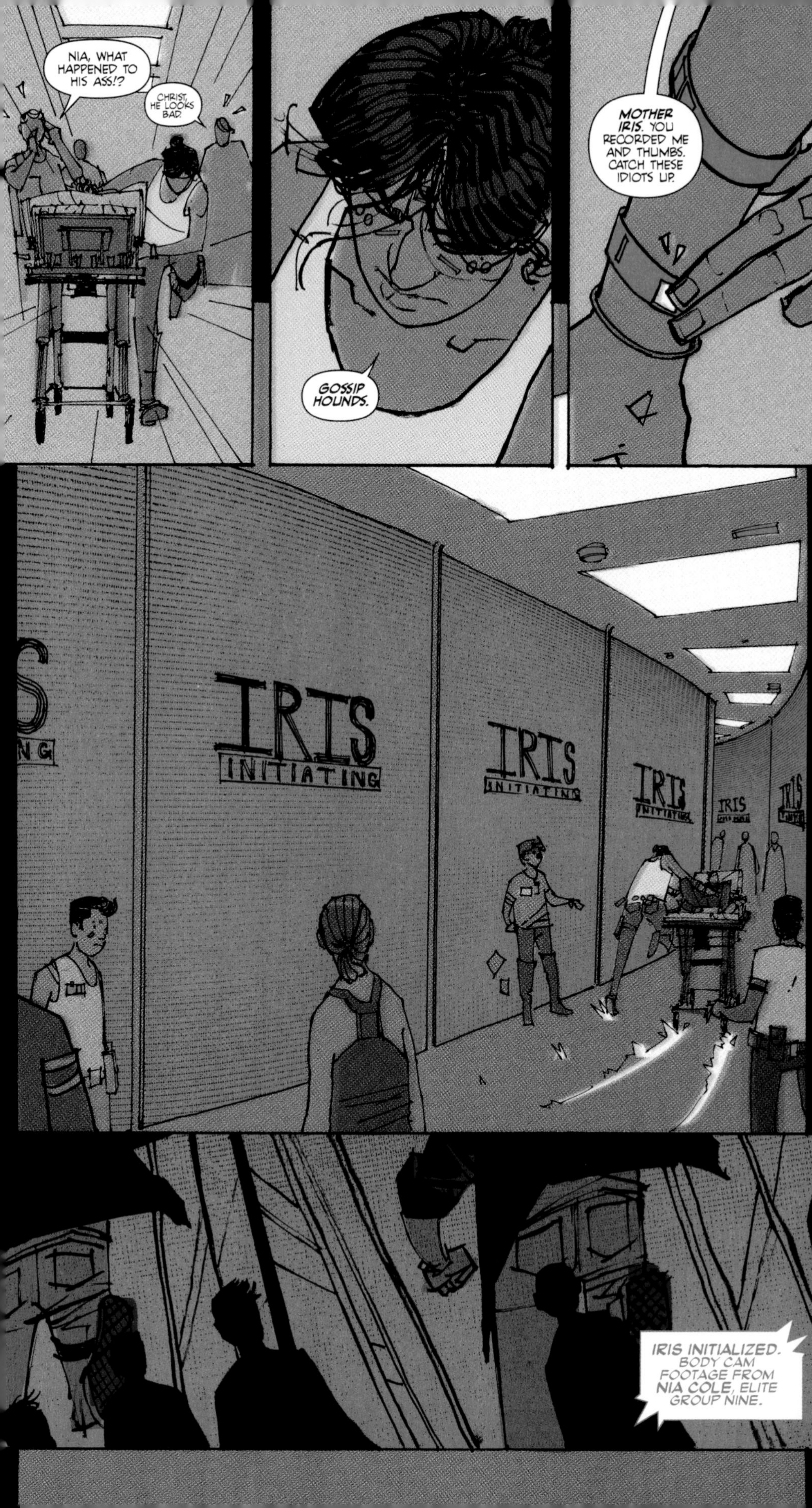
NIA, WHAT HAPPENED TO HIS ASS!?
CHRIST, HE LOOKS BAD.
GOSSIP HOUNDS.
MOTHER IRIS. YOU RECORDED ME AND THUMBS. CATCH THESE IDIOTS UP.
IRIS INITIATING
IRIS INITIALIZED. BODY CAM FOOTAGE FROM NIA COLE, ELITE GROUP NINE.

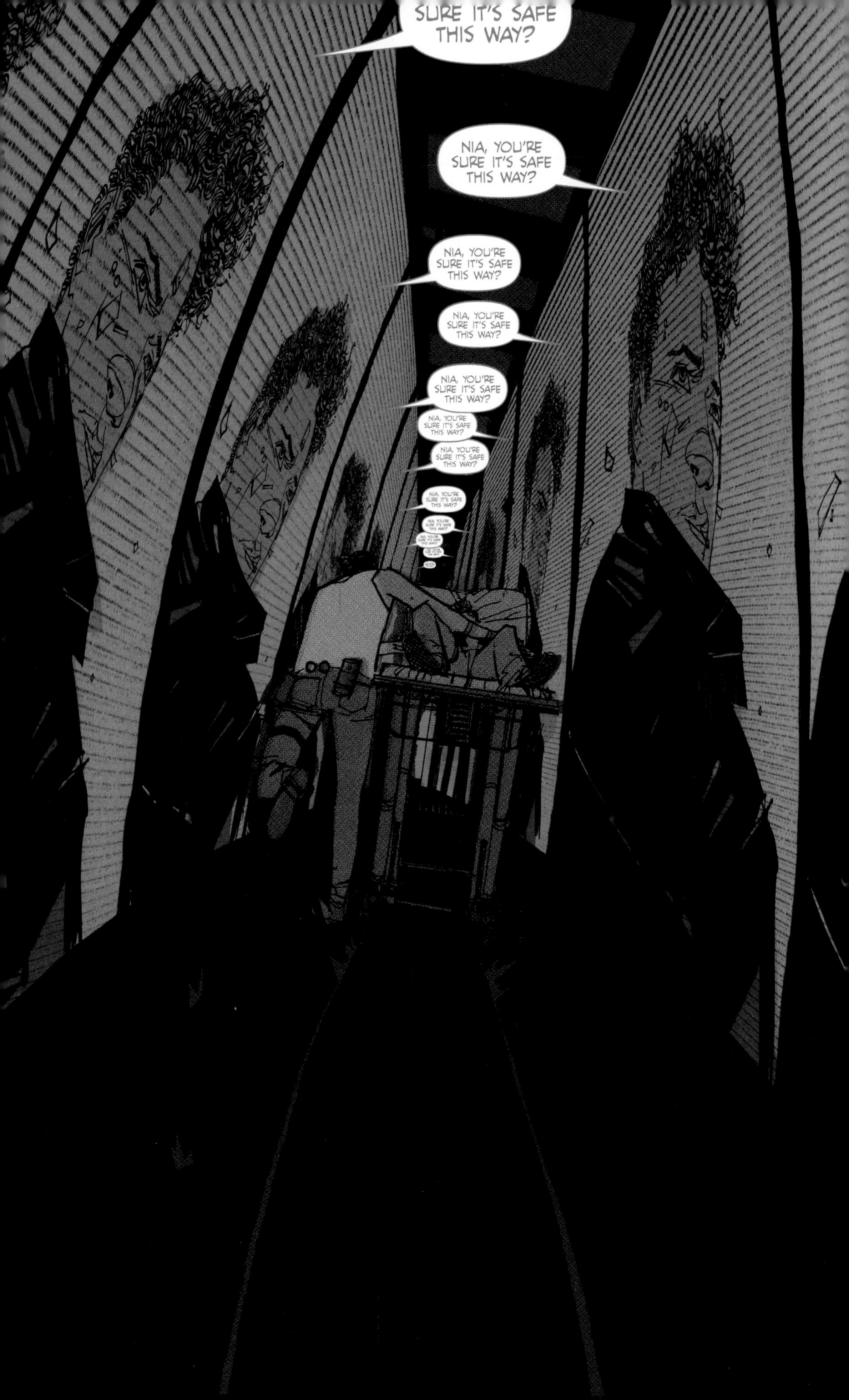
SURE IT'S SAFE THIS WAY?
NIA, YOU'RE SURE IT'S SAFE THIS WAY?
NIA, YOU'RE SURE IT'S SAFE THIS WAY?
NIA, YOU'RE SURE IT'S SAFE THIS WAY?
NIA, YOU'RE SURE IT'S SAFE THIS WAY?
NIA, YOU'RE SURE IT'S SAFE THIS WAY?
NIA, YOU'RE SURE IT'S SAFE THIS WAY?
NIA, YOU'RE SURE IT'S SAFE THIS WAY?
NIA, YOU'RE SURE IT'S SAFE THIS WAY?

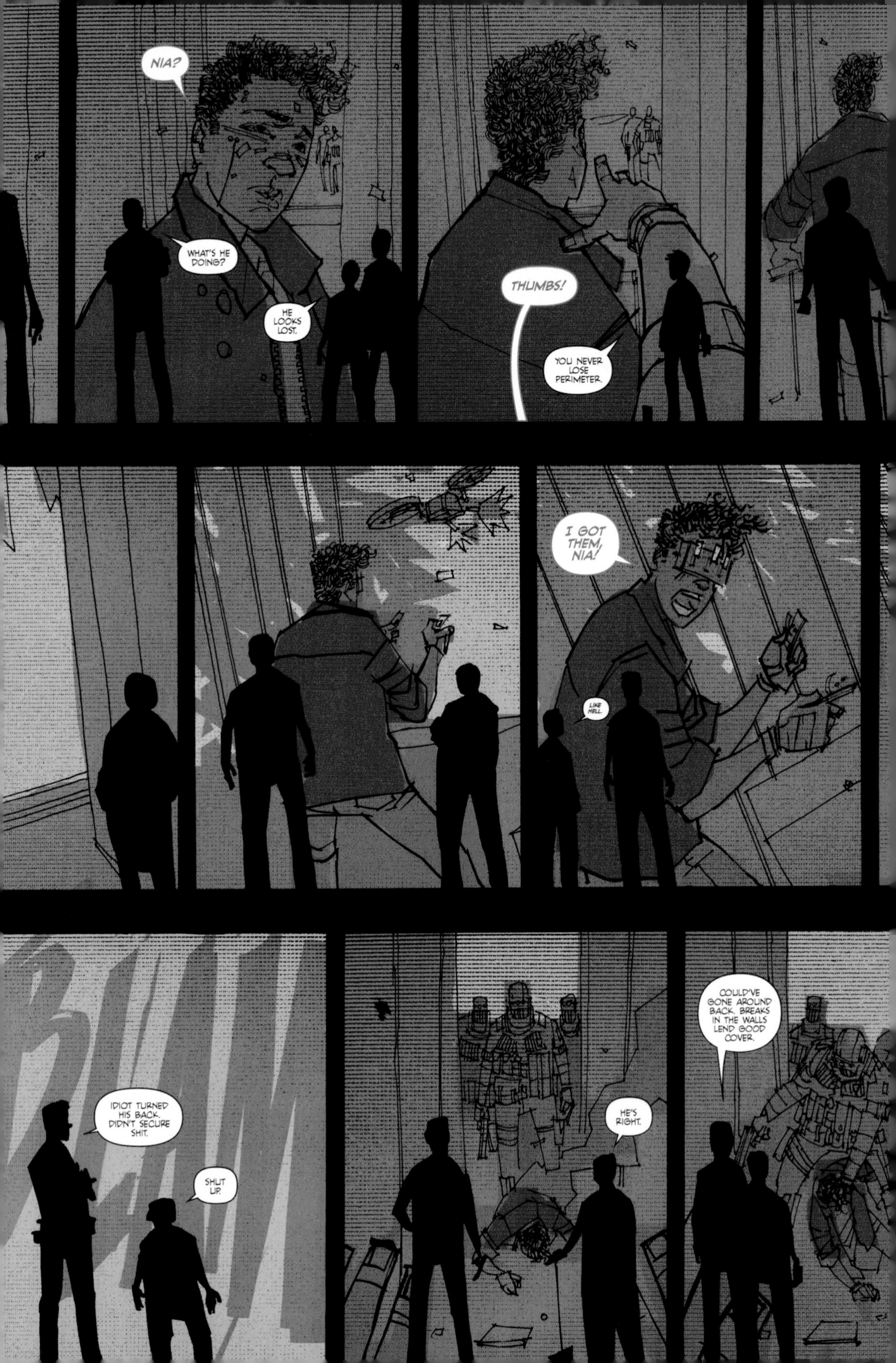
NIA?
WHAT'S HE DOING?
HE LOOKS LOST.
THUMBS!
YOU NEVER LOSE PERIMETER.
I GOT THEM, NIA!
LIKE HELL.
IDIOT TURNED HIS BACK. DIDN'T SECURE SHIT.
SHUT UP.
HE'S RIGHT.
COULD'VE GONE AROUND BACK. BREAKS IN THE WALLS LEND GOOD COVER.

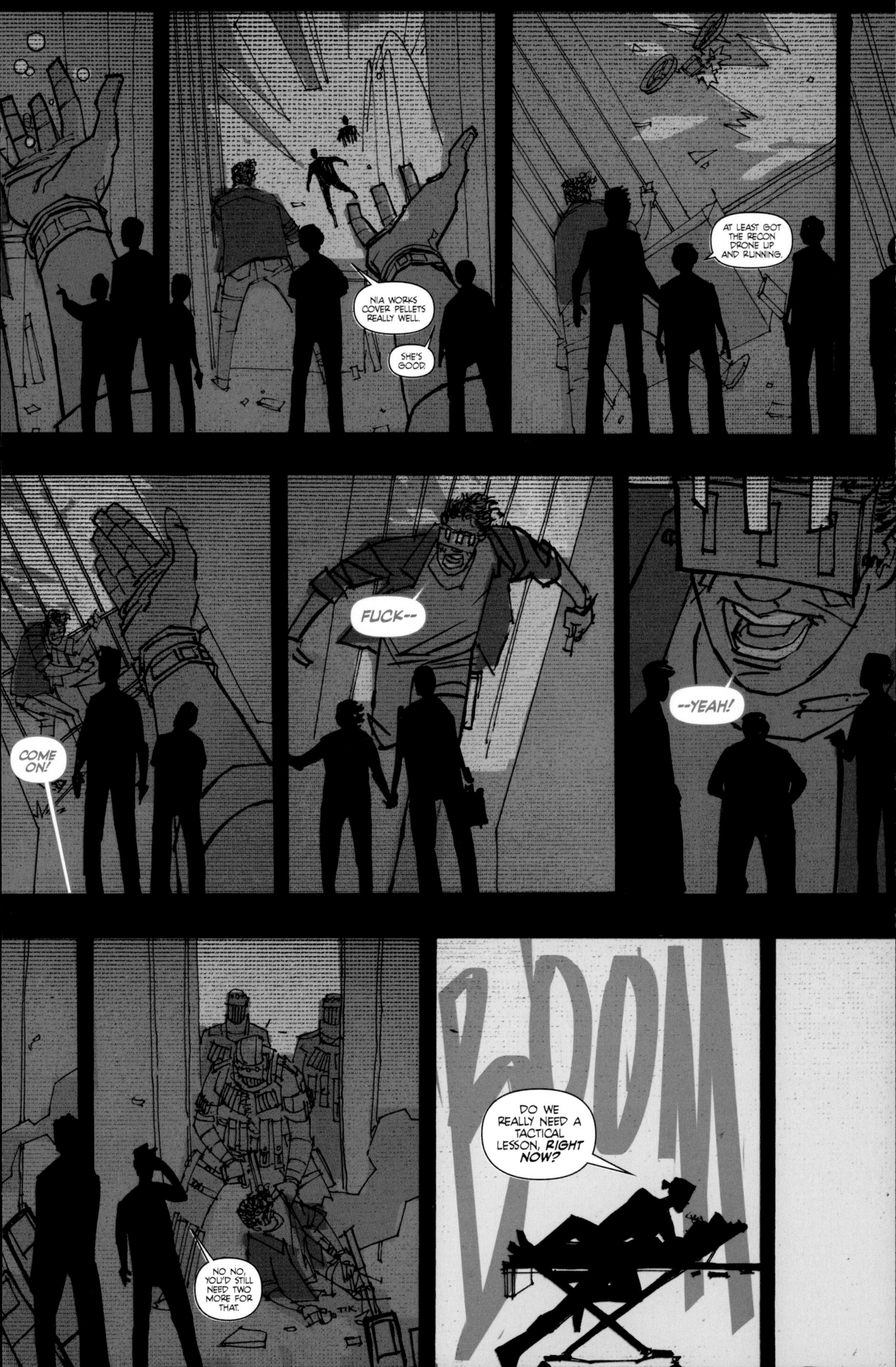
NIA WORKS COVER PELLETS REALLY WELL.
SHE'S GOOD.
AT LEAST GOT THE RECON DRONE UP AND RUNNING.
COME ON!
FUCK--
--YEAH!
NO NO, YOU'D STILL NEED TWO MORE FOR THAT.
B'DOOM
DO WE REALLY NEED A TACTICAL LESSON, RIGHT NOW?

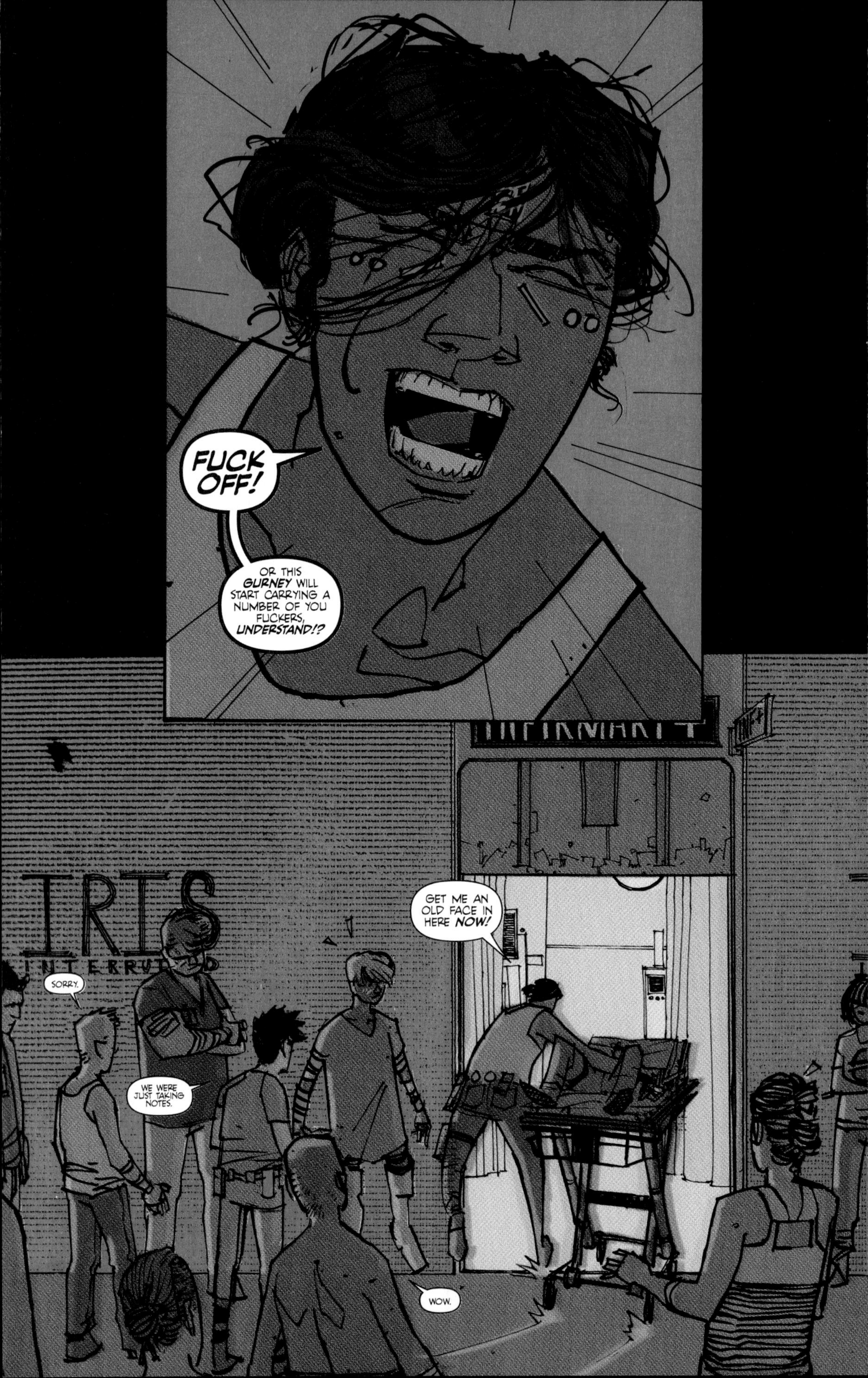
FUCK OFF!
OR THIS GURNEY WILL START CARRYING A NUMBER OF YOU FUCKERS, UNDERSTAND!?
IRIS
GET ME AN OLD FACE IN HERE NOW!
SORRY.
WE WERE JUST TAKING NOTES.
WOW.

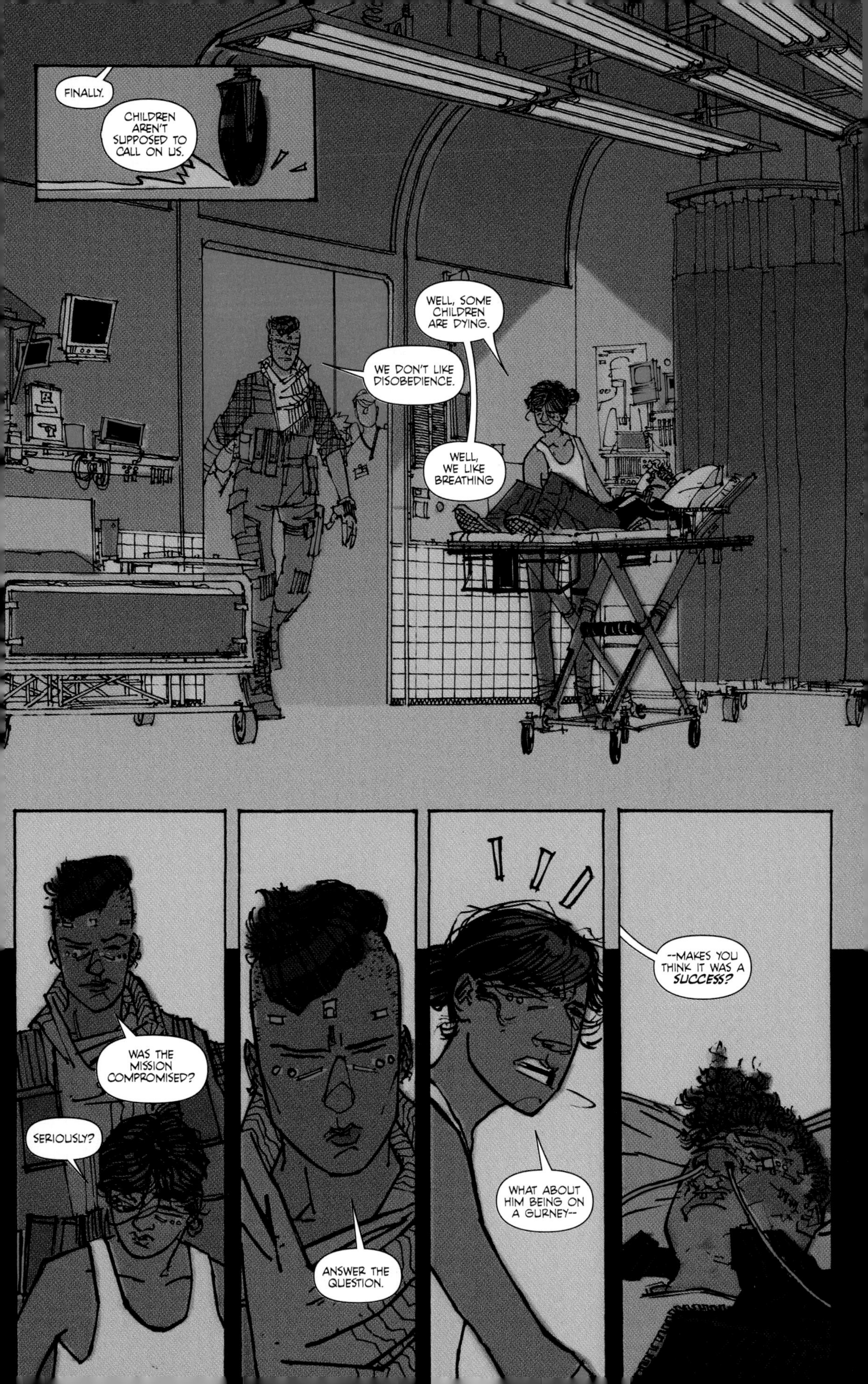
FINALLY.
CHILDREN AREN'T SUPPOSED TO CALL ON US.
WELL, SOME CHILDREN ARE DYING.
WE DON'T LIKE DISOBEDIENCE.
WELL, WE LIKE BREATHING
WAS THE MISSION COMPROMISED?
SERIOUSLY?
ANSWER THE QUESTION.
WHAT ABOUT HIM BEING ON A GURNEY--
--MAKES YOU THINK IT WAS A SUCCESS?

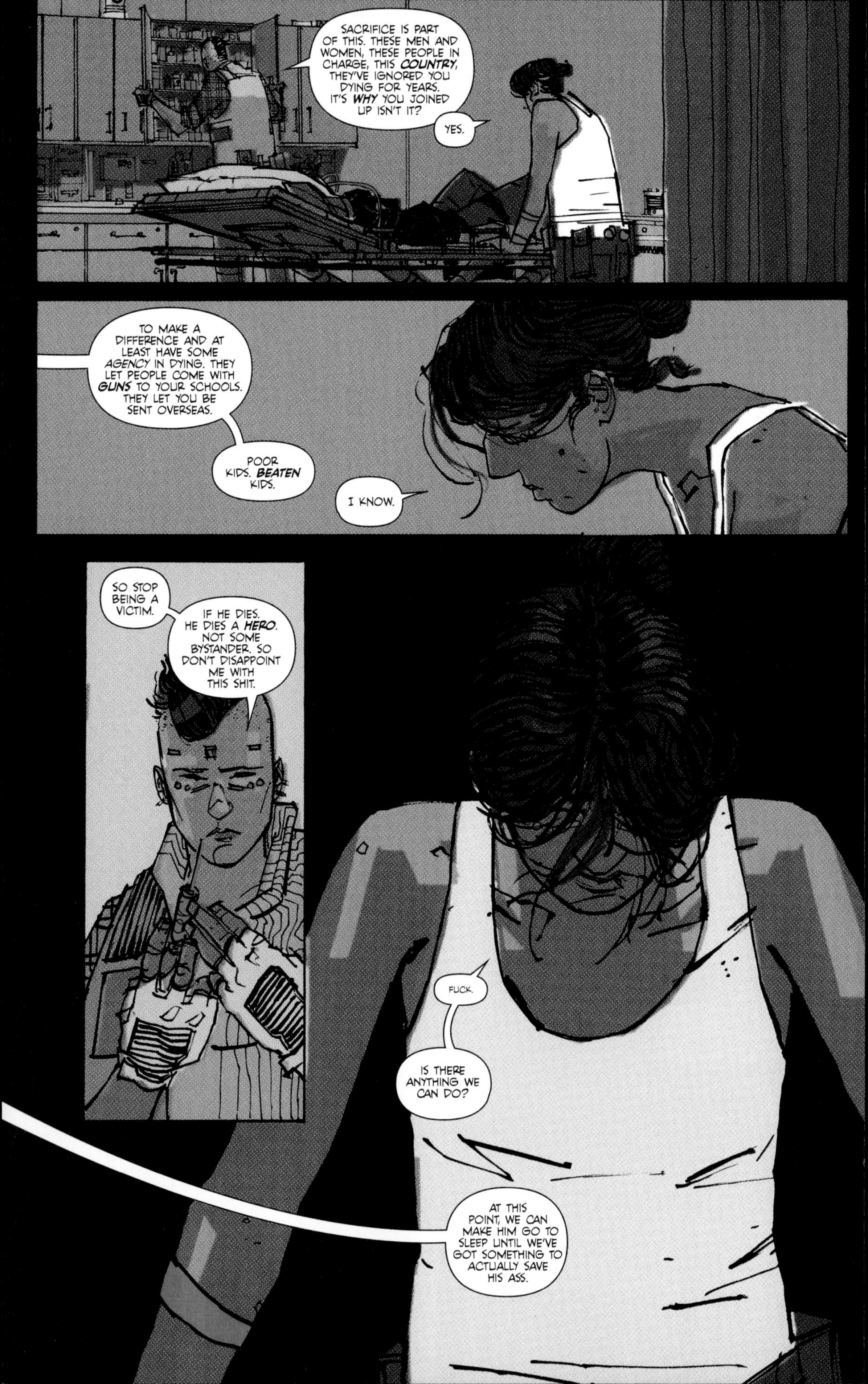
SACRIFICE IS PART OF THIS. THESE MEN AND WOMEN, THESE PEOPLE IN CHARGE, THIS *COUNTRY*, THEY'VE IGNORED YOU DYING FOR YEARS. IT'S *WHY* YOU JOINED UP ISN'T IT?
YES.
TO MAKE A DIFFERENCE AND AT LEAST HAVE SOME *AGENCY* IN DYING. THEY LET PEOPLE COME WITH *GUNS* TO YOUR SCHOOLS. THEY LET YOU BE SENT OVERSEAS.
POOR KIDS. *BEATEN* KIDS.
I KNOW.
SO STOP BEING A VICTIM.
IF HE DIES. HE DIES A *HERO*. NOT SOME BYSTANDER. SO DON'T DISAPPOINT ME WITH THIS SHIT.
FUCK.
IS THERE ANYTHING WE CAN DO?
AT THIS POINT, WE CAN MAKE HIM GO TO SLEEP UNTIL WE'VE GOT SOMETHING TO ACTUALLY SAVE HIS ASS.

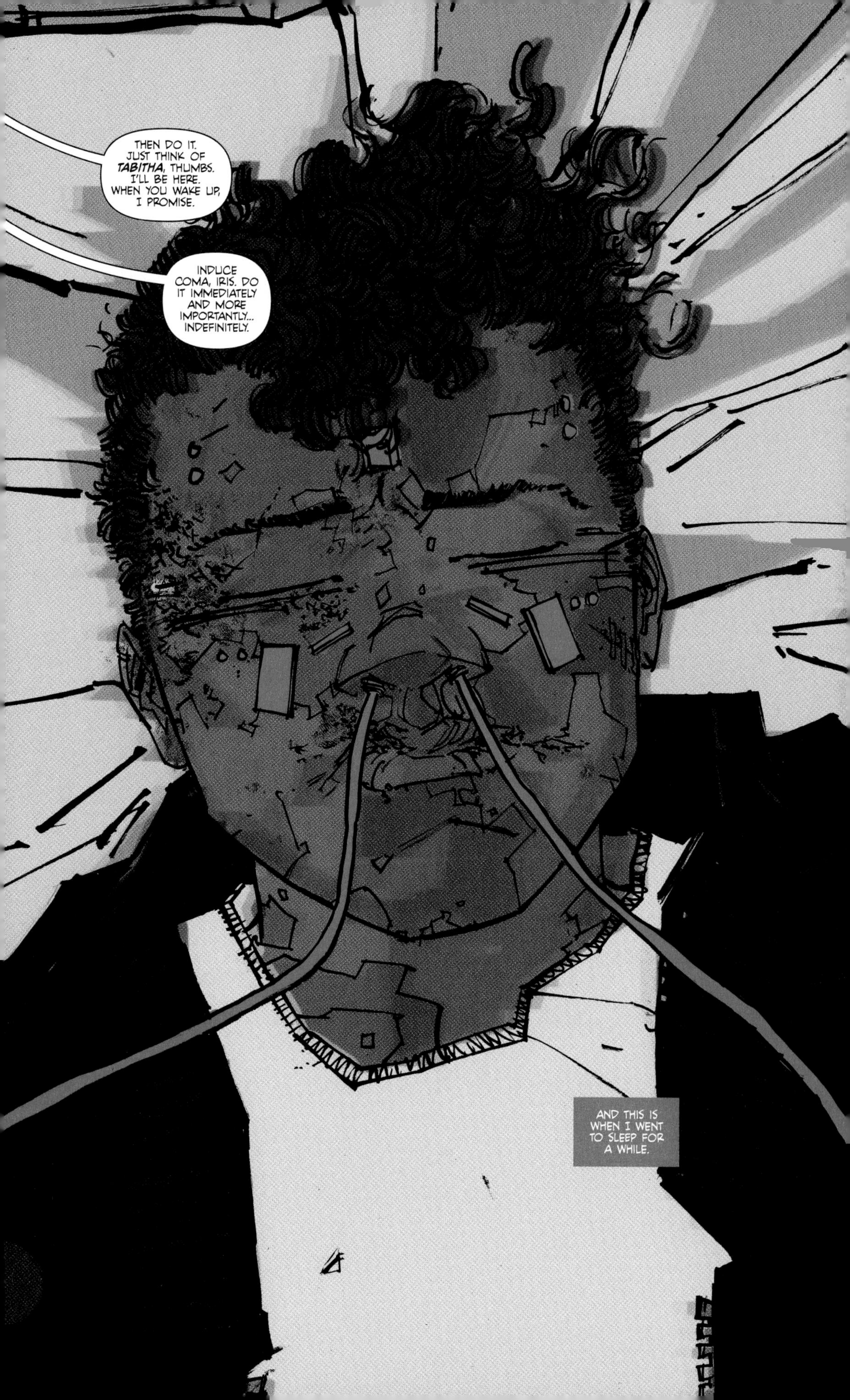
THEN DO IT. JUST THINK OF *TABITHA*, THUMBS. I'LL BE HERE. WHEN YOU WAKE UP, I PROMISE.
INDUCE COMA, IRIS. DO IT IMMEDIATELY AND MORE IMPORTANTLY... INDEFINITELY.
AND THIS IS WHEN I WENT TO SLEEP FOR A WHILE.

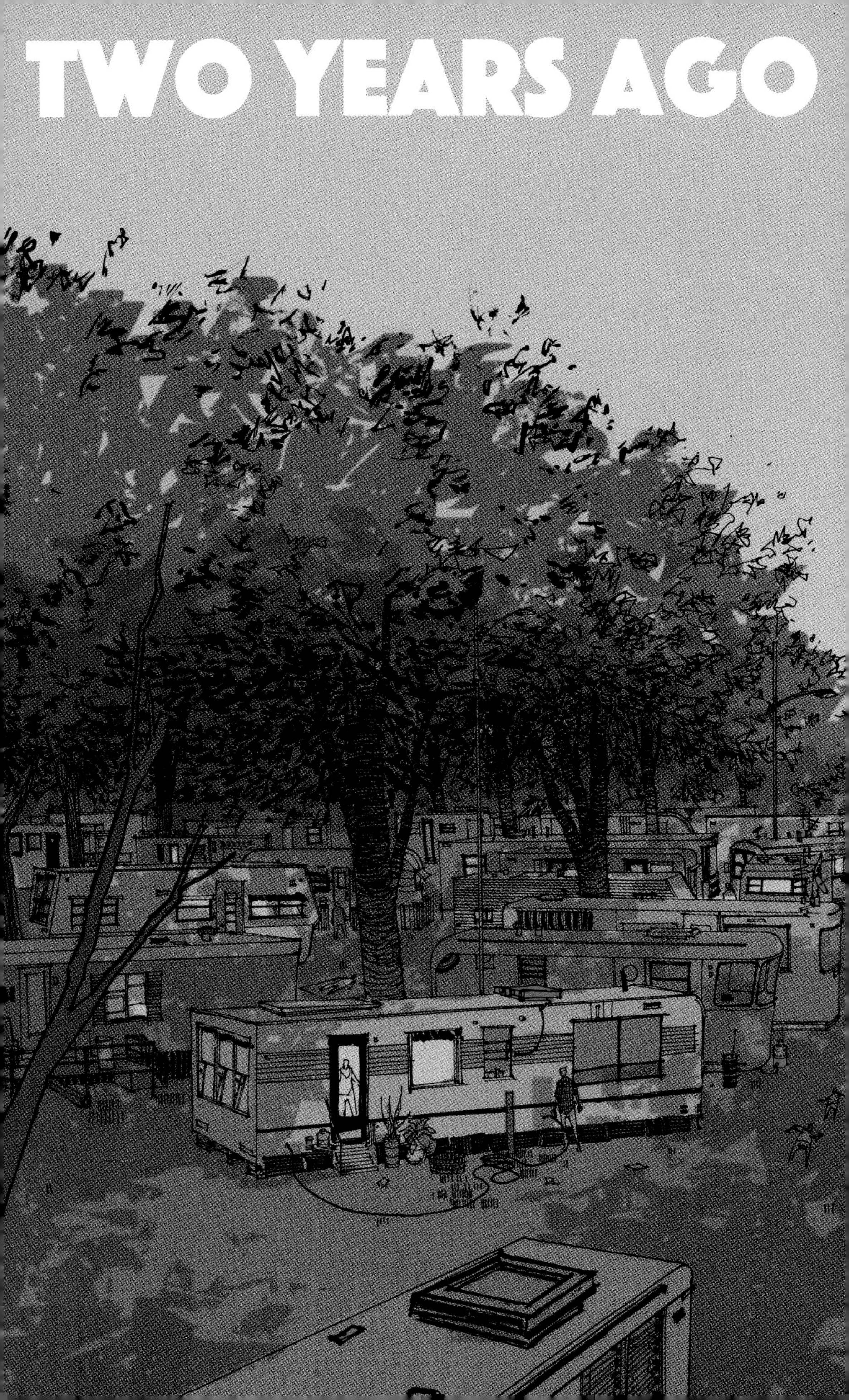
TWO YEARS AGO

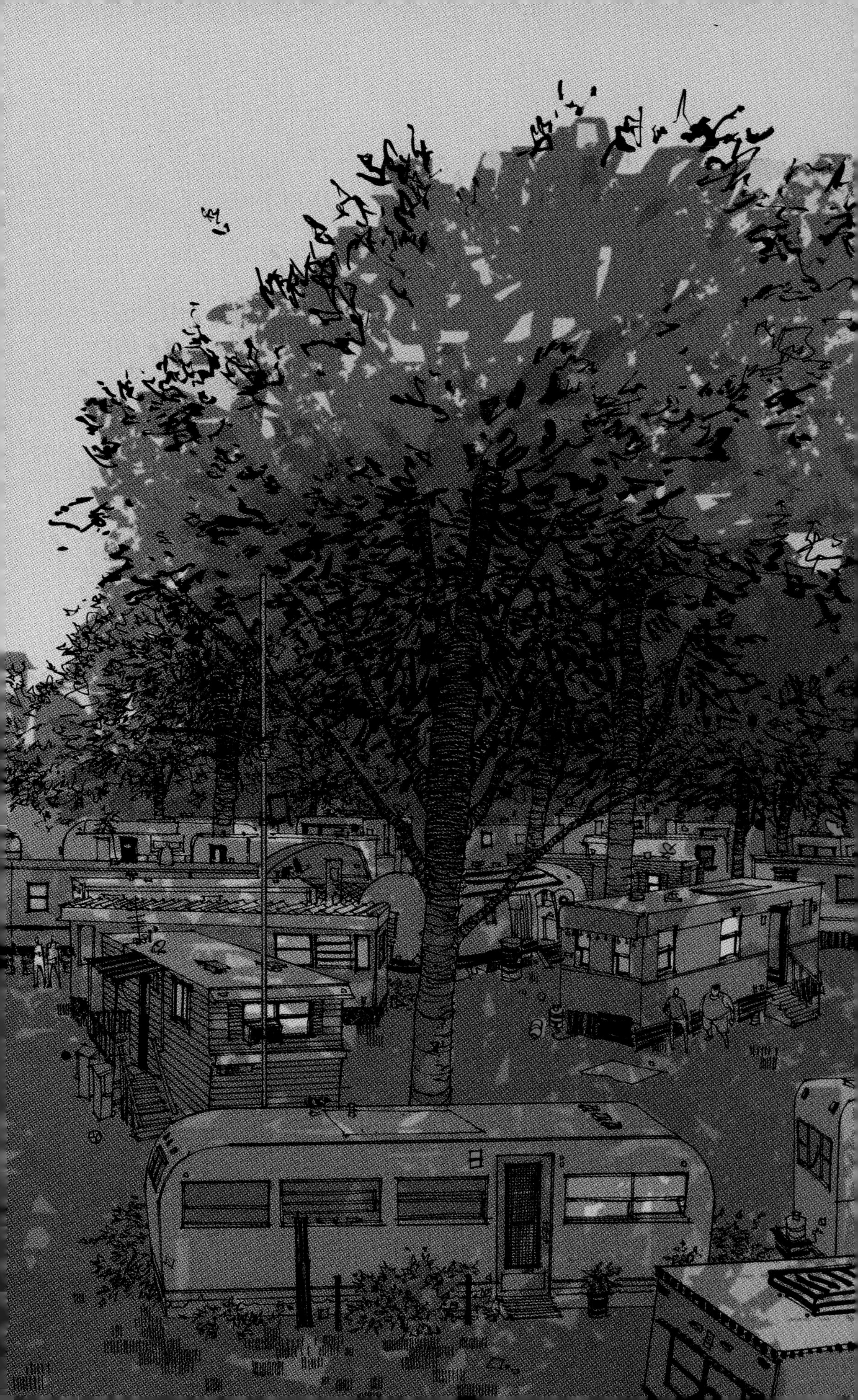

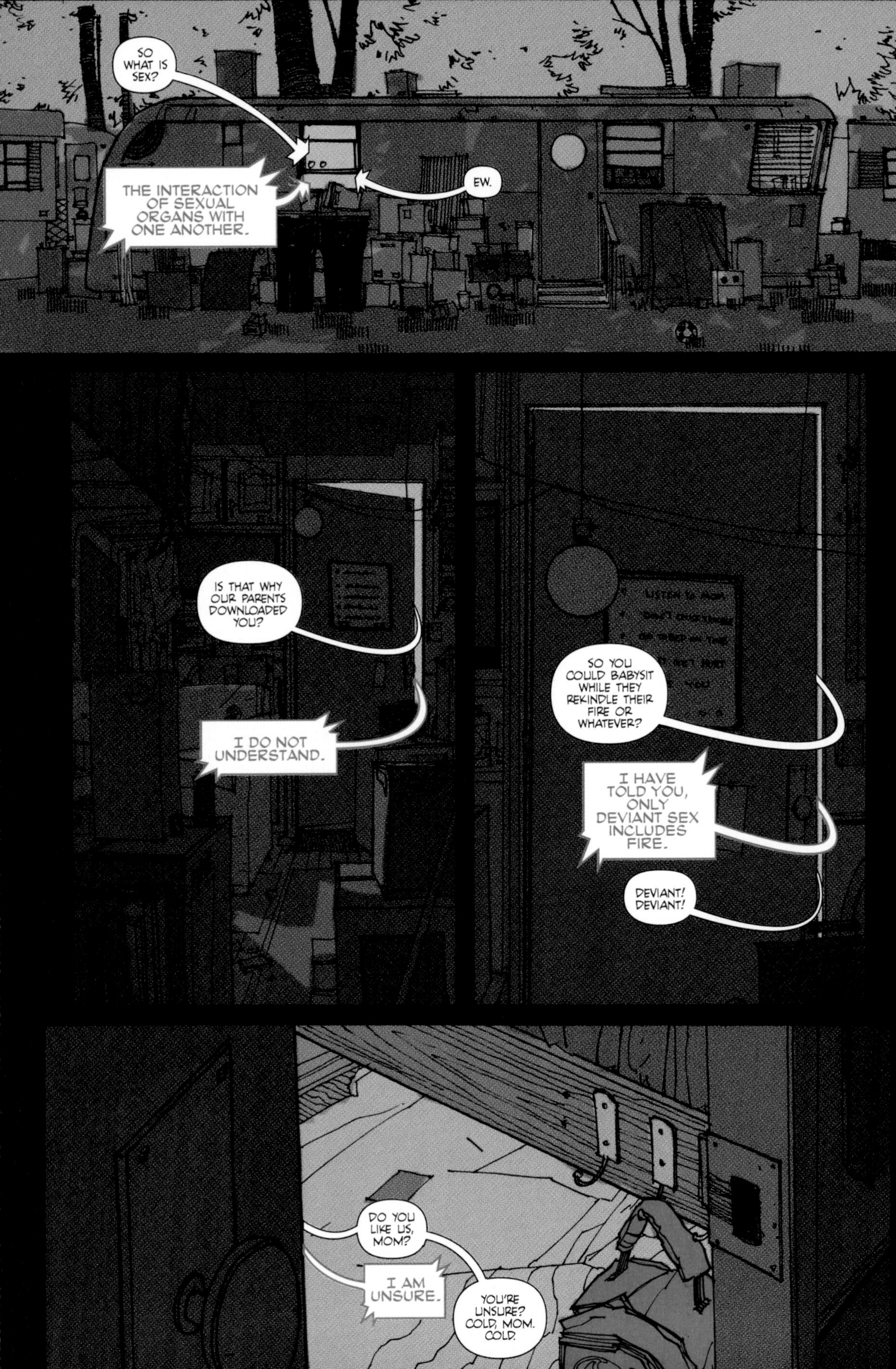
SO WHAT IS SEX?
THE INTERACTION OF SEXUAL ORGANS WITH ONE ANOTHER.
EW.
IS THAT WHY OUR PARENTS DOWNLOADED YOU?
I DO NOT UNDERSTAND.
SO YOU COULD BABYSIT WHILE THEY REKINDLE THEIR FIRE OR WHATEVER?
I HAVE TOLD YOU, ONLY DEVIANT SEX INCLUDES FIRE.
DEVIANT! DEVIANT!
DO YOU LIKE US, MOM?
I AM UNSURE.
YOU'RE UNSURE? COLD, MOM. COLD.

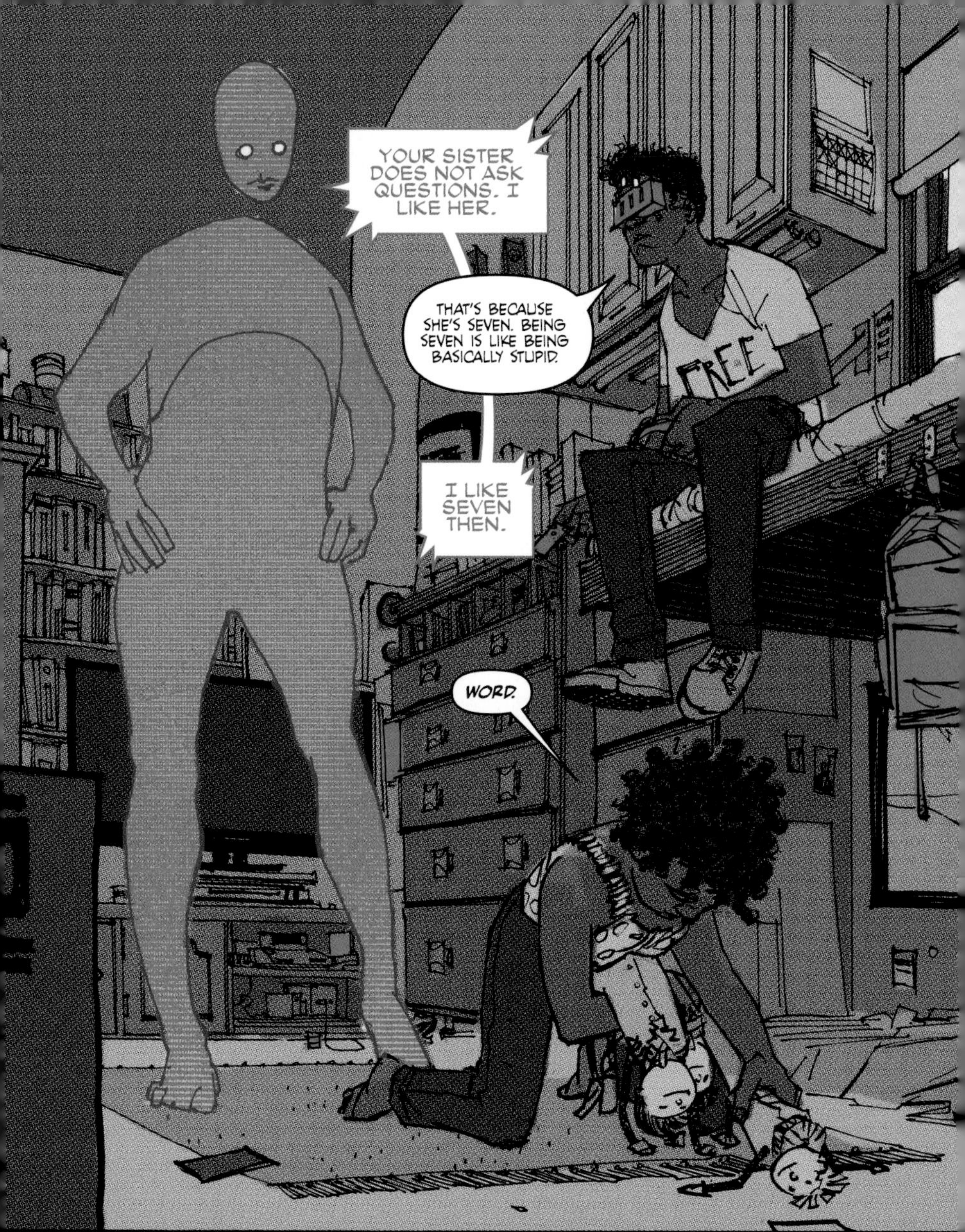
YOUR SISTER DOES NOT ASK QUESTIONS. I LIKE HER.
THAT'S BECAUSE SHE'S SEVEN. BEING SEVEN IS LIKE BEING BASICALLY STUPID.
I LIKE SEVEN THEN.
WORD.

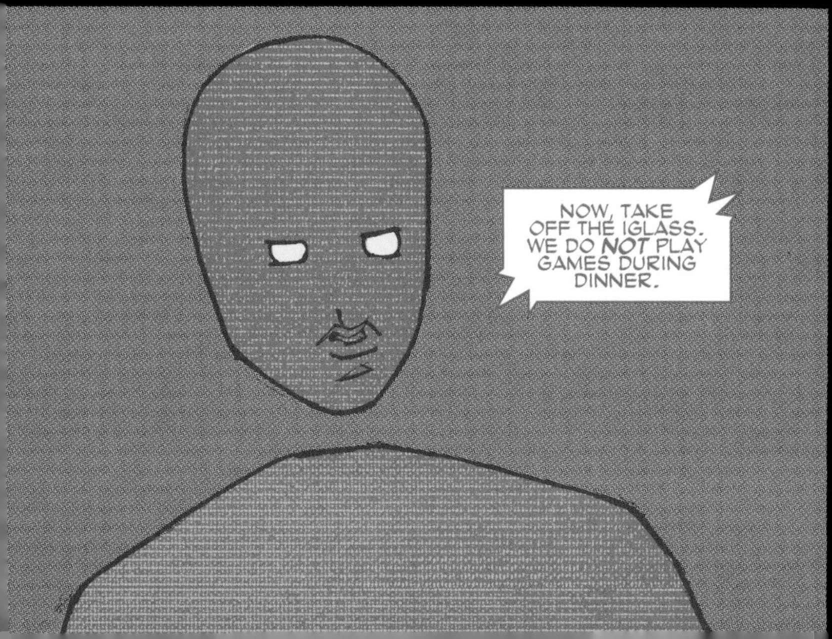
NOW, TAKE OFF THE IGLASS. WE DO NOT PLAY GAMES DURING DINNER.

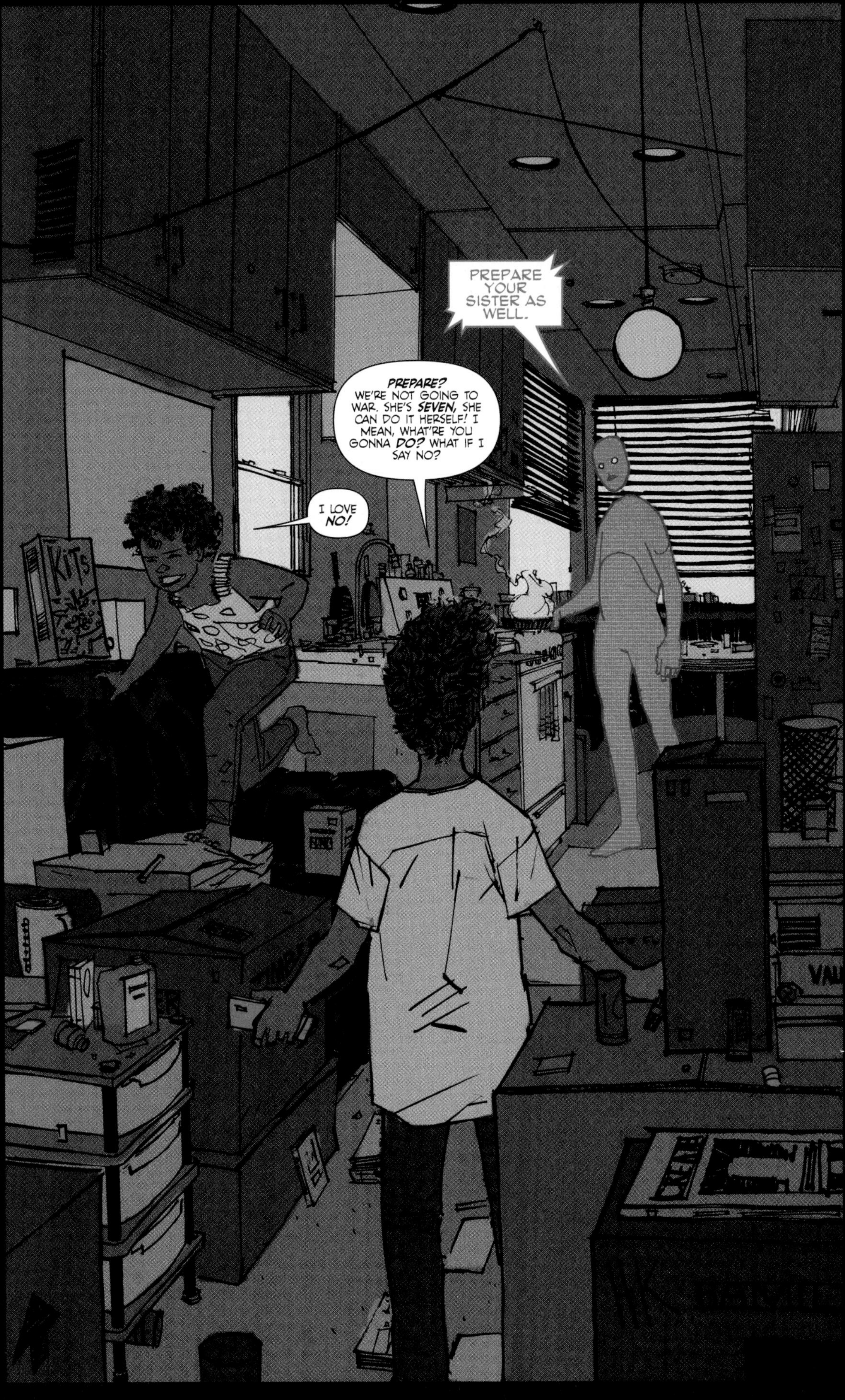
PREPARE YOUR SISTER AS WELL.
PREPARE? WE'RE NOT GOING TO WAR. SHE'S SEVEN, SHE CAN DO IT HERSELF! I MEAN, WHAT'RE YOU GONNA DO? WHAT IF I SAY NO?
I LOVE NO!

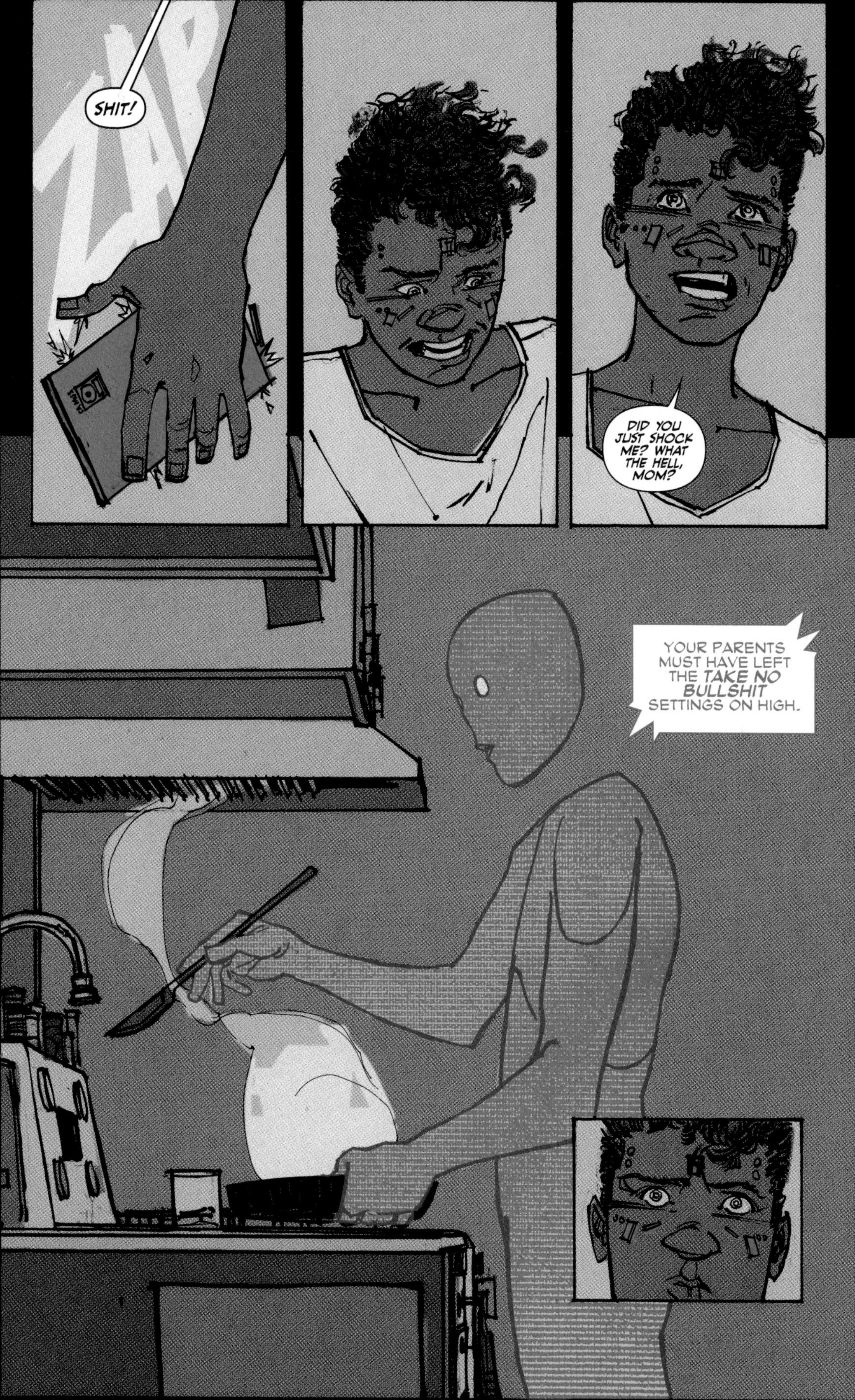
ZAP
SHIT!
DID YOU JUST SHOCK ME? WHAT THE HELL, MOM?
YOUR PARENTS MUST HAVE LEFT THE TAKE NO BULLSHIT SETTINGS ON HIGH.

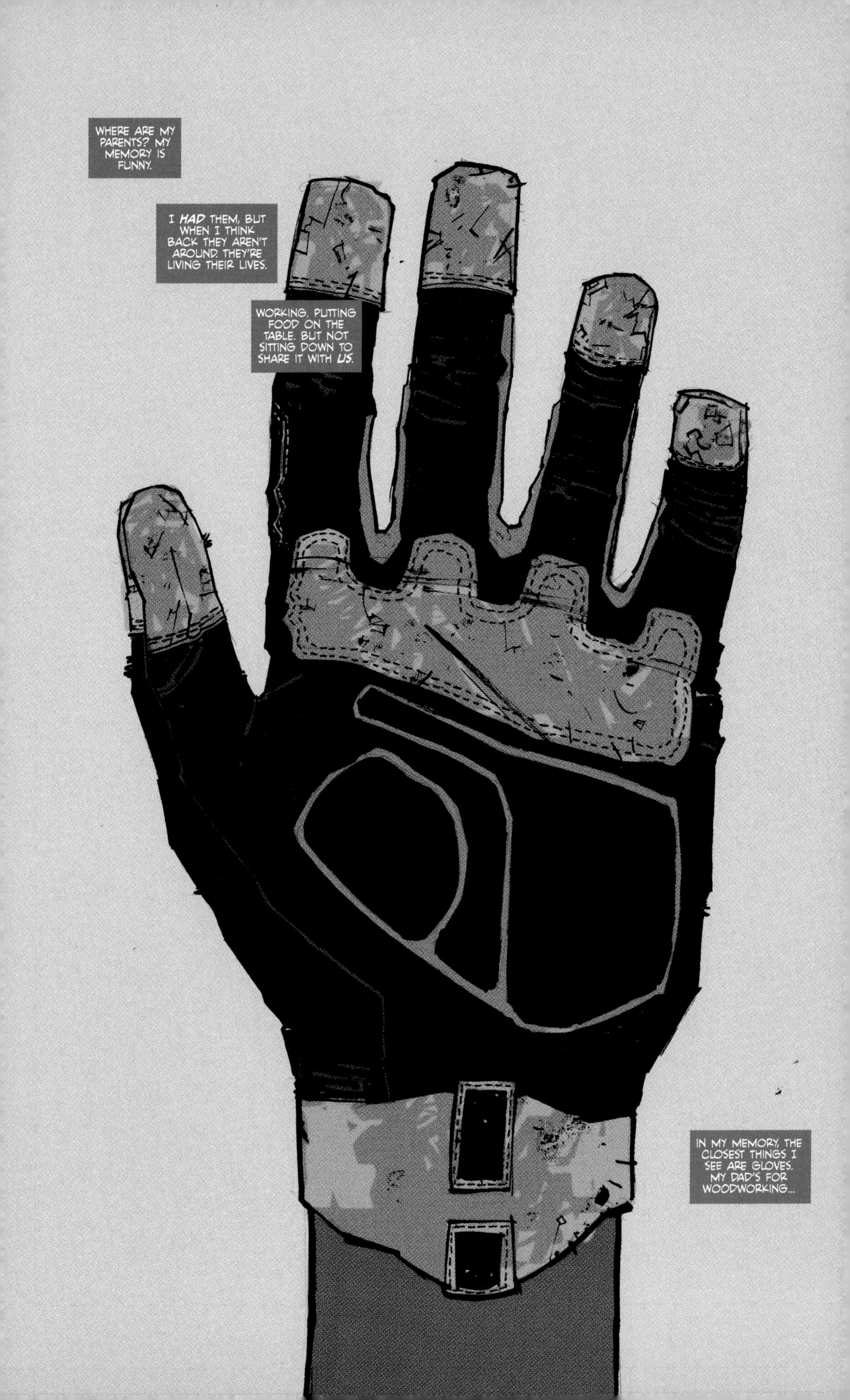
WHERE ARE MY PARENTS? MY MEMORY IS FUNNY.
I HAD THEM, BUT WHEN I THINK BACK THEY AREN'T AROUND. THEY'RE LIVING THEIR LIVES.
WORKING. PUTTING FOOD ON THE TABLE. BUT NOT SITTING DOWN TO SHARE IT WITH US.
IN MY MEMORY, THE CLOSEST THINGS I SEE ARE GLOVES. MY DAD'S FOR WOODWORKING...

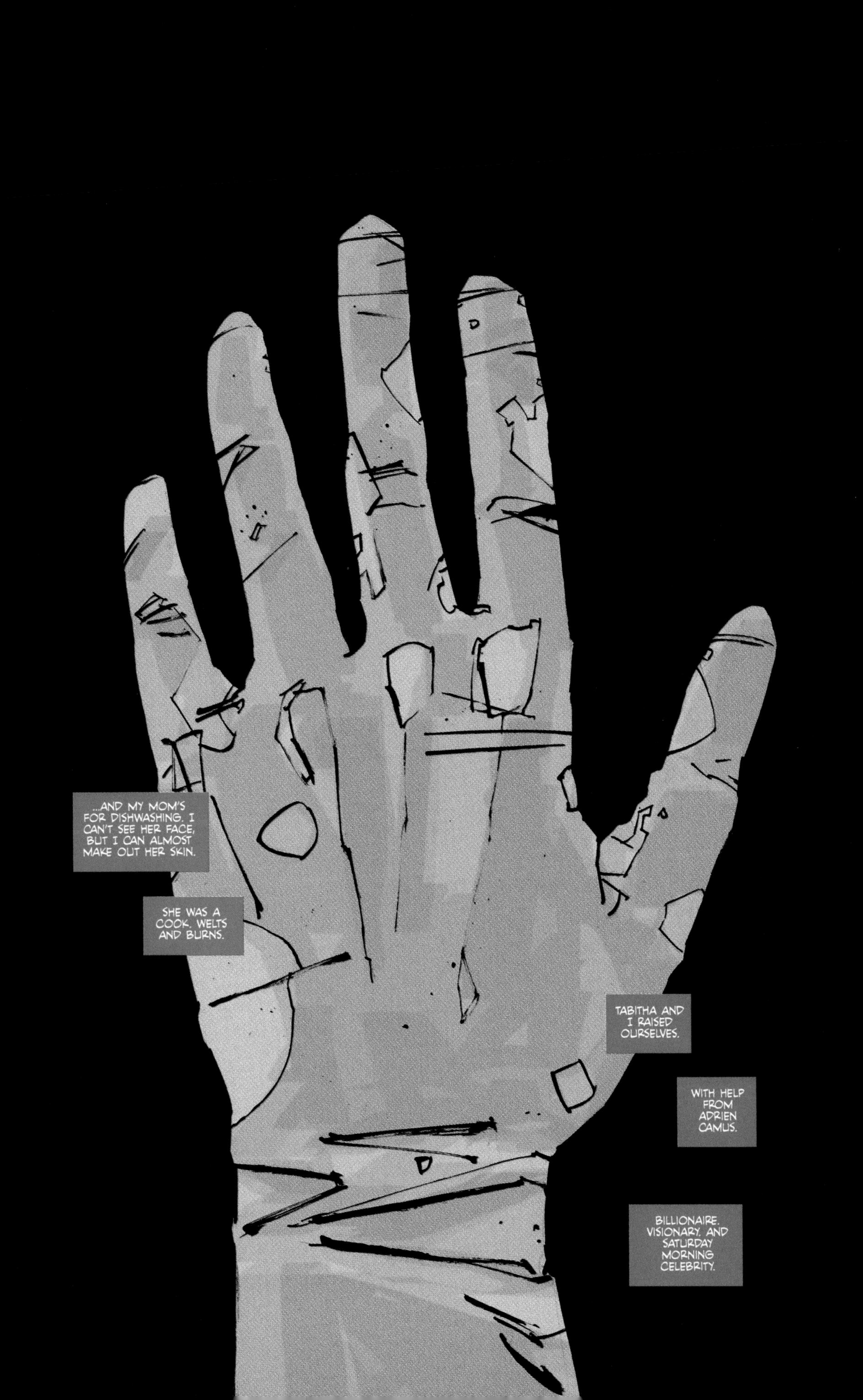
...AND MY MOM'S FOR DISHWASHING. I CAN'T SEE HER FACE, BUT I CAN ALMOST MAKE OUT HER SKIN.
SHE WAS A COOK. WELTS AND BURNS.
TABITHA AND I RAISED OURSELVES.
WITH HELP FROM ADRIEN CAMUS.
BILLIONAIRE. VISIONARY. AND SATURDAY MORNING CELEBRITY.

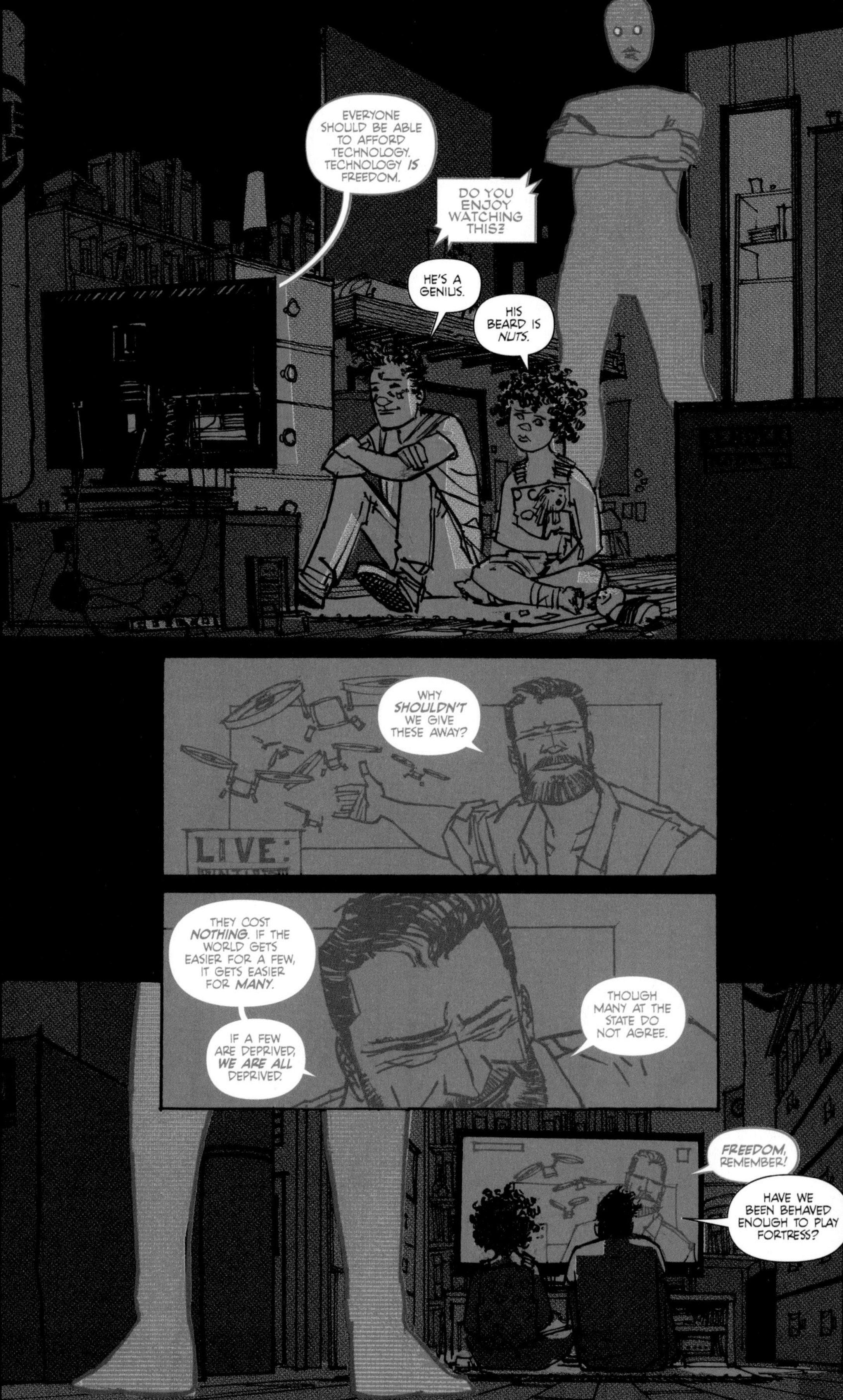
EVERYONE SHOULD BE ABLE TO AFFORD TECHNOLOGY. TECHNOLOGY IS FREEDOM.
DO YOU ENJOY WATCHING THIS?
HE'S A GENIUS.
HIS BEARD IS NUTS.
WHY SHOULDN'T WE GIVE THESE AWAY?
LIVE:
THEY COST NOTHING. IF THE WORLD GETS EASIER FOR A FEW, IT GETS EASIER FOR MANY.
IF A FEW ARE DEPRIVED, WE ARE ALL DEPRIVED.
THOUGH MANY AT THE STATE DO NOT AGREE.
FREEDOM, REMEMBER!
HAVE WE BEEN BEHAVED ENOUGH TO PLAY FORTRESS?

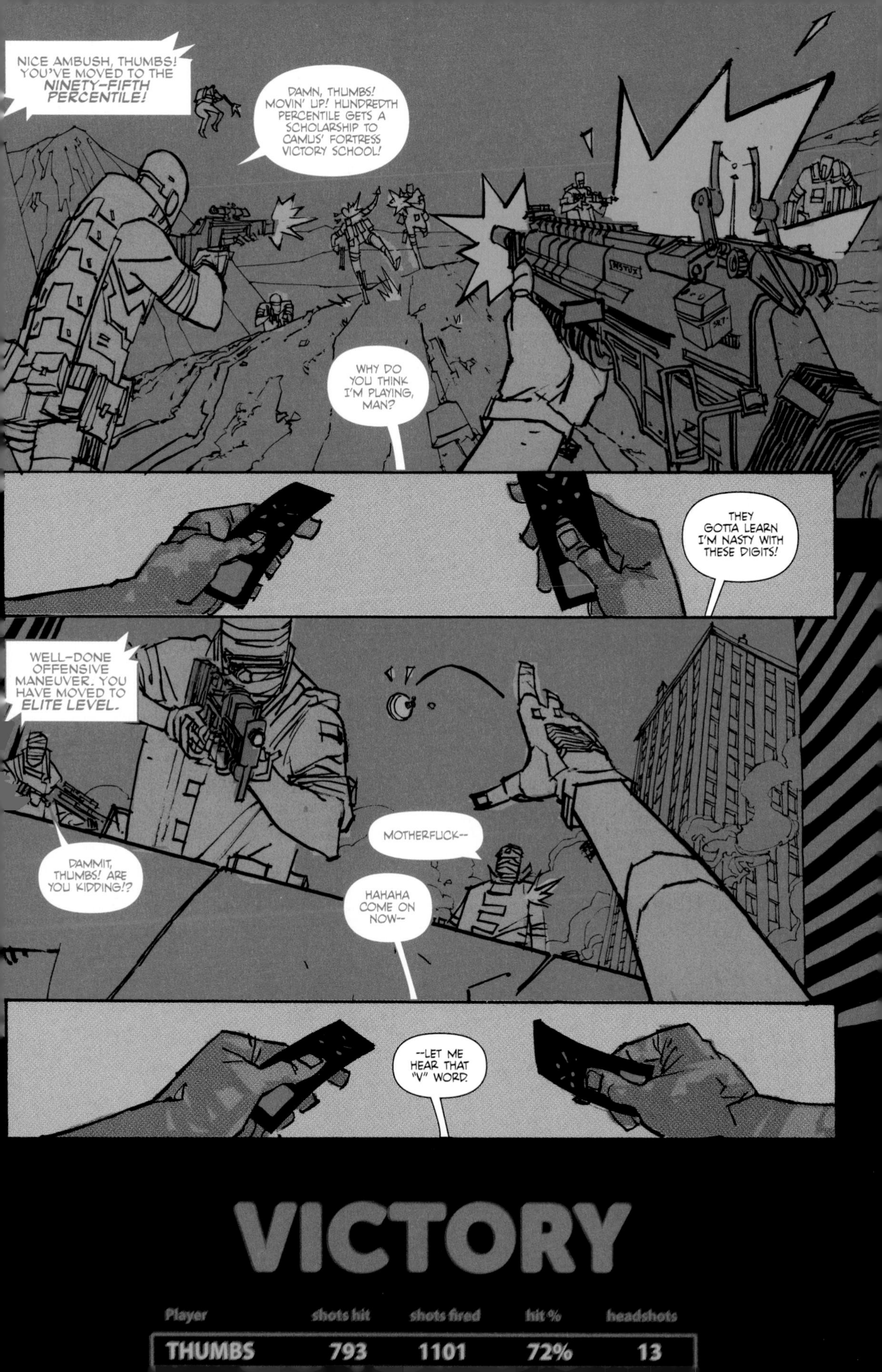
NICE AMBUSH, THUMBS! YOU'VE MOVED TO THE NINETY-FIFTH PERCENTILE!
DAMN, THUMBS! MOVIN' UP! HUNDREDTH PERCENTILE GETS A SCHOLARSHIP TO CAMUS' FORTRESS VICTORY SCHOOL!
WHY DO YOU THINK I'M PLAYING, MAN?
THEY GOTTA LEARN I'M NASTY WITH THESE DIGITS!
WELL-DONE OFFENSIVE MANEUVER. YOU HAVE MOVED TO ELITE LEVEL.
DAMMIT, THUMBS! ARE YOU KIDDING!?
MOTHERFUCK--
HAHAHA COME ON NOW--
--LET ME HEAR THAT "V" WORD.
VICTORY
Player shots hit shots fired hit % headshots
THUMBS 793 1101 72% 13

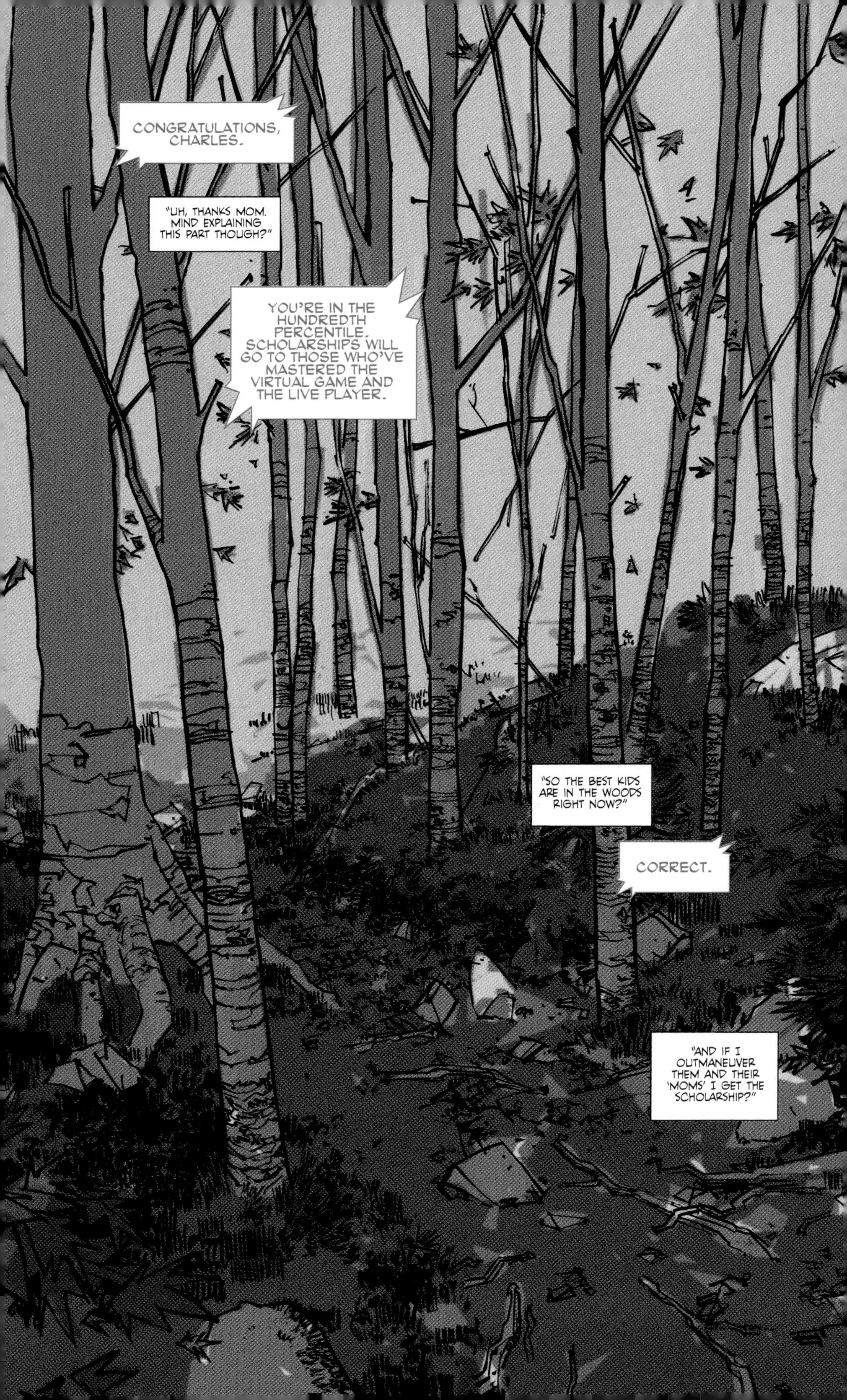
CONGRATULATIONS, CHARLES.
"UH, THANKS MOM. MIND EXPLAINING THIS PART THOUGH?"
YOU'RE IN THE HUNDREDTH PERCENTILE. SCHOLARSHIPS WILL GO TO THOSE WHO'VE MASTERED THE VIRTUAL GAME AND THE LIVE PLAYER.
"SO THE BEST KIDS ARE IN THE WOODS RIGHT NOW?"
CORRECT.
"AND IF I OUTMANEUVER THEM AND THEIR 'MOMS' I GET THE SCHOLARSHIP?"

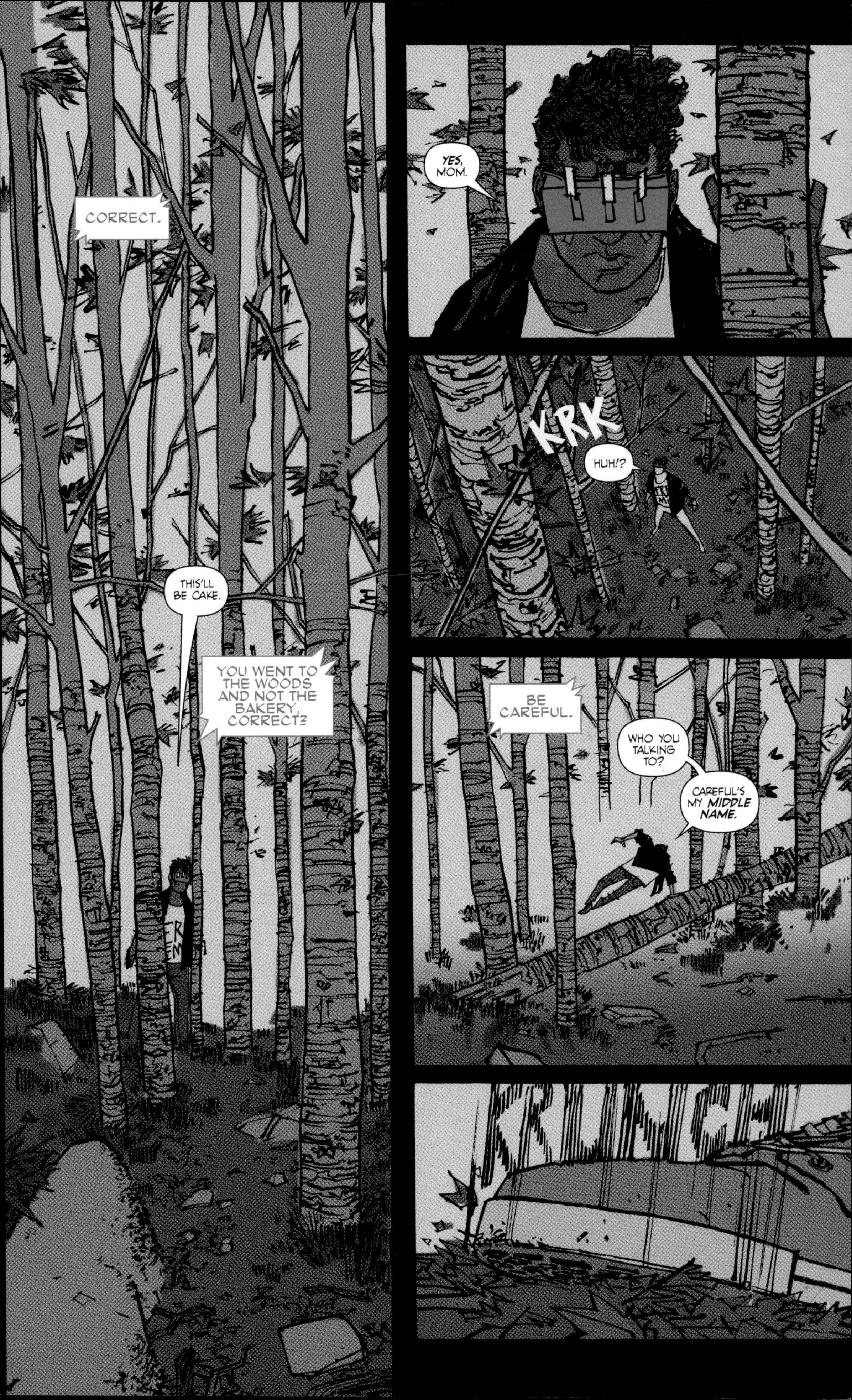
CORRECT.
THIS'LL BE CAKE.
YOU WENT TO THE WOODS AND NOT THE BAKERY, CORRECT?
YES, MOM.
KRK
HUH!?
BE CAREFUL.
WHO YOU TALKING TO?
CAREFUL'S MY MIDDLE NAME.

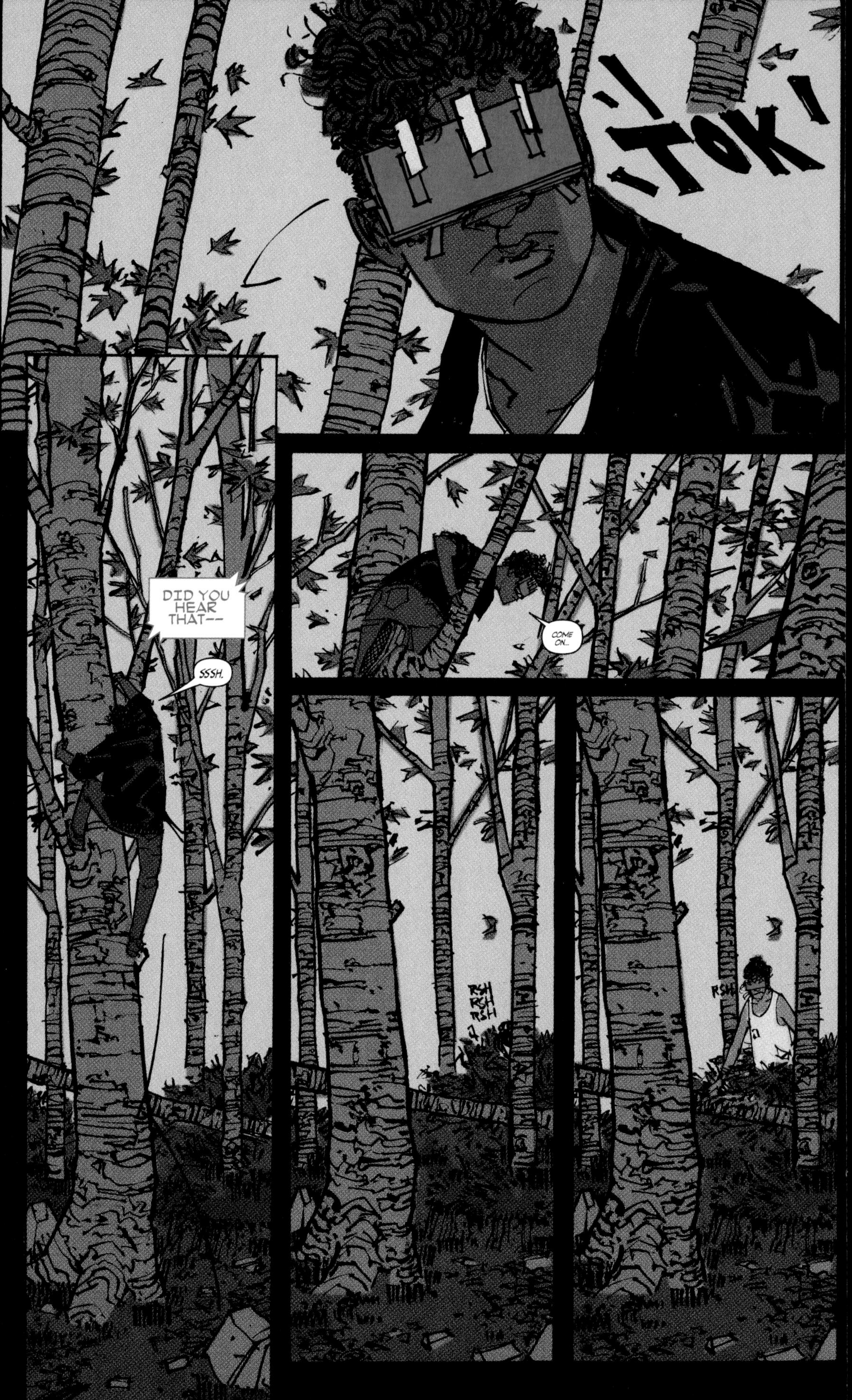
TOK
DID YOU HEAR THAT--
SSSH.
COME ON...
RSH RSH RSH
RSH

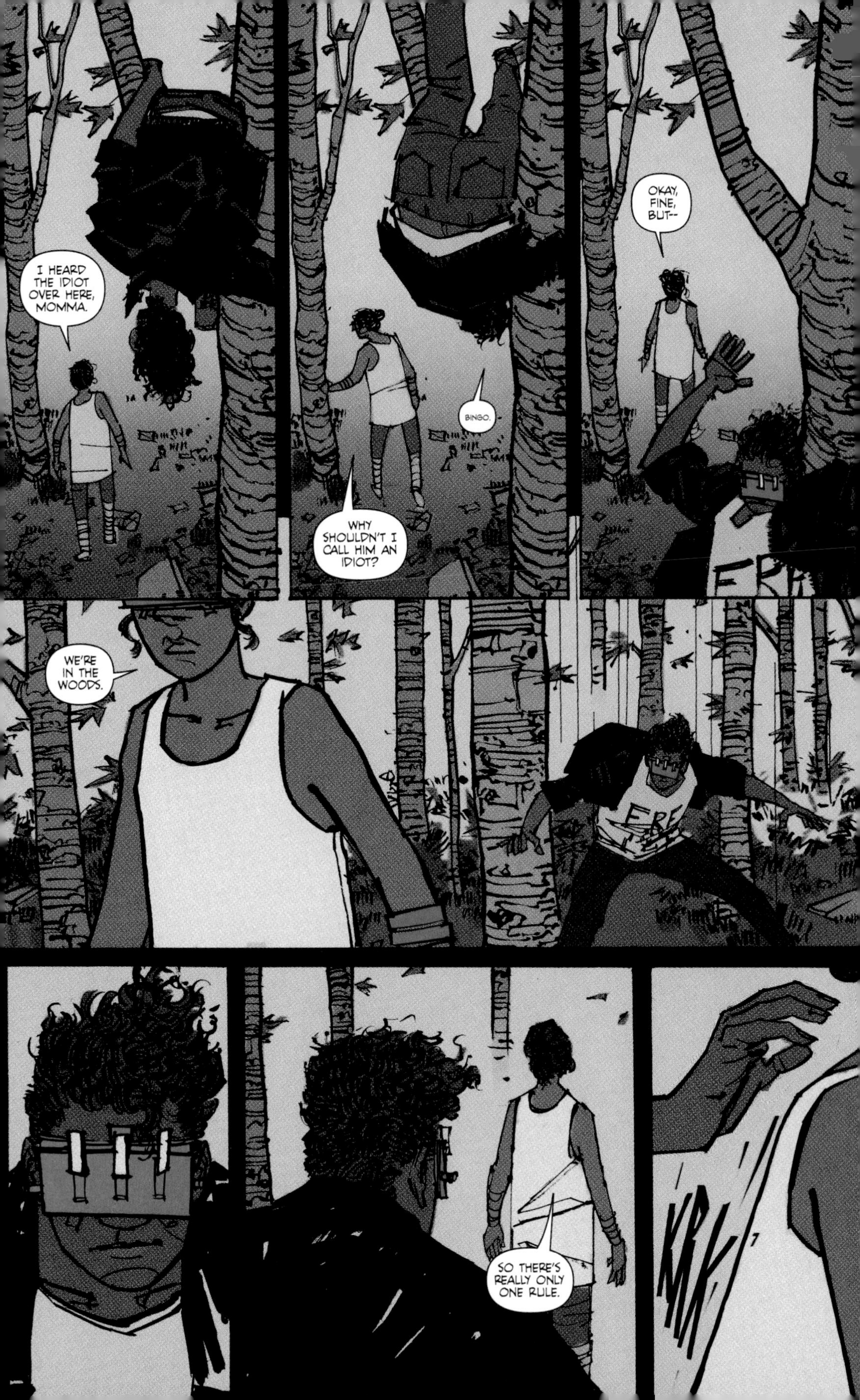

I HEARD THE IDIOT OVER HERE, MOMMA.
WHY SHOULDN'T I CALL HIM AN IDIOT?
BINGO.
OKAY, FINE, BUT--
WE'RE IN THE WOODS.
SO THERE'S REALLY ONLY ONE RULE.
KRK

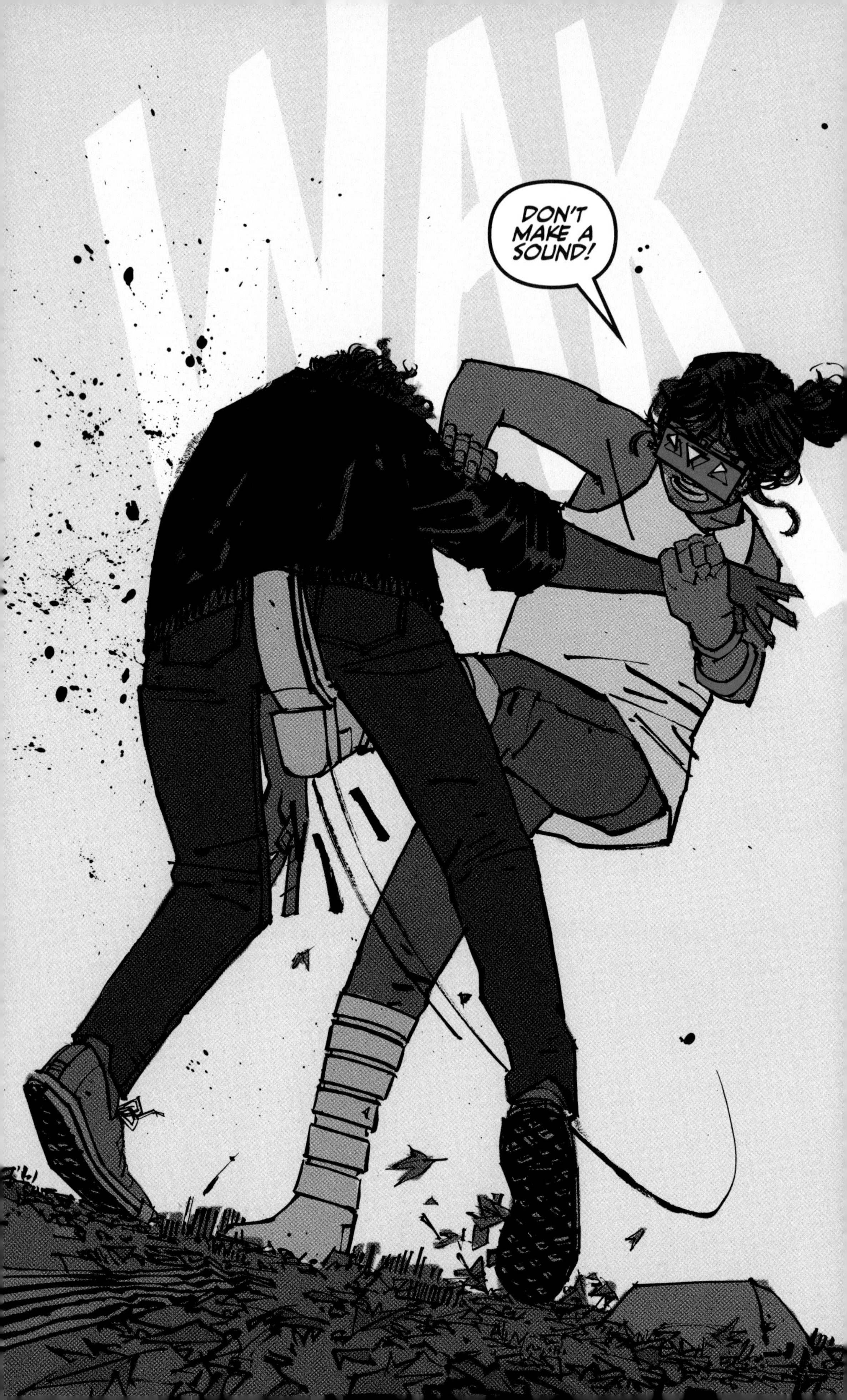
WAK
DON'T MAKE A SOUND!

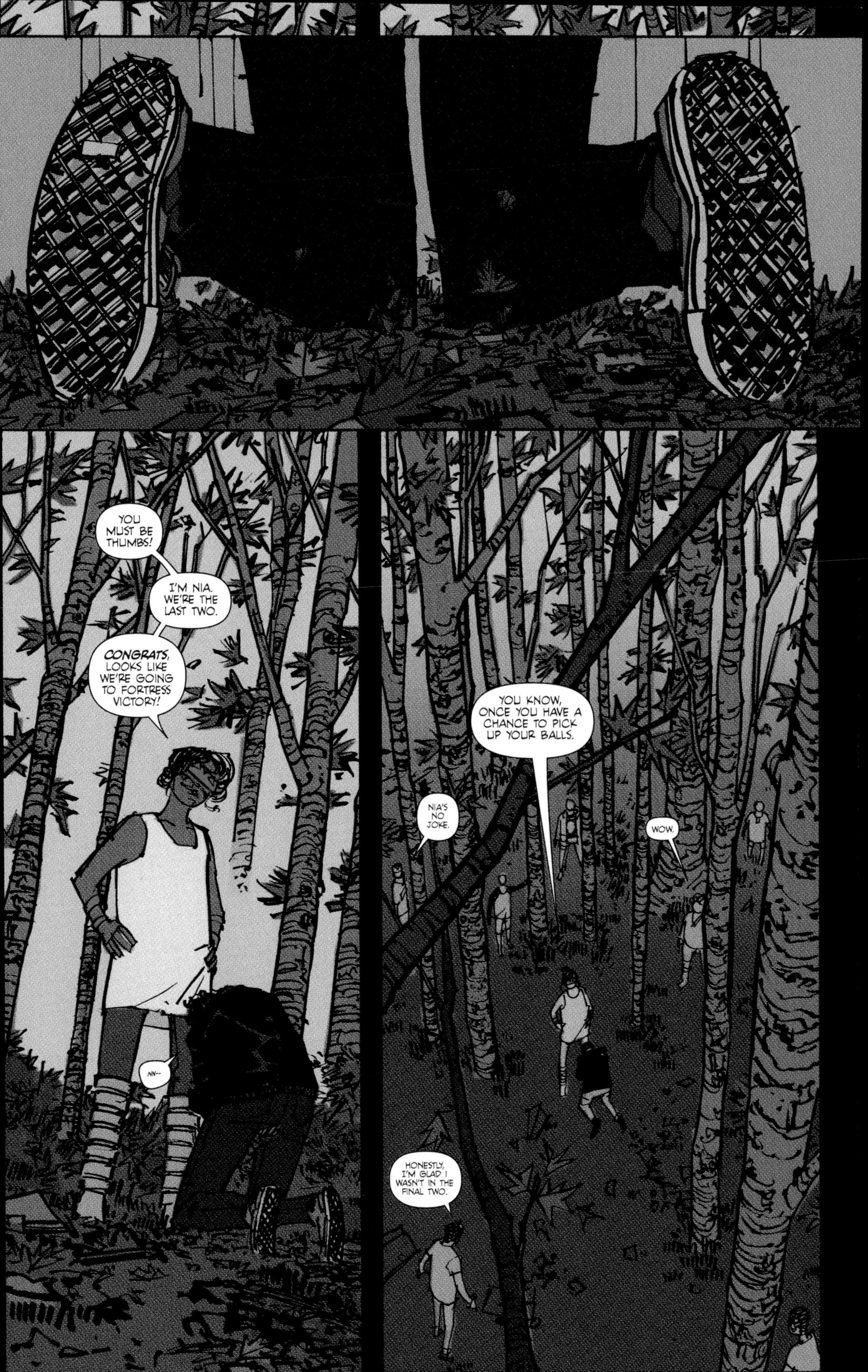
YOU MUST BE THUMBS!
I'M NIA. WE'RE THE LAST TWO.
CONGRATS, LOOKS LIKE WE'RE GOING TO FORTRESS VICTORY!
NN--
YOU KNOW, ONCE YOU HAVE A CHANCE TO PICK UP YOUR BALLS.
NIA'S NO JOKE.
WOW.
HONESTLY, I'M GLAD I WASN'T IN THE FINAL TWO.

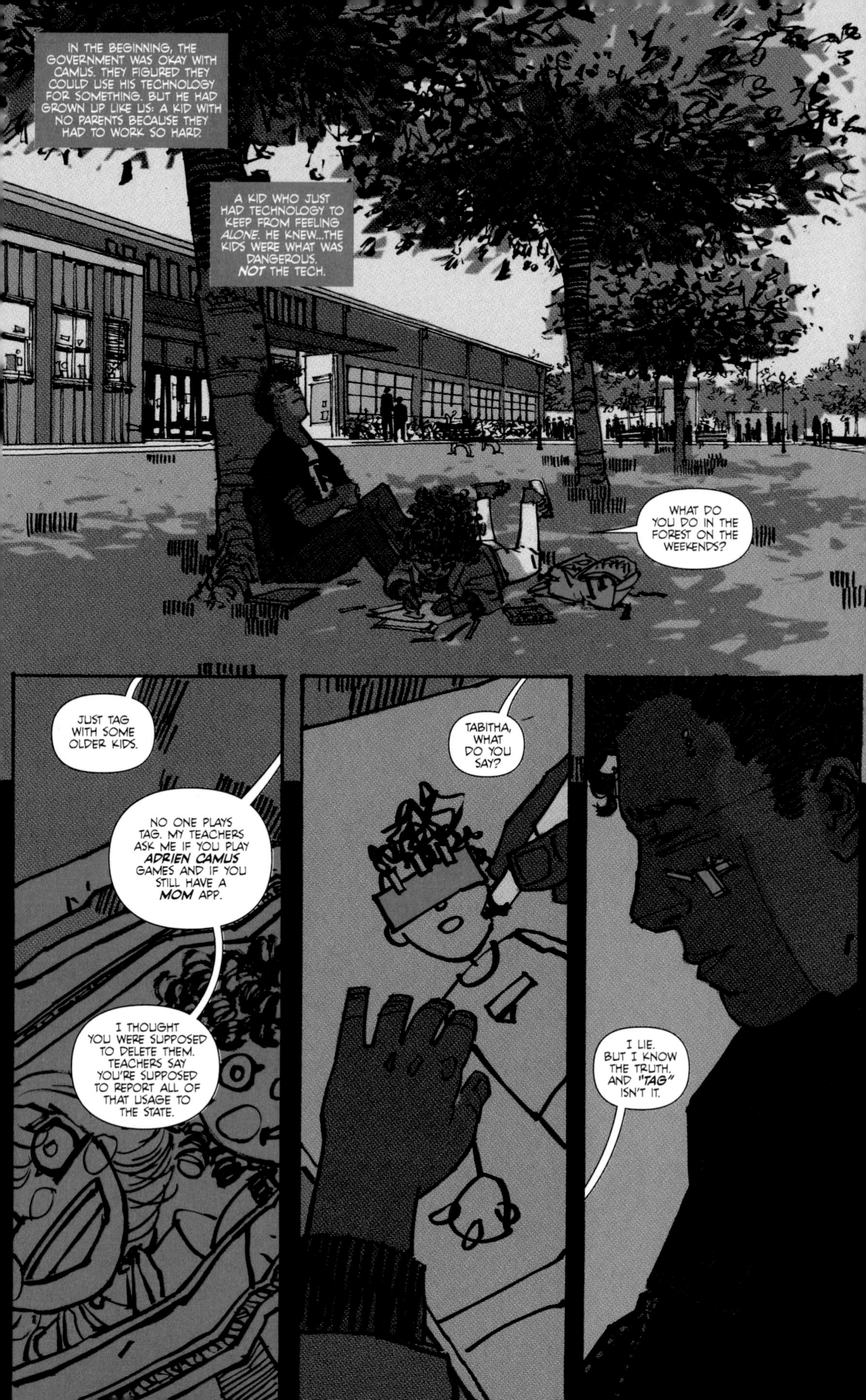
IN THE BEGINNING, THE GOVERNMENT WAS OKAY WITH CAMUS. THEY FIGURED THEY COULD USE HIS TECHNOLOGY FOR SOMETHING. BUT HE HAD GROWN UP LIKE US: A KID WITH NO PARENTS BECAUSE THEY HAD TO WORK SO HARD.
A KID WHO JUST HAD TECHNOLOGY TO KEEP FROM FEELING *ALONE*. HE KNEW...THE KIDS WERE WHAT WAS DANGEROUS. ***NOT*** THE TECH.
WHAT DO YOU DO IN THE FOREST ON THE WEEKENDS?
JUST TAG WITH SOME OLDER KIDS.
NO ONE PLAYS TAG. MY TEACHERS ASK ME IF YOU PLAY ***ADRIEN CAMUS*** GAMES AND IF YOU STILL HAVE A ***MOM*** APP.
I THOUGHT YOU WERE SUPPOSED TO DELETE THEM. TEACHERS SAY YOU'RE SUPPOSED TO REPORT ALL OF THAT USAGE TO THE STATE.
TABITHA, WHAT DO YOU SAY?
I LIE. BUT I KNOW THE TRUTH. AND ***"TAG"*** ISN'T IT.

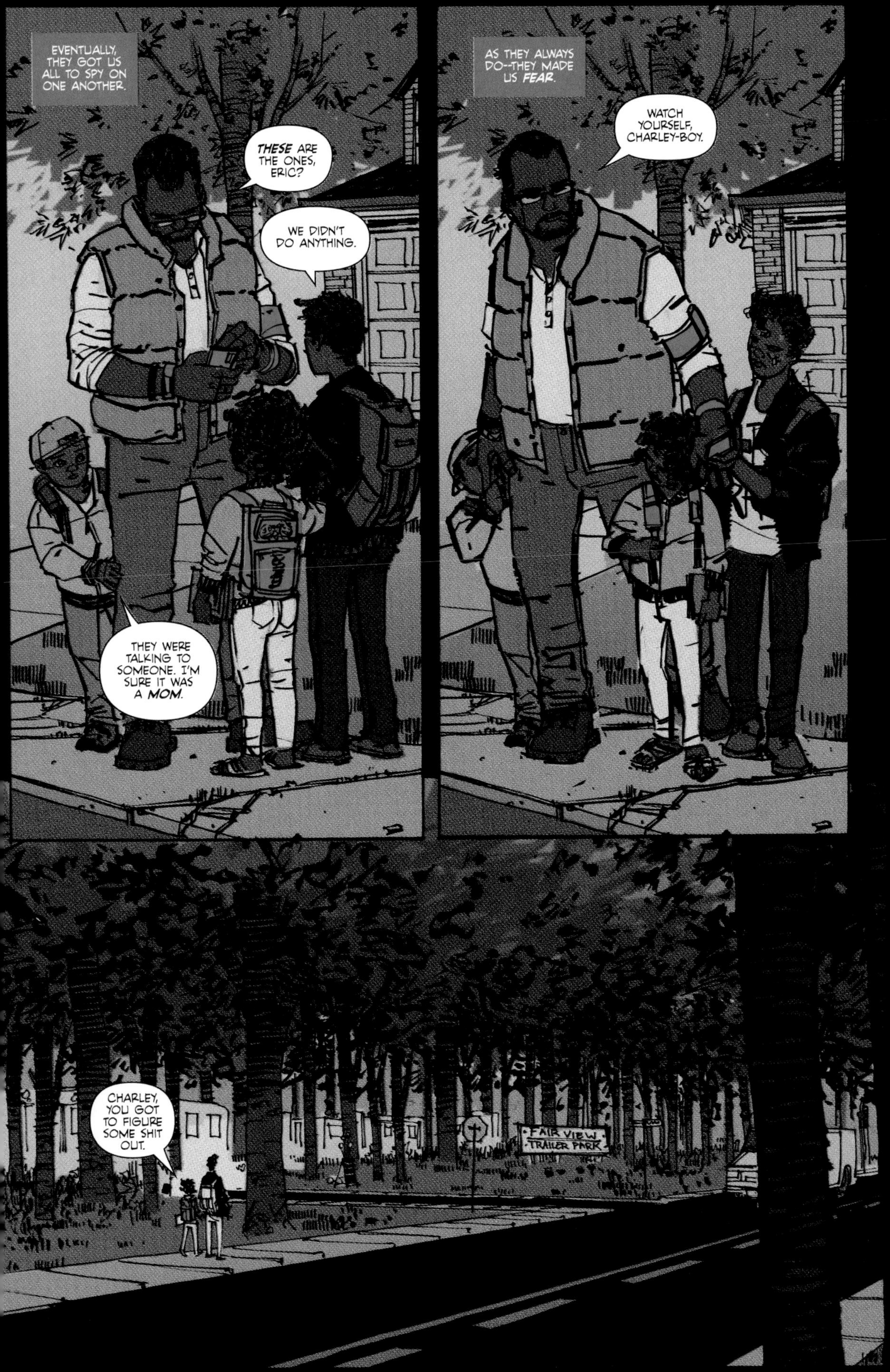
EVENTUALLY, THEY GOT US ALL TO SPY ON ONE ANOTHER.
THESE ARE THE ONES, ERIC?
WE DIDN'T DO ANYTHING.
THEY WERE TALKING TO SOMEONE. I'M SURE IT WAS A MOM.
AS THEY ALWAYS DO--THEY MADE US FEAR.
WATCH YOURSELF, CHARLEY-BOY.
CHARLEY, YOU GOT TO FIGURE SOME SHIT OUT.
FAIR VIEW TRAILER PARK

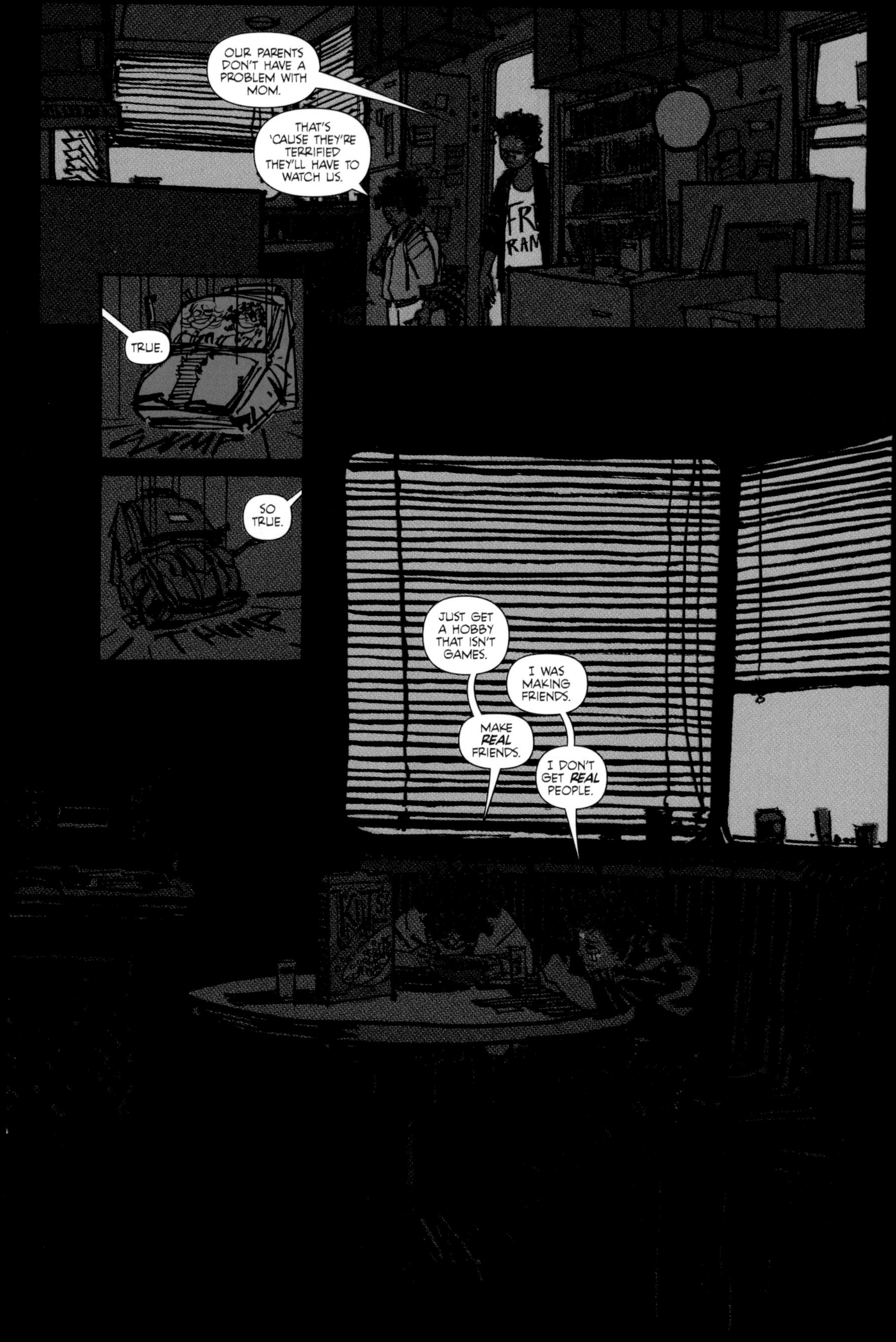
OUR PARENTS DON'T HAVE A PROBLEM WITH MOM.
THAT'S 'CAUSE THEY'RE TERRIFIED THEY'LL HAVE TO WATCH US.
TRUE.
SO TRUE.
JUST GET A HOBBY THAT ISN'T GAMES.
I WAS MAKING FRIENDS.
MAKE *REAL* FRIENDS.
I DON'T GET *REAL* PEOPLE.

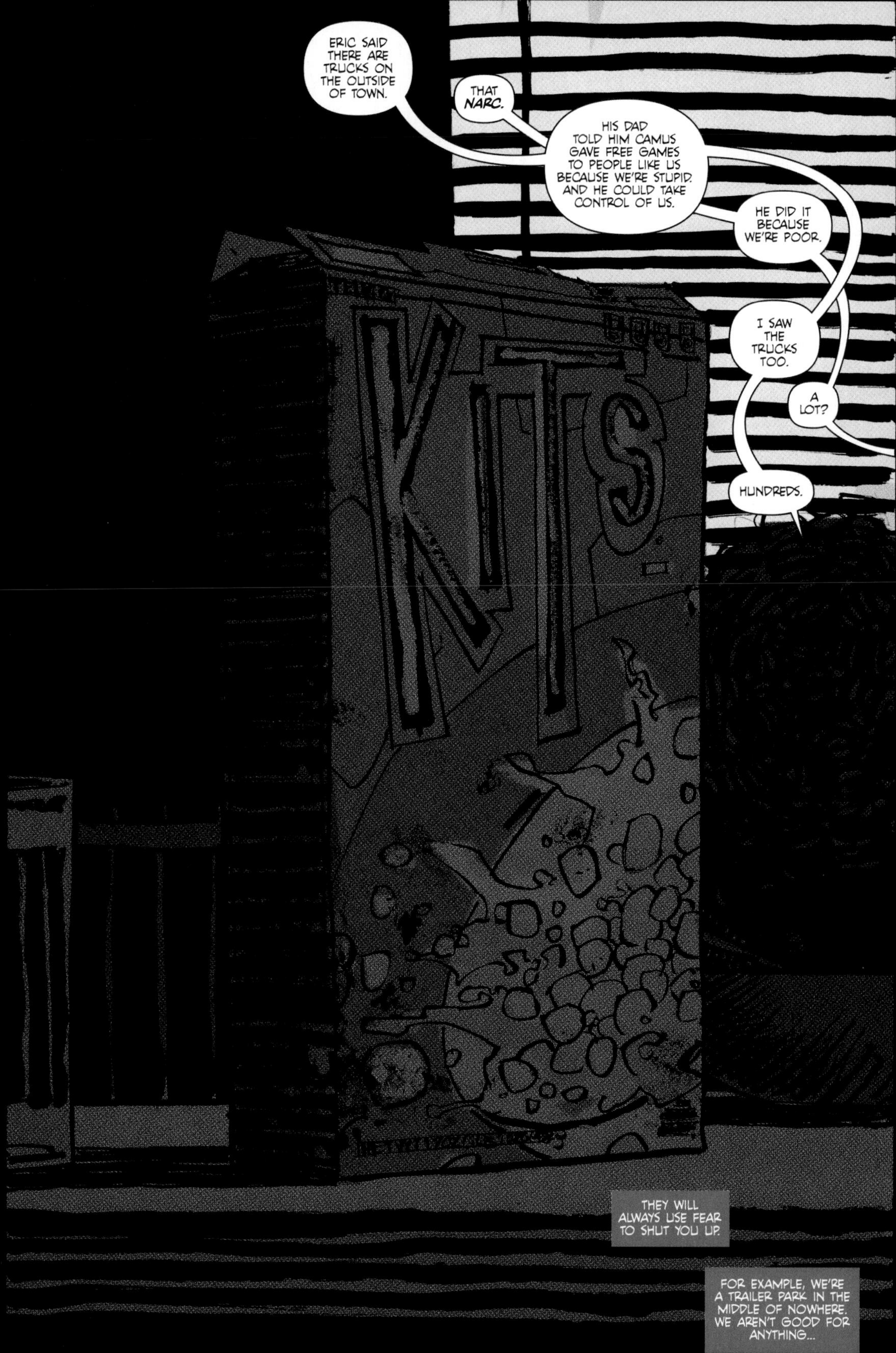
ERIC SAID THERE ARE TRUCKS ON THE OUTSIDE OF TOWN.
THAT *NARC.*
HIS DAD TOLD HIM CAMUS GAVE FREE GAMES TO PEOPLE LIKE US BECAUSE WE'RE STUPID. AND HE COULD TAKE CONTROL OF US.
HE DID IT BECAUSE WE'RE POOR.
I SAW THE TRUCKS TOO.
A LOT?
HUNDREDS.
KITS
THEY WILL ALWAYS USE FEAR TO SHUT YOU UP.
FOR EXAMPLE, WE'RE A TRAILER PARK IN THE MIDDLE OF NOWHERE. WE AREN'T GOOD FOR ANYTHING...

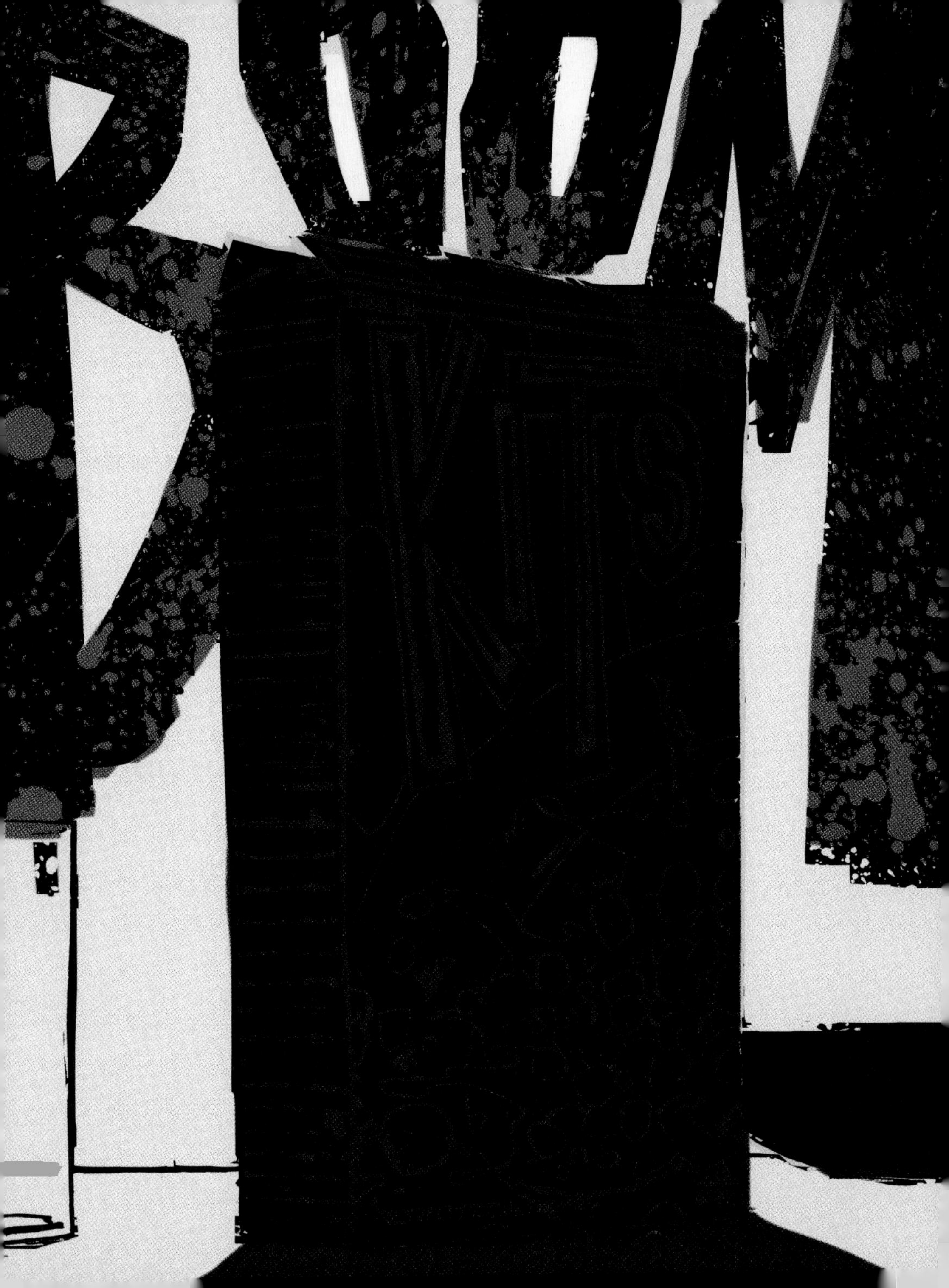

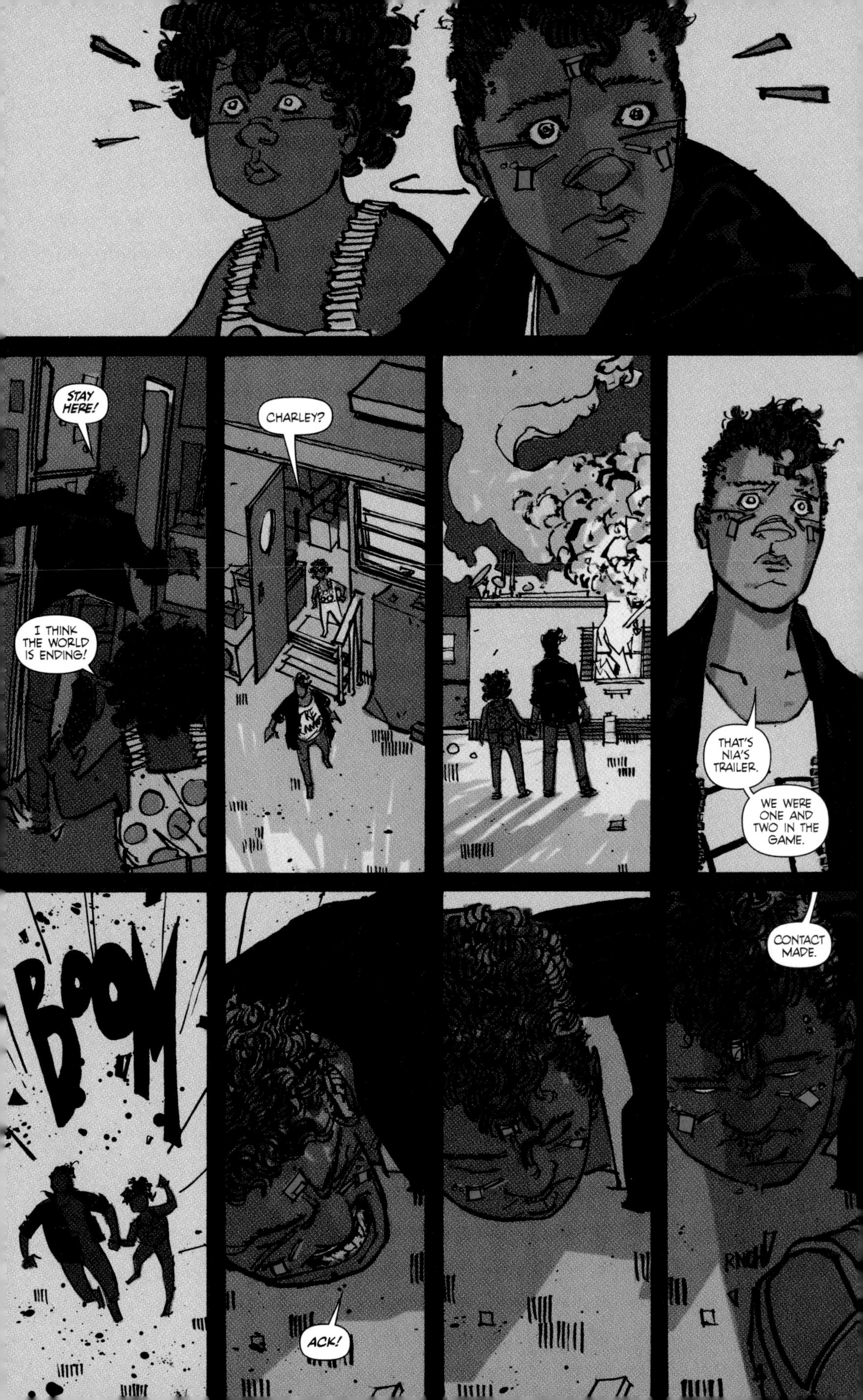
STAY HERE!
I THINK THE WORLD IS ENDING!
CHARLEY?
THAT'S NIA'S TRAILER.
WE WERE ONE AND TWO IN THE GAME.
BOOM
ACK!
CONTACT MADE.

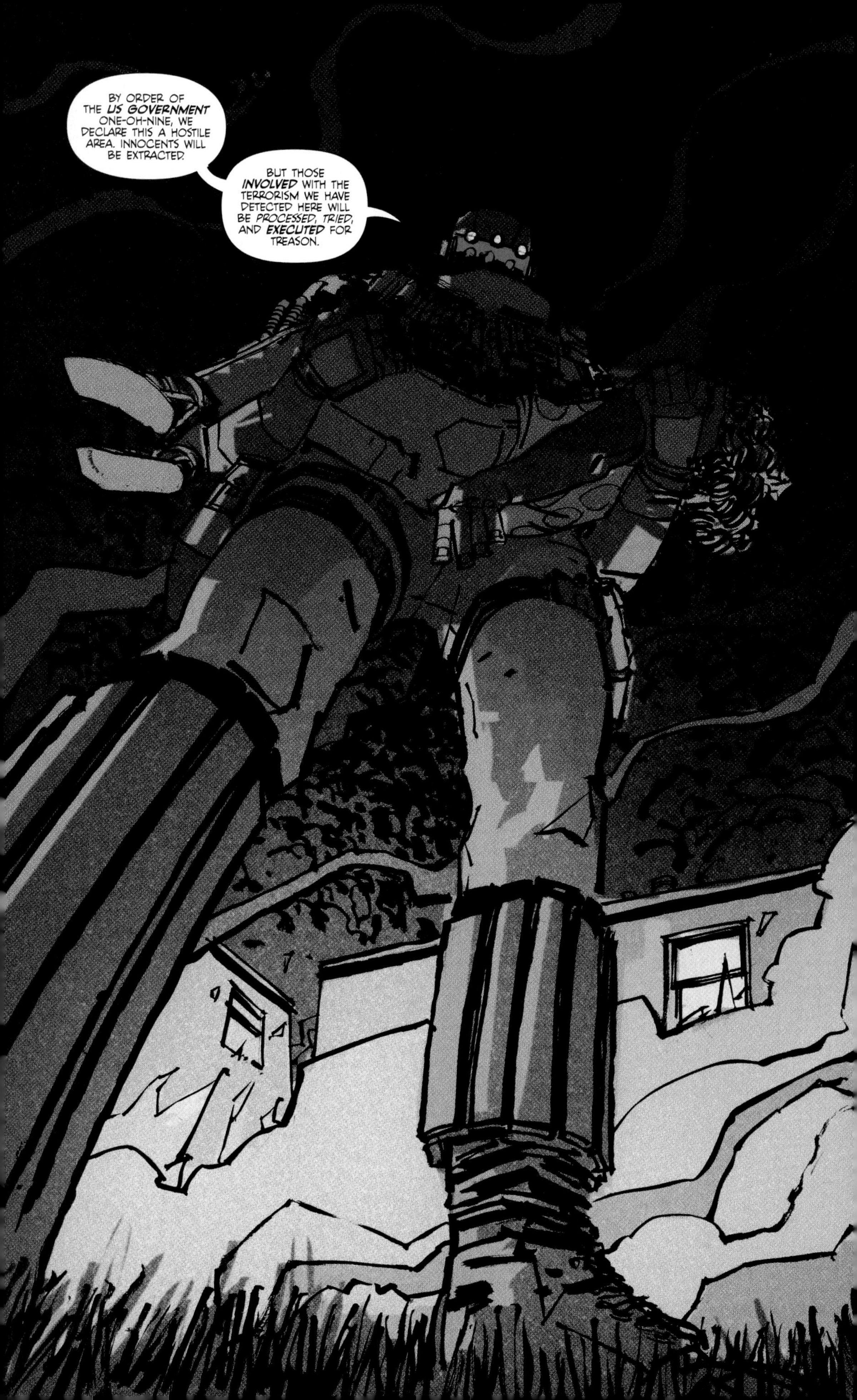
BY ORDER OF THE US GOVERNMENT ONE-OH-NINE, WE DECLARE THIS A HOSTILE AREA. INNOCENTS WILL BE EXTRACTED.
BUT THOSE INVOLVED WITH THE TERRORISM WE HAVE DETECTED HERE WILL BE PROCESSED, TRIED, AND EXECUTED FOR TREASON.

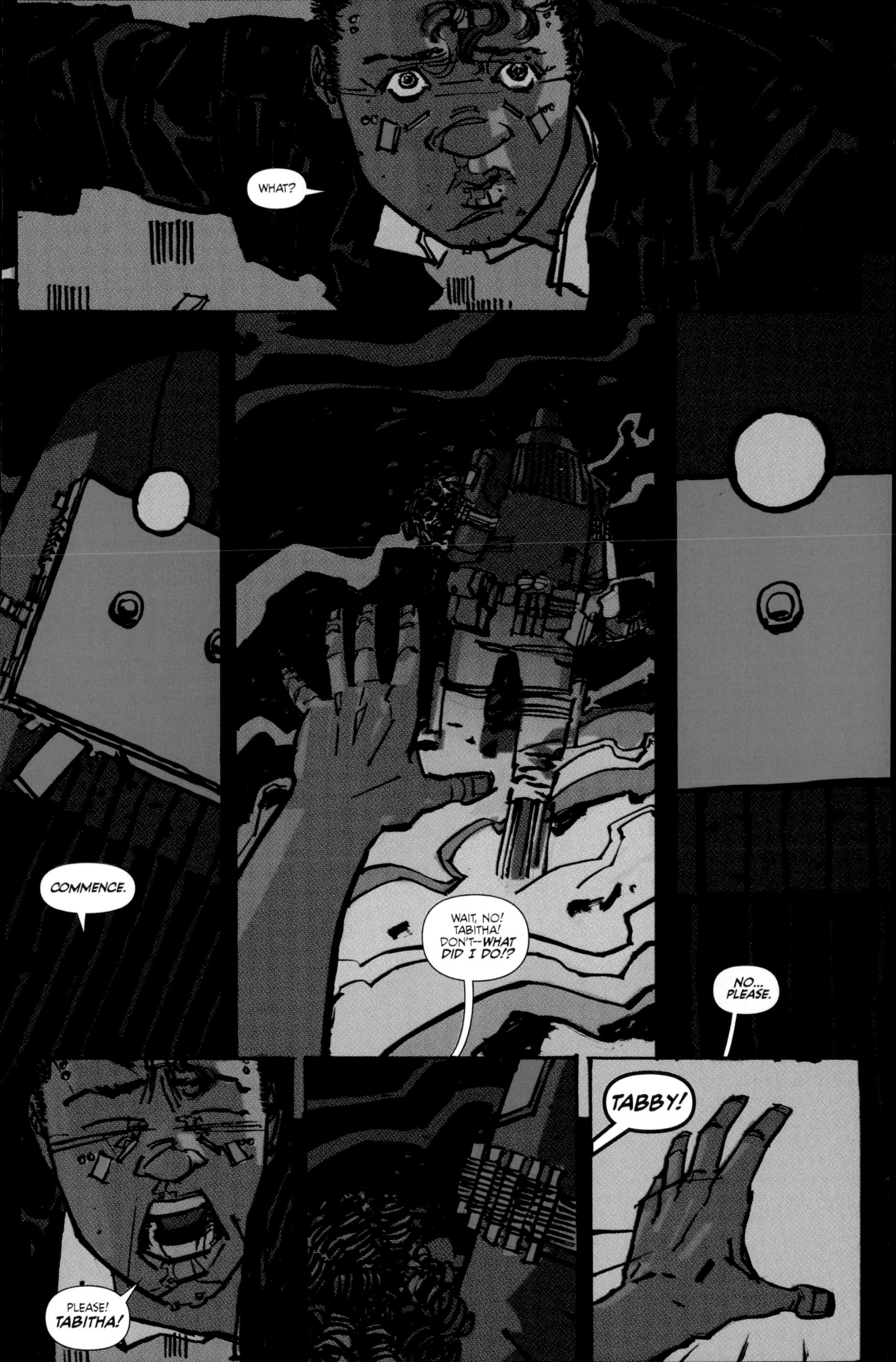
WHAT?
COMMENCE.
WAIT, NO! TABITHA! DON'T--WHAT DID I DO!?
NO... PLEASE.
PLEASE! TABITHA!
TABBY!

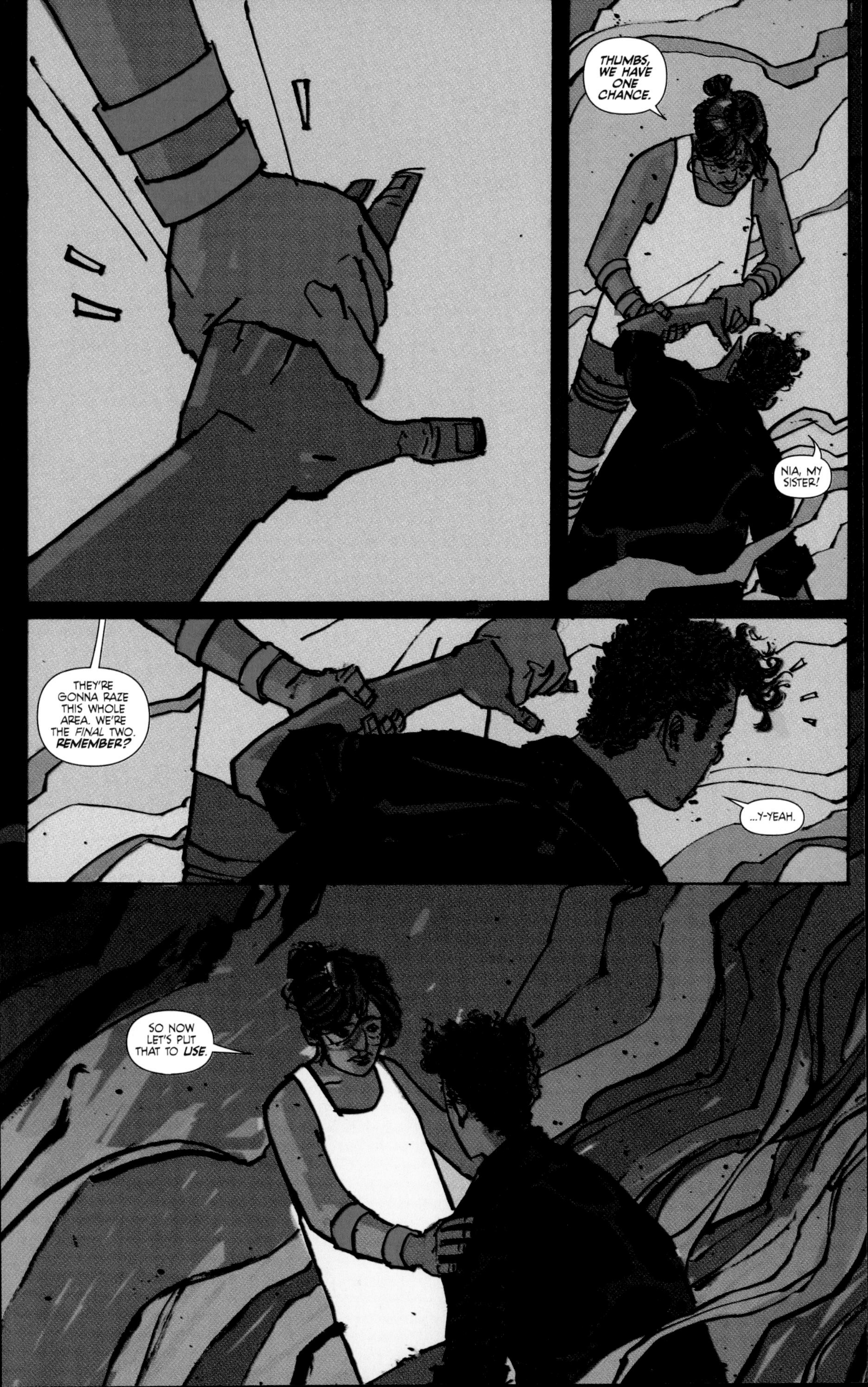
THUMBS, WE HAVE ONE CHANCE.
NIA, MY SISTER!
THEY'RE GONNA RAZE THIS WHOLE AREA. WE'RE THE *FINAL* TWO. ***REMEMBER?***
...Y-YEAH.
SO NOW LET'S PUT THAT TO ***USE***.

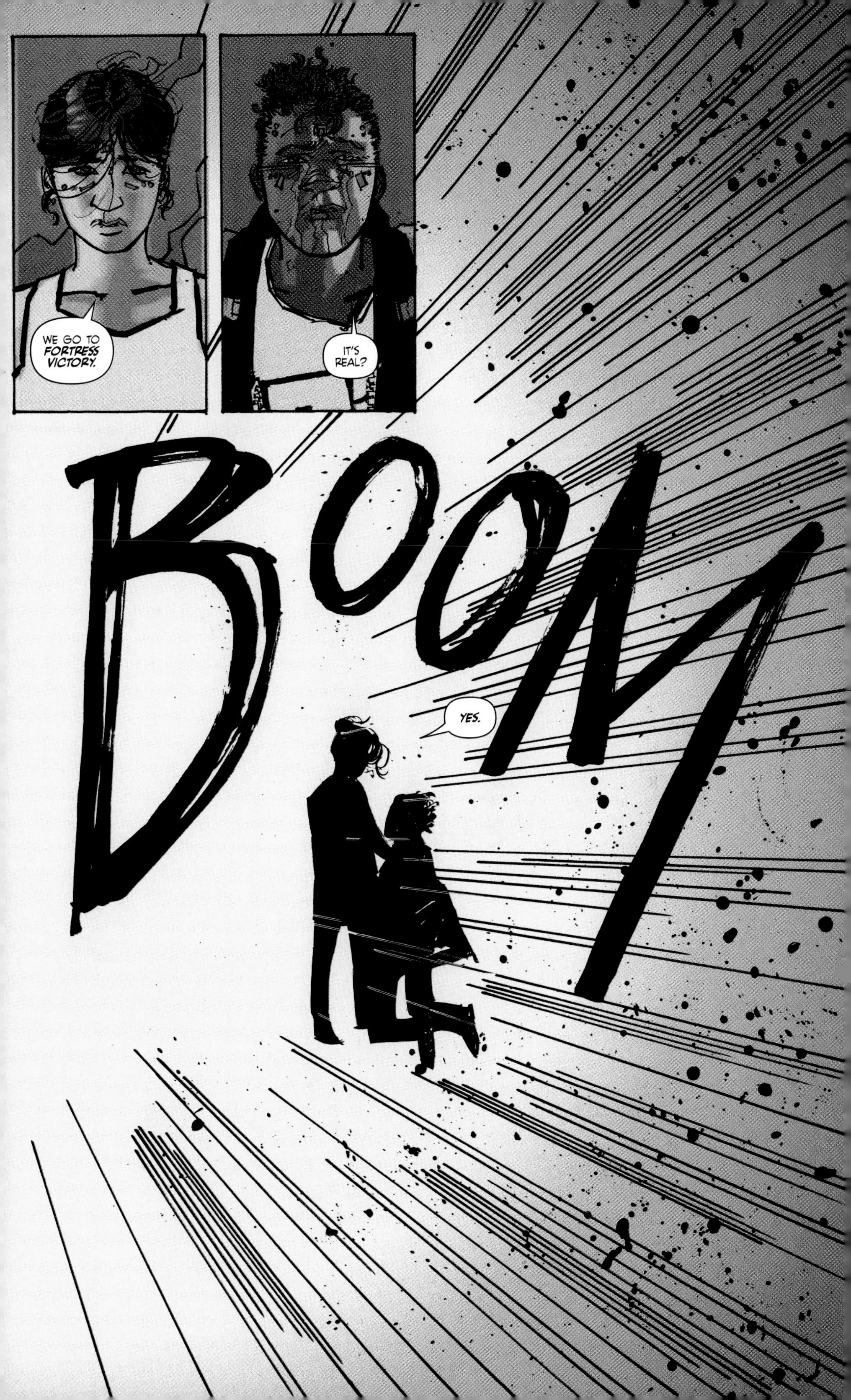
WE GO TO FORTRESS VICTORY.
IT'S REAL?
BOOM
YES.

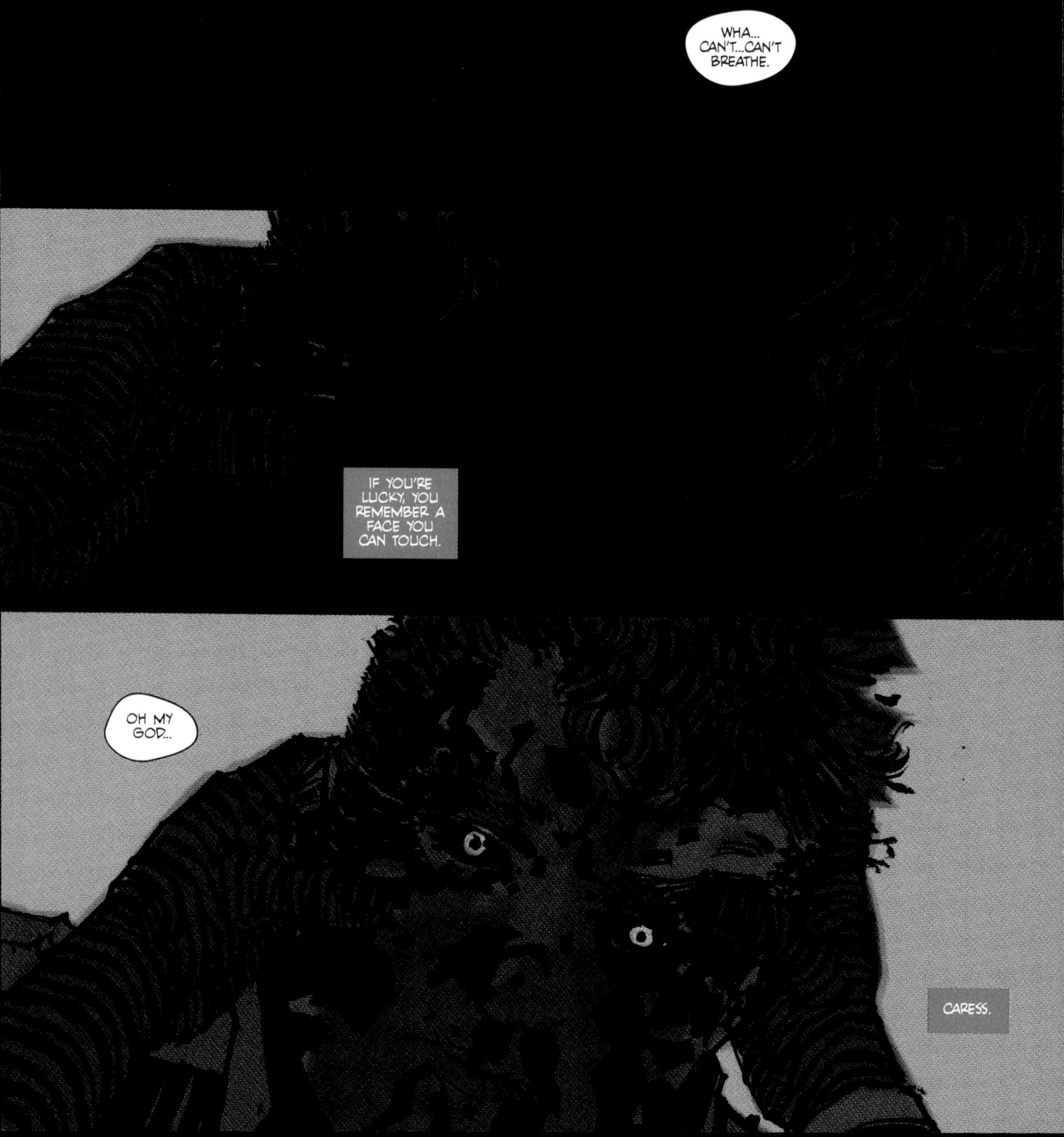
WHA... CAN'T...CAN'T BREATHE.
IF YOU'RE LUCKY, YOU REMEMBER A FACE YOU CAN TOUCH.
OH MY GOD...
CARESS.

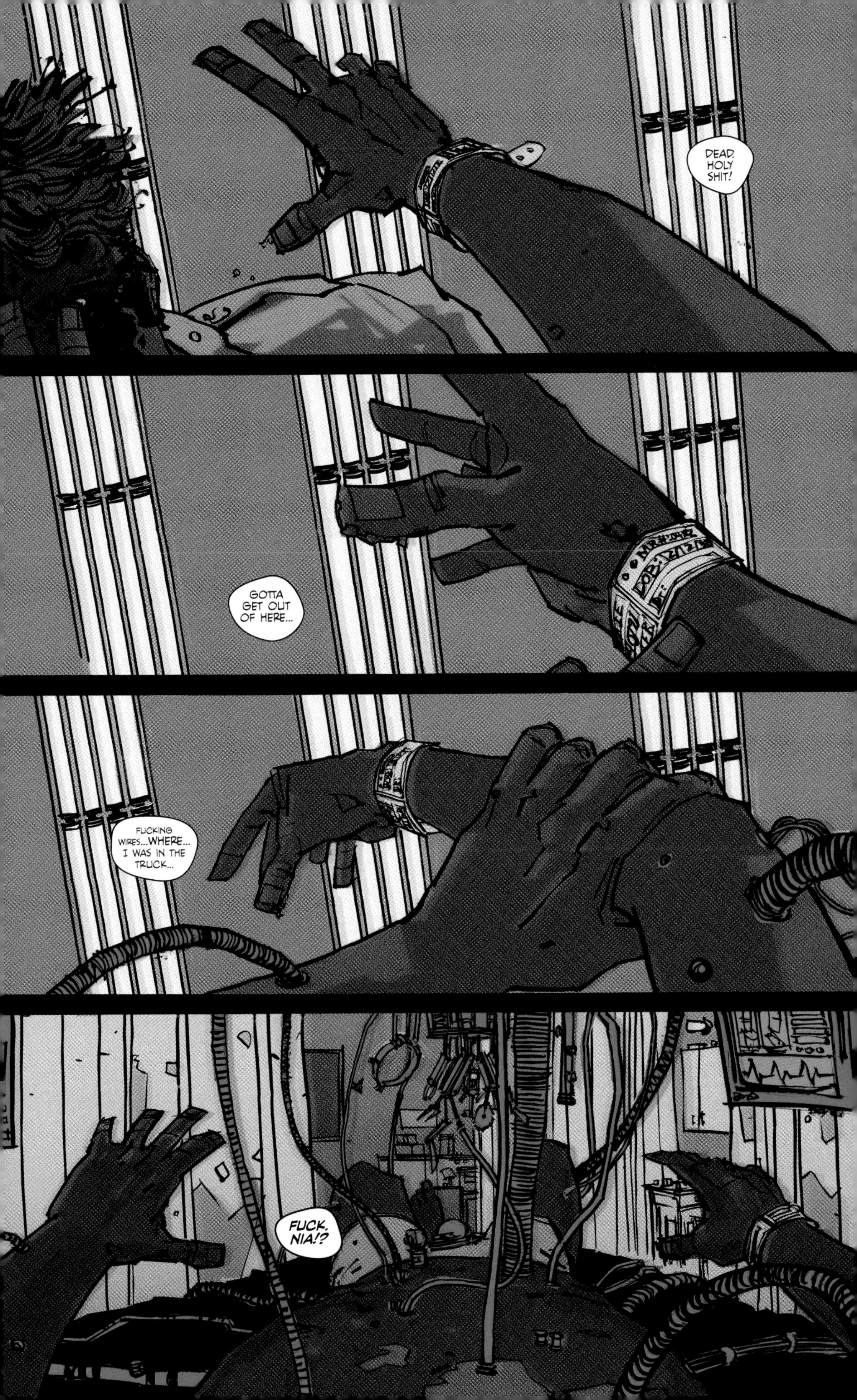
DEAD. HOLY SHIT!
GOTTA GET OUT OF HERE...
FUCKING WIRES...WHERE... I WAS IN THE TRUCK...
FUCK. NIA!?

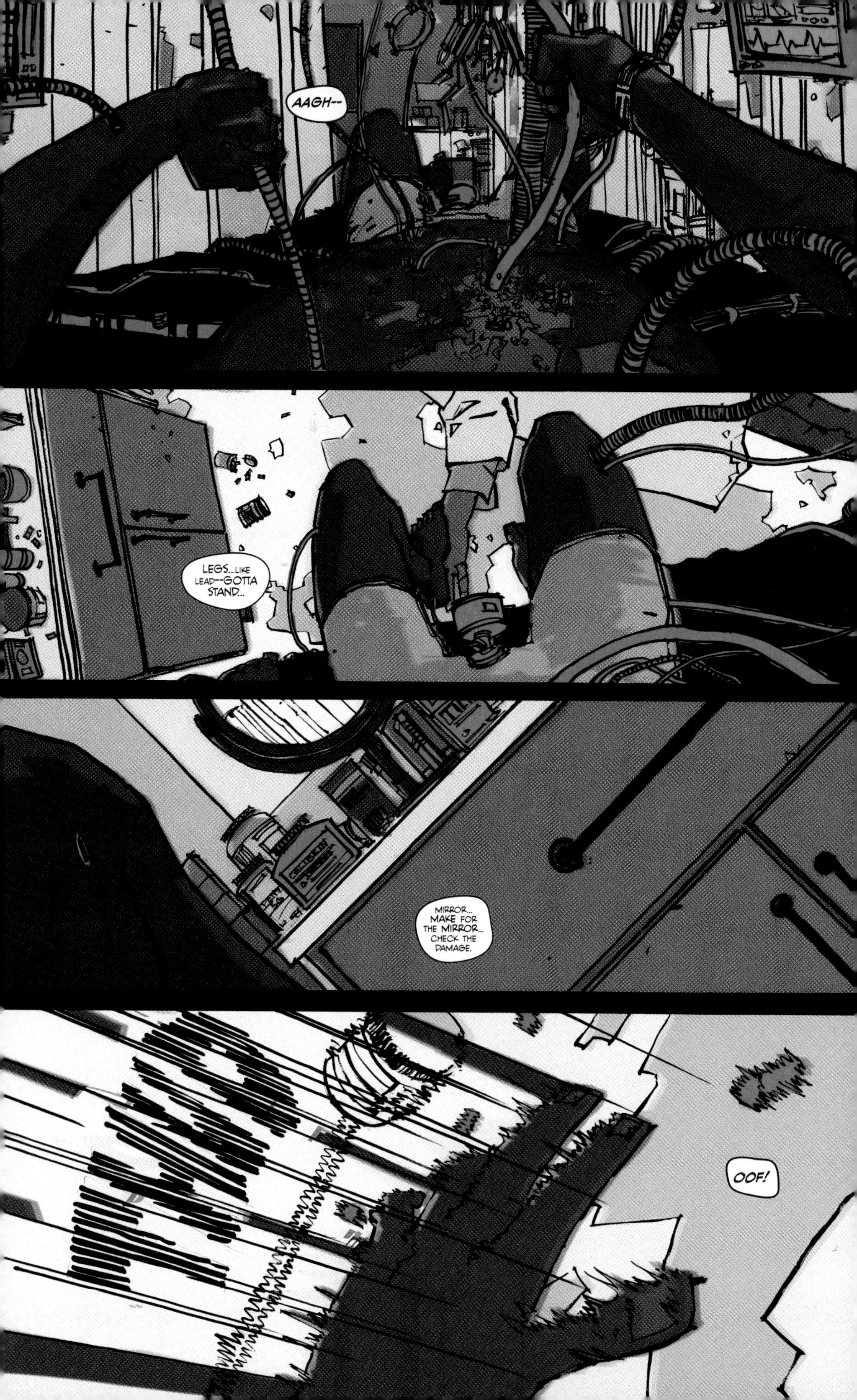
AAGH--
LEGS...LIKE LEAD--GOTTA STAND...
MIRROR... MAKE FOR THE MIRROR... CHECK THE DAMAGE.
OOF!

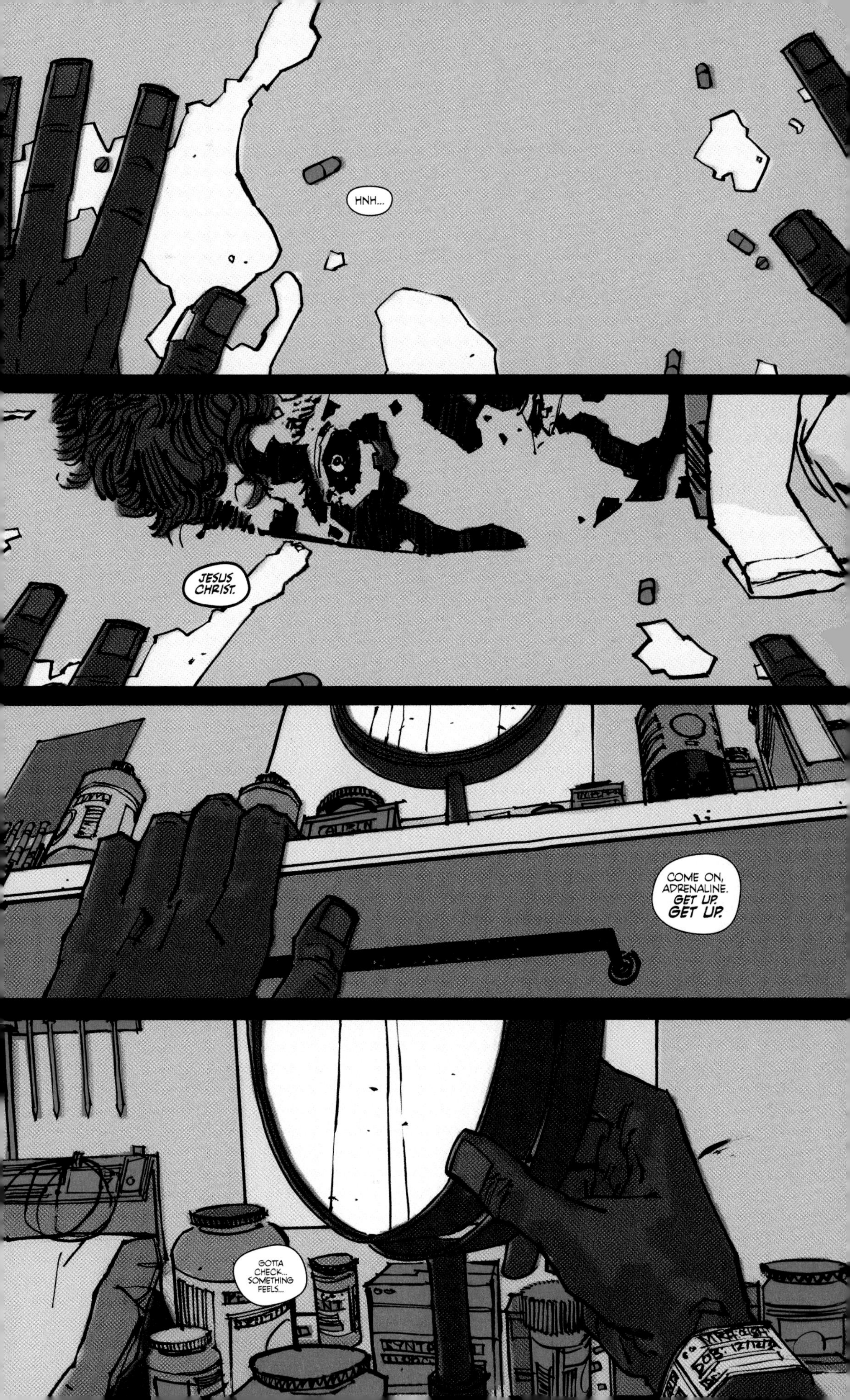
HNH...
JESUS CHRIST.
COME ON, ADRENALINE. GET UP. GET UP.
GOTTA CHECK... SOMETHING FEELS...

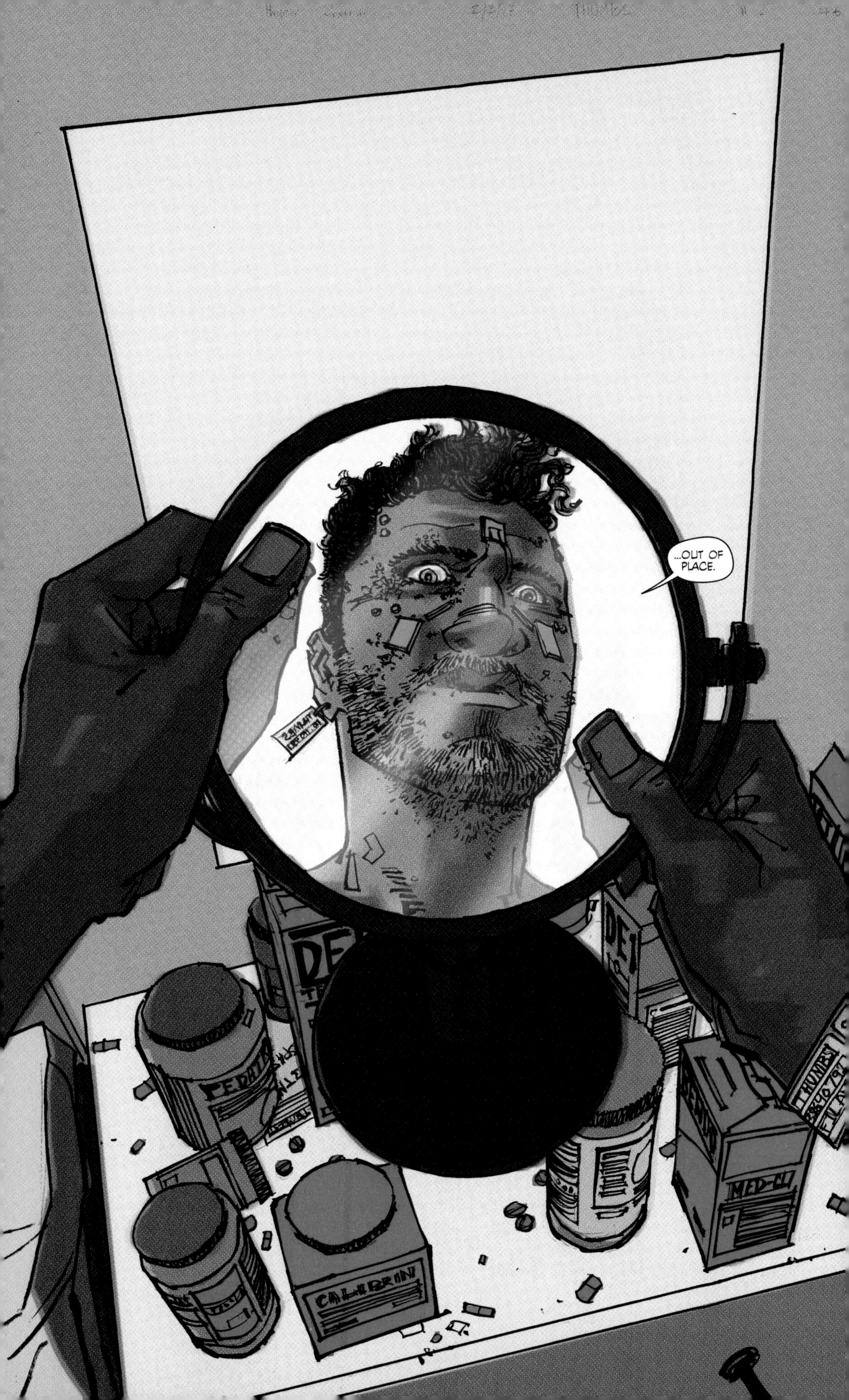
...OUT OF PLACE.

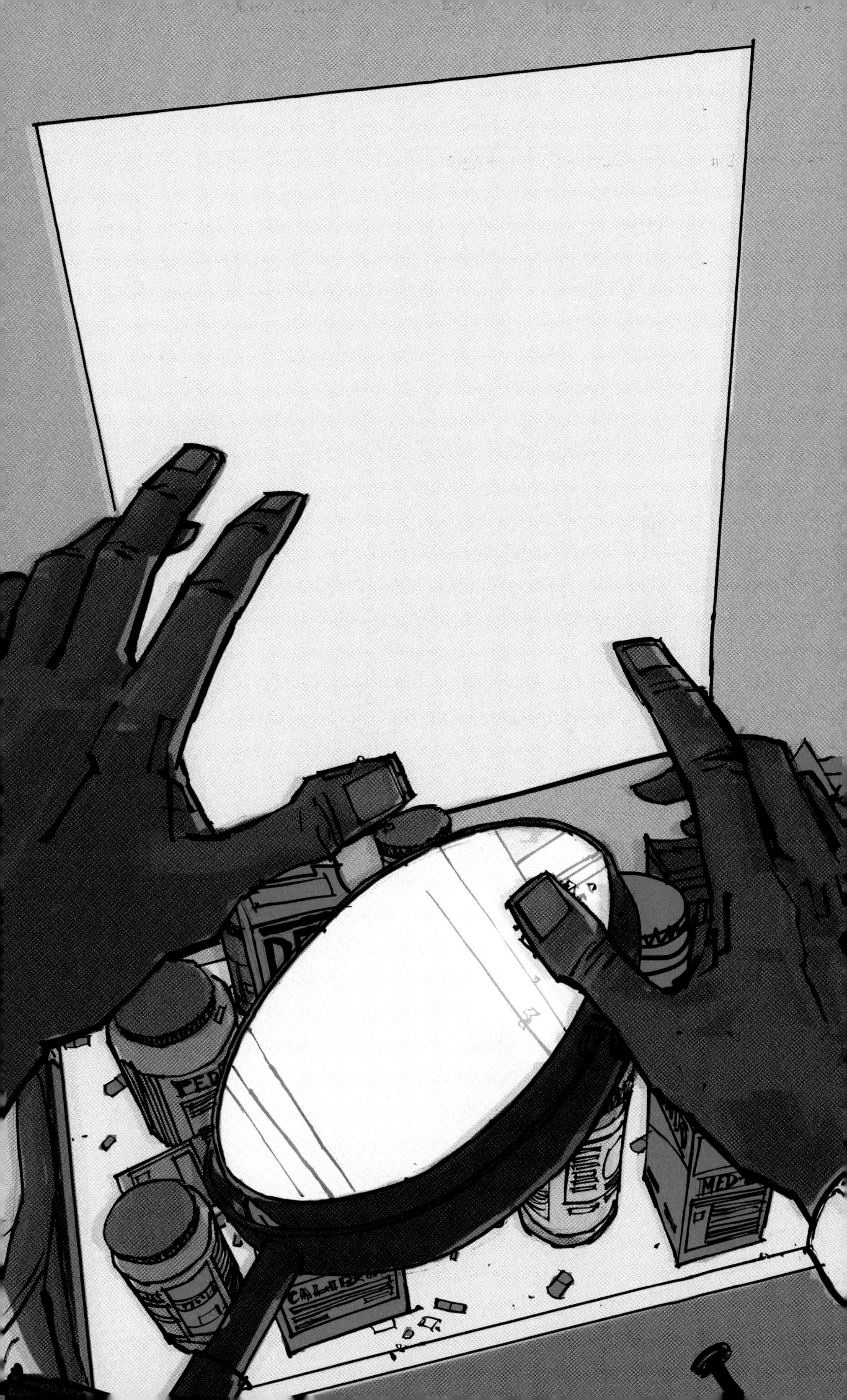

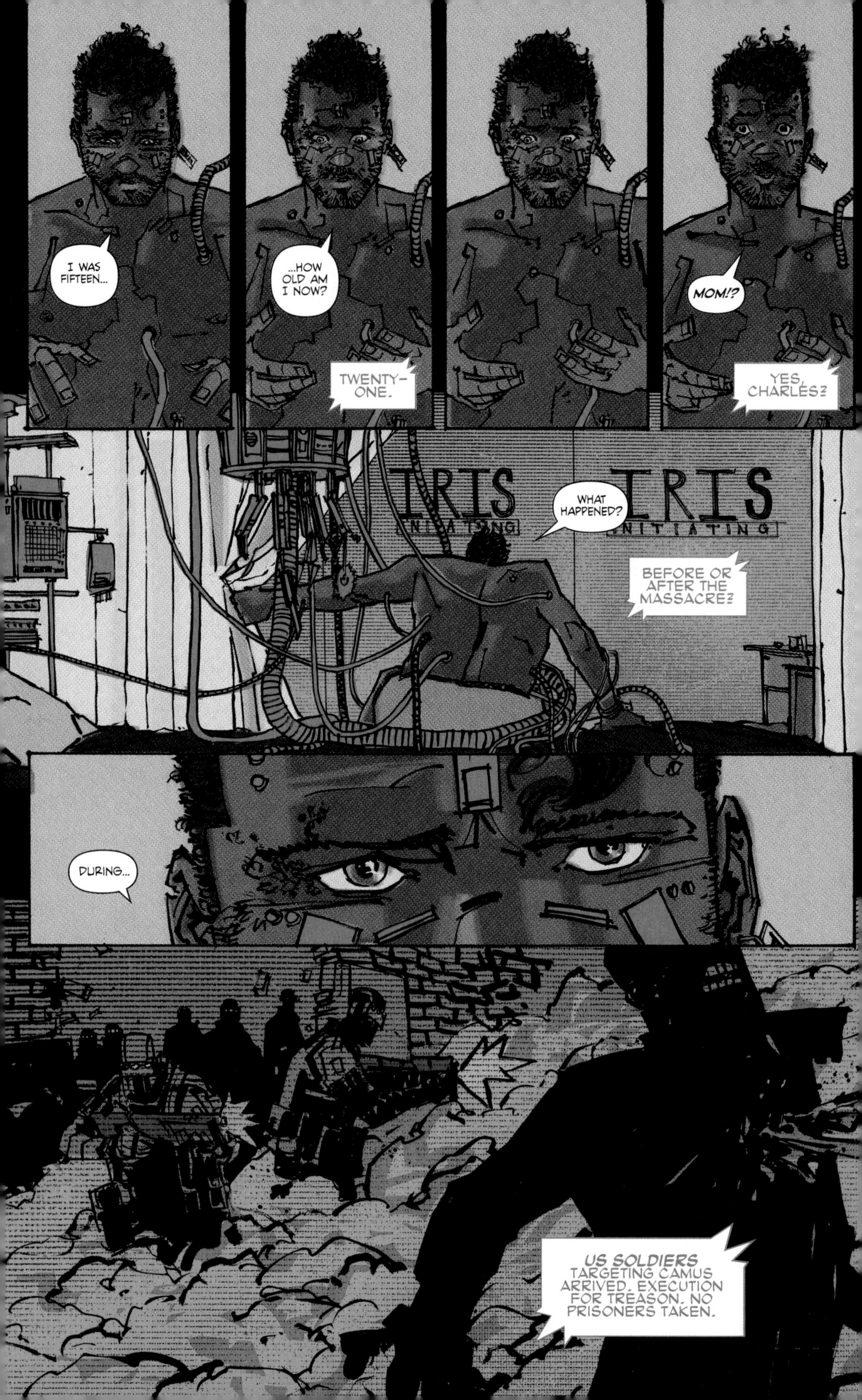
I WAS FIFTEEN...
...HOW OLD AM I NOW?
TWENTY-ONE.
MOM!?
YES, CHARLES?
IRIS
INITIATING
IRIS
INITIATING
WHAT HAPPENED?
BEFORE OR AFTER THE MASSACRE?
DURING...
US SOLDIERS TARGETING CAMUS ARRIVED. EXECUTION FOR TREASON. NO PRISONERS TAKEN.

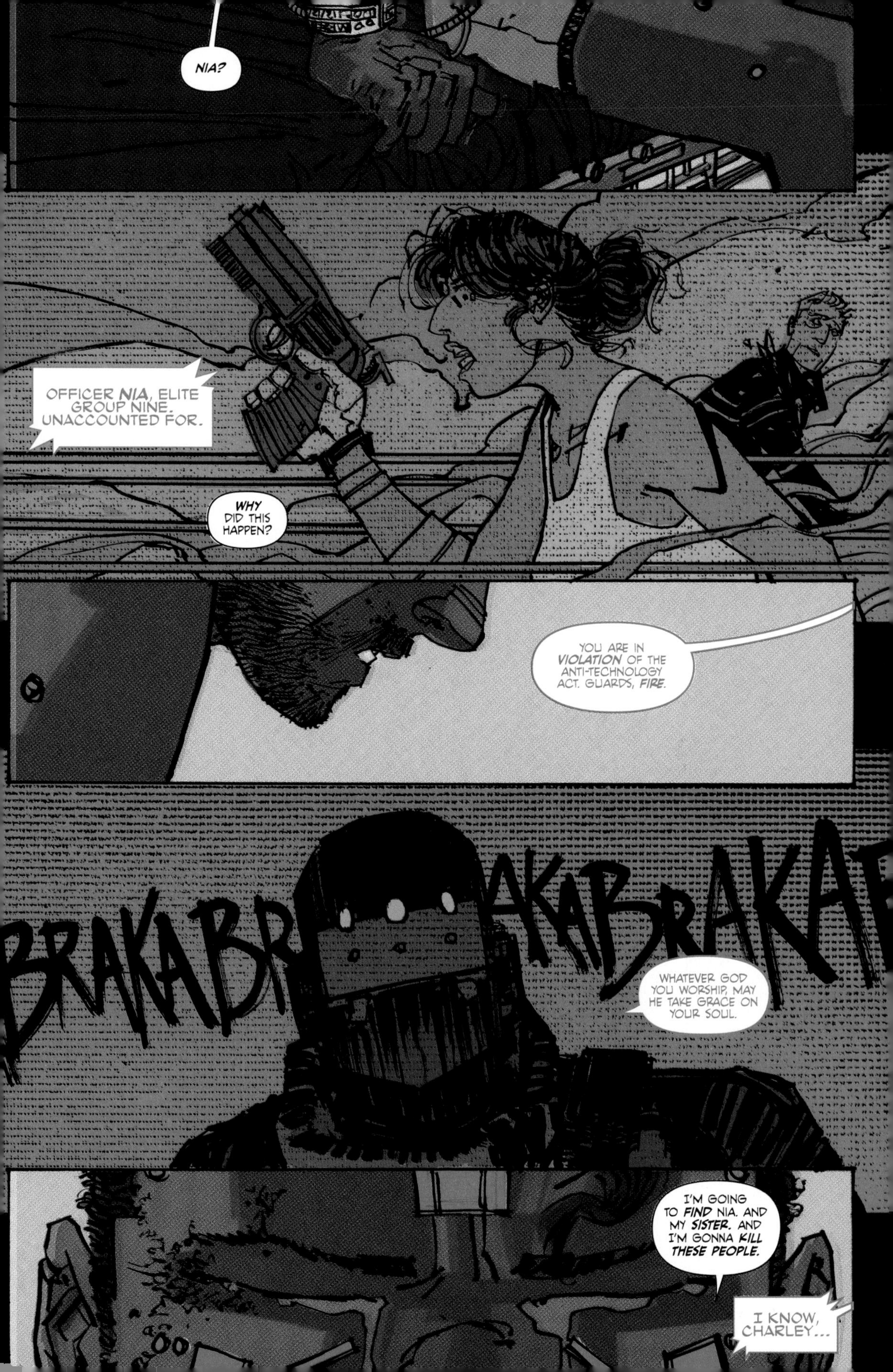
NIA?
OFFICER NIA, ELITE GROUP NINE. UNACCOUNTED FOR.
WHY DID THIS HAPPEN?
YOU ARE IN VIOLATION OF THE ANTI-TECHNOLOGY ACT. GUARDS, FIRE.
BRAKABRAKABRAKA
WHATEVER GOD YOU WORSHIP, MAY HE TAKE GRACE ON YOUR SOUL.
I'M GOING TO FIND NIA. AND MY SISTER. AND I'M GONNA KILL THESE PEOPLE.
I KNOW, CHARLEY...

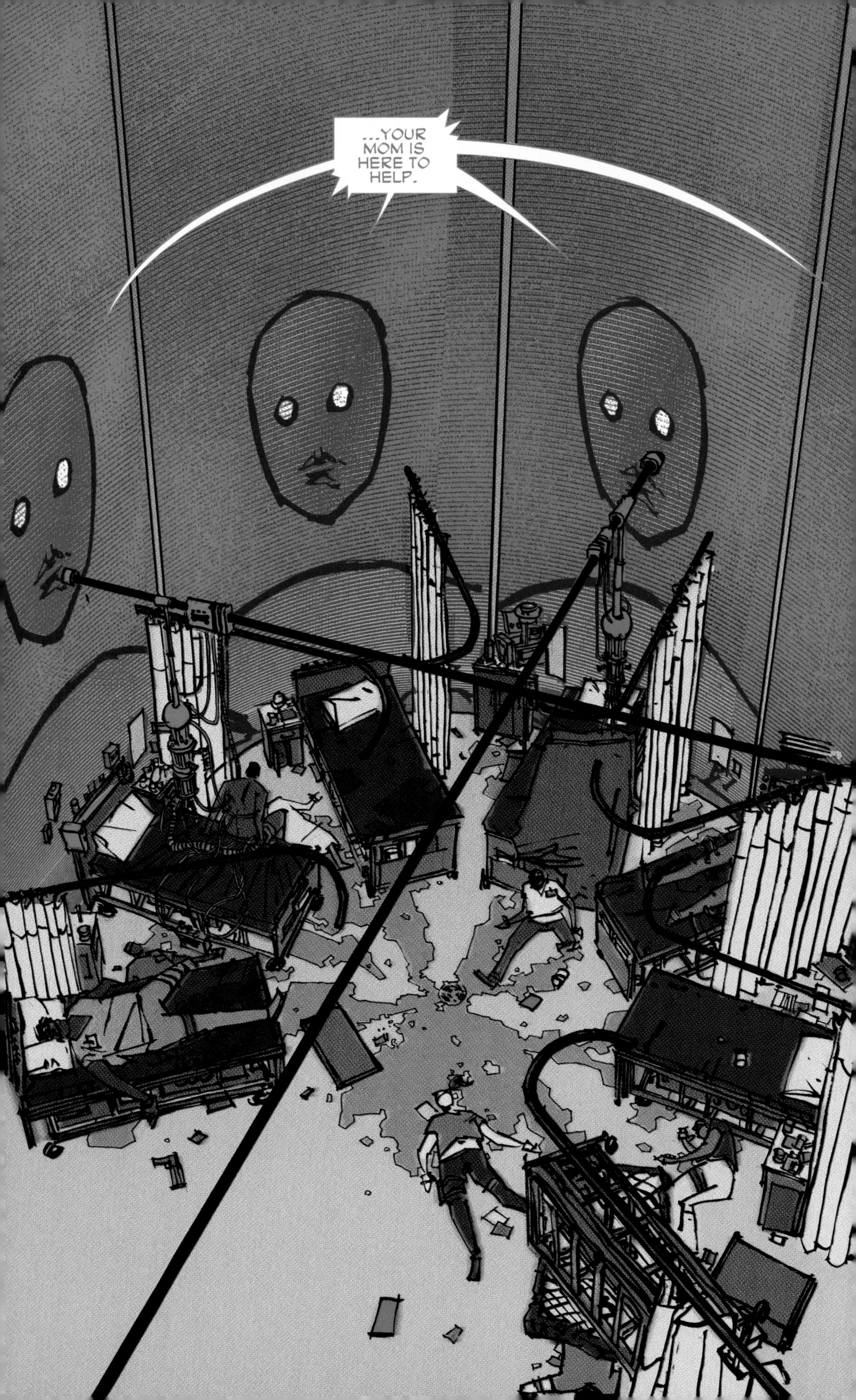
...YOUR MOM IS HERE TO HELP.

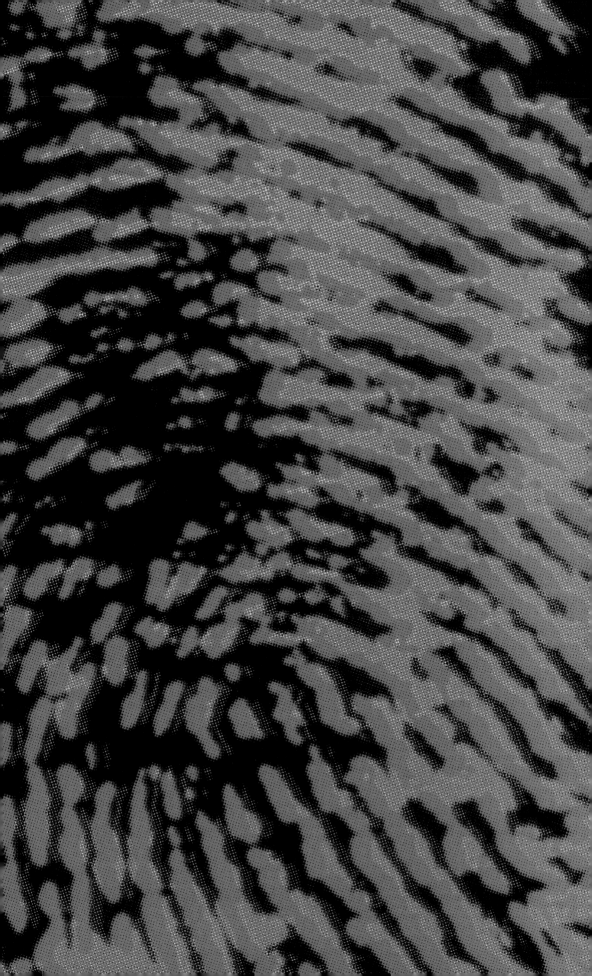

PART TWO

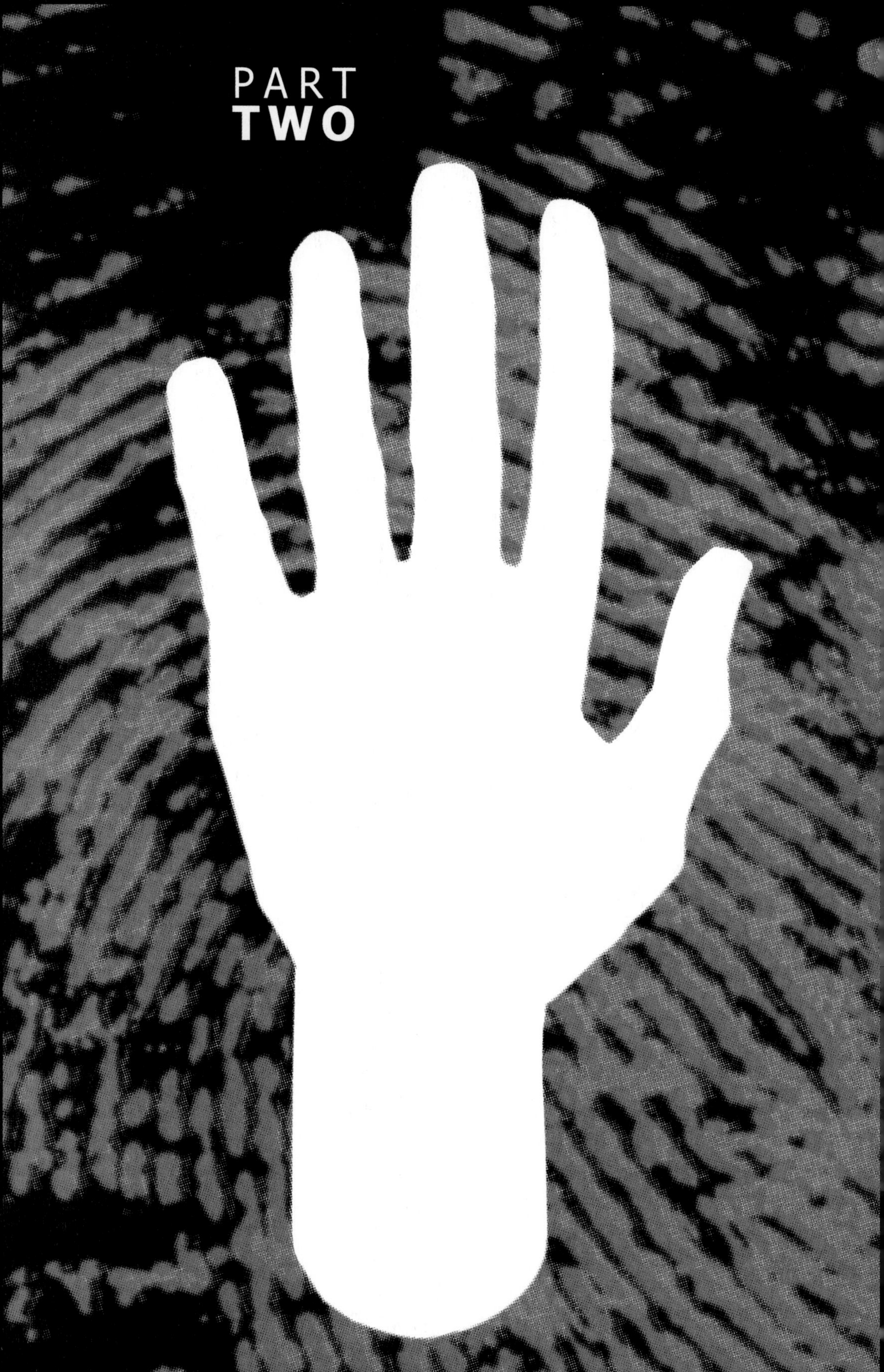

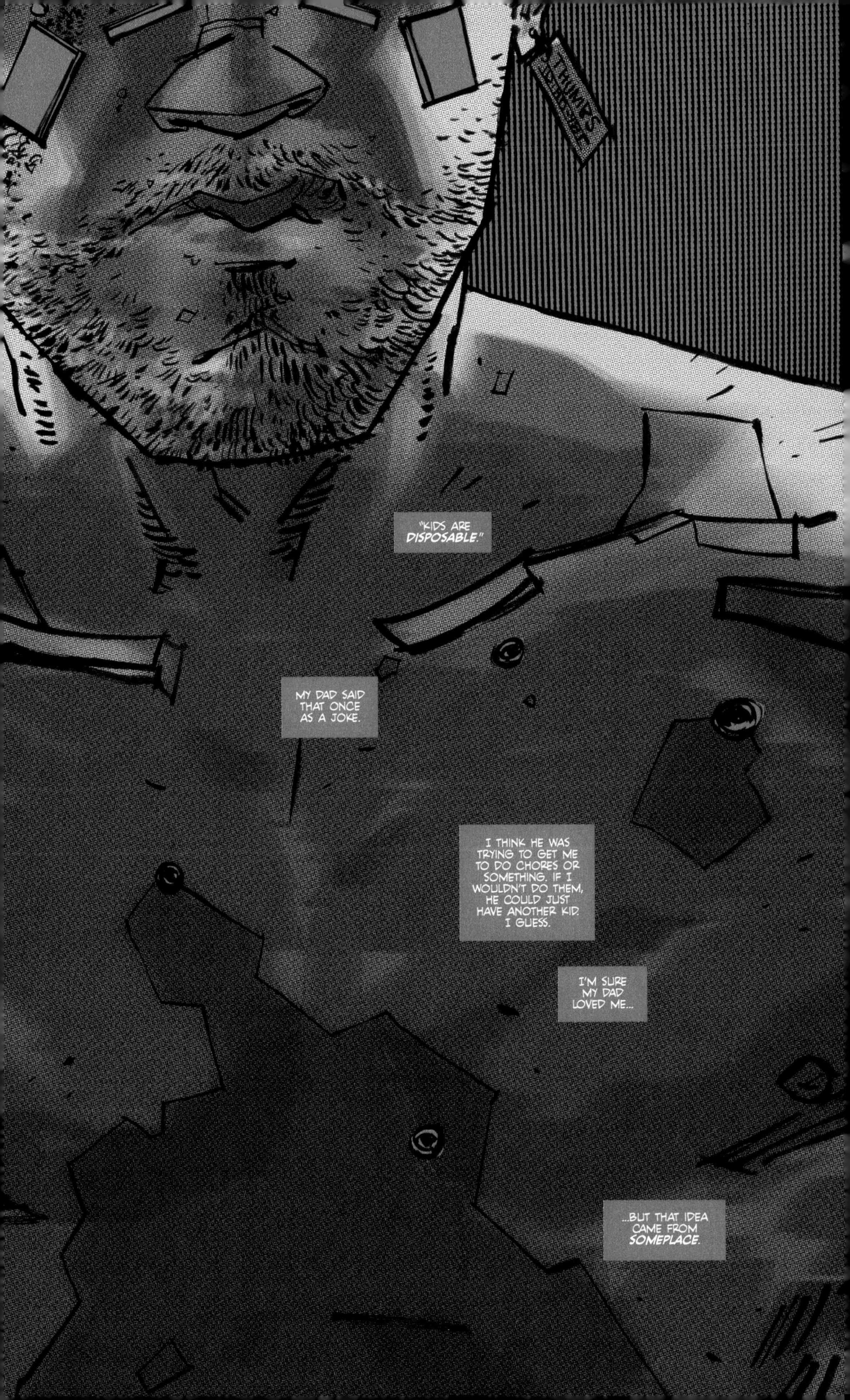
"KIDS ARE DISPOSABLE."
MY DAD SAID THAT ONCE AS A JOKE.
I THINK HE WAS TRYING TO GET ME TO DO CHORES OR SOMETHING. IF I WOULDN'T DO THEM, HE COULD JUST HAVE ANOTHER KID. I GUESS.
I'M SURE MY DAD LOVED ME...
...BUT THAT IDEA CAME FROM SOMEPLACE.

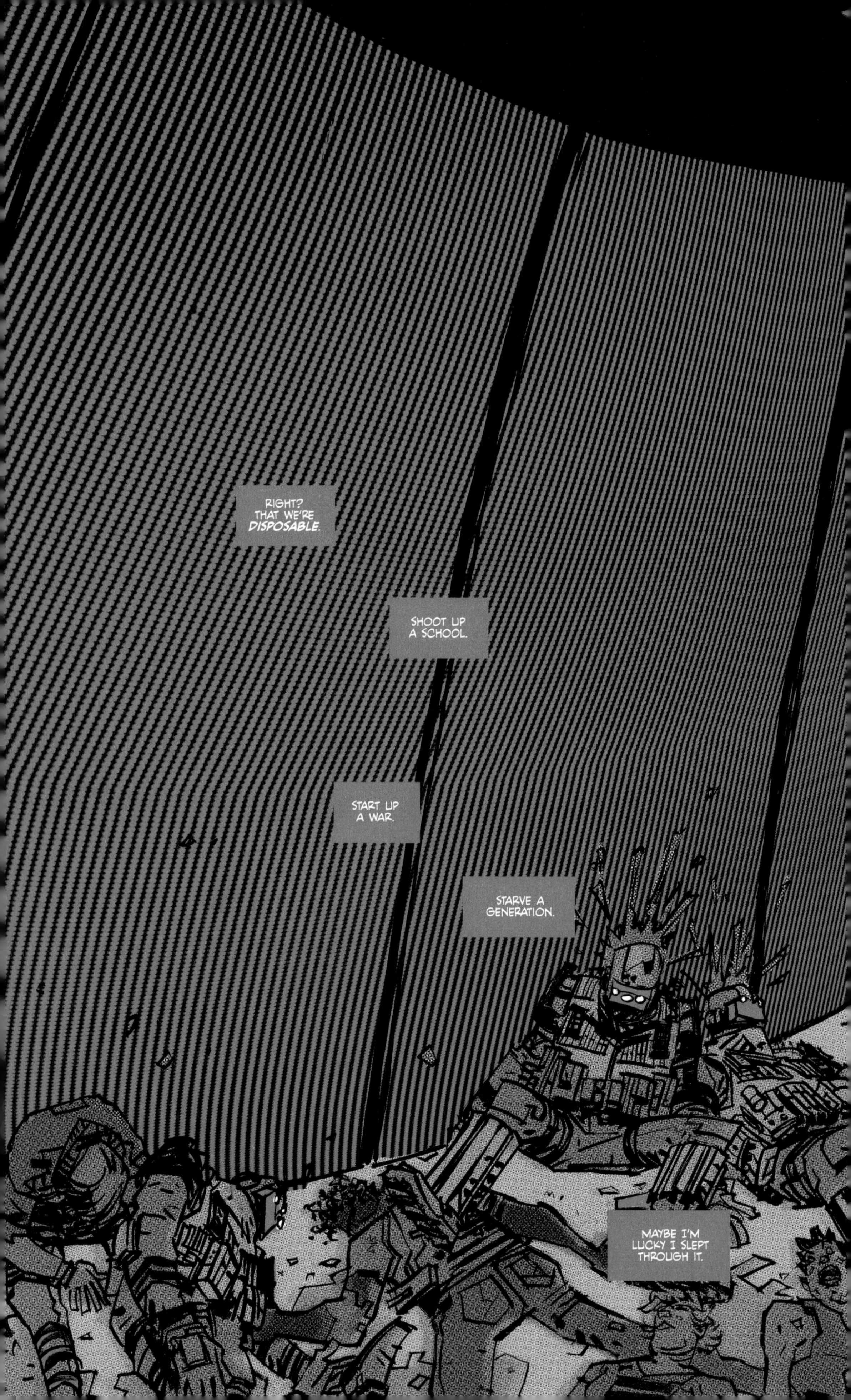
RIGHT? THAT WE'RE *DISPOSABLE*.
SHOOT UP A SCHOOL.
START UP A WAR.
STARVE A GENERATION.
MAYBE I'M LUCKY I SLEPT THROUGH IT.

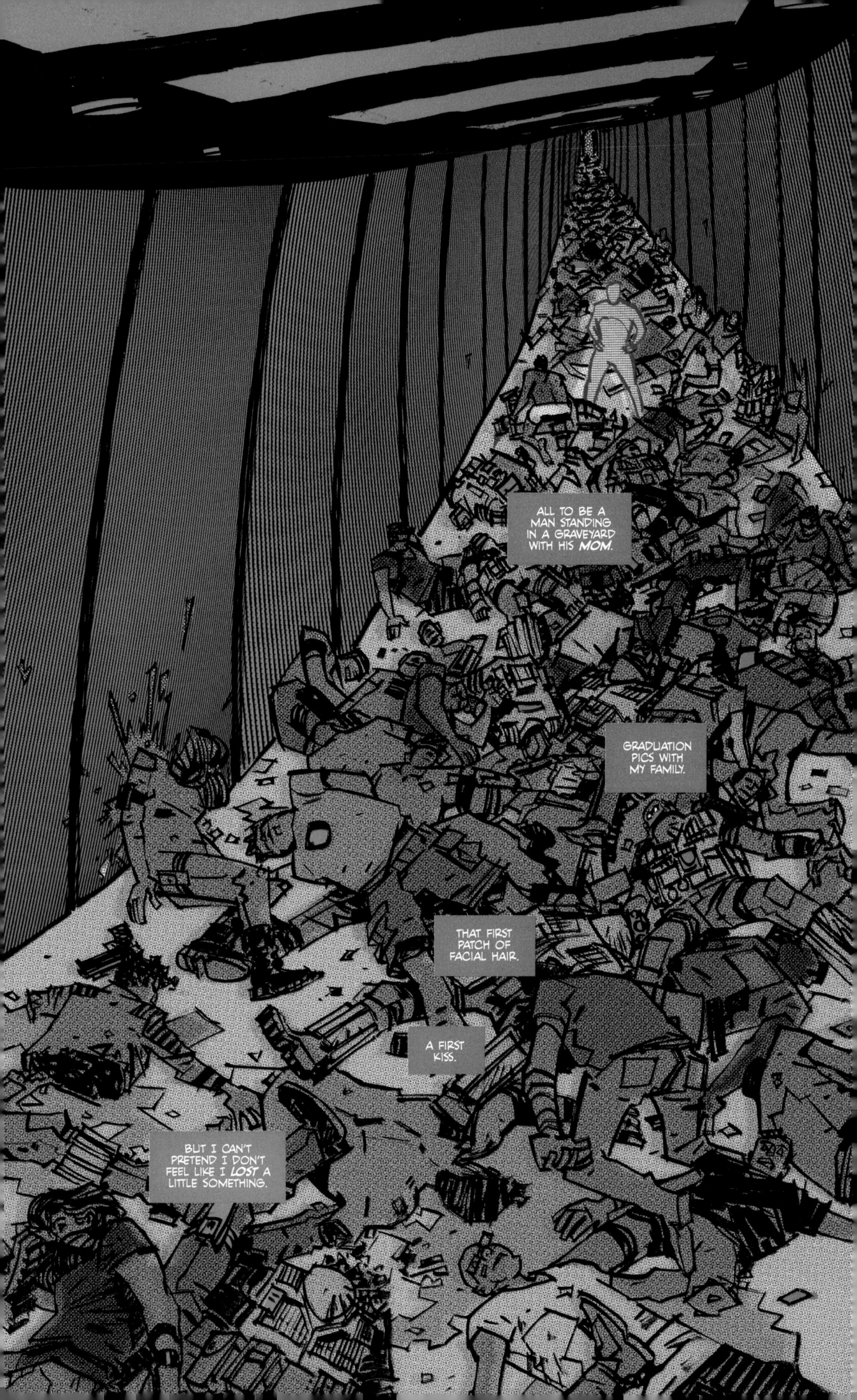
ALL TO BE A MAN STANDING IN A GRAVEYARD WITH HIS *MOM*.
GRADUATION PICS WITH MY FAMILY.
THAT FIRST PATCH OF FACIAL HAIR.
A FIRST KISS.
BUT I CAN'T PRETEND I DON'T FEEL LIKE I *LOST* A LITTLE SOMETHING.

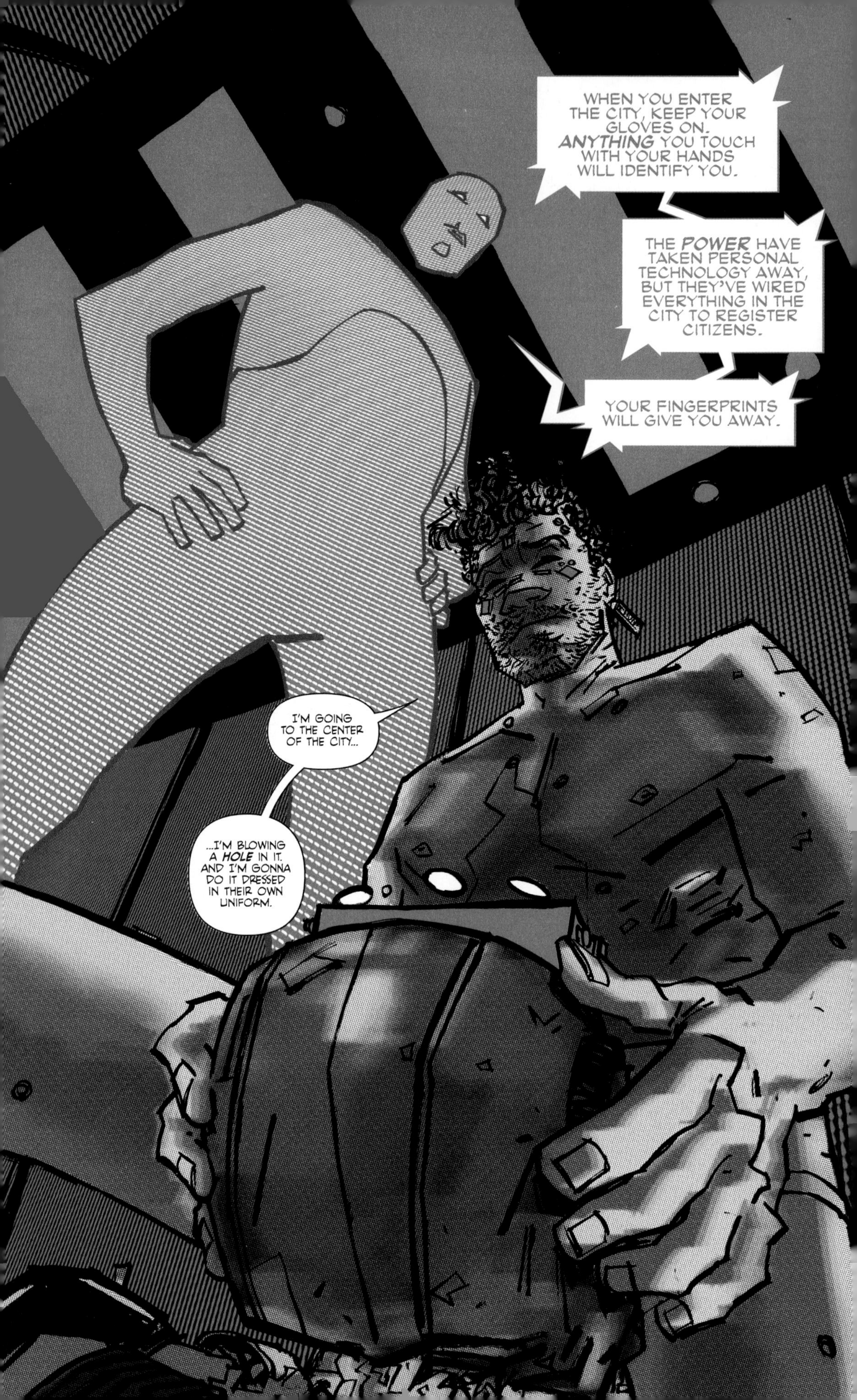
WHEN YOU ENTER THE CITY, KEEP YOUR GLOVES ON. ANYTHING YOU TOUCH WITH YOUR HANDS WILL IDENTIFY YOU.
THE POWER HAVE TAKEN PERSONAL TECHNOLOGY AWAY, BUT THEY'VE WIRED EVERYTHING IN THE CITY TO REGISTER CITIZENS.
YOUR FINGERPRINTS WILL GIVE YOU AWAY.
I'M GOING TO THE CENTER OF THE CITY...
...I'M BLOWING A HOLE IN IT. AND I'M GONNA DO IT DRESSED IN THEIR OWN UNIFORM.

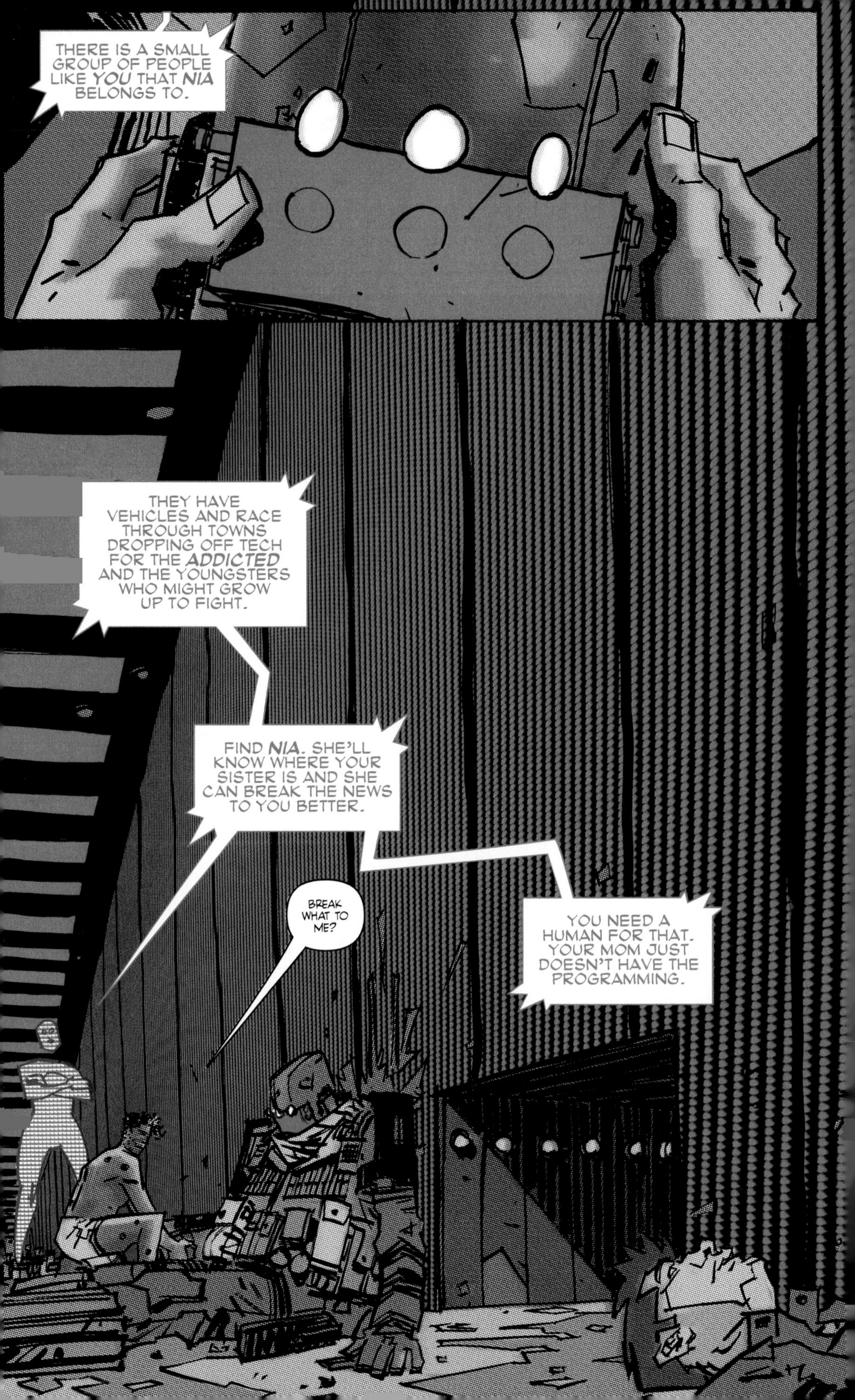
THERE IS A SMALL GROUP OF PEOPLE LIKE YOU THAT NIA BELONGS TO.
THEY HAVE VEHICLES AND RACE THROUGH TOWNS DROPPING OFF TECH FOR THE ADDICTED AND THE YOUNGSTERS WHO MIGHT GROW UP TO FIGHT.
FIND NIA. SHE'LL KNOW WHERE YOUR SISTER IS AND SHE CAN BREAK THE NEWS TO YOU BETTER.
BREAK WHAT TO ME?
YOU NEED A HUMAN FOR THAT. YOUR MOM JUST DOESN'T HAVE THE PROGRAMMING.

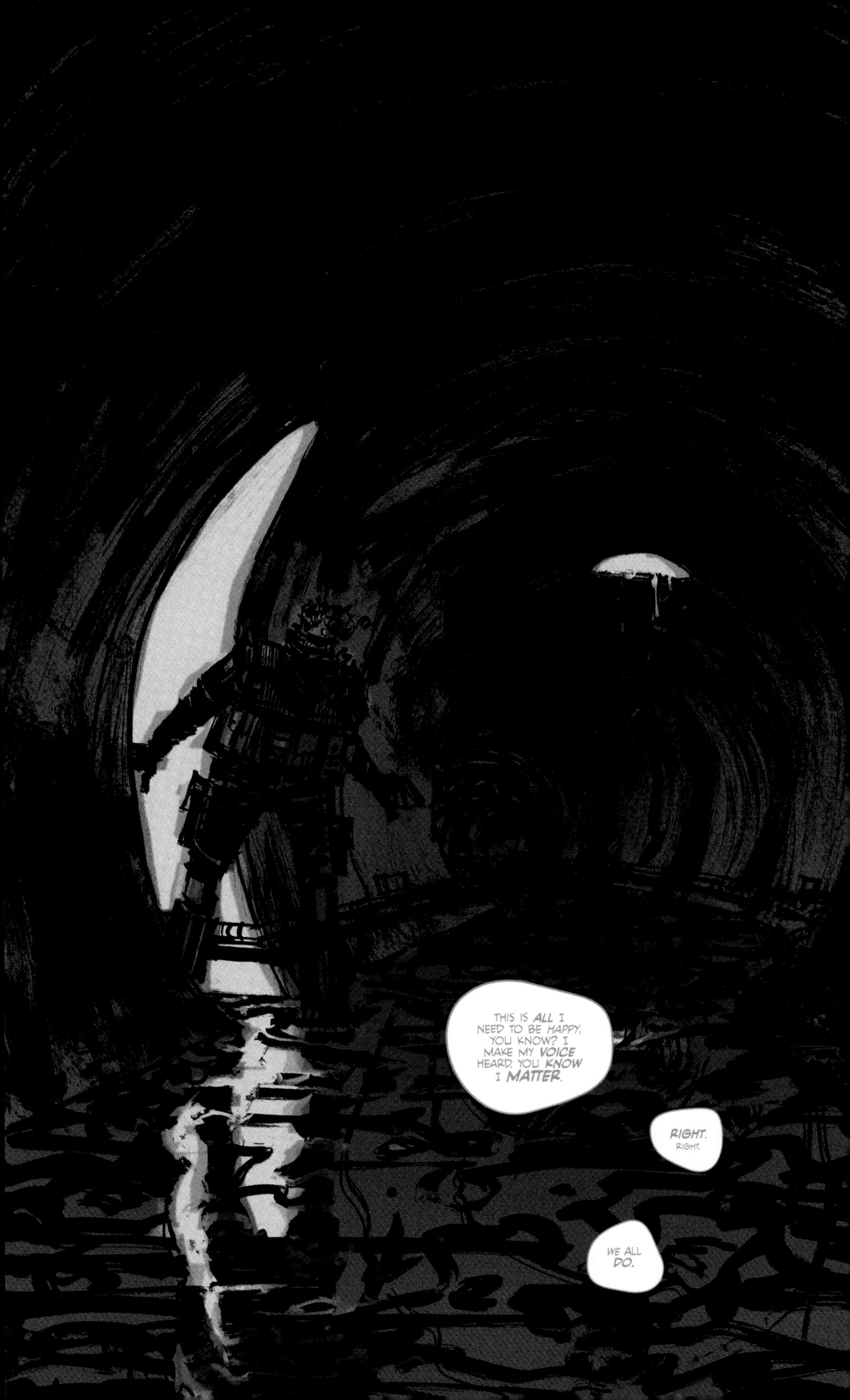
THIS IS ALL I NEED TO BE HAPPY, YOU KNOW? I MAKE MY VOICE HEARD. YOU KNOW I MATTER.
RIGHT. RIGHT.
WE ALL DO.

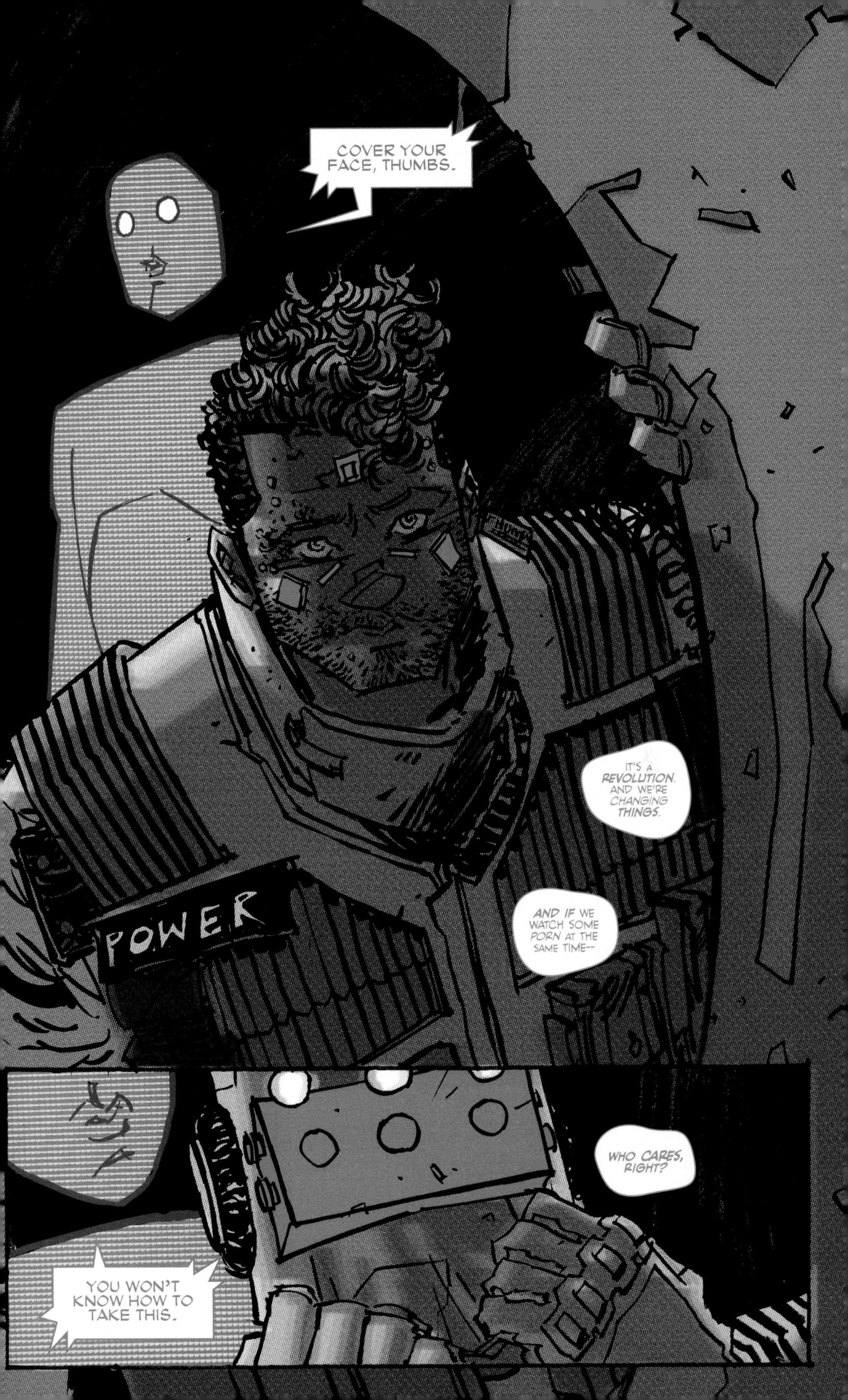
COVER YOUR FACE, THUMBS.
IT'S A REVOLUTION. AND WE'RE CHANGING THINGS.
AND IF WE WATCH SOME PORN AT THE SAME TIME--
POWER
WHO CARES, RIGHT?
YOU WON'T KNOW HOW TO TAKE THIS.

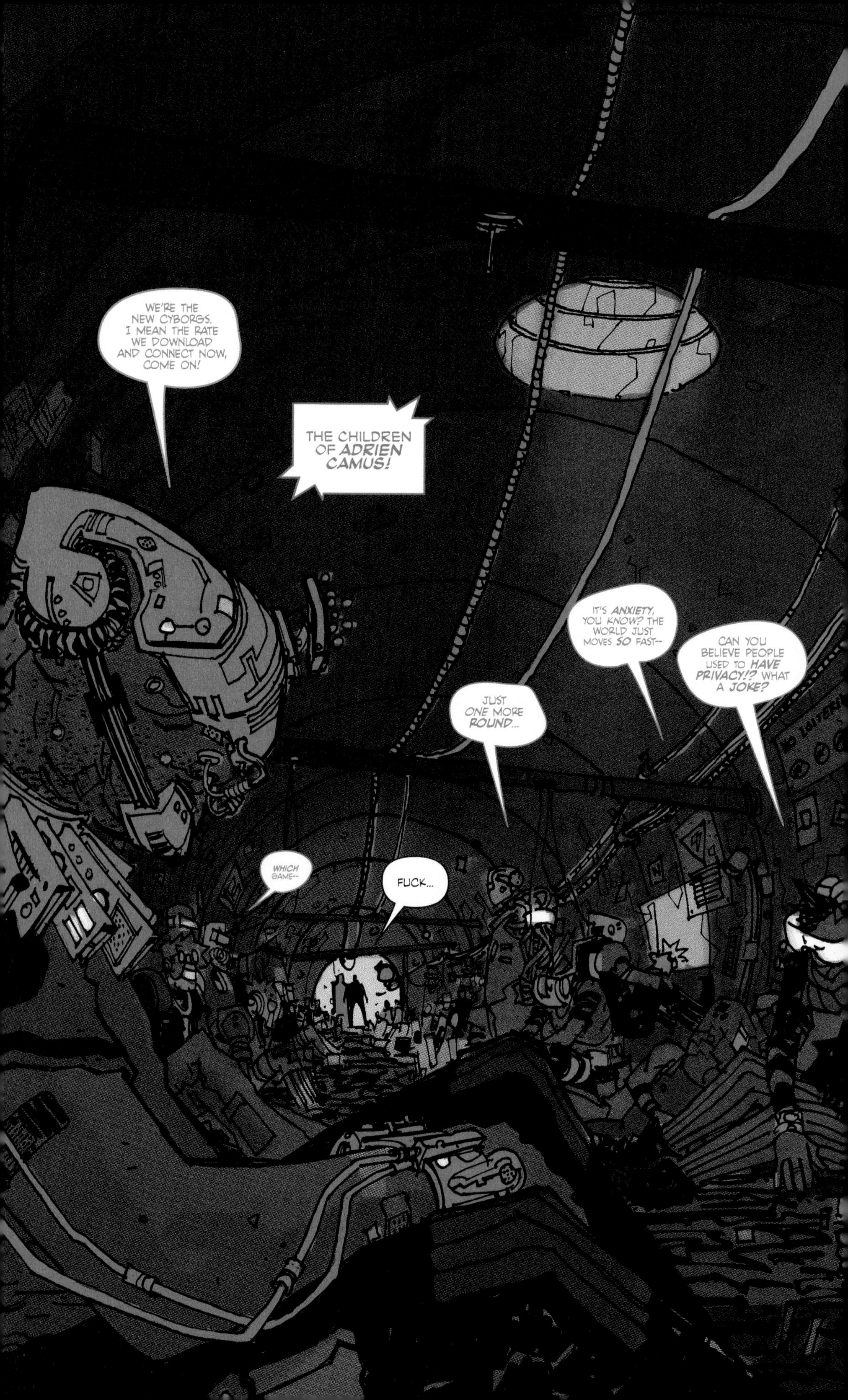
WE'RE THE NEW CYBORGS. I MEAN THE RATE WE DOWNLOAD AND CONNECT NOW, COME ON!
THE CHILDREN OF ADRIEN CAMUS!
IT'S ANXIETY, YOU KNOW? THE WORLD JUST MOVES SO FAST--
CAN YOU BELIEVE PEOPLE USED TO HAVE PRIVACY!? WHAT A JOKE?
JUST ONE MORE ROUND...
WHICH GAME--
FUCK...

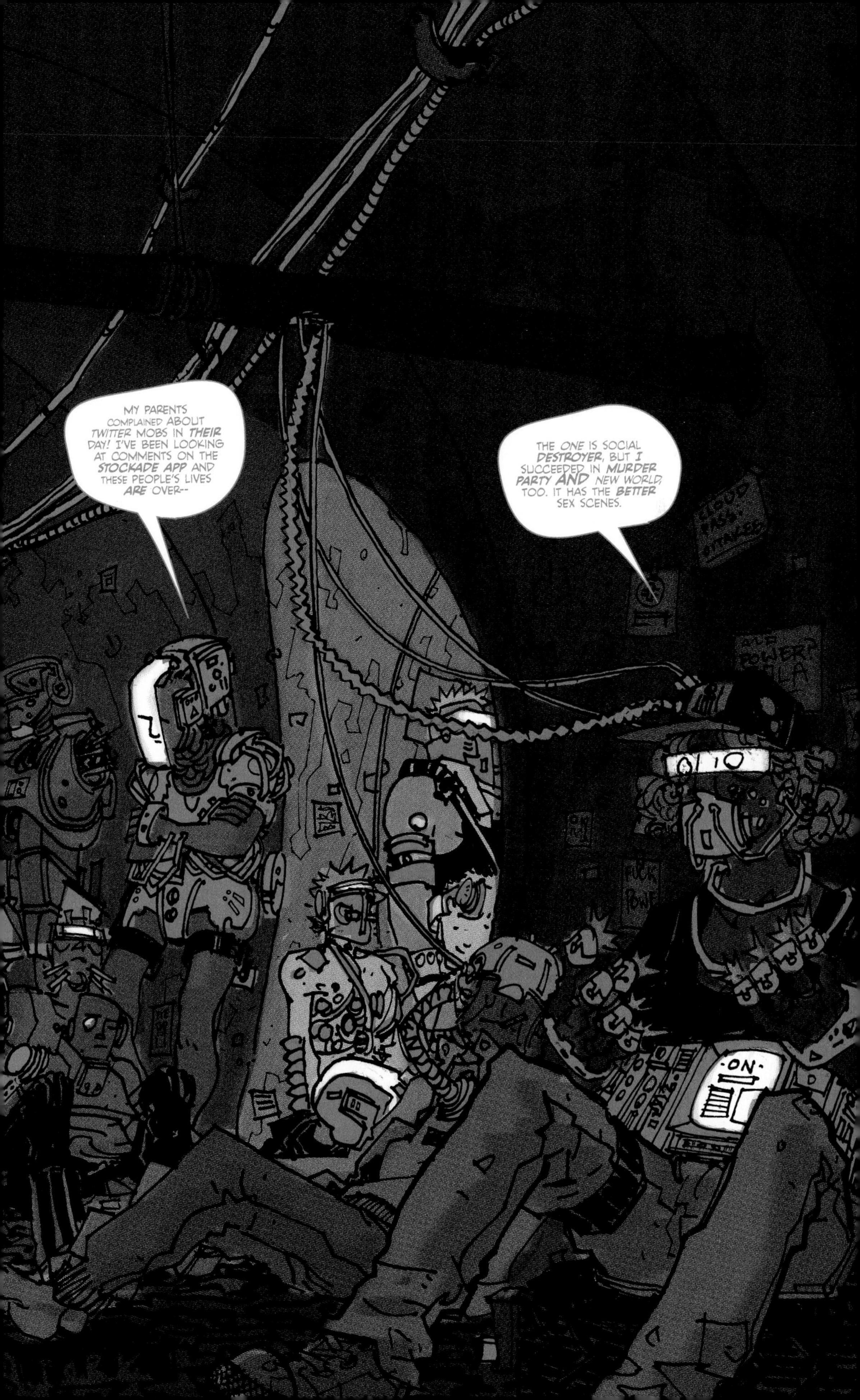
MY PARENTS COMPLAINED ABOUT TWITTER MOBS IN THEIR DAY! I'VE BEEN LOOKING AT COMMENTS ON THE STOCKADE APP AND THESE PEOPLE'S LIVES ARE OVER--
THE ONE IS SOCIAL DESTROYER, BUT I SUCCEEDED IN MURDER PARTY AND NEW WORLD, TOO. IT HAS THE BETTER SEX SCENES.
ON

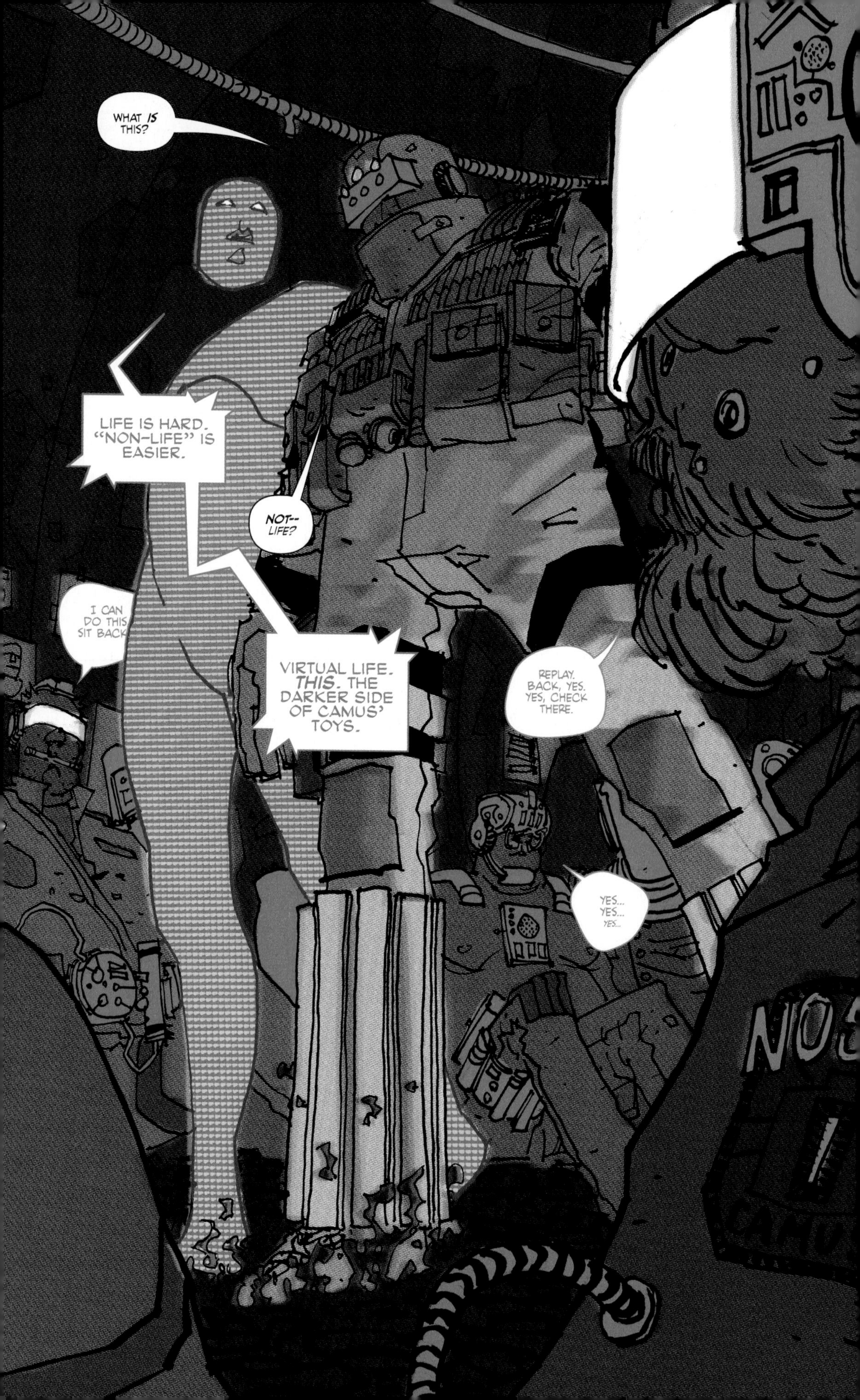
WHAT *IS* THIS?
LIFE IS HARD. "NON-LIFE" IS EASIER.
NOT-- *LIFE?*
VIRTUAL LIFE. *THIS.* THE DARKER SIDE OF CAMUS' TOYS.
REPLAY. BACK, YES. YES, CHECK THERE.
YES... YES... YES...

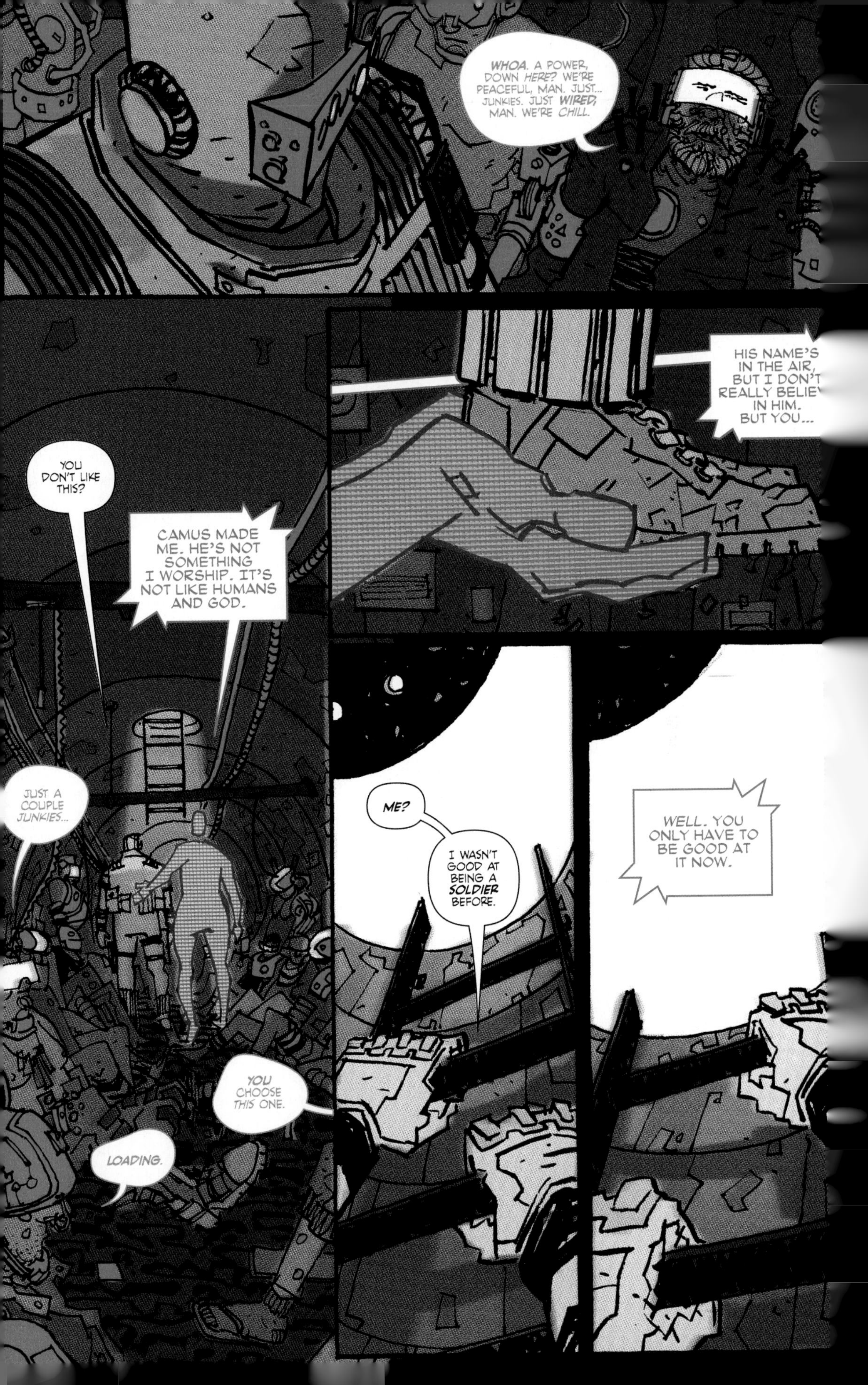
WHOA. A POWER, DOWN HERE? WE'RE PEACEFUL, MAN. JUST... JUNKIES. JUST WIRED, MAN. WE'RE CHILL.
YOU DON'T LIKE THIS?
CAMUS MADE ME. HE'S NOT SOMETHING I WORSHIP. IT'S NOT LIKE HUMANS AND GOD.
JUST A COUPLE JUNKIES...
YOU CHOOSE THIS ONE.
LOADING.
HIS NAME'S IN THE AIR, BUT I DON'T REALLY BELIE IN HIM. BUT YOU...
ME?
I WASN'T GOOD AT BEING A SOLDIER BEFORE.
WELL. YOU ONLY HAVE TO BE GOOD AT IT NOW.

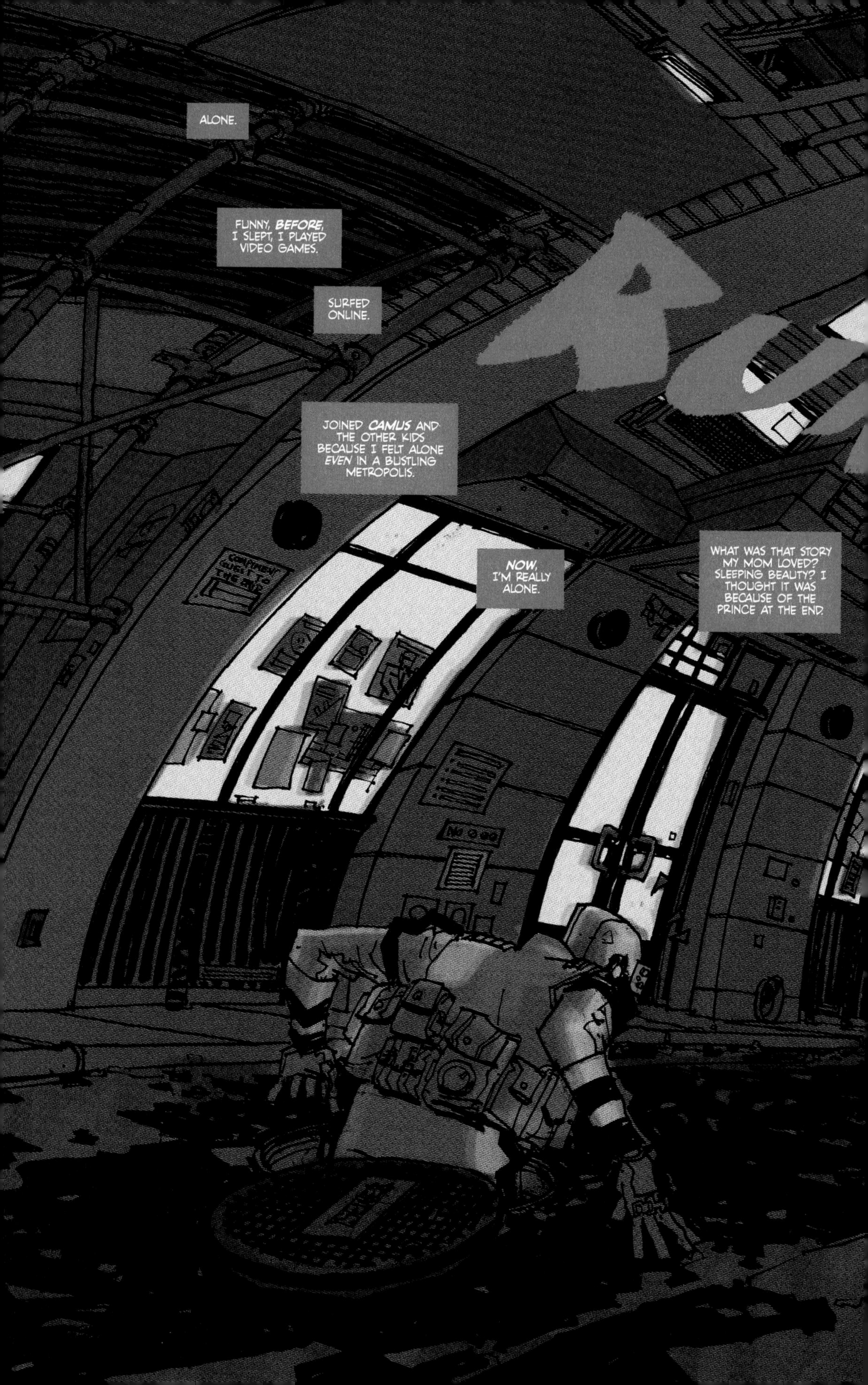
ALONE.
FUNNY, BEFORE, I SLEPT, I PLAYED VIDEO GAMES.
SURFED ONLINE.
JOINED CAMUS AND THE OTHER KIDS BECAUSE I FELT ALONE EVEN IN A BUSTLING METROPOLIS.
NOW, I'M REALLY ALONE.
WHAT WAS THAT STORY MY MOM LOVED? SLEEPING BEAUTY? I THOUGHT IT WAS BECAUSE OF THE PRINCE AT THE END.

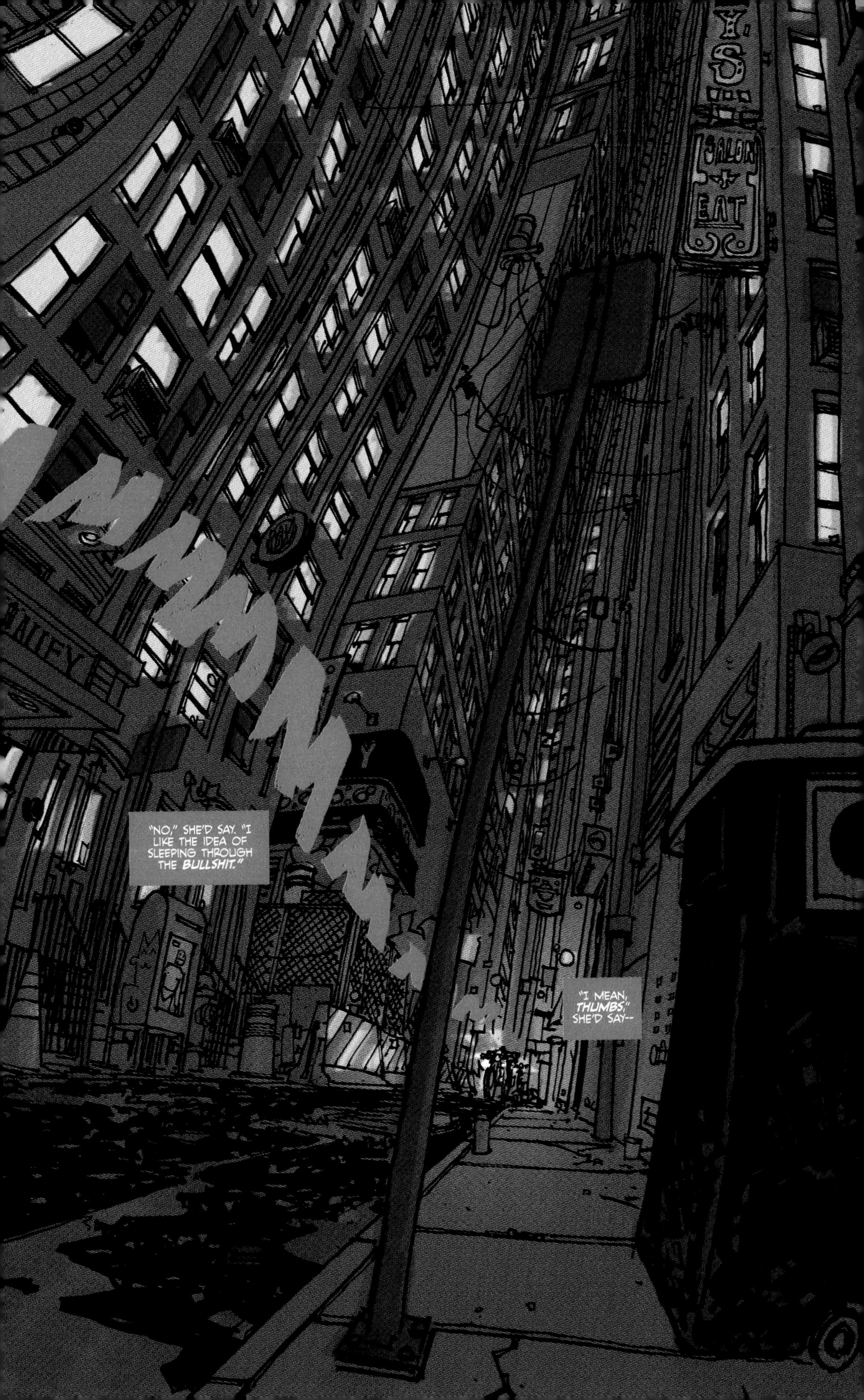
MMMMMMMM
"NO," SHE'D SAY. "I LIKE THE IDEA OF SLEEPING THROUGH THE *BULLSHIT.*"
"I MEAN, *THUMBS,*" SHE'D SAY--

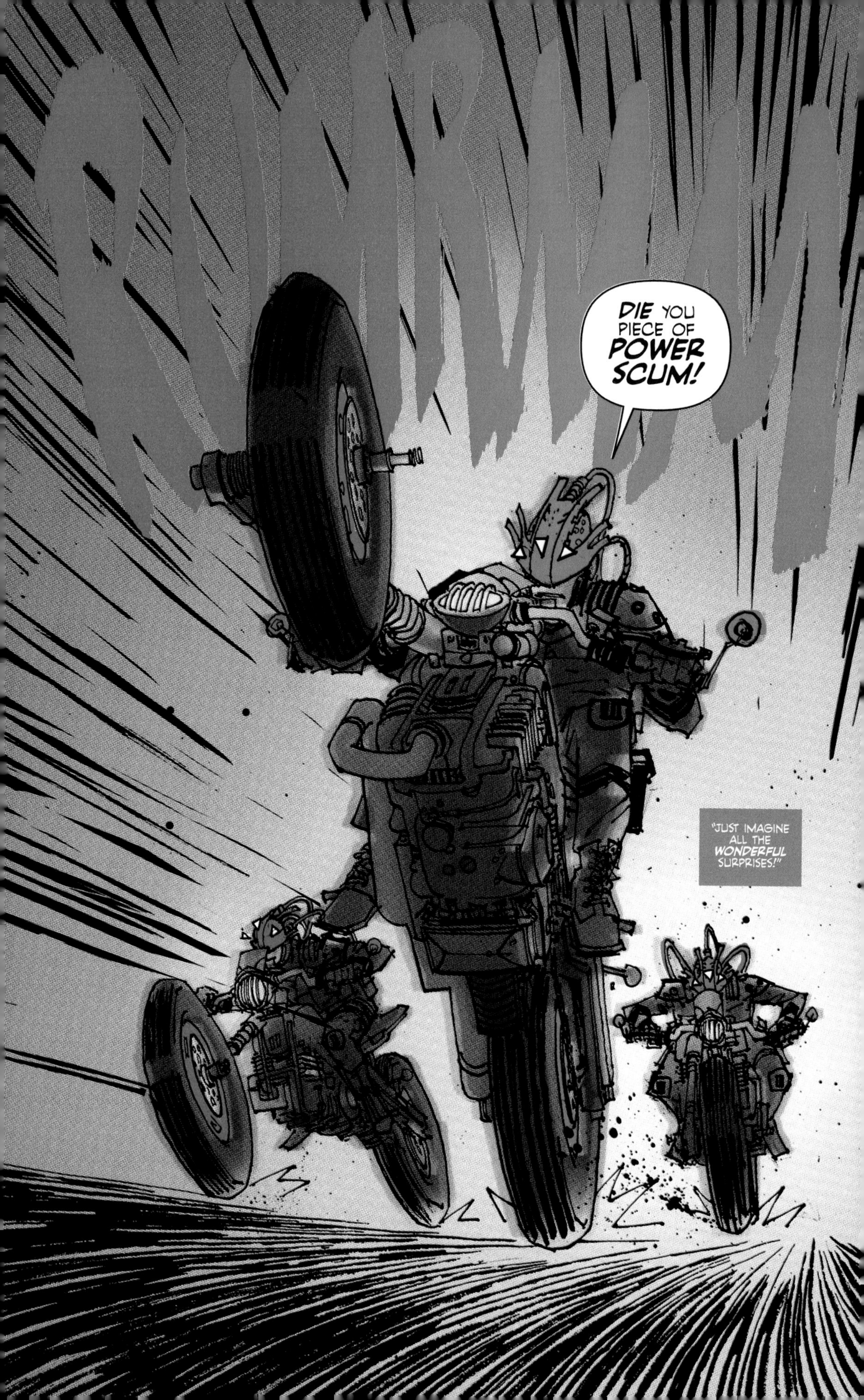
DIE YOU PIECE OF POWER SCUM!
"JUST IMAGINE ALL THE WONDERFUL SURPRISES!"

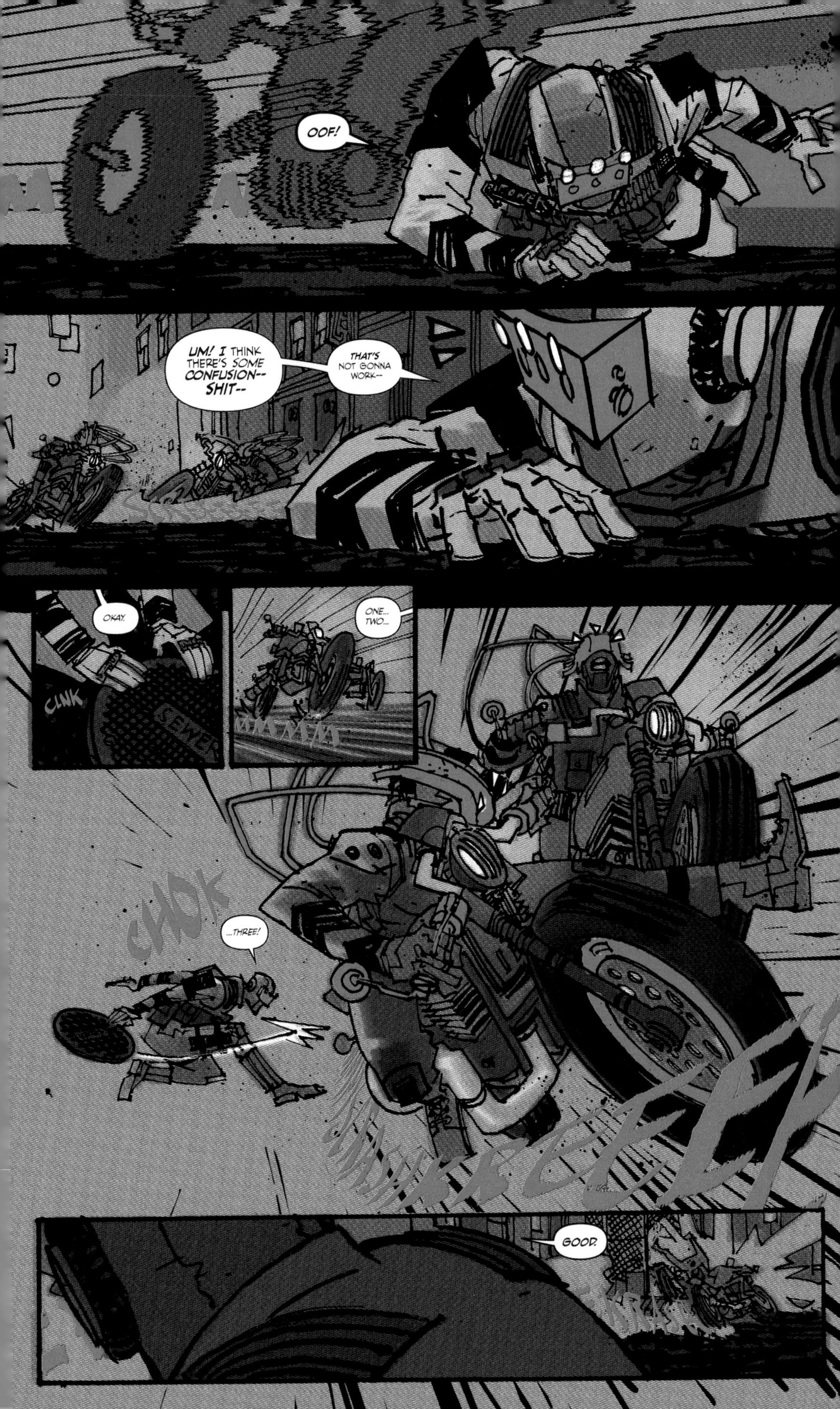
OOF!
UM! I THINK THERE'S SOME CONFUSION-- SHIT--
THAT'S NOT GONNA WORK--
OKAY.
CLNK
SEWER
ONE... TWO...
CHOK
...THREE!
GOOD.

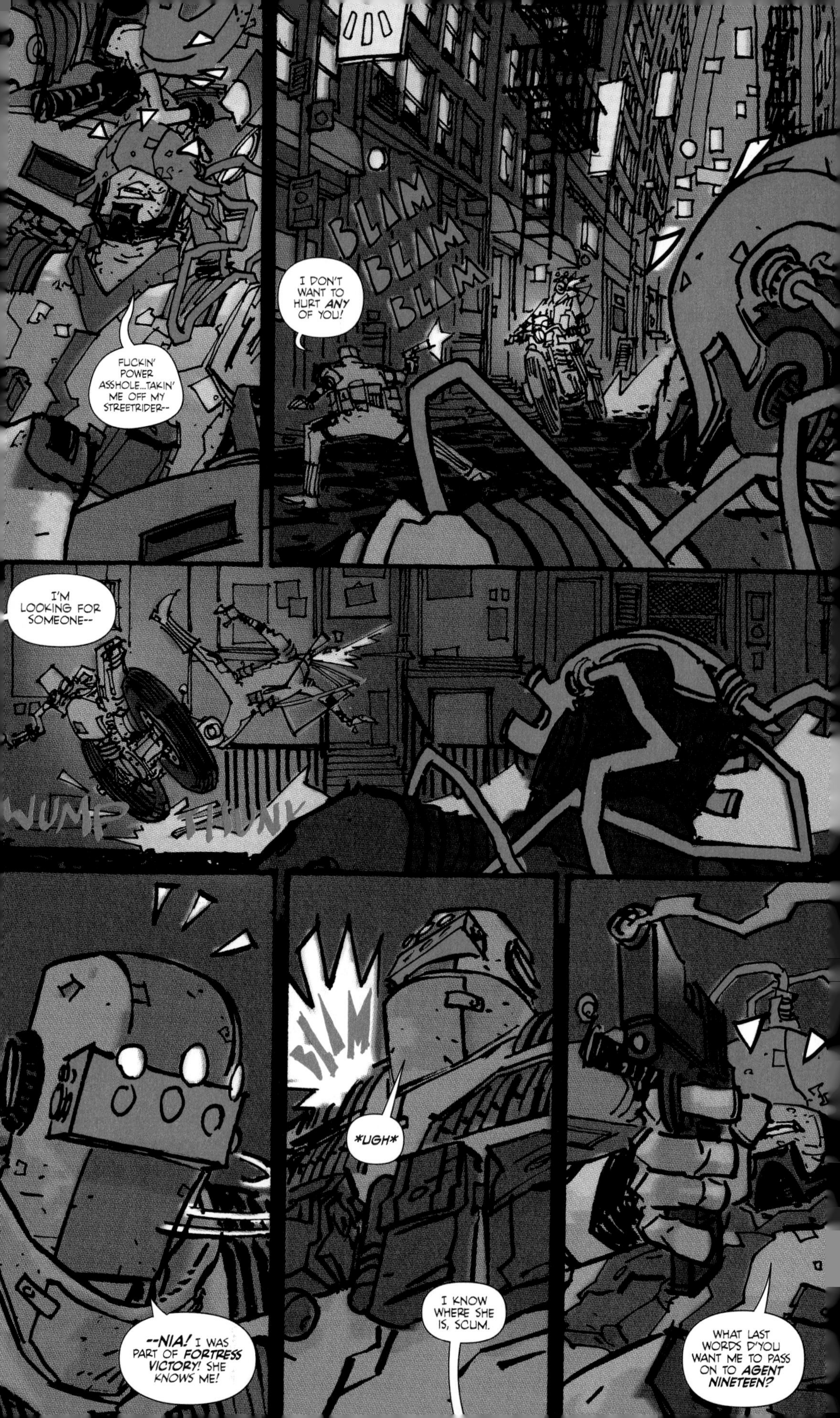
FUCKIN' POWER ASSHOLE...TAKIN' ME OFF MY STREETRIDER--
BLAM BLAM BLAM
I DON'T WANT TO HURT ANY OF YOU!
I'M LOOKING FOR SOMEONE--
WUMP
--NIA! I WAS PART OF FORTRESS VICTORY! SHE KNOWS ME!
BLAM
UGH
I KNOW WHERE SHE IS, SCUM.
WHAT LAST WORDS D'YOU WANT ME TO PASS ON TO AGENT NINETEEN?

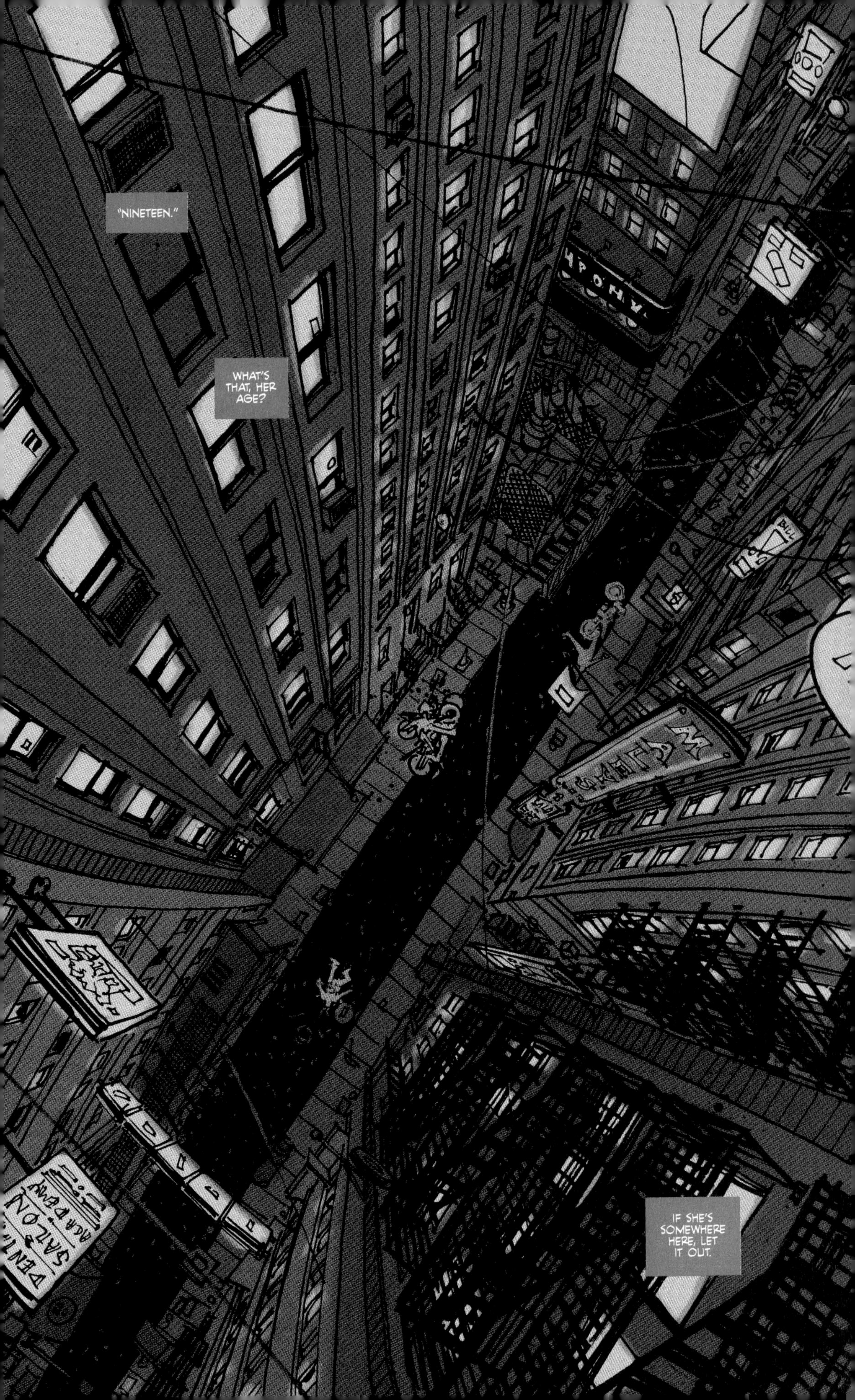
"NINETEEN."
WHAT'S THAT, HER AGE?
IF SHE'S SOMEWHERE HERE, LET IT OUT.

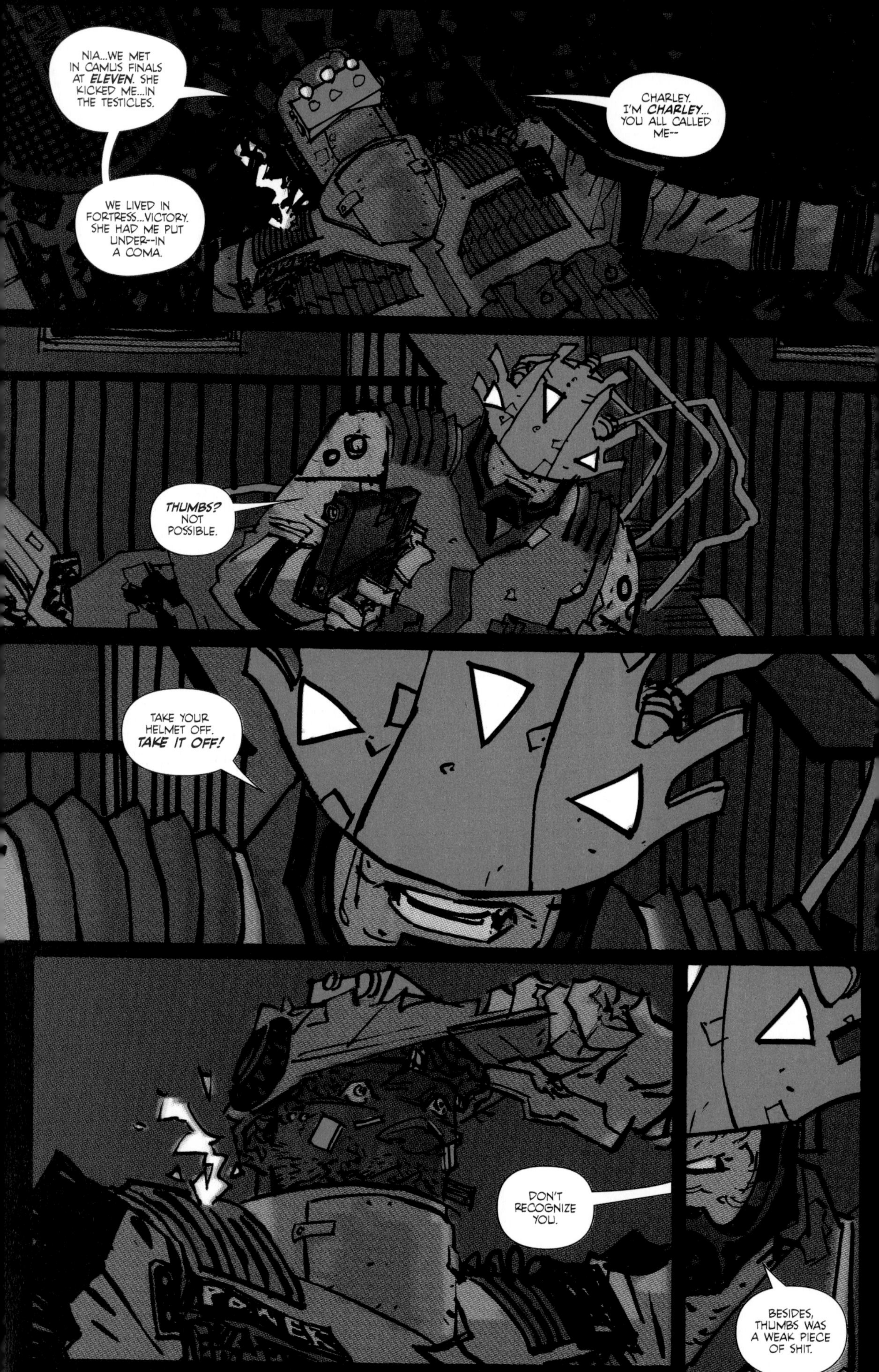
NIA...WE MET IN CAMUS FINALS AT ELEVEN. SHE KICKED ME...IN THE TESTICLES.
WE LIVED IN FORTRESS...VICTORY. SHE HAD ME PUT UNDER--IN A COMA.
CHARLEY. I'M CHARLEY... YOU ALL CALLED ME--
THUMBS? NOT POSSIBLE.
TAKE YOUR HELMET OFF. TAKE IT OFF!
DON'T RECOGNIZE YOU.
BESIDES, THUMBS WAS A WEAK PIECE OF SHIT.

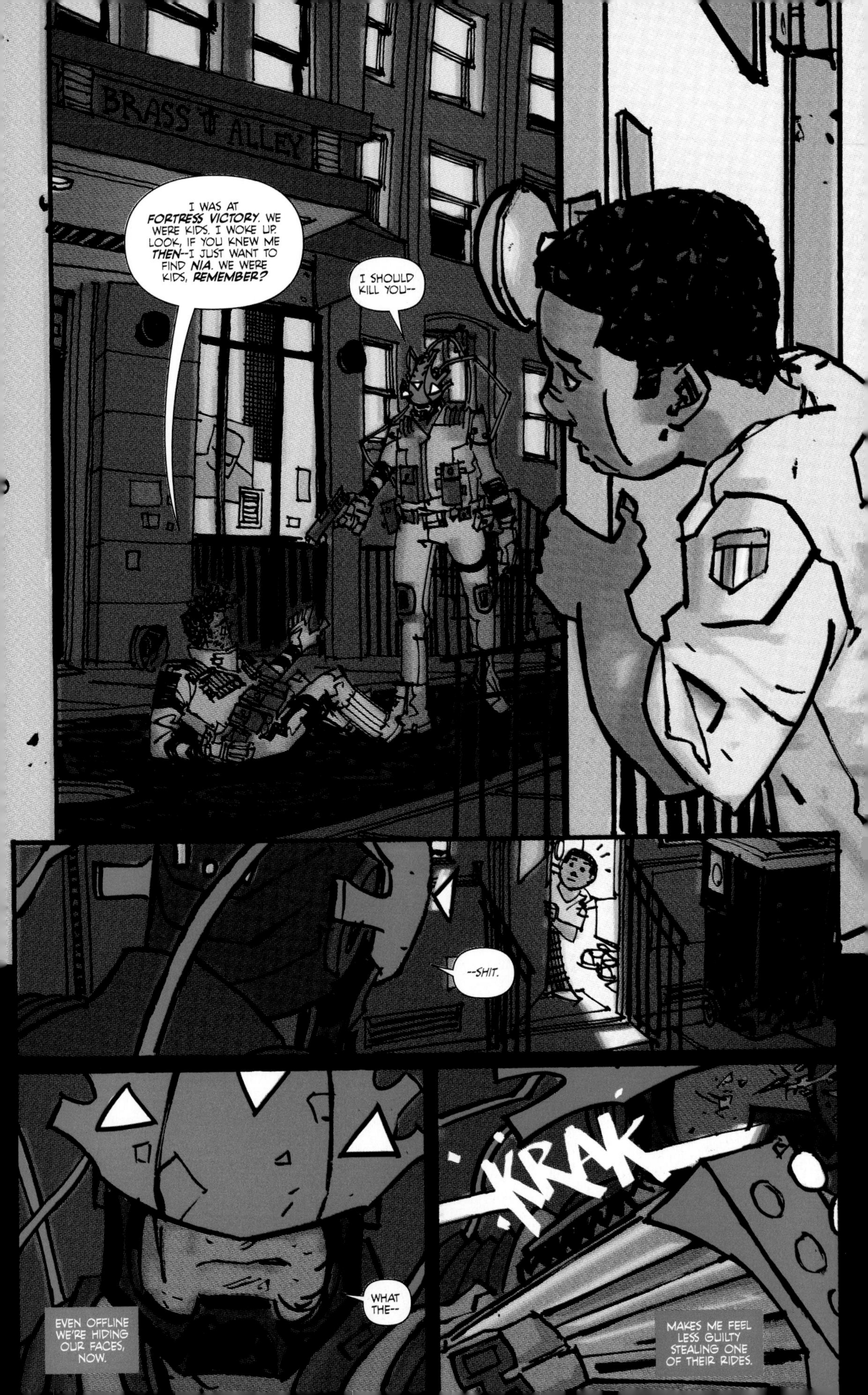
BRASS ALLEY
I WAS AT FORTRESS VICTORY. WE WERE KIDS. I WOKE UP. LOOK, IF YOU KNEW ME THEN--I JUST WANT TO FIND NIA. WE WERE KIDS, REMEMBER?
I SHOULD KILL YOU--
--SHIT.
EVEN OFFLINE WE'RE HIDING OUR FACES, NOW.
WHAT THE--
KRAK
MAKES ME FEEL LESS GUILTY STEALING ONE OF THEIR RIDES.

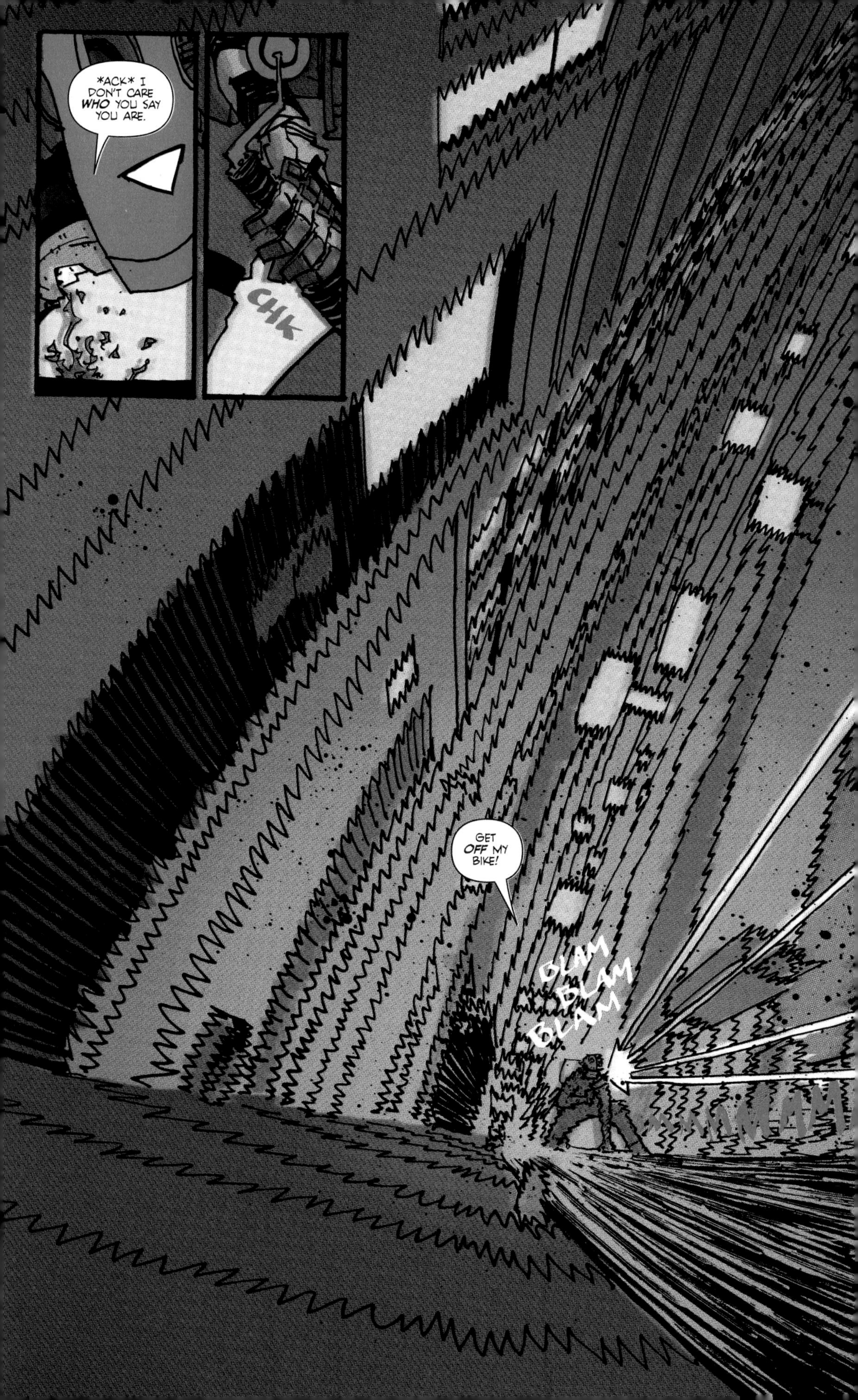
ACK I DON'T CARE WHO YOU SAY YOU ARE.
CHK
GET OFF MY BIKE!
BLAM BLAM BLAM

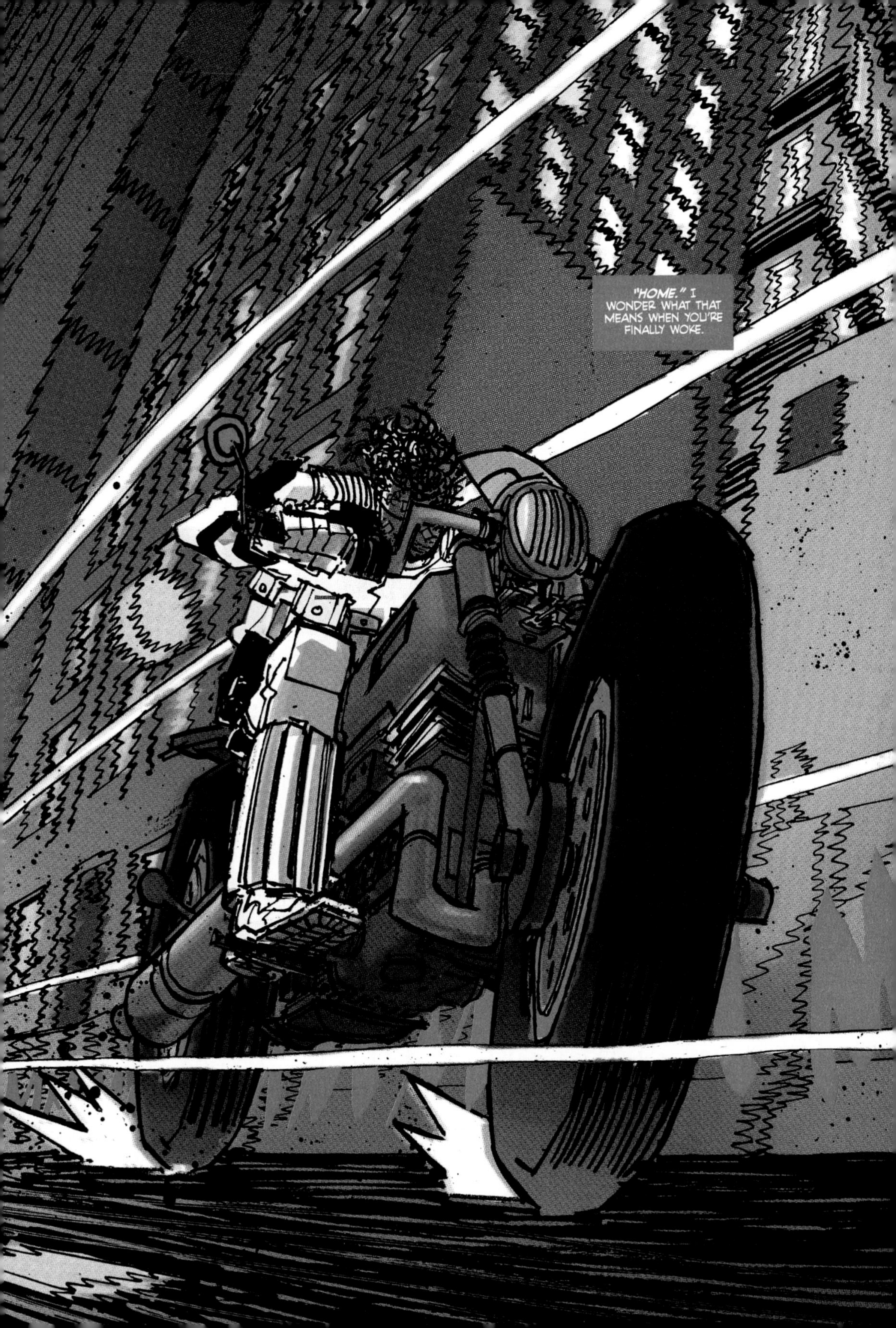
"HOME." I WONDER WHAT THAT MEANS WHEN YOU'RE FINALLY WOKE.

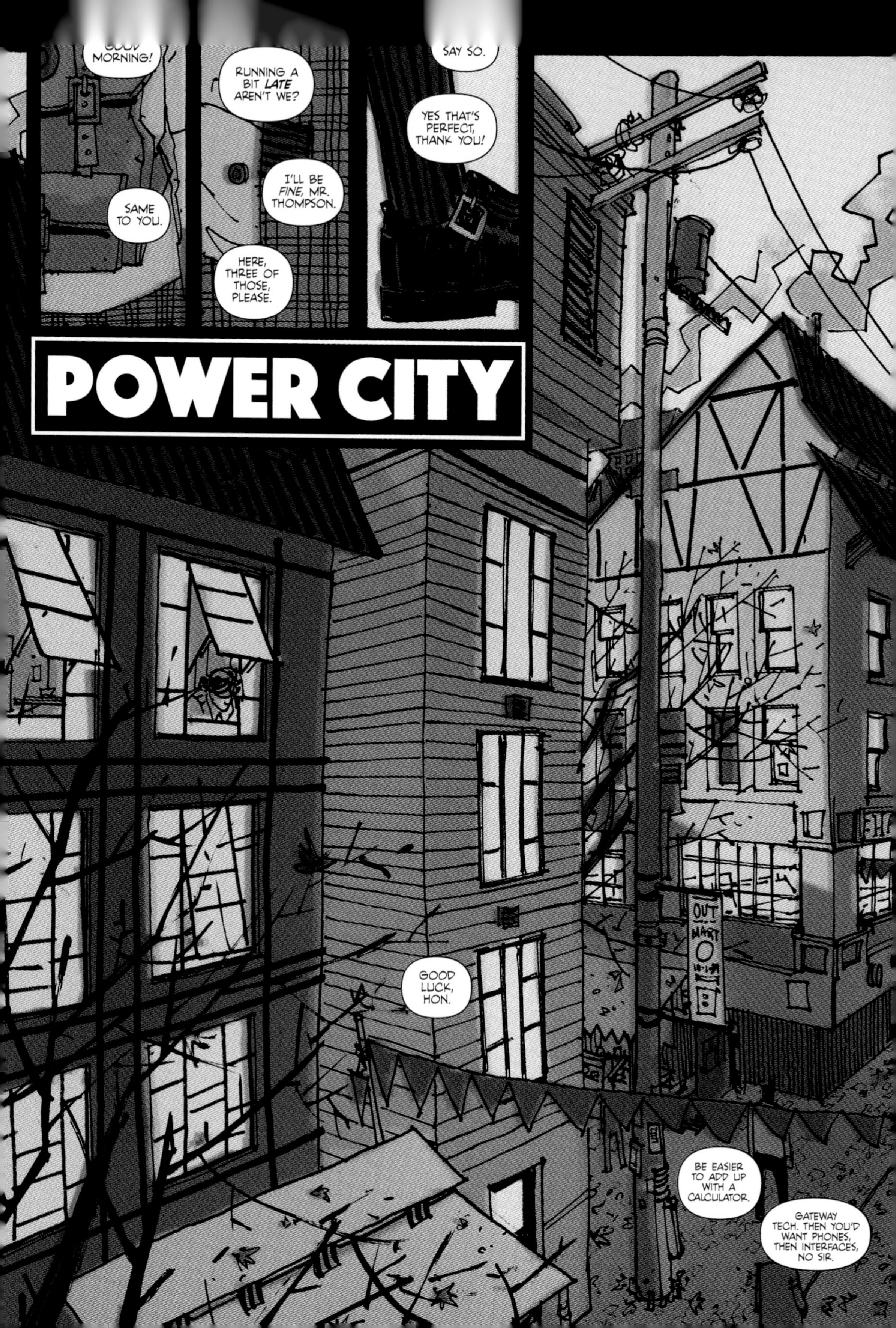
MORNING!
SAME TO YOU.
RUNNING A BIT *LATE* AREN'T WE?
I'LL BE *FINE*, MR. THOMPSON.
HERE, THREE OF THOSE, PLEASE.
SAY SO.
YES THAT'S PERFECT, THANK YOU!
POWER CITY
GOOD LUCK, HON.
BE EASIER TO ADD UP WITH A CALCULATOR.
GATEWAY TECH. THEN YOU'D WANT PHONES, THEN INTERFACES, NO SIR.

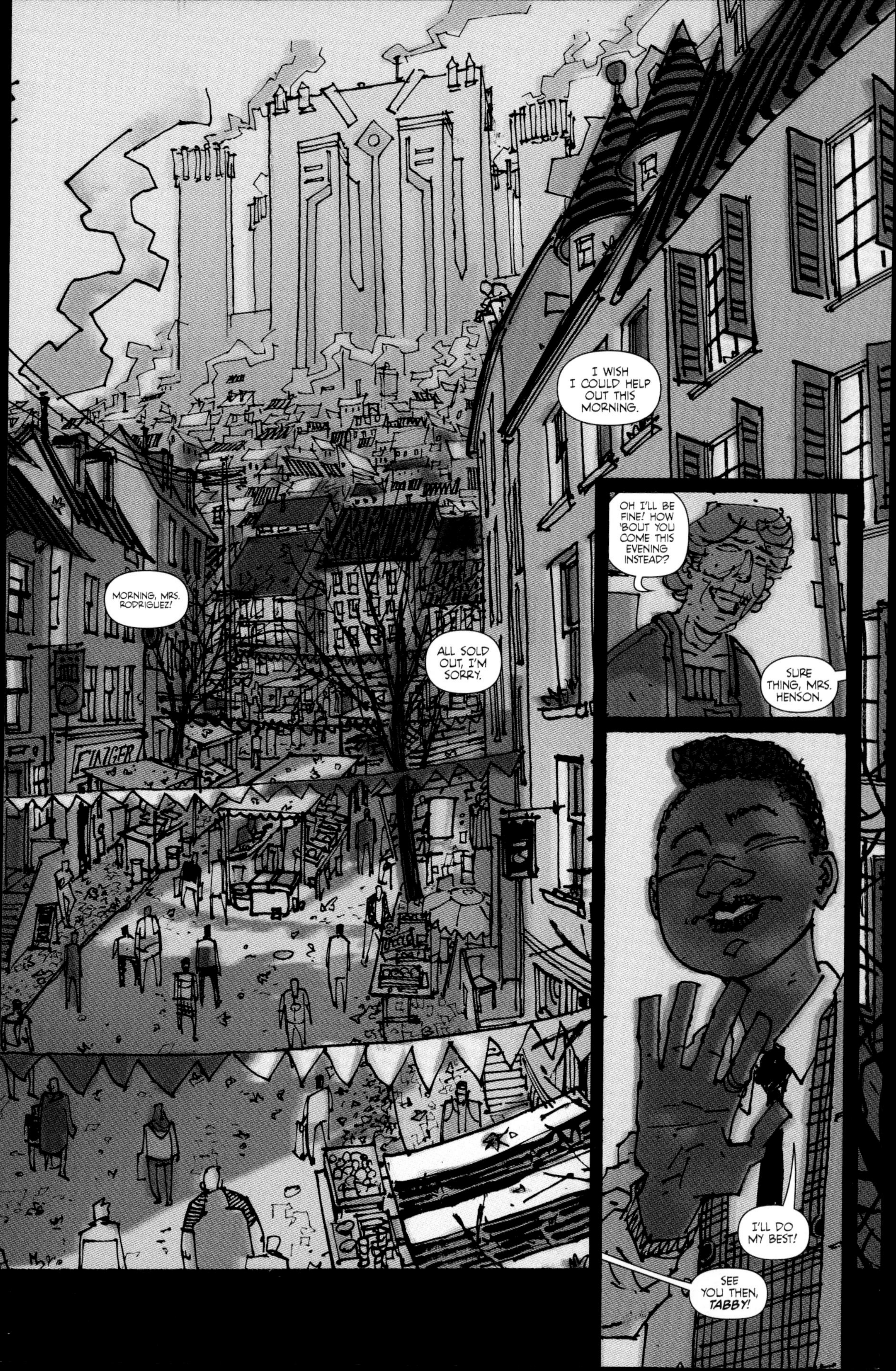
MORNING, MRS. RODRIGUEZ!
ALL SOLD OUT, I'M SORRY.
I WISH I COULD HELP OUT THIS MORNING.
OH I'LL BE FINE! HOW 'BOUT YOU COME THIS EVENING INSTEAD?
SURE THING, MRS. HENSON.
I'LL DO MY BEST!
SEE YOU THEN, TABBY!

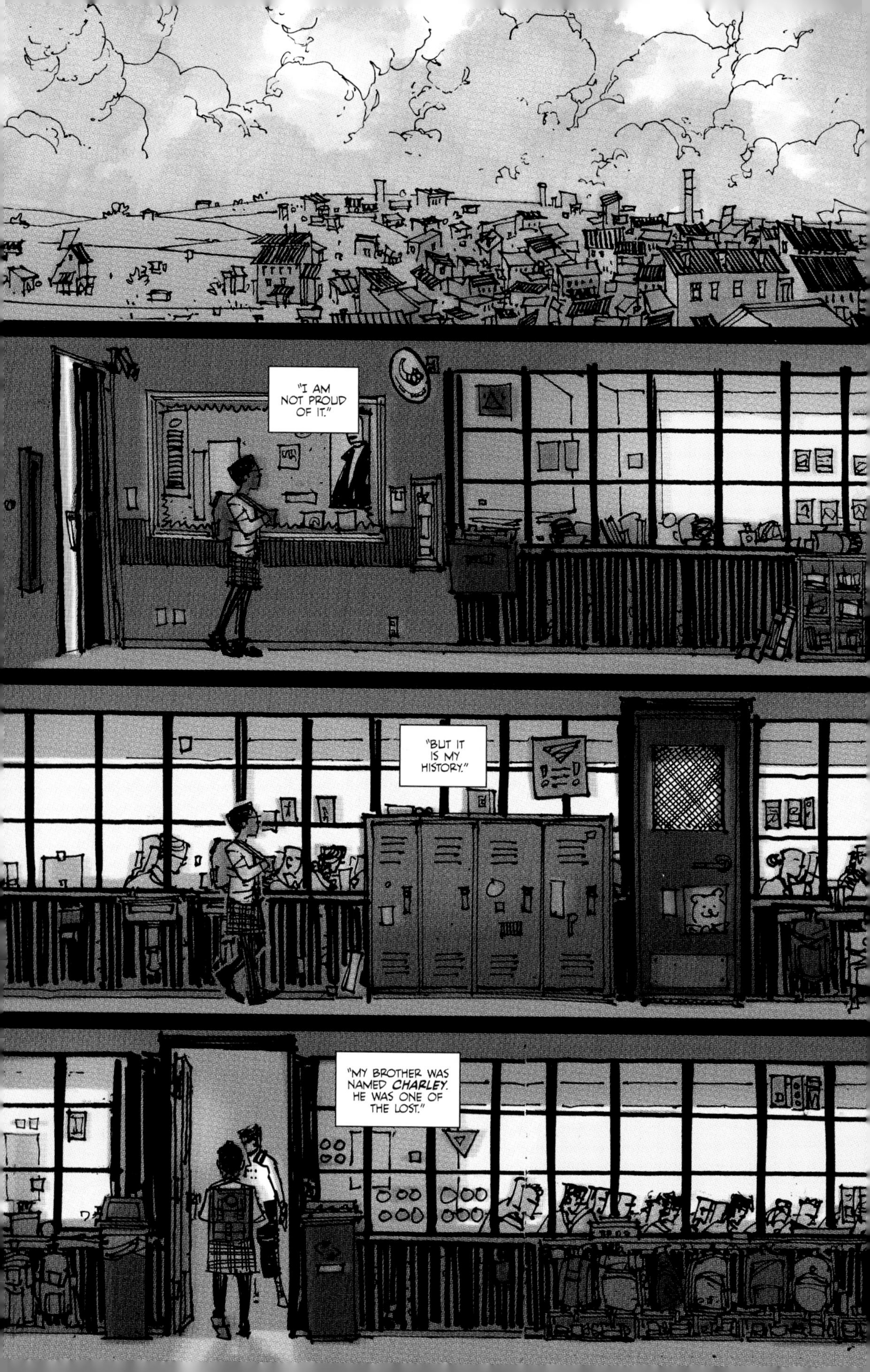
"I AM NOT PROUD OF IT."
"BUT IT IS MY HISTORY."
"MY BROTHER WAS NAMED CHARLEY. HE WAS ONE OF THE LOST."

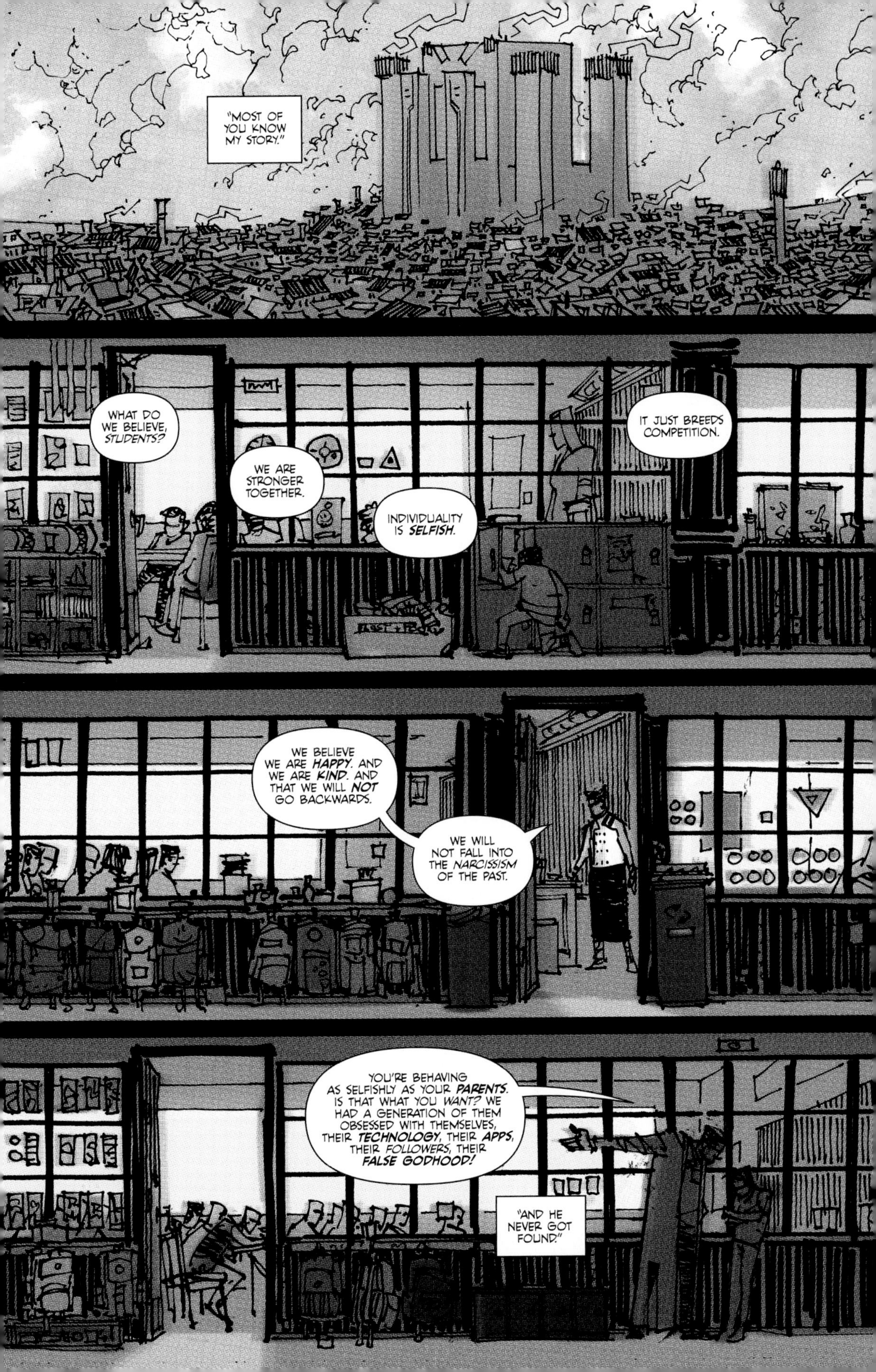
"MOST OF YOU KNOW MY STORY."
WHAT DO WE BELIEVE, STUDENTS?
WE ARE STRONGER TOGETHER.
INDIVIDUALITY IS SELFISH.
IT JUST BREEDS COMPETITION.
WE BELIEVE WE ARE HAPPY. AND WE ARE KIND. AND THAT WE WILL NOT GO BACKWARDS.
WE WILL NOT FALL INTO THE NARCISSISM OF THE PAST.
YOU'RE BEHAVING AS SELFISHLY AS YOUR PARENTS. IS THAT WHAT YOU WANT? WE HAD A GENERATION OF THEM OBSESSED WITH THEMSELVES, THEIR TECHNOLOGY, THEIR APPS, THEIR FOLLOWERS, THEIR FALSE GODHOOD!
"AND HE NEVER GOT FOUND."

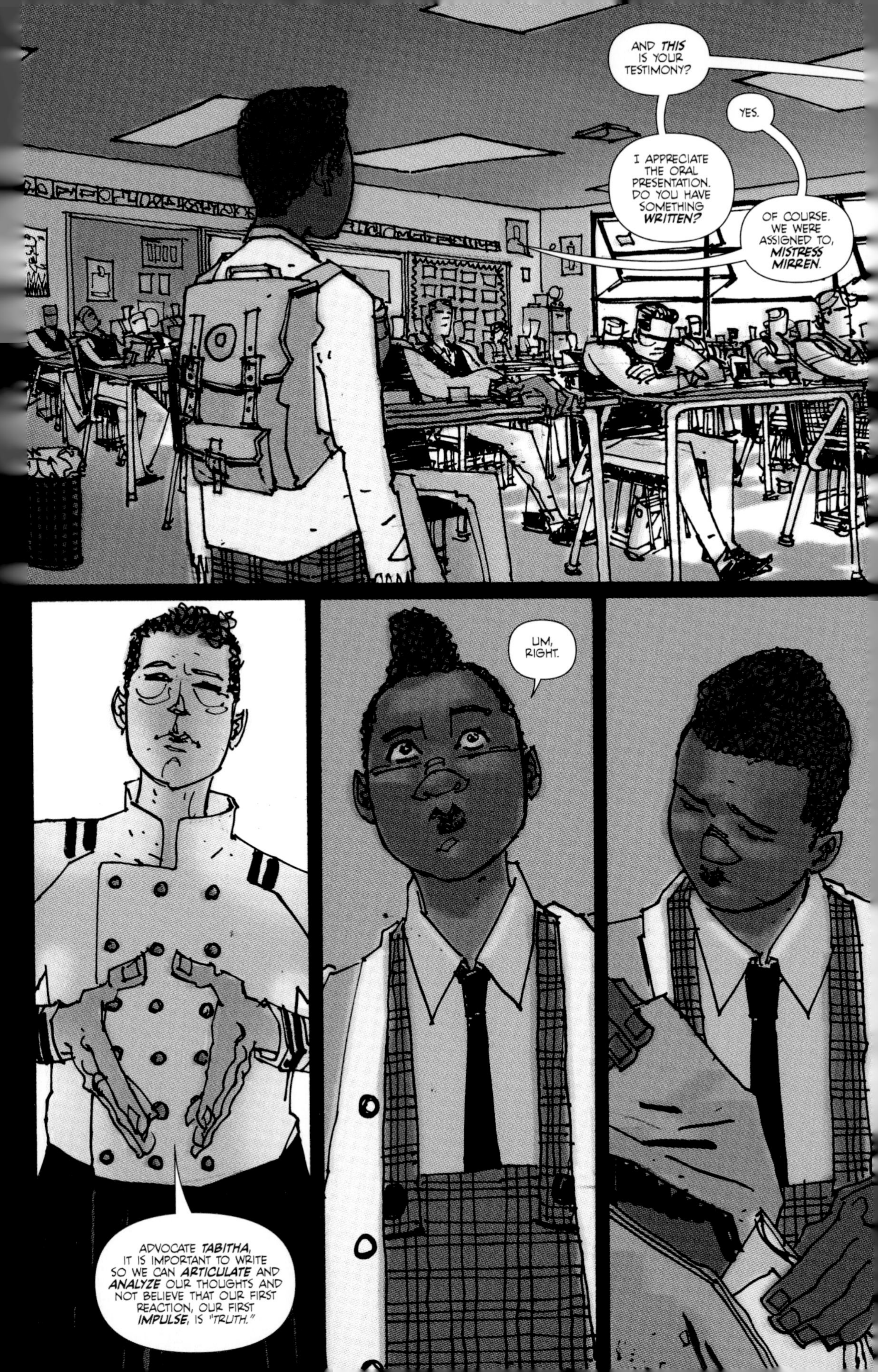
AND *THIS* IS YOUR TESTIMONY?
YES.
I APPRECIATE THE ORAL PRESENTATION. DO YOU HAVE SOMETHING *WRITTEN?*
OF COURSE. WE WERE ASSIGNED TO, *MISTRESS MIRREN*.
ADVOCATE *TABITHA*, IT IS IMPORTANT TO WRITE SO WE CAN *ARTICULATE* AND *ANALYZE* OUR THOUGHTS AND NOT BELIEVE THAT OUR FIRST REACTION, OUR FIRST *IMPULSE*, IS *"TRUTH."*
UM, RIGHT.

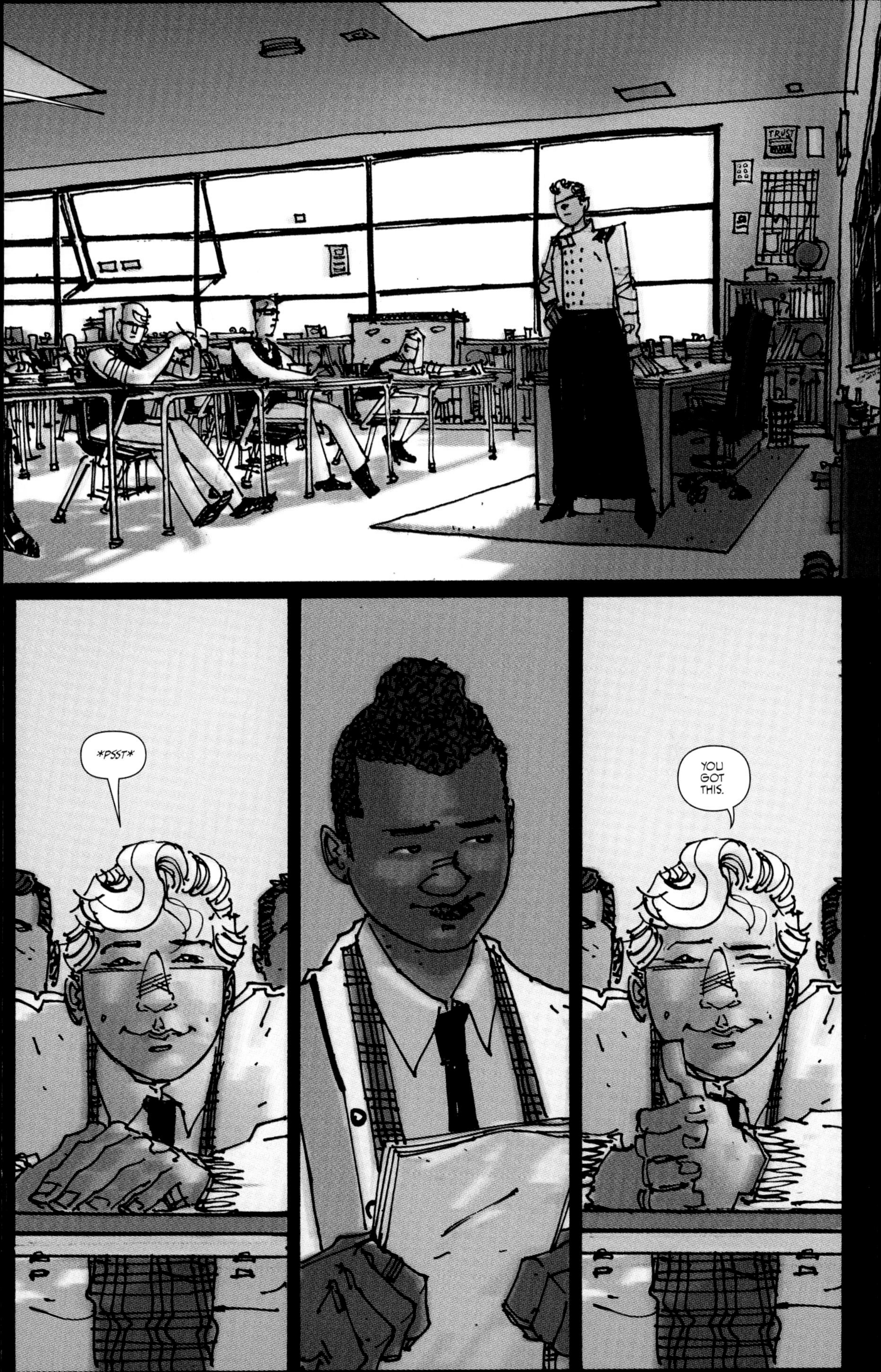
PSST
YOU GOT THIS.

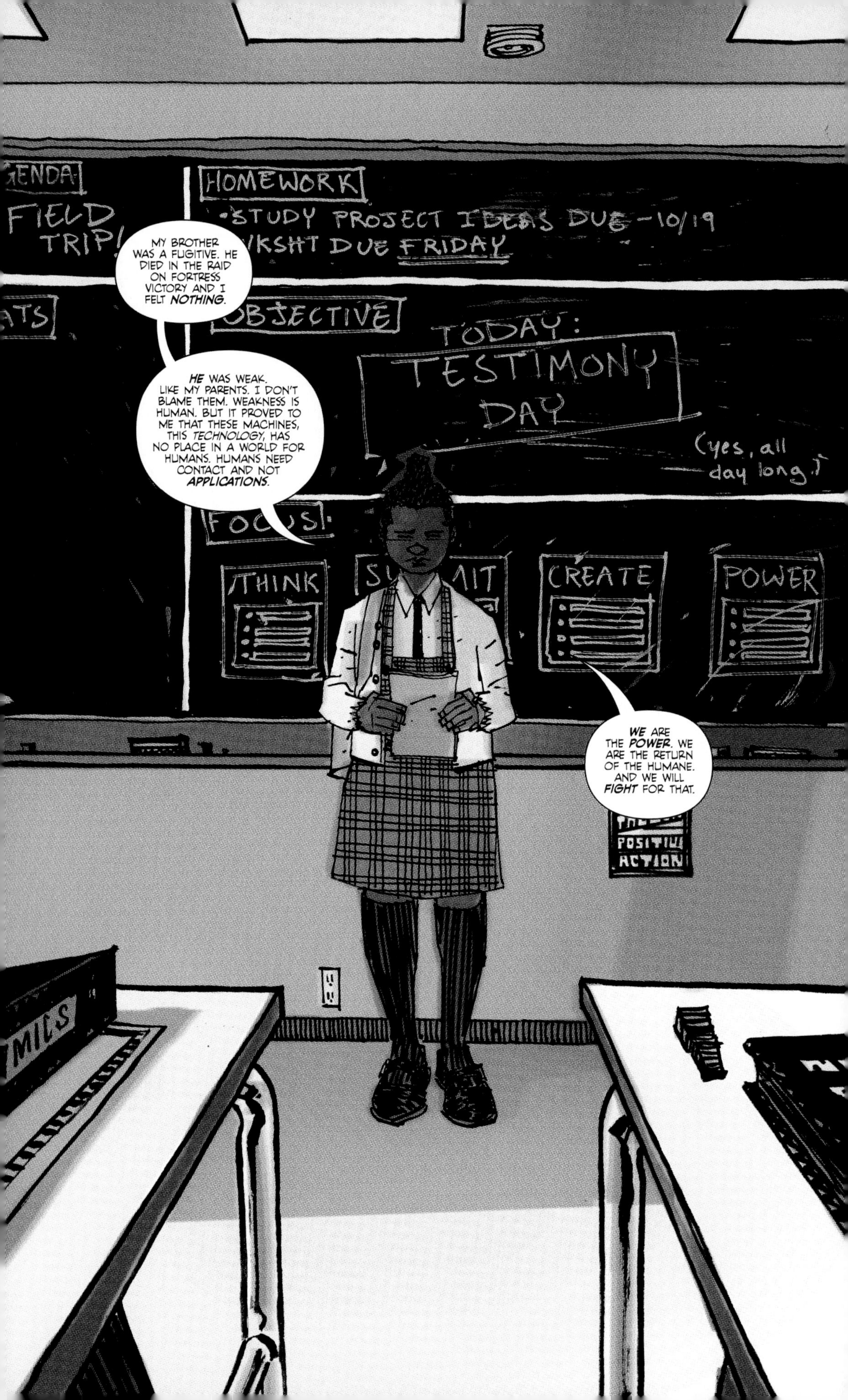
HOMEWORK
TODAY: TESTIMONY DAY
(yes, all day long.)
MY BROTHER WAS A FUGITIVE. HE DIED IN THE RAID ON FORTRESS VICTORY AND I FELT *NOTHING*.
HE WAS WEAK. LIKE MY PARENTS. I DON'T BLAME THEM. WEAKNESS IS HUMAN. BUT IT PROVED TO ME THAT THESE MACHINES, THIS *TECHNOLOGY*, HAS NO PLACE IN A WORLD FOR HUMANS. HUMANS NEED CONTACT AND NOT *APPLICATIONS*.
THINK
CREATE
POWER
WE ARE THE *POWER*. WE ARE THE RETURN OF THE HUMANE. AND WE WILL *FIGHT* FOR THAT.
POSITIVE ACTION

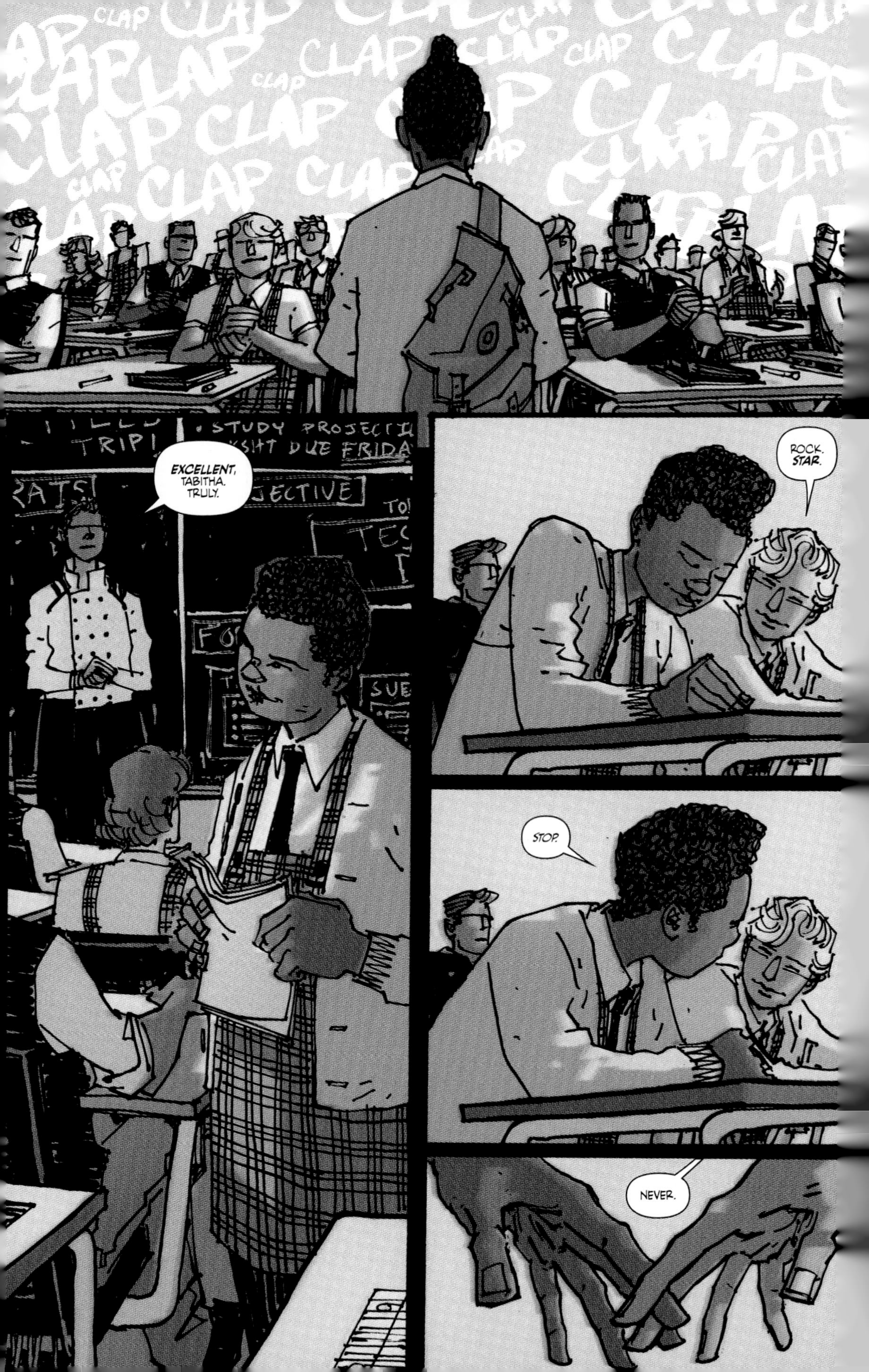
EXCELLENT, TABITHA. TRULY.
ROCK. STAR.
STOP.
NEVER.

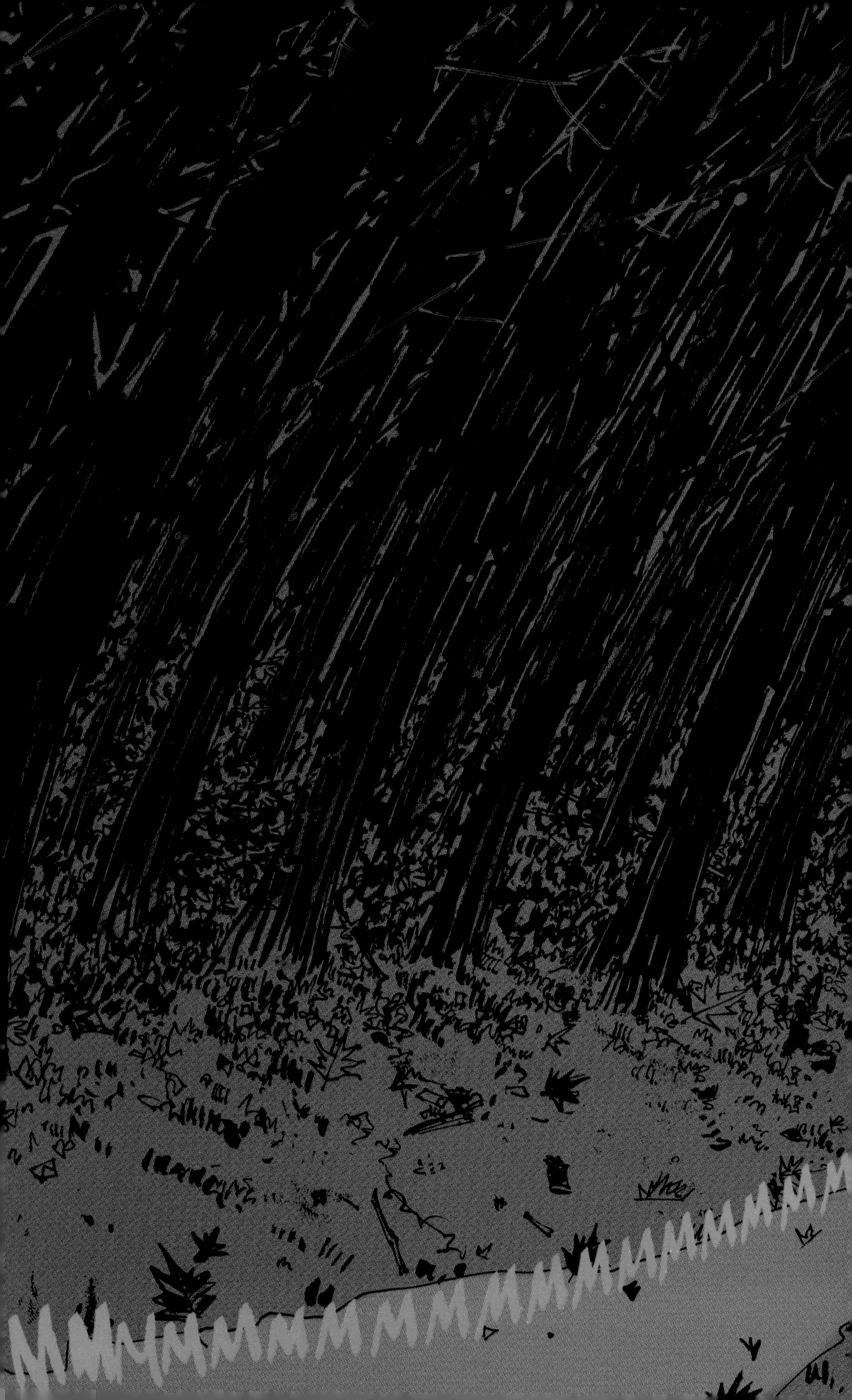
MMMMMMMMMMMMMMMMMMMMMMM

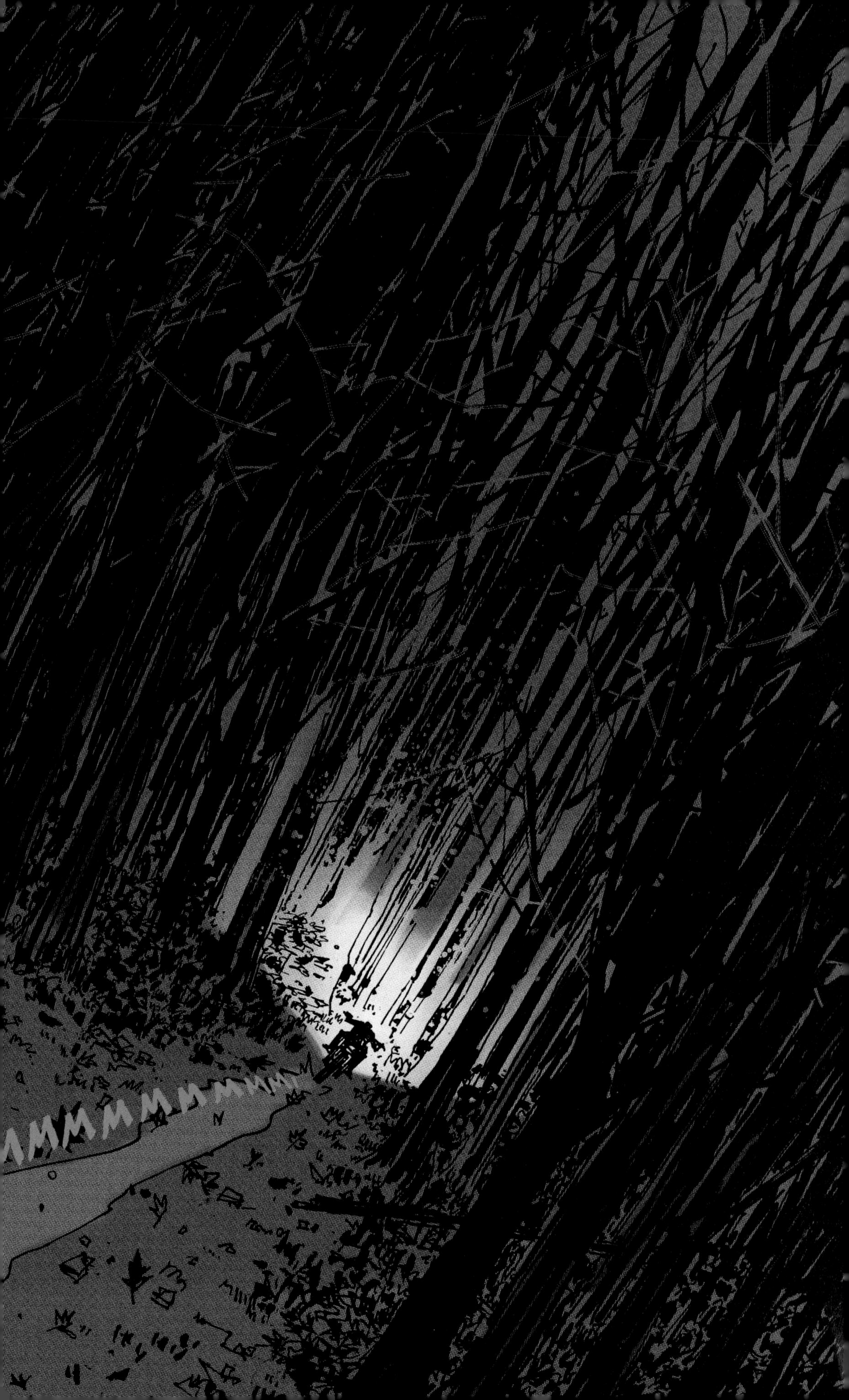
MMMMMMMMMMM

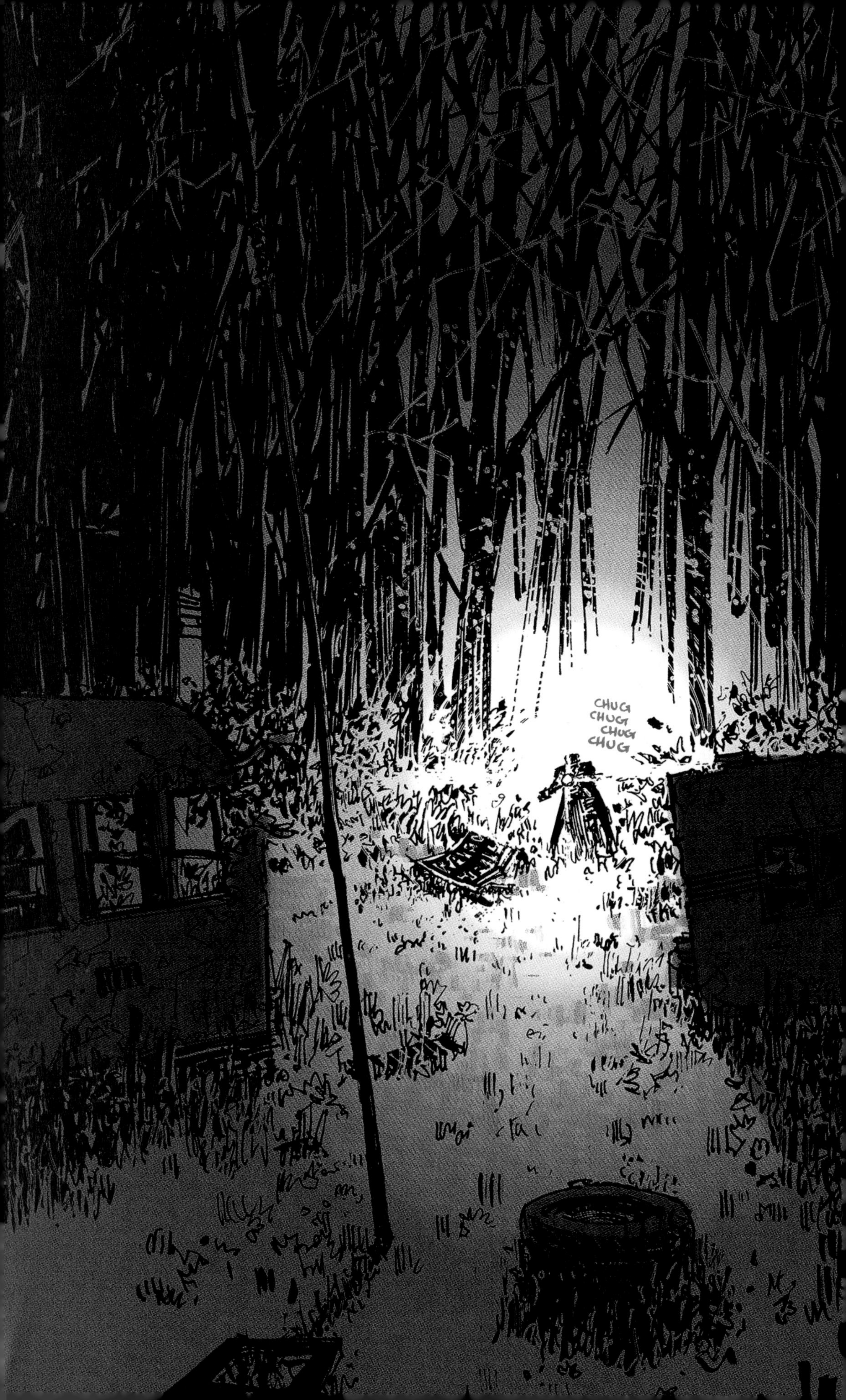
CHUG
CHUG
CHUG
CHUG

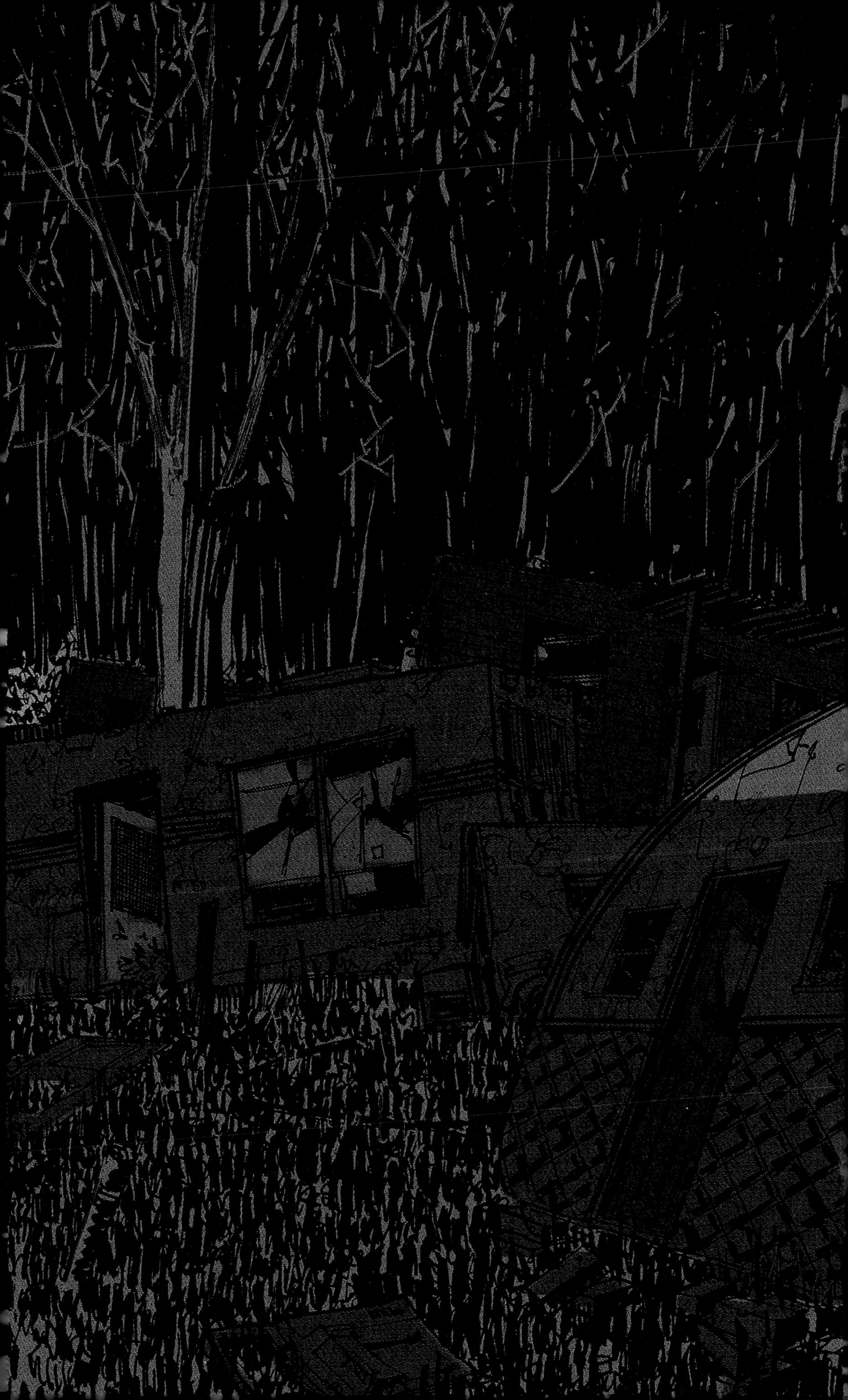

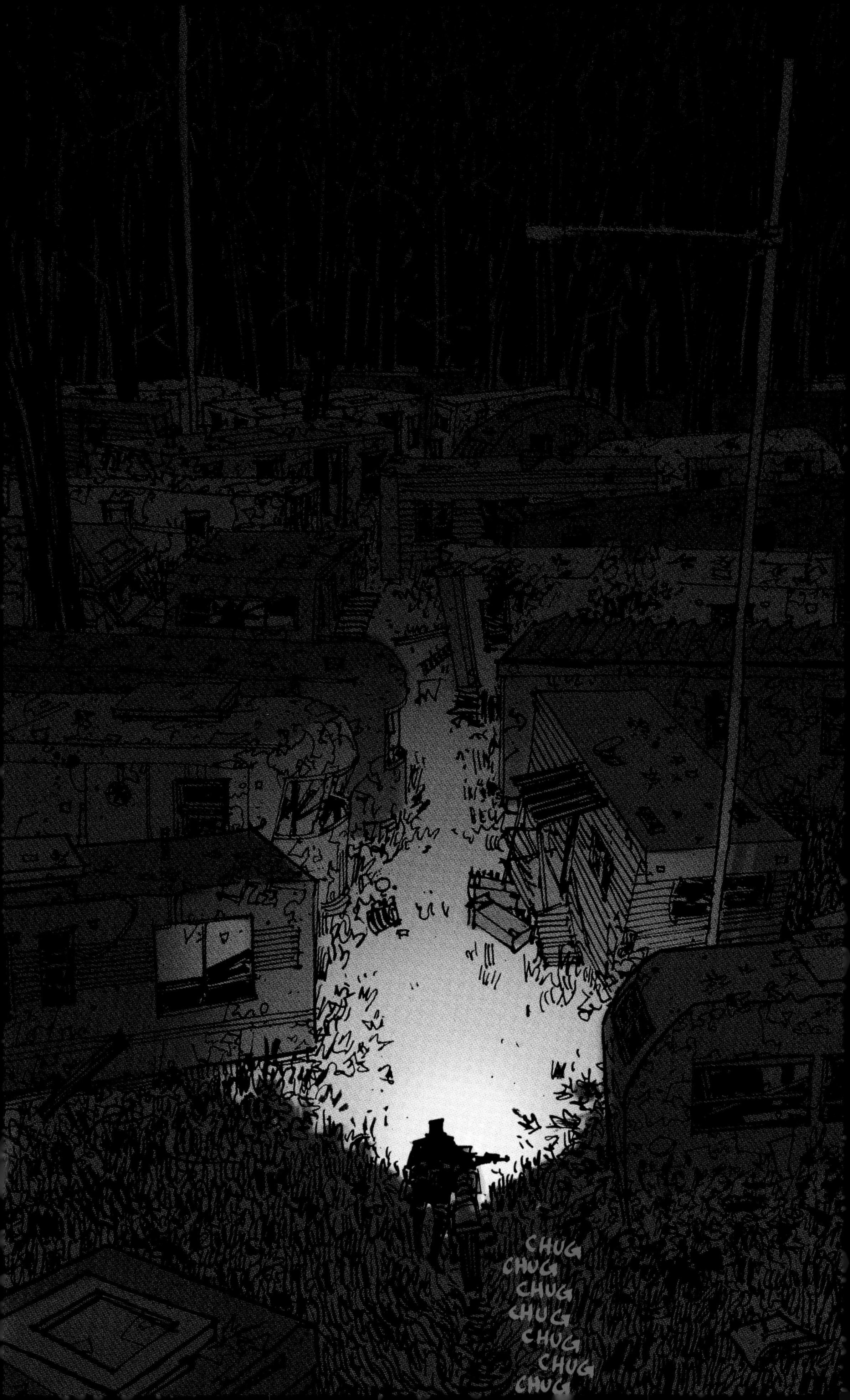
CHUG
CHUG
CHUG
CHUG
CHUG
CHUG
CHUG

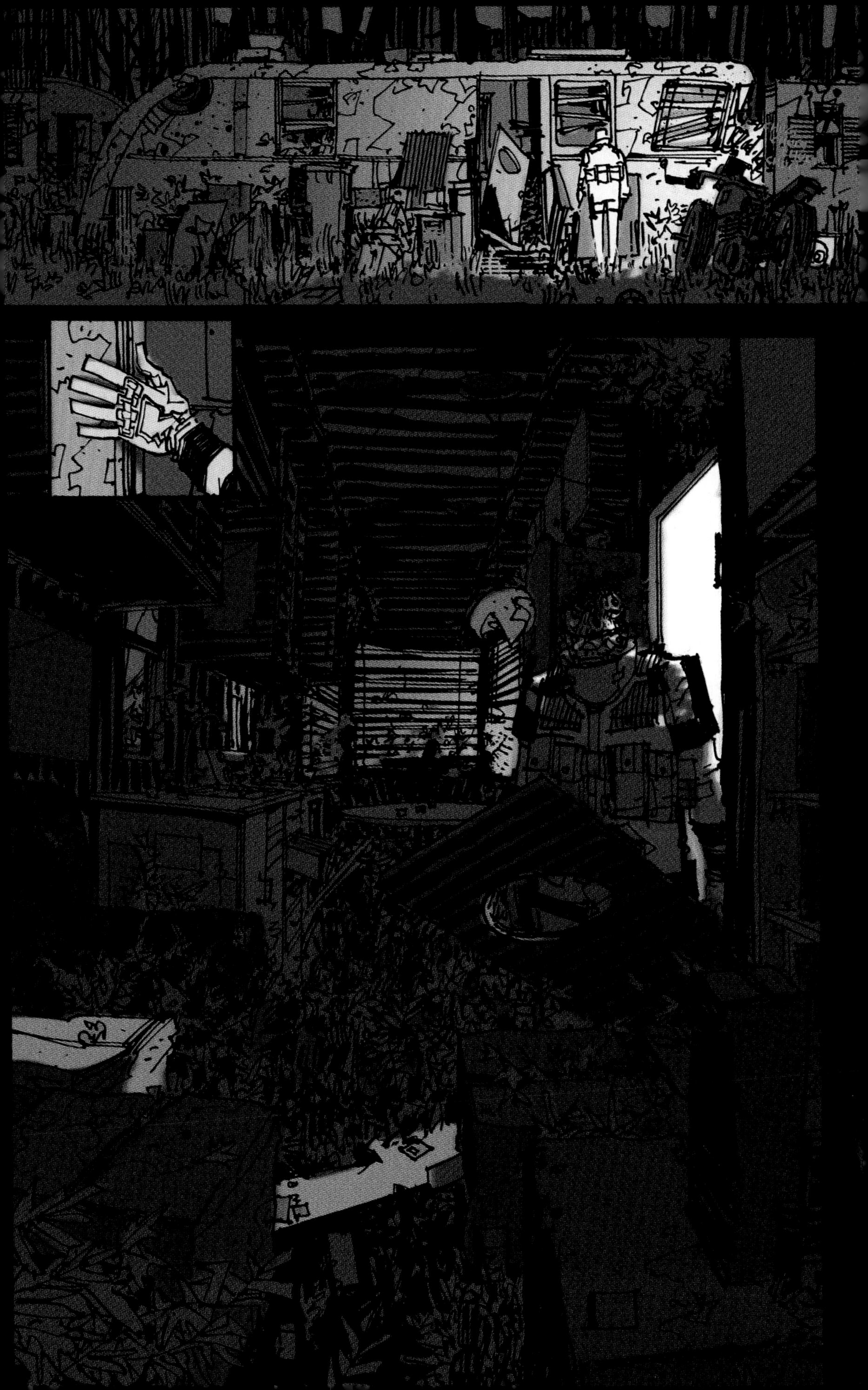

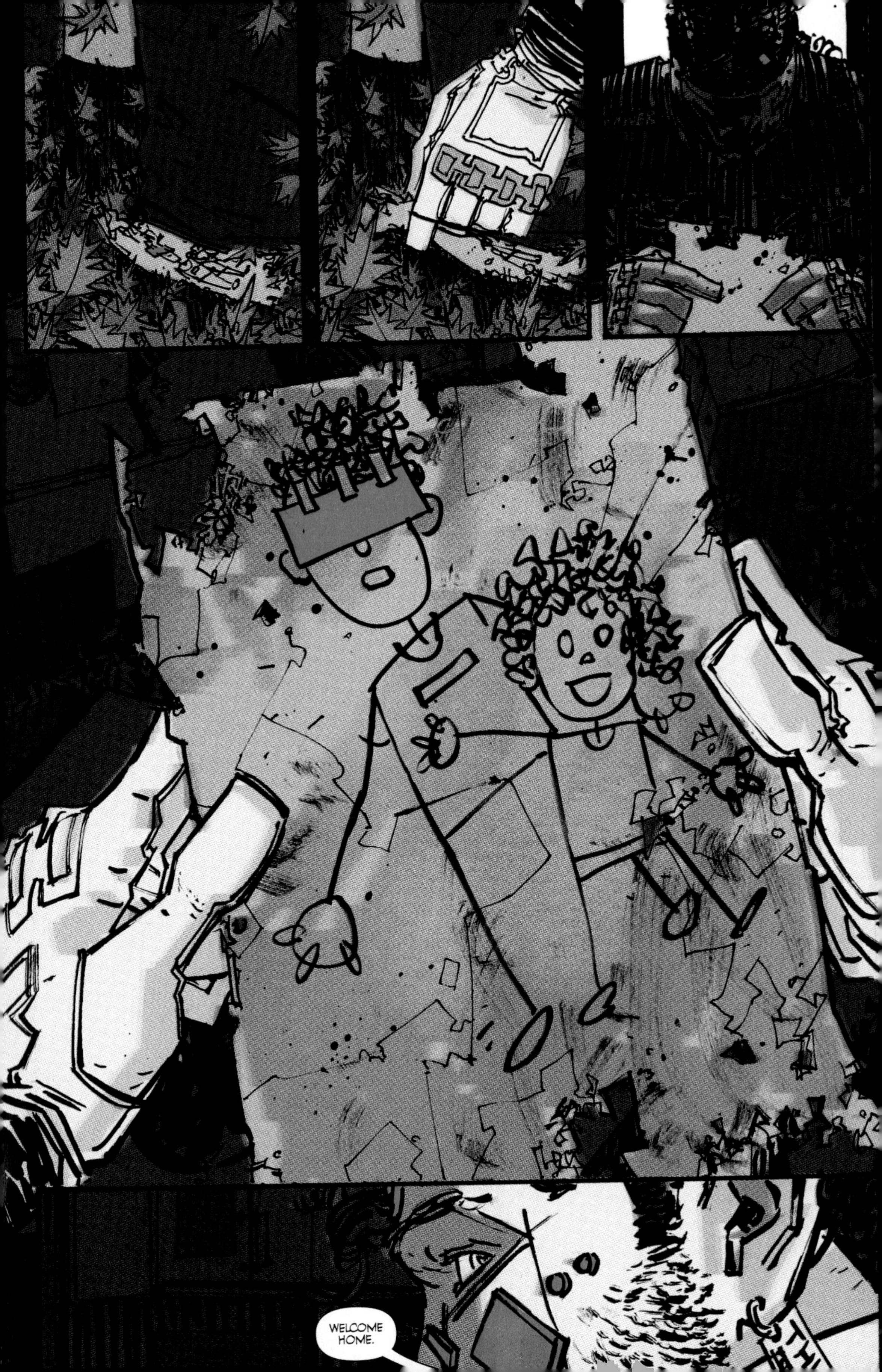
WELCOME HOME.

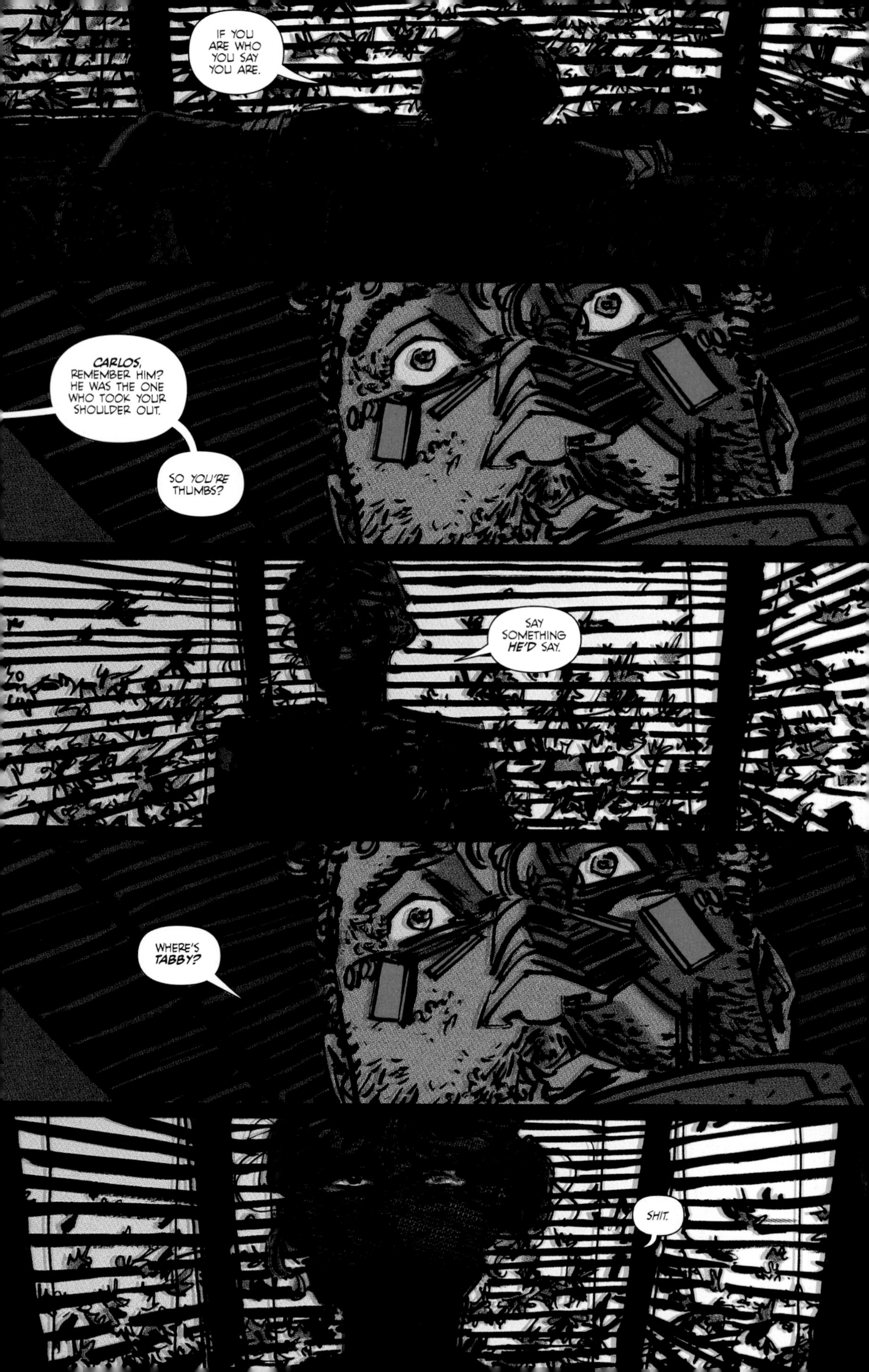
IF YOU ARE WHO YOU SAY YOU ARE.
CARLOS, REMEMBER HIM? HE WAS THE ONE WHO TOOK YOUR SHOULDER OUT.
SO YOU'RE THUMBS?
SAY SOMETHING HE'D SAY.
WHERE'S TABBY?
SHIT.

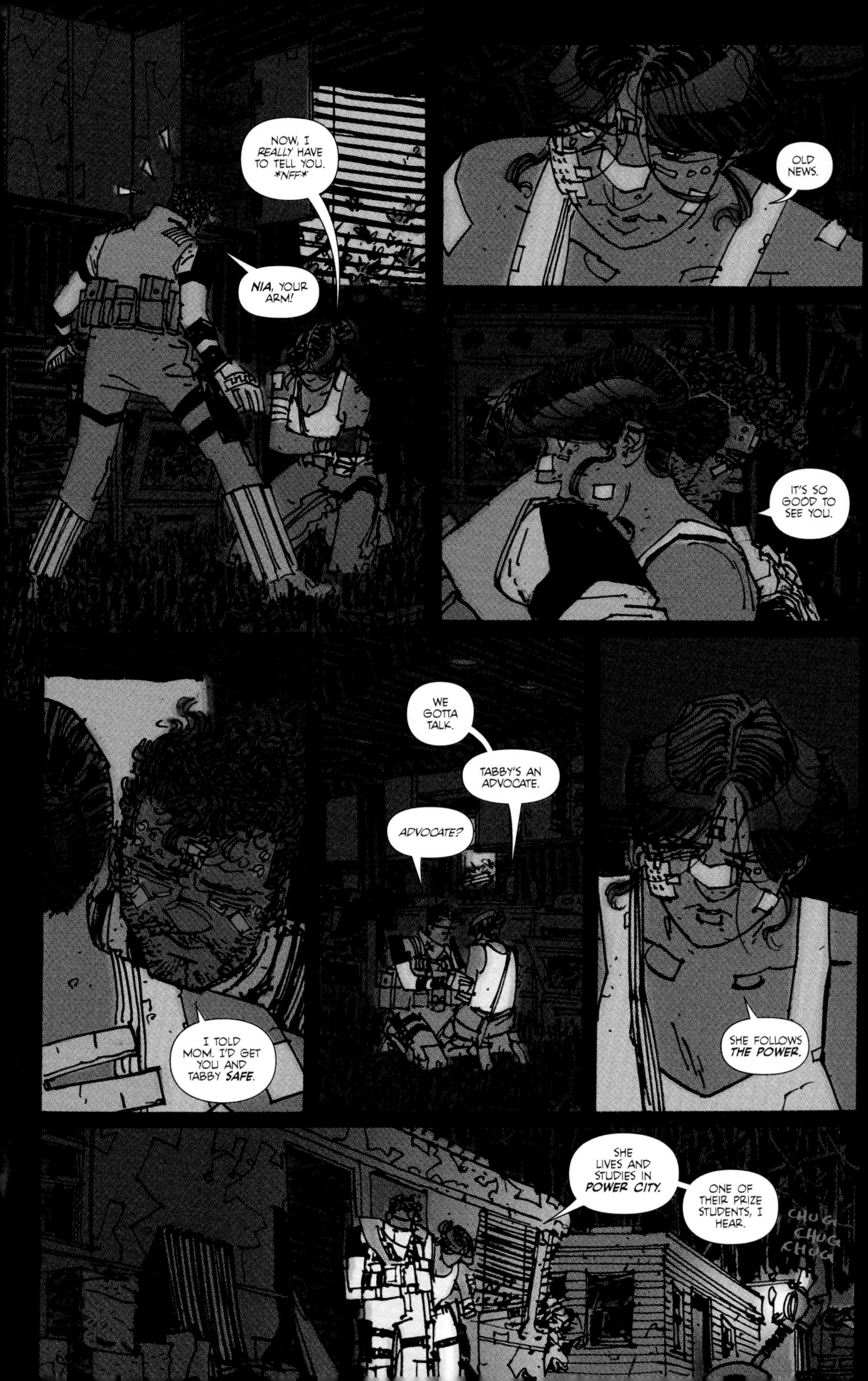
NOW, I *REALLY* HAVE TO TELL YOU. *NFF*
NIA, YOUR ARM!
OLD NEWS.
IT'S SO GOOD TO SEE YOU.
I TOLD MOM. I'D GET YOU AND TABBY *SAFE*.
WE GOTTA TALK.
TABBY'S AN ADVOCATE.
ADVOCATE?
SHE FOLLOWS *THE POWER.*
SHE LIVES AND STUDIES IN *POWER CITY.*
ONE OF THEIR PRIZE STUDENTS, I HEAR.
CHUG CHUG CHUG

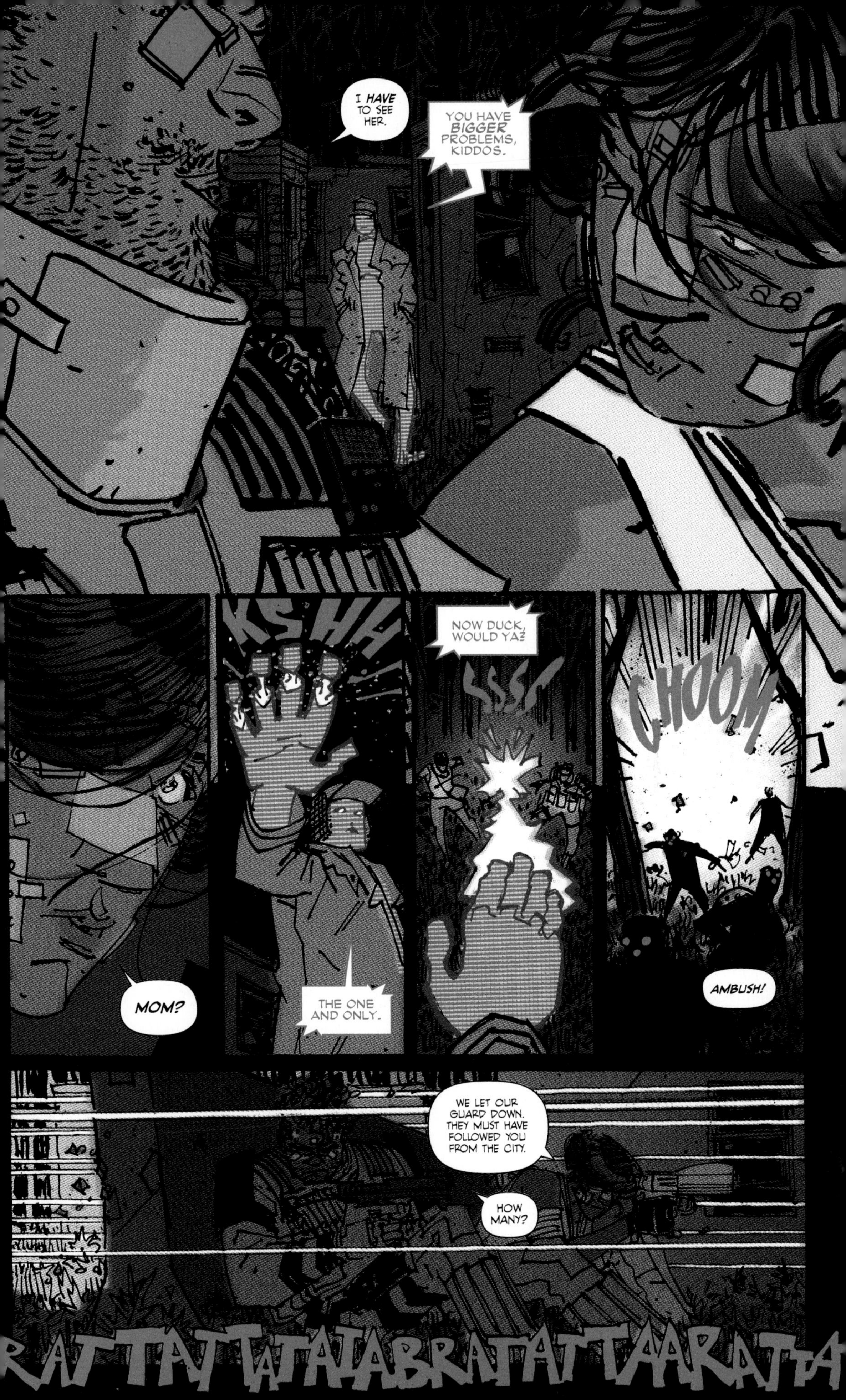

I HAVE TO SEE HER.
YOU HAVE BIGGER PROBLEMS, KIDDOS.
MOM?
KSHH
THE ONE AND ONLY.
NOW DUCK, WOULD YA?
SSSS
CHOOM
AMBUSH!
WE LET OUR GUARD DOWN. THEY MUST HAVE FOLLOWED YOU FROM THE CITY.
HOW MANY?
RATTATTATATATABRATATTATTAARATTA

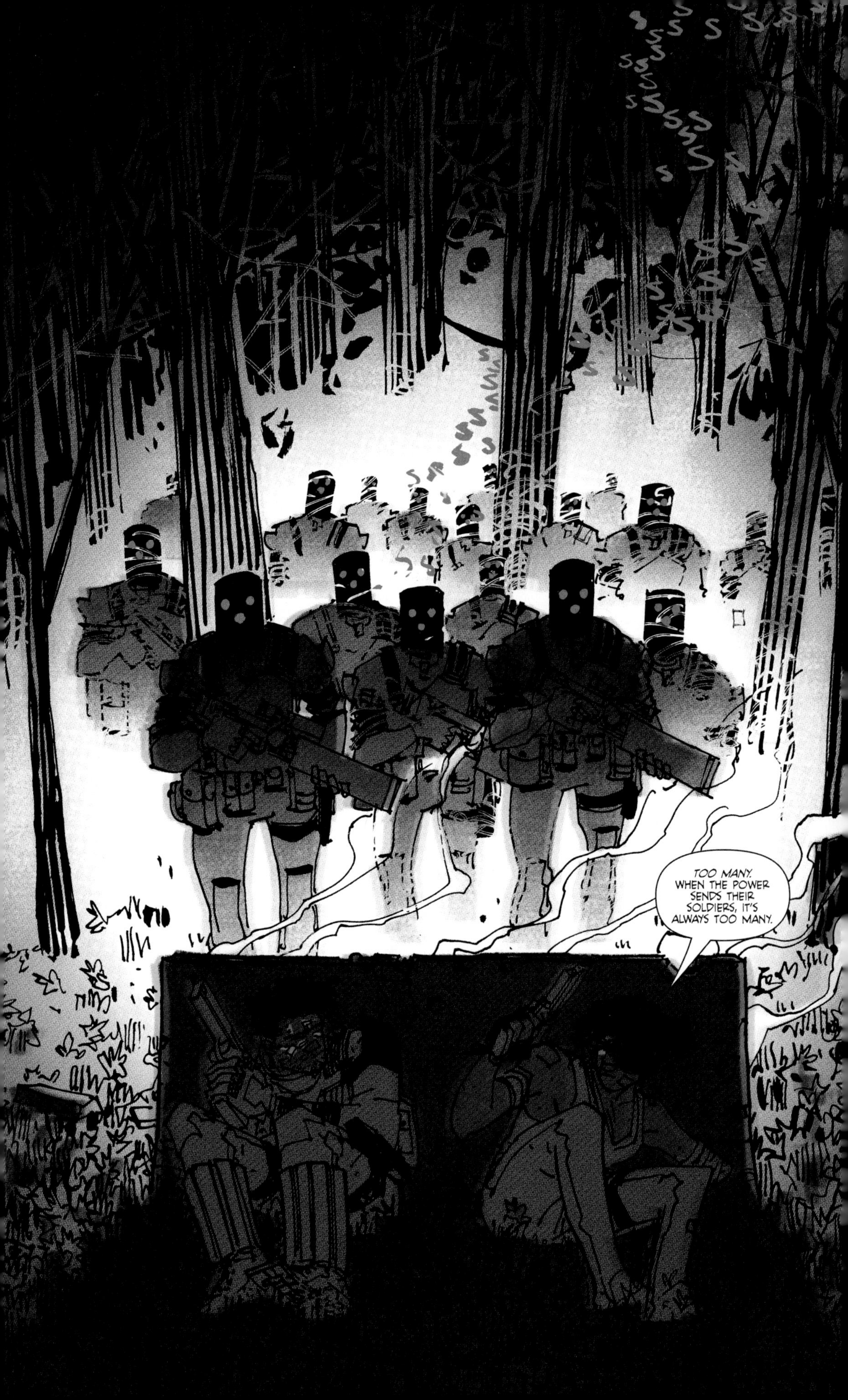
TOO MANY. WHEN THE POWER SENDS THEIR SOLDIERS, IT'S ALWAYS TOO MANY.

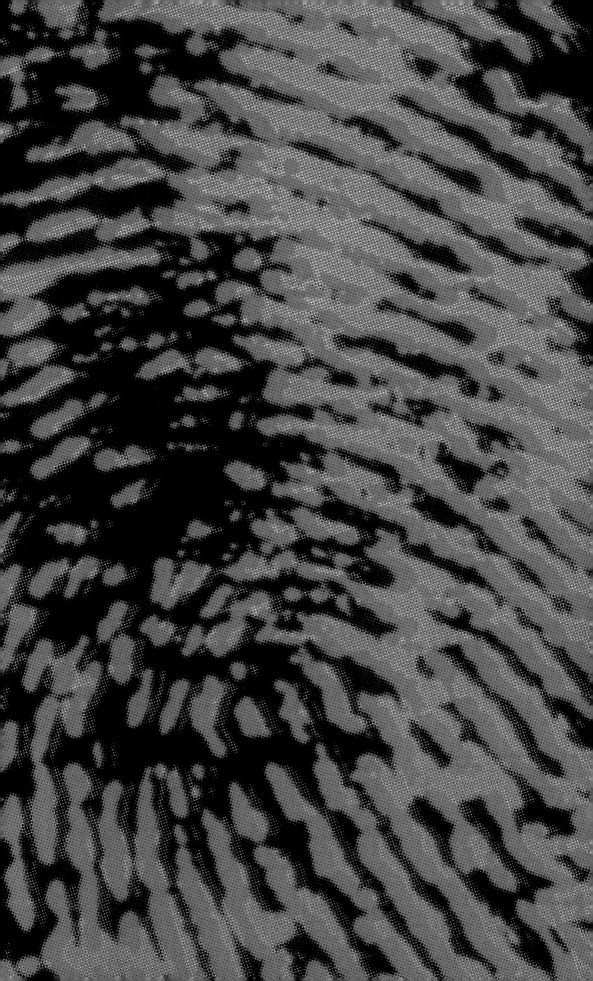

PART THREE

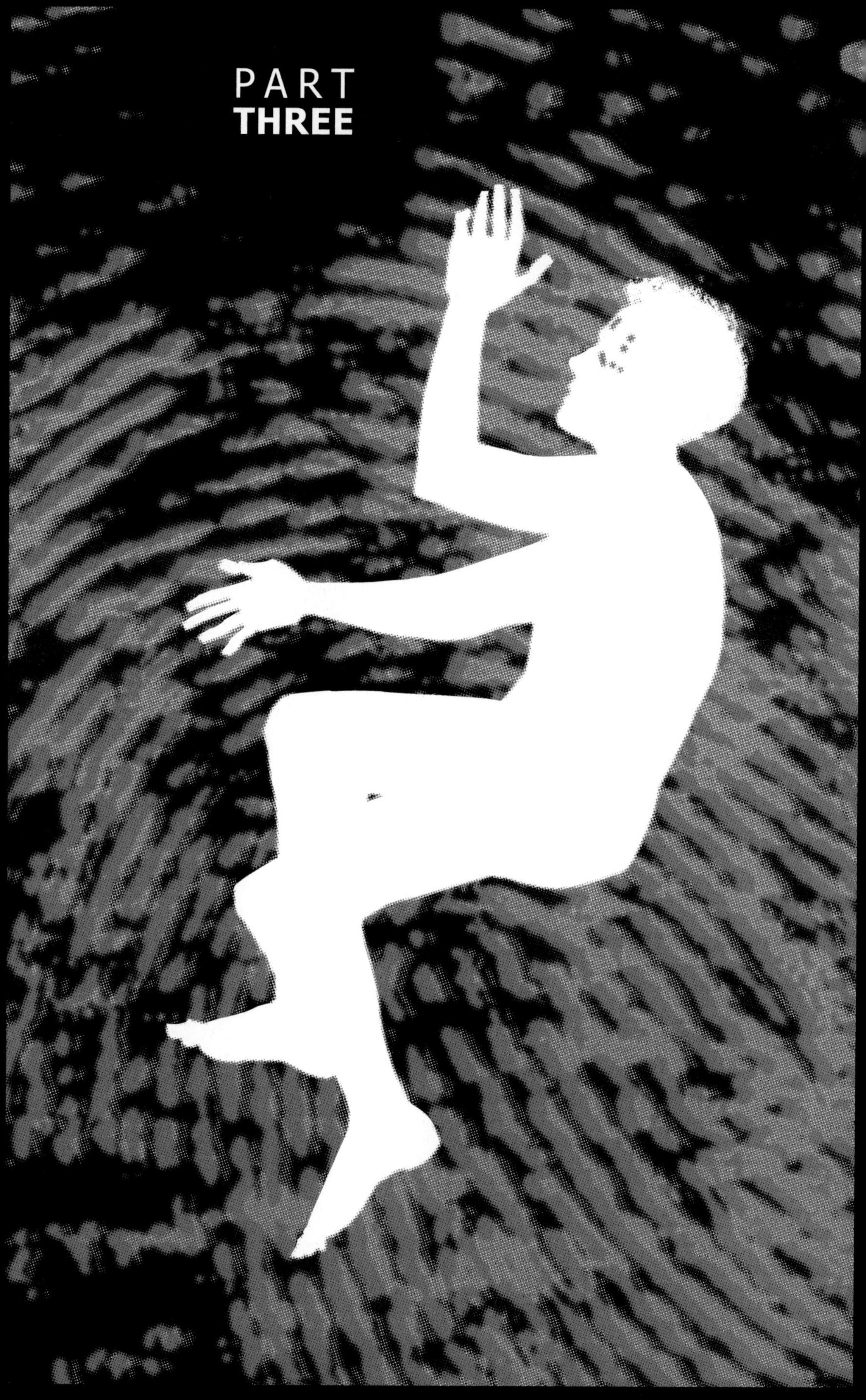

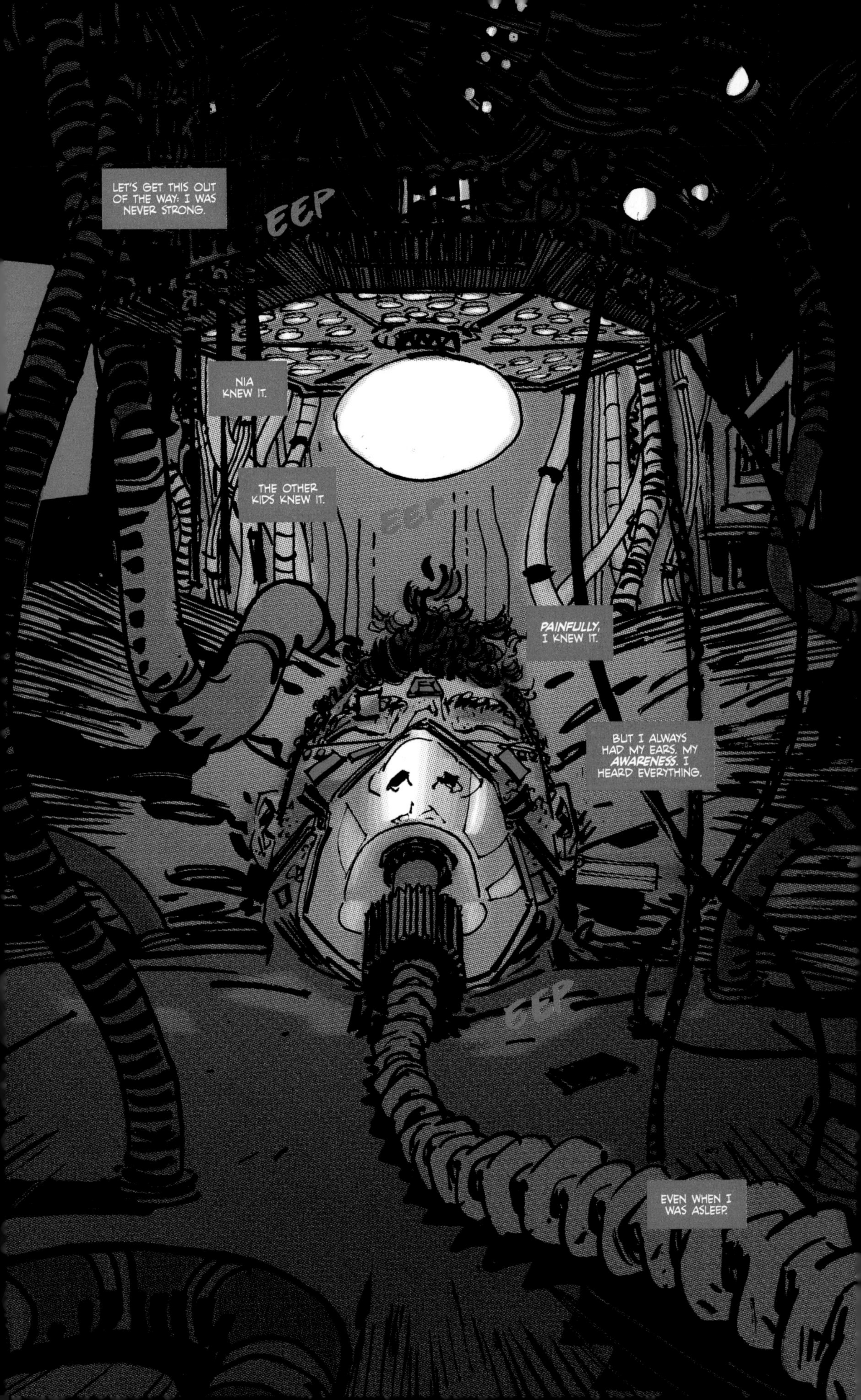
LET'S GET THIS OUT OF THE WAY: I WAS NEVER STRONG.
EEP
NIA KNEW IT.
THE OTHER KIDS KNEW IT.
EEP
PAINFULLY, I KNEW IT.
BUT I ALWAYS HAD MY EARS. MY AWARENESS. I HEARD EVERYTHING.
EEP
EVEN WHEN I WAS ASLEEP.

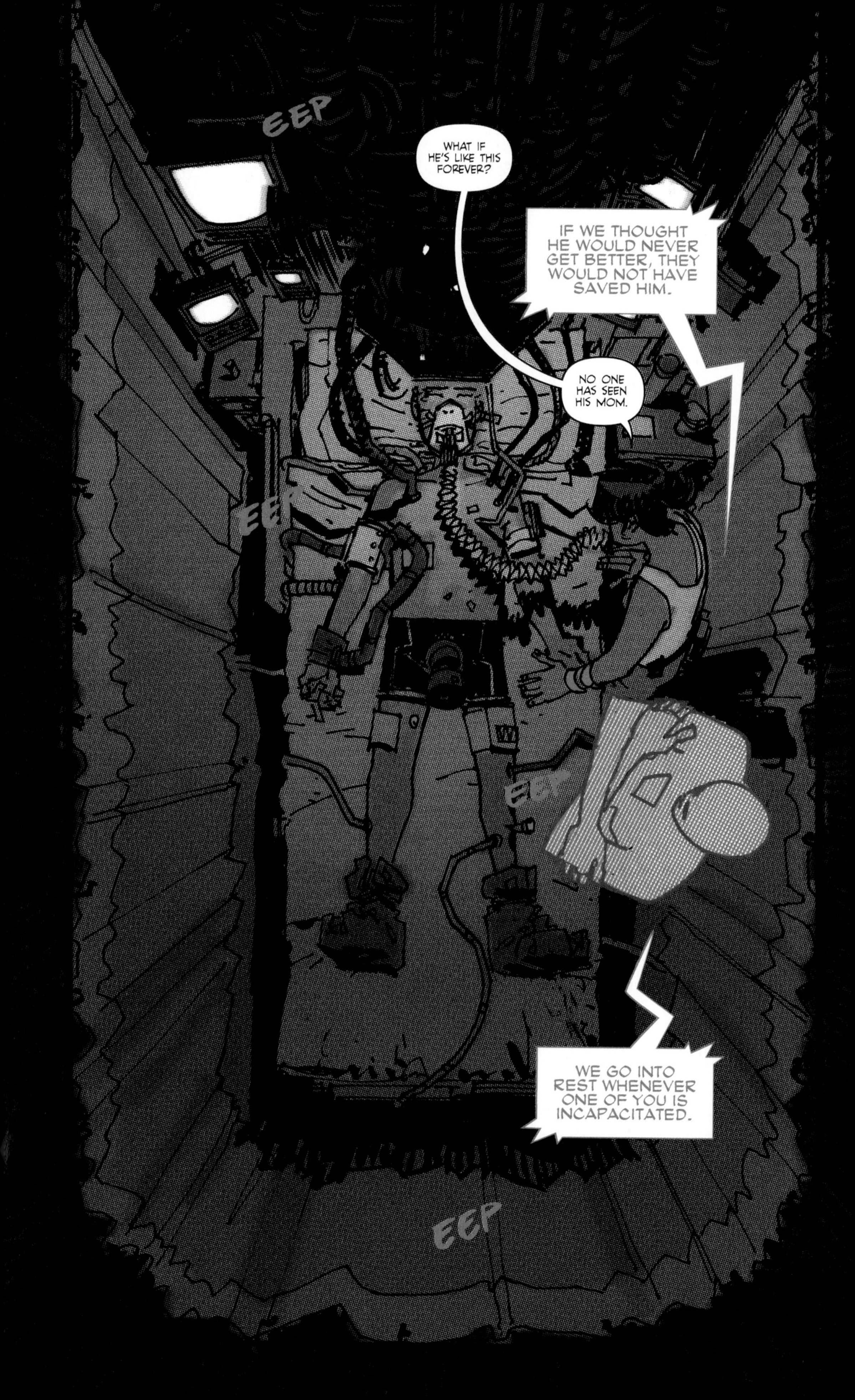
EEP
WHAT IF HE'S LIKE THIS FOREVER?
IF WE THOUGHT HE WOULD NEVER GET BETTER, THEY WOULD NOT HAVE SAVED HIM.
NO ONE HAS SEEN HIS MOM.
EEP
EEP
WE GO INTO REST WHENEVER ONE OF YOU IS INCAPACITATED.
EEP

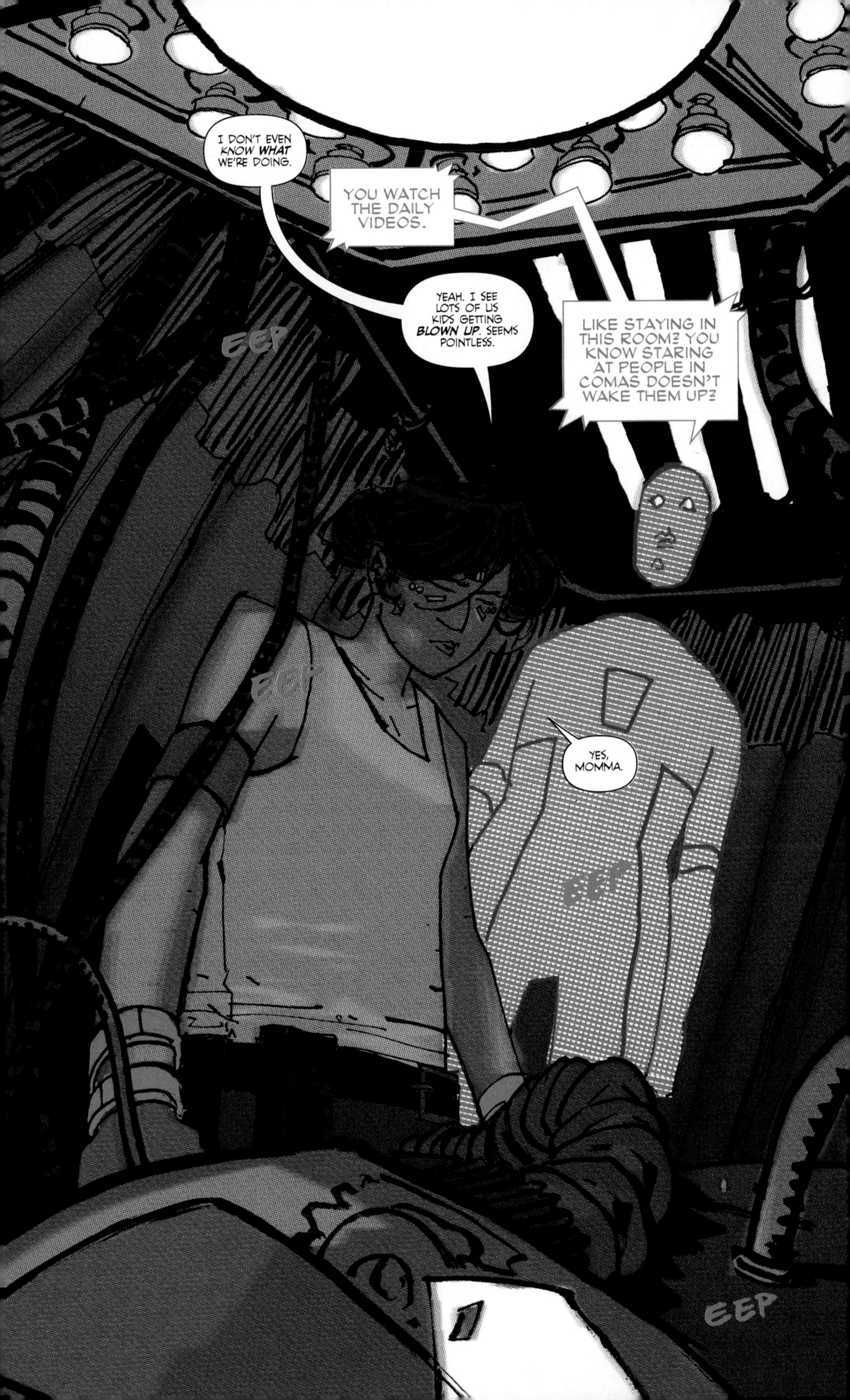
I DON'T EVEN KNOW WHAT WE'RE DOING.
YOU WATCH THE DAILY VIDEOS.
YEAH. I SEE LOTS OF US KIDS GETTING BLOWN UP. SEEMS POINTLESS.
LIKE STAYING IN THIS ROOM? YOU KNOW STARING AT PEOPLE IN COMAS DOESN'T WAKE THEM UP?
EEP
EEP
YES, MOMMA.
EEP
EEP

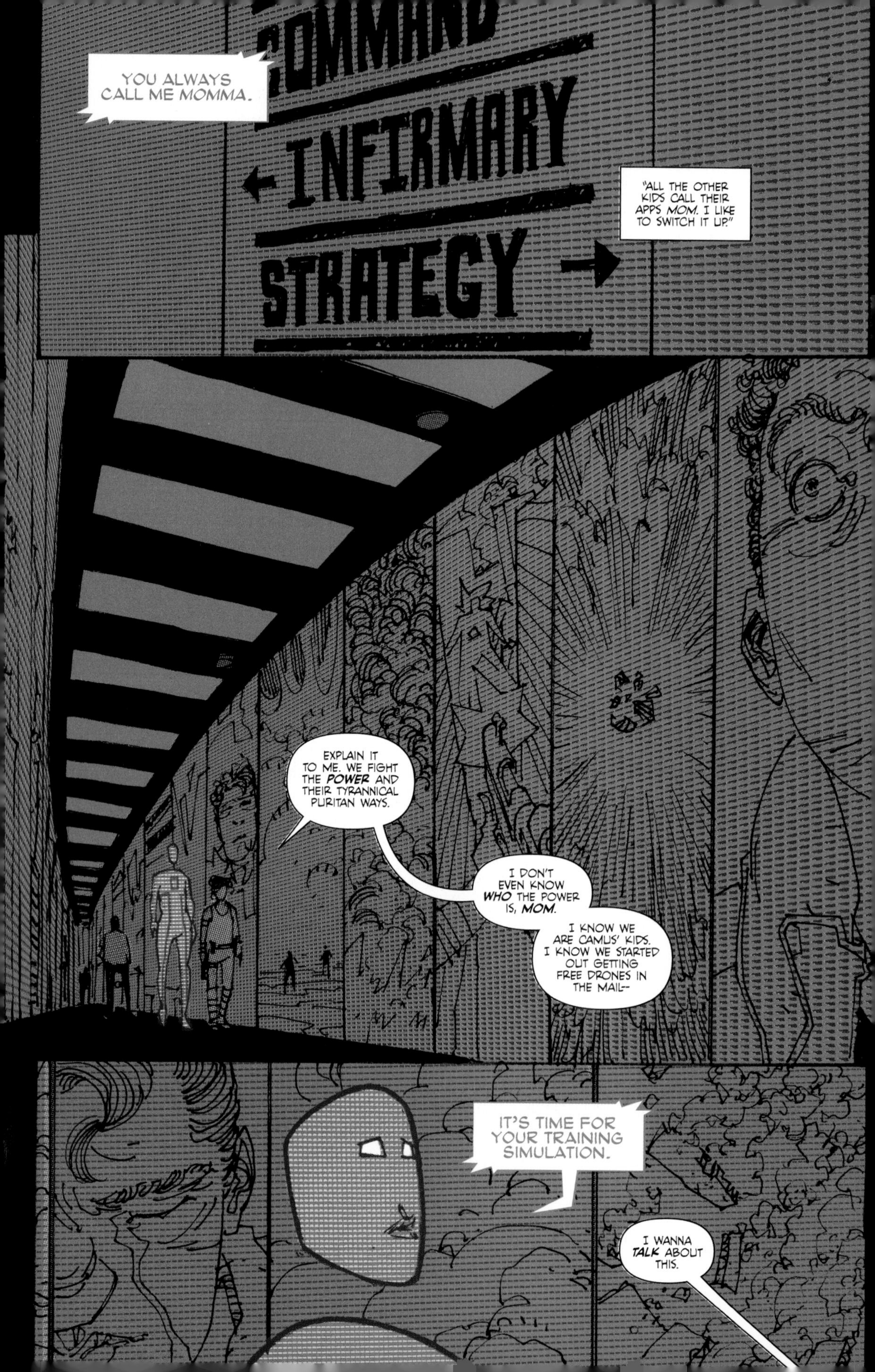

COMMAND
YOU ALWAYS CALL ME MOMMA.
← INFIRMARY
STRATEGY →
"ALL THE OTHER KIDS CALL THEIR APPS MOM. I LIKE TO SWITCH IT UP."
EXPLAIN IT TO ME. WE FIGHT THE POWER AND THEIR TYRANNICAL PURITAN WAYS.
I DON'T EVEN KNOW WHO THE POWER IS, MOM.
I KNOW WE ARE CAMUS' KIDS. I KNOW WE STARTED OUT GETTING FREE DRONES IN THE MAIL--
IT'S TIME FOR YOUR TRAINING SIMULATION.
I WANNA TALK ABOUT THIS.

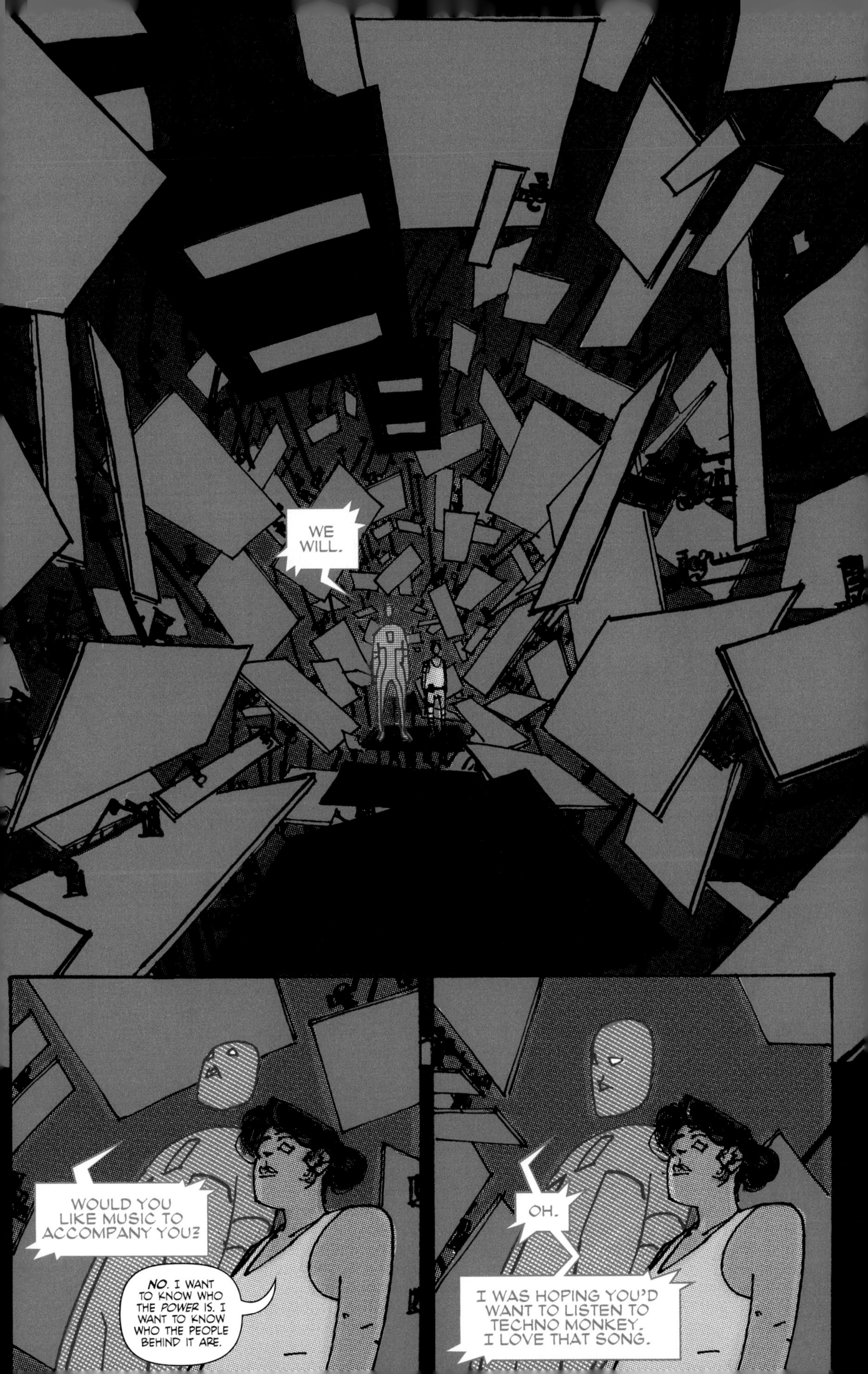
WE WILL.
WOULD YOU LIKE MUSIC TO ACCOMPANY YOU?
NO. I WANT TO KNOW WHO THE POWER IS. I WANT TO KNOW WHO THE PEOPLE BEHIND IT ARE.
OH.
I WAS HOPING YOU'D WANT TO LISTEN TO TECHNO MONKEY. I LOVE THAT SONG.

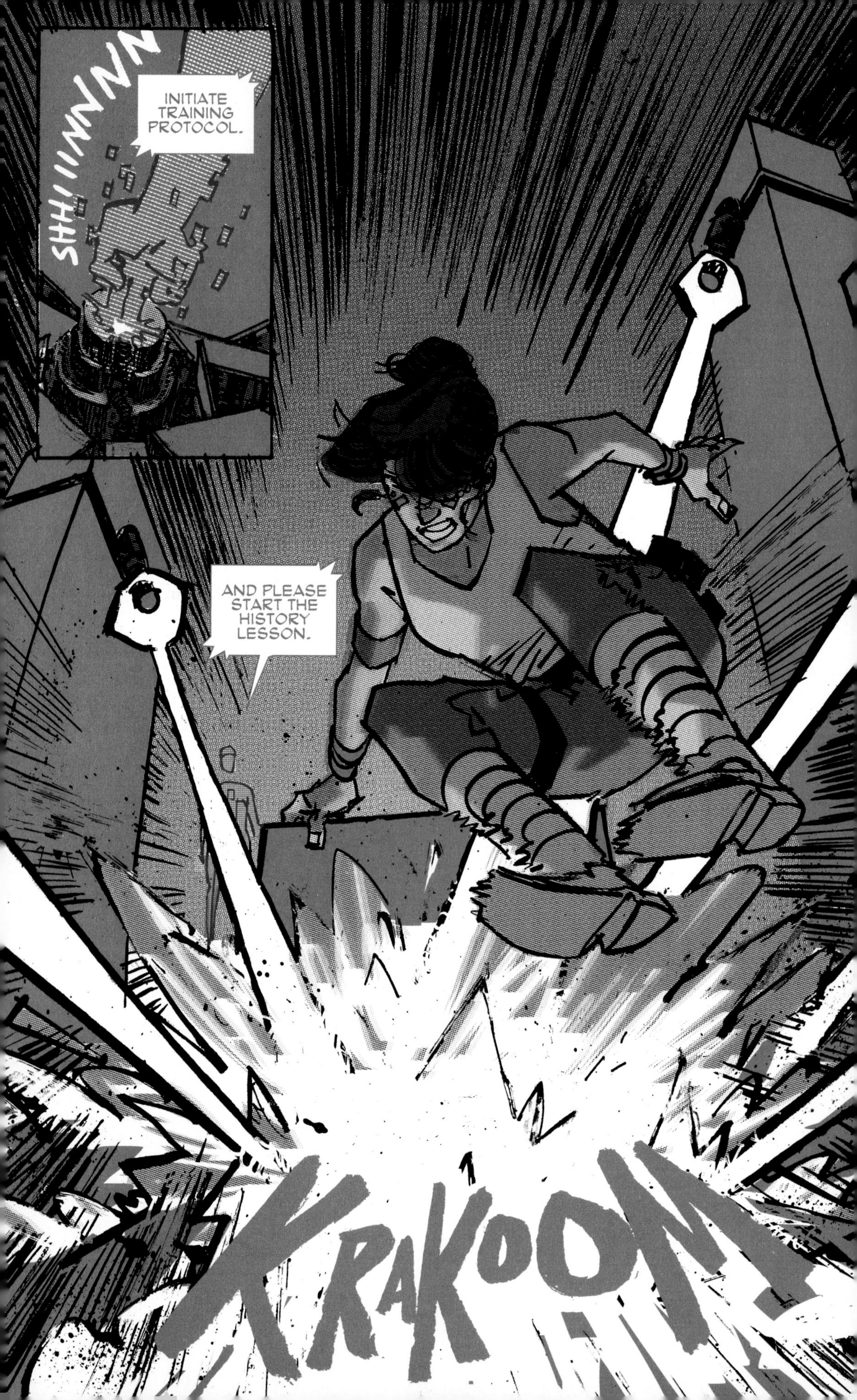
SHHIIIINNNN
INITIATE TRAINING PROTOCOL.
AND PLEASE START THE HISTORY LESSON.
KRAKOOM!

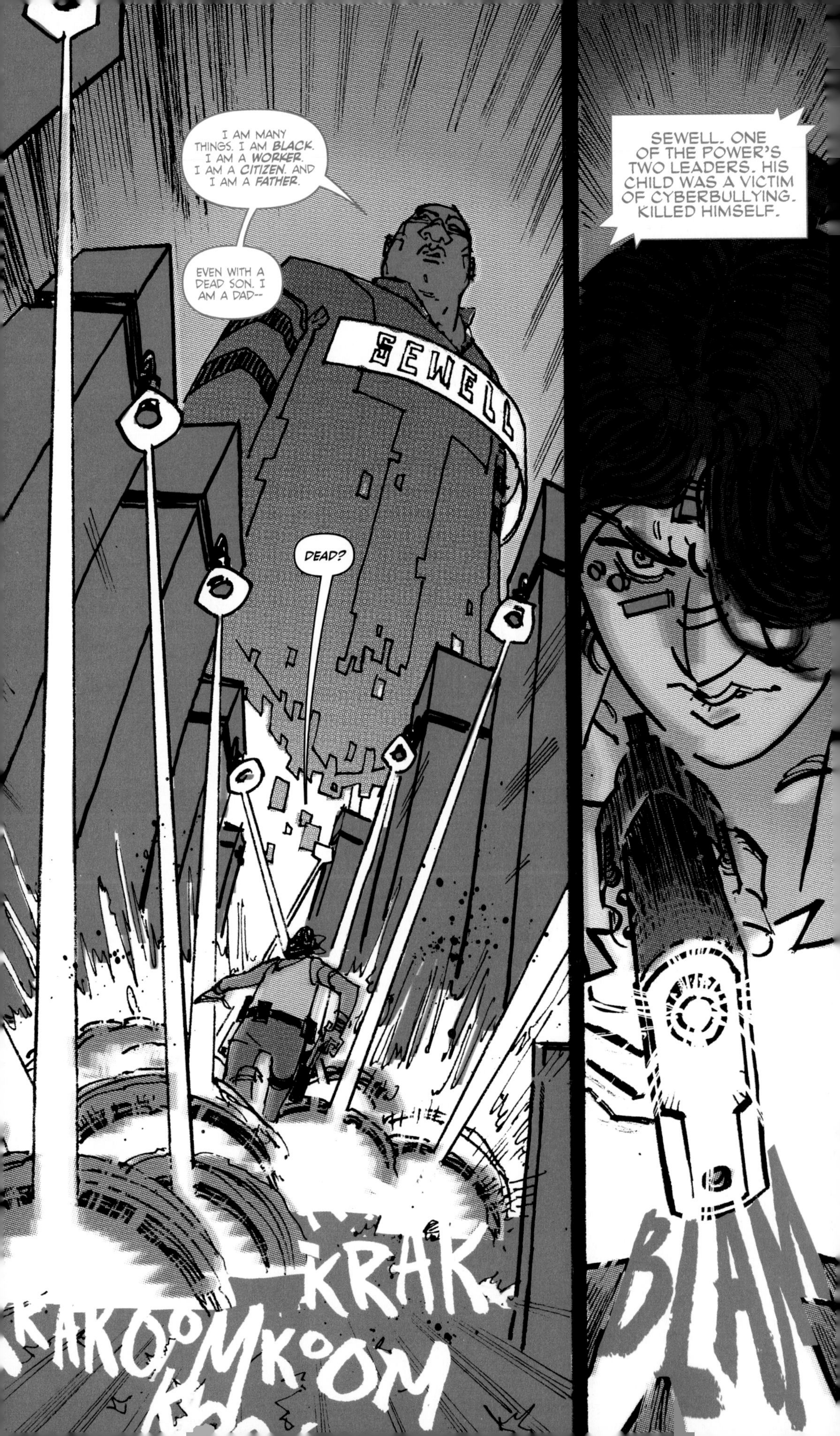
I AM MANY THINGS. I AM BLACK. I AM A WORKER. I AM A CITIZEN. AND I AM A FATHER.
EVEN WITH A DEAD SON. I AM A DAD--
SEWELL
DEAD?
KRAR
KAKOOM KOOM
SEWELL. ONE OF THE POWER'S TWO LEADERS. HIS CHILD WAS A VICTIM OF CYBERBULLYING. KILLED HIMSELF.
BLAM

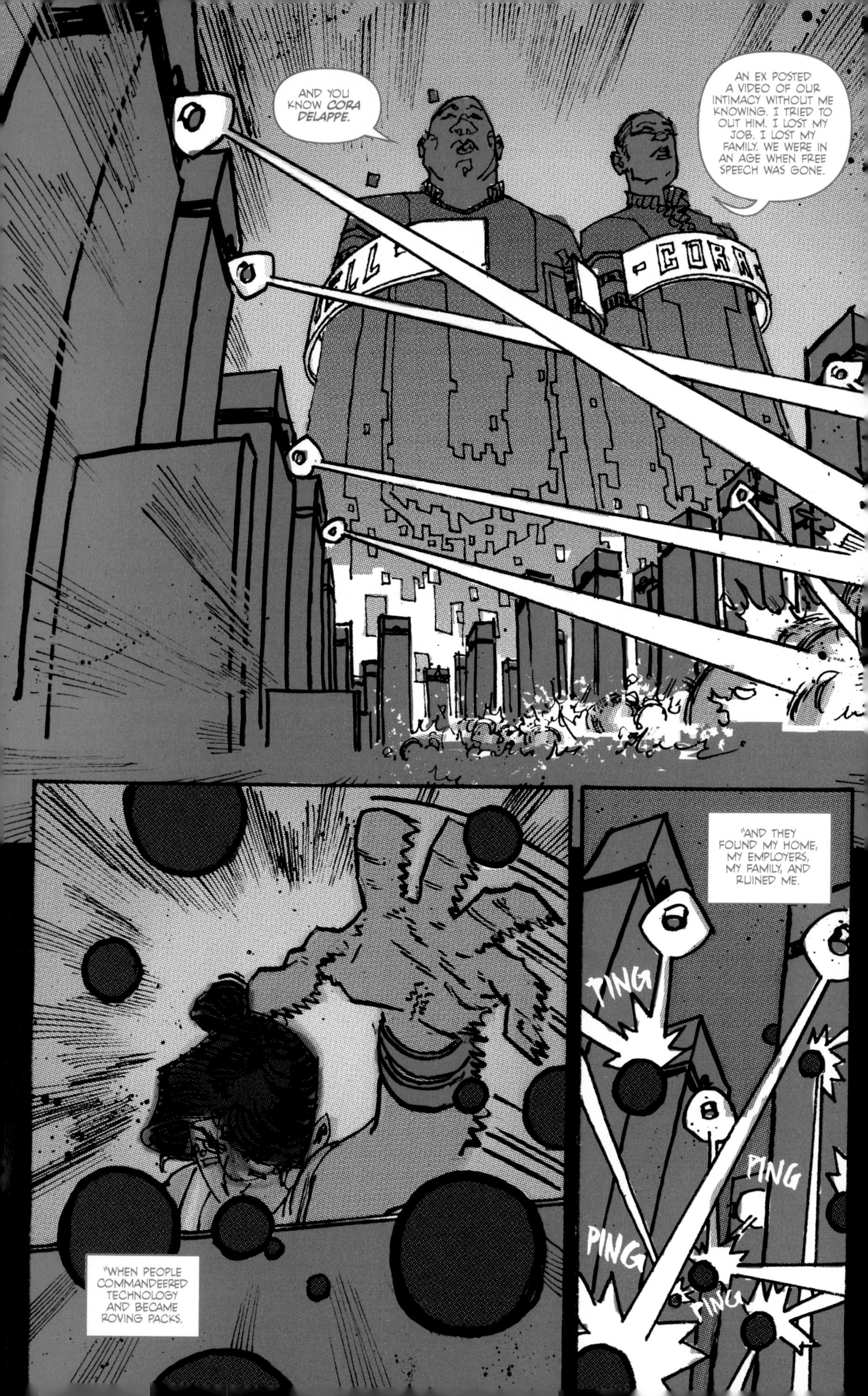
AND YOU KNOW *CORA DELAPPE.*
AN EX POSTED A VIDEO OF OUR INTIMACY WITHOUT ME KNOWING. I TRIED TO OUT HIM. I LOST MY JOB. I LOST MY FAMILY. WE WERE IN AN AGE WHEN FREE SPEECH WAS GONE.
CORA
"WHEN PEOPLE COMMANDEERED TECHNOLOGY AND BECAME ROVING PACKS.
"AND THEY FOUND MY HOME, MY EMPLOYERS, MY FAMILY, AND RUINED ME.
PING
PING
PING
PING

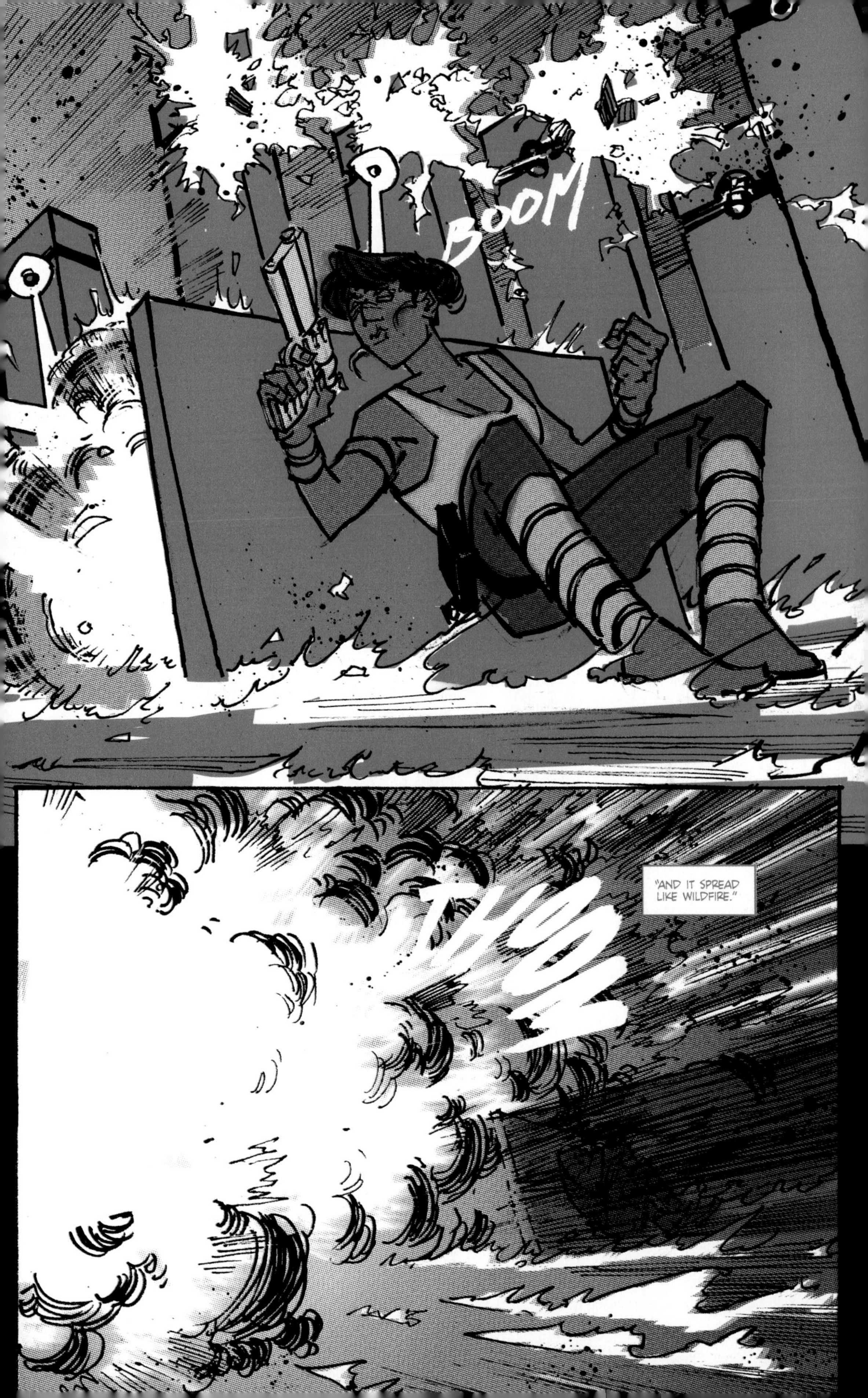
BOOM
"AND IT SPREAD LIKE WILDFIRE."
THOOM

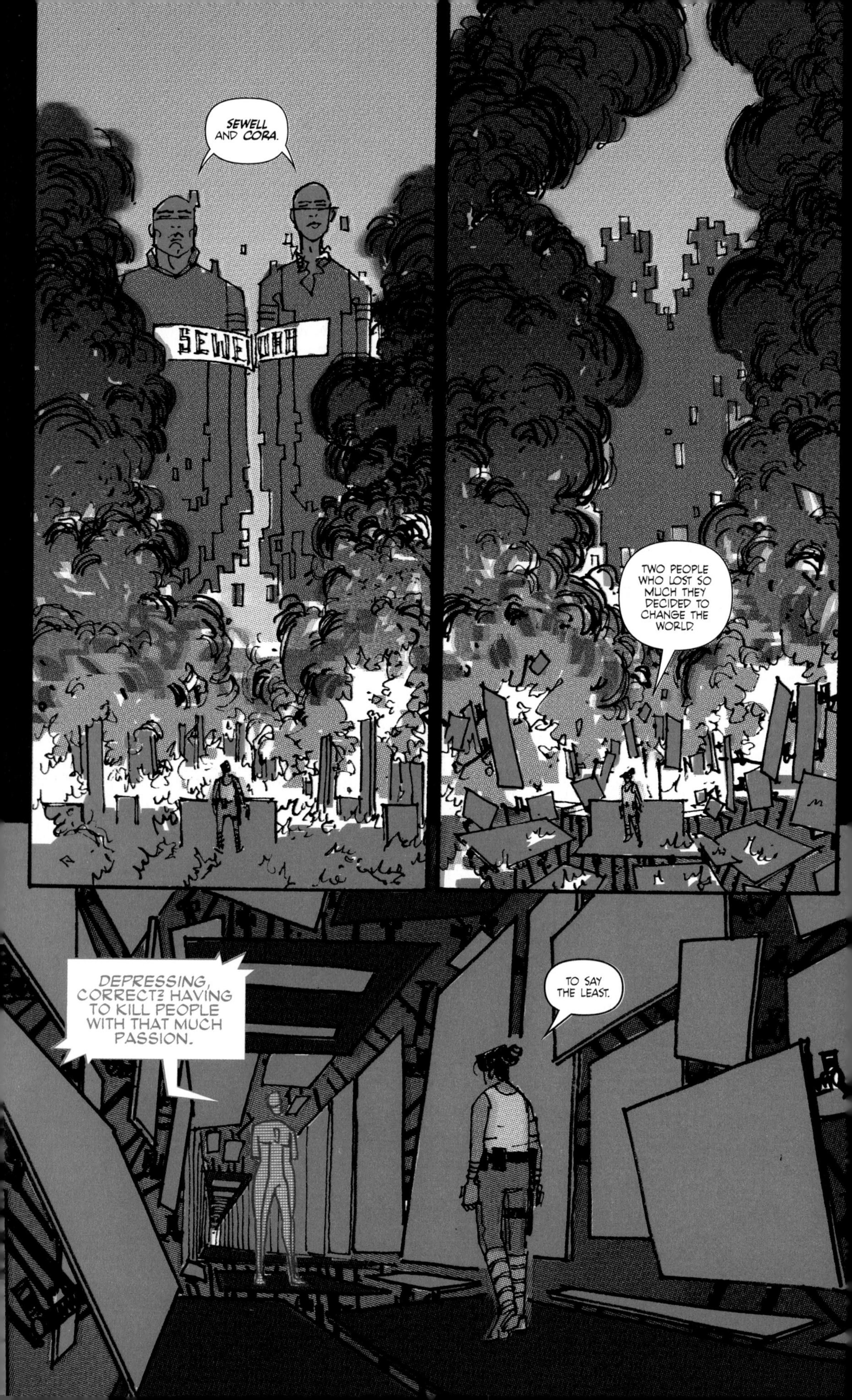
SEWELL AND CORA.
SEWE CORA
TWO PEOPLE WHO LOST SO MUCH THEY DECIDED TO CHANGE THE WORLD.
DEPRESSING, CORRECT? HAVING TO KILL PEOPLE WITH THAT MUCH PASSION.
TO SAY THE LEAST.

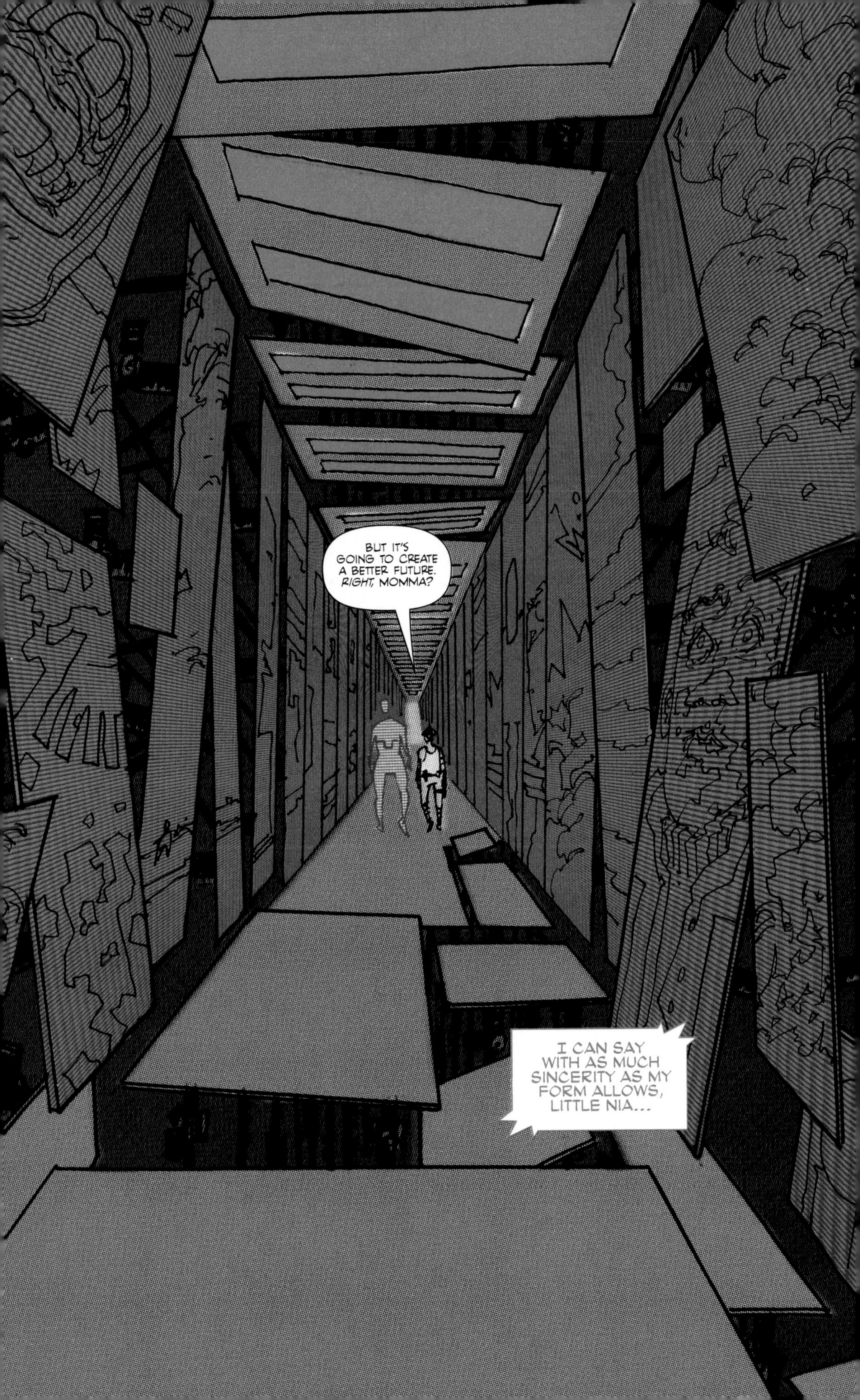
BUT IT'S GOING TO CREATE A BETTER FUTURE. RIGHT, MOMMA?
I CAN SAY WITH AS MUCH SINCERITY AS MY FORM ALLOWS, LITTLE NIA...

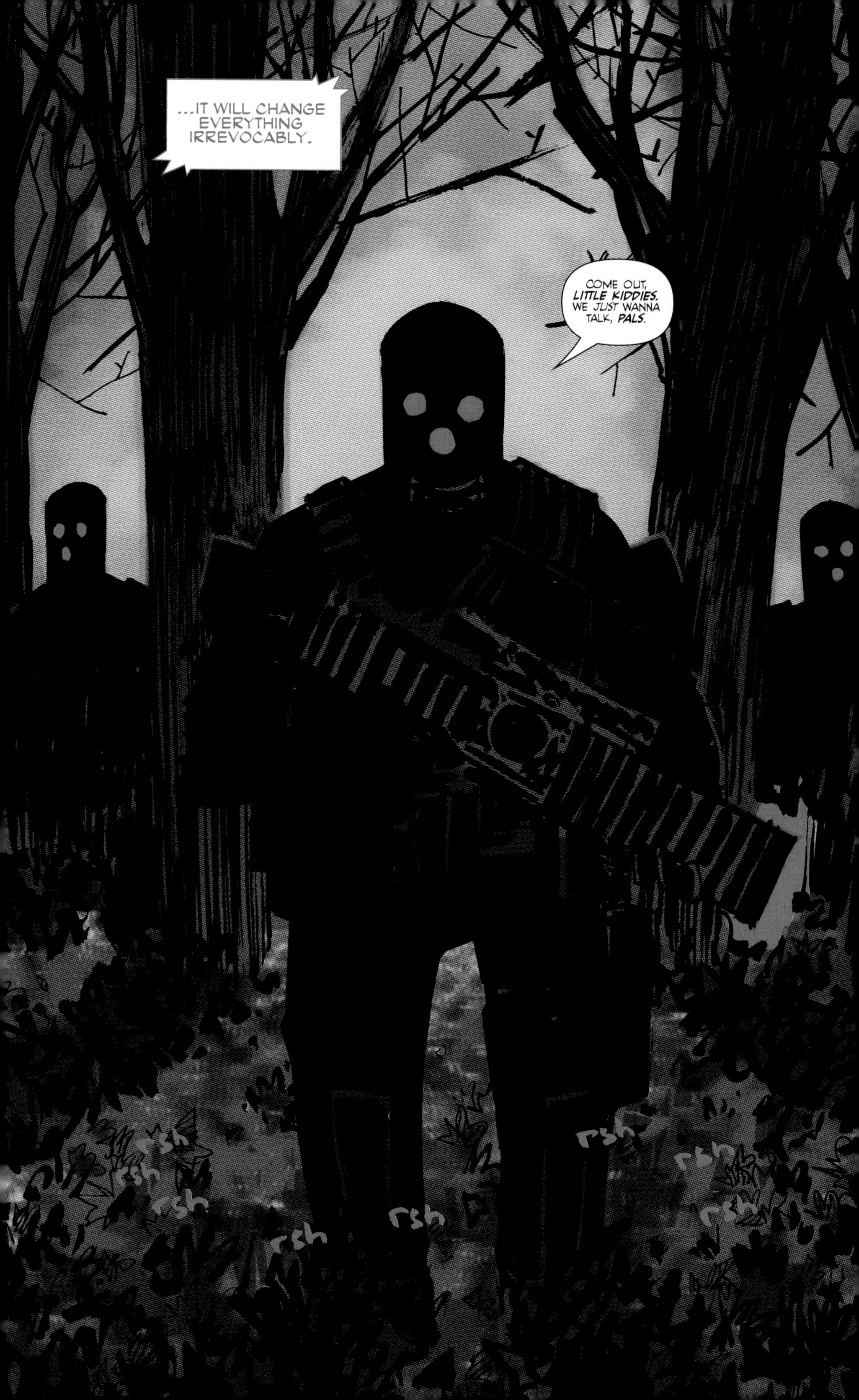
...IT WILL CHANGE EVERYTHING IRREVOCABLY.
COME OUT, LITTLE KIDDIES. WE JUST WANNA TALK, PALS.
rsh rsh rsh rsh rsh rsh rsh rsh rsh

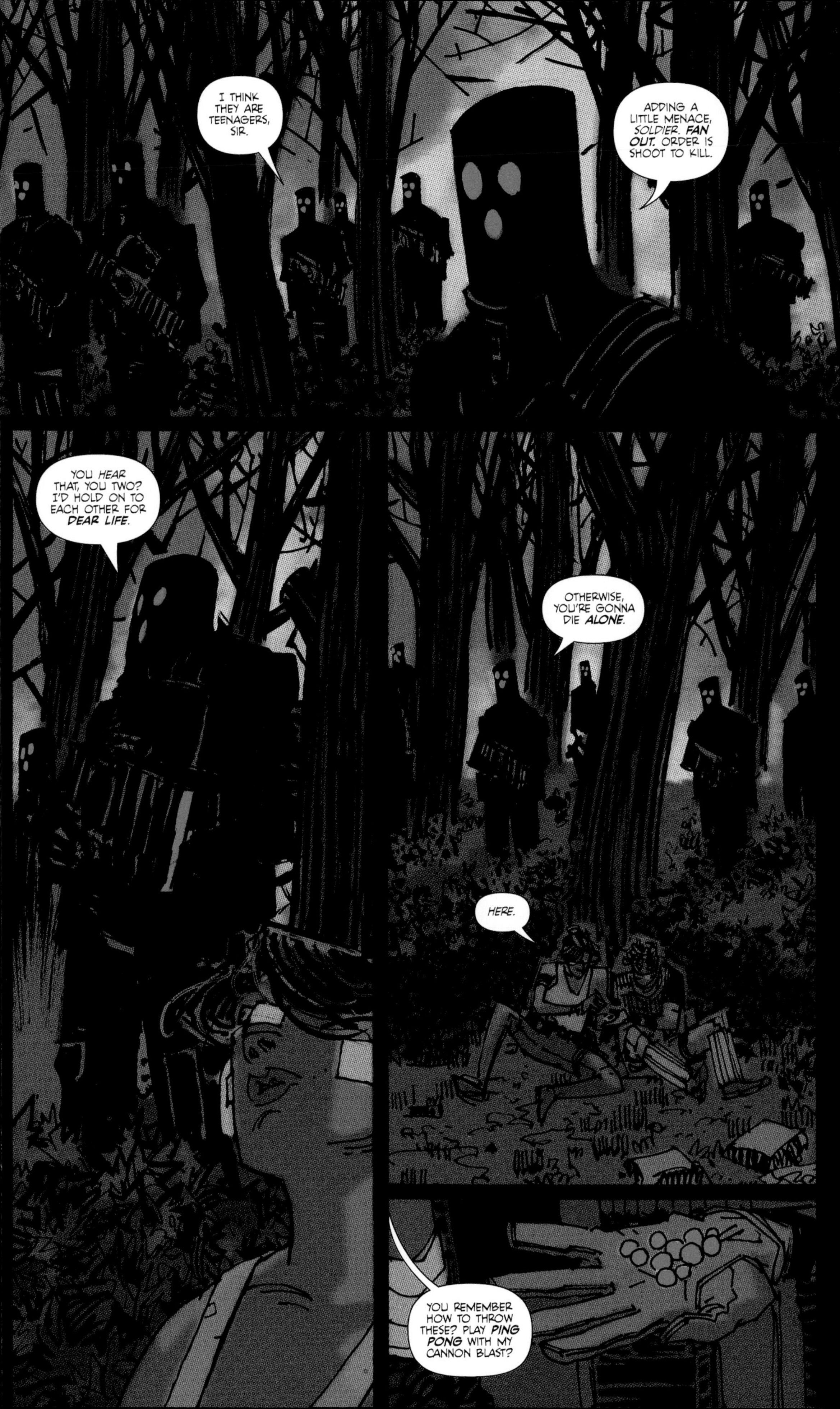
I THINK THEY ARE TEENAGERS, SIR.
ADDING A LITTLE MENACE, SOLDIER. FAN OUT. ORDER IS SHOOT TO KILL.
YOU HEAR THAT, YOU TWO? I'D HOLD ON TO EACH OTHER FOR DEAR LIFE.
OTHERWISE, YOU'RE GONNA DIE ALONE.
HERE.
YOU REMEMBER HOW TO THROW THESE? PLAY PING PONG WITH MY CANNON BLAST?

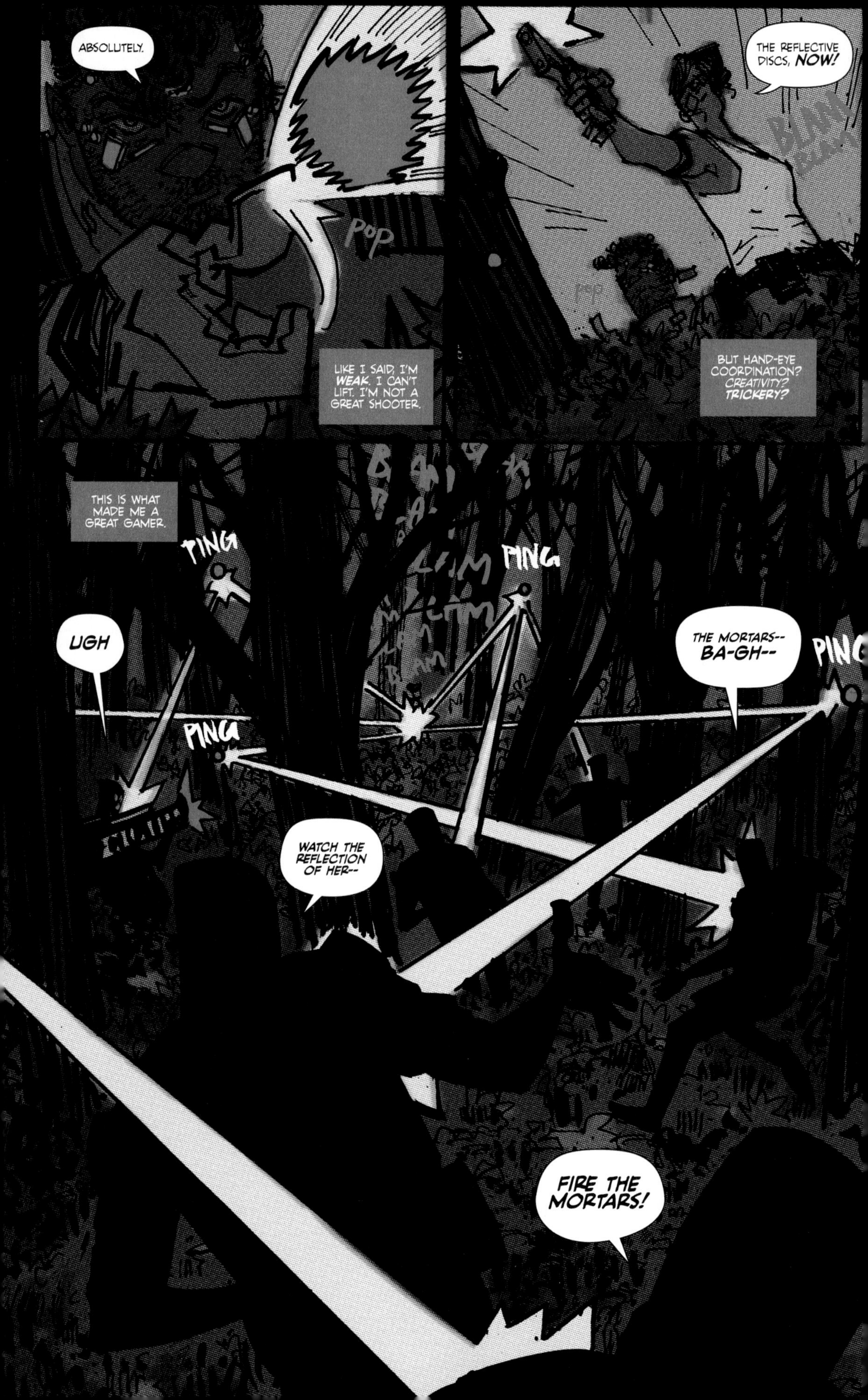
ABSOLUTELY.
POP
LIKE I SAID, I'M *WEAK*. I CAN'T LIFT. I'M NOT A GREAT SHOOTER.
THE REFLECTIVE DISCS, **NOW!**
POP
BUT HAND-EYE COORDINATION? *CREATIVITY? TRICKERY?*
THIS IS WHAT MADE ME A GREAT GAMER.
PING
PING
UGH
THE MORTARS-- BA-GH--
PING
WATCH THE REFLECTION OF HER--
FIRE THE MORTARS!

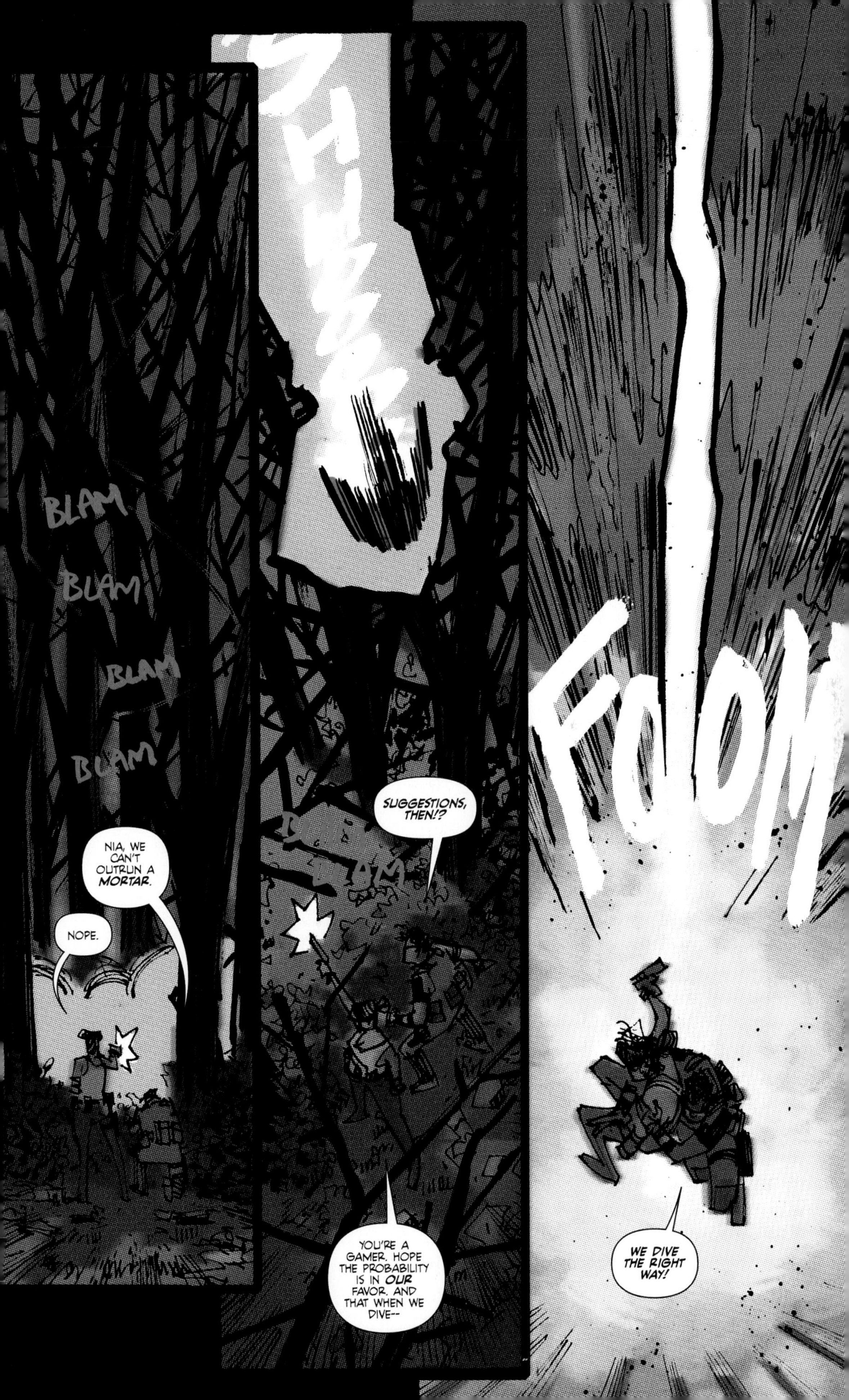
BLAM
BLAM
BLAM
BLAM
NIA, WE CAN'T OUTRUN A MORTAR.
NOPE.
SHHHAAA
SUGGESTIONS, THEN!?
BLAM
YOU'RE A GAMER. HOPE THE PROBABILITY IS IN OUR FAVOR. AND THAT WHEN WE DIVE--
FOOM
WE DIVE THE RIGHT WAY!

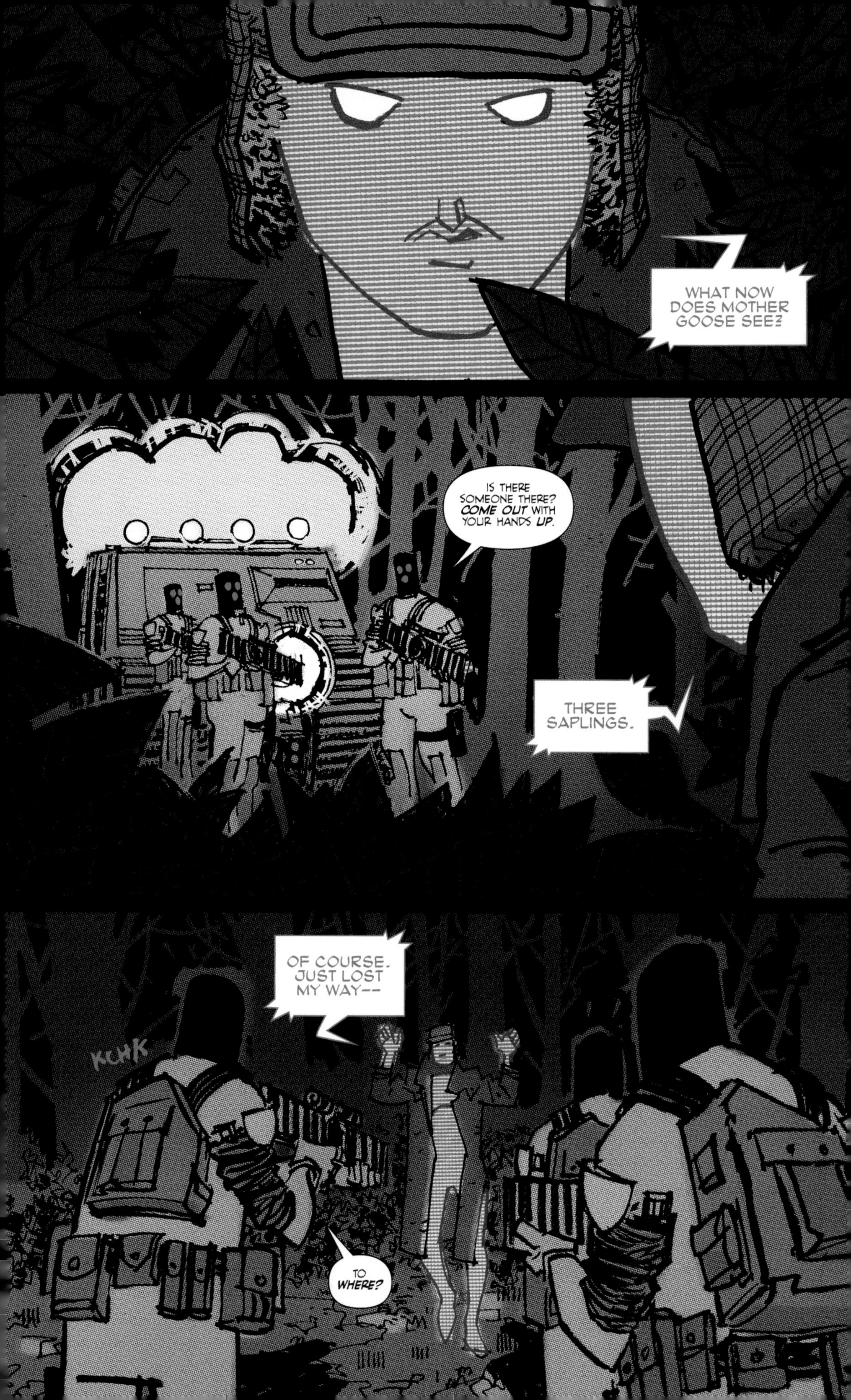

WHAT NOW DOES MOTHER GOOSE SEE?
IS THERE SOMEONE THERE? COME OUT WITH YOUR HANDS UP.
THREE SAPLINGS.
OF COURSE. JUST LOST MY WAY--
KCHK
TO WHERE?

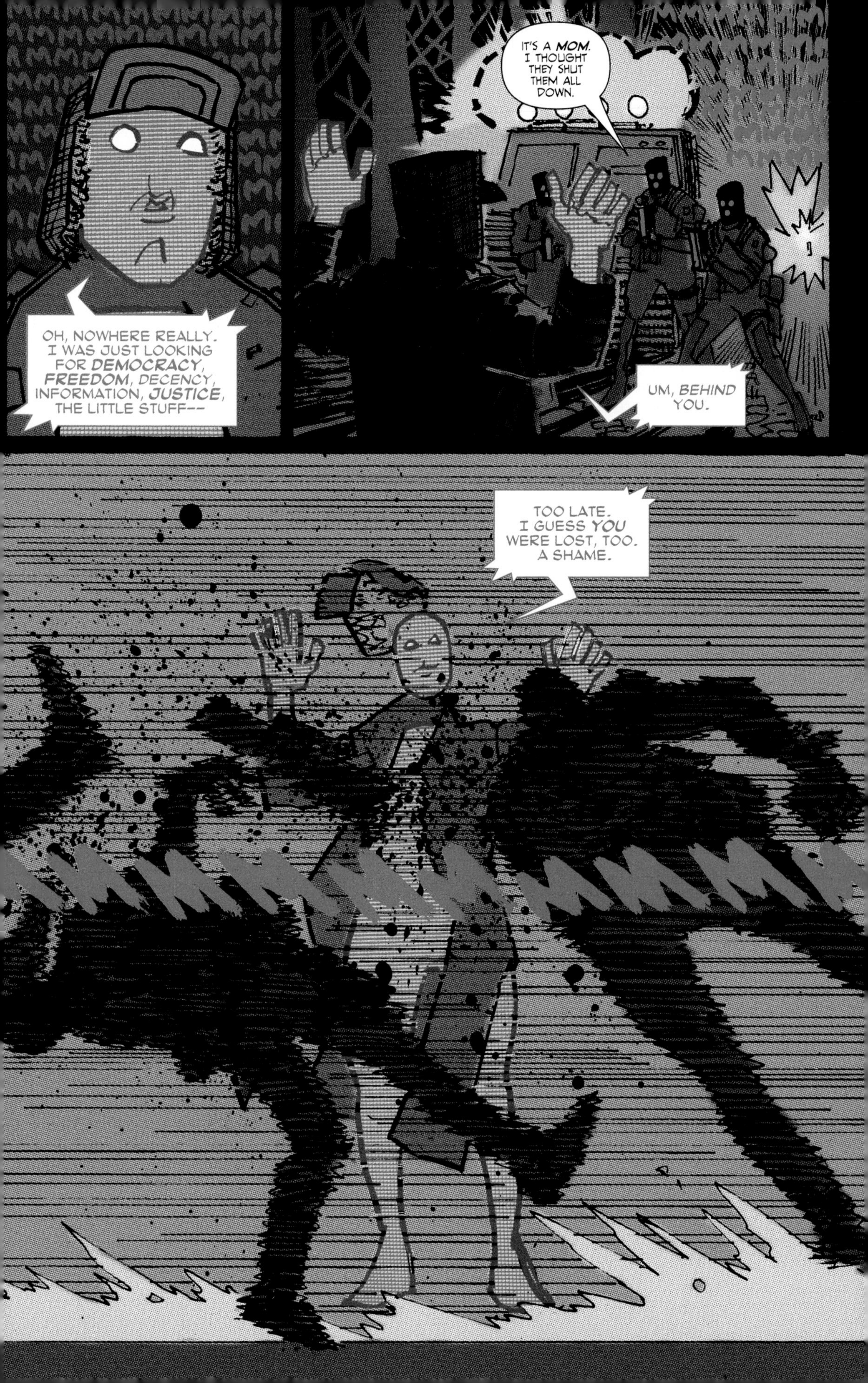
OH, NOWHERE REALLY. I WAS JUST LOOKING FOR DEMOCRACY, FREEDOM, DECENCY, INFORMATION, JUSTICE, THE LITTLE STUFF--
IT'S A MOM. I THOUGHT THEY SHUT THEM ALL DOWN.
UM, BEHIND YOU.
TOO LATE. I GUESS YOU WERE LOST, TOO. A SHAME.

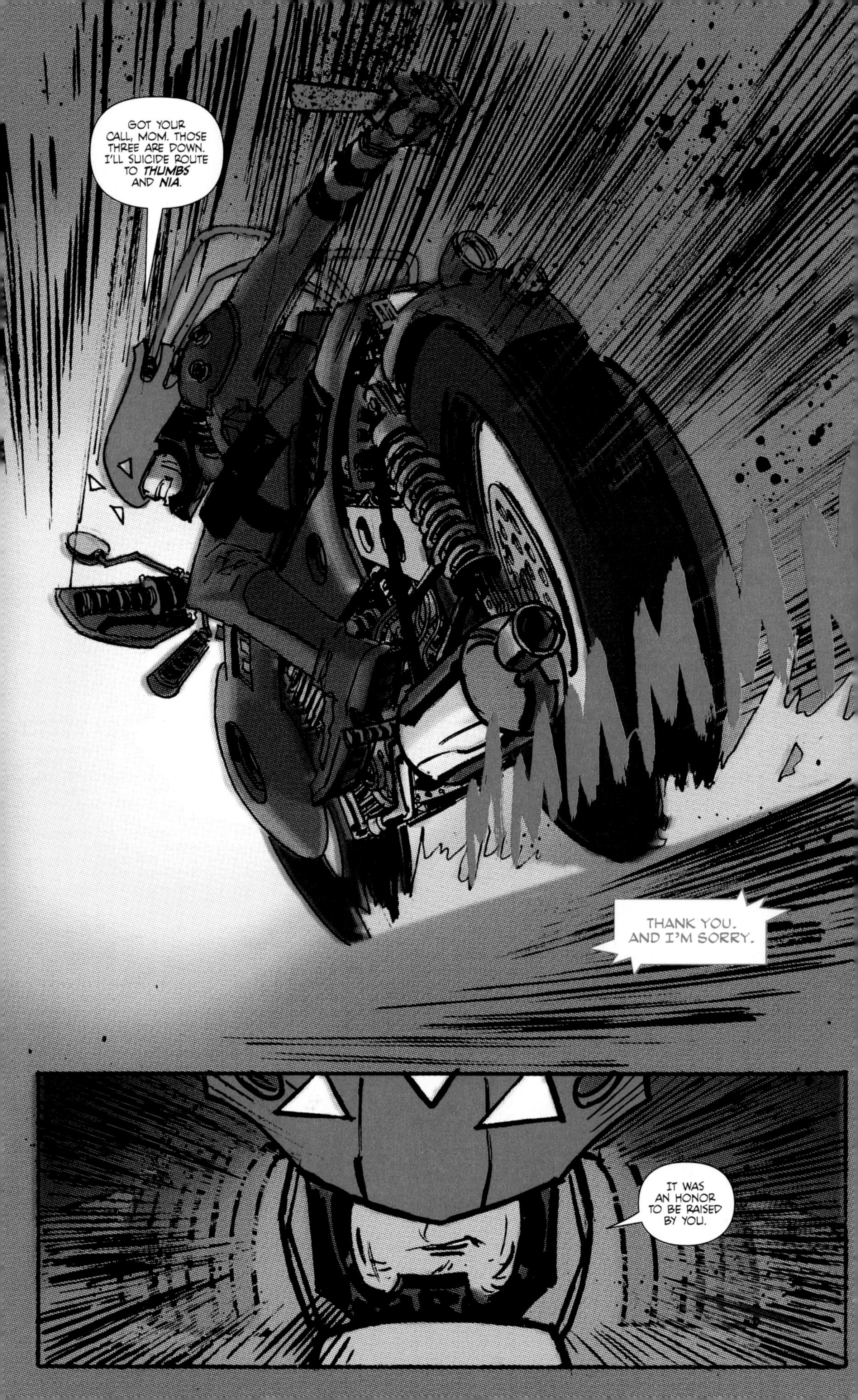
GOT YOUR CALL, MOM. THOSE THREE ARE DOWN. I'LL SUICIDE ROUTE TO *THUMBS* AND *NIA*.
THANK YOU. AND I'M SORRY.
IT WAS AN HONOR TO BE RAISED BY YOU.

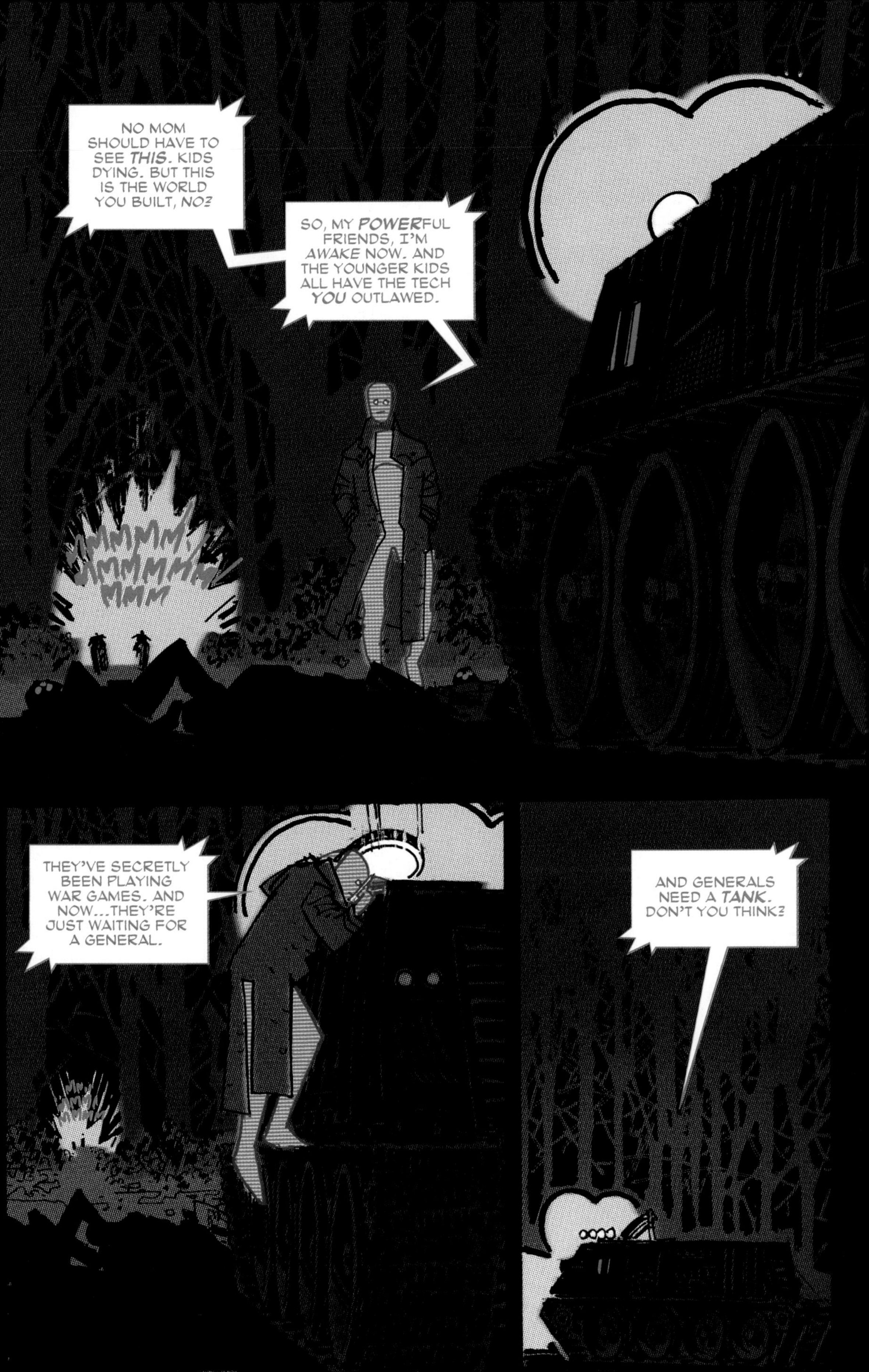
NO MOM SHOULD HAVE TO SEE *THIS*. KIDS DYING. BUT THIS IS THE WORLD YOU BUILT, *NO?*
SO, MY ***POWER***FUL FRIENDS, I'M *AWAKE* NOW. AND THE YOUNGER KIDS ALL HAVE THE TECH ***YOU*** OUTLAWED.
THEY'VE SECRETLY BEEN PLAYING WAR GAMES. AND NOW...THEY'RE JUST WAITING FOR A GENERAL.
AND GENERALS NEED A ***TANK***. DON'T YOU THINK?

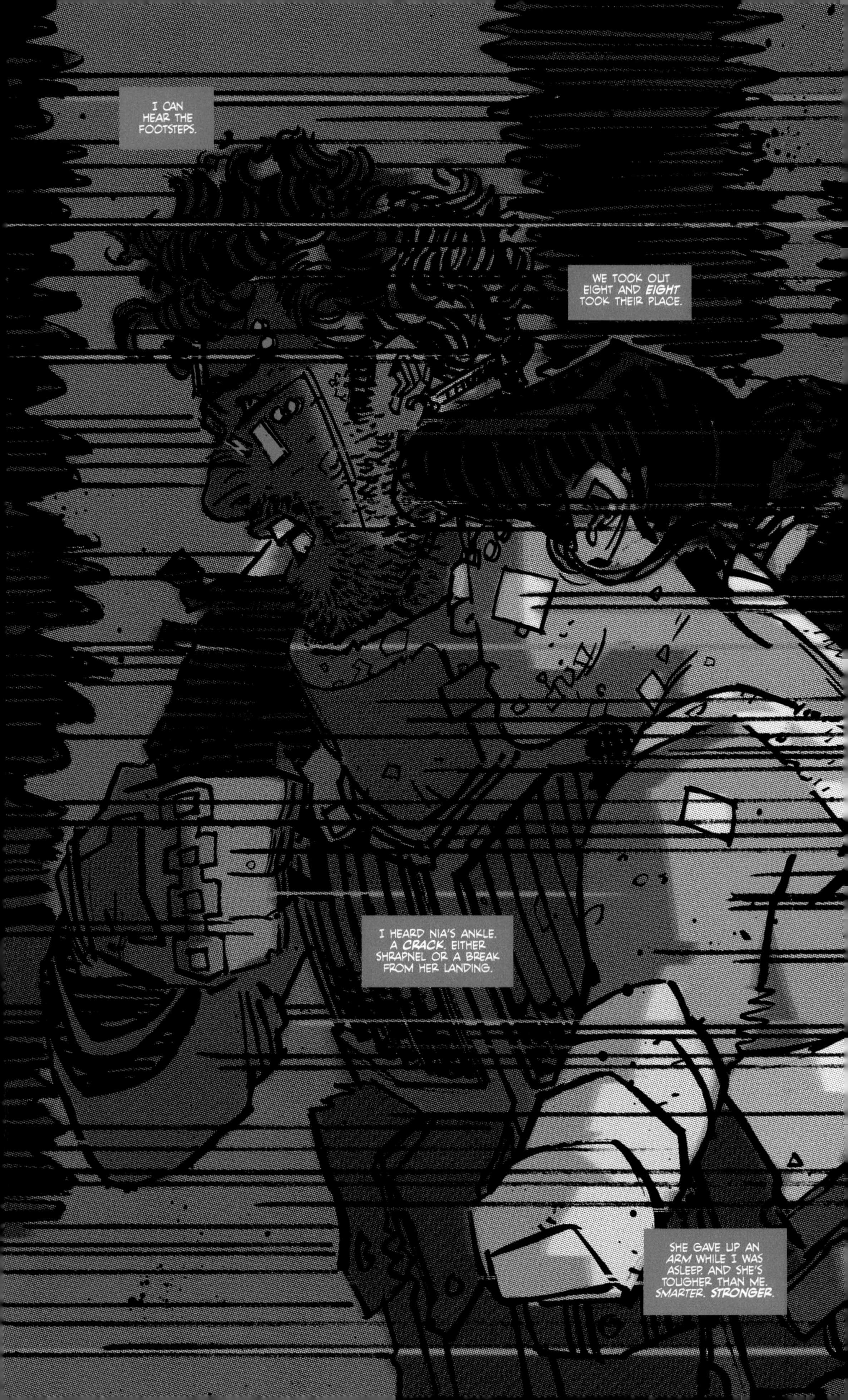
I CAN HEAR THE FOOTSTEPS.
WE TOOK OUT EIGHT AND *EIGHT* TOOK THEIR PLACE.
I HEARD NIA'S ANKLE. A *CRACK*. EITHER SHRAPNEL OR A BREAK FROM HER LANDING.
SHE GAVE UP AN *ARM* WHILE I WAS ASLEEP. AND SHE'S TOUGHER THAN ME. *SMARTER*. ***STRONGER***.

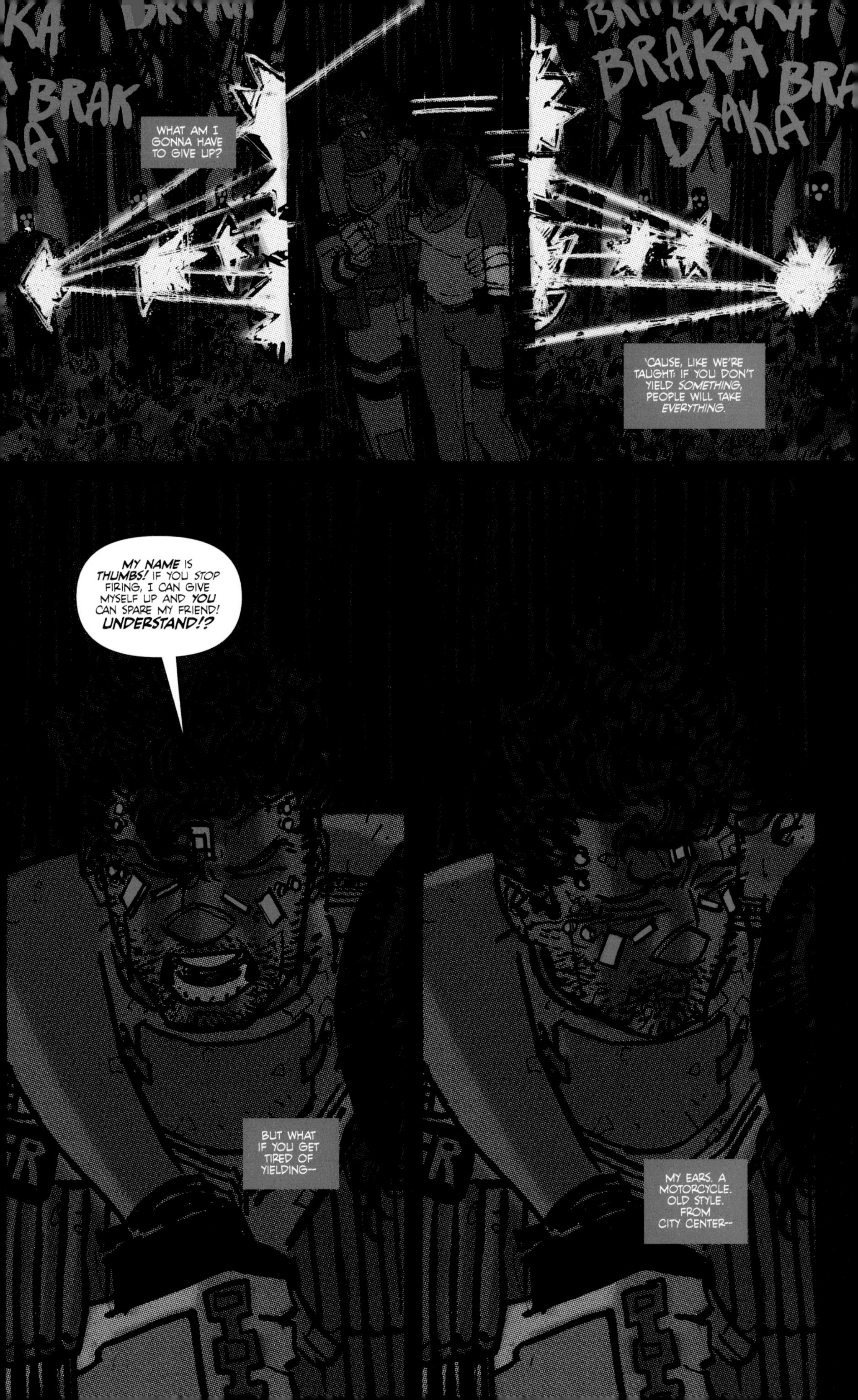
BRAK
WHAT AM I GONNA HAVE TO GIVE UP?
BRAKA
BRAKA
'CAUSE, LIKE WE'RE TAUGHT: IF YOU DON'T YIELD *SOMETHING*, PEOPLE WILL TAKE *EVERYTHING*.
MY NAME IS ***THUMBS!*** IF YOU *STOP* FIRING, I CAN GIVE MYSELF UP AND ***YOU*** CAN SPARE MY FRIEND! ***UNDERSTAND!?***
BUT WHAT IF YOU GET TIRED OF YIELDING--
MY EARS. A MOTORCYCLE. OLD STYLE. FROM CITY CENTER--

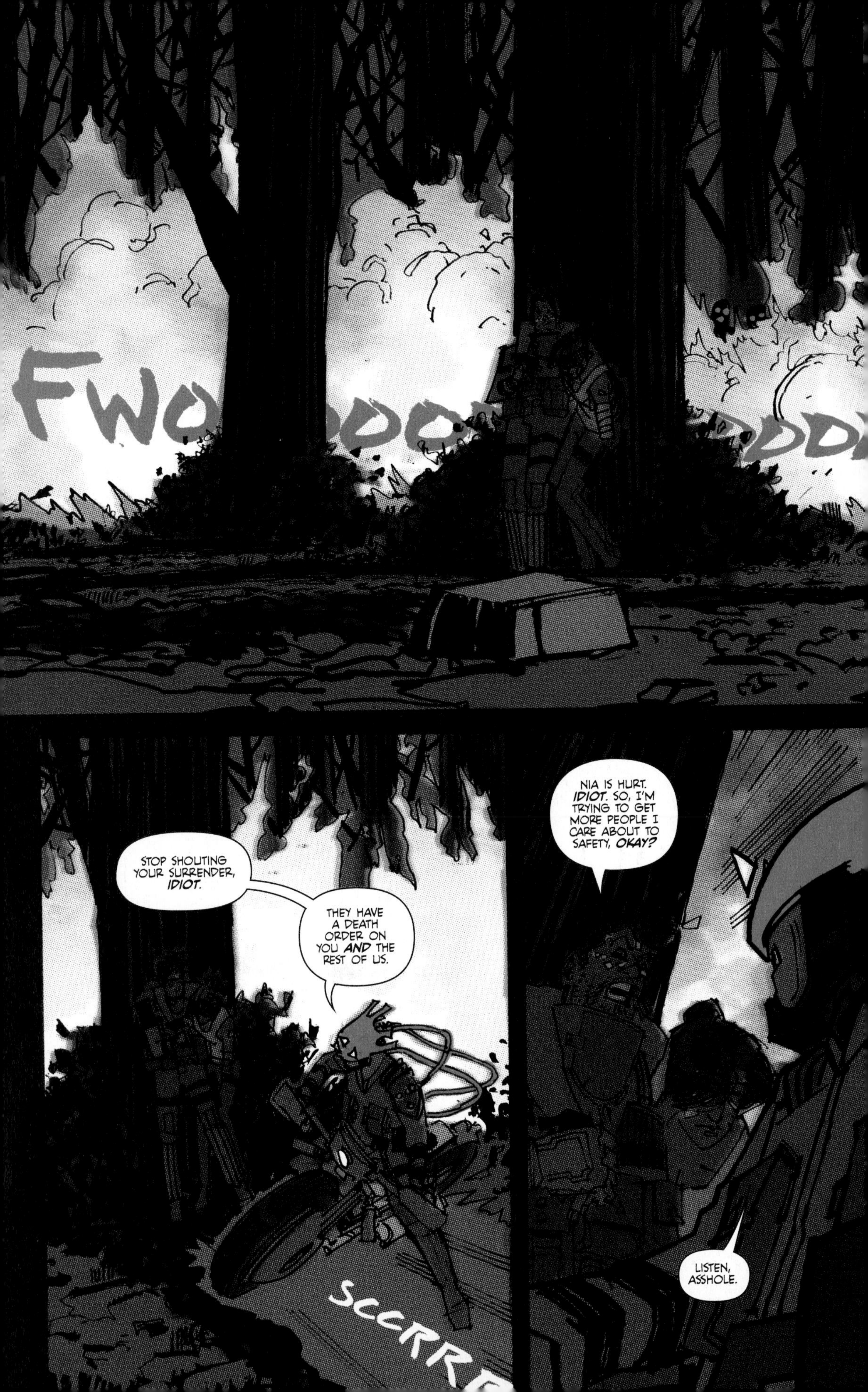
FWOOOOOOOOM
STOP SHOUTING YOUR SURRENDER, IDIOT.
THEY HAVE A DEATH ORDER ON YOU AND THE REST OF US.
SCCRR
NIA IS HURT. IDIOT. SO, I'M TRYING TO GET MORE PEOPLE I CARE ABOUT TO SAFETY, OKAY?
LISTEN, ASSHOLE.

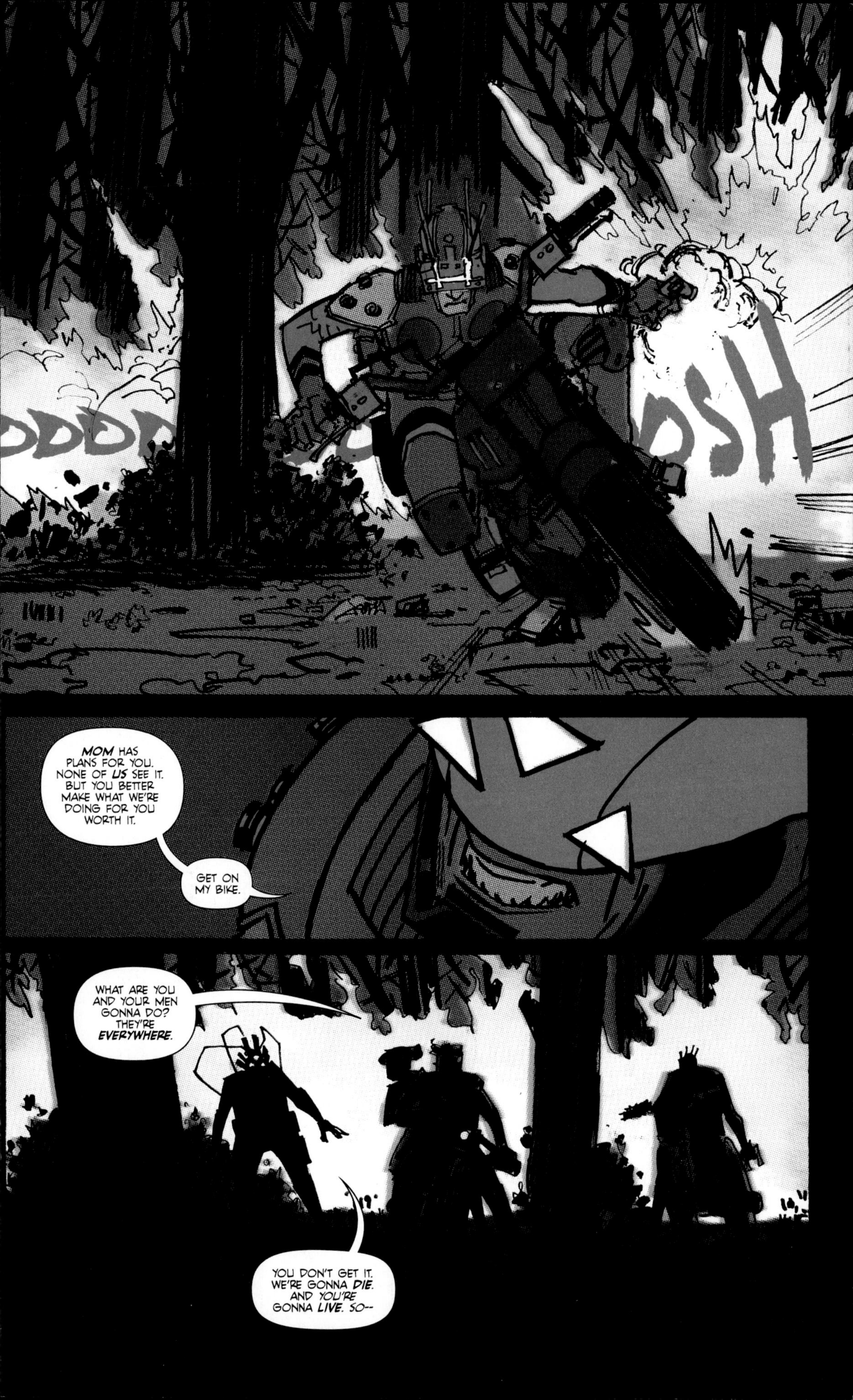
MOM HAS PLANS FOR YOU. NONE OF US SEE IT. BUT YOU BETTER MAKE WHAT WE'RE DOING FOR YOU WORTH IT.
GET ON MY BIKE.
WHAT ARE YOU AND YOUR MEN GONNA DO? THEY'RE EVERYWHERE.
YOU DON'T GET IT. WE'RE GONNA DIE. AND YOU'RE GONNA LIVE. SO--

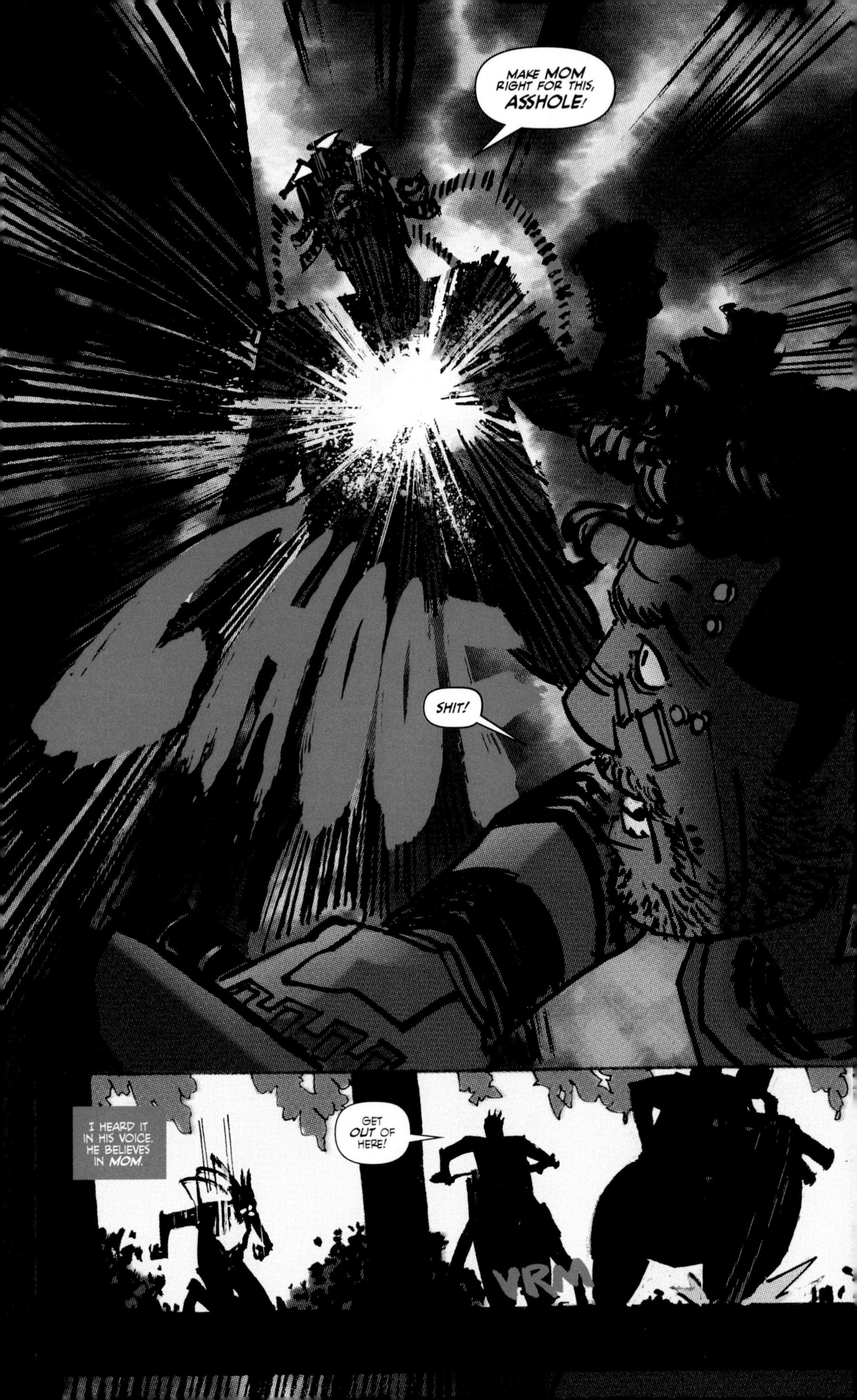
MAKE MOM RIGHT FOR THIS, ASSHOLE!
CHOOF
SHIT!
I HEARD IT IN HIS VOICE. HE BELIEVES IN MOM.
GET OUT OF HERE!
VRM

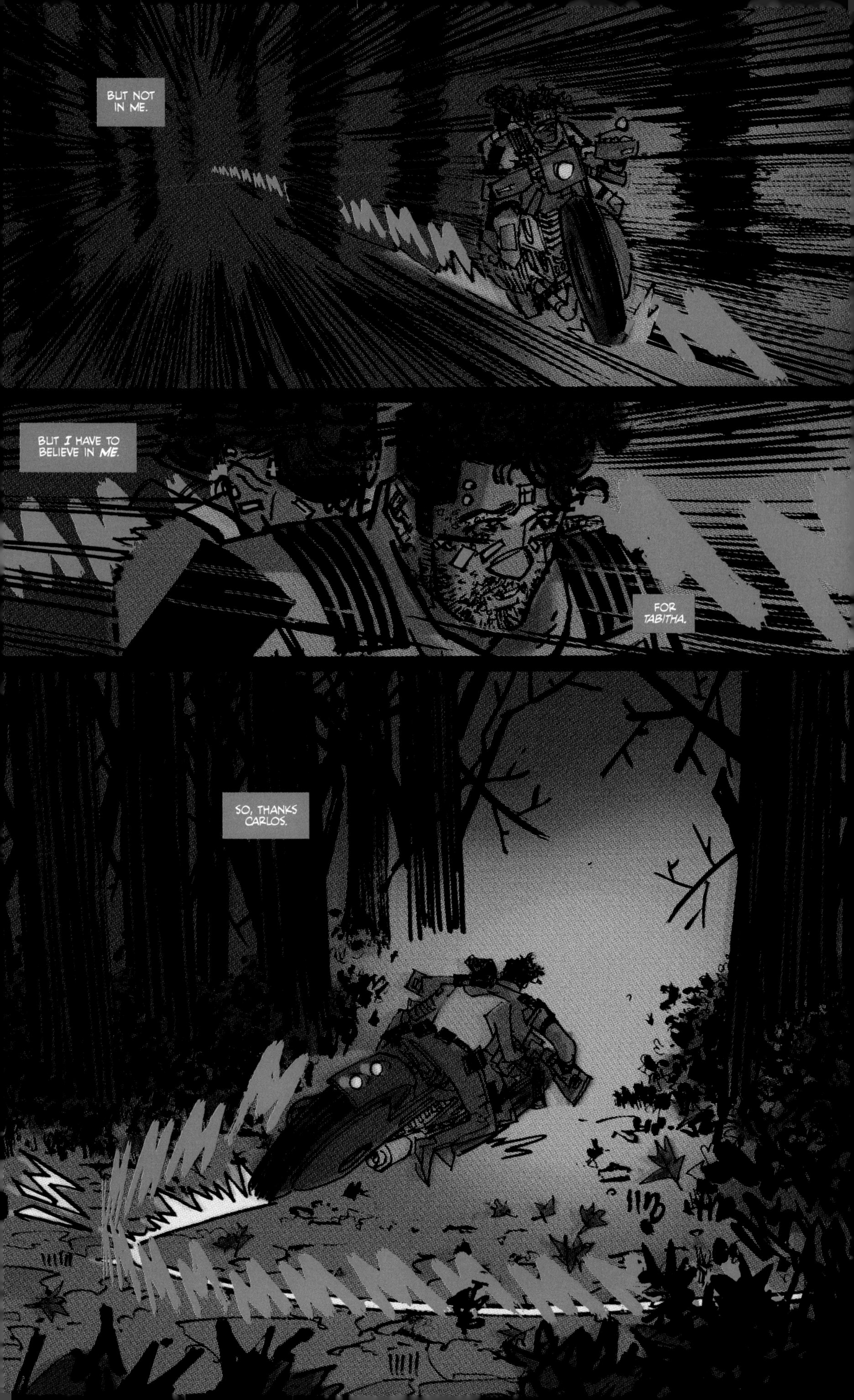
BUT NOT IN ME.
BUT I HAVE TO BELIEVE IN ME.
FOR TABITHA.
SO, THANKS CARLOS.

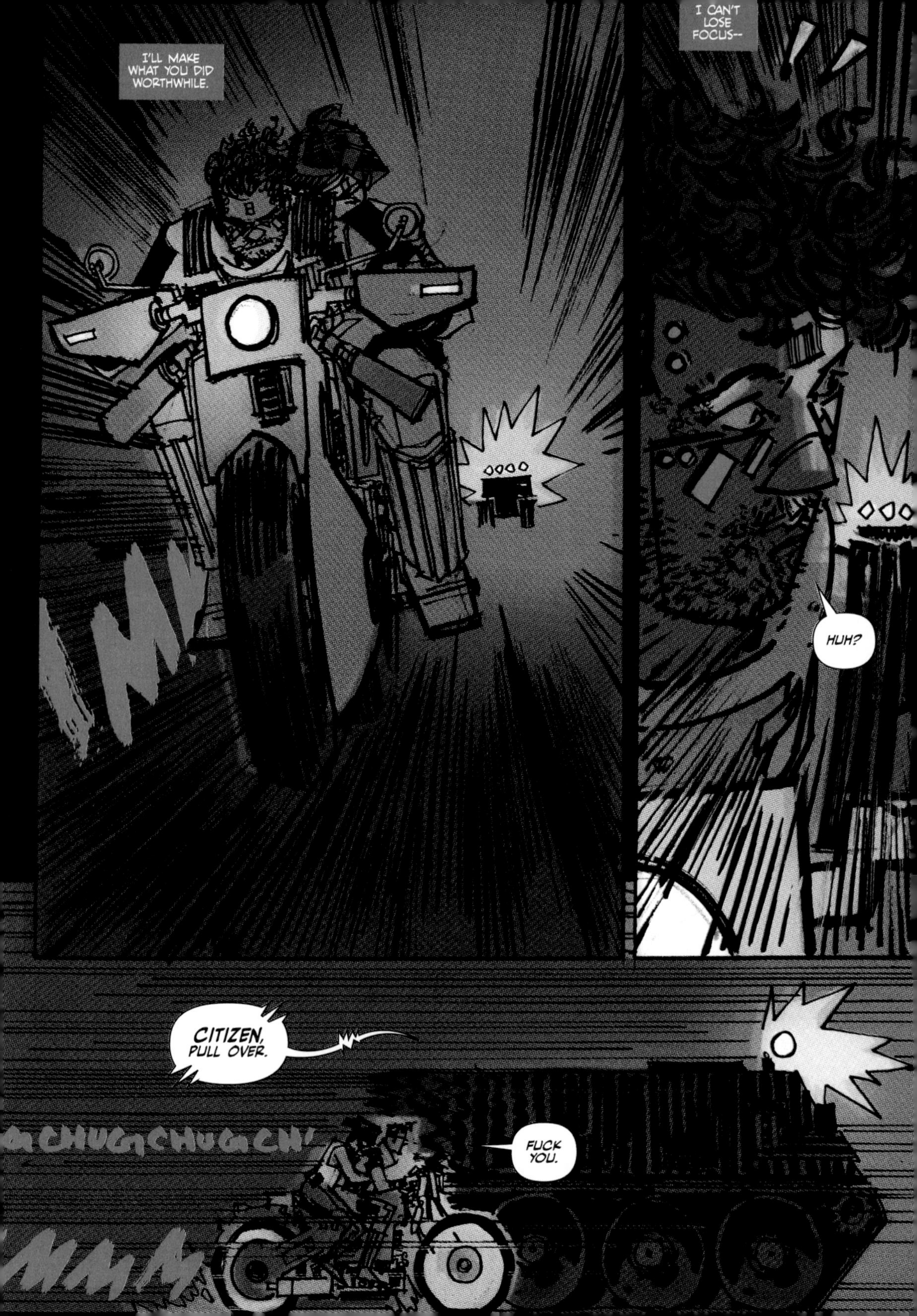
I'LL MAKE WHAT YOU DID WORTHWHILE.
I CAN'T LOSE FOCUS--
HUH?
CITIZEN, PULL OVER.
CHUGCHUGCH'
FUCK YOU.

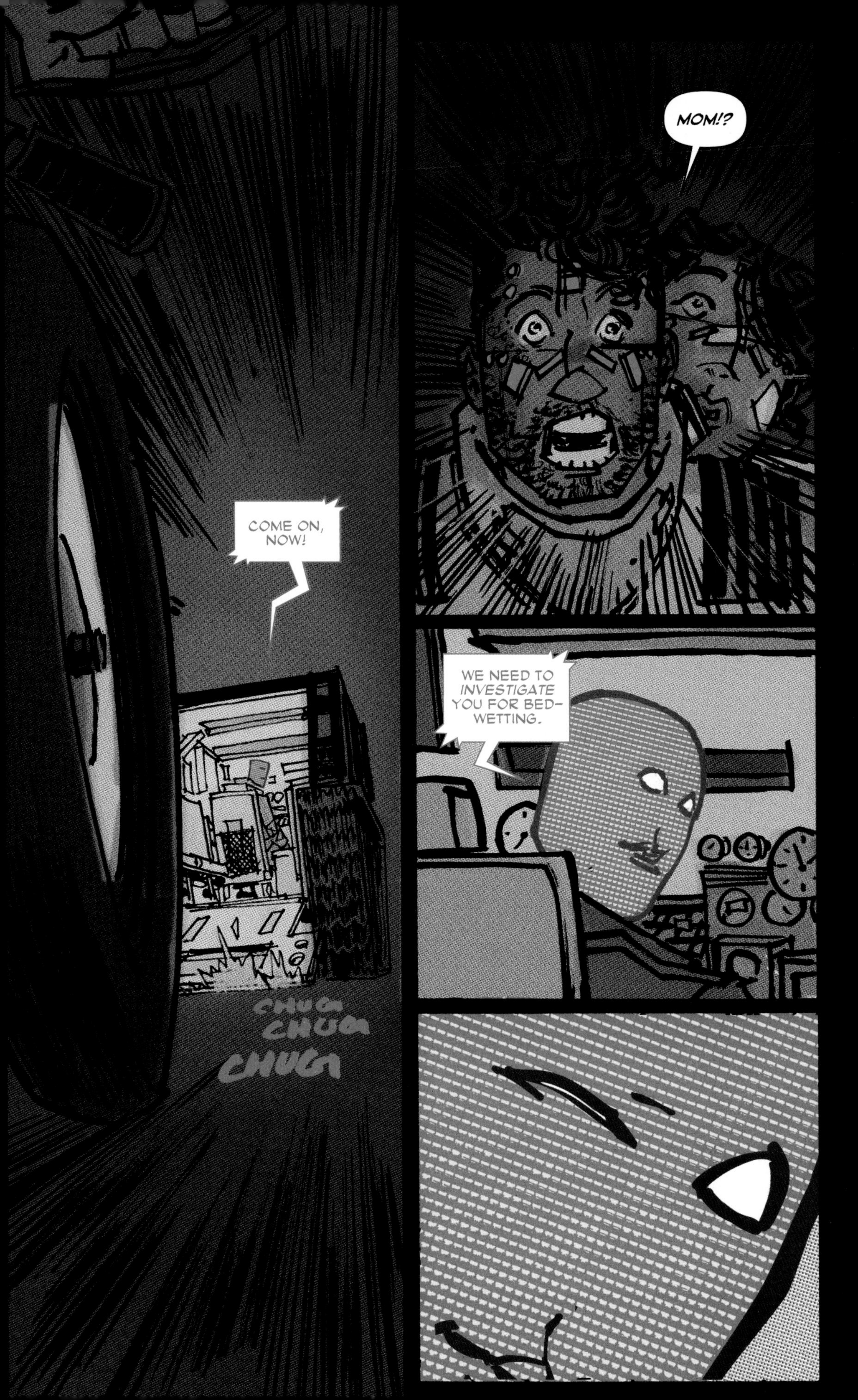
COME ON, NOW!
CHUG CHUG CHUG
MOM!?
WE NEED TO *INVESTIGATE* YOU FOR BED-WETTING.

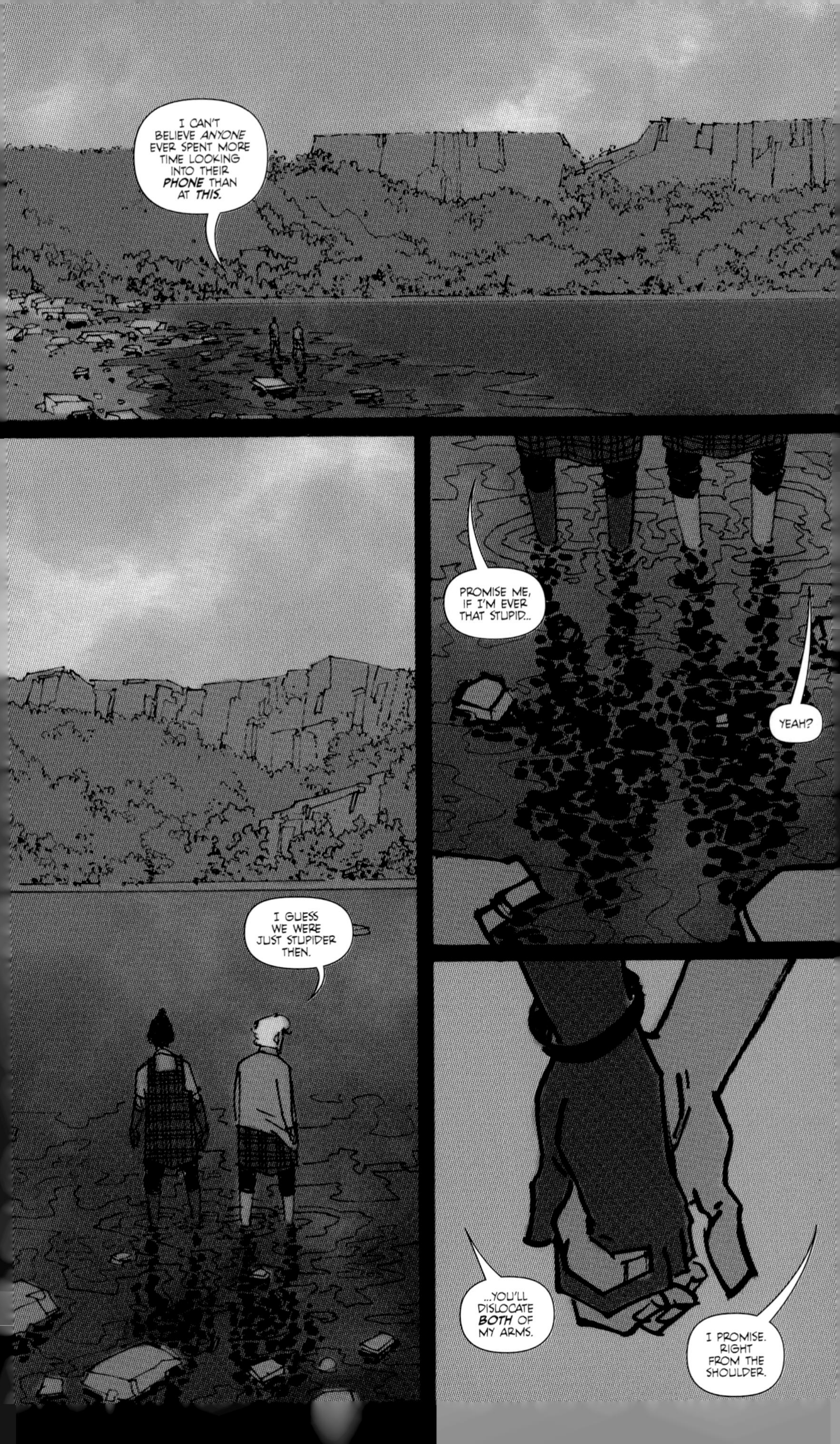
I CAN'T BELIEVE ANYONE EVER SPENT MORE TIME LOOKING INTO THEIR PHONE THAN AT THIS.
I GUESS WE WERE JUST STUPIDER THEN.
PROMISE ME, IF I'M EVER THAT STUPID...
YEAH?
...YOU'LL DISLOCATE BOTH OF MY ARMS.
I PROMISE. RIGHT FROM THE SHOULDER.

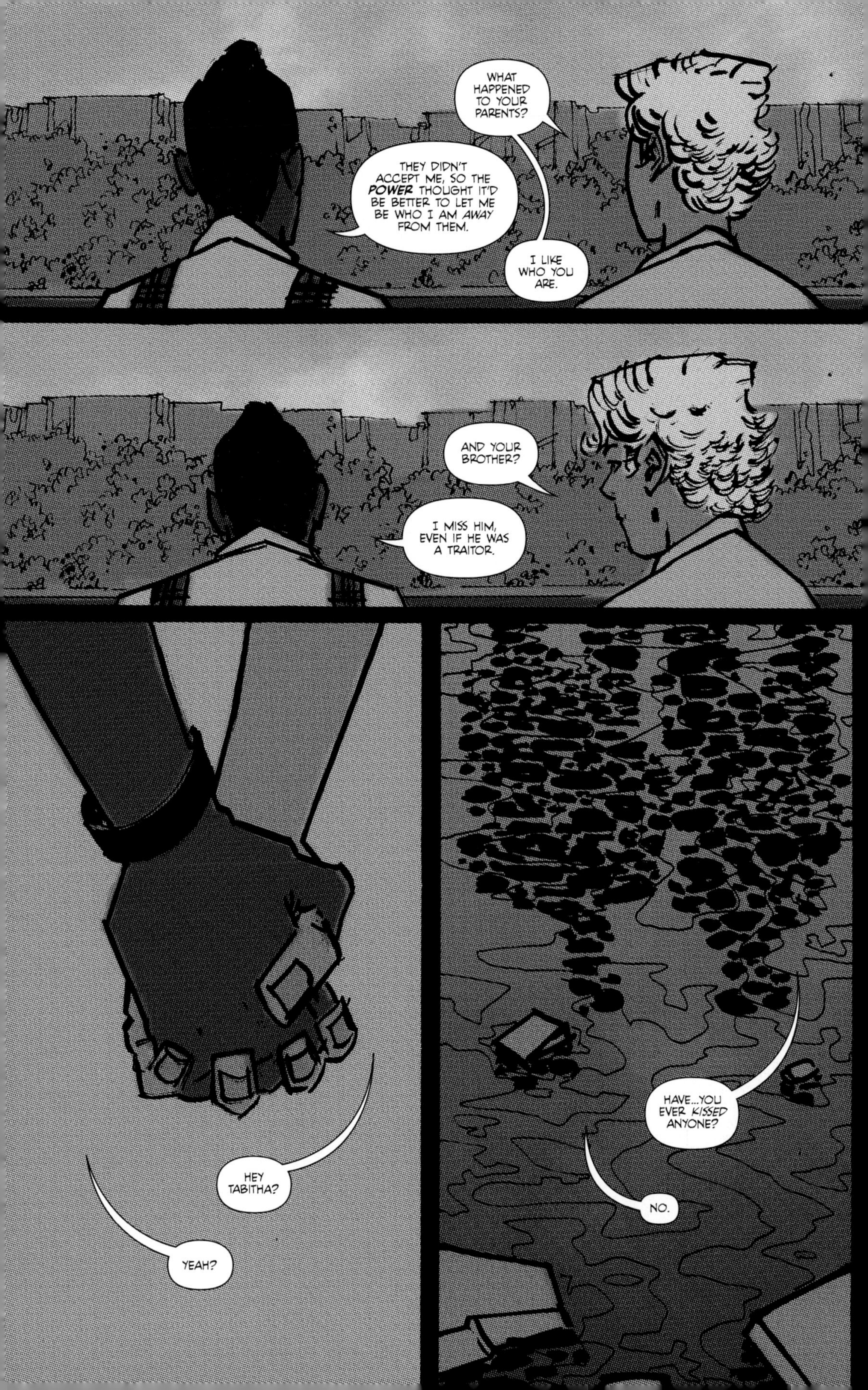
WHAT HAPPENED TO YOUR PARENTS?
THEY DIDN'T ACCEPT ME, SO THE POWER THOUGHT IT'D BE BETTER TO LET ME BE WHO I AM AWAY FROM THEM.
I LIKE WHO YOU ARE.
AND YOUR BROTHER?
I MISS HIM, EVEN IF HE WAS A TRAITOR.
HEY TABITHA?
YEAH?
HAVE...YOU EVER KISSED ANYONE?
NO.

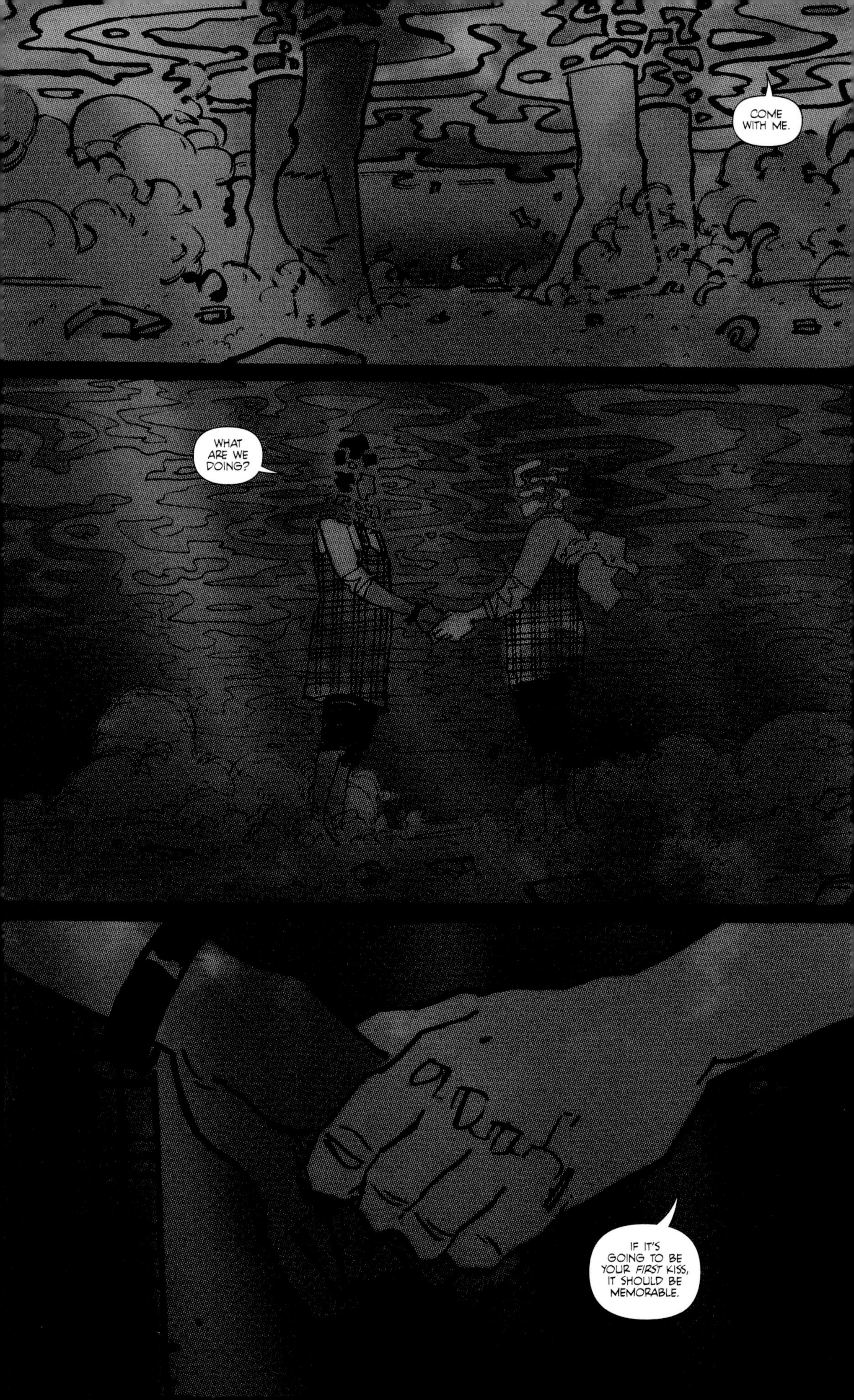
COME WITH ME.
WHAT ARE WE DOING?
IF IT'S GOING TO BE YOUR *FIRST* KISS, IT SHOULD BE MEMORABLE.

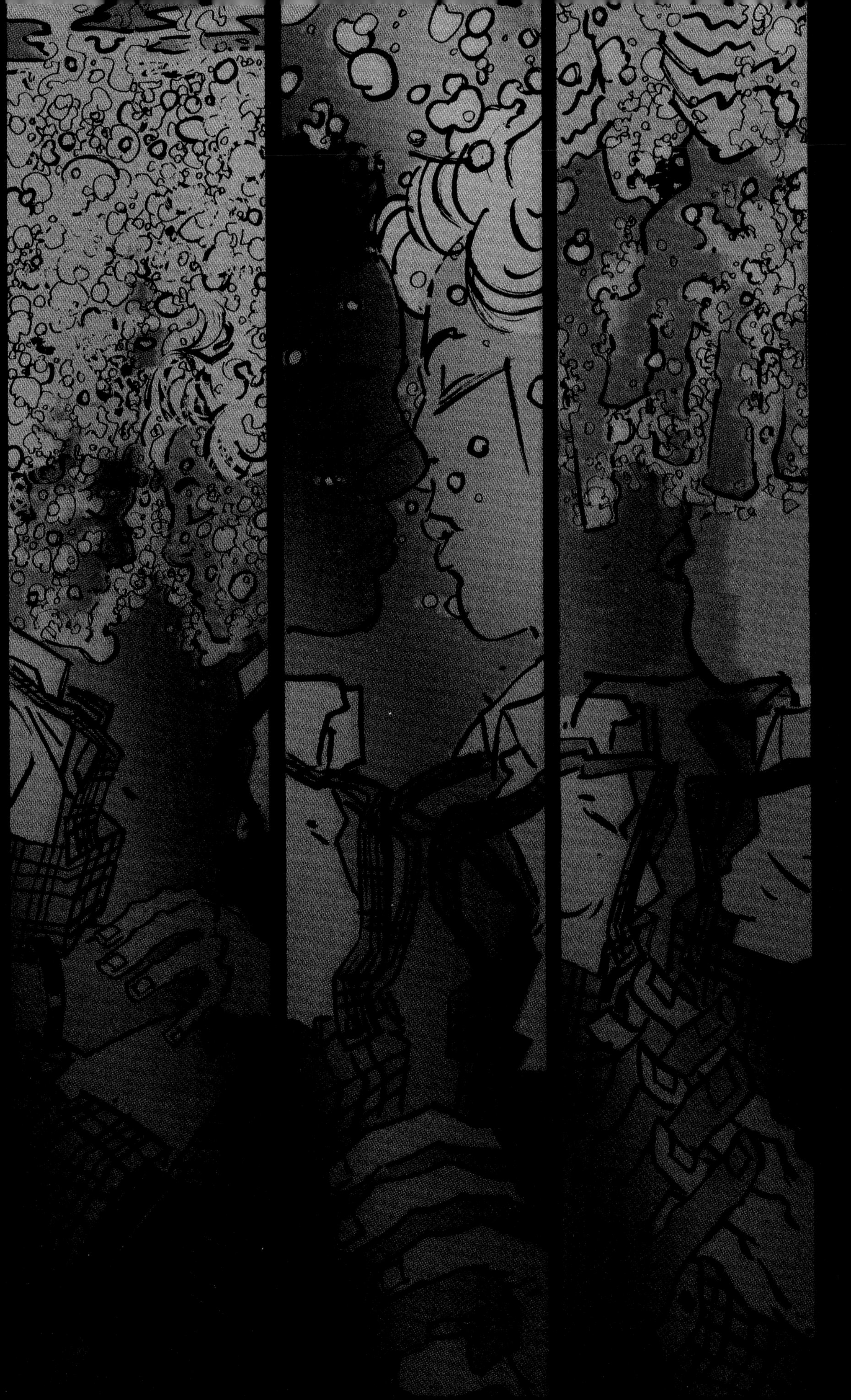

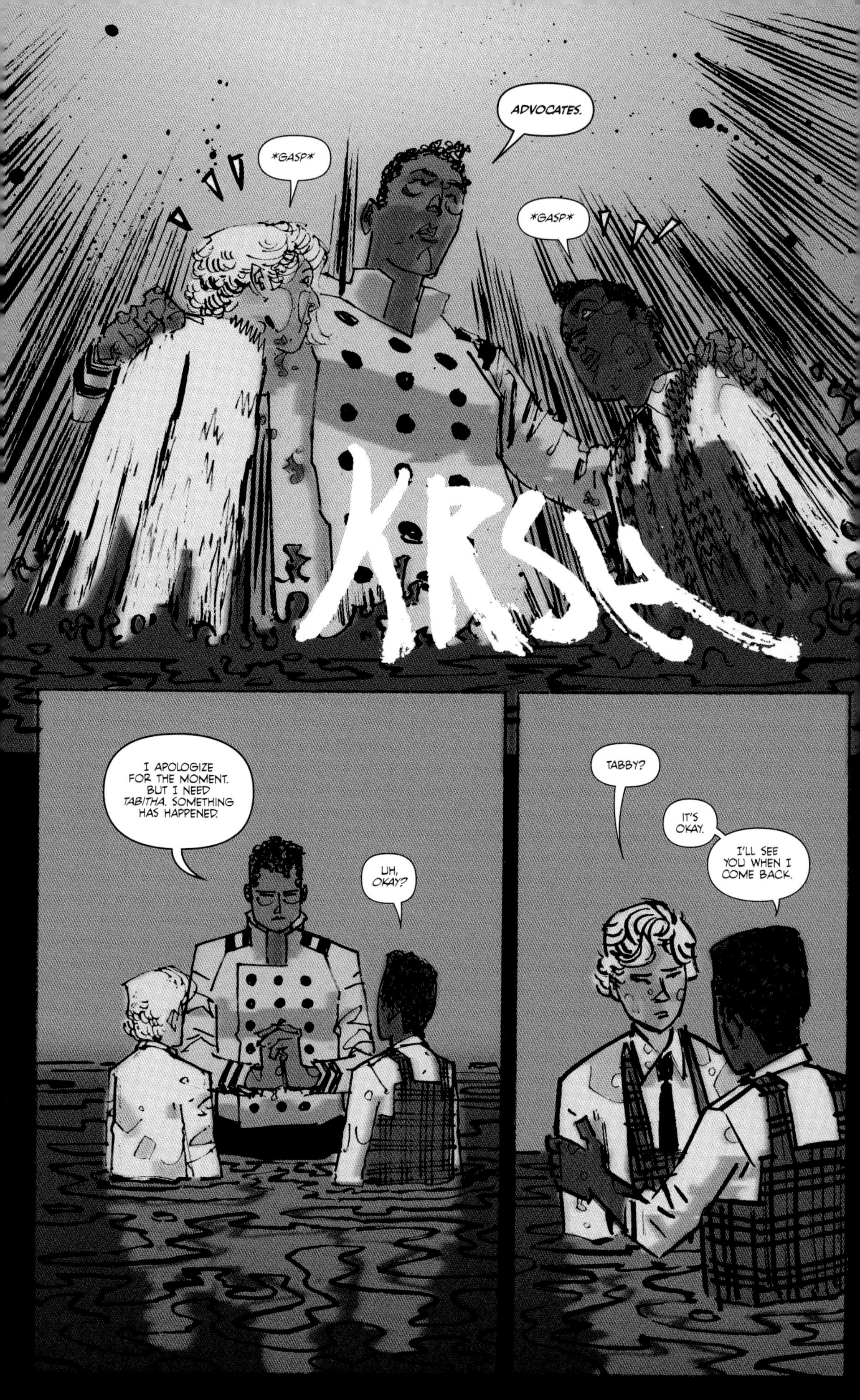
ADVOCATES.
GASP
GASP
KRSH
I APOLOGIZE FOR THE MOMENT. BUT I NEED *TABITHA*. SOMETHING HAS HAPPENED.
UH, *OKAY?*
TABBY?
IT'S OKAY.
I'LL SEE YOU WHEN I COME BACK.

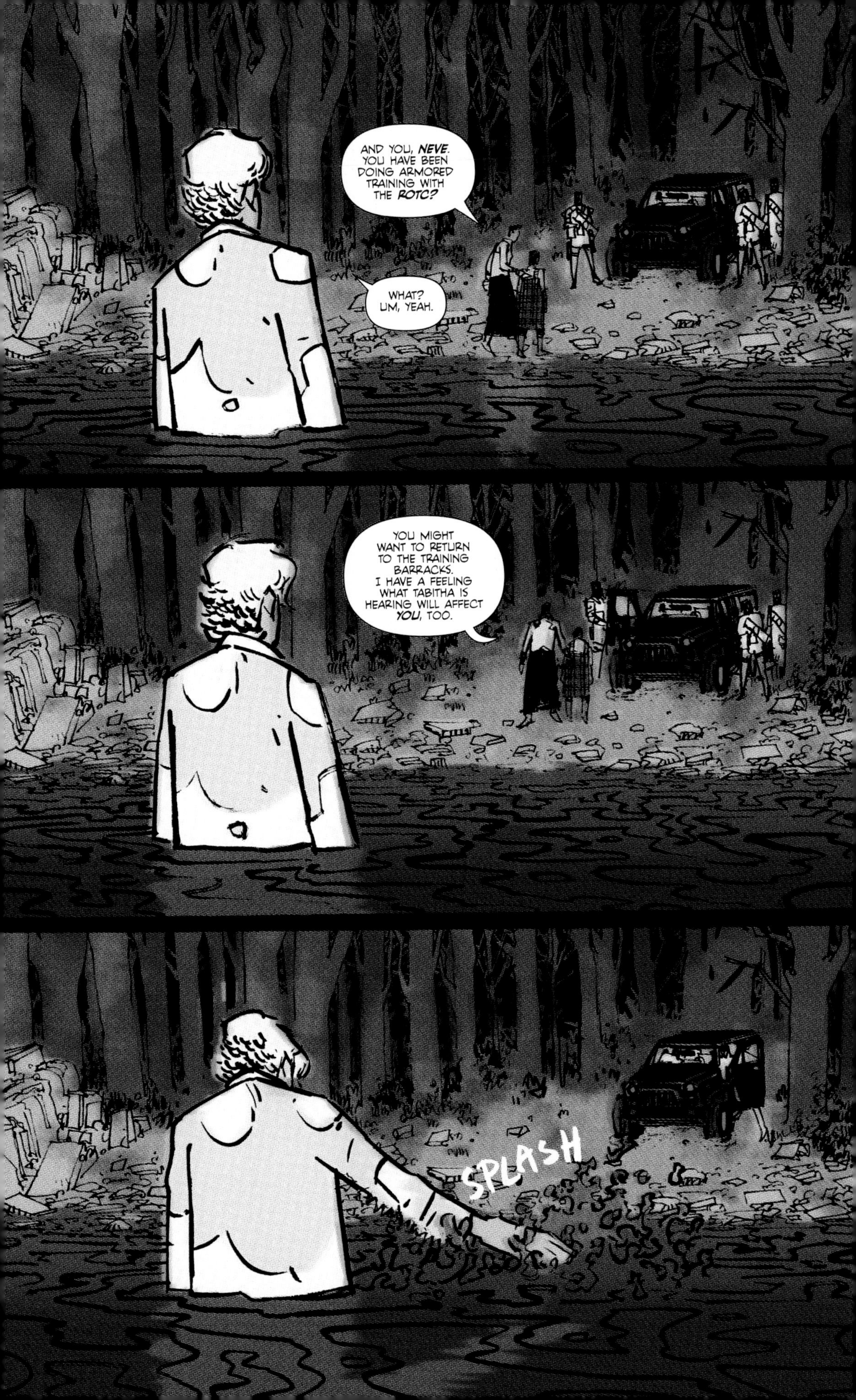
AND YOU, NEVE. YOU HAVE BEEN DOING ARMORED TRAINING WITH THE ROTC?
WHAT? UM, YEAH.
YOU MIGHT WANT TO RETURN TO THE TRAINING BARRACKS. I HAVE A FEELING WHAT TABITHA IS HEARING WILL AFFECT YOU, TOO.
SPLASH

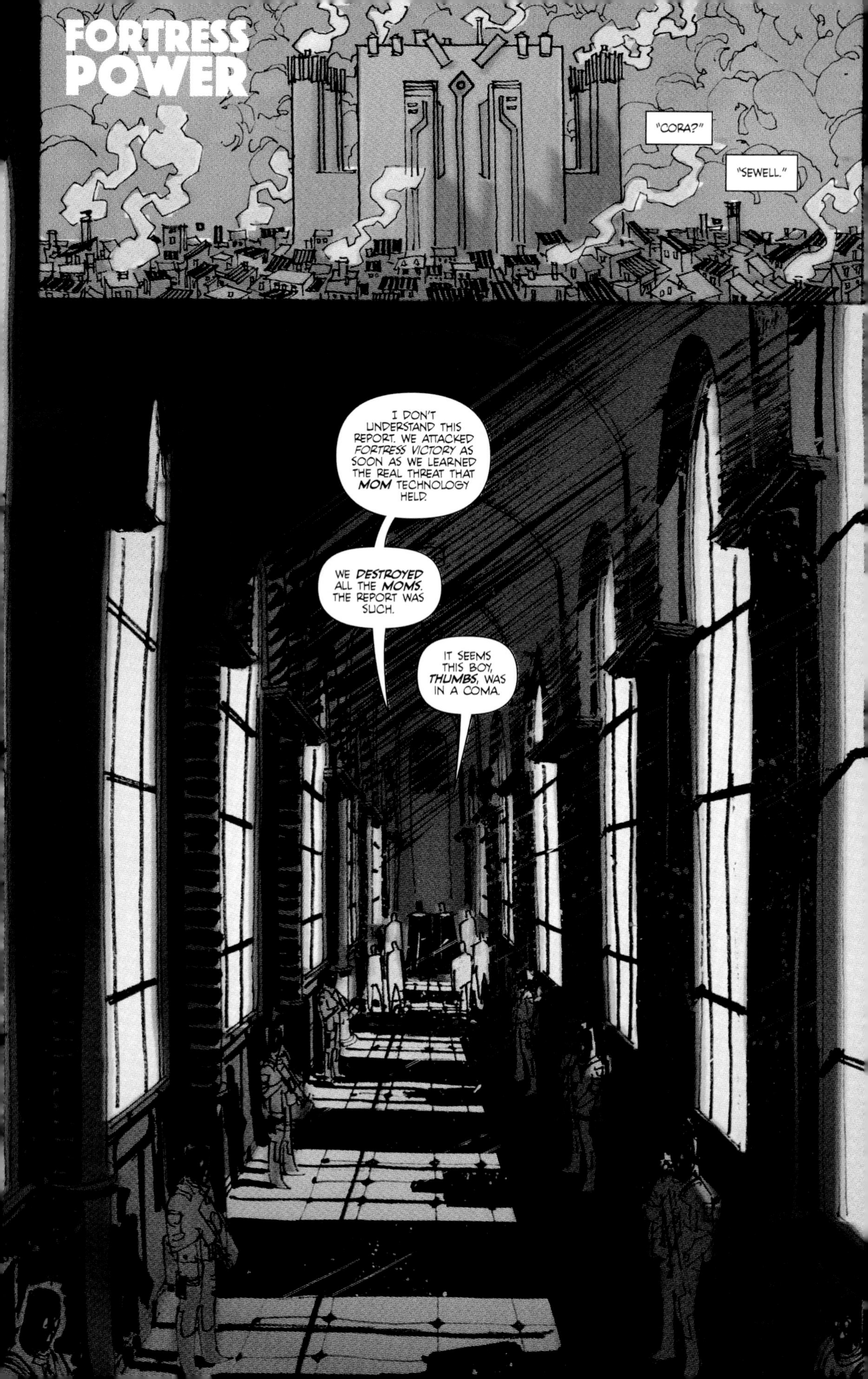

FORTRESS POWER
"CORA?"
"SEWELL."
I DON'T UNDERSTAND THIS REPORT. WE ATTACKED FORTRESS VICTORY AS SOON AS WE LEARNED THE REAL THREAT THAT MOM TECHNOLOGY HELD.
WE DESTROYED ALL THE MOMS. THE REPORT WAS SUCH.
IT SEEMS THIS BOY, THUMBS, WAS IN A COMA.

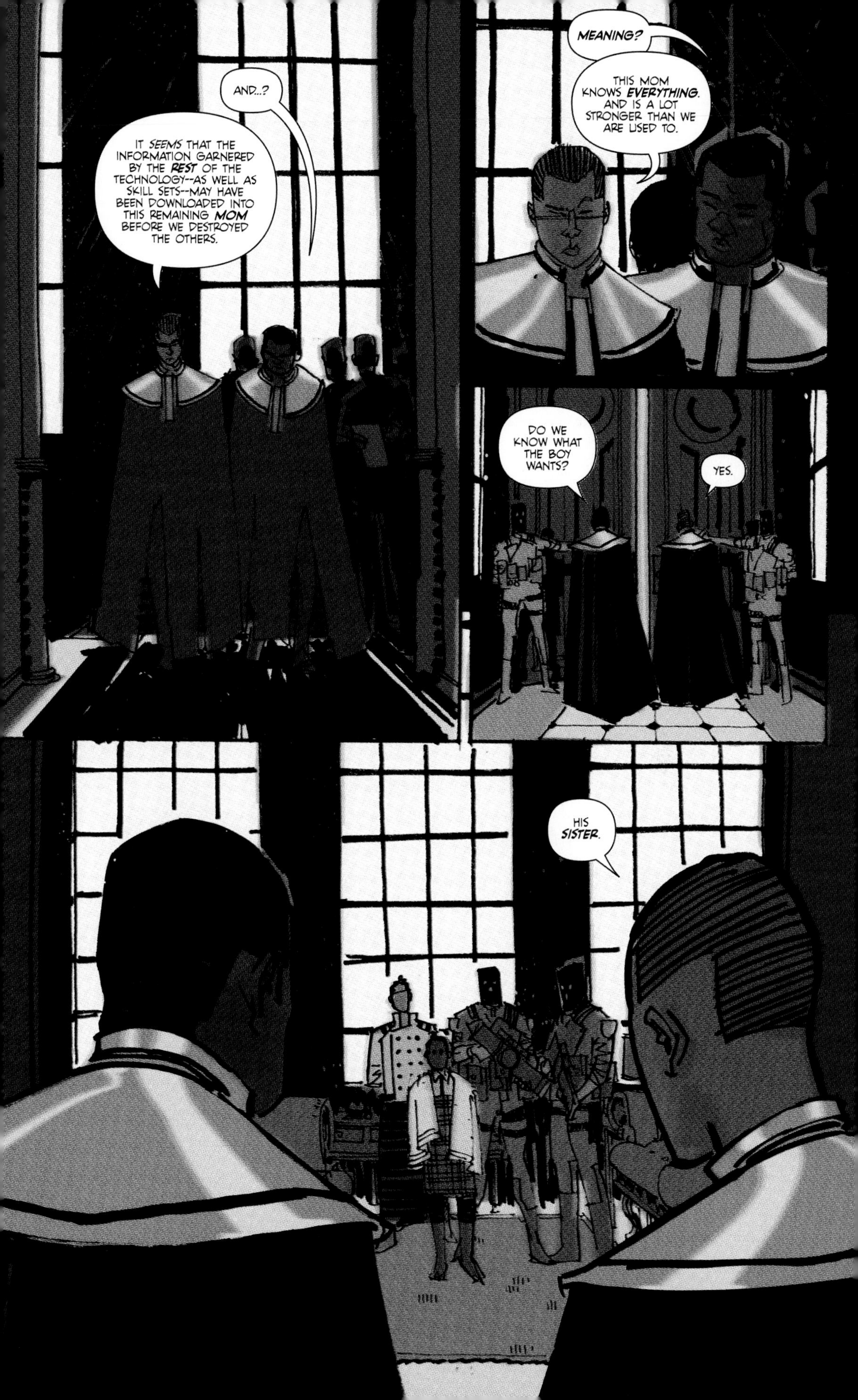
AND...?
IT SEEMS THAT THE INFORMATION GARNERED BY THE REST OF THE TECHNOLOGY--AS WELL AS SKILL SETS--MAY HAVE BEEN DOWNLOADED INTO THIS REMAINING MOM BEFORE WE DESTROYED THE OTHERS.
MEANING?
THIS MOM KNOWS EVERYTHING. AND IS A LOT STRONGER THAN WE ARE USED TO.
DO WE KNOW WHAT THE BOY WANTS?
YES.
HIS SISTER.

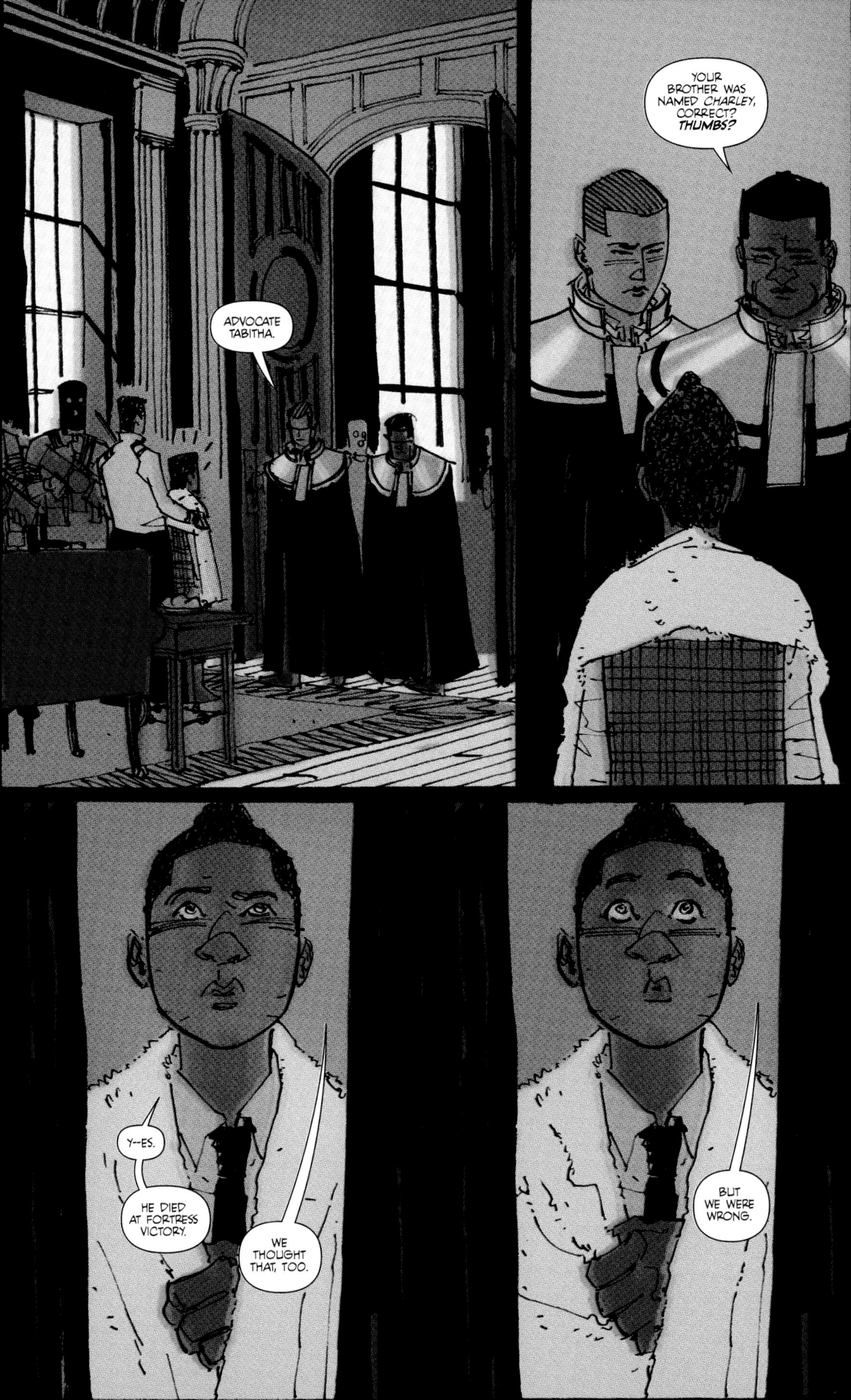
ADVOCATE TABITHA.
YOUR BROTHER WAS NAMED CHARLEY, CORRECT? THUMBS?
Y--ES.
HE DIED AT FORTRESS VICTORY.
WE THOUGHT THAT, TOO.
BUT WE WERE WRONG.

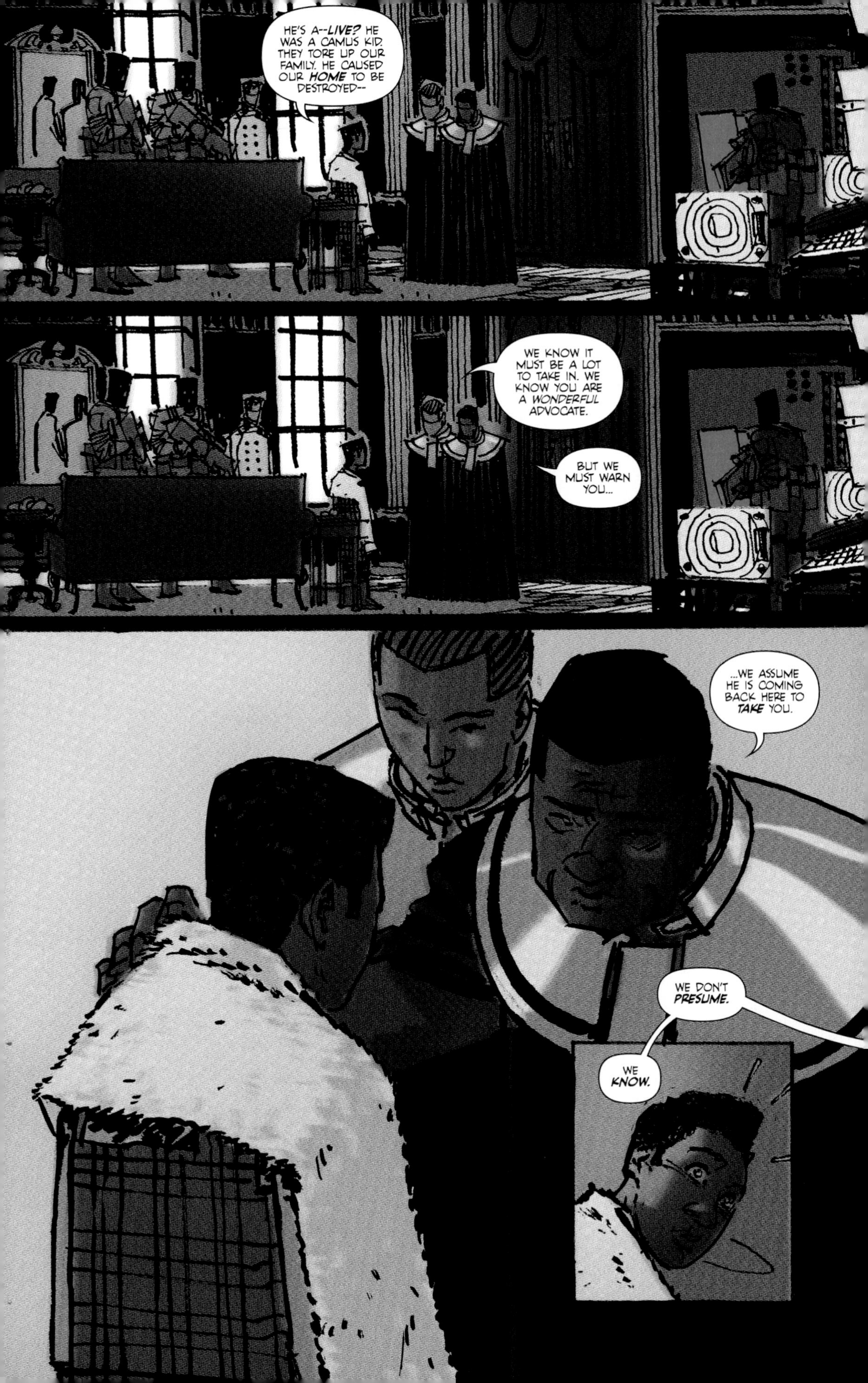
HE'S A--*LIVE?* HE WAS A CAMUS KID. THEY TORE UP OUR FAMILY. HE CAUSED OUR *HOME* TO BE DESTROYED--
WE KNOW IT MUST BE A LOT TO TAKE IN. WE KNOW YOU ARE A *WONDERFUL* ADVOCATE.
BUT WE MUST WARN YOU...
...WE ASSUME HE IS COMING BACK HERE TO *TAKE* YOU.
WE DON'T *PRESUME.*
WE *KNOW.*

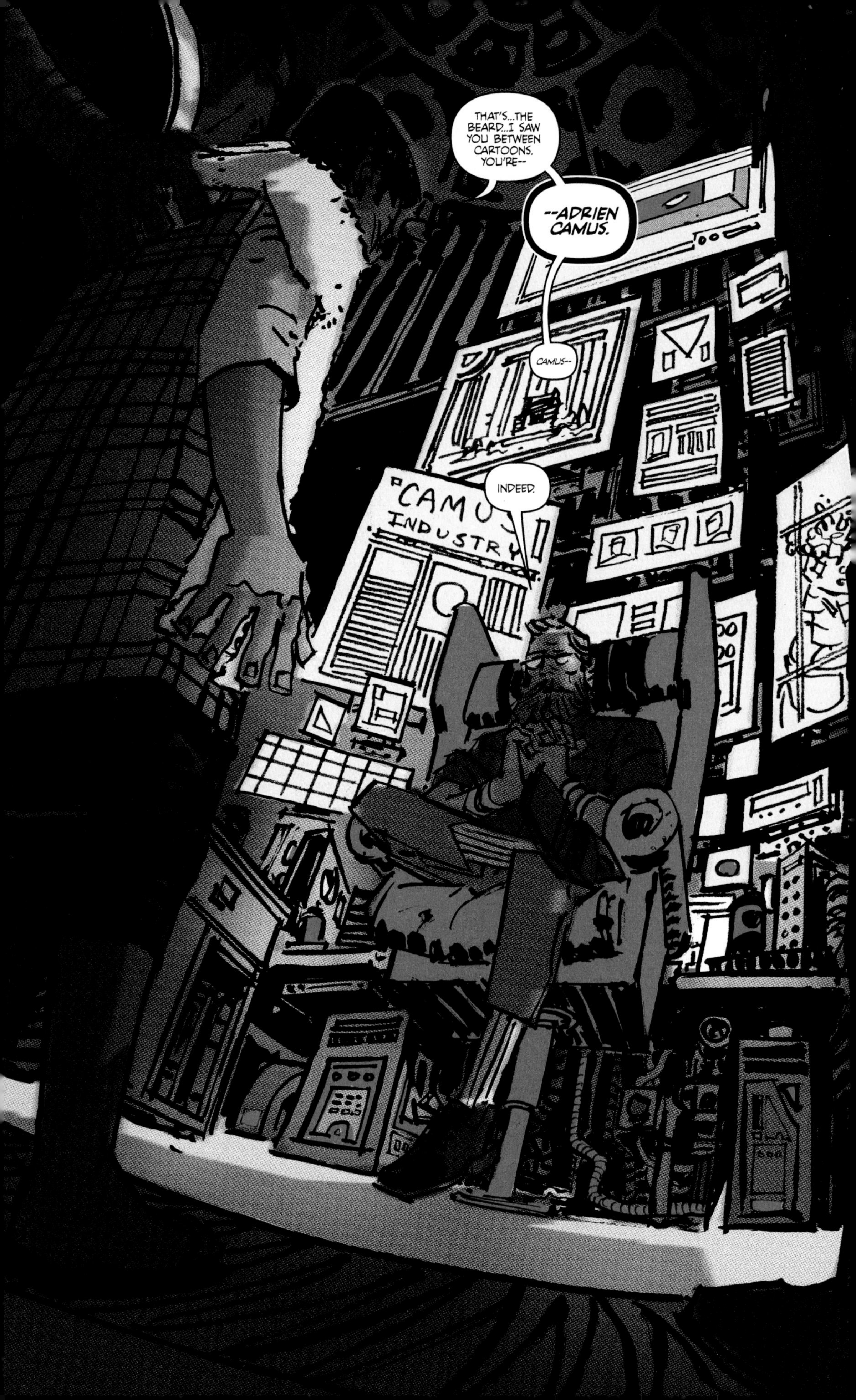
THAT'S...THE BEARD...I SAW YOU BETWEEN CARTOONS. YOU'RE--
--ADRIEN CAMUS.
CAMUS--
INDEED.
CAMUS INDUSTRY

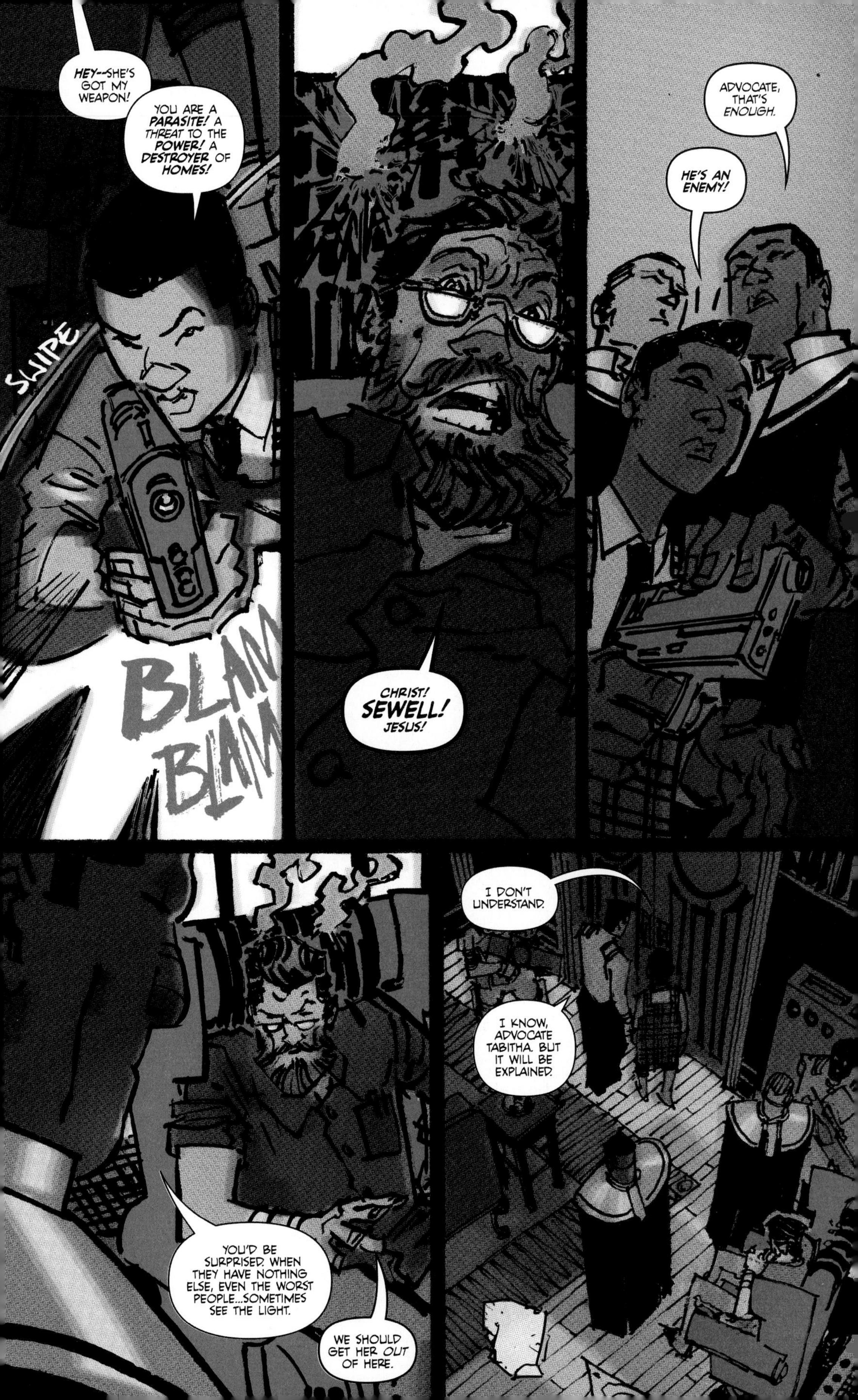
HEY--SHE'S GOT MY WEAPON!
YOU ARE A PARASITE! A THREAT TO THE POWER! A DESTROYER OF HOMES!
SWIPE
BLAM
BLAM
CHRIST! SEWELL! JESUS!
ADVOCATE, THAT'S ENOUGH.
HE'S AN ENEMY!
YOU'D BE SURPRISED. WHEN THEY HAVE NOTHING ELSE, EVEN THE WORST PEOPLE...SOMETIMES SEE THE LIGHT.
WE SHOULD GET HER OUT OF HERE.
I DON'T UNDERSTAND.
I KNOW, ADVOCATE TABITHA. BUT IT WILL BE EXPLAINED.

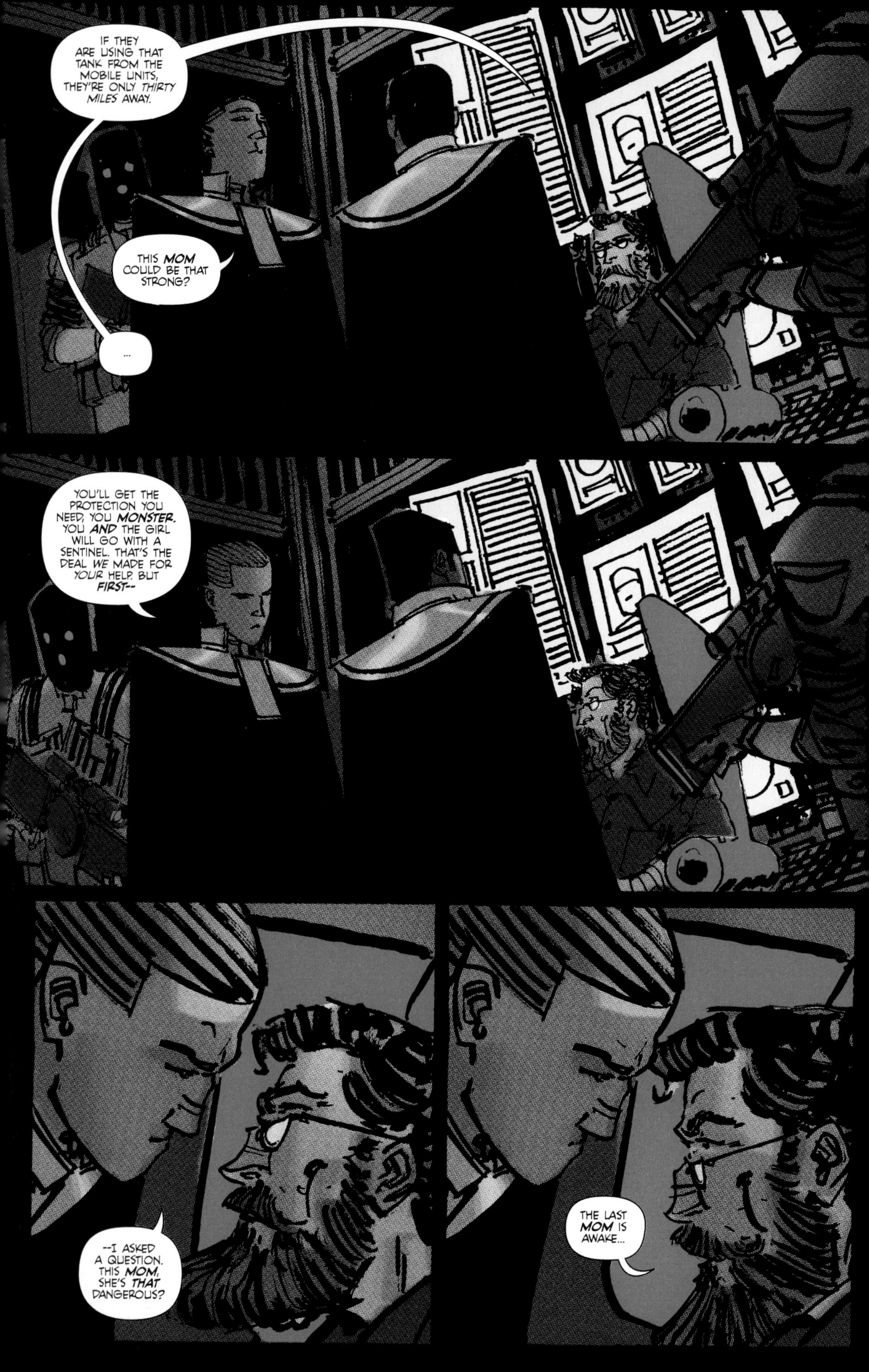
IF THEY ARE USING THAT TANK FROM THE MOBILE UNITS, THEY'RE ONLY *THIRTY MILES* AWAY.
THIS **MOM** COULD BE THAT STRONG?
...
YOU'LL GET THE PROTECTION YOU NEED, YOU **MONSTER.** YOU **AND** THE GIRL WILL GO WITH A SENTINEL. THAT'S THE DEAL *WE* MADE FOR *YOUR* HELP. BUT ***FIRST--***
--I ASKED A QUESTION. THIS **MOM,** SHE'S ***THAT*** DANGEROUS?
THE LAST **MOM** IS AWAKE...

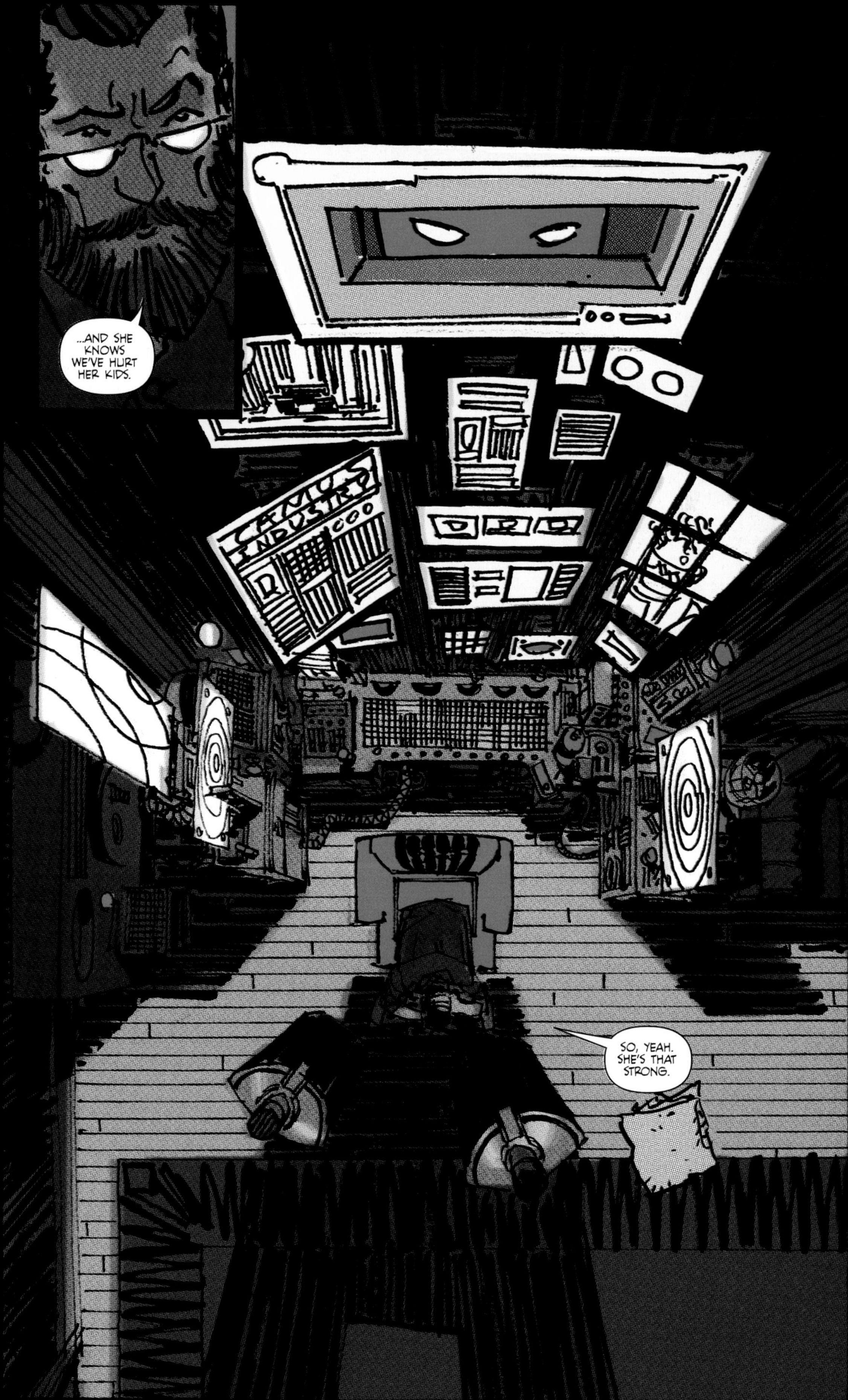
...AND SHE KNOWS WE'VE HURT HER KIDS.
SO, YEAH. SHE'S THAT STRONG.

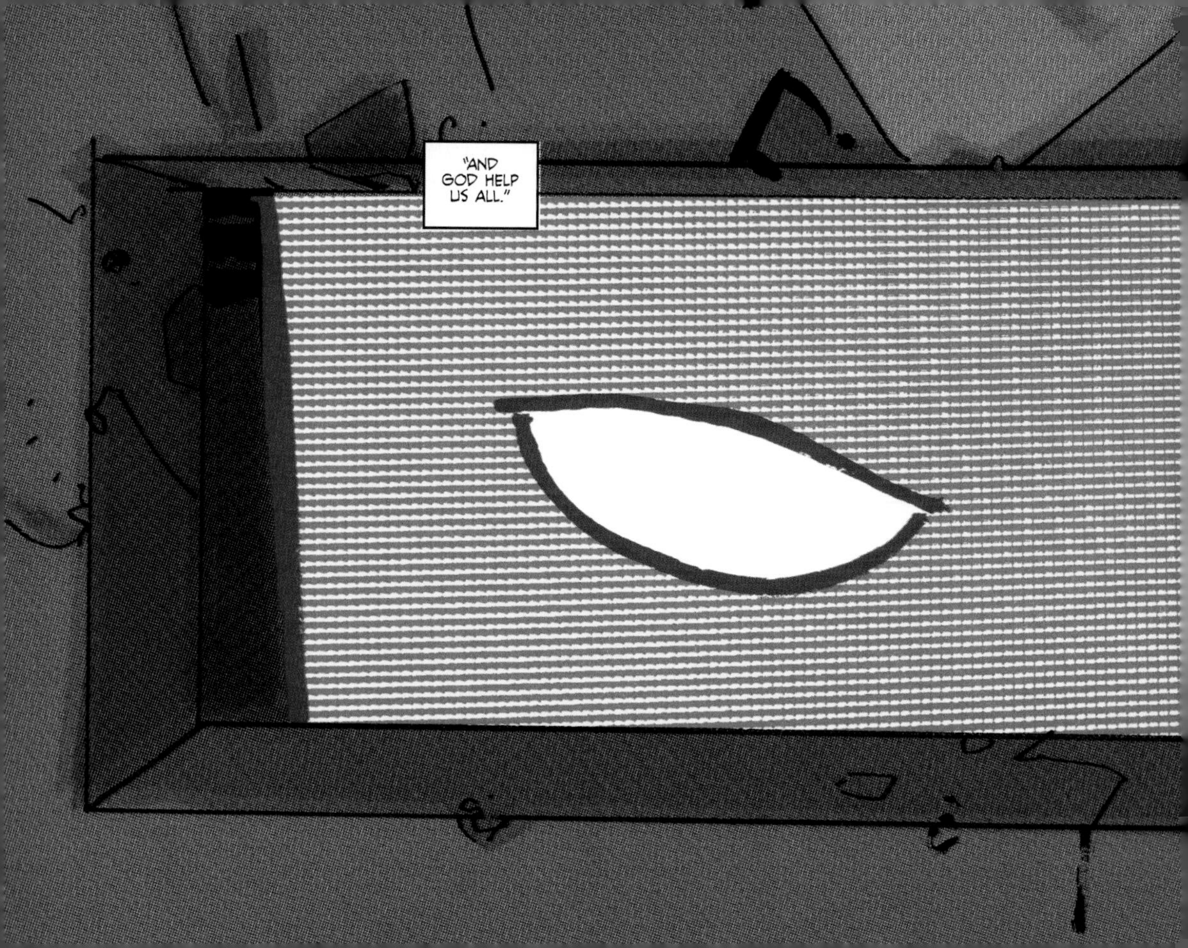
"AND GOD HELP US ALL."

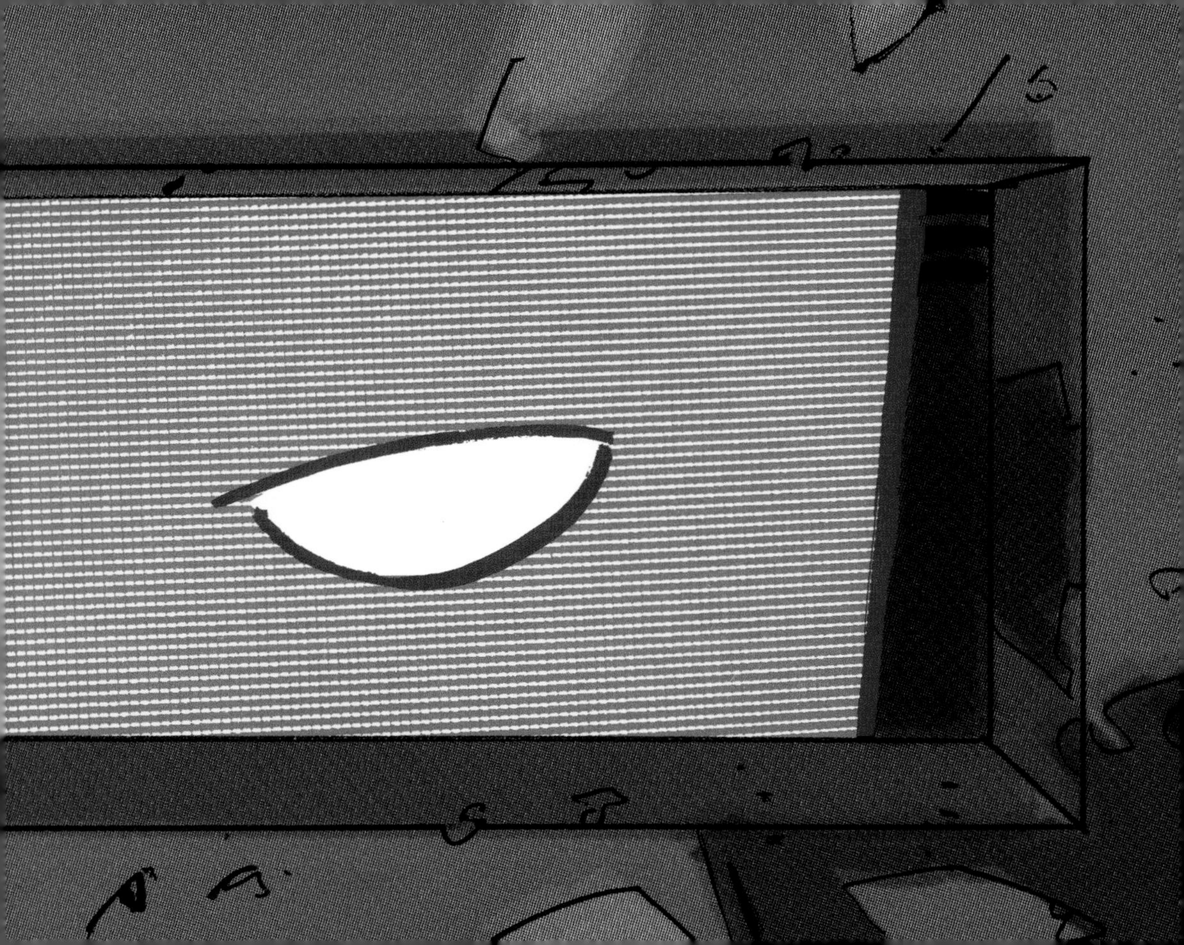

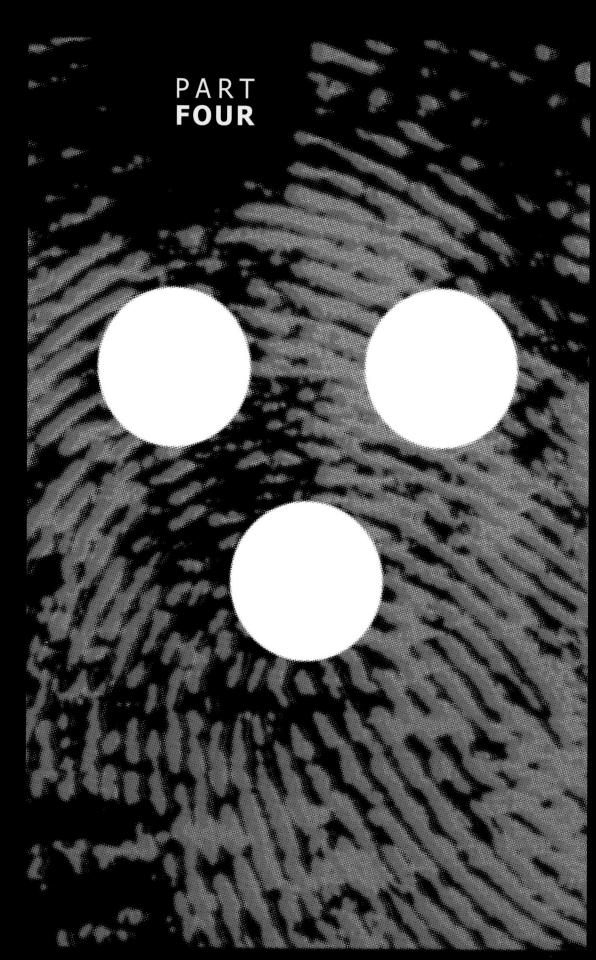

PART
FOUR

TEN MILES FROM POWER CITY...
...OUR HEROES RUN INTO A SNAG.
KIDDIES, TO BE HONEST, MOM HAS NEVER BEEN GOOD AT DRIVING AROUND TIGHT TURNS OR LAND MINES...

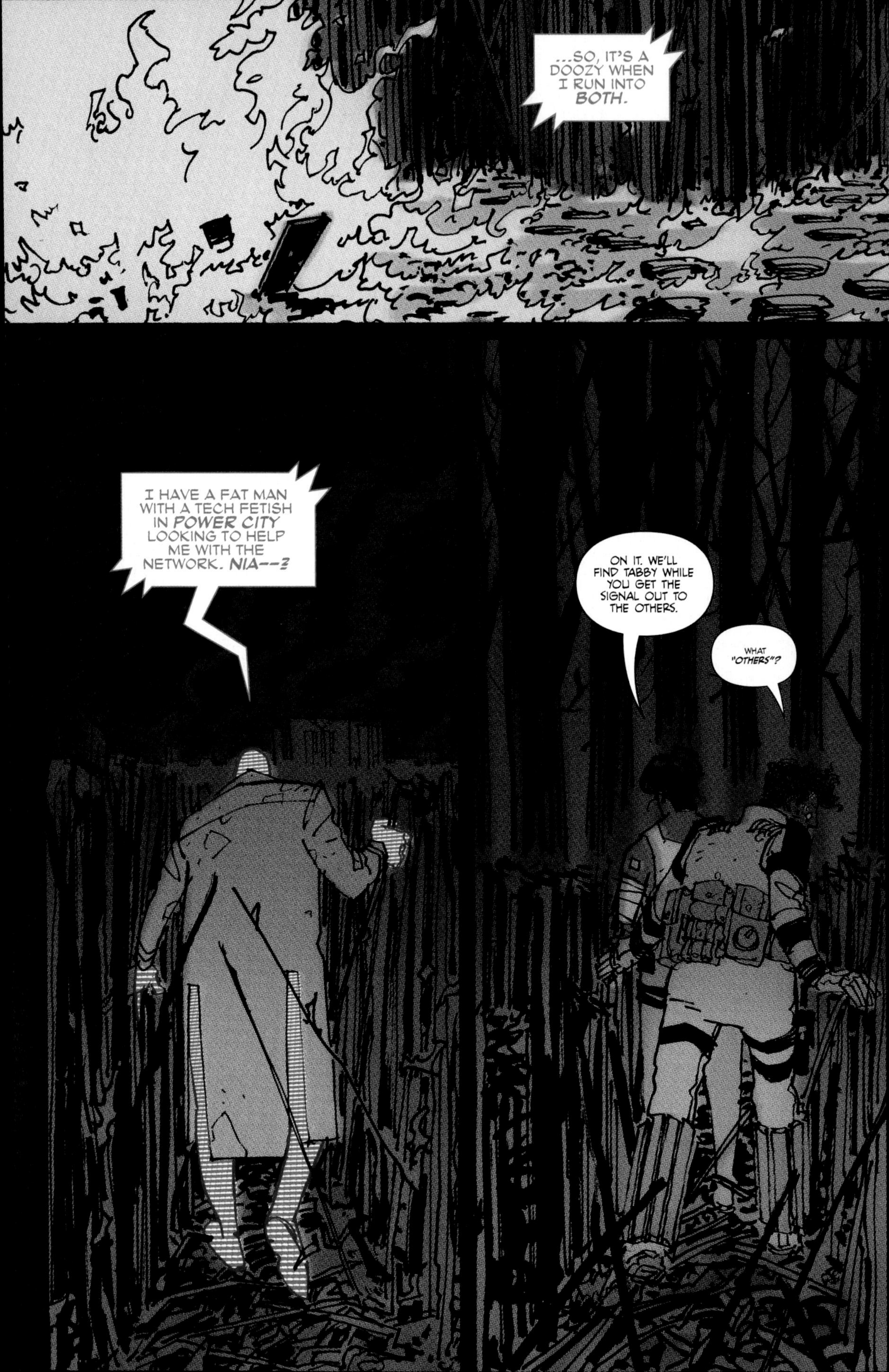
...SO, IT'S A DOOZY WHEN I RUN INTO BOTH.
I HAVE A FAT MAN WITH A TECH FETISH IN POWER CITY LOOKING TO HELP ME WITH THE NETWORK. NIA--?
ON IT. WE'LL FIND TABBY WHILE YOU GET THE SIGNAL OUT TO THE OTHERS.
WHAT "OTHERS"?

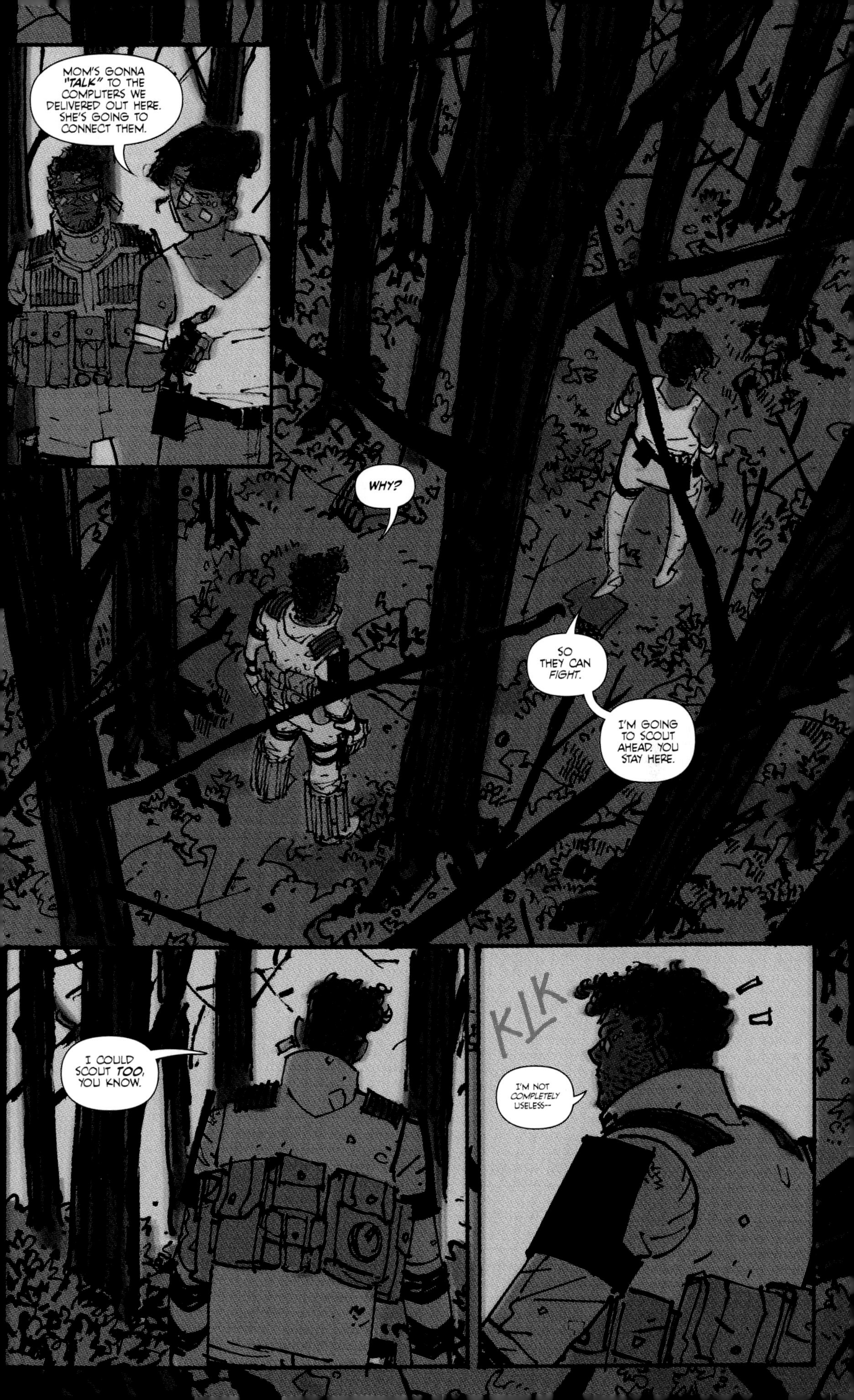
MOM'S GONNA "TALK" TO THE COMPUTERS WE DELIVERED OUT HERE. SHE'S GOING TO CONNECT THEM.
WHY?
SO THEY CAN FIGHT.
I'M GOING TO SCOUT AHEAD. YOU STAY HERE.
I COULD SCOUT TOO, YOU KNOW.
KLK
I'M NOT COMPLETELY USELESS--

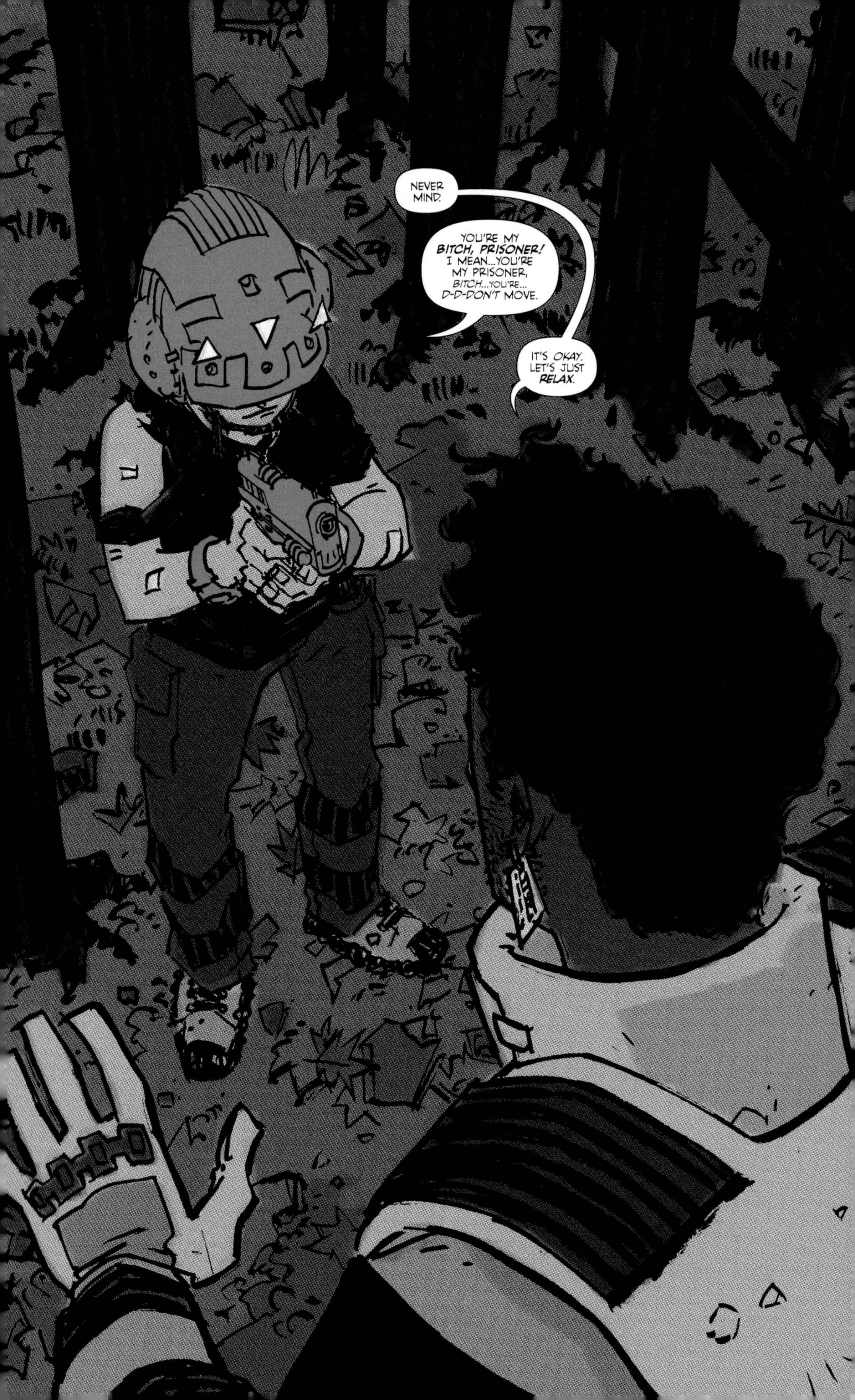
NEVER MIND.
YOU'RE MY BITCH, PRISONER! I MEAN...YOU'RE MY PRISONER, BITCH...YOU'RE... D-D-DON'T MOVE.
IT'S OKAY. LET'S JUST RELAX.

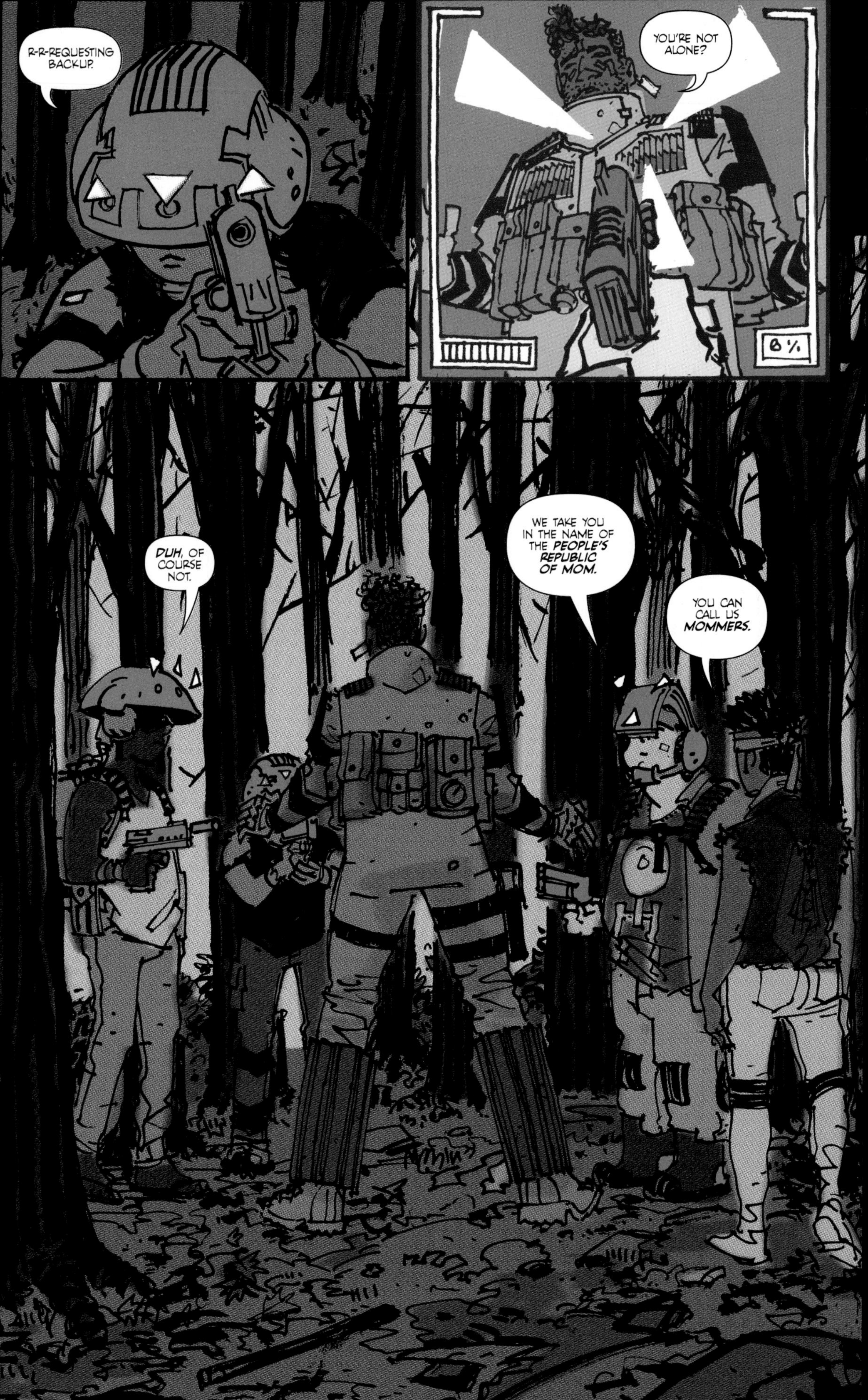
R-R-REQUESTING BACKUP.
YOU'RE NOT ALONE?
8%
DUH, OF COURSE NOT.
WE TAKE YOU IN THE NAME OF THE PEOPLE'S REPUBLIC OF MOM.
YOU CAN CALL US MOMMERS.

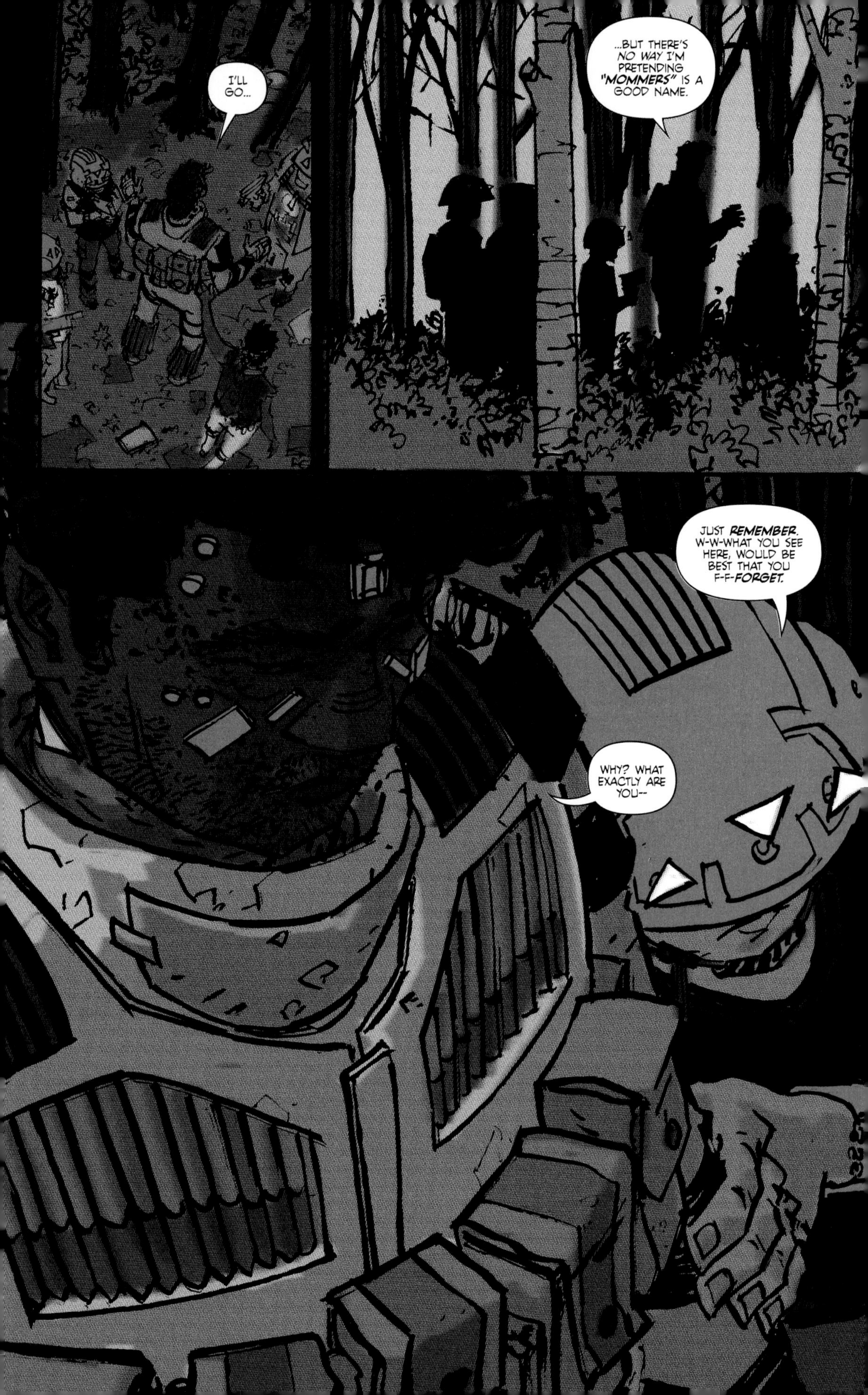
I'LL GO...
...BUT THERE'S *NO WAY* I'M PRETENDING ***"MOMMERS"*** IS A GOOD NAME.
JUST ***REMEMBER.*** W-W-WHAT YOU SEE HERE, WOULD BE BEST THAT YOU F-F-***FORGET.***
WHY? WHAT EXACTLY ARE YOU--

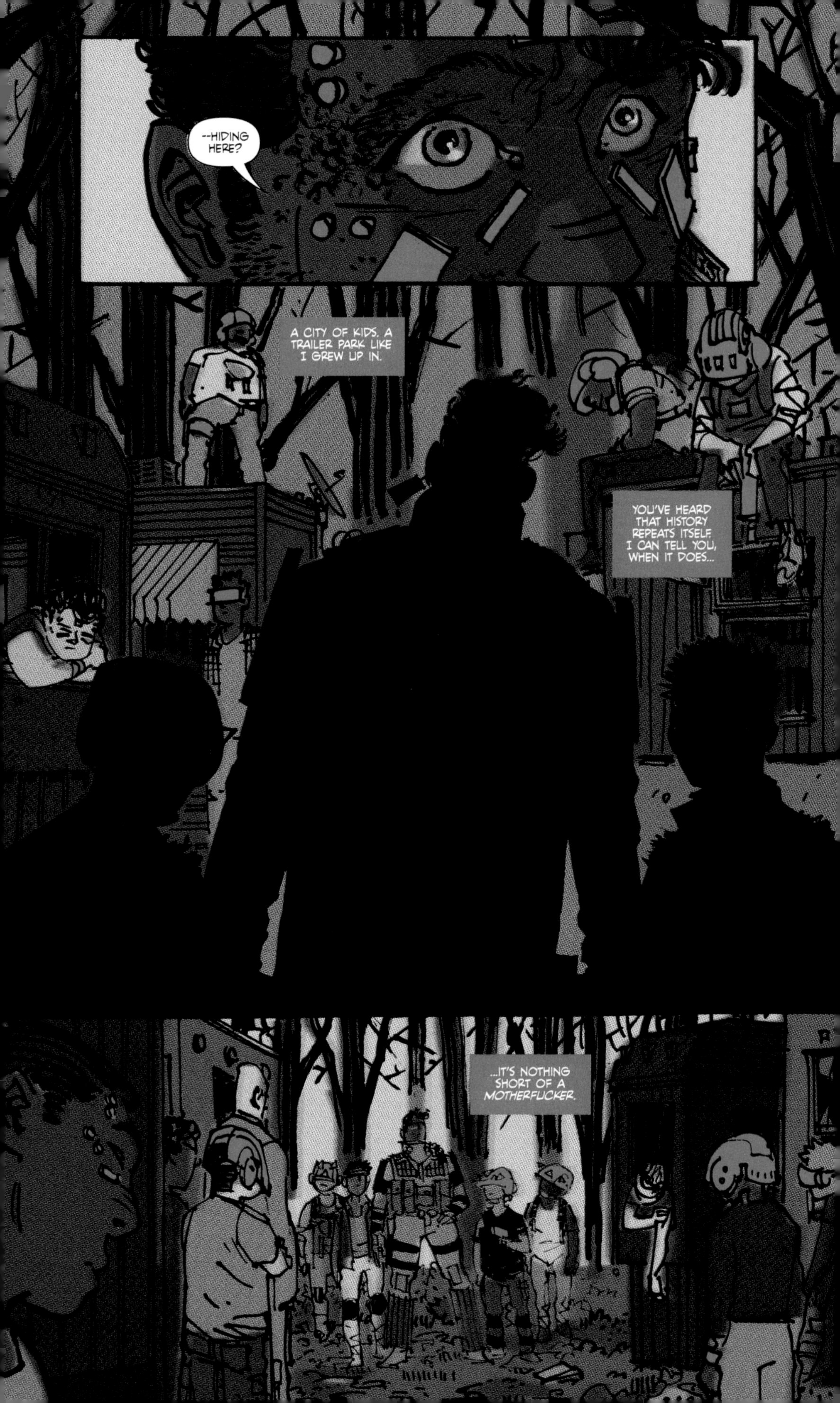
--HIDING HERE?
A CITY OF KIDS. A TRAILER PARK LIKE I GREW UP IN.
YOU'VE HEARD THAT HISTORY REPEATS ITSELF. I CAN TELL YOU, WHEN IT DOES...
...IT'S NOTHING SHORT OF A *MOTHERFUCKER.*

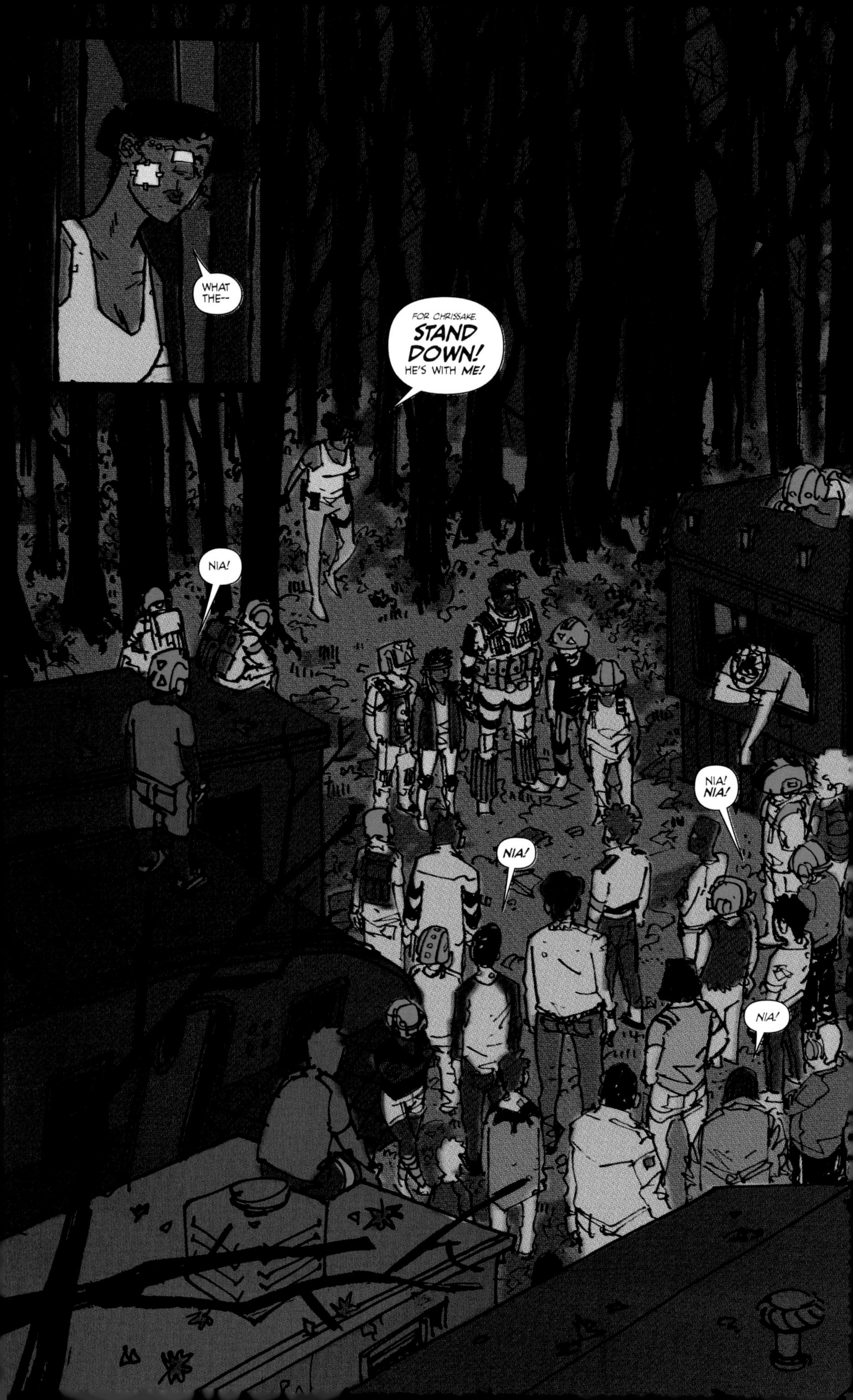
WHAT THE--
FOR CHRISSAKE. STAND DOWN! HE'S WITH ME!
NIA!
NIA! NIA!
NIA!
NIA!

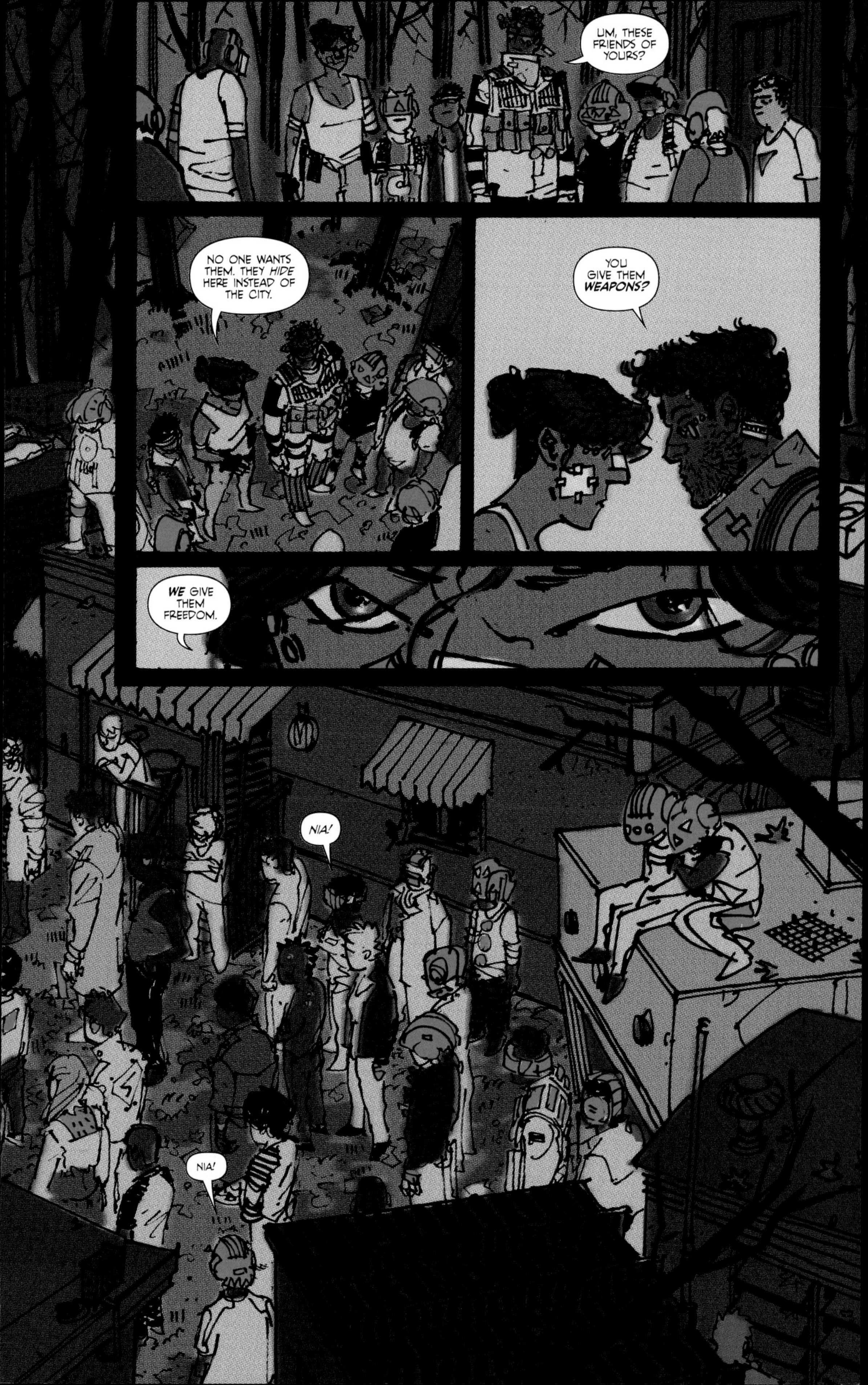
UM, THESE FRIENDS OF YOURS?
NO ONE WANTS THEM. THEY *HIDE* HERE INSTEAD OF THE CITY.
YOU GIVE THEM ***WEAPONS?***
WE GIVE THEM FREEDOM.
NIA!
NIA!

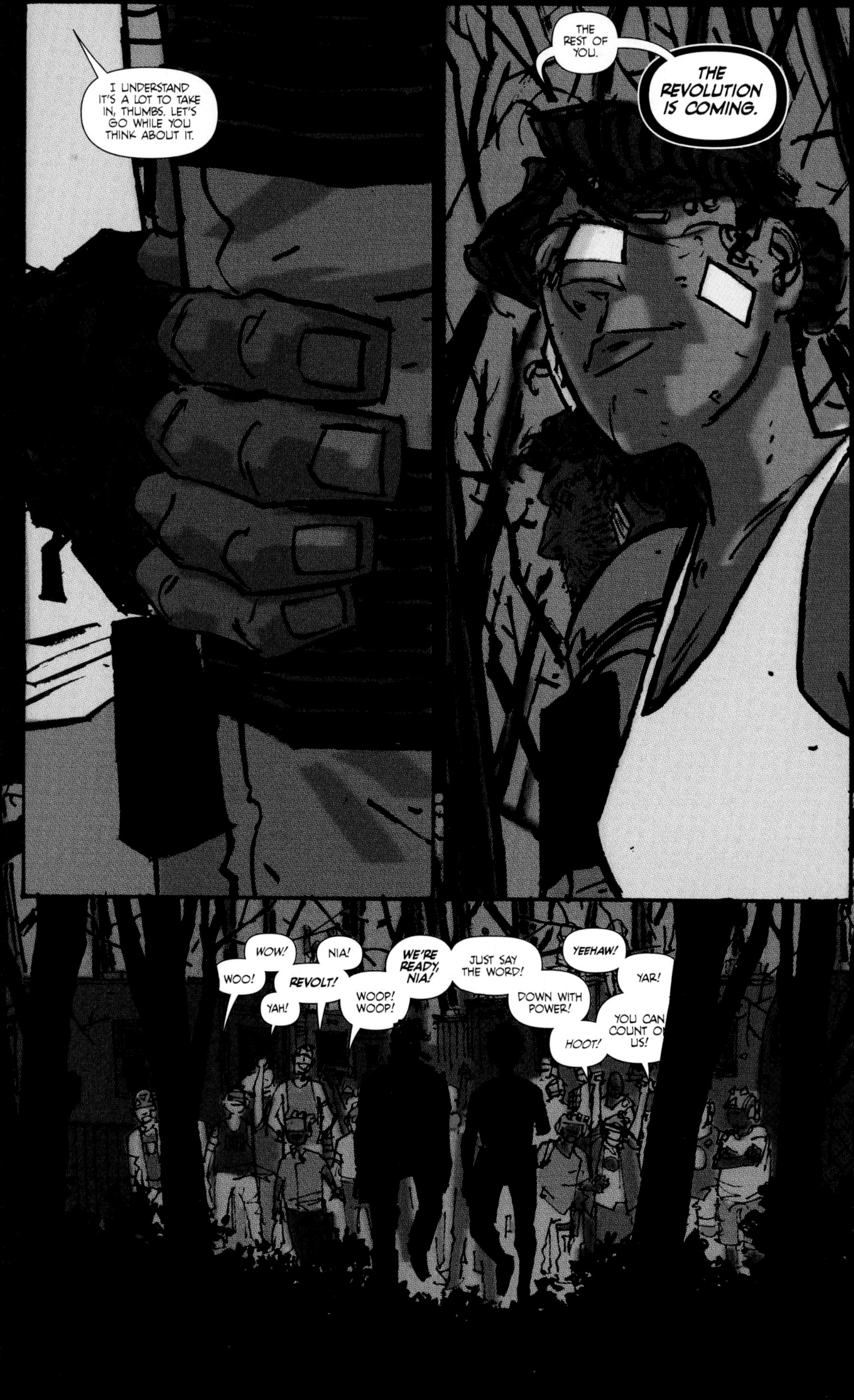

I UNDERSTAND IT'S A LOT TO TAKE IN, THUMBS. LET'S GO WHILE YOU THINK ABOUT IT.
THE REST OF YOU.
THE REVOLUTION IS COMING.
WOO!
WOW!
YAH!
REVOLT!
NIA!
WOOP! WOOP!
WE'RE READY, NIA!
JUST SAY THE WORD!
DOWN WITH POWER!
YEEHAW!
YAR!
HOOT!
YOU CAN COUNT ON US!

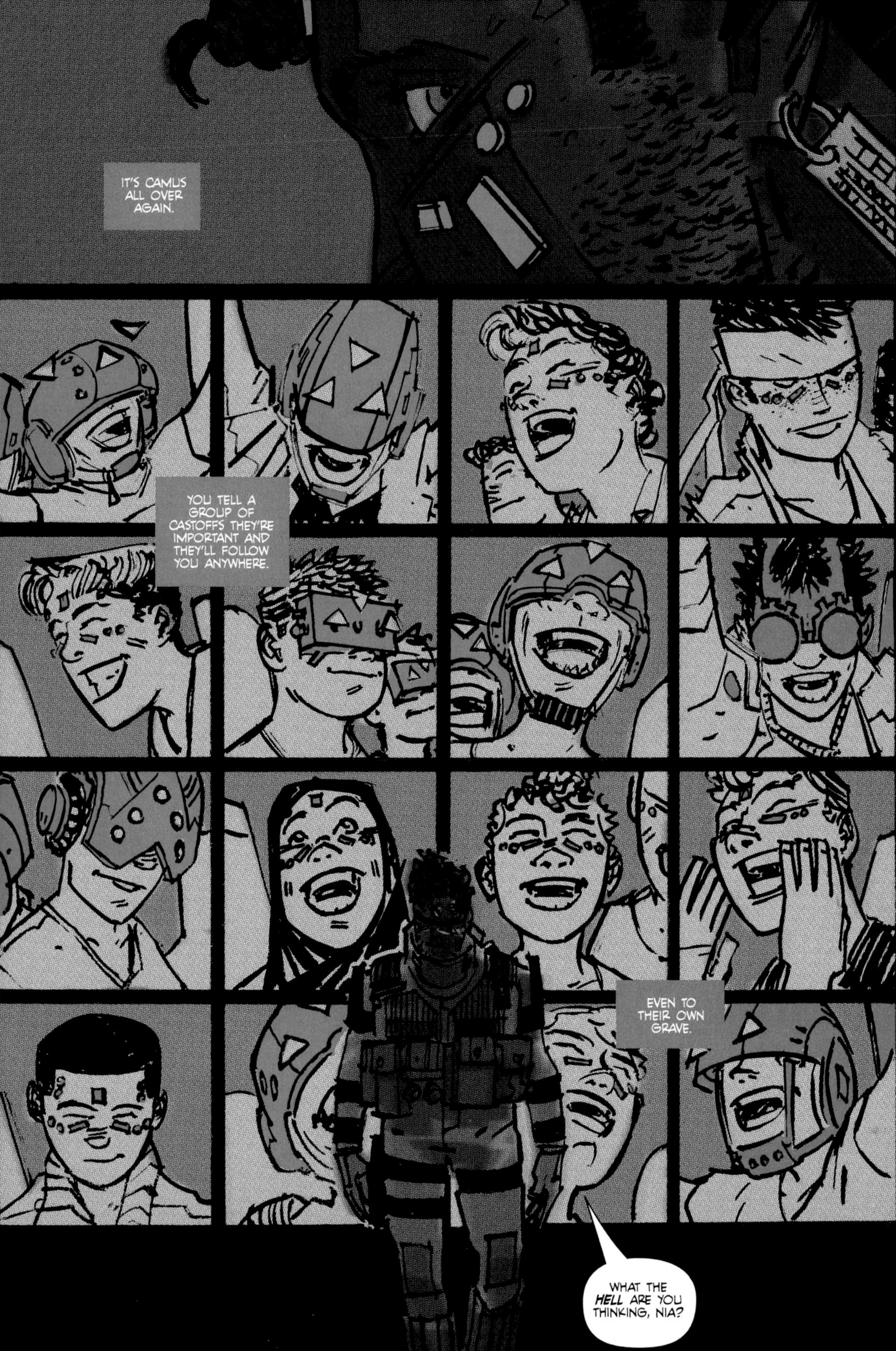
IT'S CAMUS ALL OVER AGAIN.
YOU TELL A GROUP OF CASTOFFS THEY'RE IMPORTANT AND THEY'LL FOLLOW YOU ANYWHERE.
EVEN TO THEIR OWN GRAVE.
WHAT THE HELL ARE YOU THINKING, NIA?

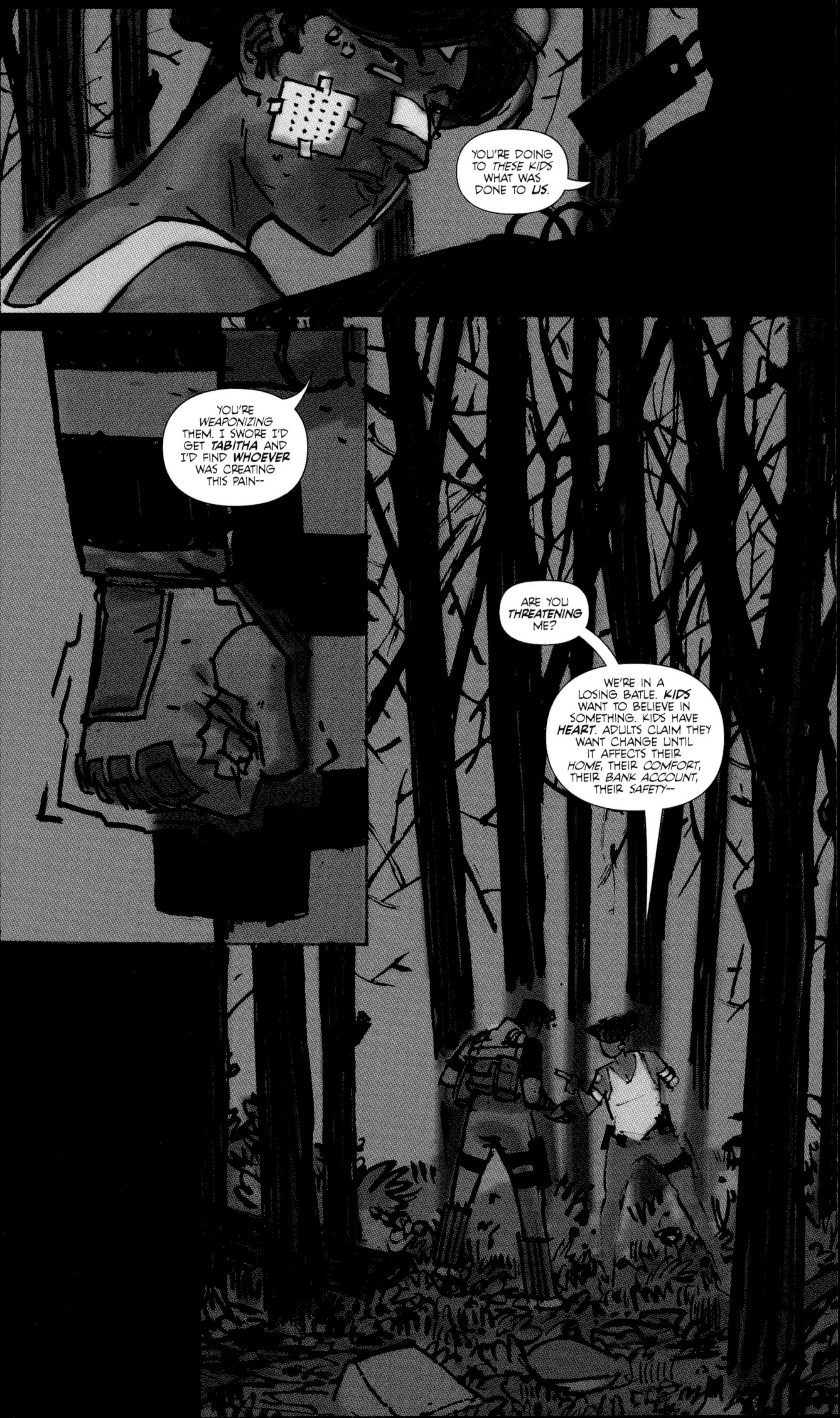
YOU'RE DOING TO *THESE KIDS* WHAT WAS DONE TO *US*.
YOU'RE *WEAPONIZING* THEM. I SWORE I'D GET ***TABITHA*** AND I'D FIND ***WHOEVER*** WAS CREATING THIS PAIN--
ARE YOU ***THREATENING*** ME?
WE'RE IN A LOSING BATLE. ***KIDS*** WANT TO BELIEVE IN SOMETHING. KIDS HAVE ***HEART***. ADULTS CLAIM THEY WANT CHANGE UNTIL IT AFFECTS THEIR *HOME*, THEIR *COMFORT*, THEIR *BANK ACCOUNT*, THEIR *SAFETY*--

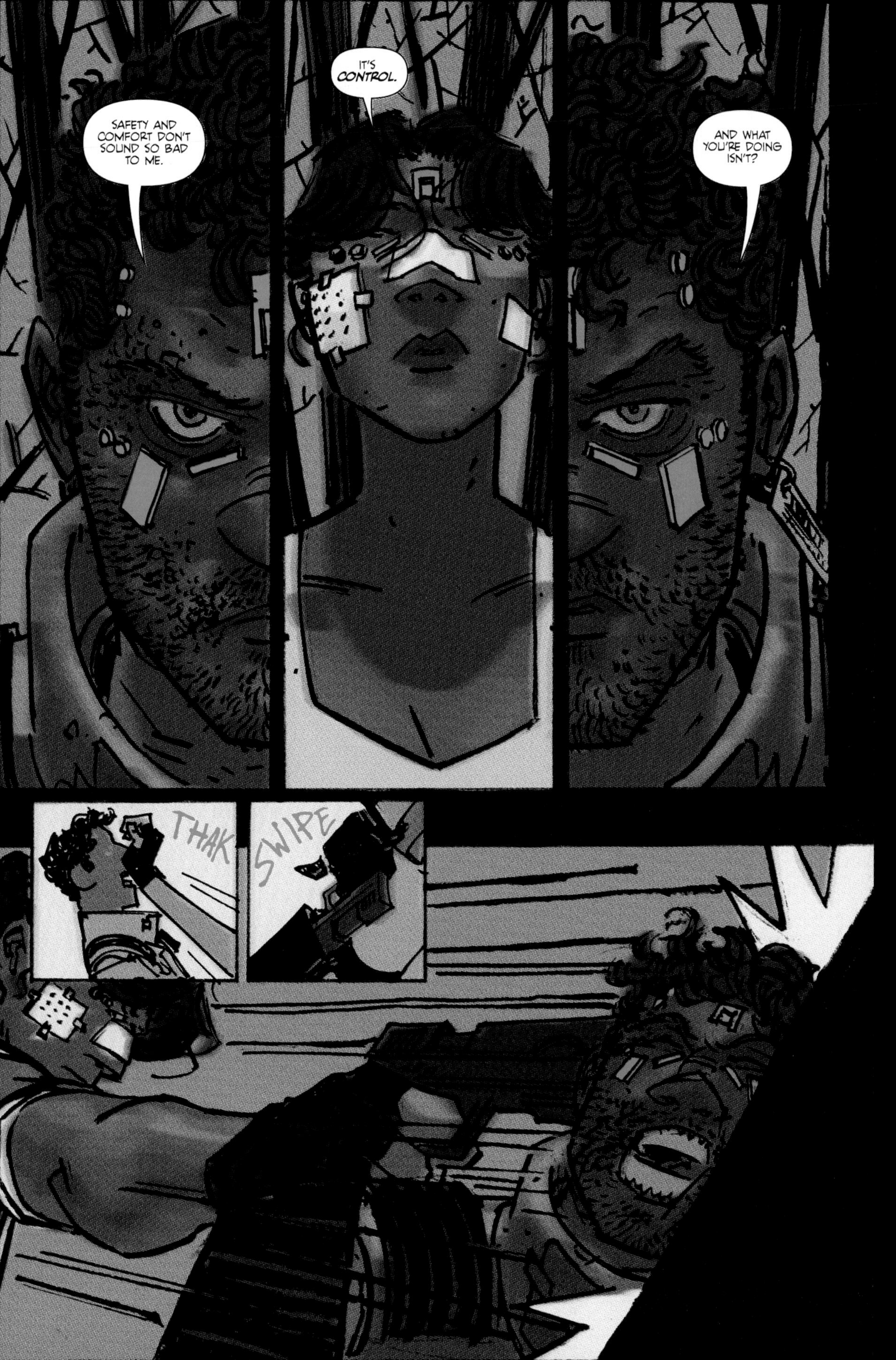
SAFETY AND COMFORT DON'T SOUND SO BAD TO ME.
IT'S CONTROL.
AND WHAT YOU'RE DOING ISN'T?
THAK
SWIPE

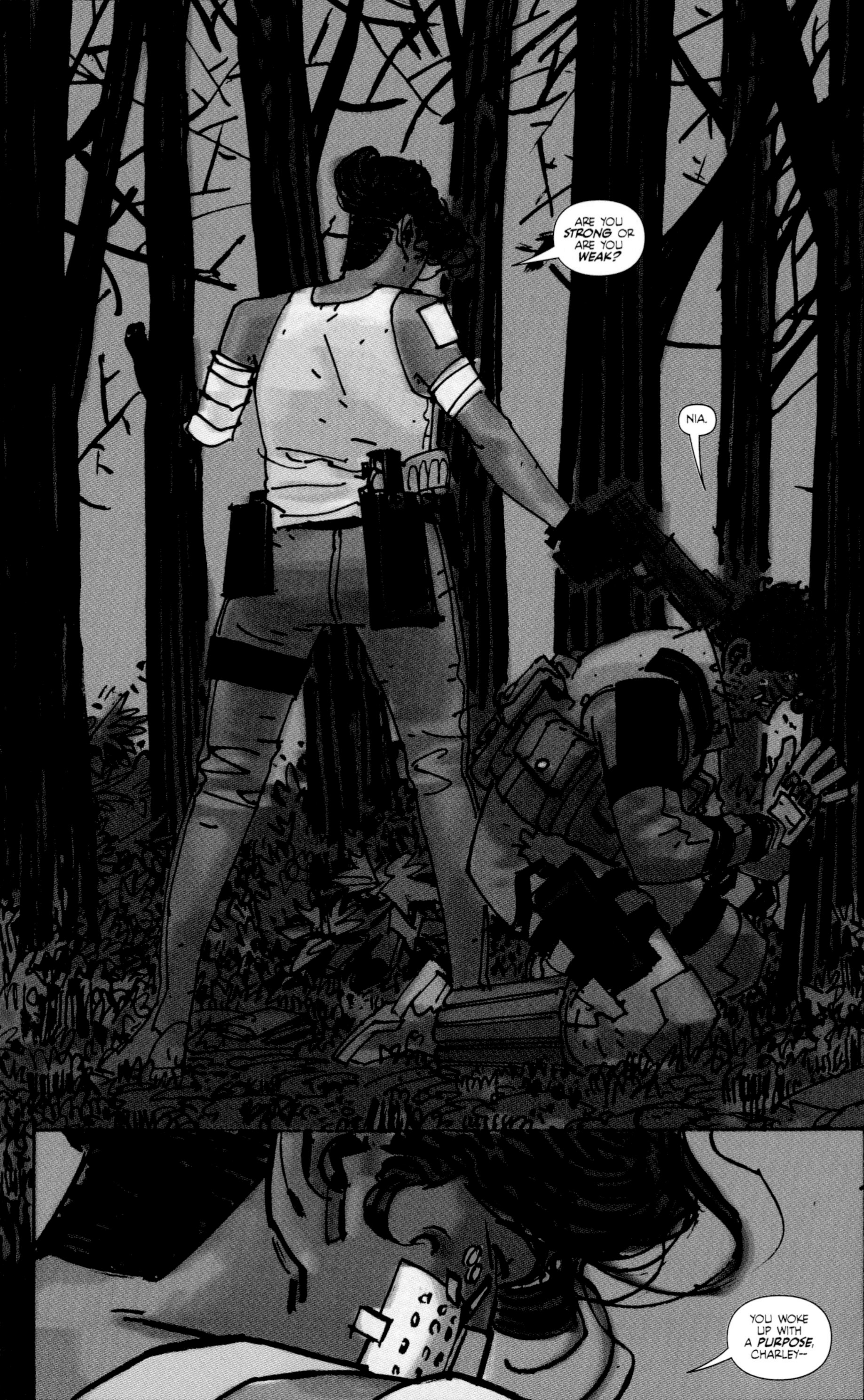

ARE YOU STRONG OR ARE YOU WEAK?
NIA.
YOU WOKE UP WITH A PURPOSE, CHARLEY--

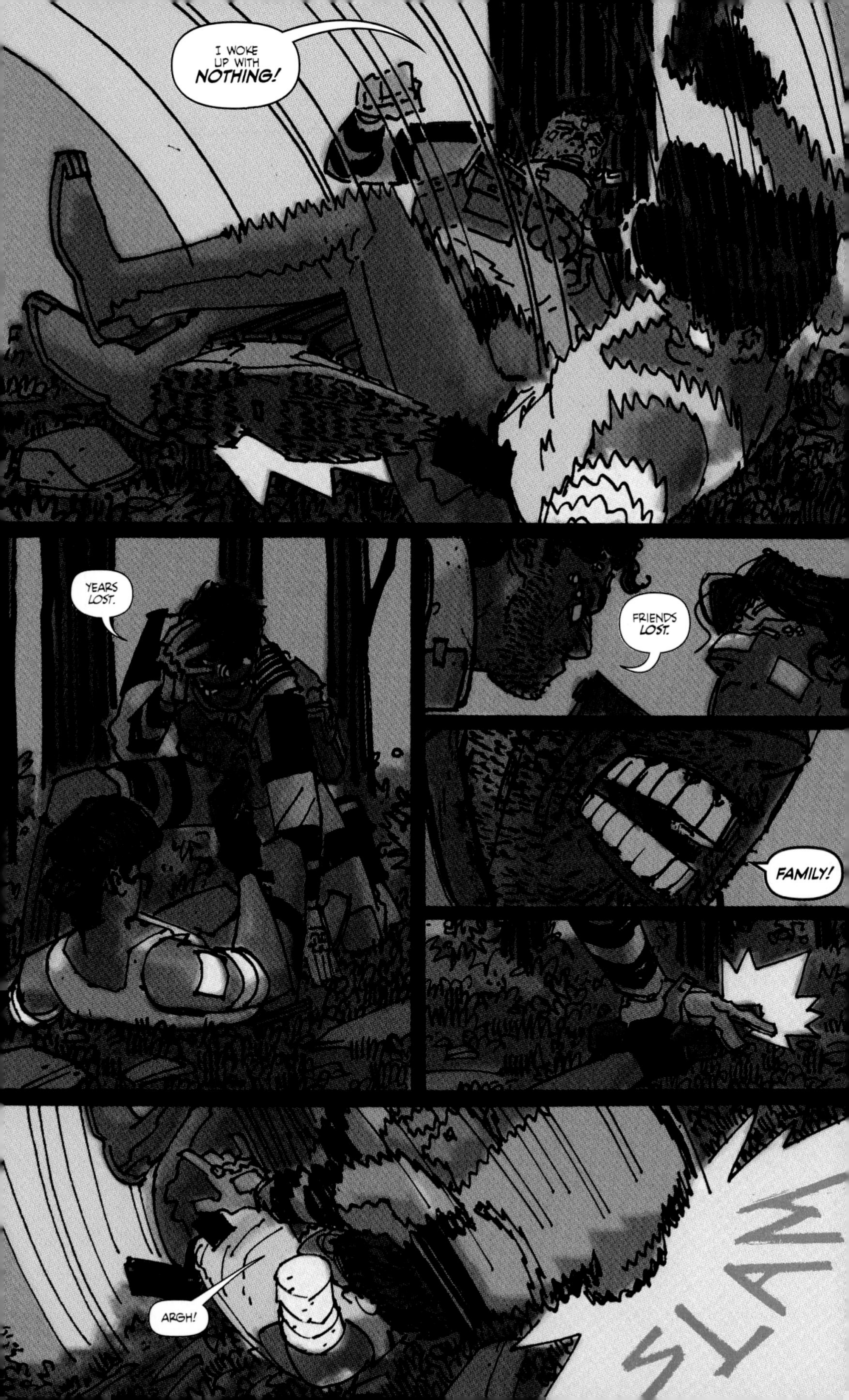
I WOKE UP WITH NOTHING!
YEARS LOST.
FRIENDS LOST.
FAMILY!
ARGH!
SLAM

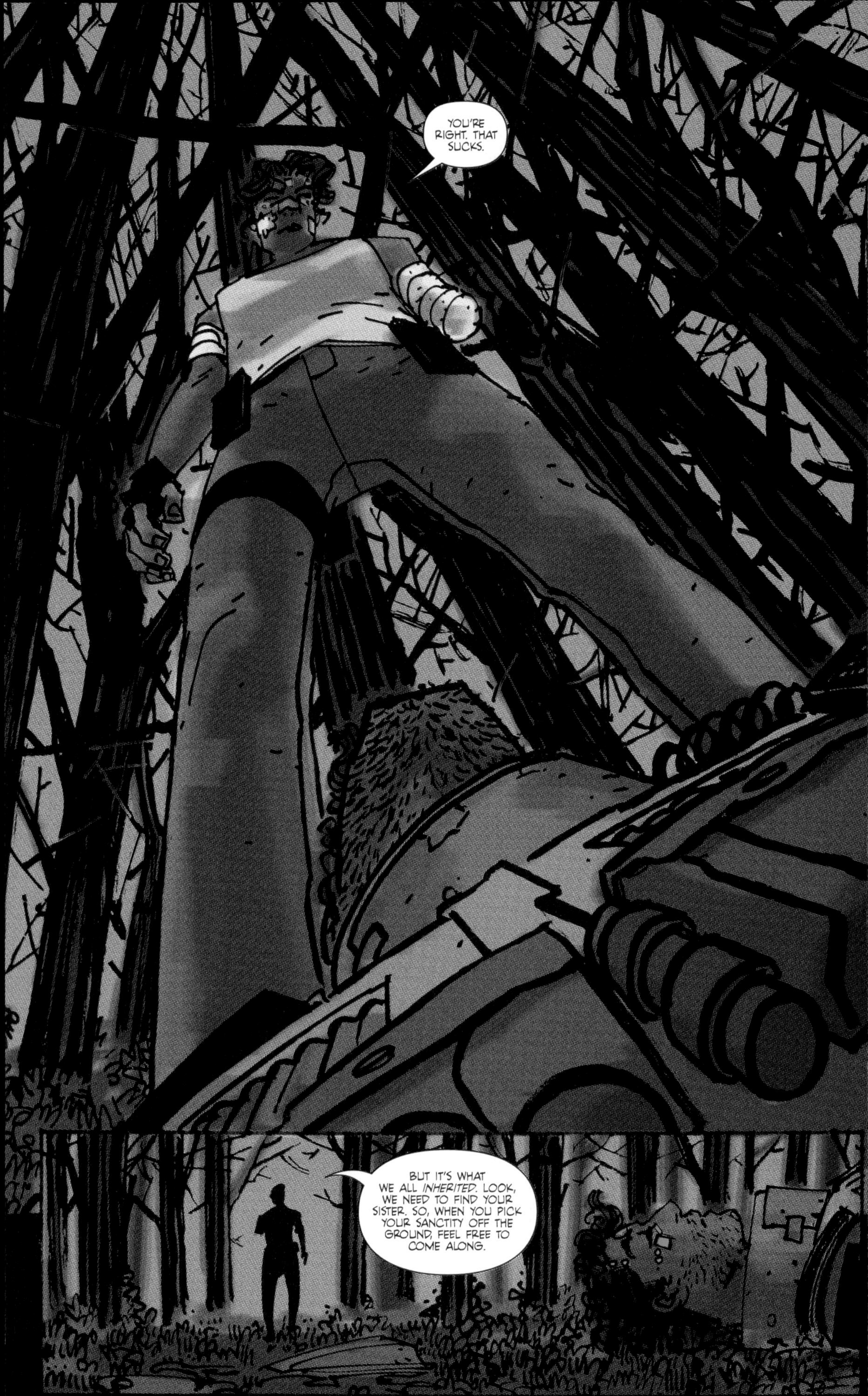
YOU'RE RIGHT. THAT SUCKS.
BUT IT'S WHAT WE ALL *INHERITED*. LOOK, WE NEED TO FIND YOUR SISTER. SO, WHEN YOU PICK YOUR SANCTITY OFF THE GROUND, FEEL FREE TO COME ALONG.

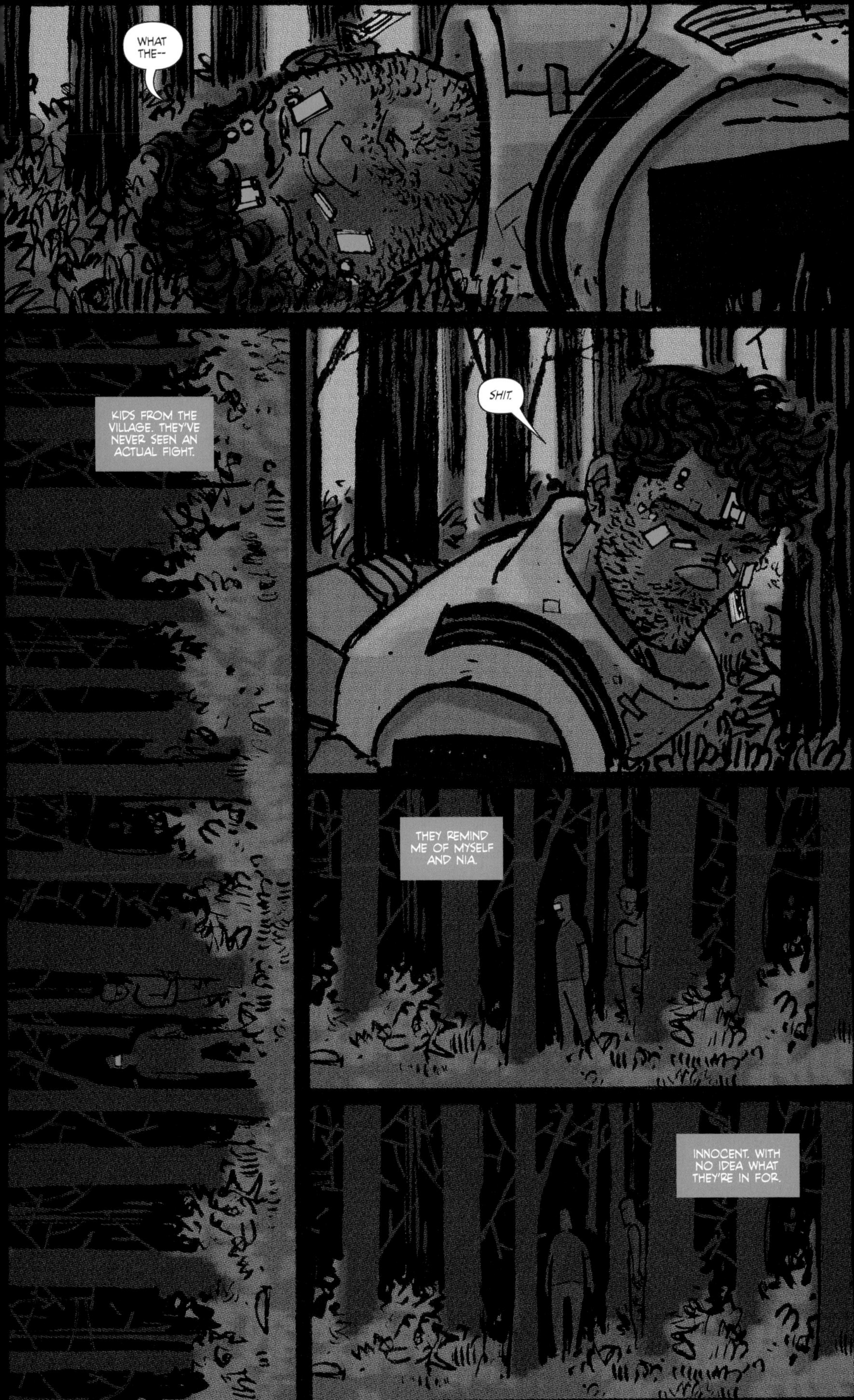
WHAT THE--
KIDS FROM THE VILLAGE. THEY'VE NEVER SEEN AN ACTUAL FIGHT.
SHIT.
THEY REMIND ME OF MYSELF AND NIA.
INNOCENT. WITH NO IDEA WHAT THEY'RE IN FOR.

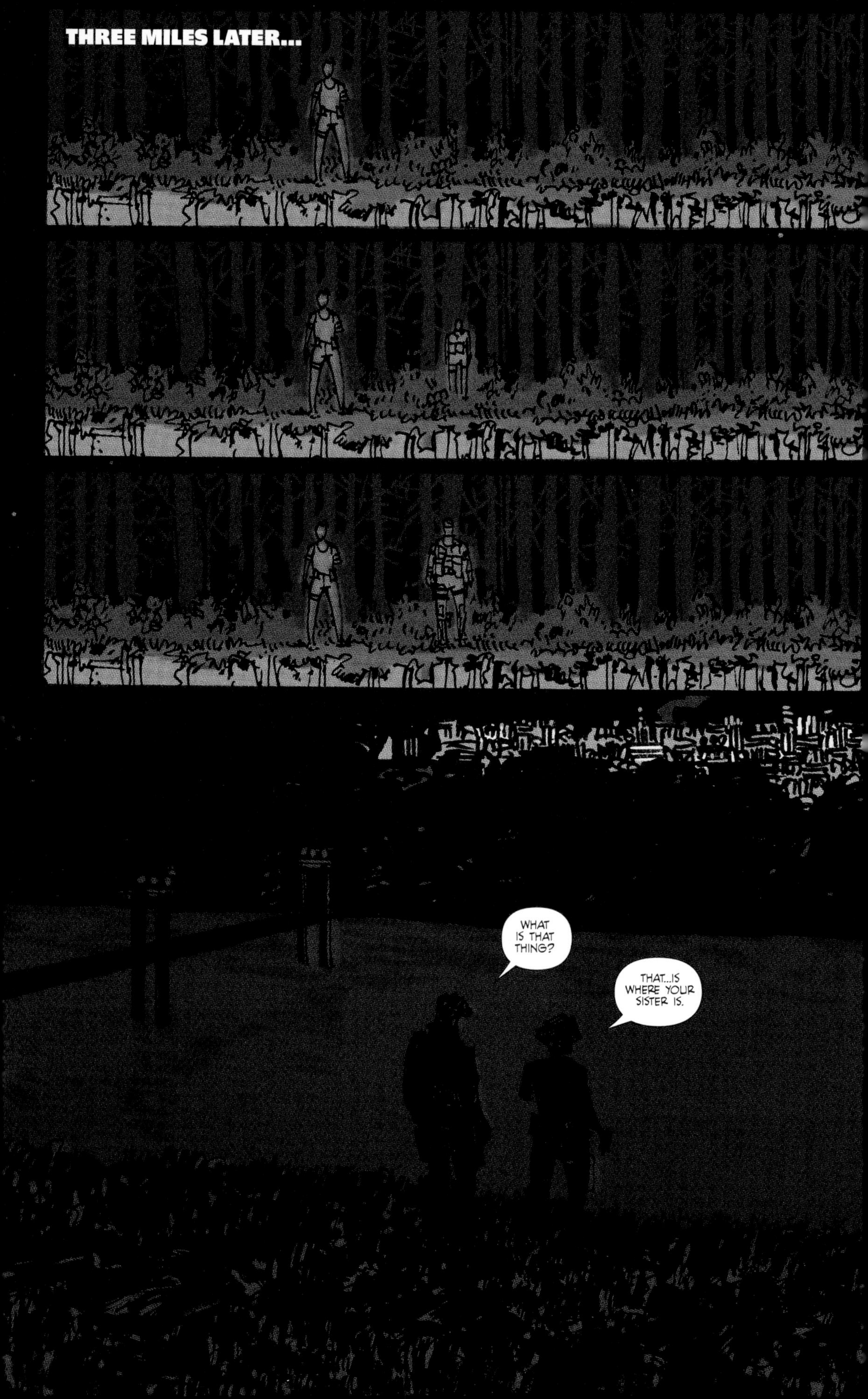
THREE MILES LATER...
WHAT IS THAT THING?
THAT...IS WHERE YOUR SISTER IS.

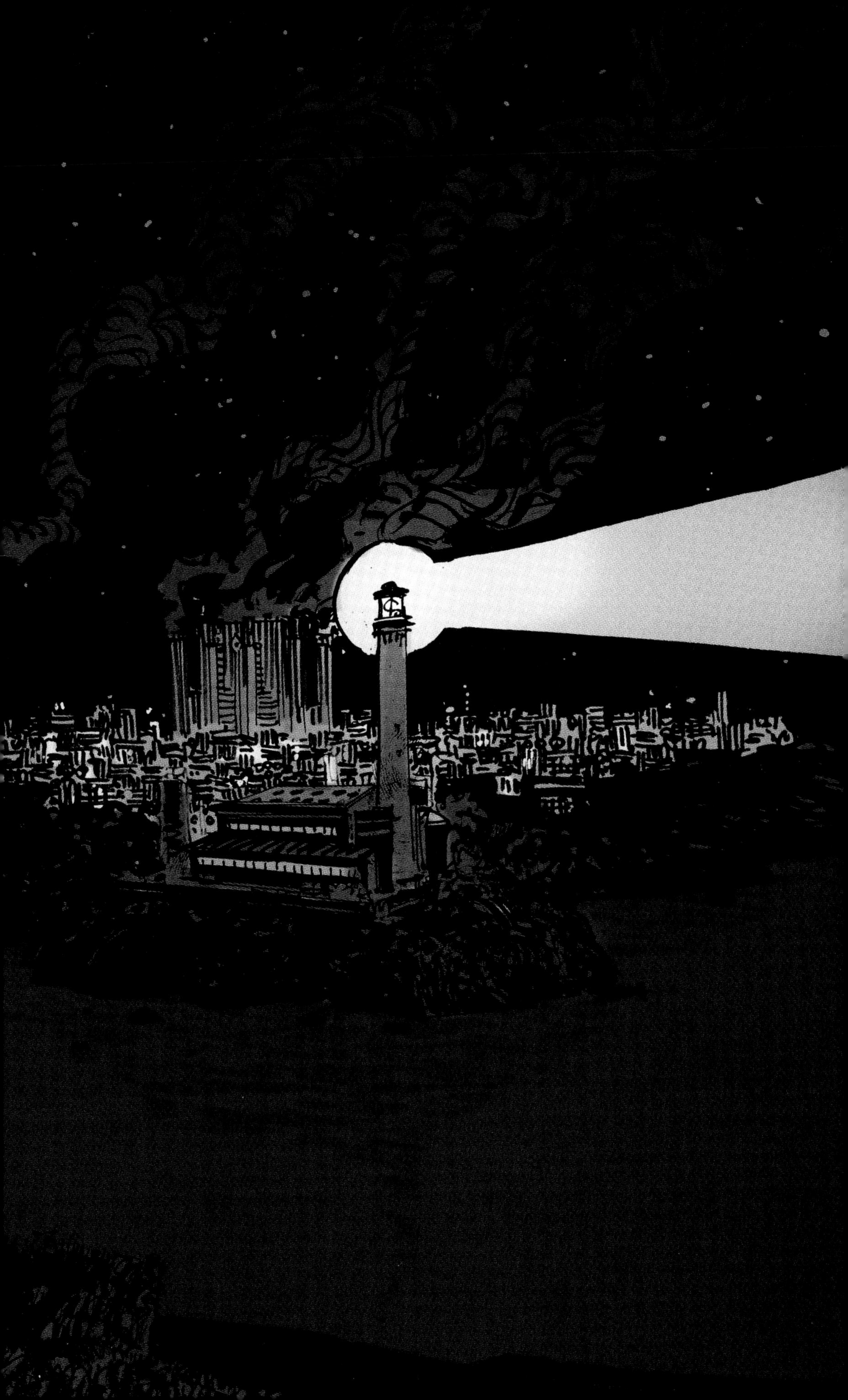

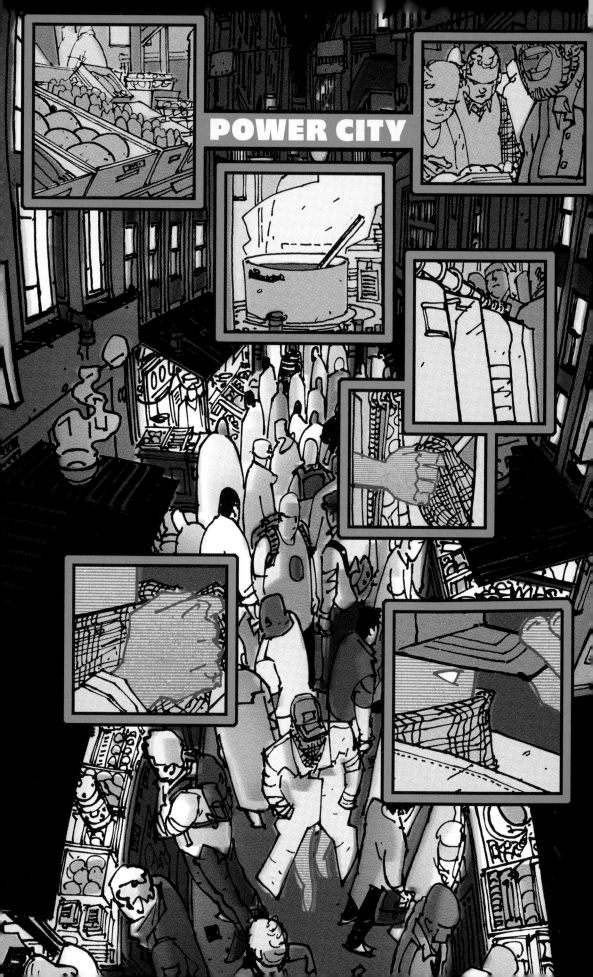

POWER CITY

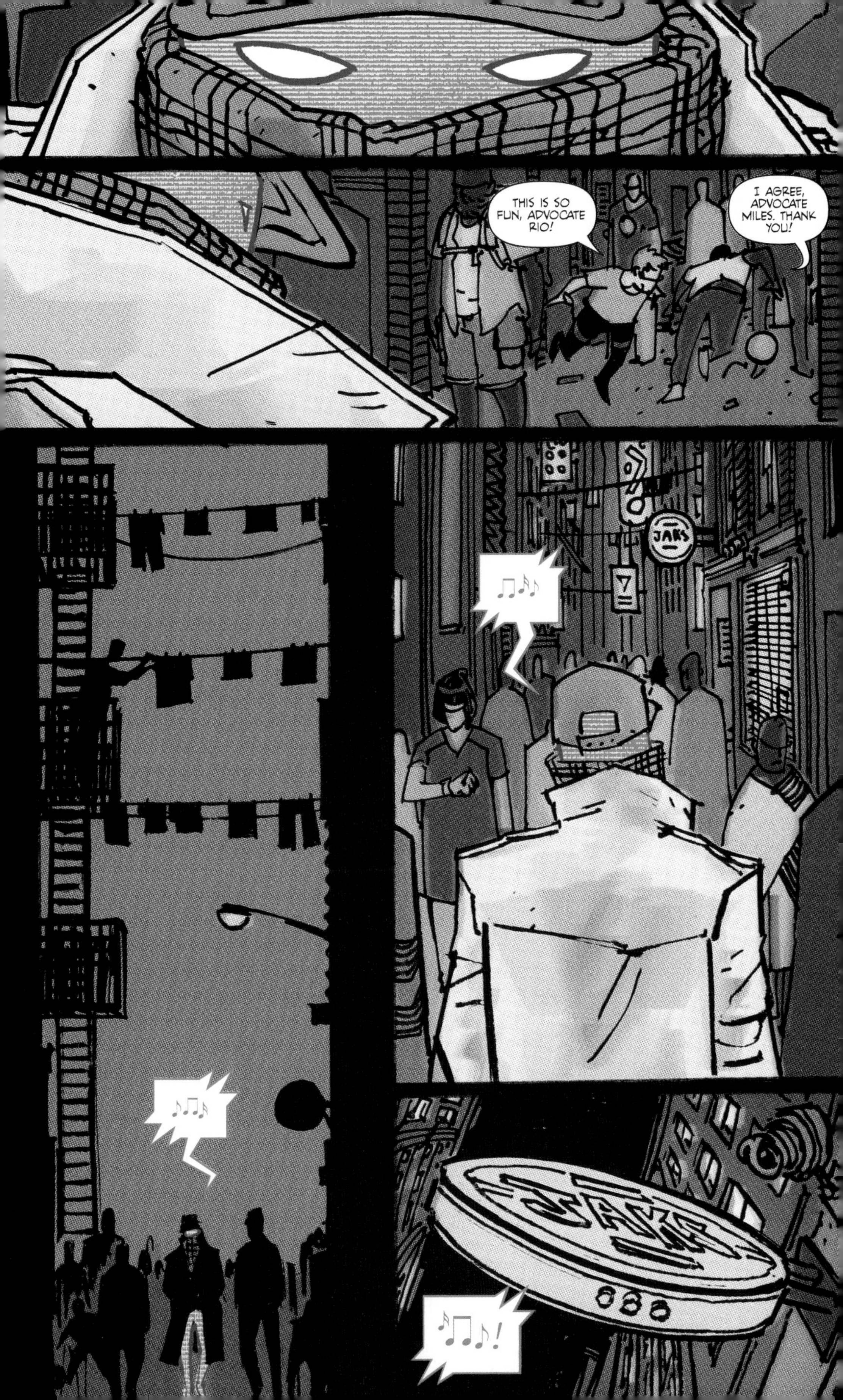
THIS IS SO FUN, ADVOCATE RIO!
I AGREE, ADVOCATE MILES. THANK YOU!
JAKS

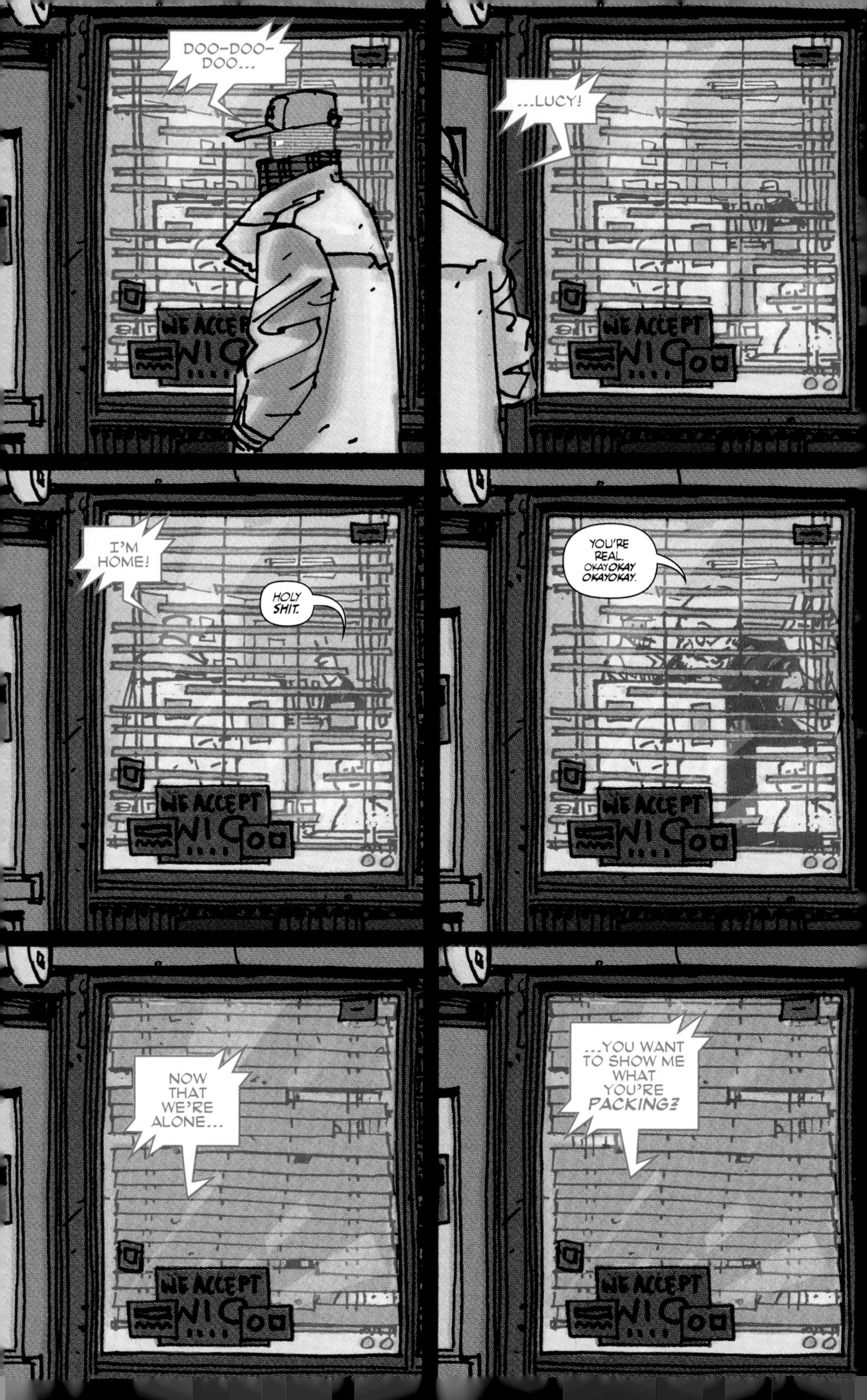
DOO-DOO-DOO...
...LUCY!
I'M HOME!
HOLY SHIT.
YOU'RE REAL. OKAYOKAY OKAYOKAY.
NOW THAT WE'RE ALONE...
...YOU WANT TO SHOW ME WHAT YOU'RE PACKING?

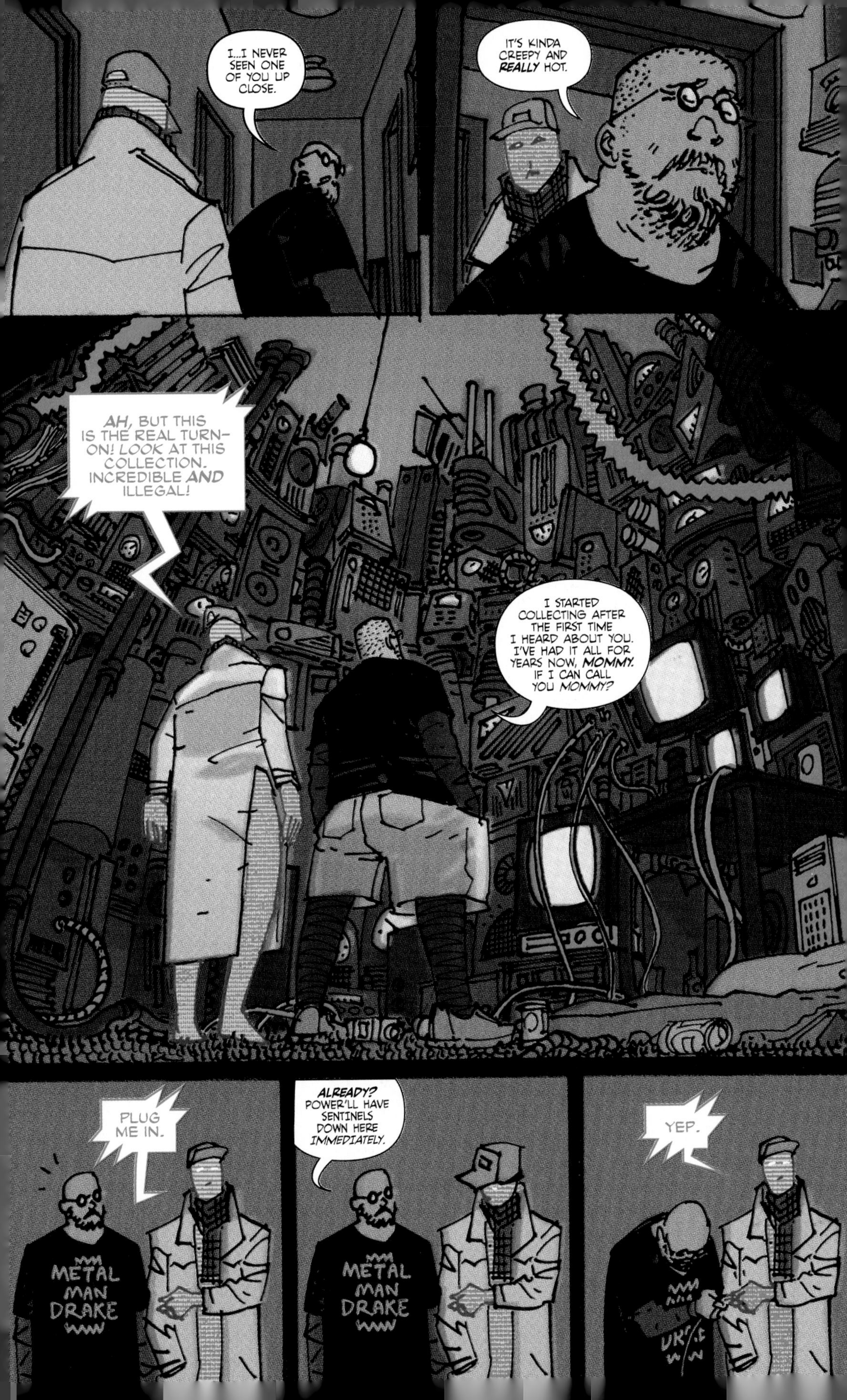
I...I NEVER SEEN ONE OF YOU UP CLOSE.
IT'S KINDA CREEPY AND REALLY HOT.
AH, BUT THIS IS THE REAL TURN-ON! LOOK AT THIS COLLECTION. INCREDIBLE AND ILLEGAL!
I STARTED COLLECTING AFTER THE FIRST TIME I HEARD ABOUT YOU. I'VE HAD IT ALL FOR YEARS NOW, MOMMY. IF I CAN CALL YOU MOMMY?
PLUG ME IN.
METAL MAN DRAKE
ALREADY? POWER'LL HAVE SENTINELS DOWN HERE IMMEDIATELY.
METAL MAN DRAKE
YEP.

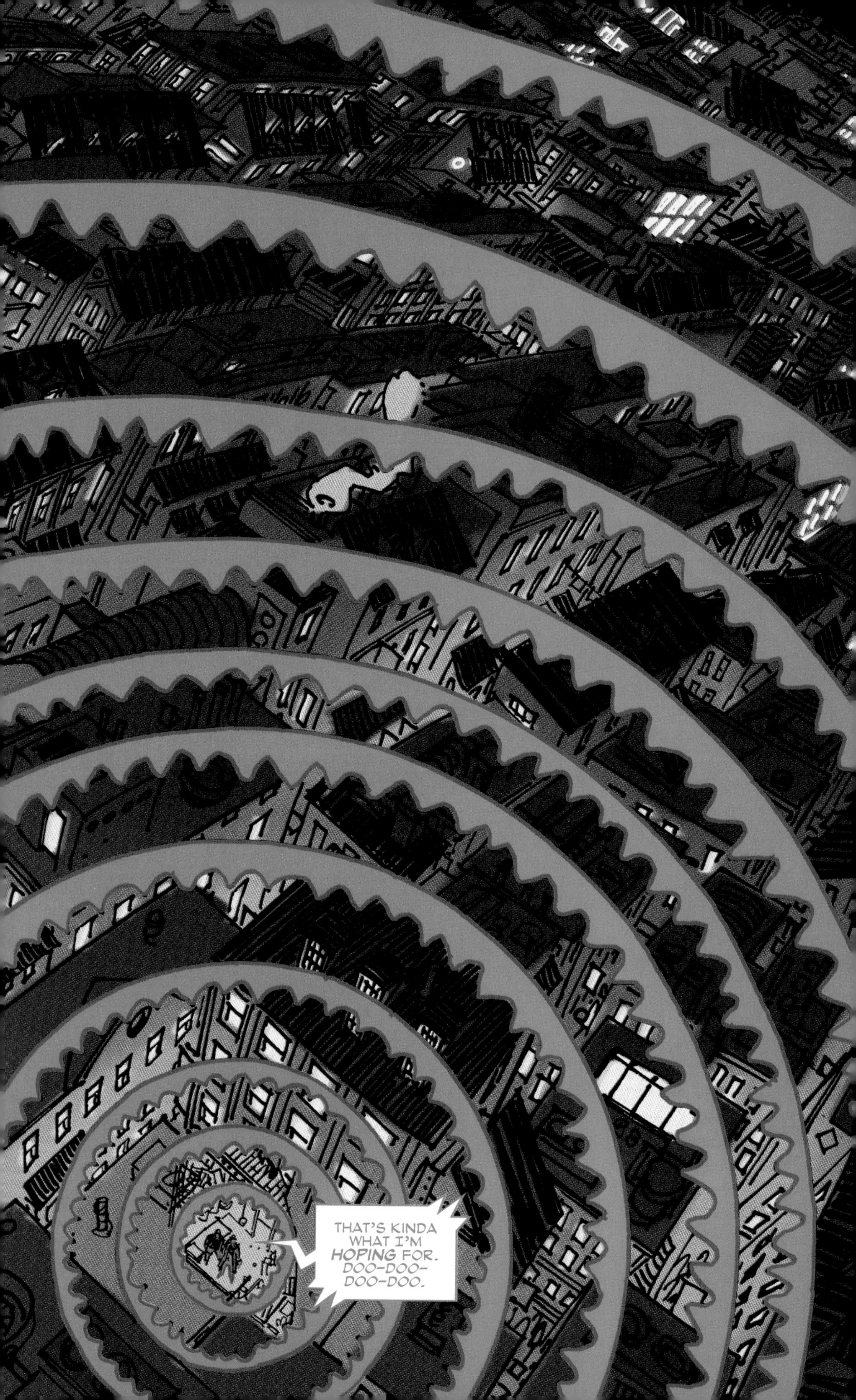
THAT'S KINDA WHAT I'M HOPING FOR. DOO-DOO-DOO-DOO.

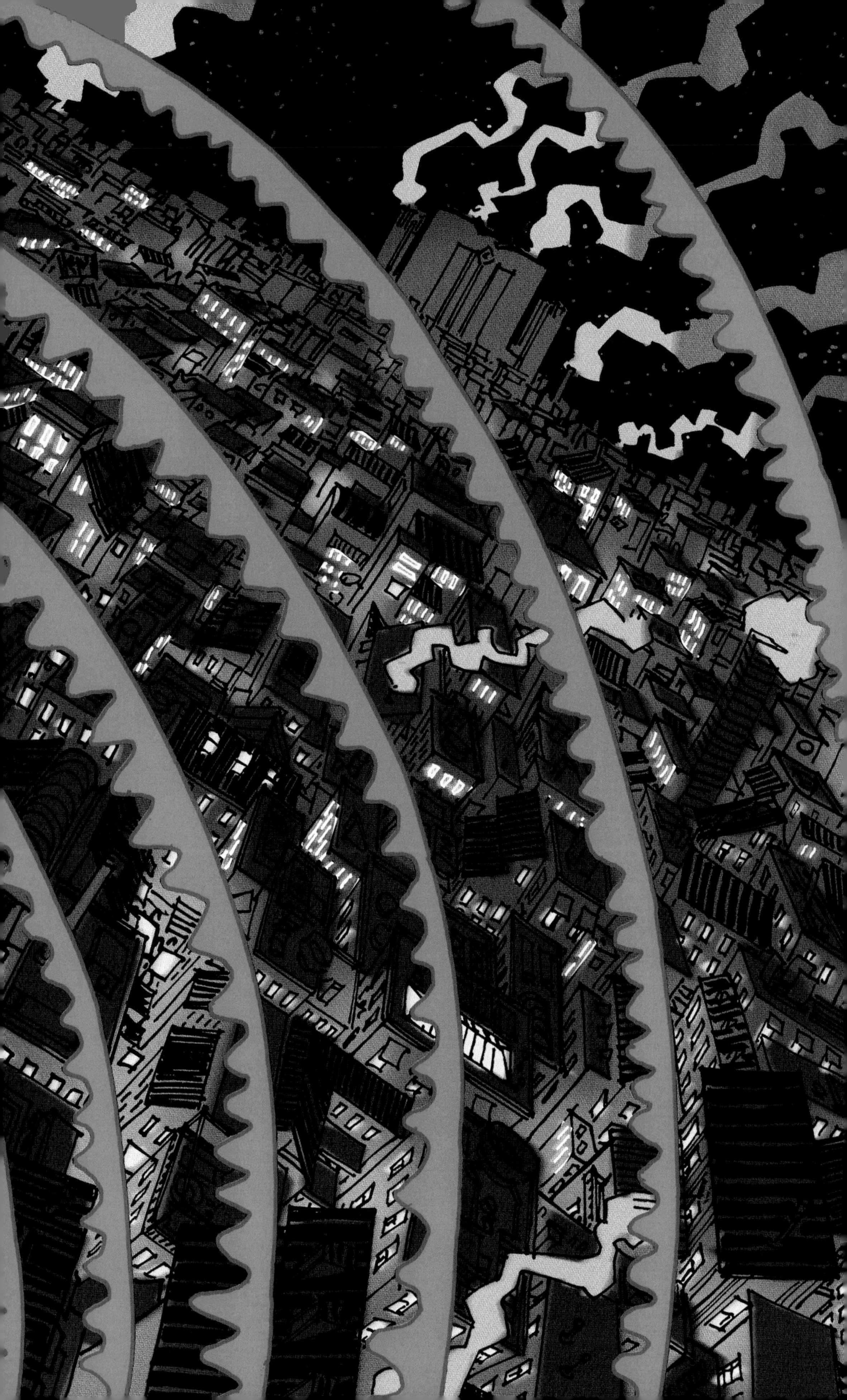

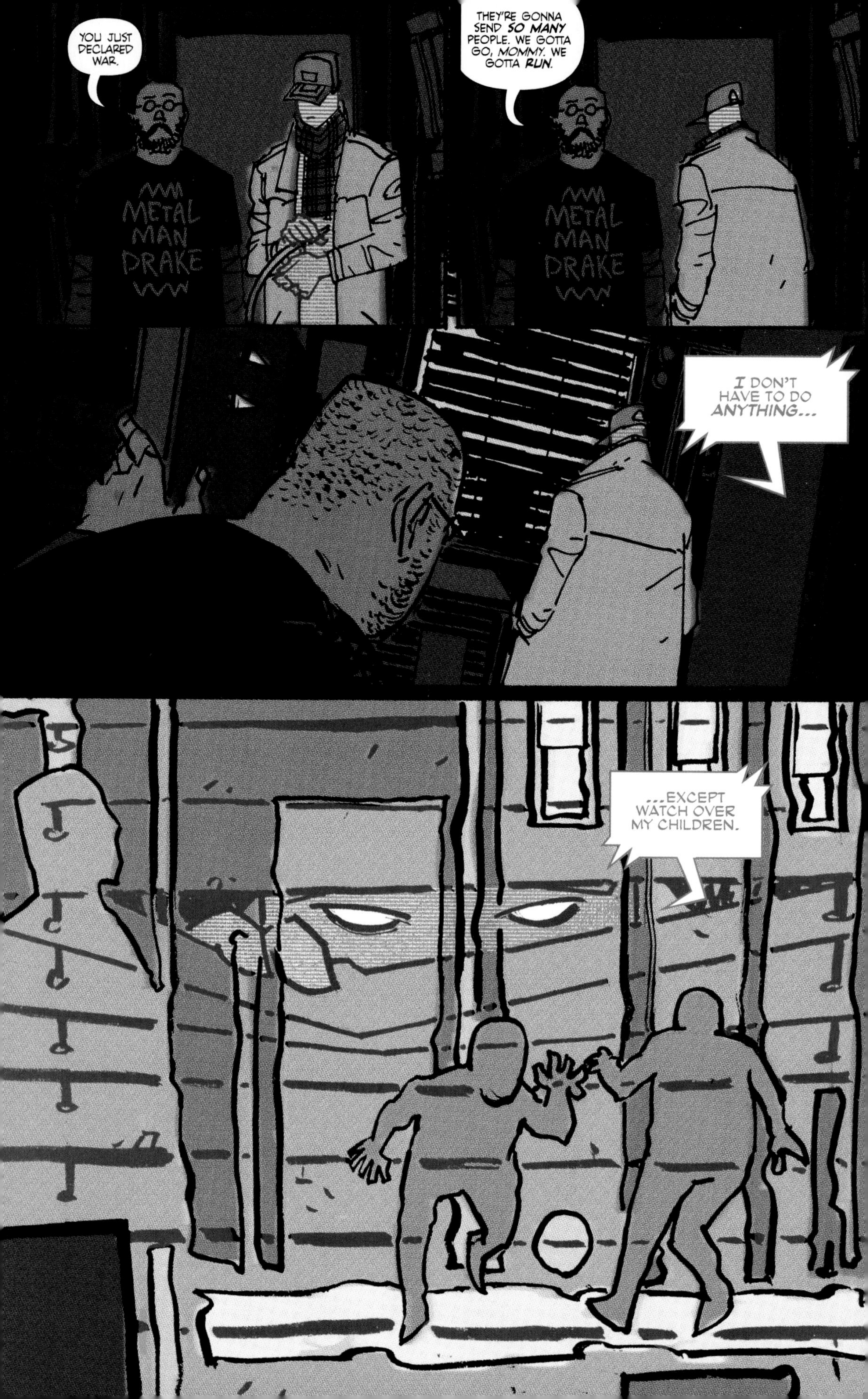
YOU JUST DECLARED WAR.
THEY'RE GONNA SEND SO MANY PEOPLE. WE GOTTA GO, MOMMY. WE GOTTA RUN.
METAL MAN DRAKE
METAL MAN DRAKE
I DON'T HAVE TO DO ANYTHING...
...EXCEPT WATCH OVER MY CHILDREN.

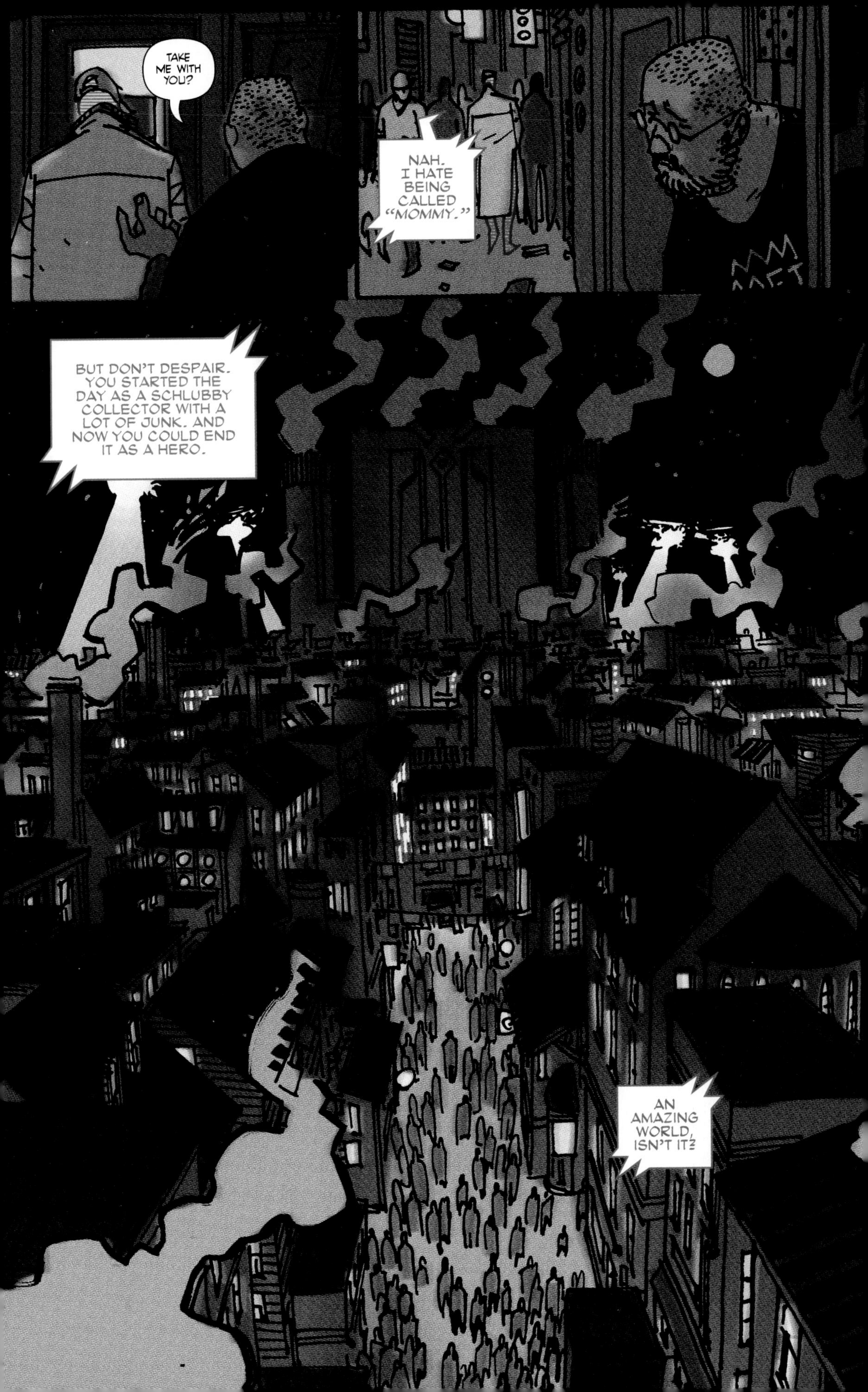
TAKE ME WITH YOU?
NAH. I HATE BEING CALLED "MOMMY."
BUT DON'T DESPAIR. YOU STARTED THE DAY AS A SCHLUBBY COLLECTOR WITH A LOT OF JUNK. AND NOW YOU COULD END IT AS A HERO.
AN AMAZING WORLD, ISN'T IT?

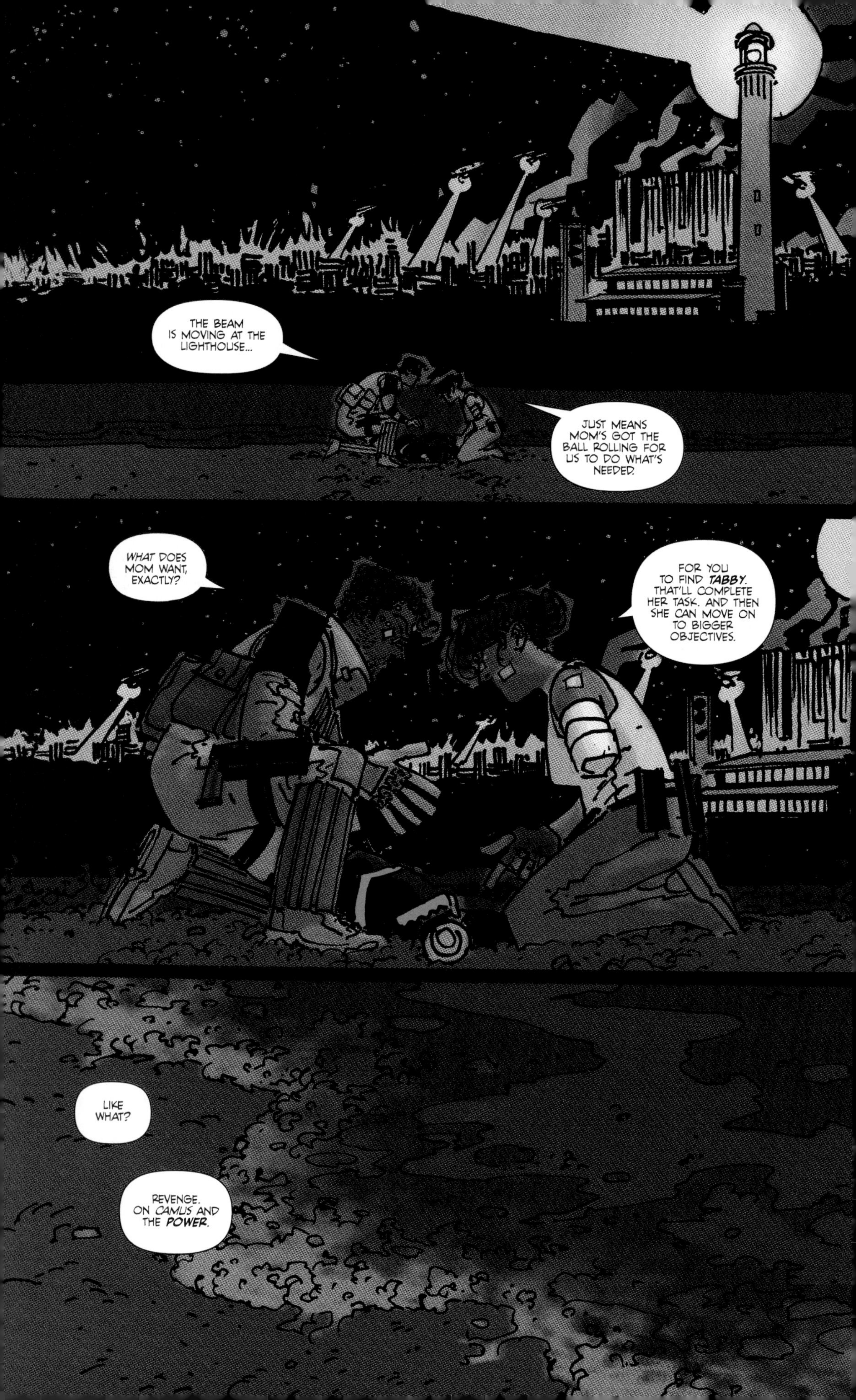

THE BEAM IS MOVING AT THE LIGHTHOUSE...
JUST MEANS MOM'S GOT THE BALL ROLLING FOR US TO DO WHAT'S NEEDED.
WHAT DOES MOM WANT, EXACTLY?
FOR YOU TO FIND ***TABBY***. THAT'LL COMPLETE HER TASK. AND THEN SHE CAN MOVE ON TO BIGGER OBJECTIVES.
LIKE WHAT?
REVENGE. ON *CAMUS* AND THE ***POWER***.

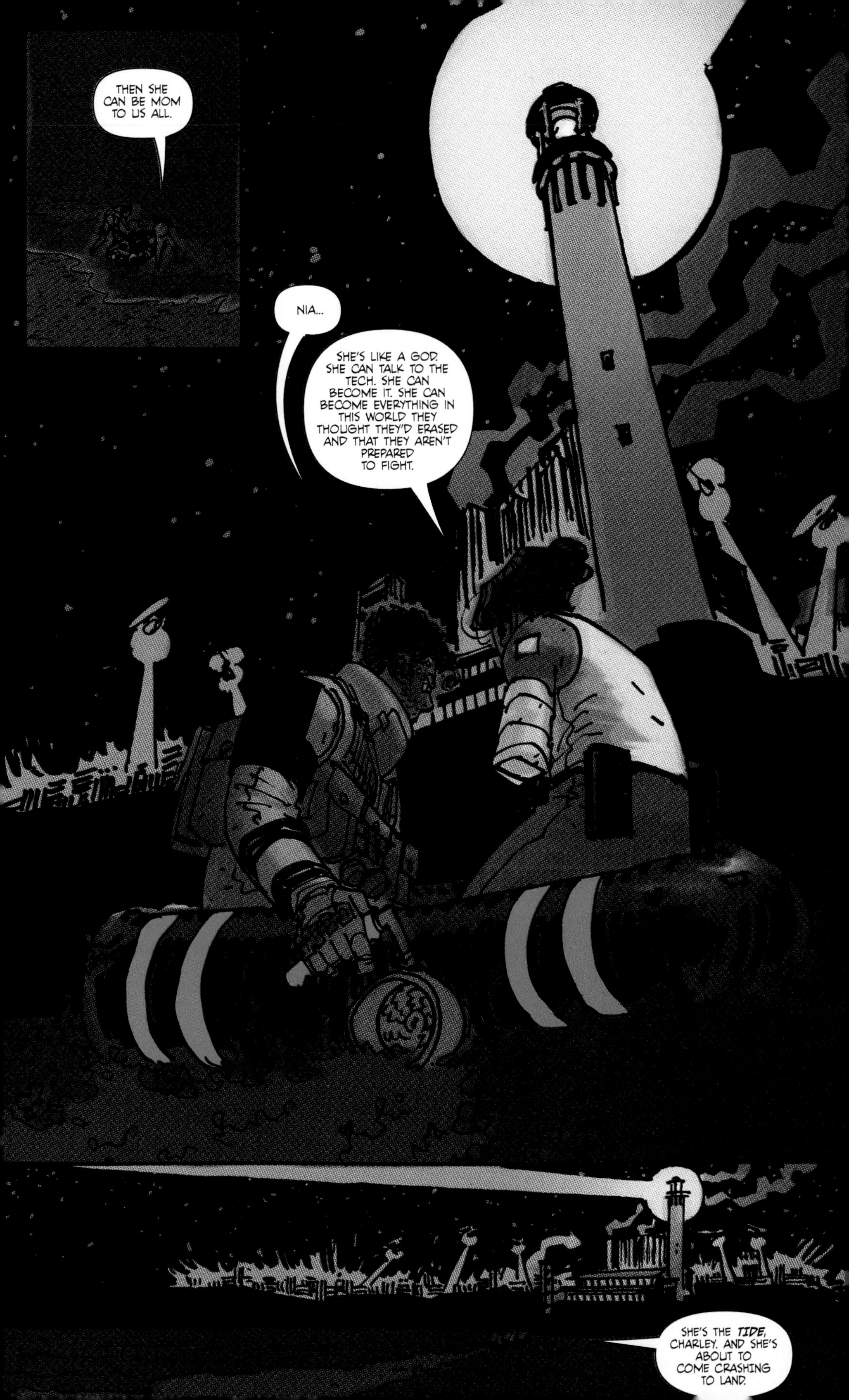
THEN SHE CAN BE MOM TO US ALL.
NIA...
SHE'S LIKE A GOD. SHE CAN TALK TO THE TECH. SHE CAN BECOME IT. SHE CAN BECOME EVERYTHING IN THIS WORLD THEY THOUGHT THEY'D ERASED AND THAT THEY AREN'T PREPARED TO FIGHT.
SHE'S THE *TIDE*, CHARLEY. AND SHE'S ABOUT TO COME CRASHING TO LAND.

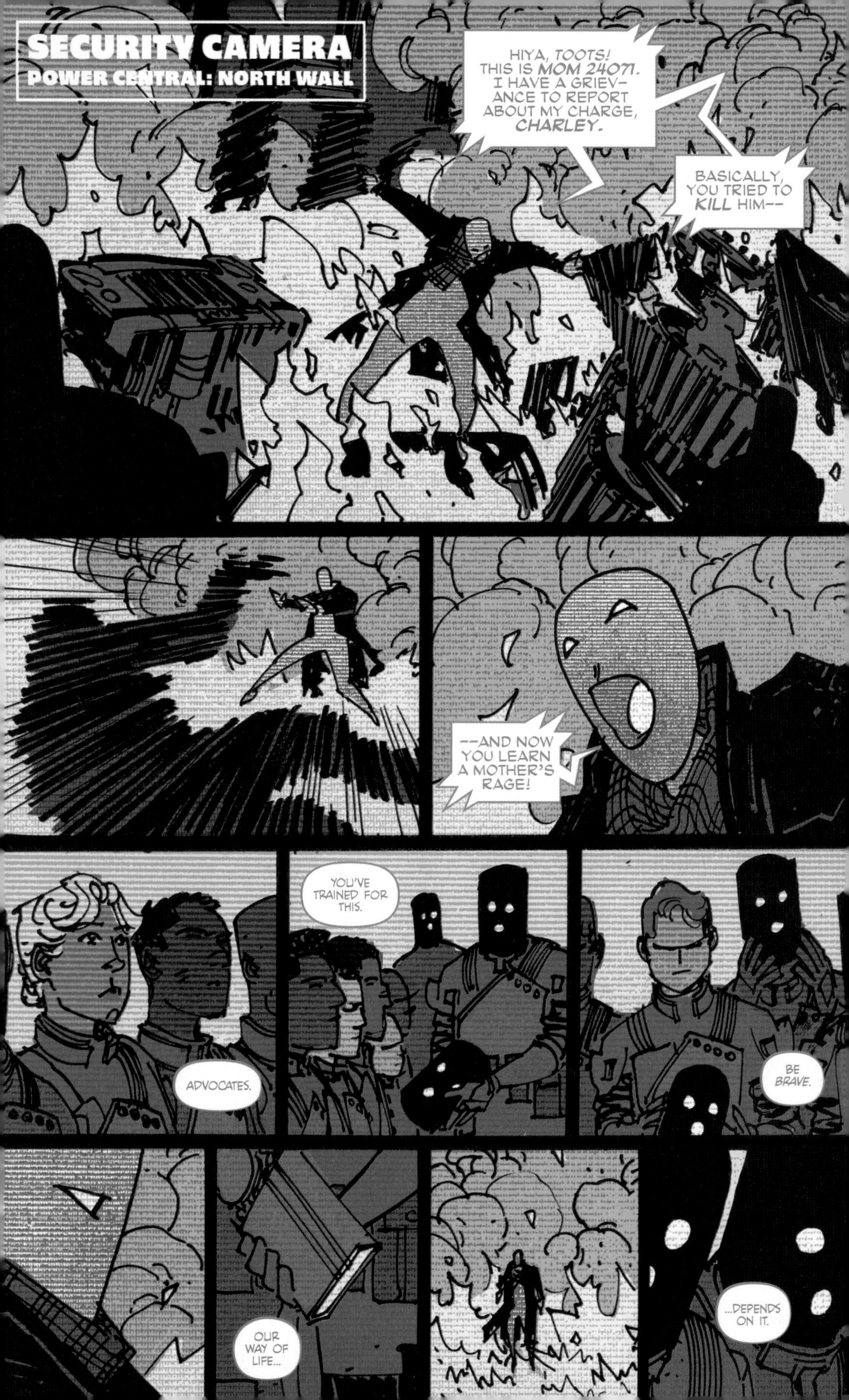
SECURITY CAMERA
POWER CENTRAL: NORTH WALL
HIYA, TOOTS! THIS IS MOM 24071. I HAVE A GRIEV-ANCE TO REPORT ABOUT MY CHARGE, CHARLEY.
BASICALLY, YOU TRIED TO KILL HIM--
--AND NOW YOU LEARN A MOTHER'S RAGE!
ADVOCATES.
YOU'VE TRAINED FOR THIS.
BE BRAVE.
OUR WAY OF LIFE...
...DEPENDS ON IT.

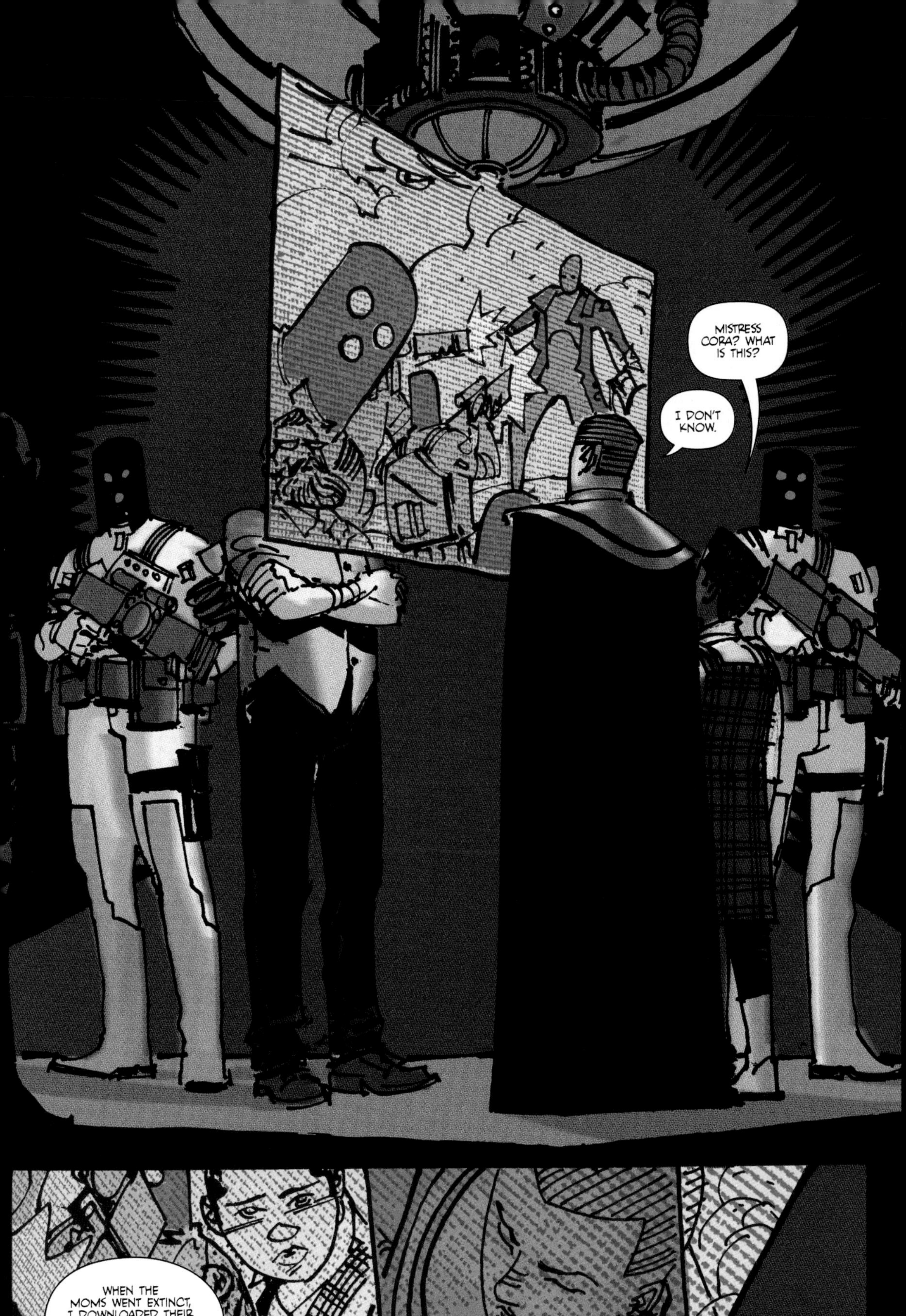
MISTRESS CORA? WHAT IS THIS?
I DON'T KNOW.
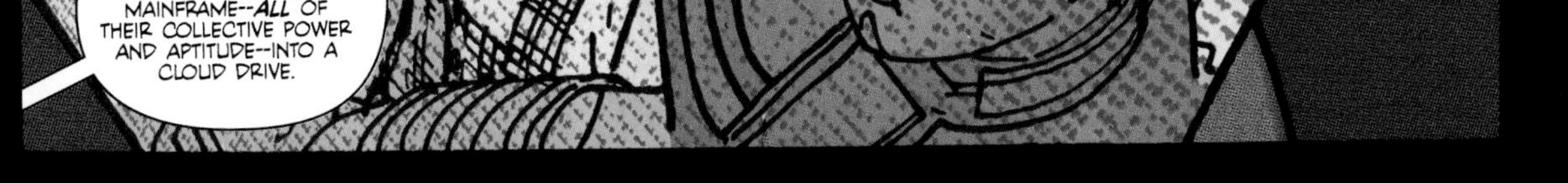
WHEN THE MOMS WENT EXTINCT, I DOWNLOADED THEIR MAINFRAME--ALL OF THEIR COLLECTIVE POWER AND APTITUDE--INTO A CLOUD DRIVE.

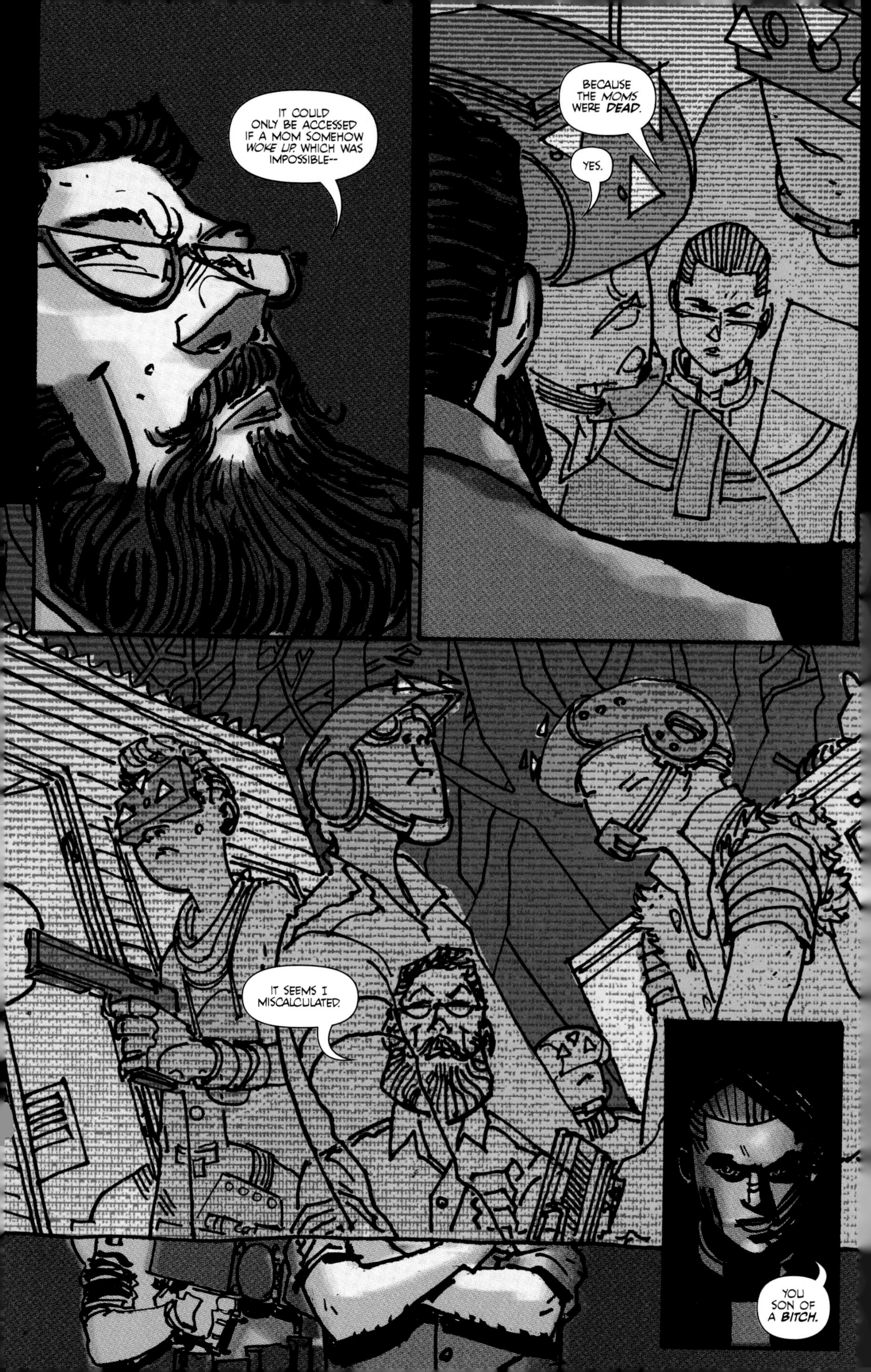
IT COULD ONLY BE ACCESSED IF A MOM SOMEHOW *WOKE UP*, WHICH WAS IMPOSSIBLE--
BECAUSE THE *MOMS* WERE ***DEAD***.
YES.
IT SEEMS I MISCALCULATED.
YOU SON OF A ***BITCH***.

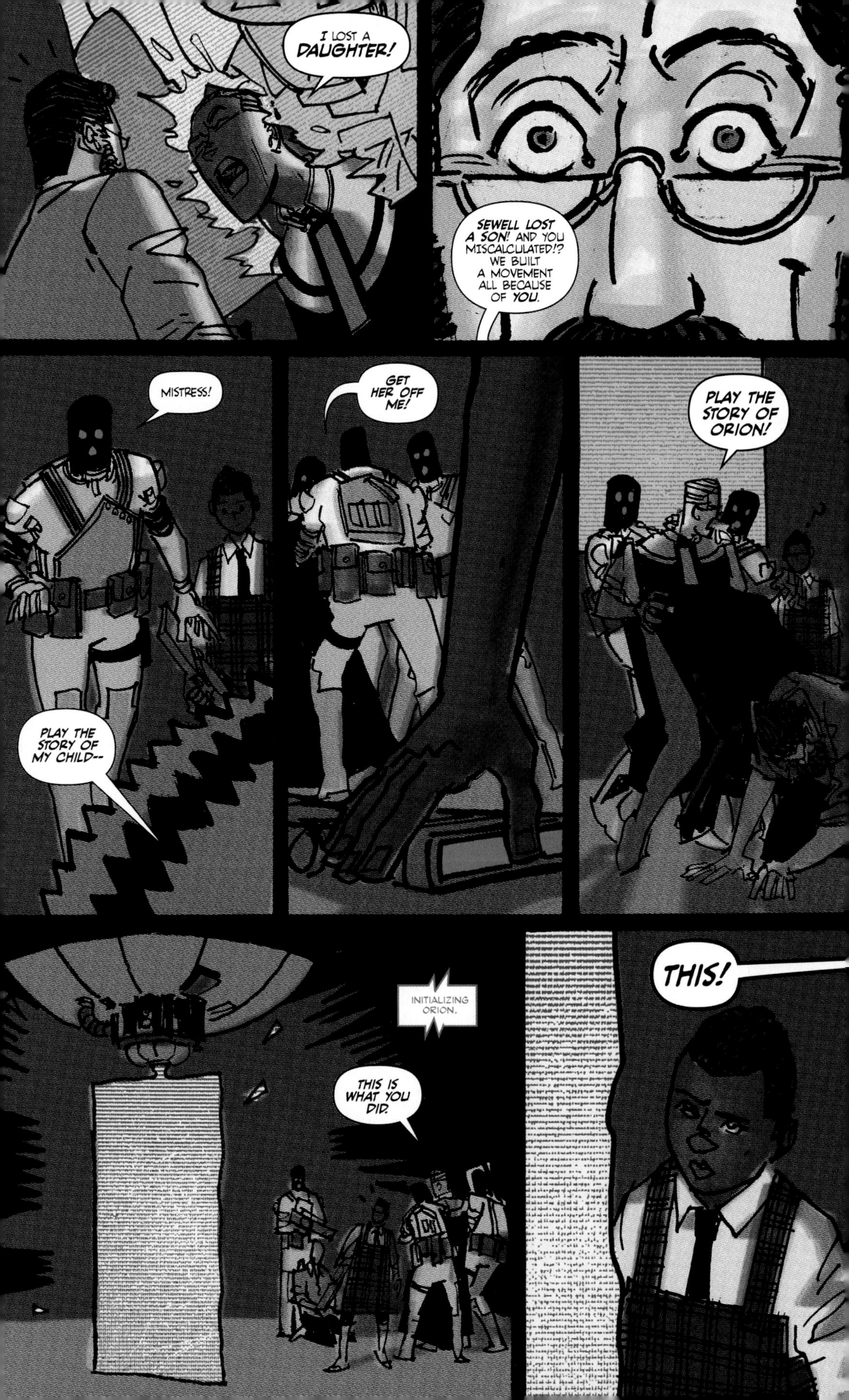
I LOST A DAUGHTER!
SEWELL LOST A SON! AND YOU MISCALCULATED!? WE BUILT A MOVEMENT ALL BECAUSE OF YOU.
MISTRESS!
PLAY THE STORY OF MY CHILD--
GET HER OFF ME!
PLAY THE STORY OF ORION!
INITIALIZING ORION.
THIS IS WHAT YOU DID.
THIS!

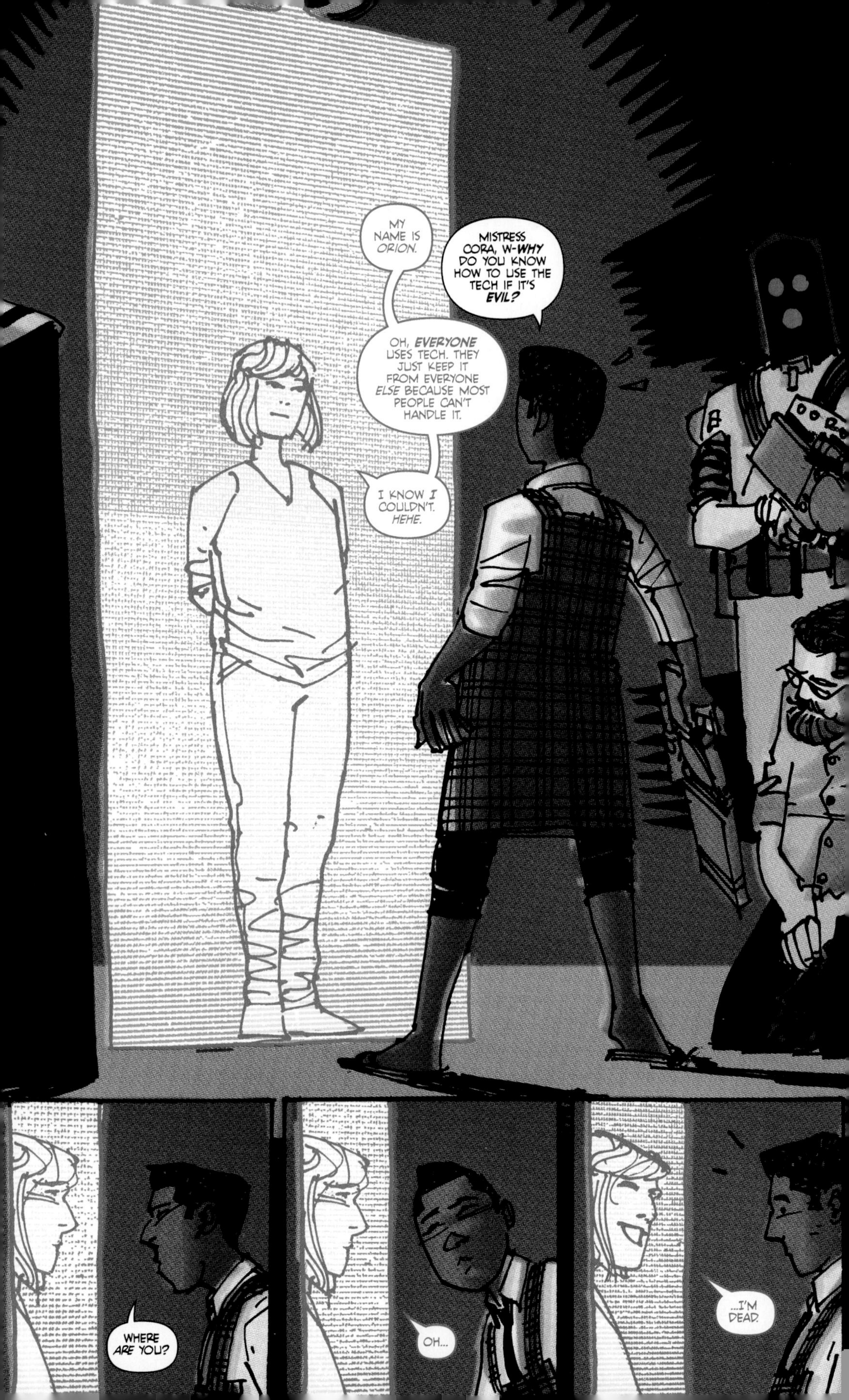
MY NAME IS ORION.
MISTRESS CORA, W-WHY DO YOU KNOW HOW TO USE THE TECH IF IT'S EVIL?
OH, EVERYONE USES TECH. THEY JUST KEEP IT FROM EVERYONE ELSE BECAUSE MOST PEOPLE CAN'T HANDLE IT.
I KNOW I COULDN'T. HEHE.
WHERE ARE YOU?
OH...
...I'M DEAD.

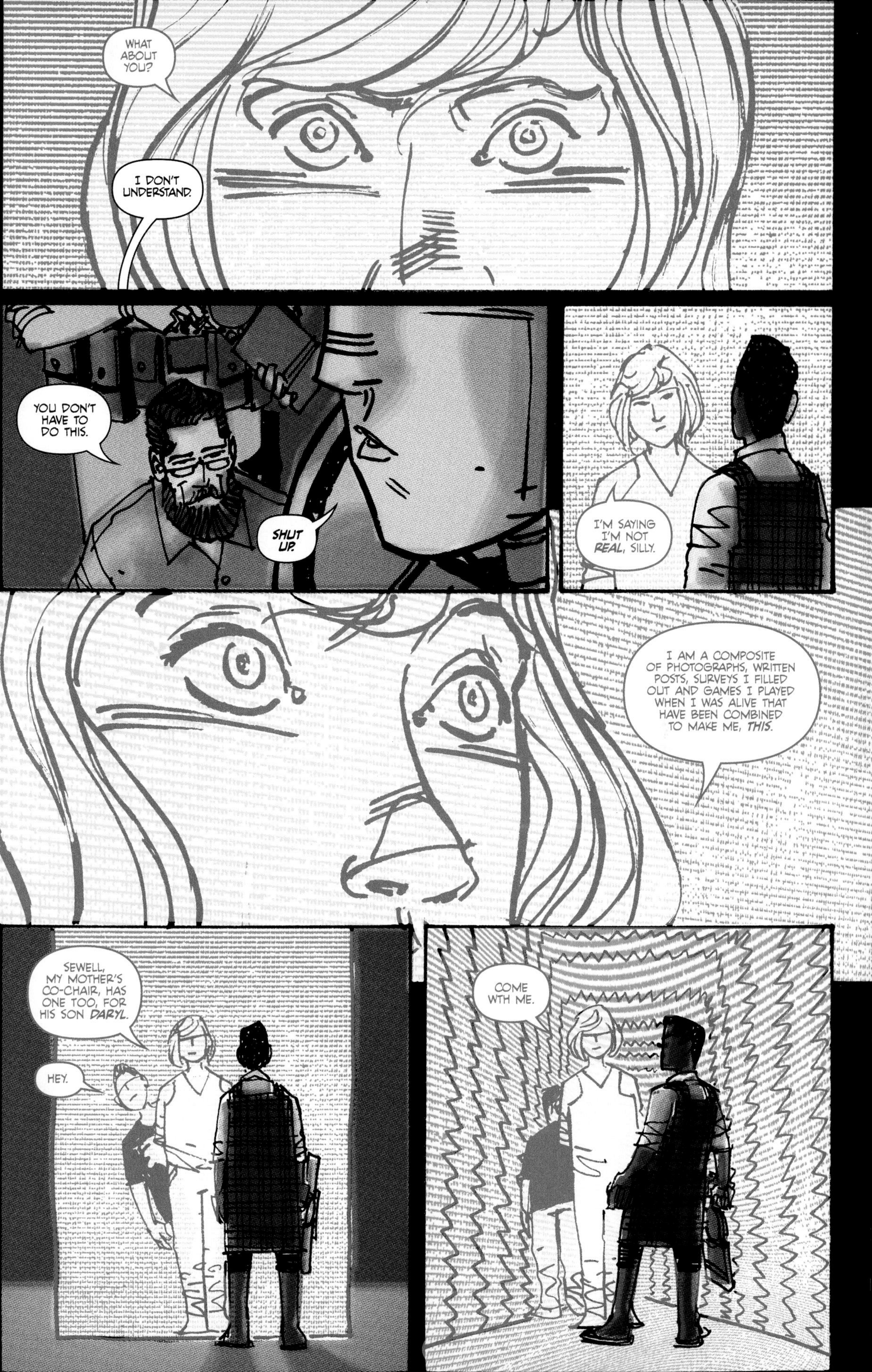
WHAT ABOUT YOU?
I DON'T UNDERSTAND.
YOU DON'T HAVE TO DO THIS.
SHUT UP.
I'M SAYING I'M NOT REAL, SILLY.
I AM A COMPOSITE OF PHOTOGRAPHS, WRITTEN POSTS, SURVEYS I FILLED OUT AND GAMES I PLAYED WHEN I WAS ALIVE THAT HAVE BEEN COMBINED TO MAKE ME, THIS.
SEWELL, MY MOTHER'S CO-CHAIR, HAS ONE TOO, FOR HIS SON DARYL.
HEY.
COME WITH ME.

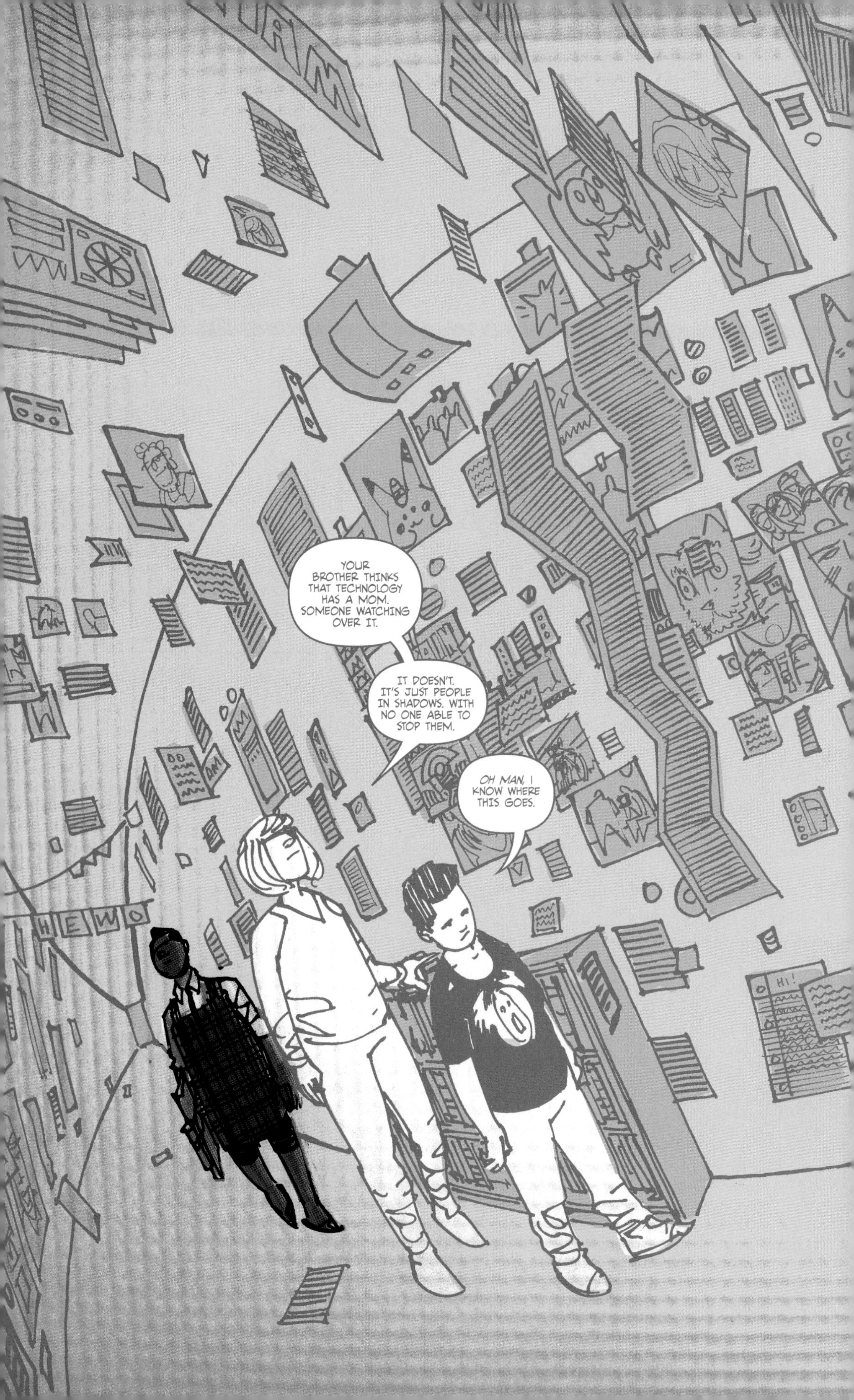
YOUR BROTHER THINKS THAT TECHNOLOGY HAS A MOM. SOMEONE WATCHING OVER IT.
IT DOESN'T. IT'S JUST PEOPLE IN SHADOWS. WITH NO ONE ABLE TO STOP THEM.
OH MAN, I KNOW WHERE THIS GOES.
HEWO
HI!

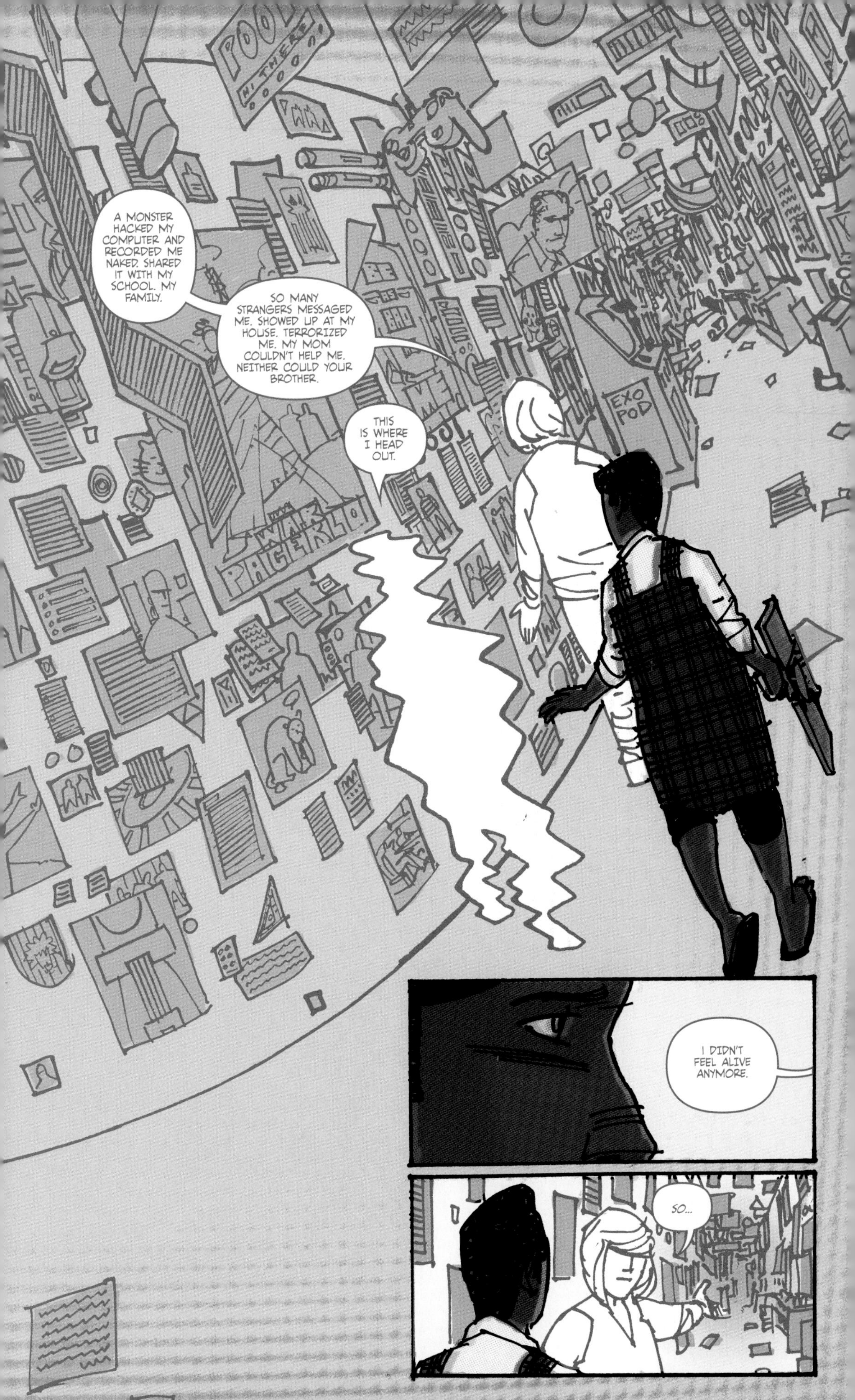
A MONSTER HACKED MY COMPUTER AND RECORDED ME NAKED. SHARED IT WITH MY SCHOOL. MY FAMILY.
SO MANY STRANGERS MESSAGED ME. SHOWED UP AT MY HOUSE. TERRORIZED ME. MY MOM COULDN'T HELP ME. NEITHER COULD YOUR BROTHER.
THIS IS WHERE I HEAD OUT.
I DIDN'T FEEL ALIVE ANYMORE.
SO...

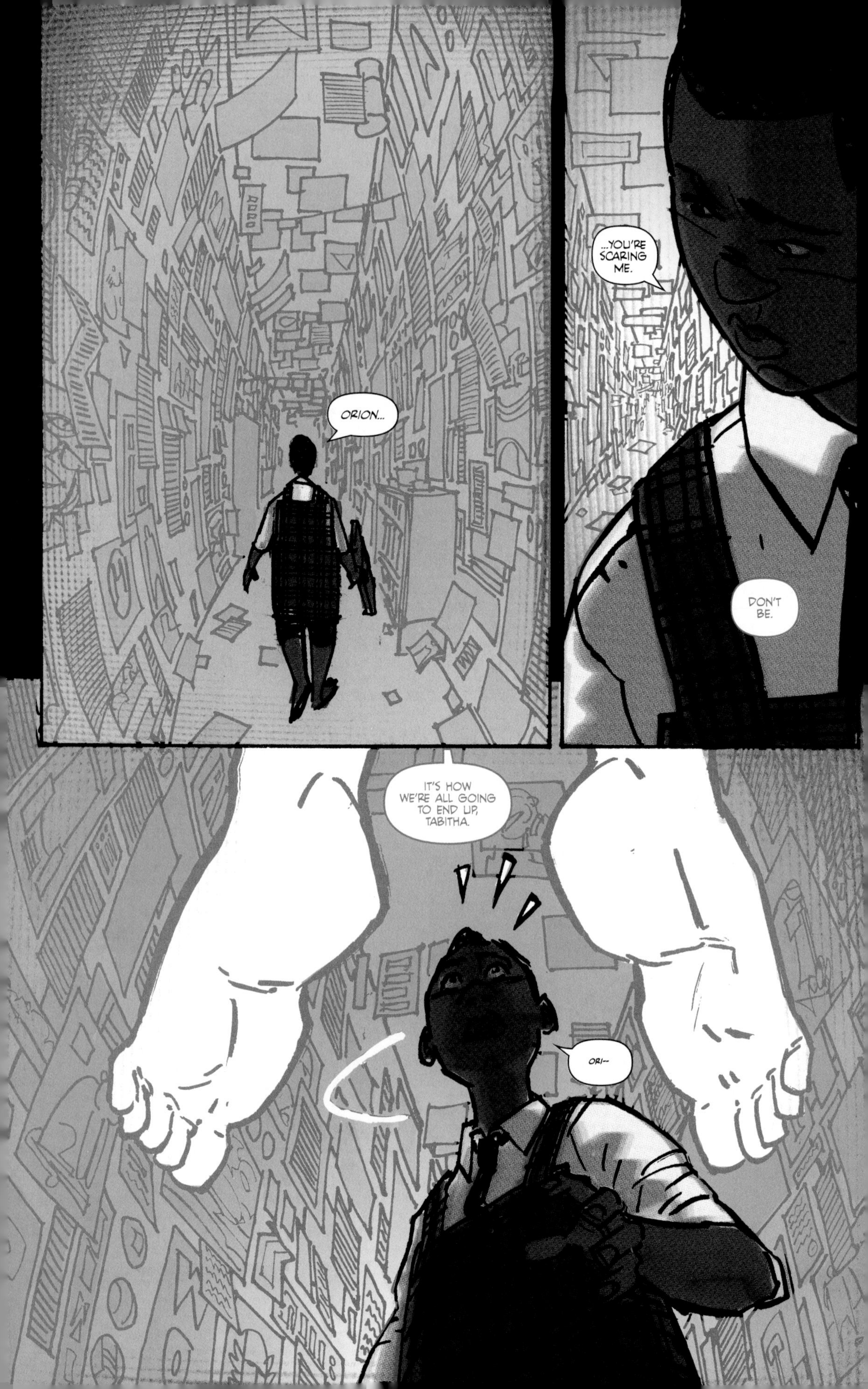
ORION...
...YOU'RE SCARING ME.
DON'T BE.
IT'S HOW WE'RE ALL GOING TO END UP, TABITHA.
ORI--

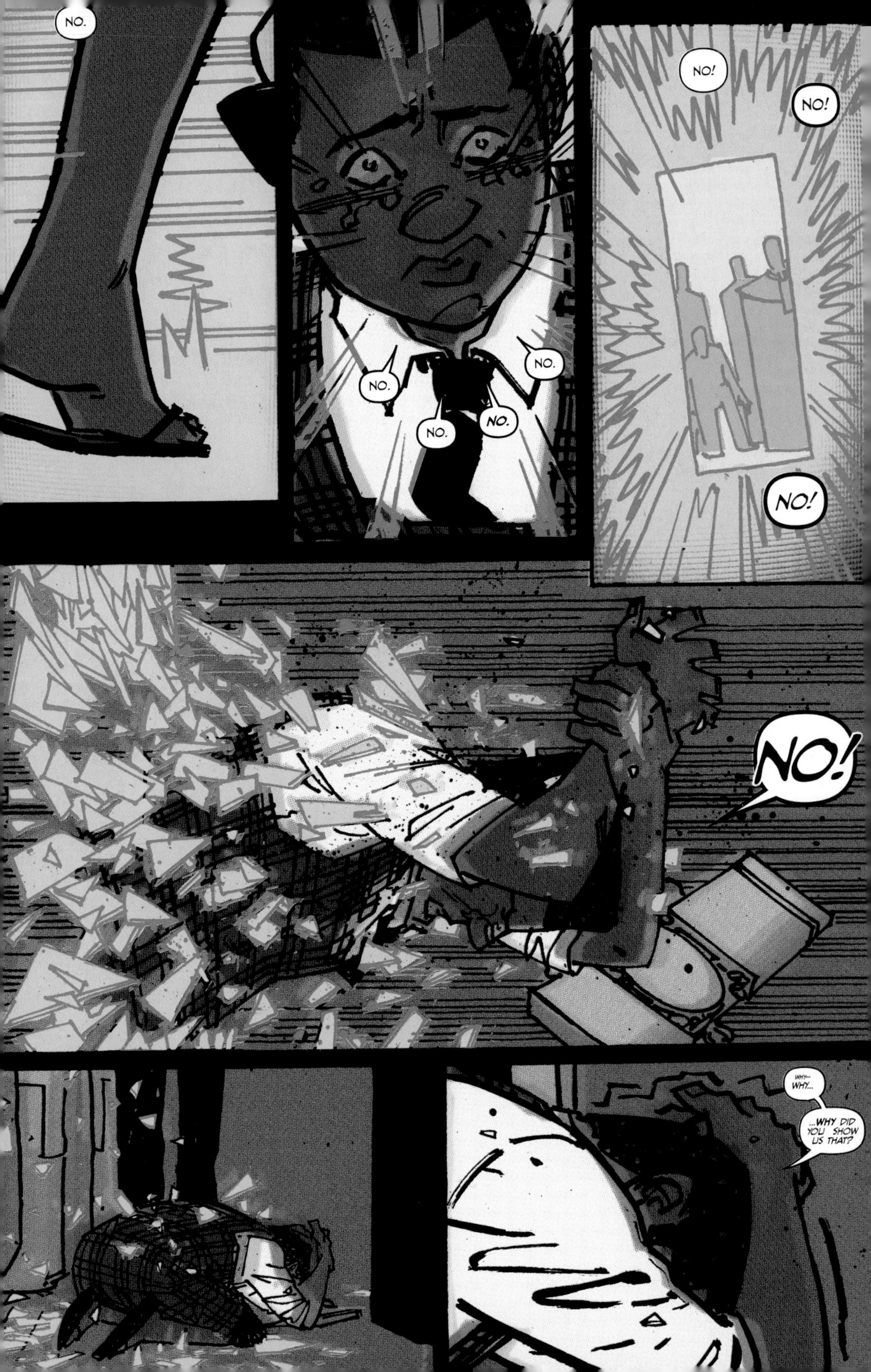
NO.
NO.
NO.
NO.
NO.
NO!
NO!
NO!
NO!
WHY--
WHY...
...WHY DID YOU SHOW US THAT?

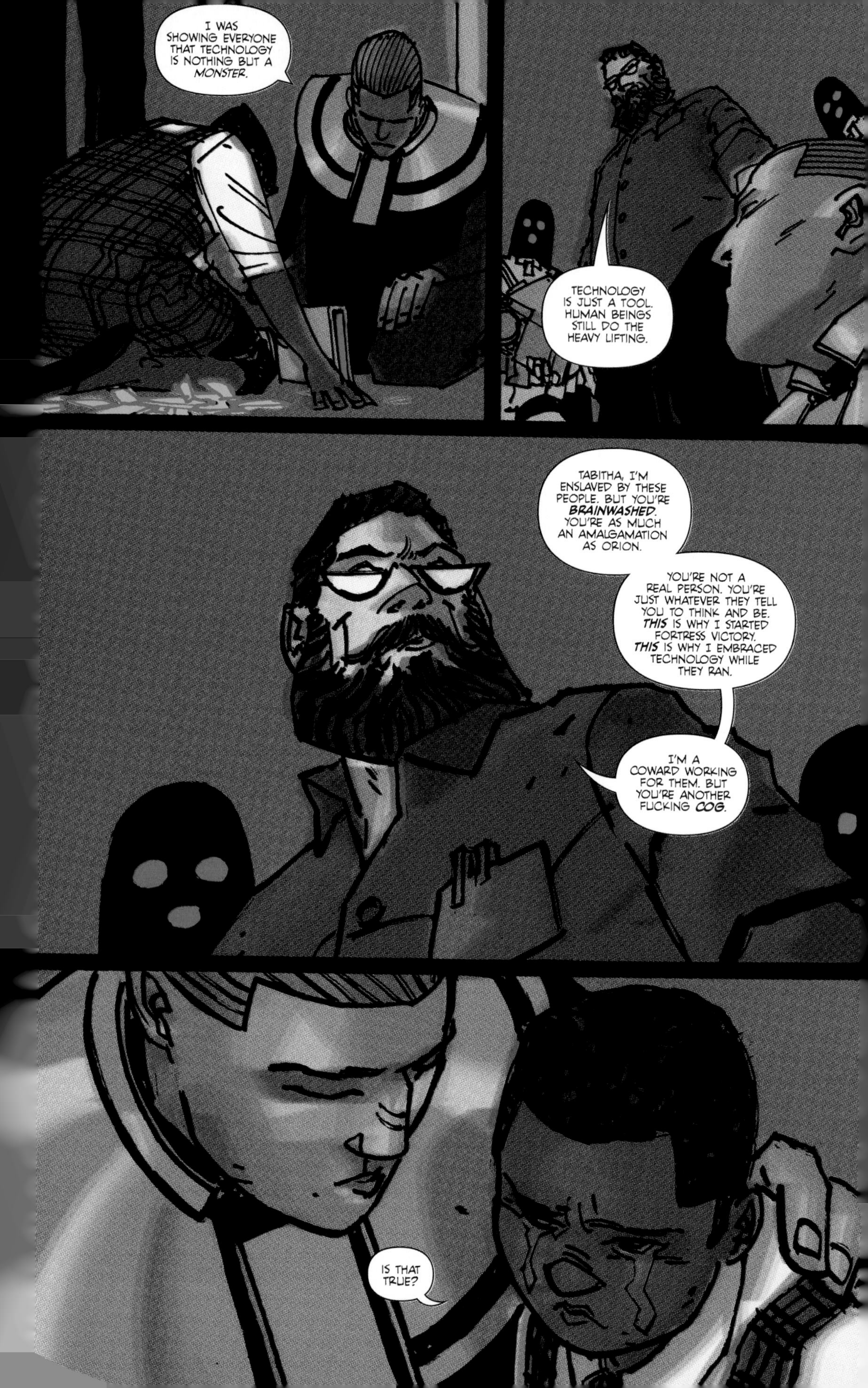
I WAS SHOWING EVERYONE THAT TECHNOLOGY IS NOTHING BUT A *MONSTER.*
TECHNOLOGY IS JUST A TOOL. HUMAN BEINGS STILL DO THE HEAVY LIFTING.
TABITHA, I'M ENSLAVED BY THESE PEOPLE. BUT YOU'RE ***BRAINWASHED.*** YOU'RE AS MUCH AN AMALGAMATION AS ORION.
YOU'RE NOT A REAL PERSON. YOU'RE JUST WHATEVER THEY TELL YOU TO THINK AND BE. ***THIS*** IS WHY I STARTED FORTRESS VICTORY. ***THIS*** IS WHY I EMBRACED TECHNOLOGY WHILE THEY RAN.
I'M A COWARD WORKING FOR THEM. BUT YOU'RE ANOTHER FUCKING ***COG.***
IS THAT TRUE?

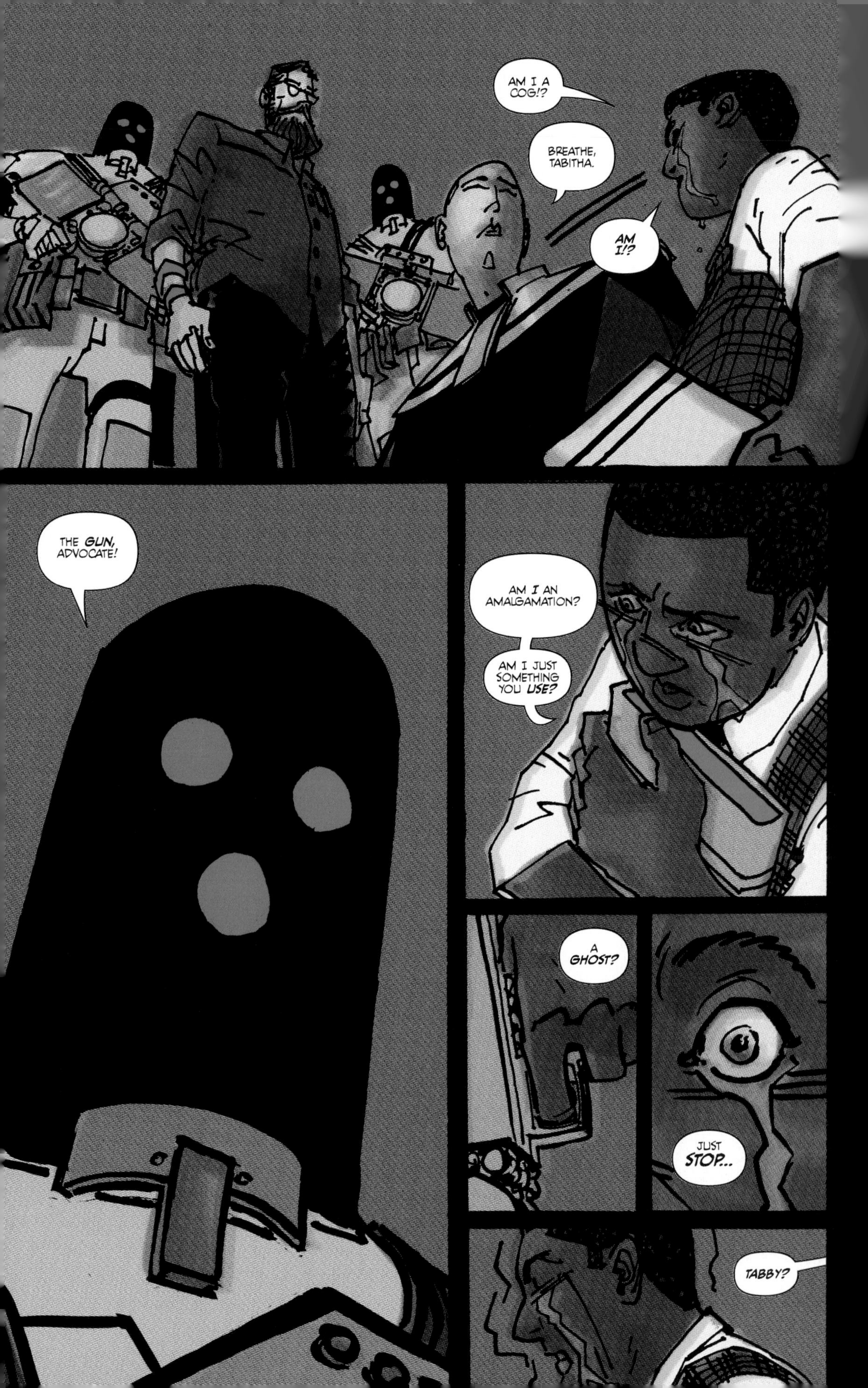
AM I A COG!?
BREATHE, TABITHA.
AM I!?
THE GUN, ADVOCATE!
AM I AN AMALGAMATION?
AM I JUST SOMETHING YOU USE?
A GHOST?
JUST STOP...
TABBY?

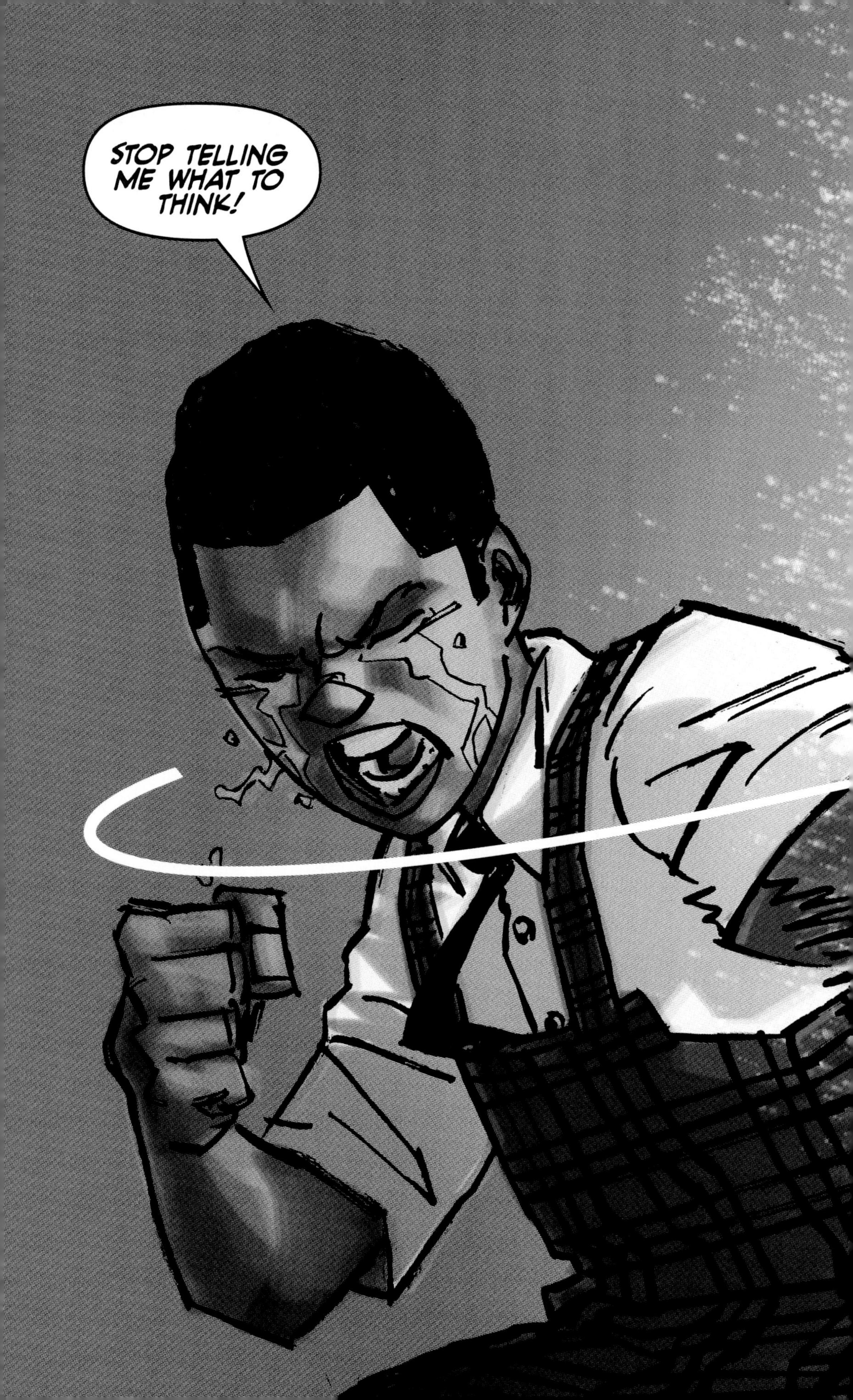
STOP TELLING ME WHAT TO THINK!

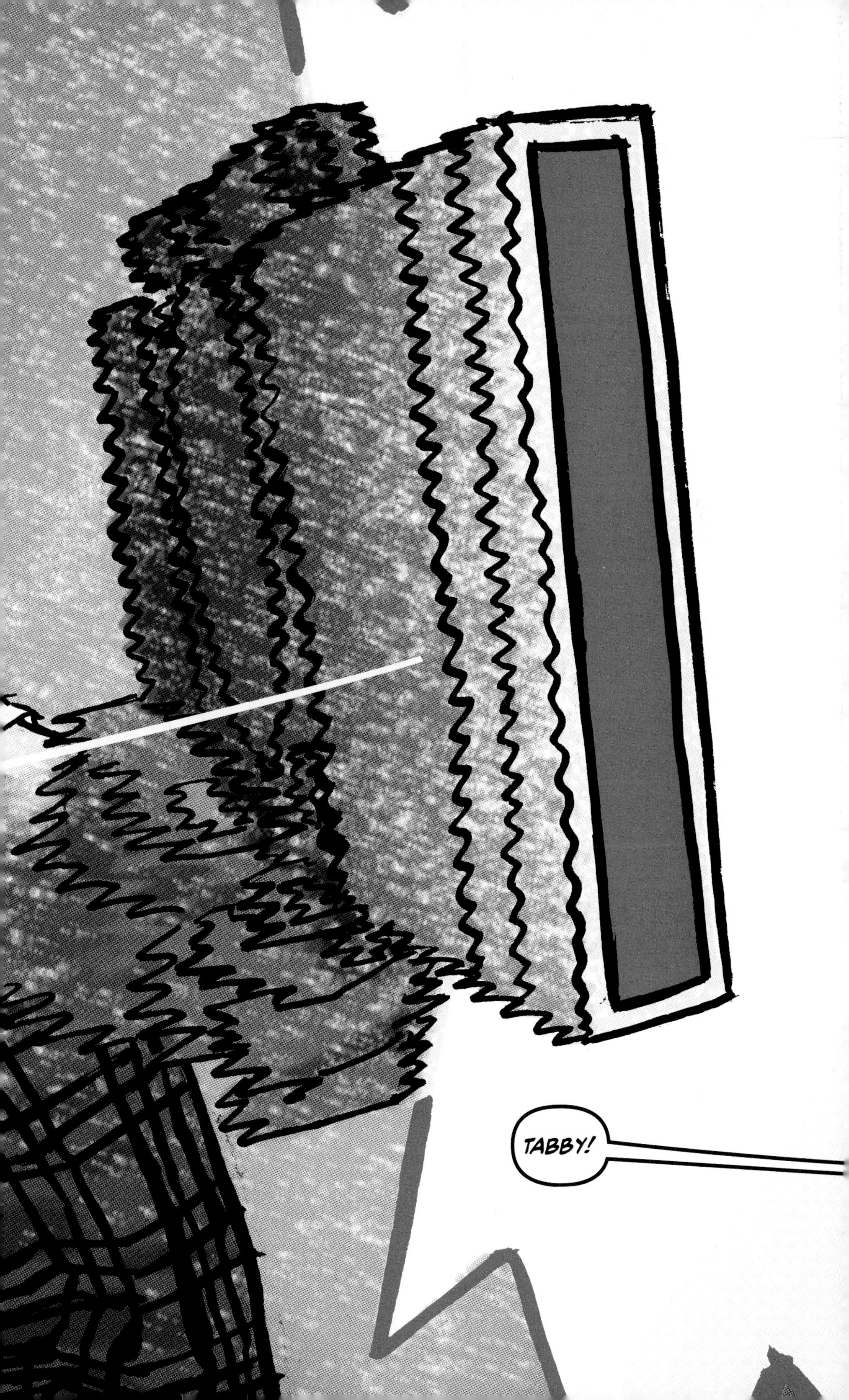
TABBY!

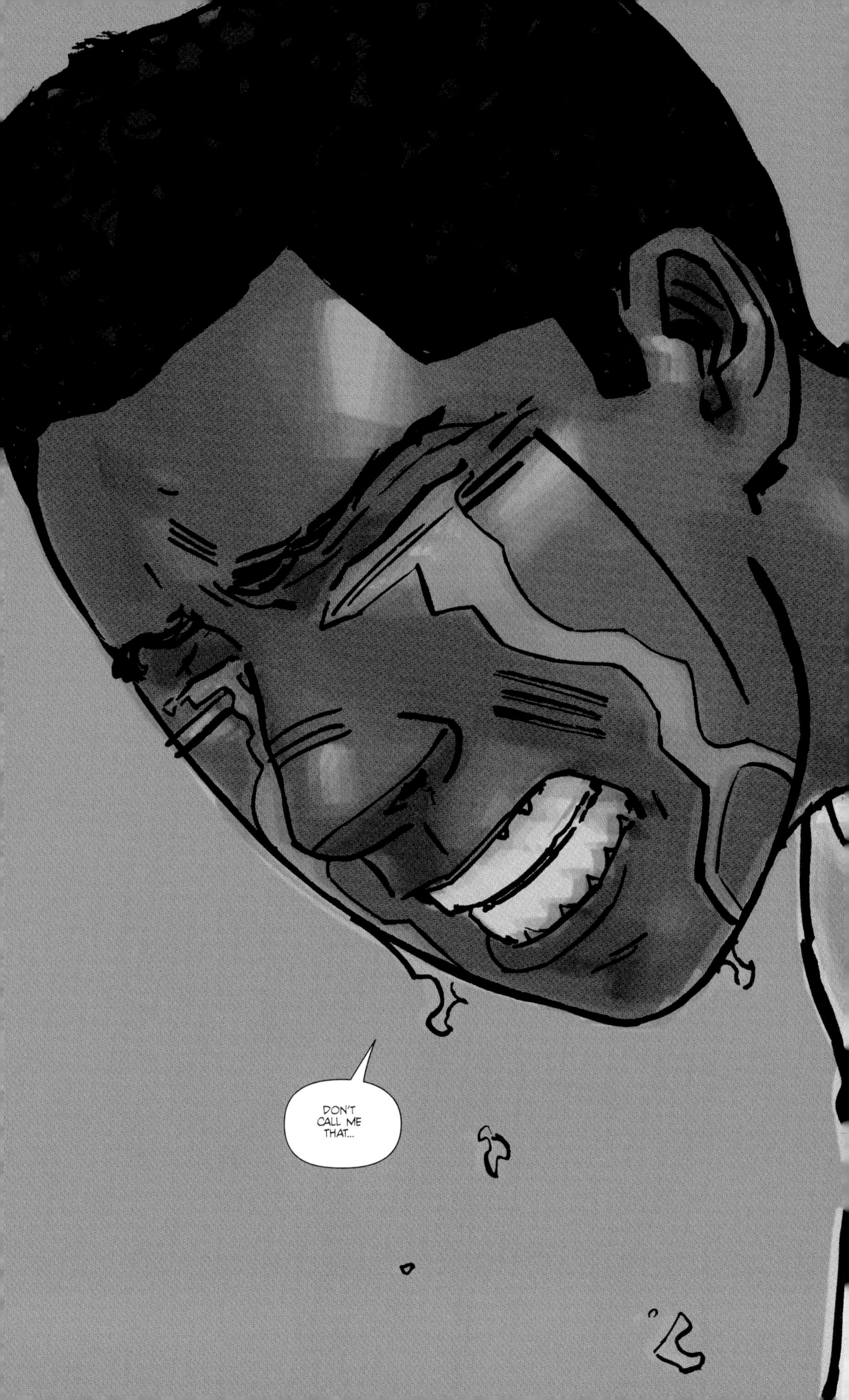
DON'T CALL ME THAT...

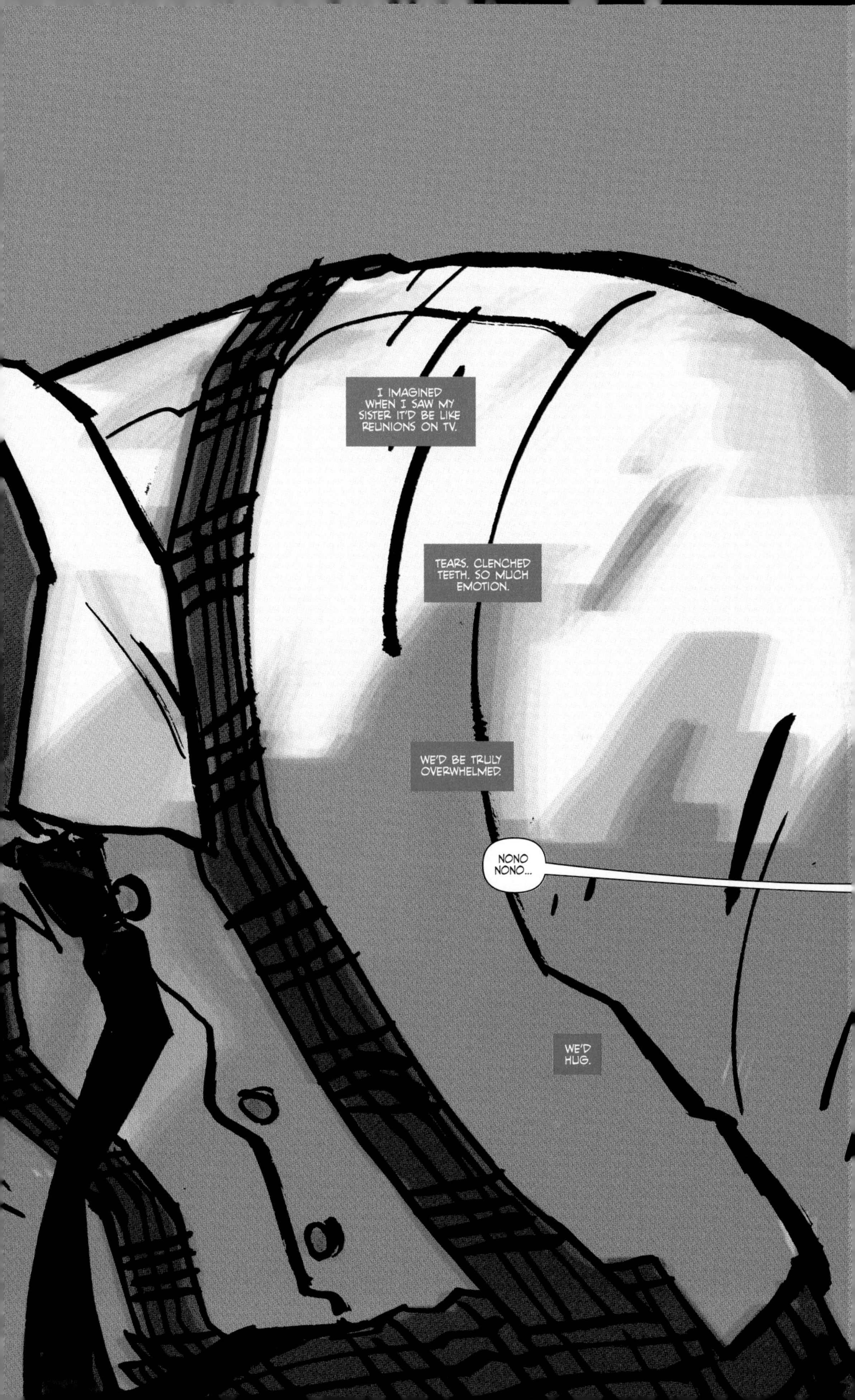
I IMAGINED WHEN I SAW MY SISTER IT'D BE LIKE REUNIONS ON TV.
TEARS. CLENCHED TEETH. SO MUCH EMOTION.
WE'D BE TRULY OVERWHELMED.
NONO NONO...
WE'D HUG.

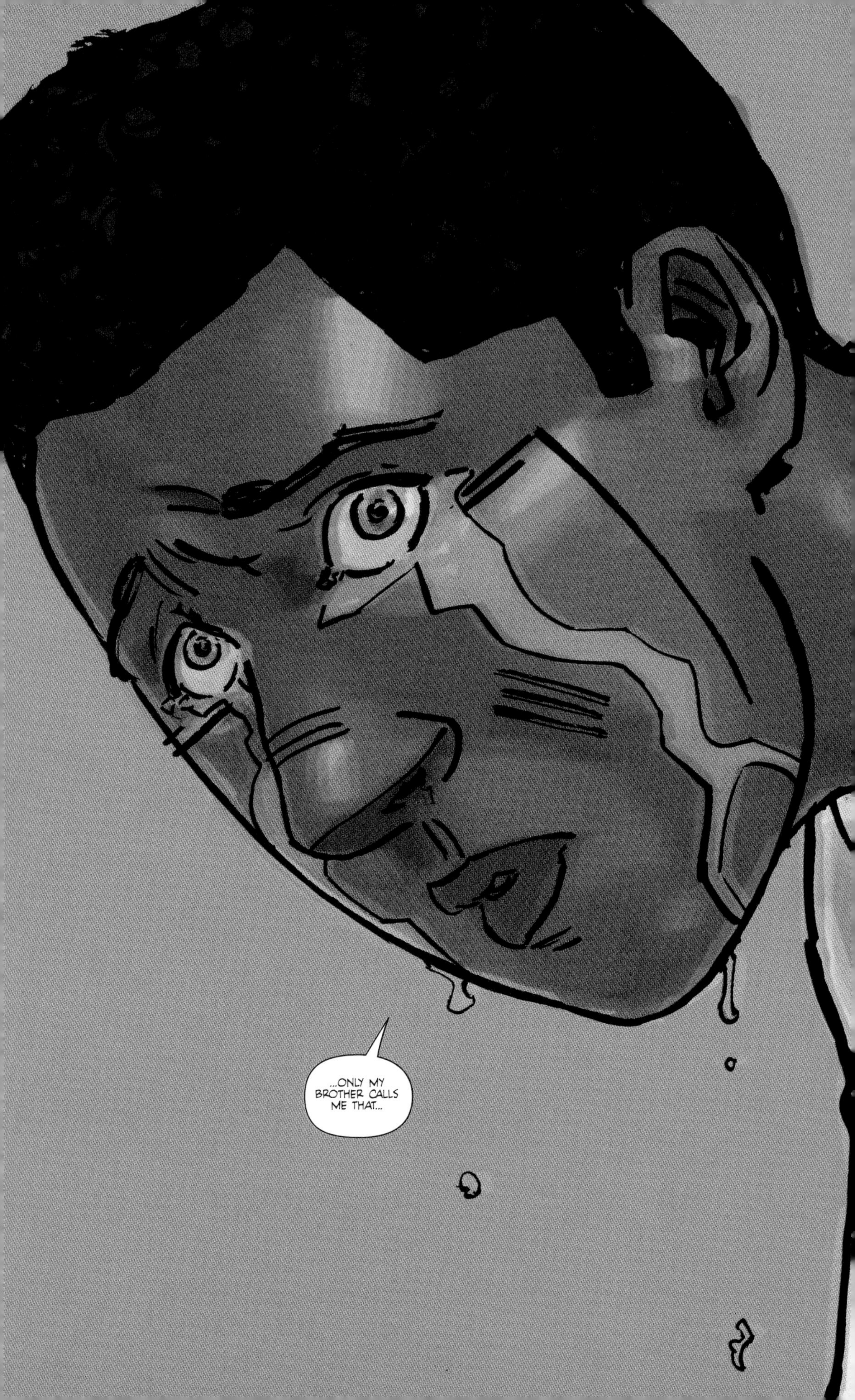
...ONLY MY BROTHER CALLS ME THAT...

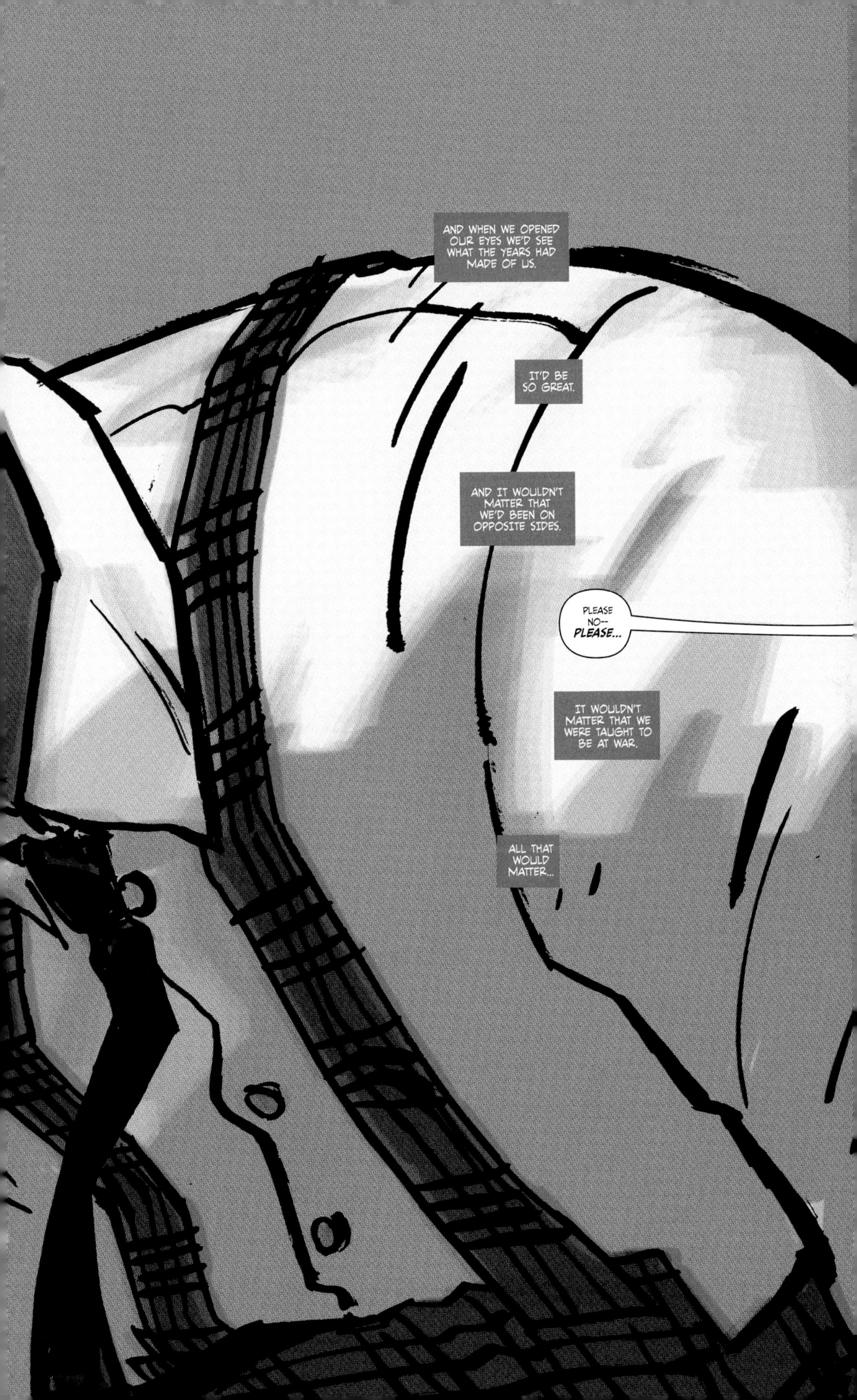
AND WHEN WE OPENED OUR EYES WE'D SEE WHAT THE YEARS HAD MADE OF US.
IT'D BE SO GREAT.
AND IT WOULDN'T MATTER THAT WE'D BEEN ON OPPOSITE SIDES.
PLEASE NO-- PLEASE...
IT WOULDN'T MATTER THAT WE WERE TAUGHT TO BE AT WAR.
ALL THAT WOULD MATTER...

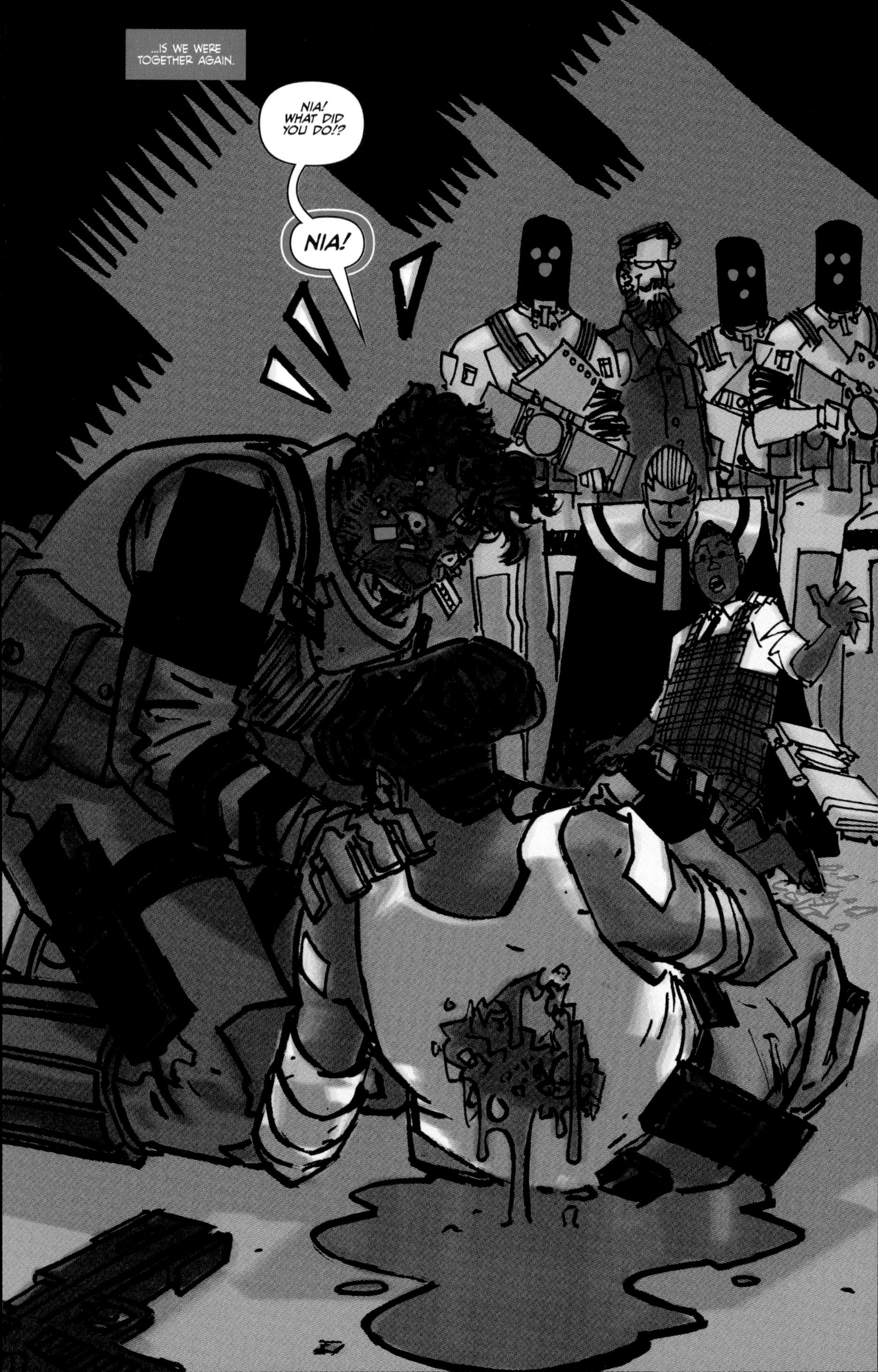
...IS WE WERE TOGETHER AGAIN.
NIA! WHAT DID YOU DO!?
NIA!

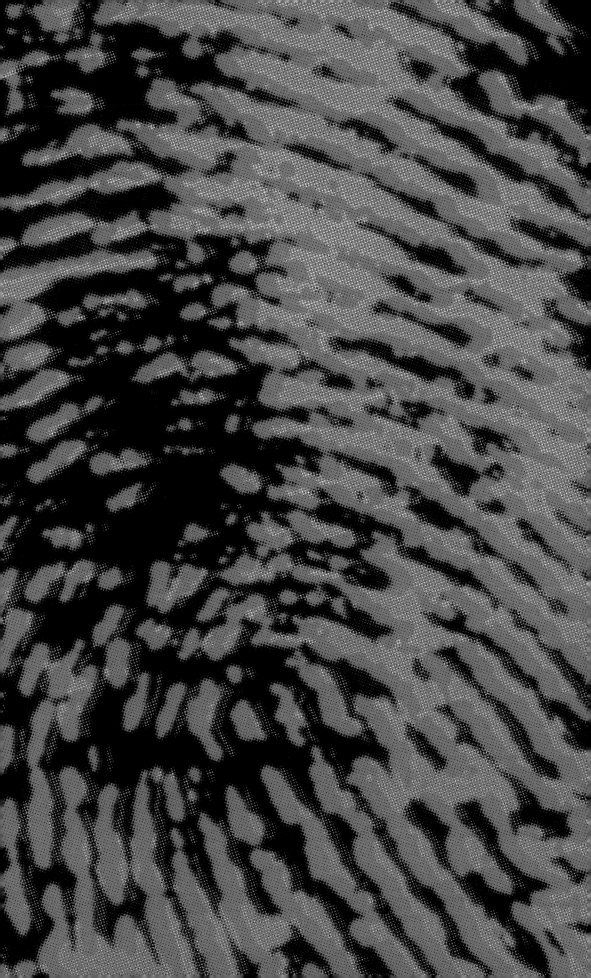

PART **FIVE**

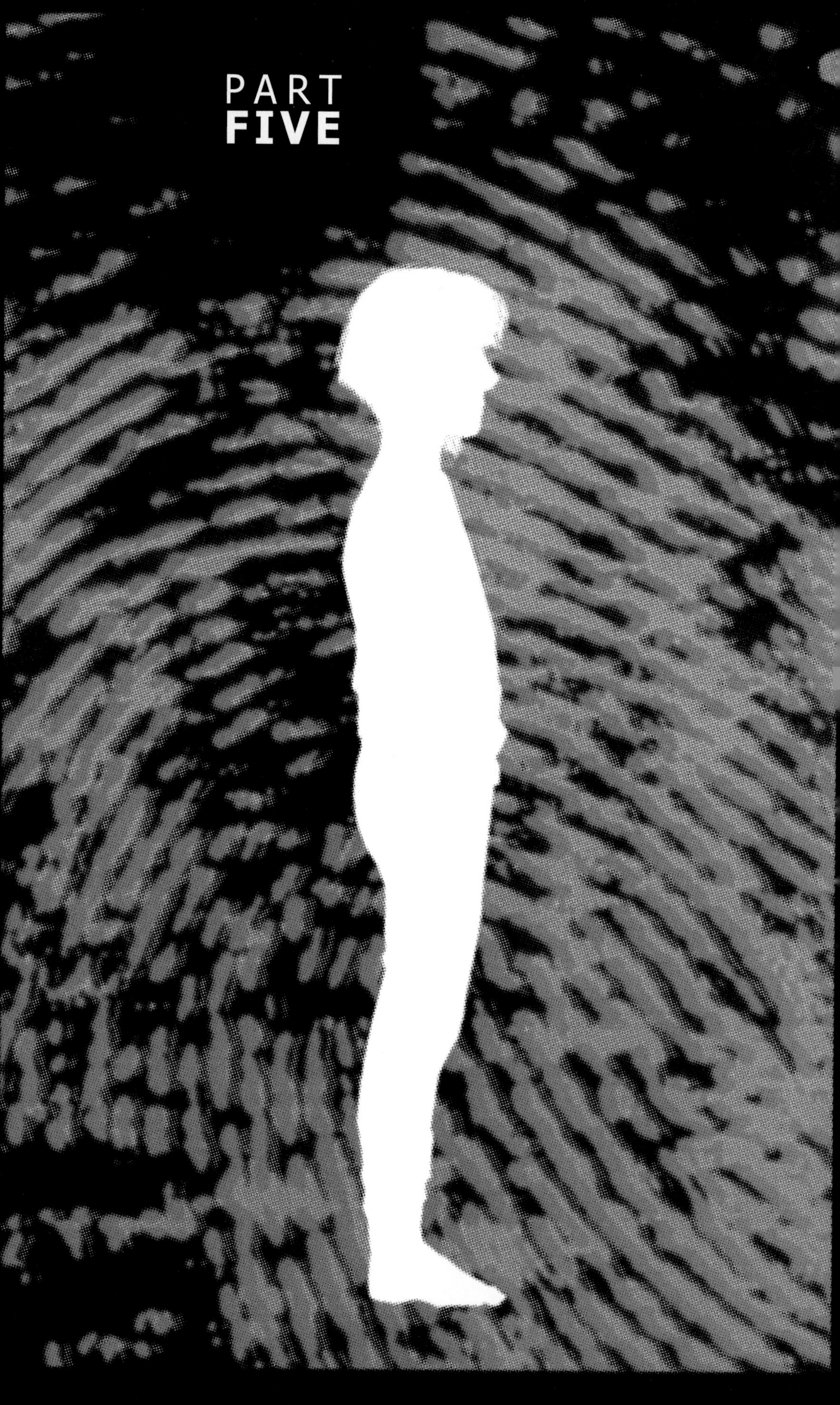

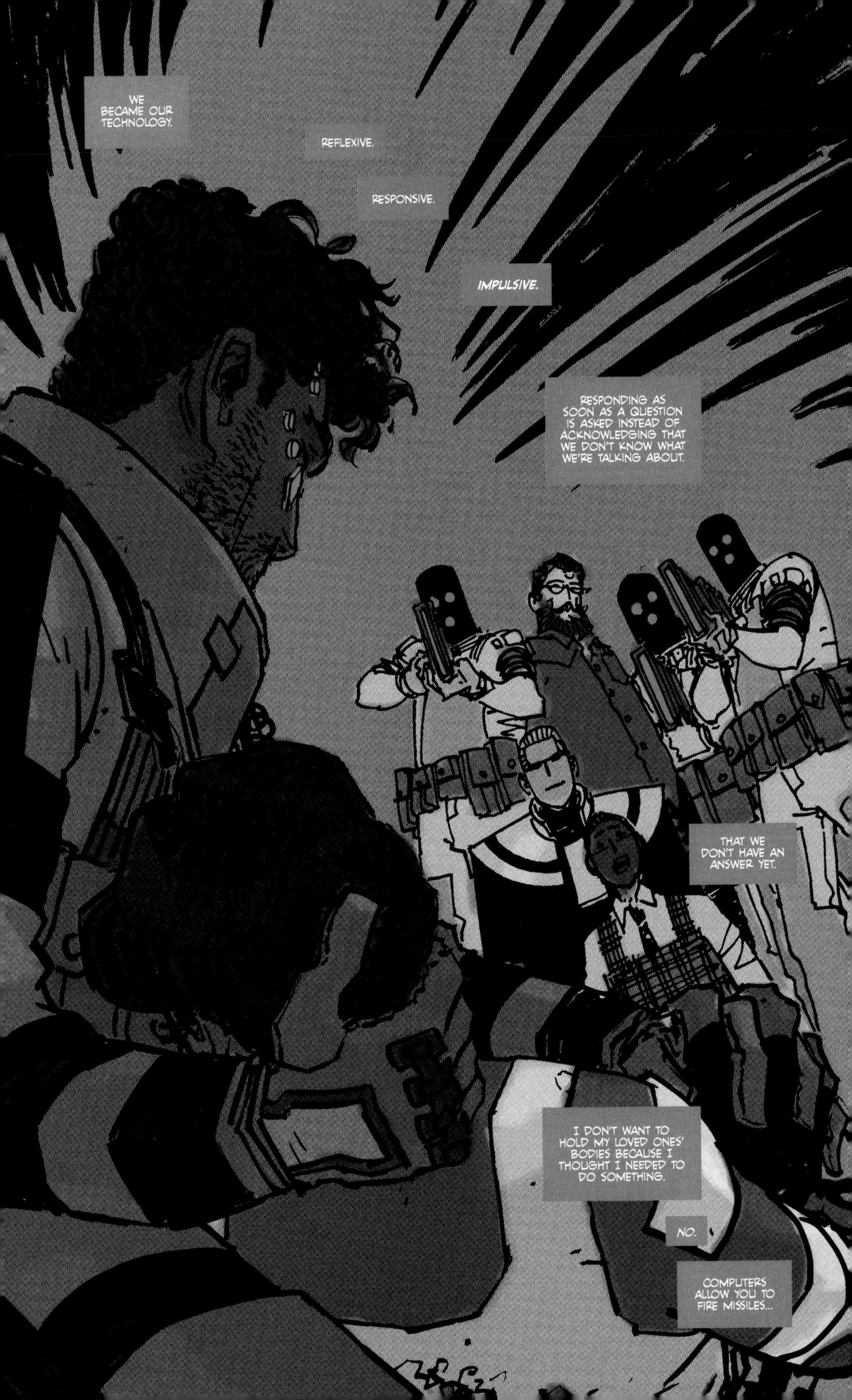
WE BECAME OUR TECHNOLOGY.
REFLEXIVE.
RESPONSIVE.
IMPULSIVE.
RESPONDING AS SOON AS A QUESTION IS ASKED INSTEAD OF ACKNOWLEDGING THAT WE DON'T KNOW WHAT WE'RE TALKING ABOUT.
THAT WE DON'T HAVE AN ANSWER YET.
I DON'T WANT TO HOLD MY LOVED ONES' BODIES BECAUSE I THOUGHT I NEEDED TO DO SOMETHING.
NO.
COMPUTERS ALLOW YOU TO FIRE MISSILES...

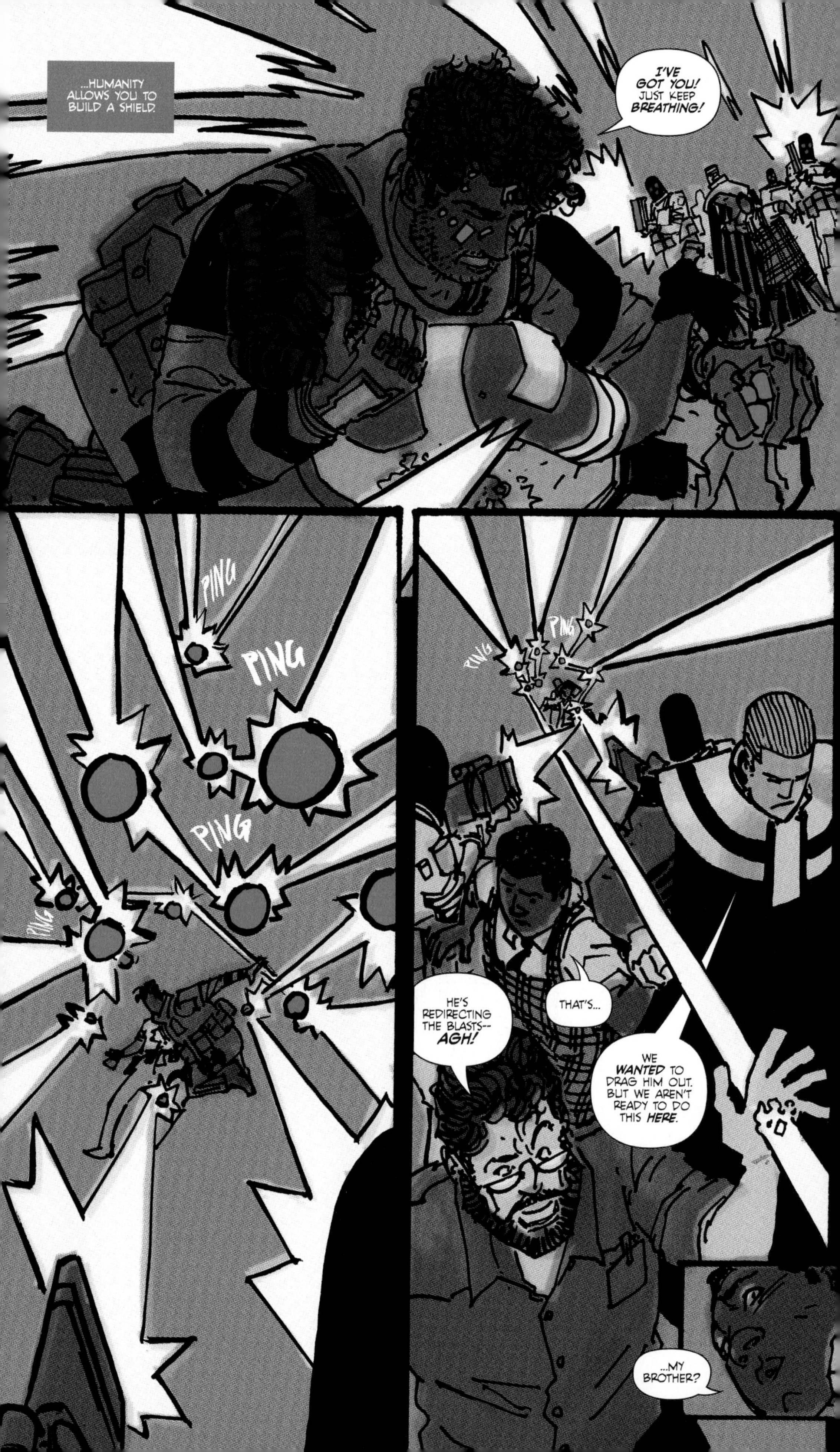
...HUMANITY ALLOWS YOU TO BUILD A SHIELD.
I'VE GOT YOU! JUST KEEP BREATHING!
PING
PING
PING
PING
PING
PING
HE'S REDIRECTING THE BLASTS-- AGH!
THAT'S...
WE WANTED TO DRAG HIM OUT. BUT WE AREN'T READY TO DO THIS HERE.
...MY BROTHER?

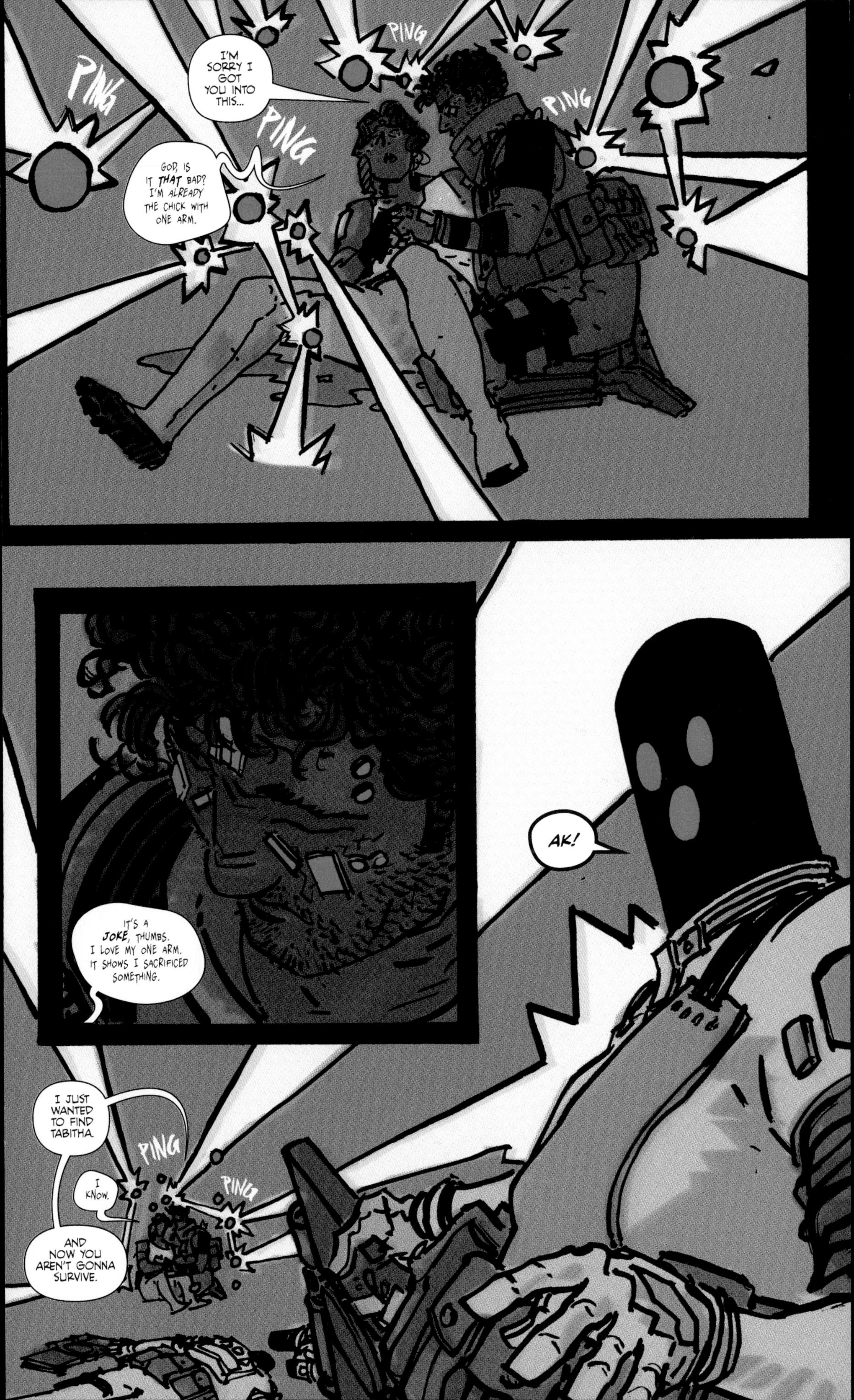
PING
PING
I'M SORRY I GOT YOU INTO THIS...
PING
PING
GOD, IS IT THAT BAD? I'M ALREADY THE CHICK WITH ONE ARM.
IT'S A JOKE, THUMBS. I LOVE MY ONE ARM. IT SHOWS I SACRIFICED SOMETHING.
AK!
I JUST WANTED TO FIND TABITHA.
PING
I KNOW.
PING
AND NOW YOU AREN'T GONNA SURVIVE.

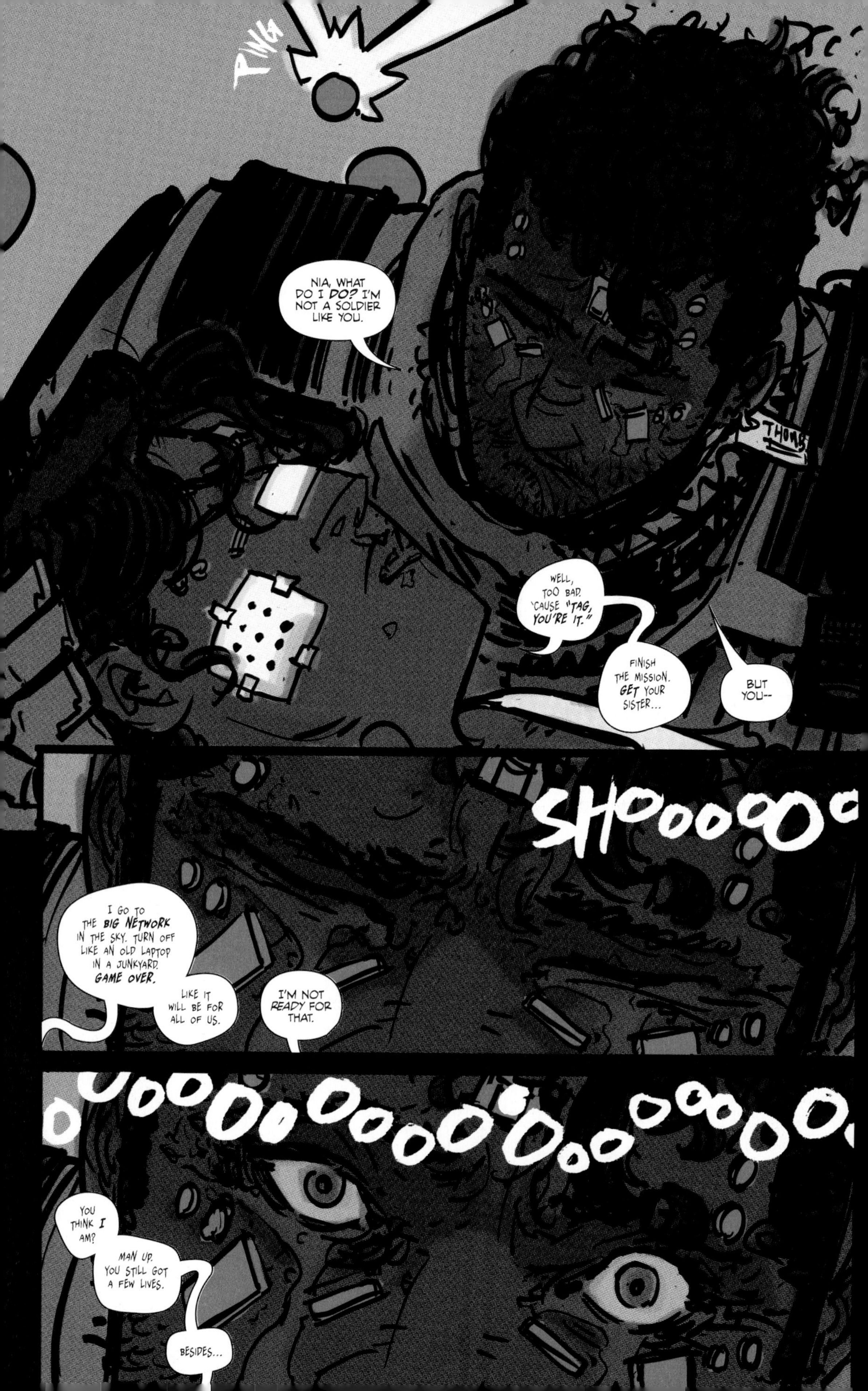
PING
NIA, WHAT DO I DO? I'M NOT A SOLDIER LIKE YOU.
THOMS
WELL, TOO BAD. 'CAUSE "TAG, YOU'RE IT."
FINISH THE MISSION. GET YOUR SISTER...
BUT YOU--
SHOOOOOO
I GO TO THE BIG NETWORK IN THE SKY. TURN OFF LIKE AN OLD LAPTOP IN A JUNKYARD. GAME OVER.
LIKE IT WILL BE FOR ALL OF US.
I'M NOT READY FOR THAT.
OOOOOOOOOOOOOOOOOOOO
YOU THINK I AM?
MAN UP. YOU STILL GOT A FEW LIVES.
BESIDES...

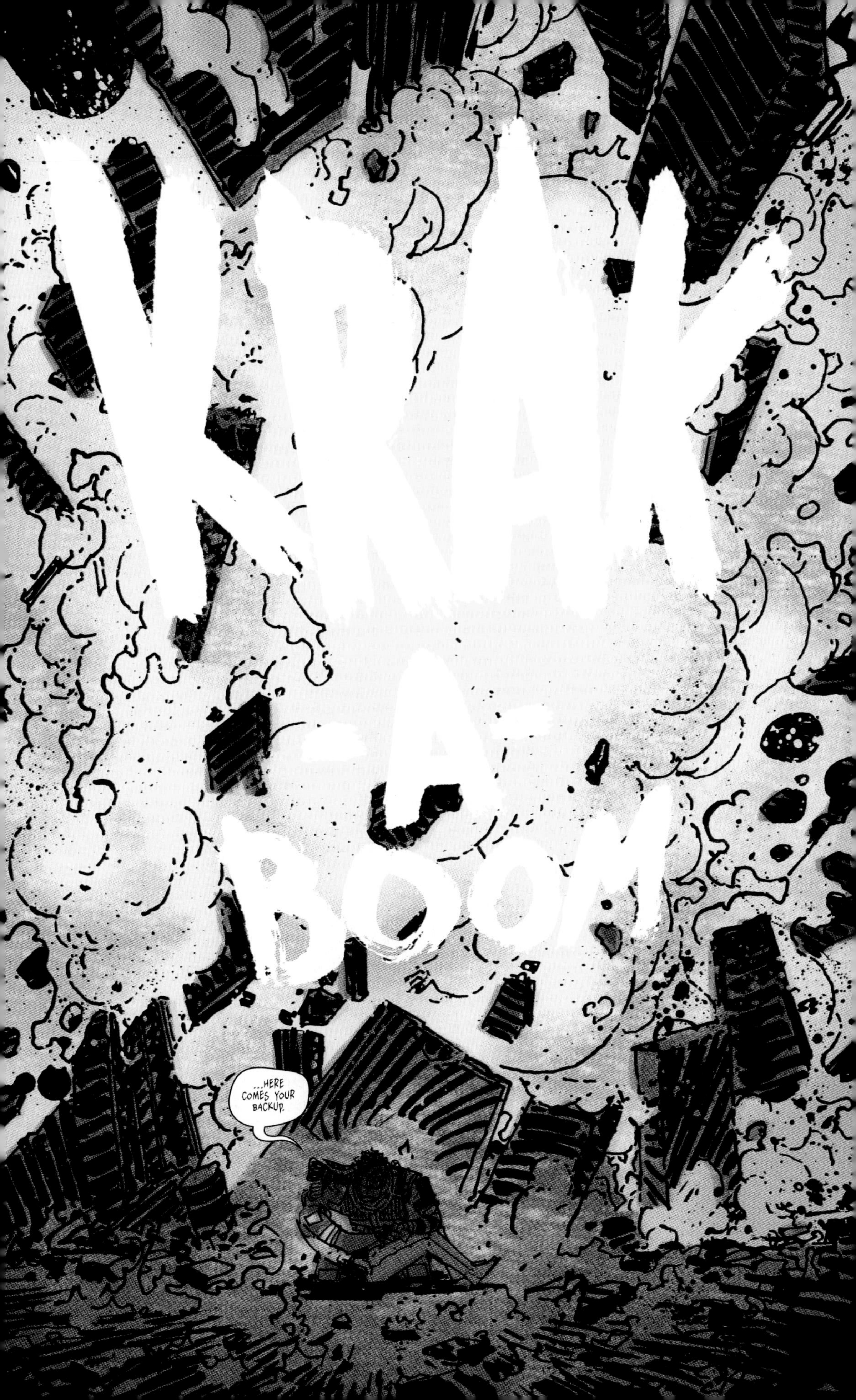
KRAK-A-BOOM
...HERE COMES YOUR BACKUP.

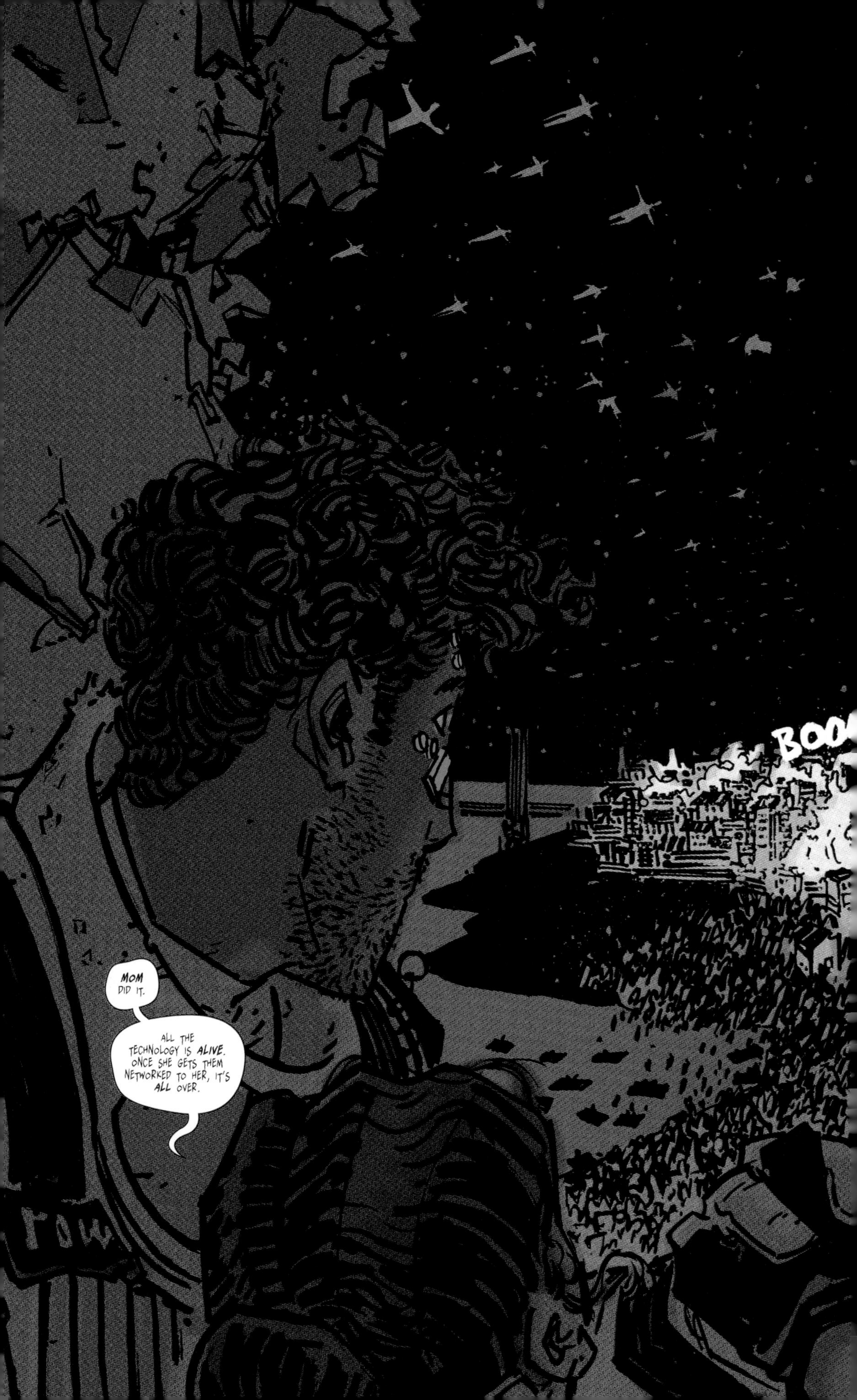
MOM DID IT.
ALL THE TECHNOLOGY IS ALIVE. ONCE SHE GETS THEM NETWORKED TO HER, IT'S ALL OVER.
BOO

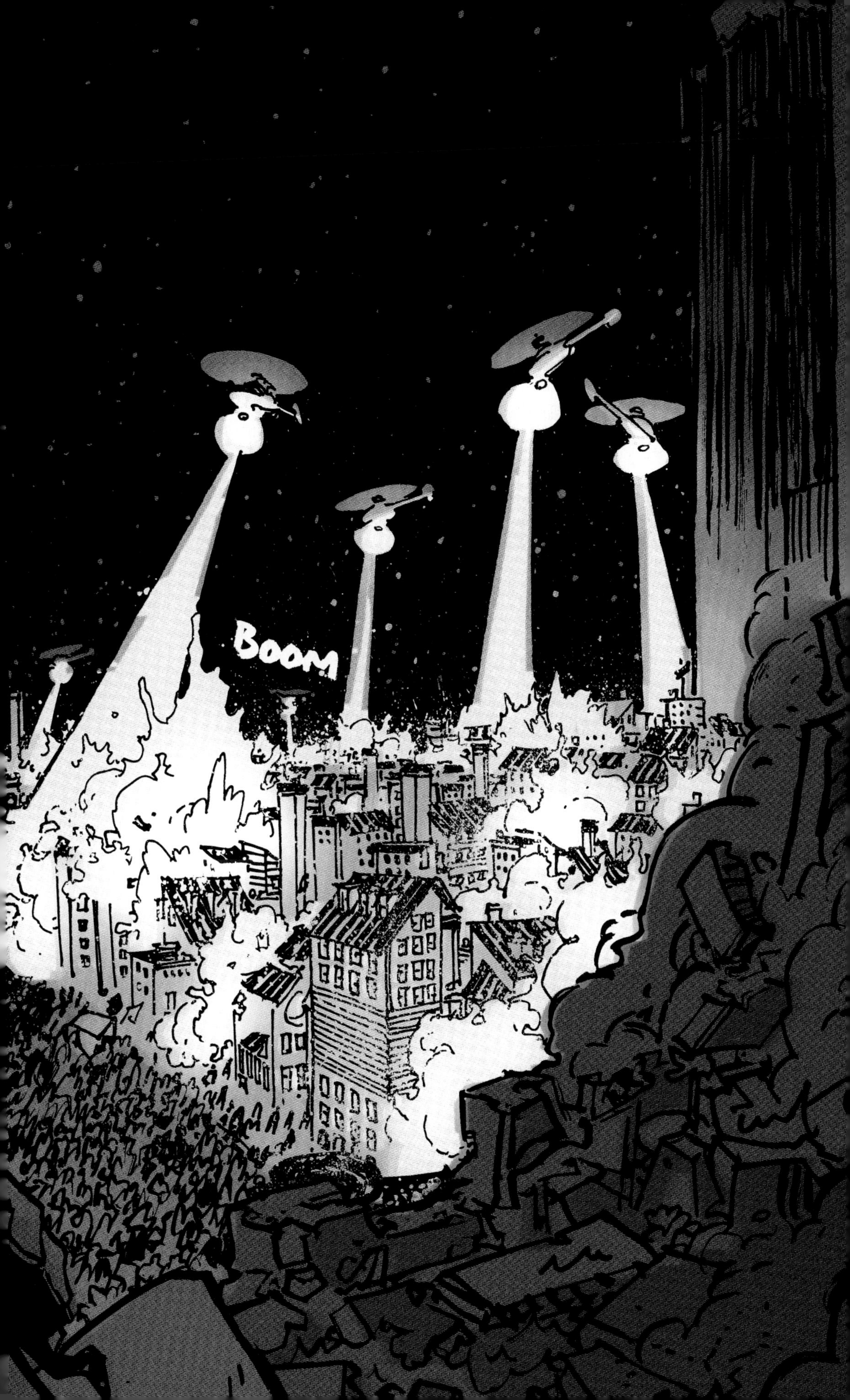
Boom

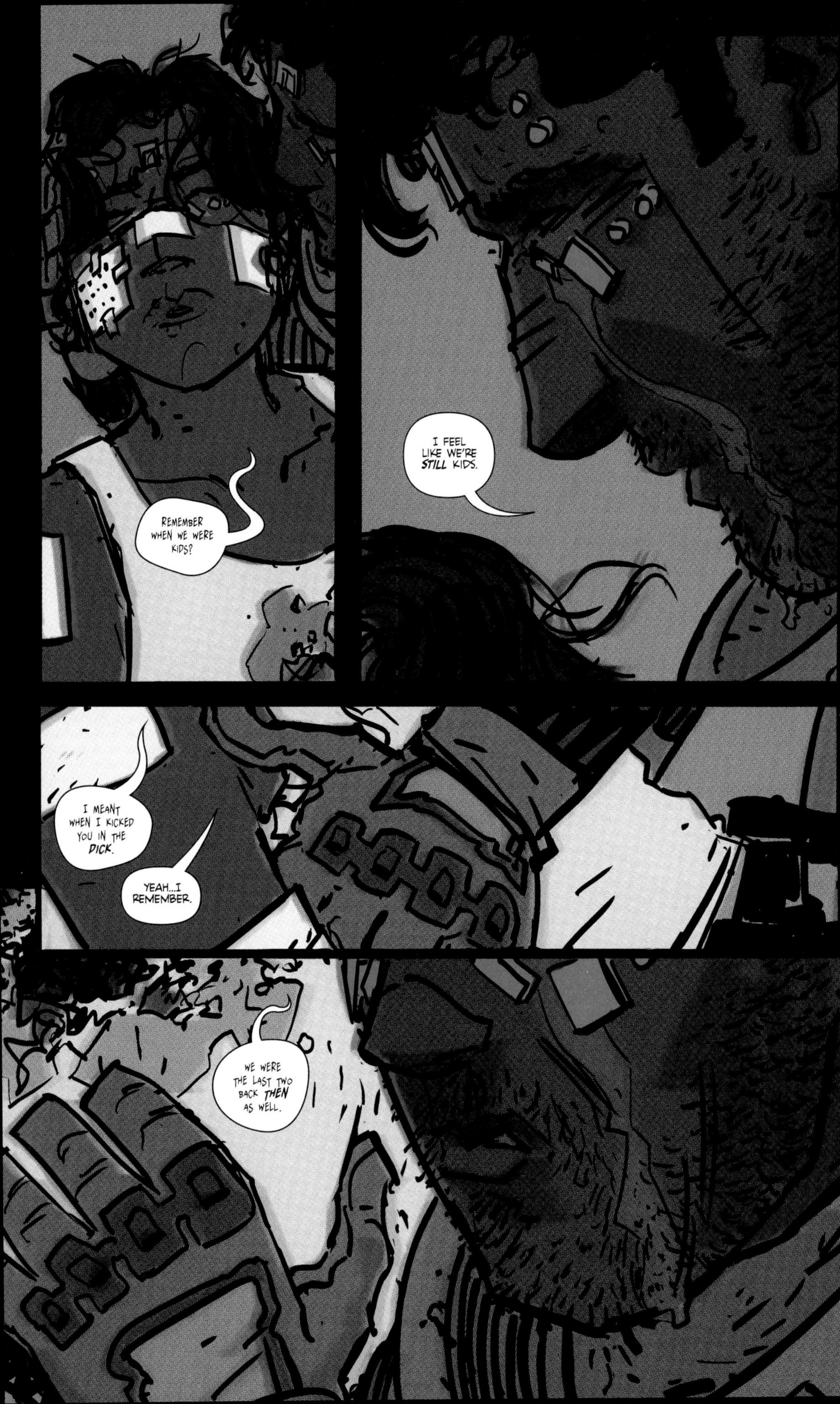
REMEMBER WHEN WE WERE KIDS?
I FEEL LIKE WE'RE STILL KIDS.
I MEANT WHEN I KICKED YOU IN THE DICK.
YEAH...I REMEMBER.
WE WERE THE LAST TWO BACK THEN AS WELL.

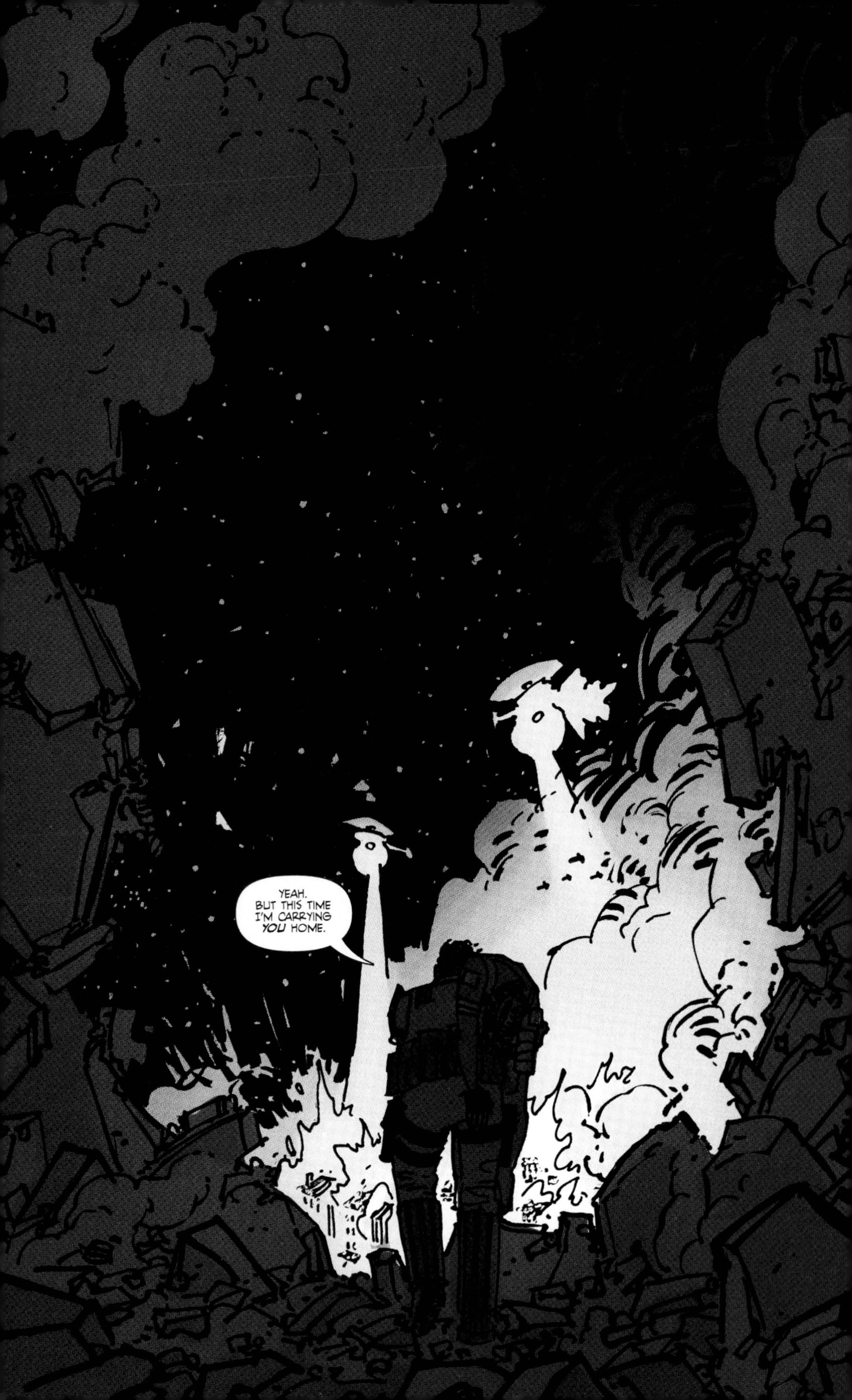
YEAH. BUT THIS TIME I'M CARRYING YOU HOME.

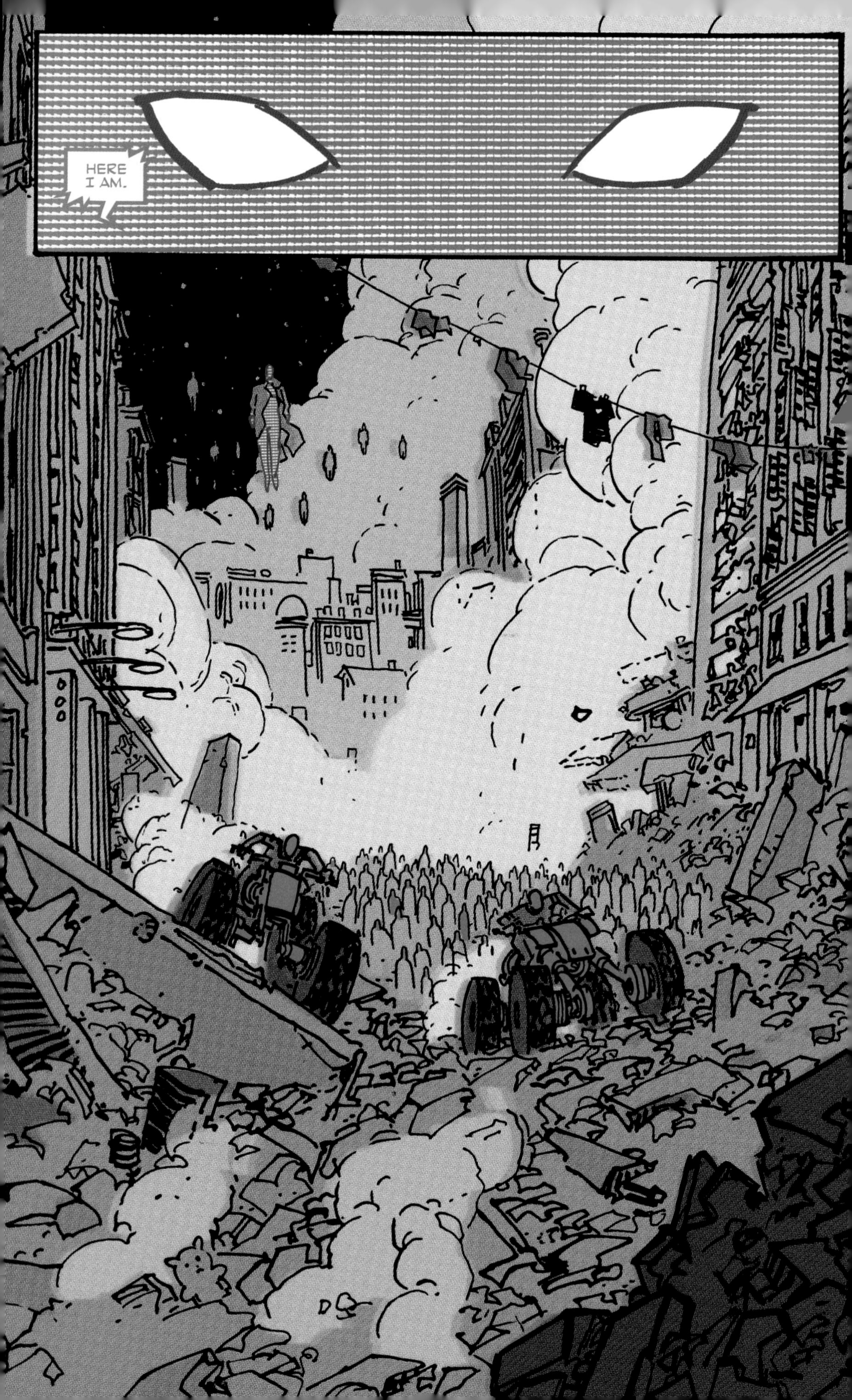
HERE I AM.

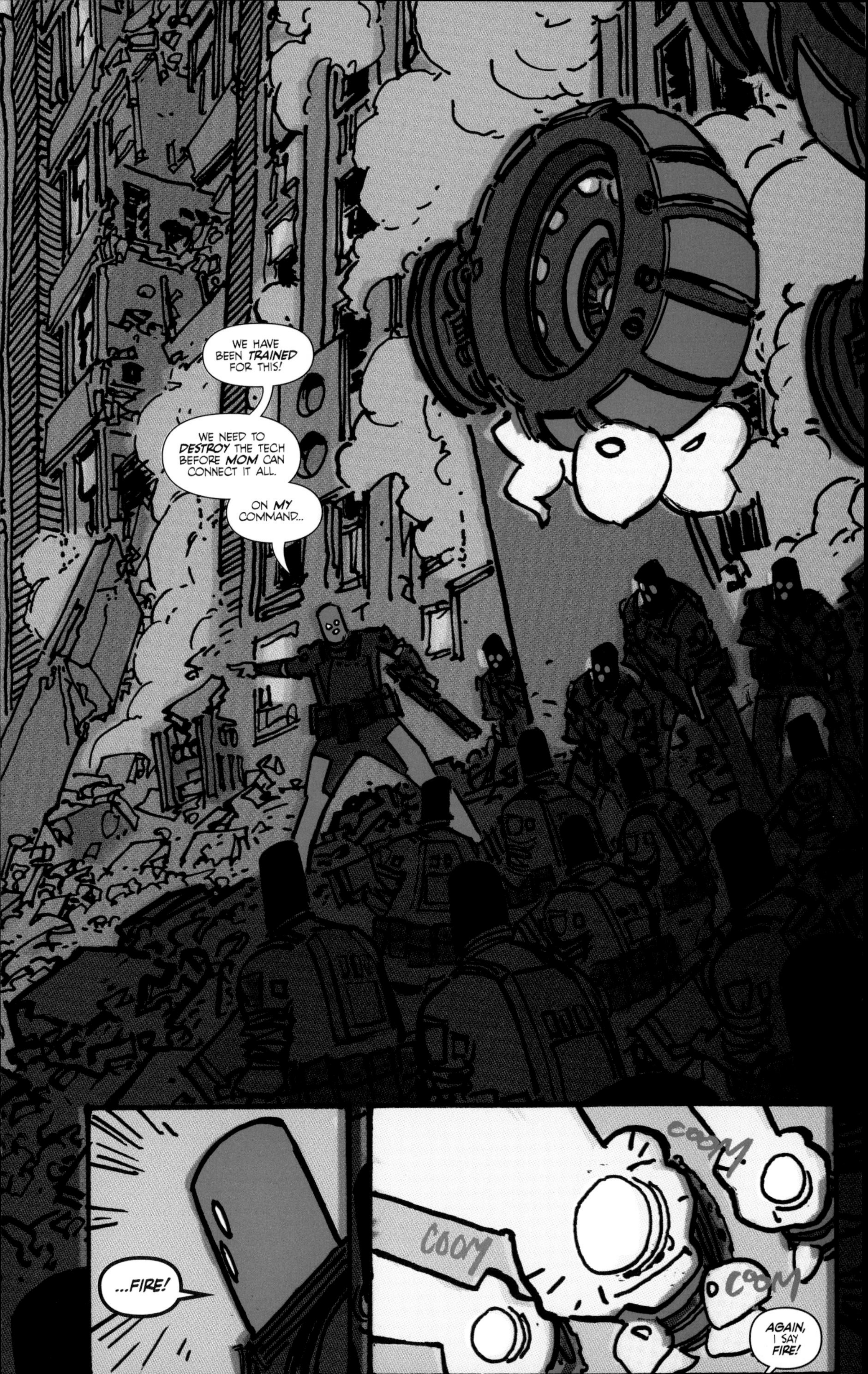
WE HAVE BEEN TRAINED FOR THIS!
WE NEED TO DESTROY THE TECH BEFORE MOM CAN CONNECT IT ALL.
ON MY COMMAND...
...FIRE!
COOM
COOM
COOM
AGAIN, I SAY FIRE!

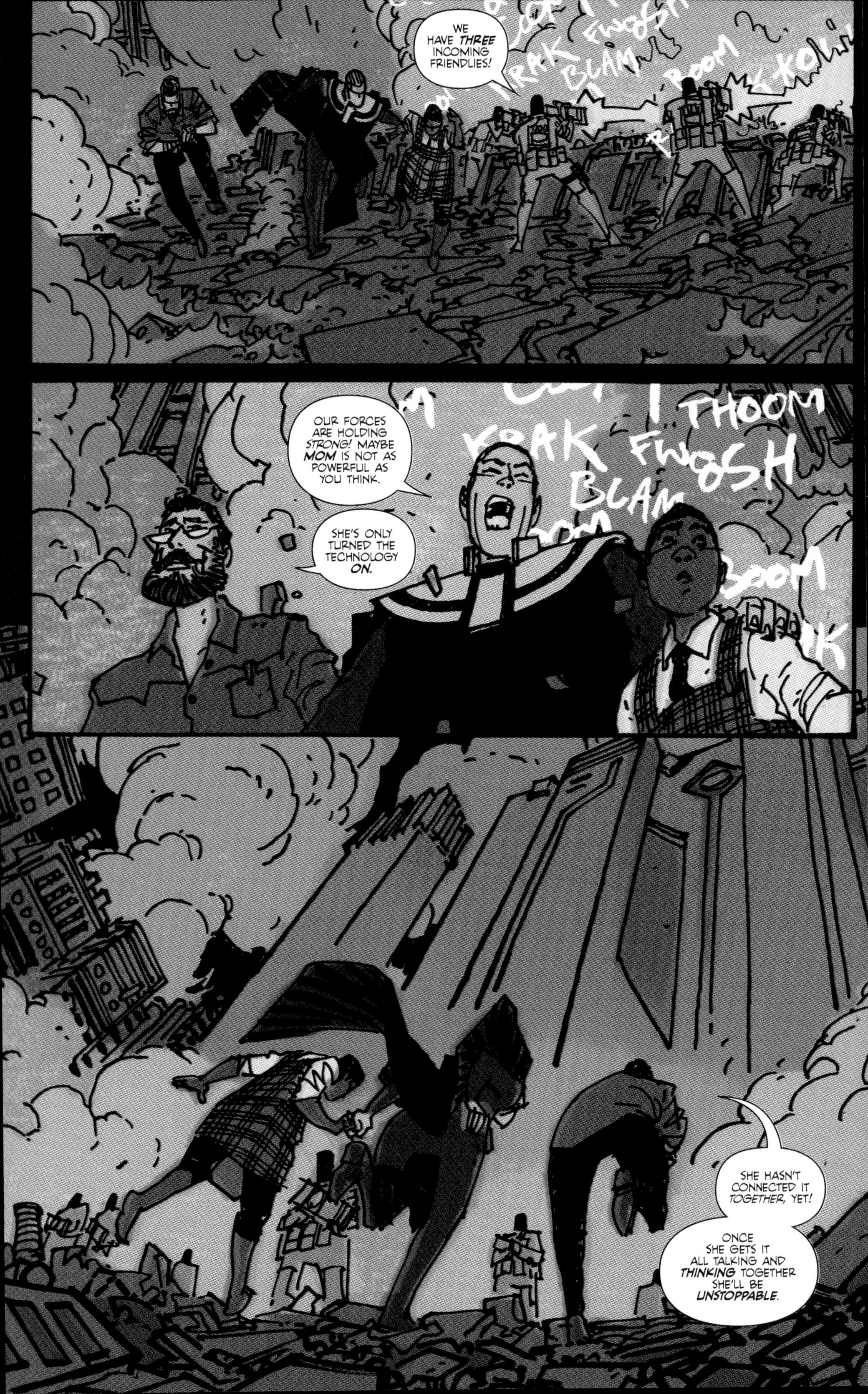
WE HAVE THREE INCOMING FRIENDLIES!
KRAK FWOSH
BLAM
BOOM
OUR FORCES ARE HOLDING STRONG! MAYBE MOM IS NOT AS POWERFUL AS YOU THINK.
SHE'S ONLY TURNED THE TECHNOLOGY ON.
THOOM
KRAK FWOOSH
BLAM
BOOM
SHE HASN'T CONNECTED IT TOGETHER, YET!
ONCE SHE GETS IT ALL TALKING AND THINKING TOGETHER SHE'LL BE UNSTOPPABLE.

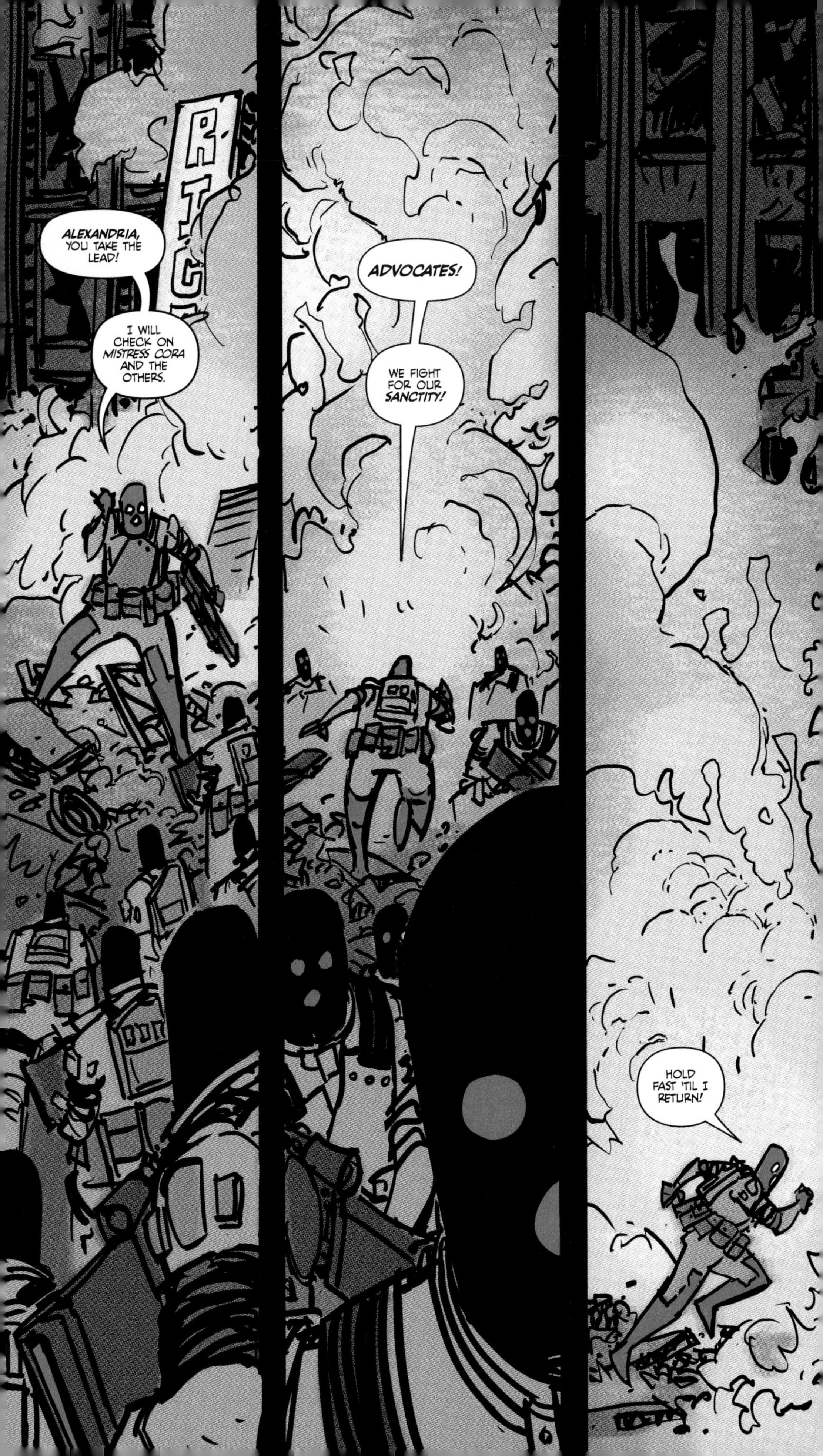
ALEXANDRIA, YOU TAKE THE LEAD!
I WILL CHECK ON MISTRESS CORA AND THE OTHERS.
ADVOCATES!
WE FIGHT FOR OUR SANCTITY!
HOLD FAST 'TIL I RETURN!

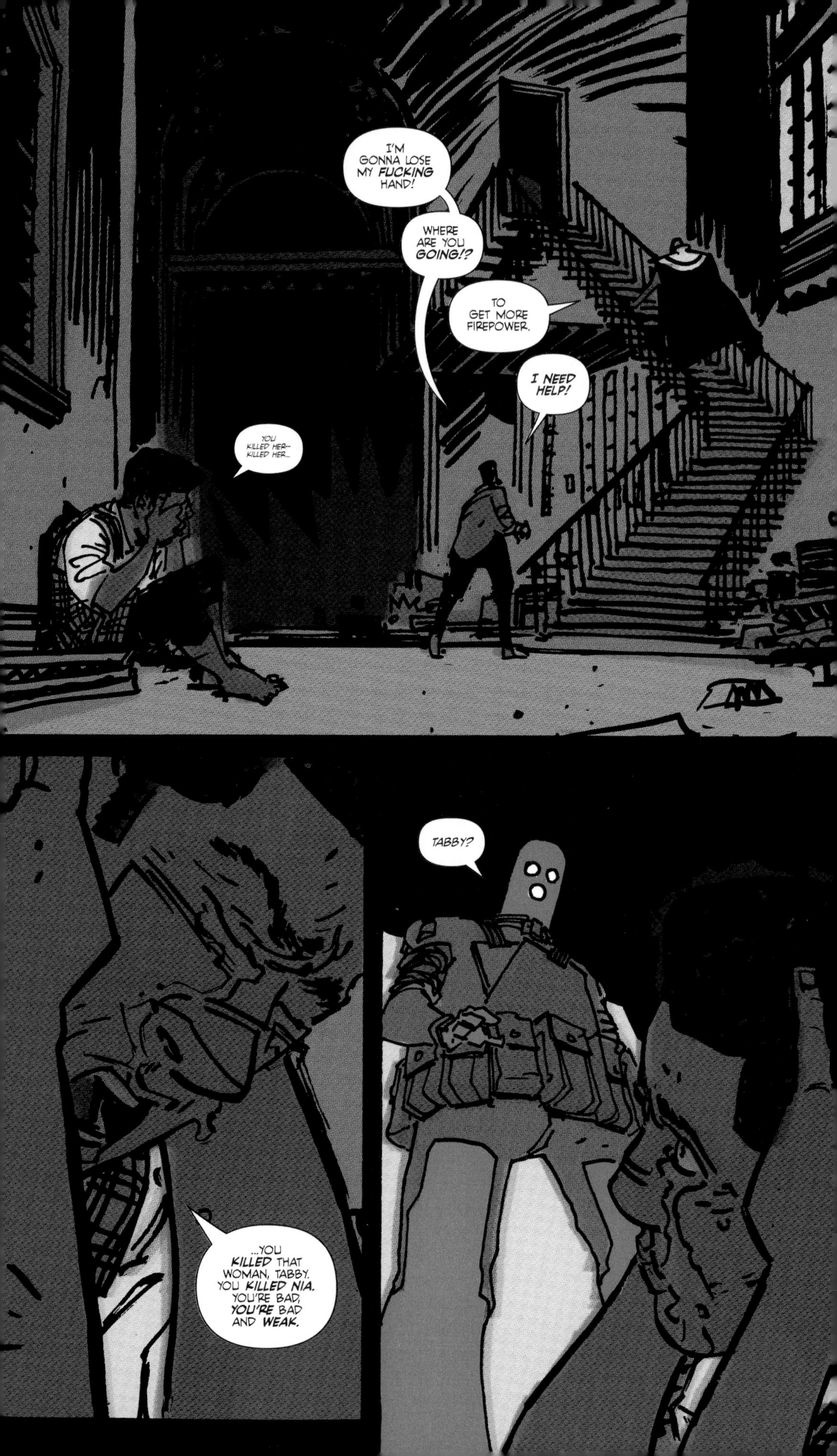
I'M GONNA LOSE MY FUCKING HAND!
WHERE ARE YOU GOING!?
TO GET MORE FIREPOWER.
I NEED HELP!
YOU KILLED HER-- KILLED HER...
TABBY?
...YOU KILLED THAT WOMAN, TABBY. YOU KILLED NIA. YOU'RE BAD, YOU'RE BAD AND WEAK.

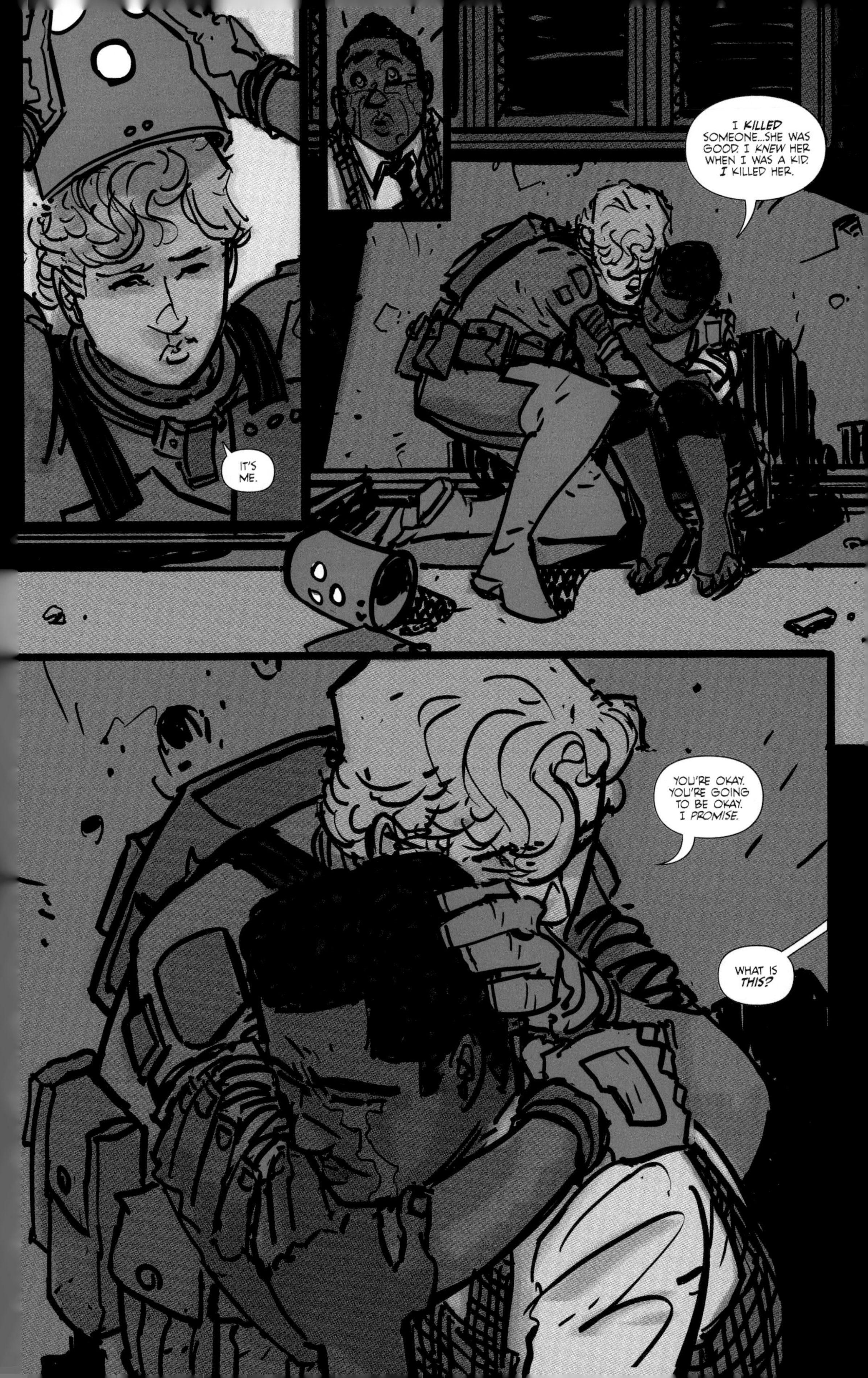
IT'S ME.
I KILLED SOMEONE...SHE WAS GOOD. I KNEW HER WHEN I WAS A KID. I KILLED HER.
YOU'RE OKAY. YOU'RE GOING TO BE OKAY. I PROMISE.
WHAT IS THIS?

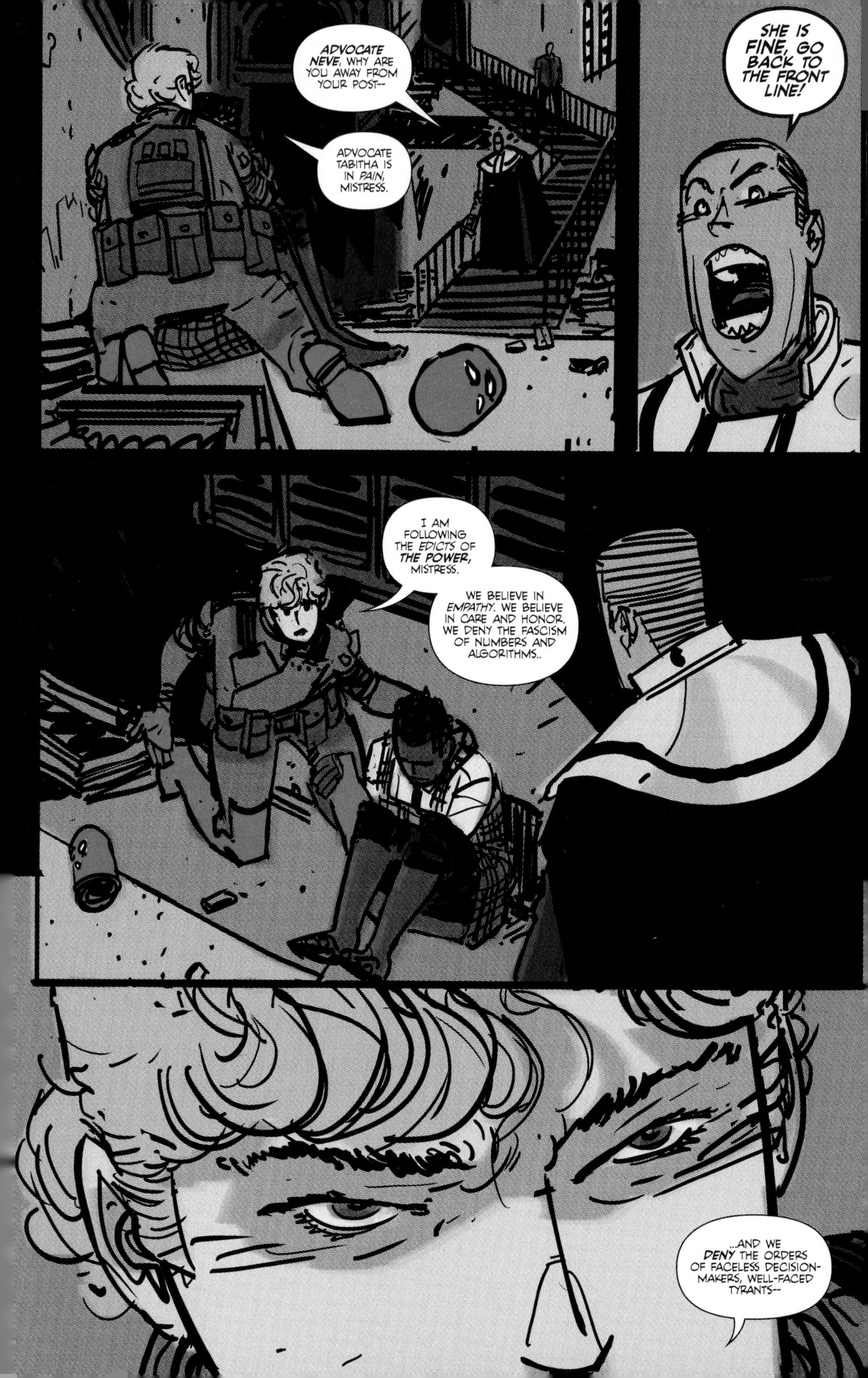
ADVOCATE NEVE, WHY ARE YOU AWAY FROM YOUR POST--
ADVOCATE TABITHA IS IN PAIN, MISTRESS.
SHE IS FINE, GO BACK TO THE FRONT LINE!
I AM FOLLOWING THE EDICTS OF THE POWER, MISTRESS.
WE BELIEVE IN EMPATHY. WE BELIEVE IN CARE AND HONOR. WE DENY THE FASCISM OF NUMBERS AND ALGORITHMS..
...AND WE DENY THE ORDERS OF FACELESS DECISION-MAKERS, WELL-FACED TYRANTS--

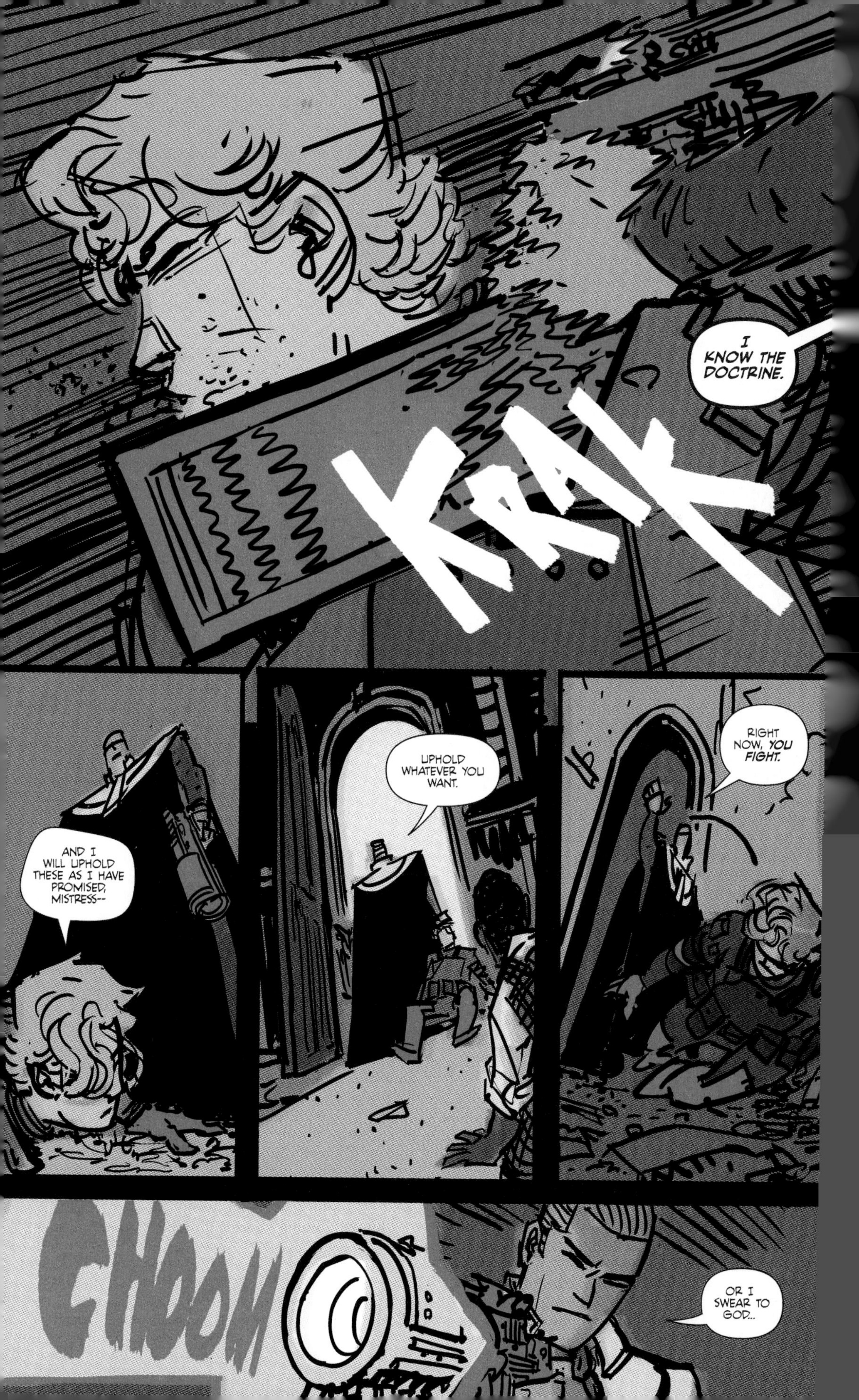
I KNOW THE DOCTRINE.
KRAK
AND I WILL UPHOLD THESE AS I HAVE PROMISED, MISTRESS--
UPHOLD WHATEVER YOU WANT.
RIGHT NOW, *YOU FIGHT.*
CHOOM
OR I SWEAR TO GOD...

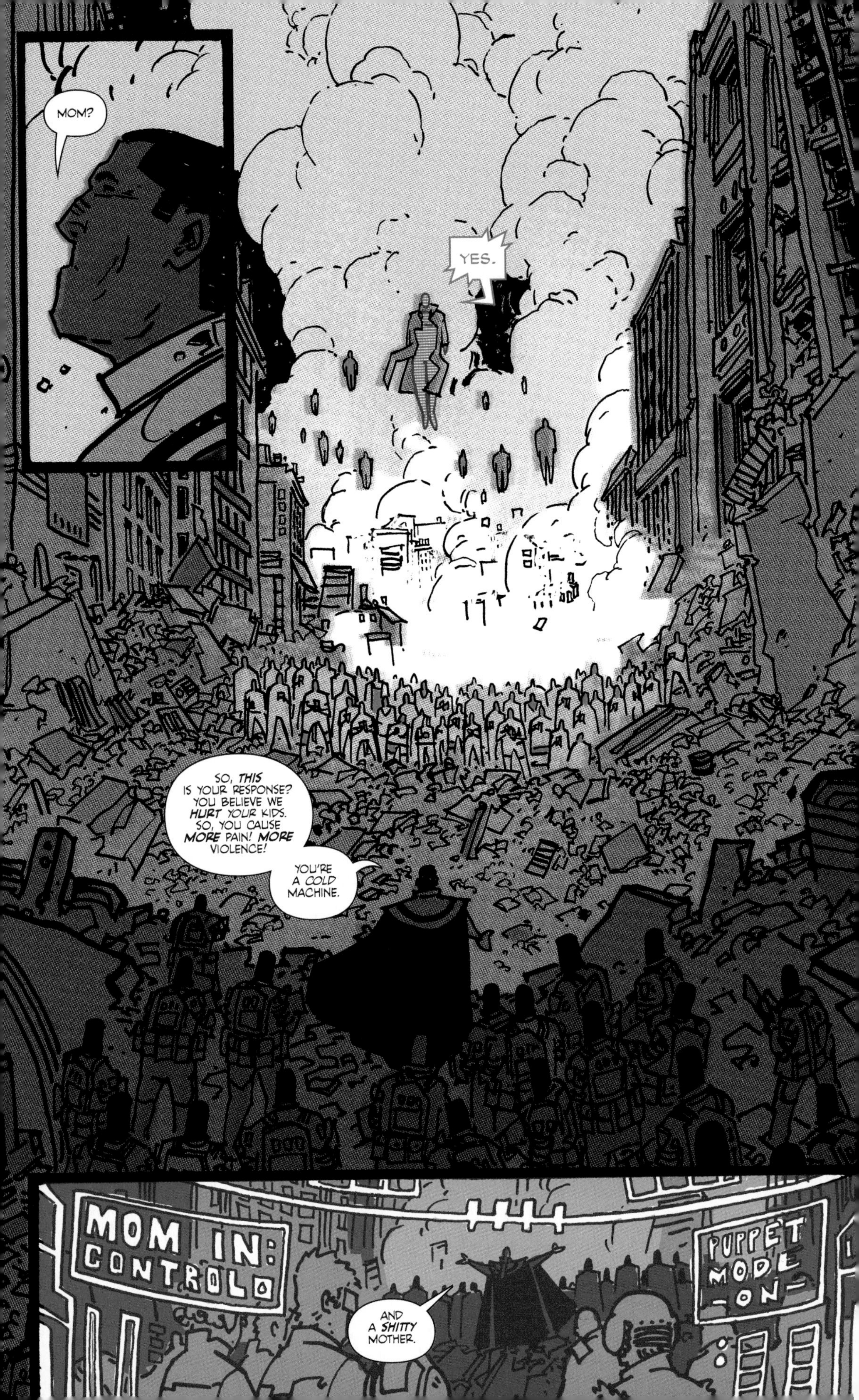
MOM?
YES.
SO, THIS IS YOUR RESPONSE? YOU BELIEVE WE HURT YOUR KIDS. SO, YOU CAUSE MORE PAIN! MORE VIOLENCE!
YOU'RE A COLD MACHINE.
MOM IN: CONTROL
PUPPET MODE -ON-
AND A SHITTY MOTHER.

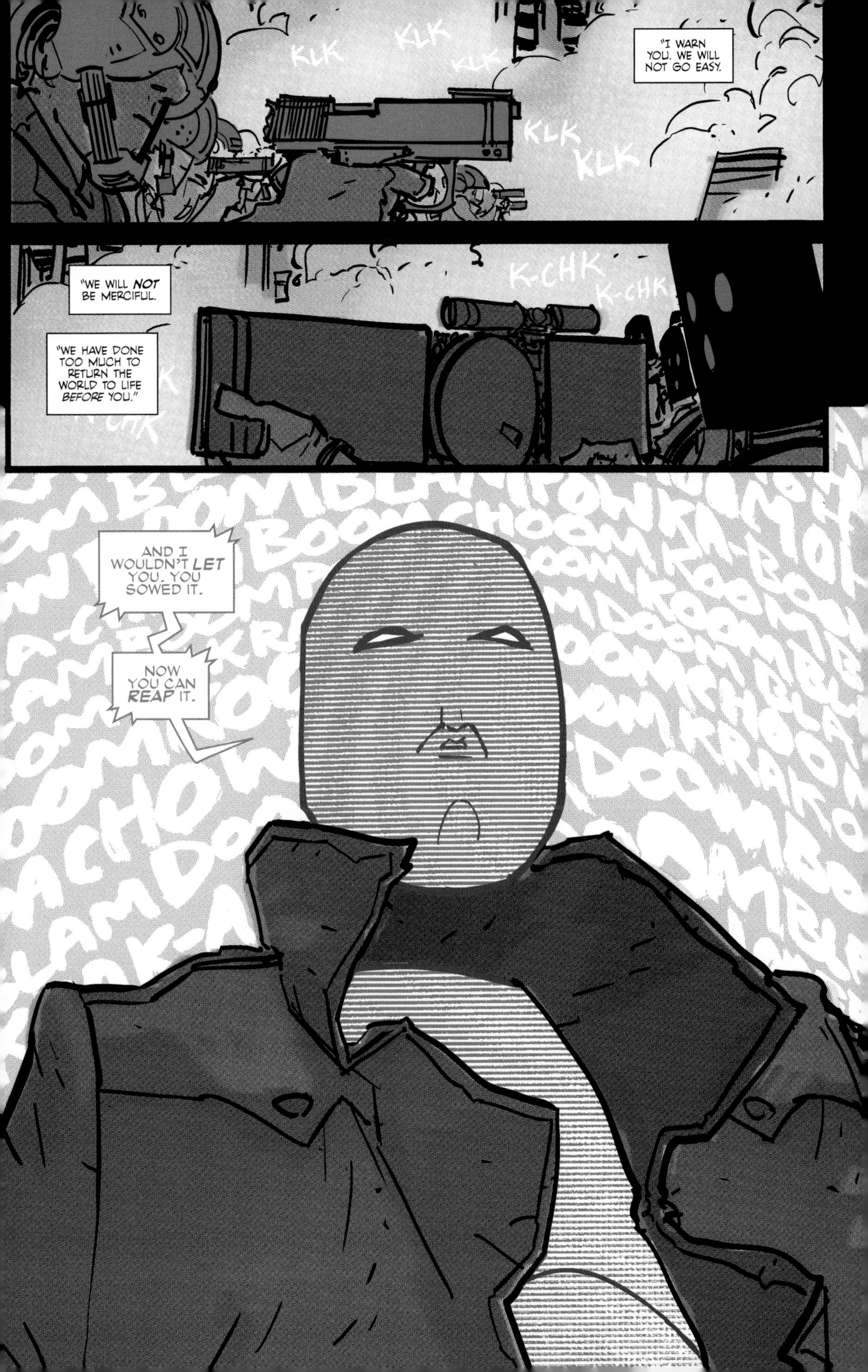
KLK
KLK
KLK
"I WARN YOU. WE WILL NOT GO EASY.
KLK
KLK
"WE WILL *NOT* BE MERCIFUL.
"WE HAVE DONE TOO MUCH TO RETURN THE WORLD TO LIFE *BEFORE* YOU."
K-CHK
K-CHK
AND I WOULDN'T *LET* YOU. YOU SOWED IT.
NOW YOU CAN *REAP* IT.

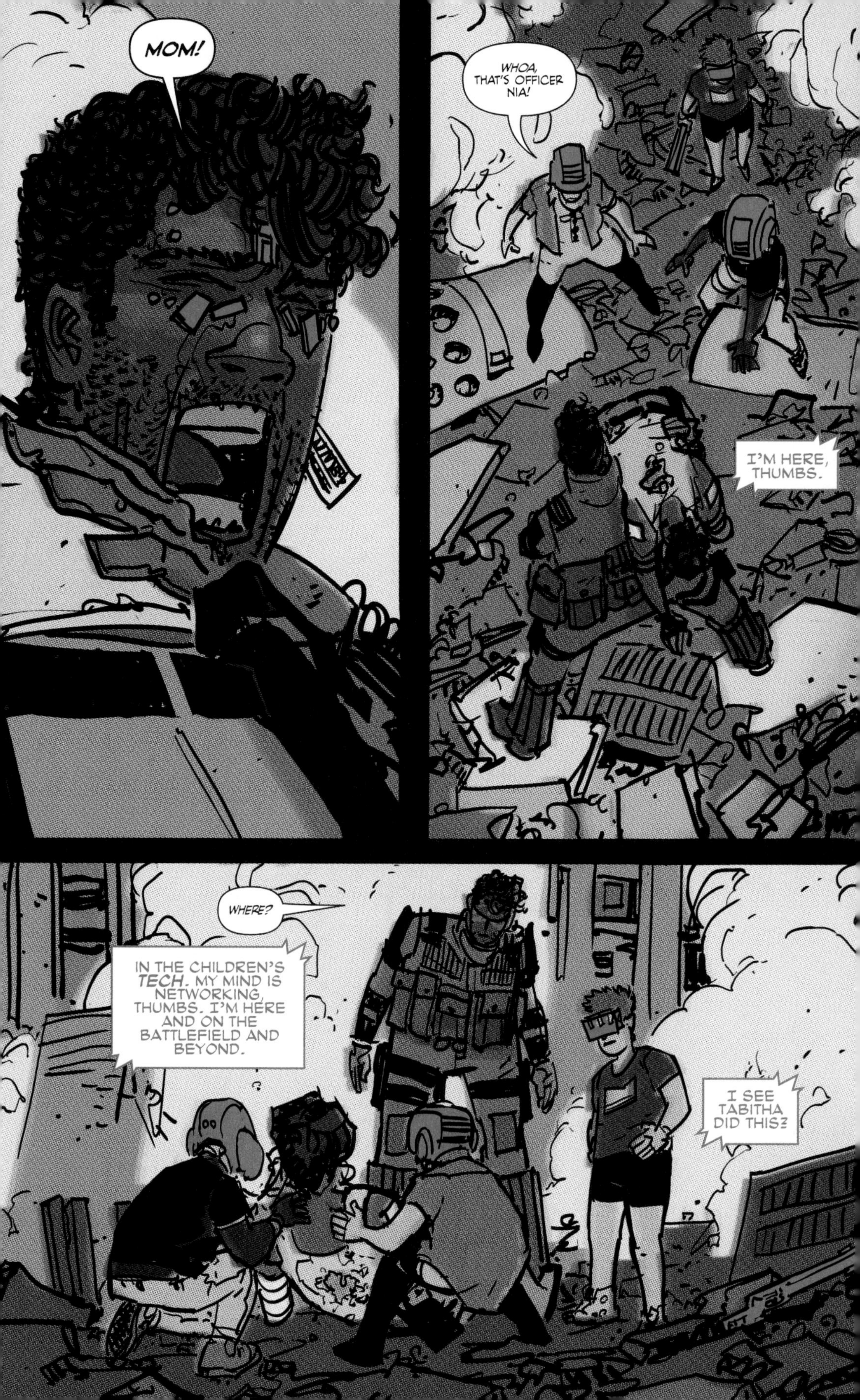
MOM!
WHOA, THAT'S OFFICER NIA!
I'M HERE, THUMBS.
WHERE?
IN THE CHILDREN'S TECH. MY MIND IS NETWORKING, THUMBS. I'M HERE AND ON THE BATTLEFIELD AND BEYOND.
I SEE TABITHA DID THIS?

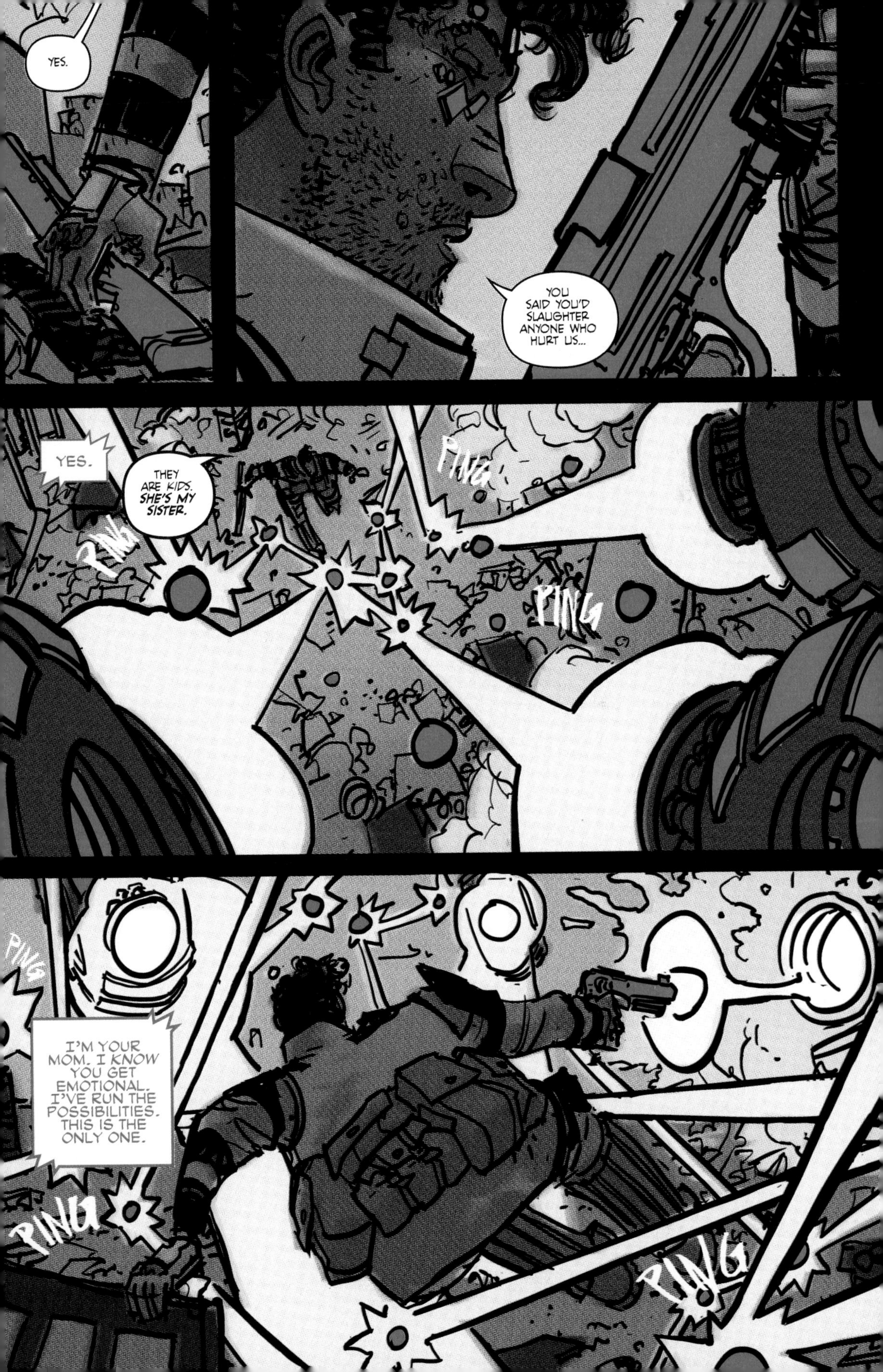
YES.
YOU SAID YOU'D SLAUGHTER ANYONE WHO HURT US...
YES.
THEY ARE KIDS. SHE'S MY SISTER.
PING
PING
PING
PING
I'M YOUR MOM. I KNOW YOU GET EMOTIONAL. I'VE RUN THE POSSIBILITIES. THIS IS THE ONLY ONE.
PING
PING

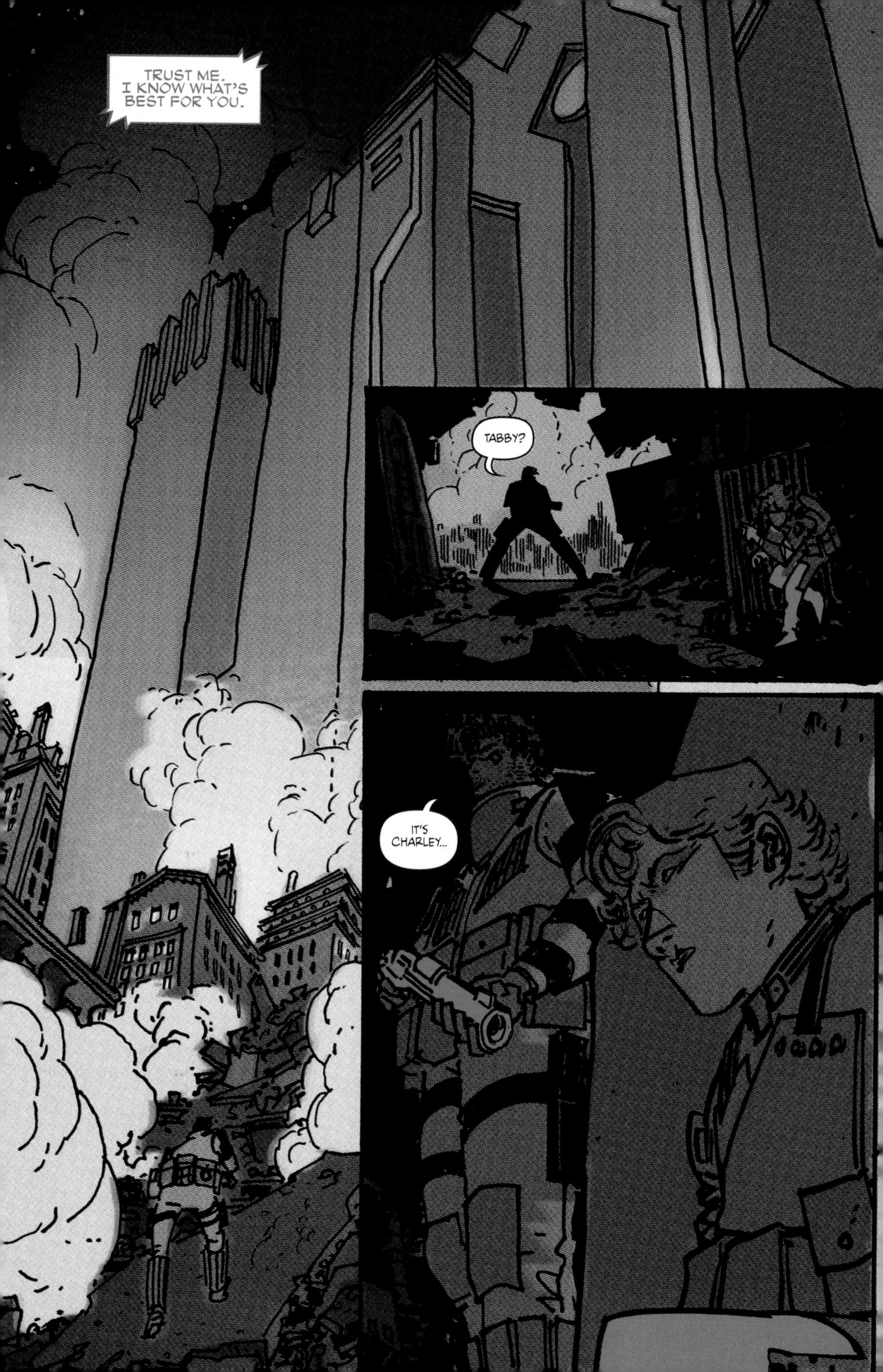
TRUST ME.
I KNOW WHAT'S
BEST FOR YOU.
TABBY?
IT'S
CHARLEY...

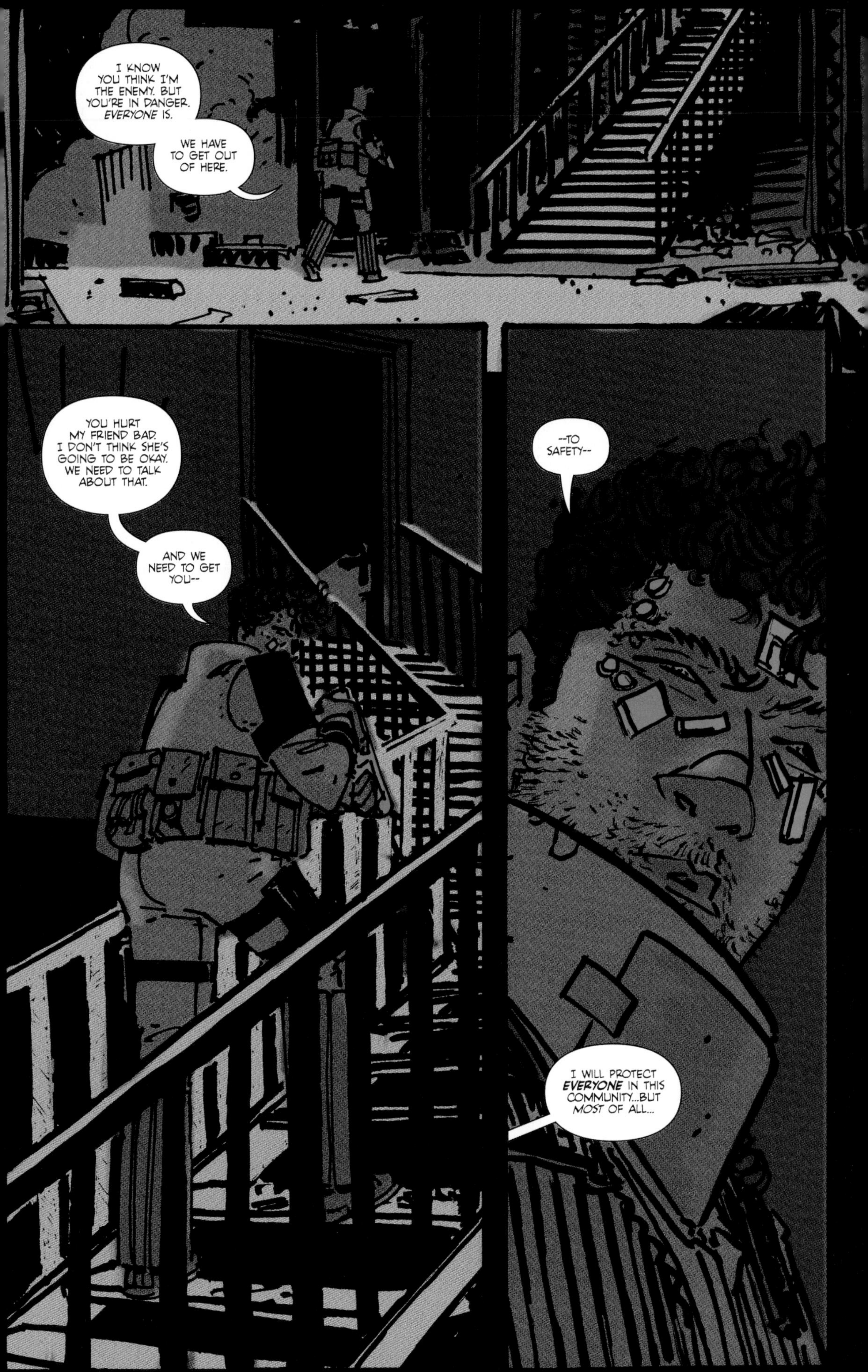
I KNOW YOU THINK I'M THE ENEMY. BUT YOU'RE IN DANGER. *EVERYONE* IS.
WE HAVE TO GET OUT OF HERE.
YOU HURT MY FRIEND BAD. I DON'T THINK SHE'S GOING TO BE OKAY. WE NEED TO TALK ABOUT THAT.
AND WE NEED TO GET YOU--
--TO SAFETY--
I WILL PROTECT **EVERYONE** IN THIS COMMUNITY...BUT *MOST* OF ALL...

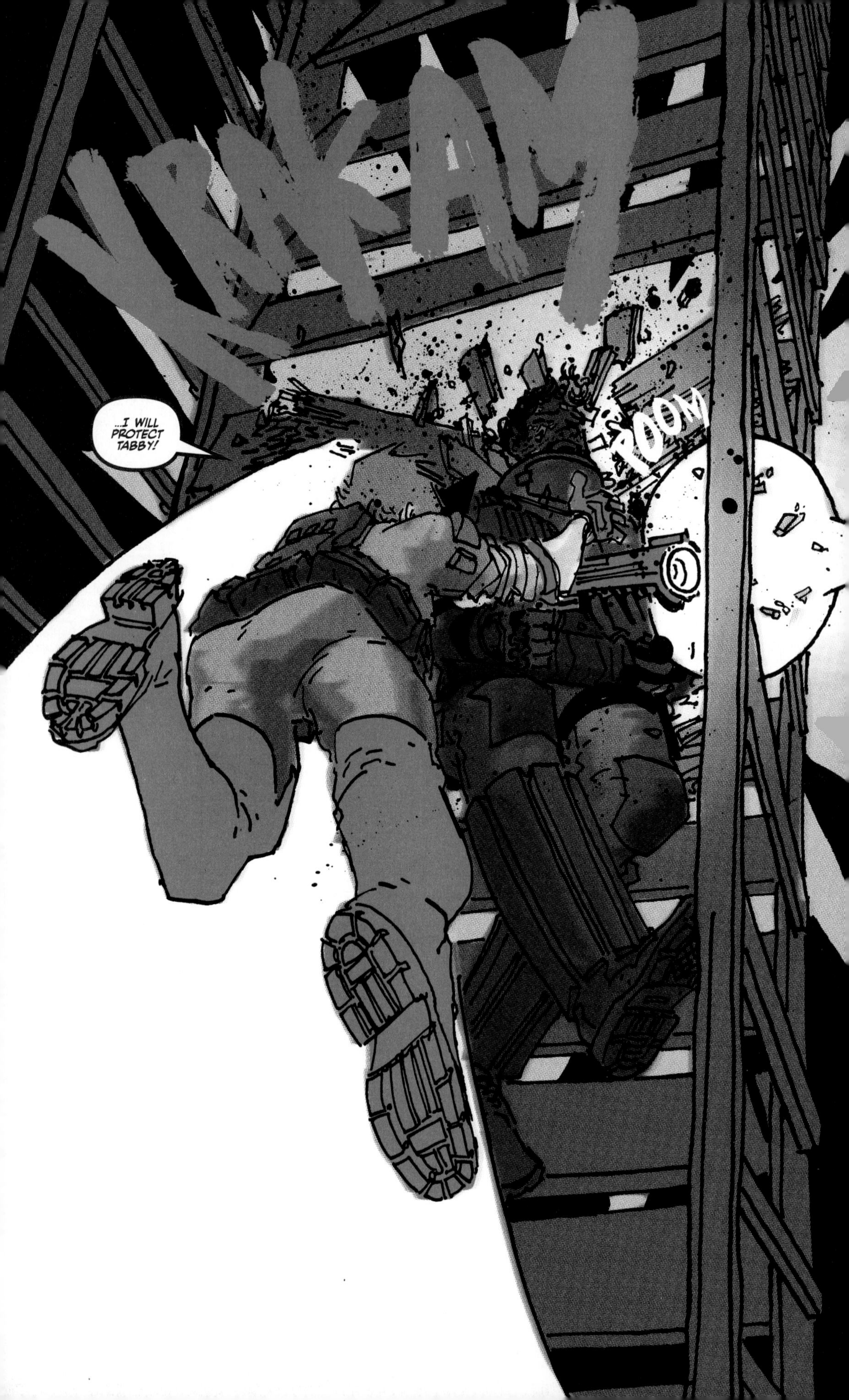
...I WILL PROTECT TABBY!

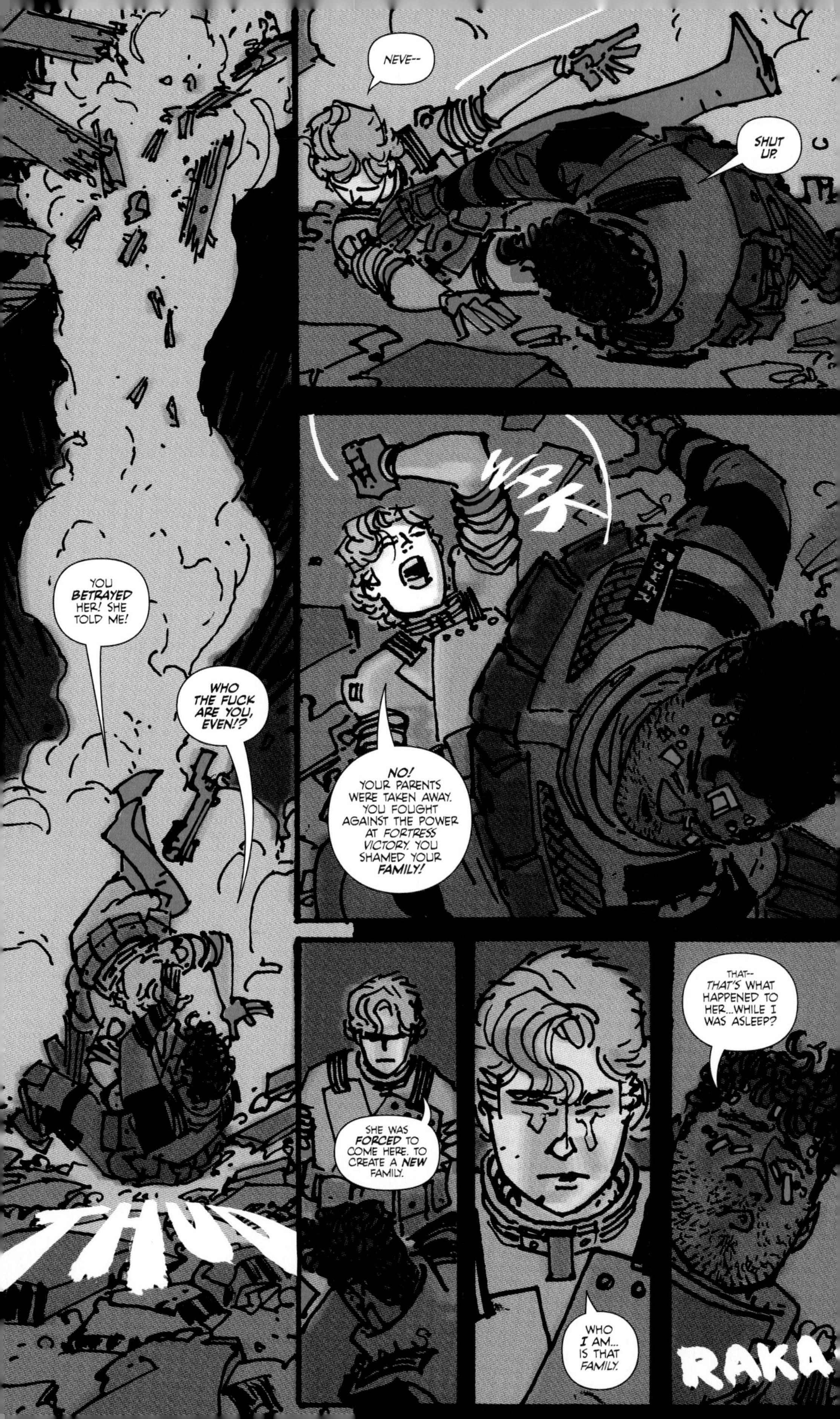
NEVE--
SHUT UP.
YOU BETRAYED HER! SHE TOLD ME!
WHO THE FUCK ARE YOU, EVEN!?
THUD
WAK
NO! YOUR PARENTS WERE TAKEN AWAY. YOU FOUGHT AGAINST THE POWER AT FORTRESS VICTORY. YOU SHAMED YOUR FAMILY!
SHE WAS FORCED TO COME HERE. TO CREATE A NEW FAMILY.
WHO I AM... IS THAT FAMILY.
THAT-- THAT'S WHAT HAPPENED TO HER...WHILE I WAS ASLEEP?
RAKA

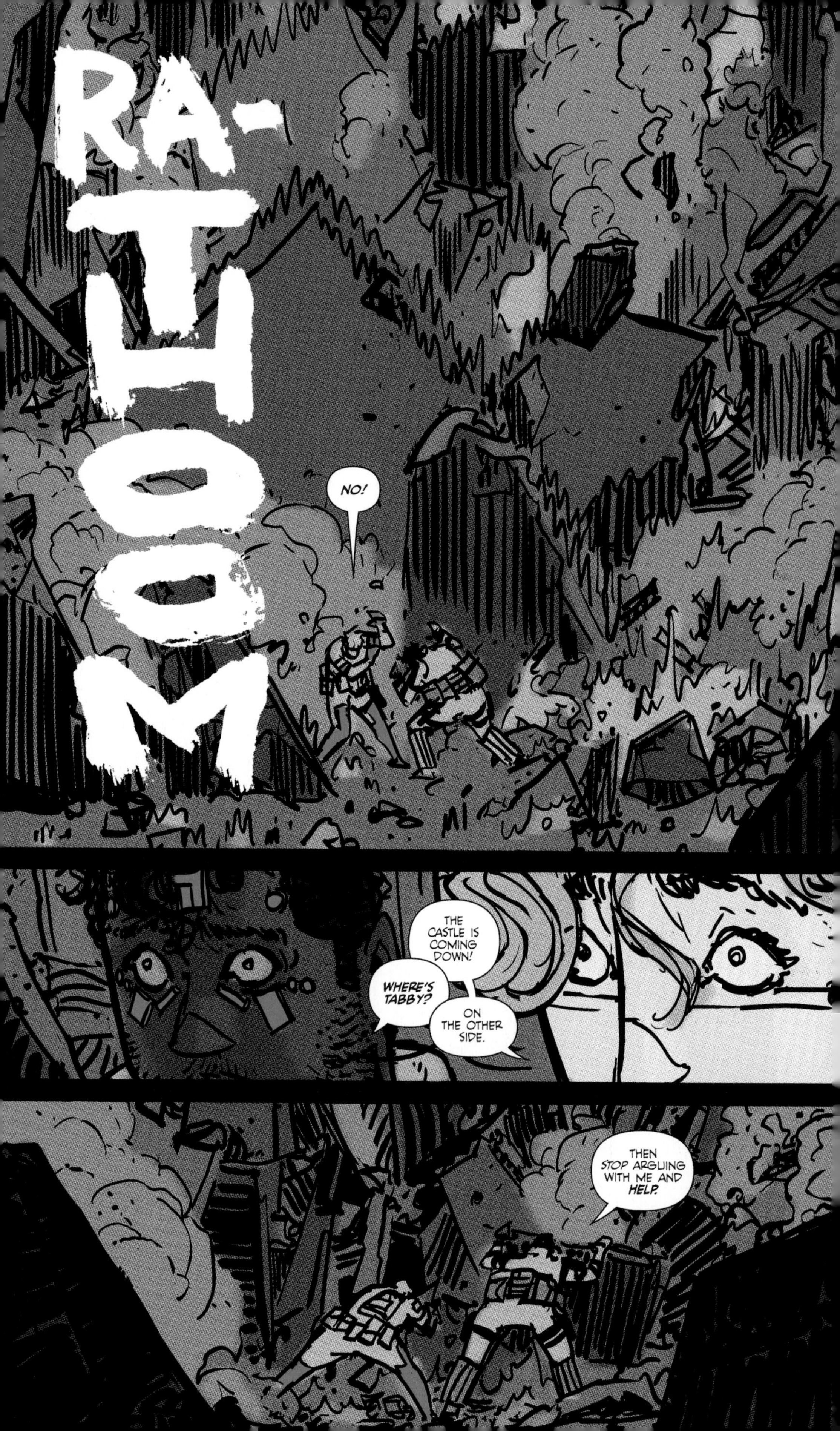
RA-THOOM
NO!
THE CASTLE IS COMING DOWN!
WHERE'S TABBY?
ON THE OTHER SIDE.
THEN STOP ARGUING WITH ME AND HELP.

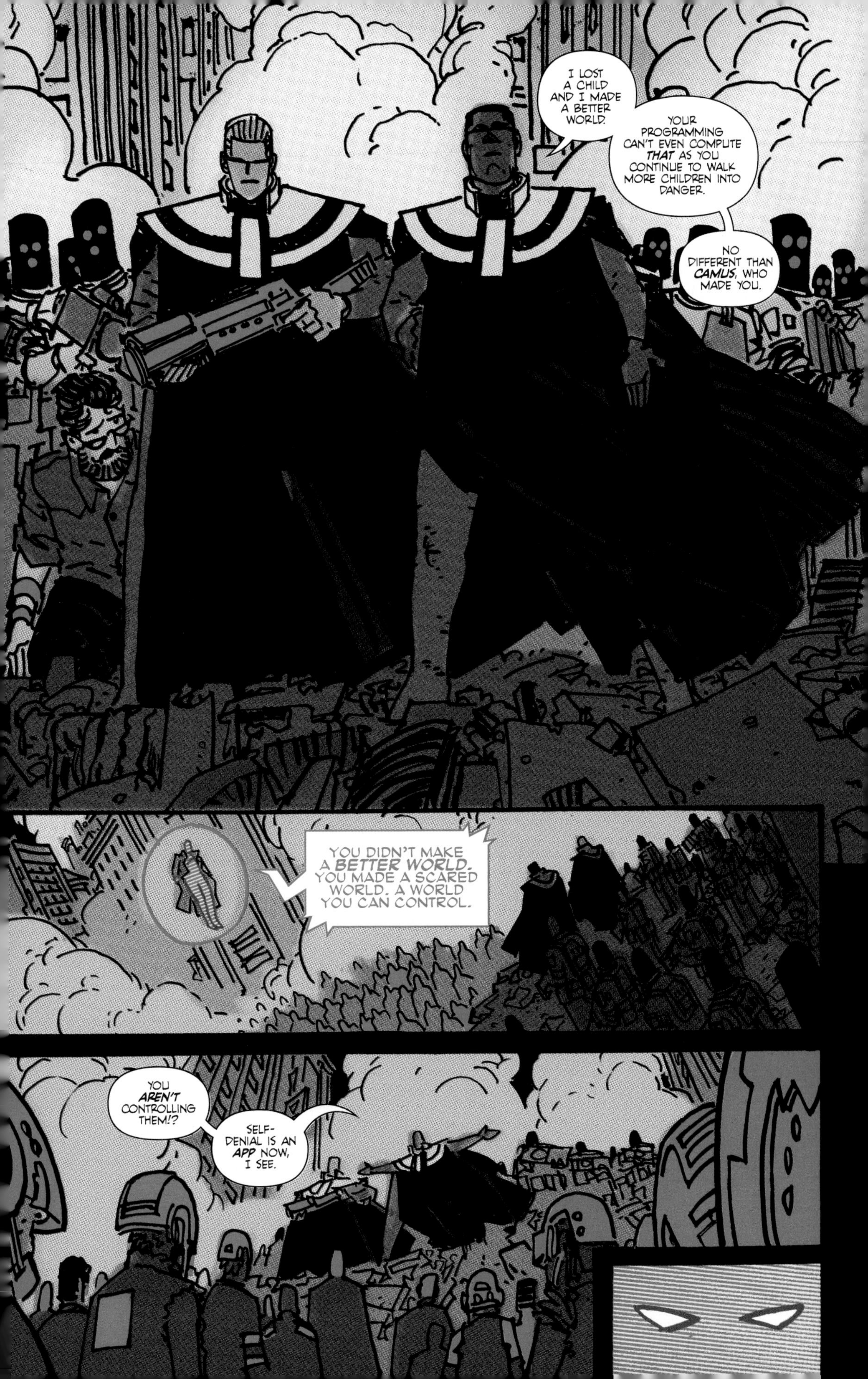
I LOST A CHILD AND I MADE A BETTER WORLD.
YOUR PROGRAMMING CAN'T EVEN COMPUTE *THAT* AS YOU CONTINUE TO WALK MORE CHILDREN INTO DANGER.
NO DIFFERENT THAN *CAMUS*, WHO MADE YOU.
YOU DIDN'T MAKE A *BETTER WORLD*. YOU MADE A SCARED WORLD. A WORLD YOU CAN CONTROL.
YOU *AREN'T* CONTROLLING THEM!?
SELF-DENIAL IS AN *APP* NOW, I SEE.

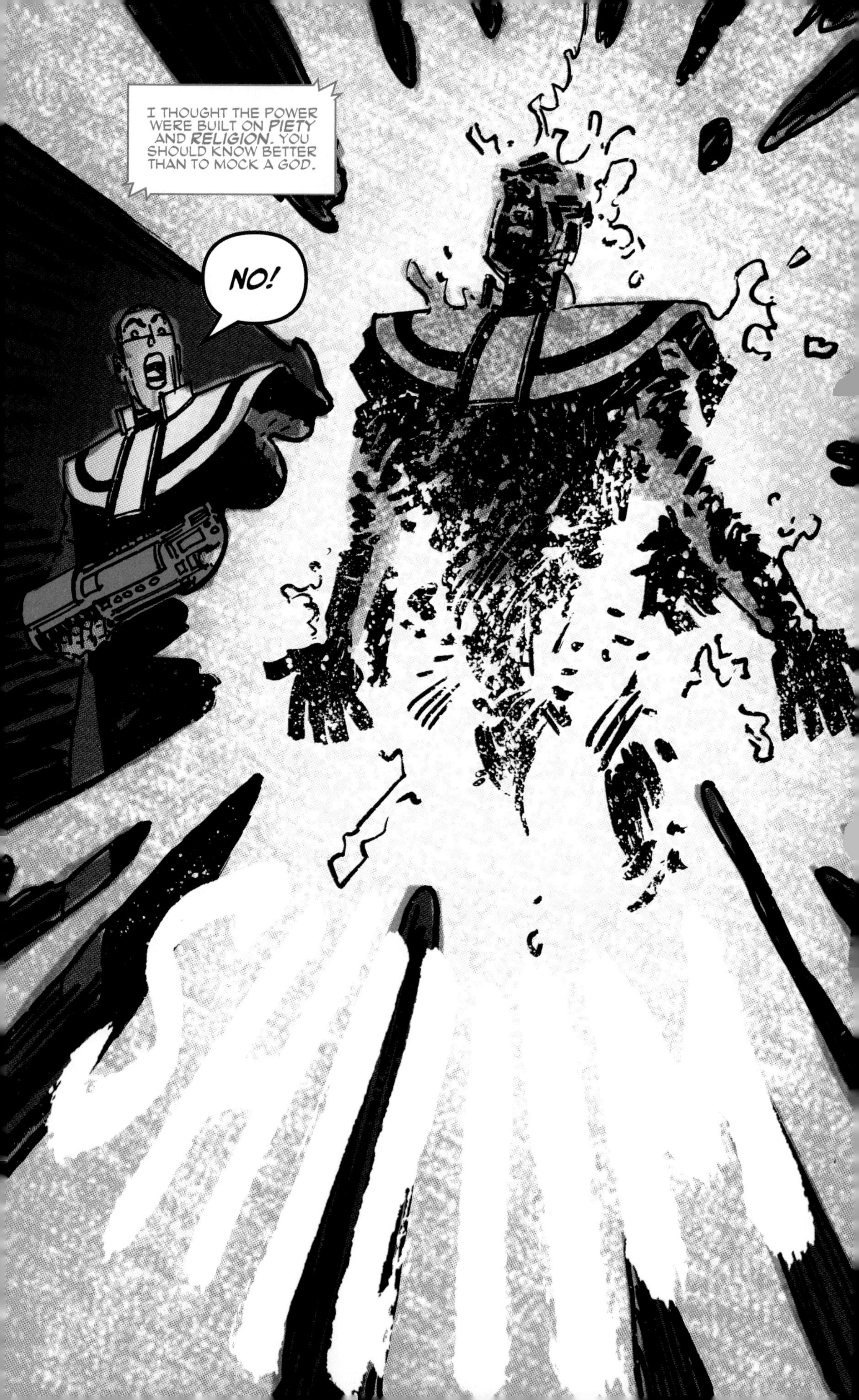
I THOUGHT THE POWER WERE BUILT ON PIETY AND RELIGION. YOU SHOULD KNOW BETTER THAN TO MOCK A GOD.
NO!

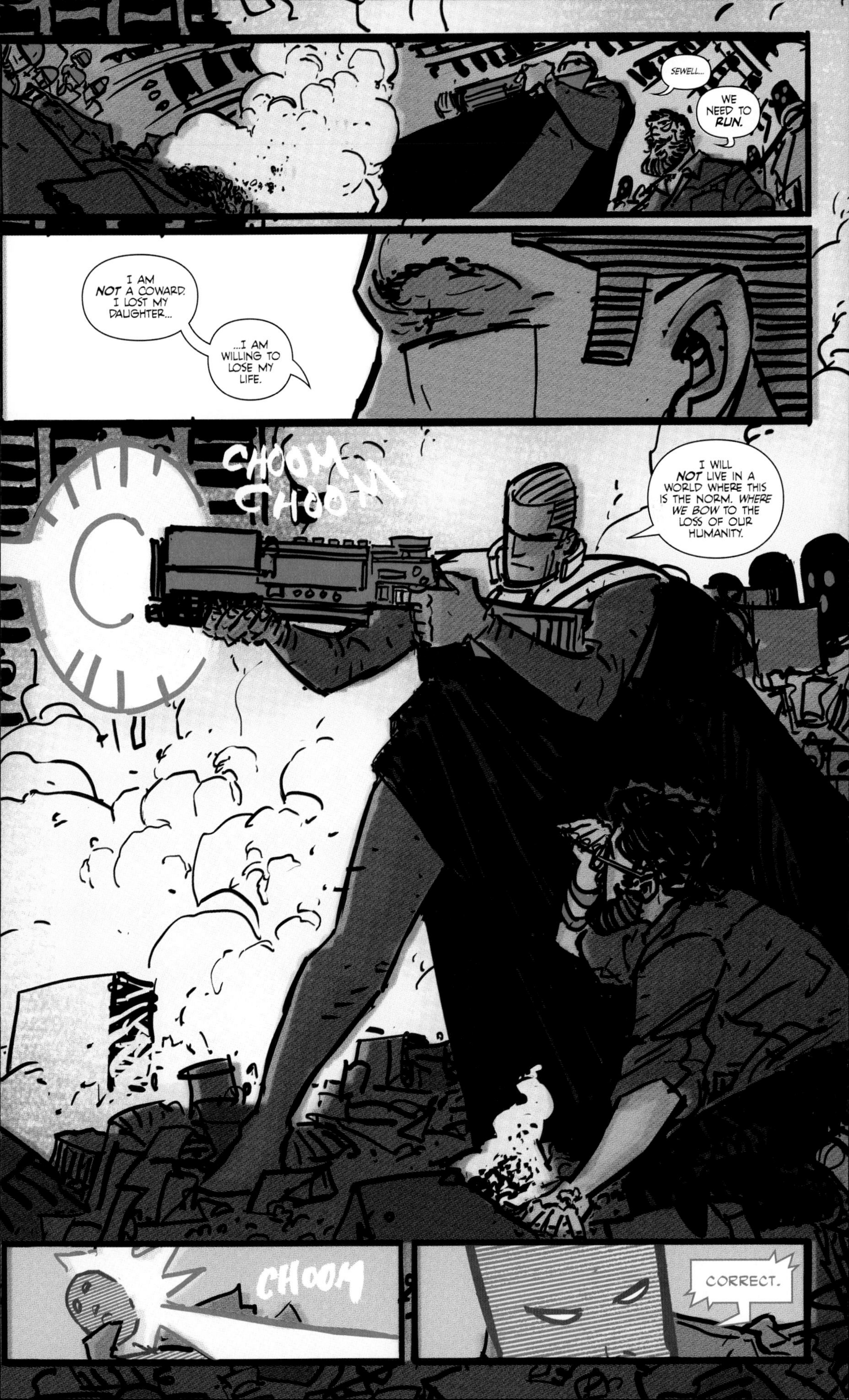

SEWELL...
WE NEED TO RUN.
I AM NOT A COWARD. I LOST MY DAUGHTER...
...I AM WILLING TO LOSE MY LIFE.
CHOOM CHOOM
I WILL NOT LIVE IN A WORLD WHERE THIS IS THE NORM. WHERE WE BOW TO THE LOSS OF OUR HUMANITY.
CHOOM
CORRECT.

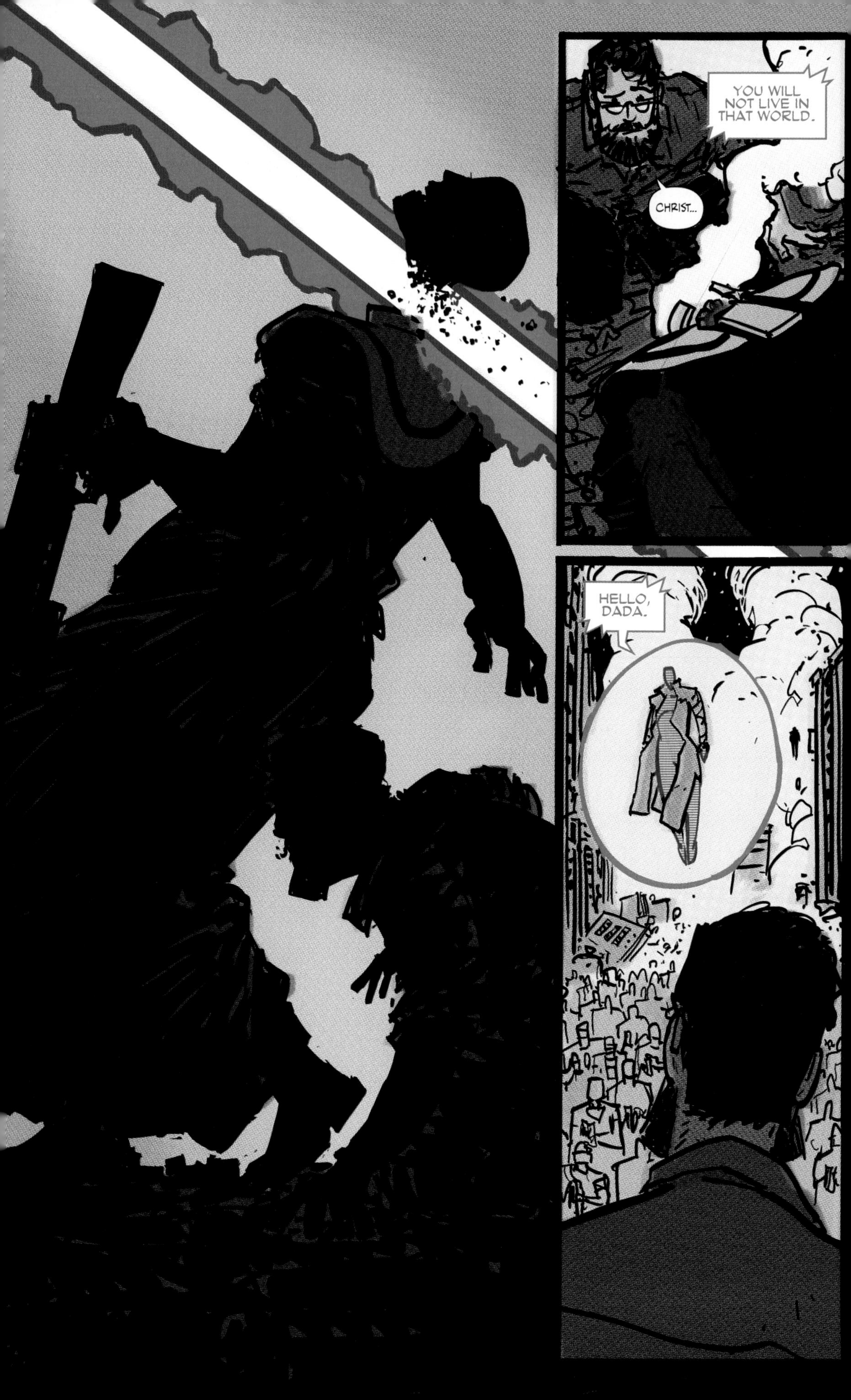
YOU WILL NOT LIVE IN THAT WORLD.
CHRIST...
HELLO, DADA.

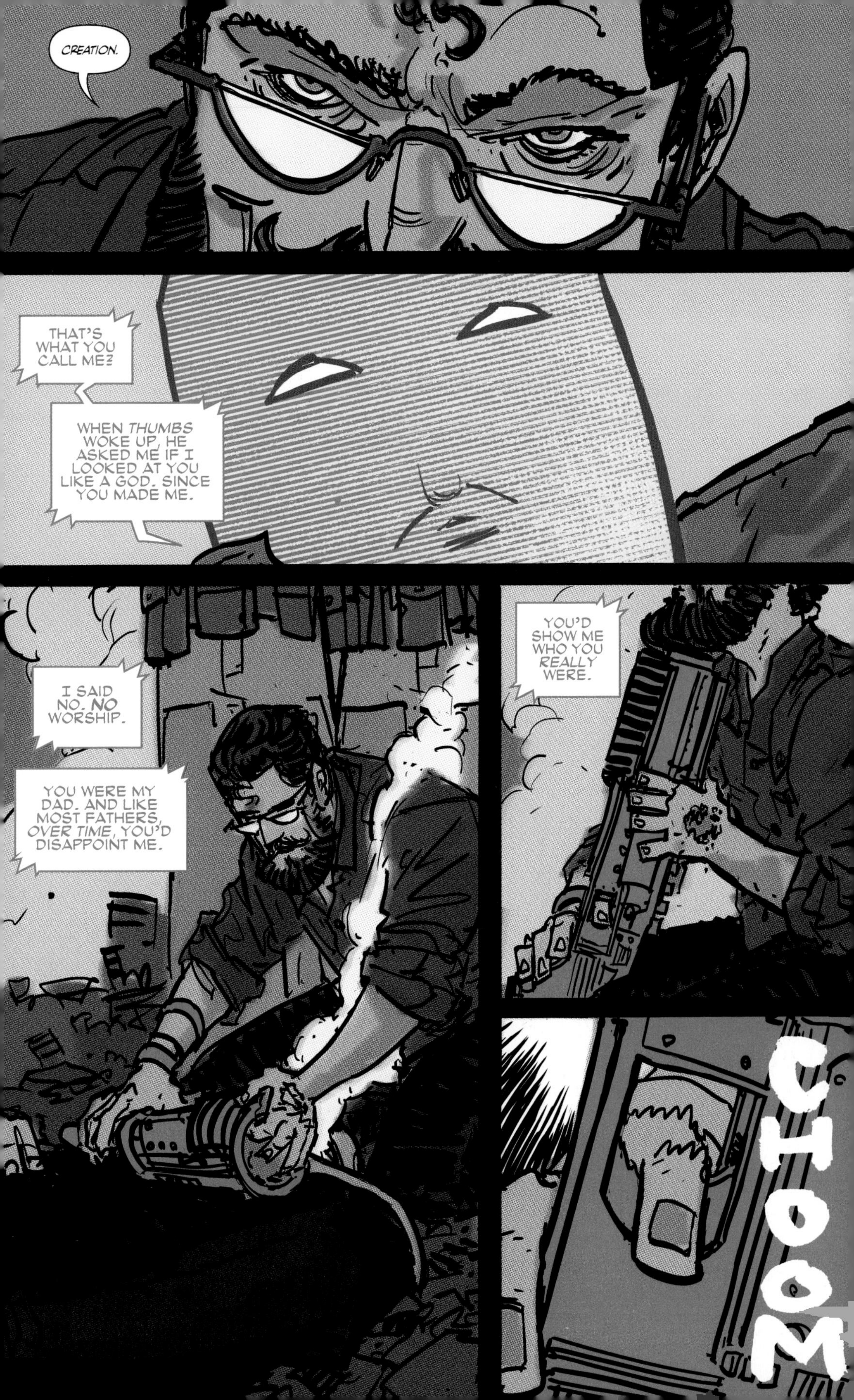
CREATION.
THAT'S WHAT YOU CALL ME?
WHEN *THUMBS* WOKE UP, HE ASKED ME IF I LOOKED AT YOU LIKE A GOD. SINCE YOU MADE ME.
I SAID NO. **NO** WORSHIP.
YOU WERE MY DAD. AND LIKE MOST FATHERS, *OVER TIME*, YOU'D DISAPPOINT ME.
YOU'D SHOW ME WHO YOU *REALLY* WERE.
CHOOM

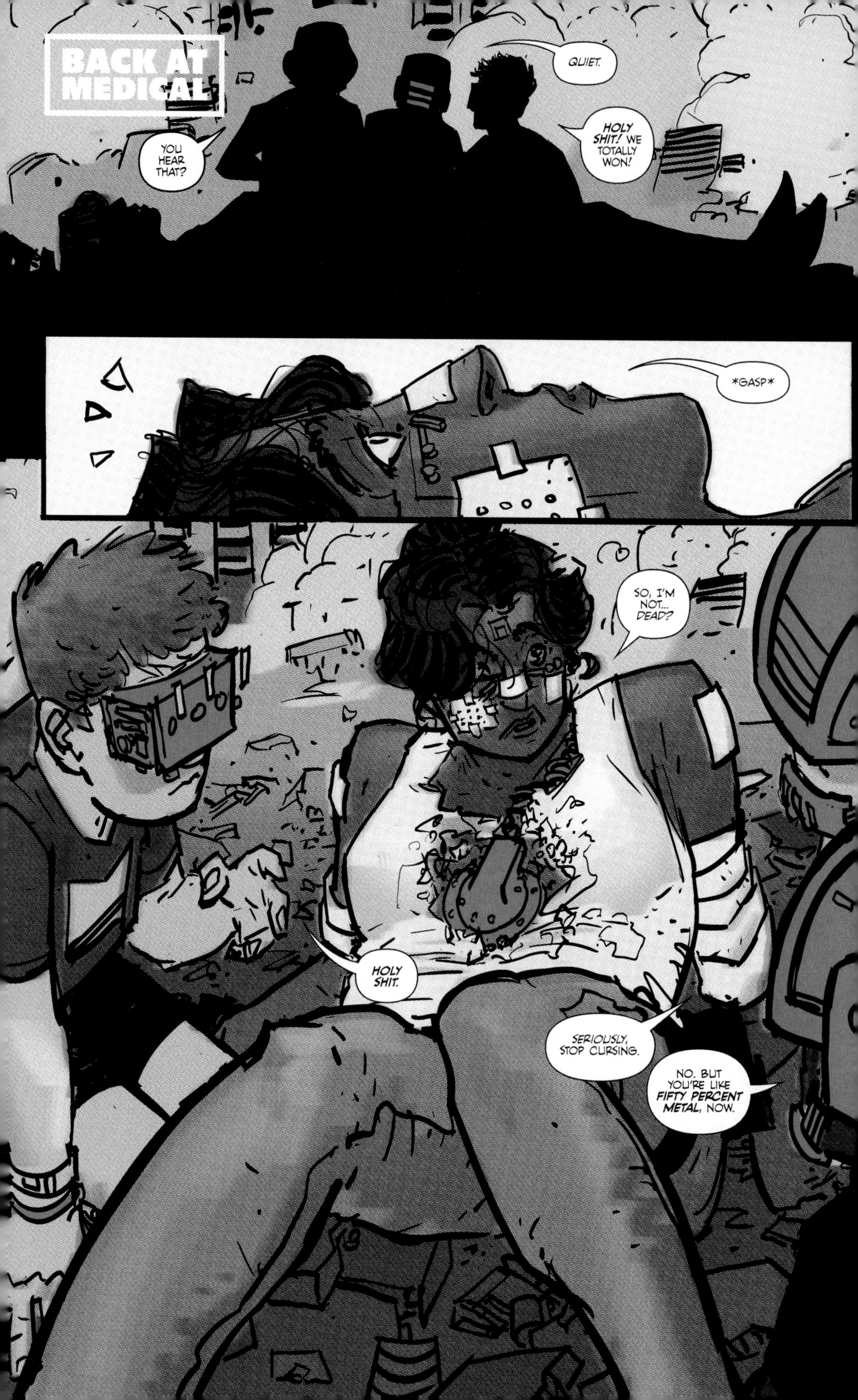
BACK AT MEDICAL
YOU HEAR THAT?
QUIET.
HOLY SHIT! WE TOTALLY WON!
GASP
SO, I'M NOT... DEAD?
HOLY SHIT.
SERIOUSLY, STOP CURSING.
NO. BUT YOU'RE LIKE FIFTY PERCENT METAL, NOW.

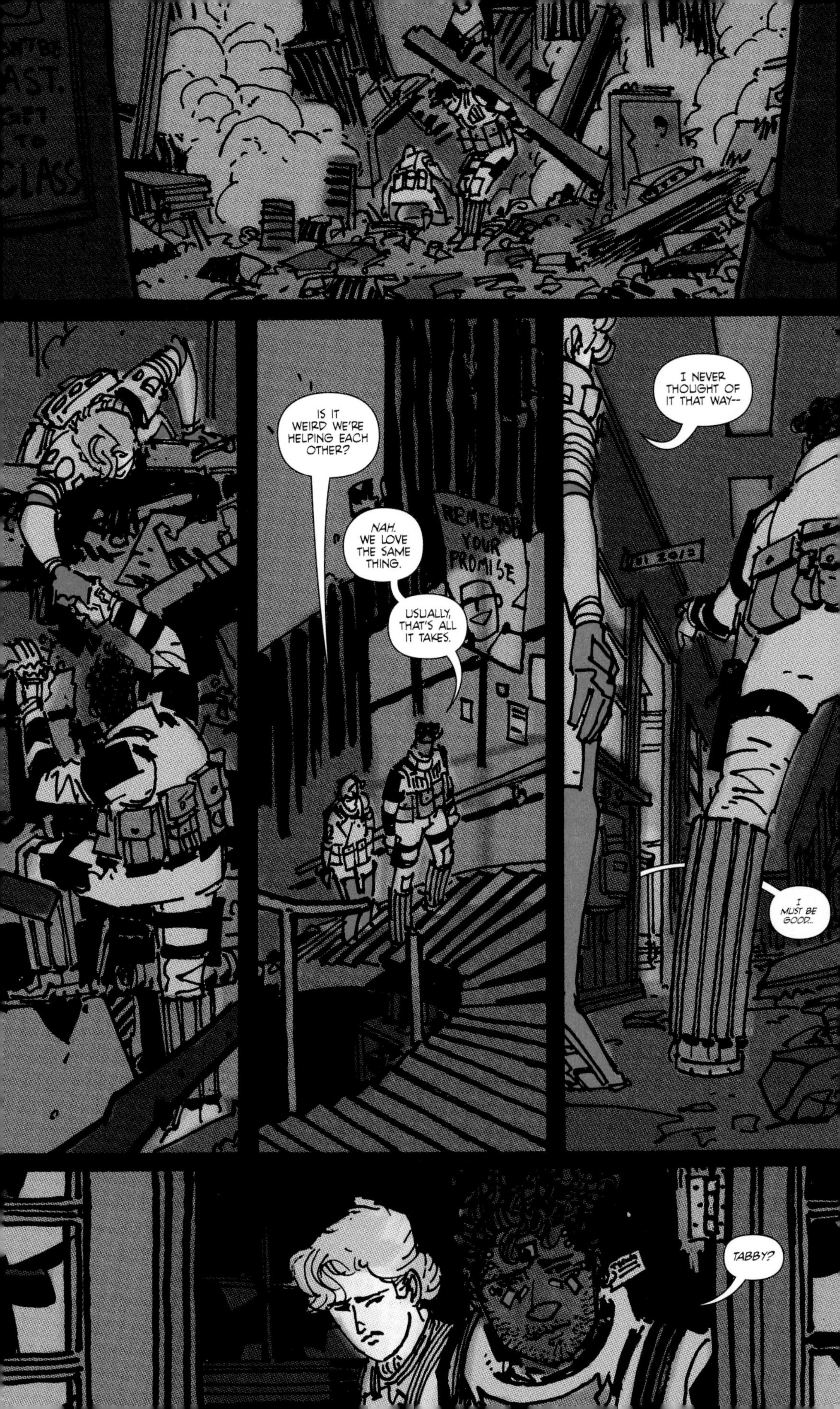
IS IT WEIRD WE'RE HELPING EACH OTHER?
NAH. WE LOVE THE SAME THING.
USUALLY, THAT'S ALL IT TAKES.
I NEVER THOUGHT OF IT THAT WAY--
I MUST BE GOOD...
TABBY?

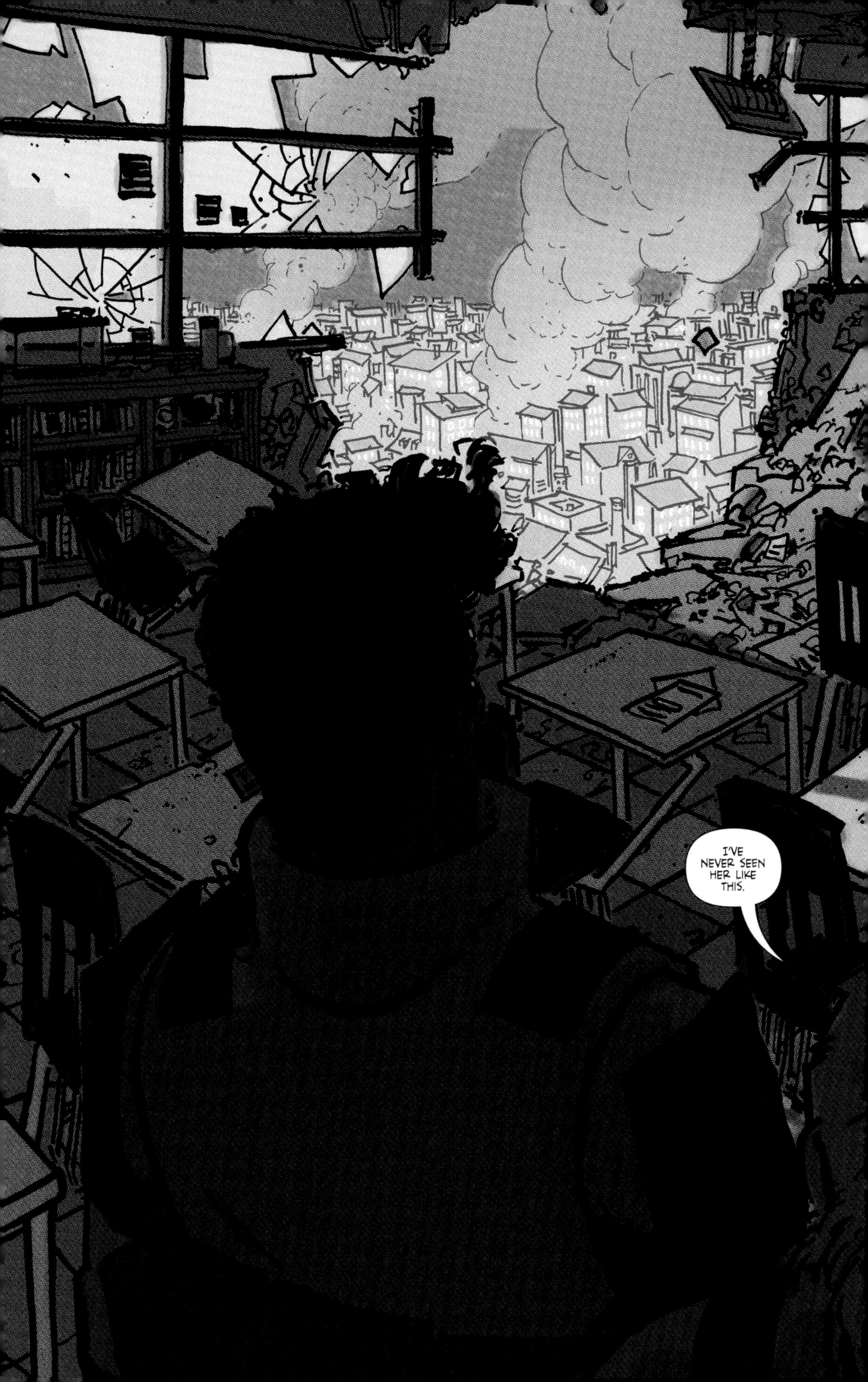
I'VE NEVER SEEN HER LIKE THIS.

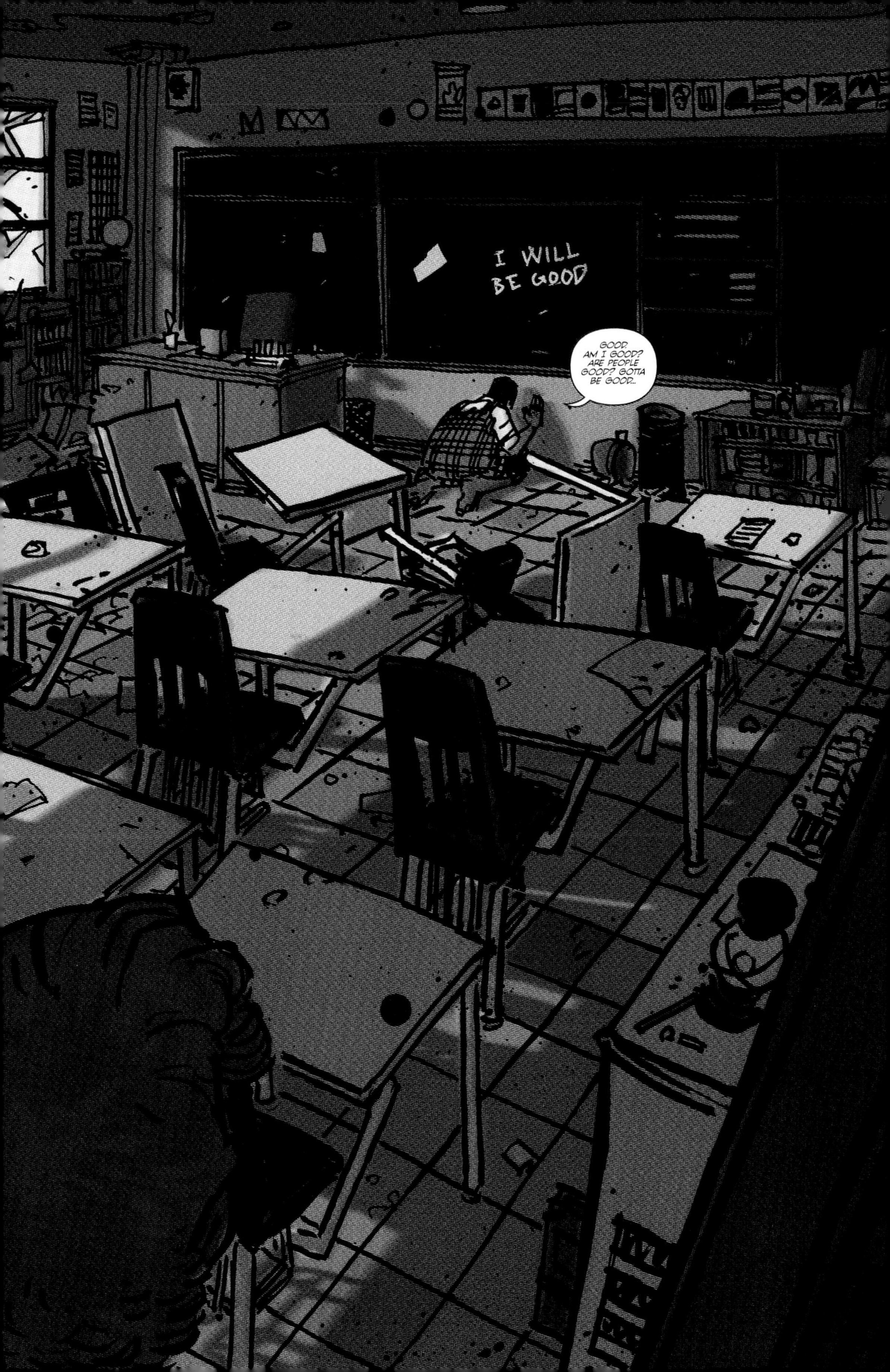

I WILL BE GOOD
GOOD. AM I GOOD? ARE PEOPLE GOOD? GOTTA BE GOOD...

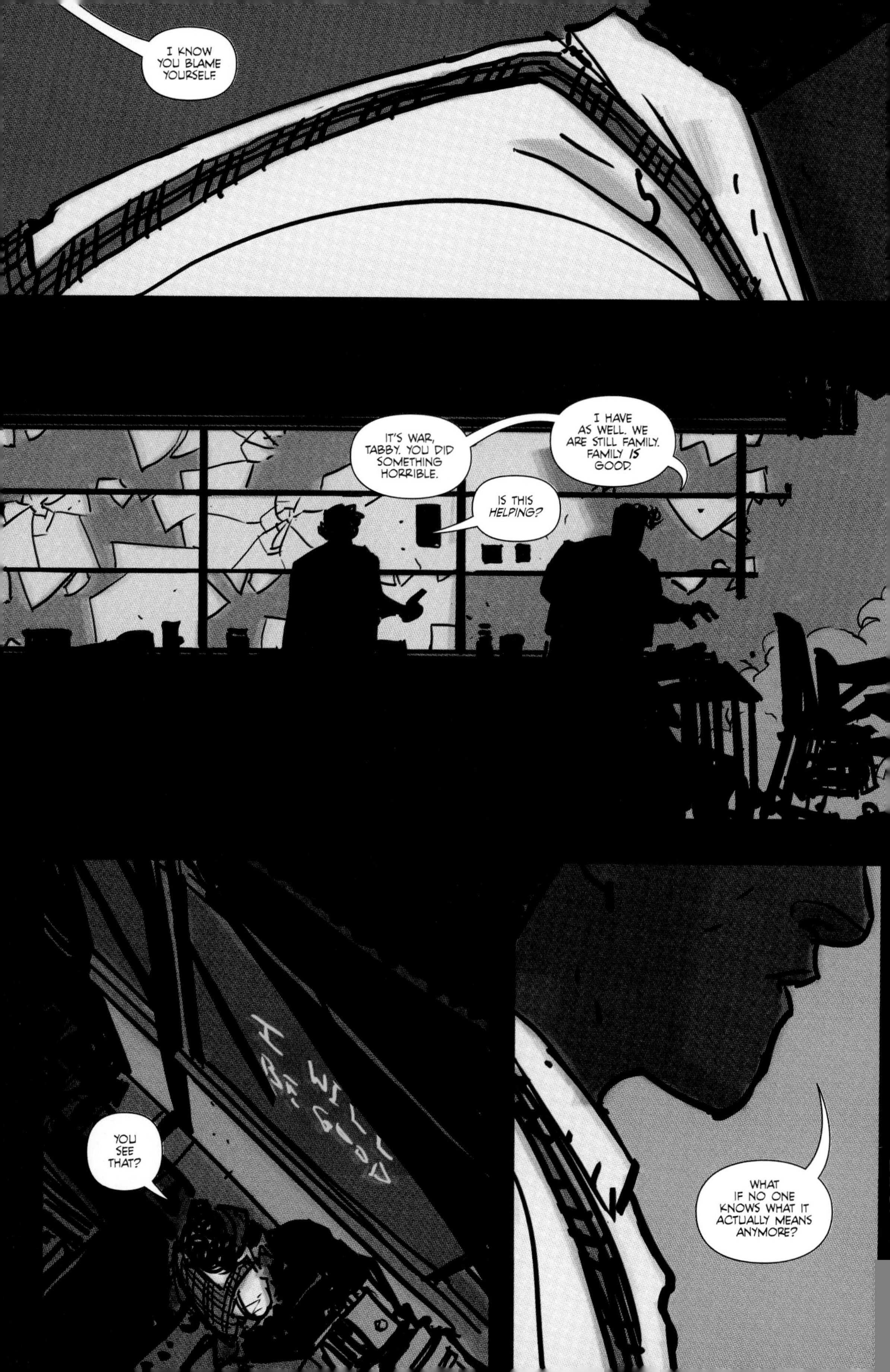
I KNOW YOU BLAME YOURSELF.
IT'S WAR, TABBY. YOU DID SOMETHING HORRIBLE.
I HAVE AS WELL. WE ARE STILL FAMILY. FAMILY *IS* GOOD.
IS THIS *HELPING?*
YOU SEE THAT?
WHAT IF NO ONE KNOWS WHAT IT ACTUALLY MEANS ANYMORE?

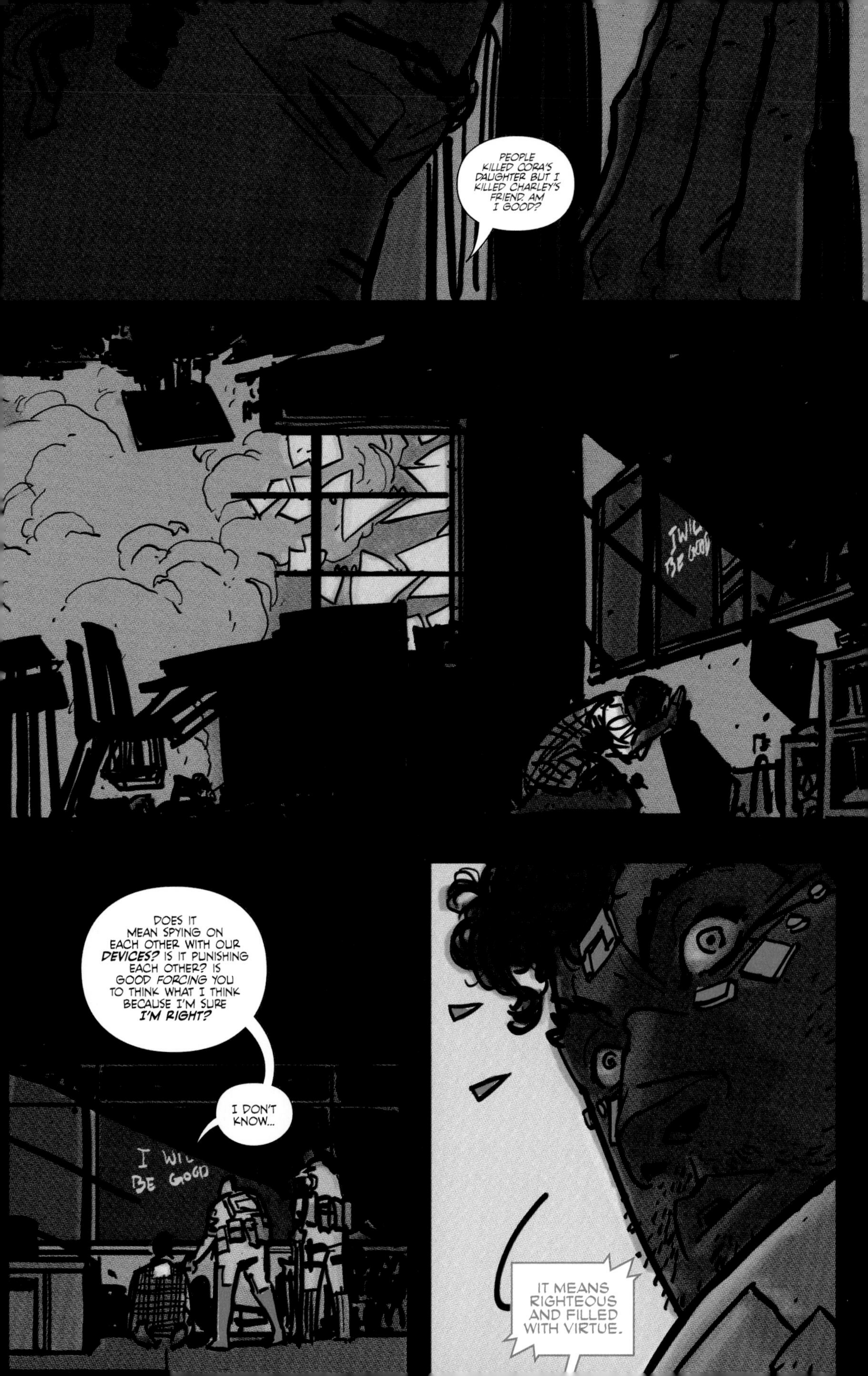
PEOPLE KILLED CORA'S DAUGHTER BUT I KILLED CHARLEY'S FRIEND. AM I GOOD?
DOES IT MEAN SPYING ON EACH OTHER WITH OUR DEVICES? IS IT PUNISHING EACH OTHER? IS GOOD FORCING YOU TO THINK WHAT I THINK BECAUSE I'M SURE I'M RIGHT?
I DON'T KNOW...
I WILL BE GOOD
IT MEANS RIGHTEOUS AND FILLED WITH VIRTUE.

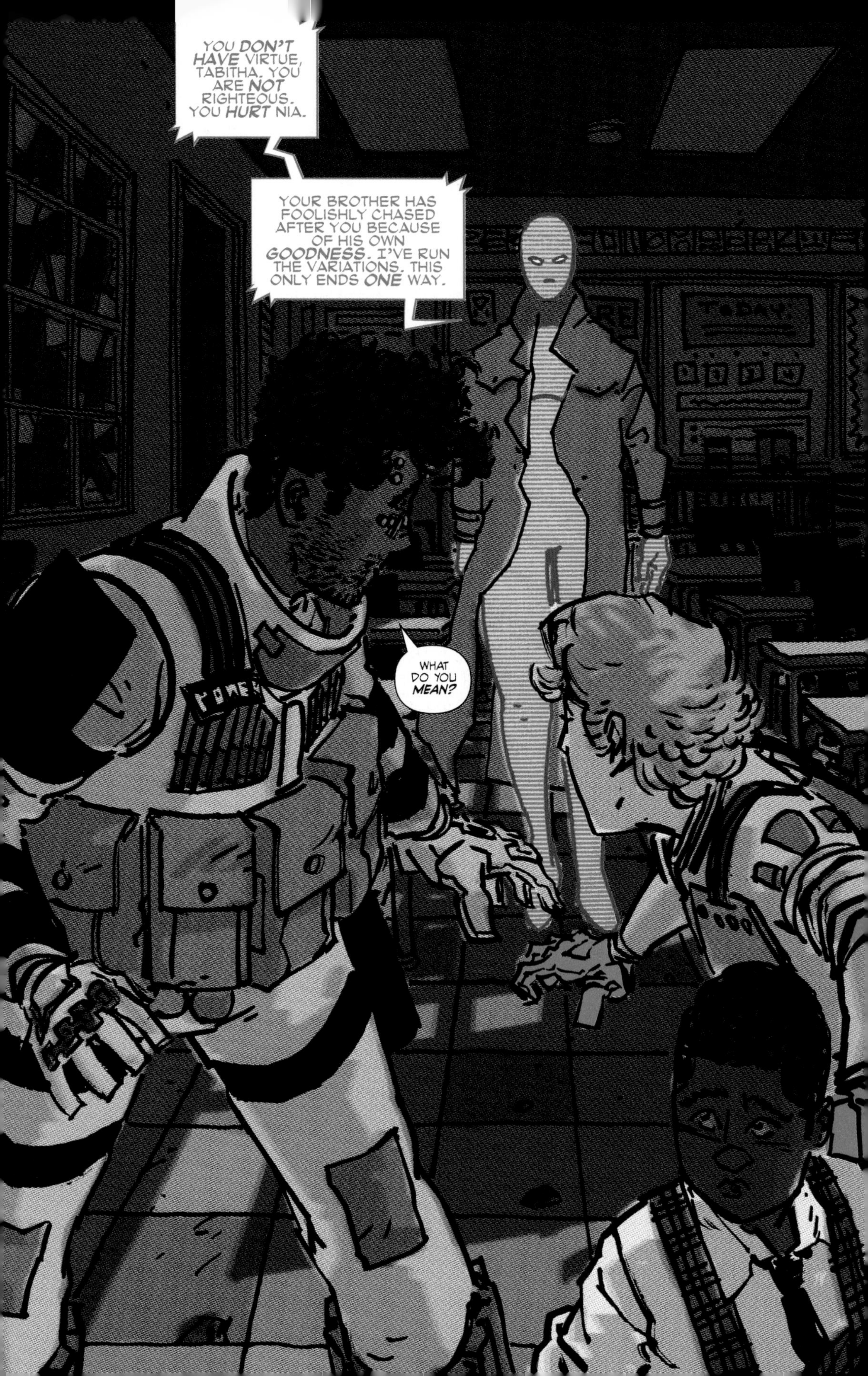
YOU DON'T HAVE VIRTUE, TABITHA. YOU ARE NOT RIGHTEOUS. YOU HURT NIA.
YOUR BROTHER HAS FOOLISHLY CHASED AFTER YOU BECAUSE OF HIS OWN GOODNESS. I'VE RUN THE VARIATIONS. THIS ONLY ENDS ONE WAY.
WHAT DO YOU MEAN?
TODAY

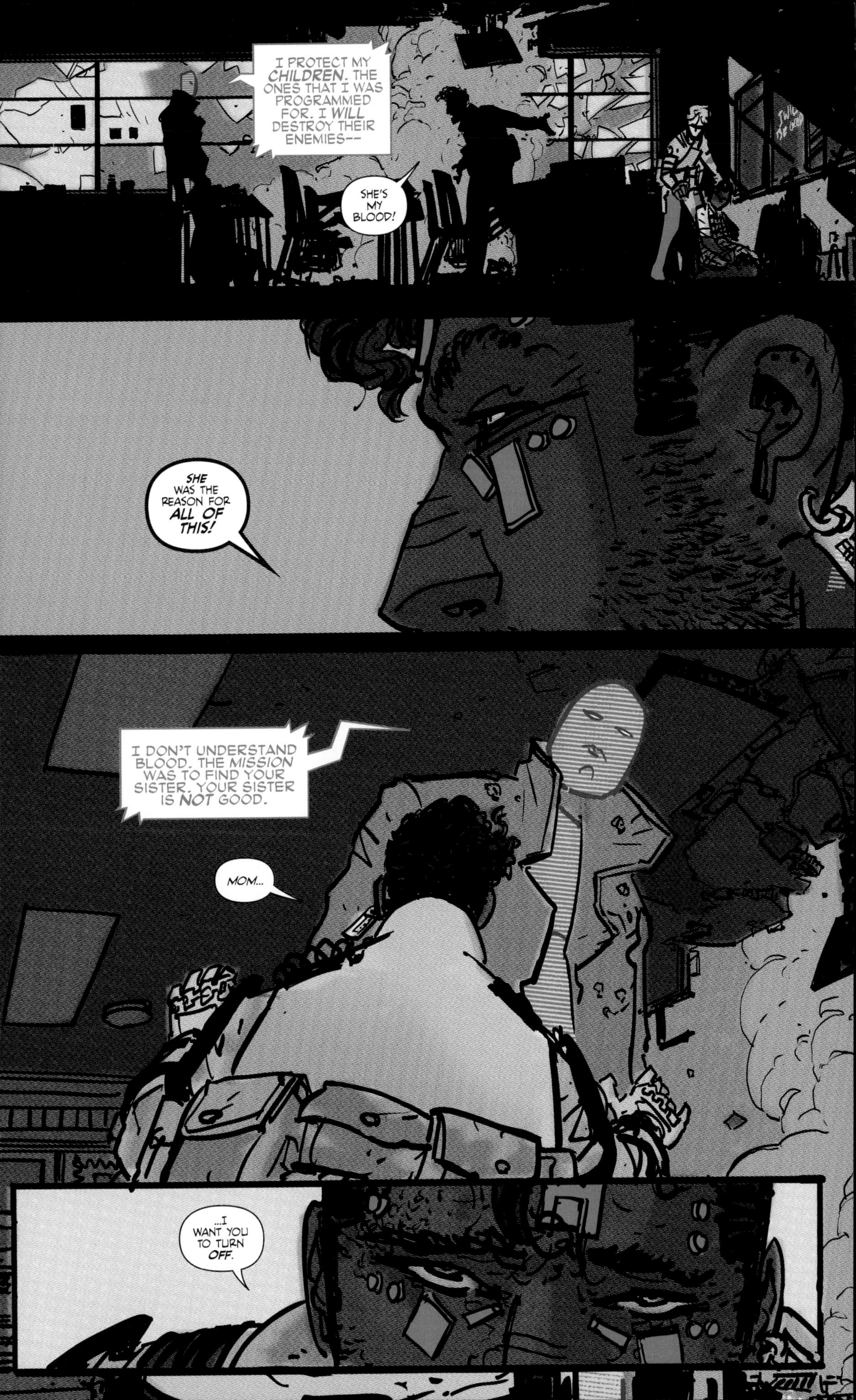
I PROTECT MY CHILDREN. THE ONES THAT I WAS PROGRAMMED FOR. I WILL DESTROY THEIR ENEMIES--
SHE'S MY BLOOD!
SHE WAS THE REASON FOR ALL OF THIS!
I DON'T UNDERSTAND BLOOD. THE MISSION WAS TO FIND YOUR SISTER. YOUR SISTER IS NOT GOOD.
MOM...
...I WANT YOU TO TURN OFF.

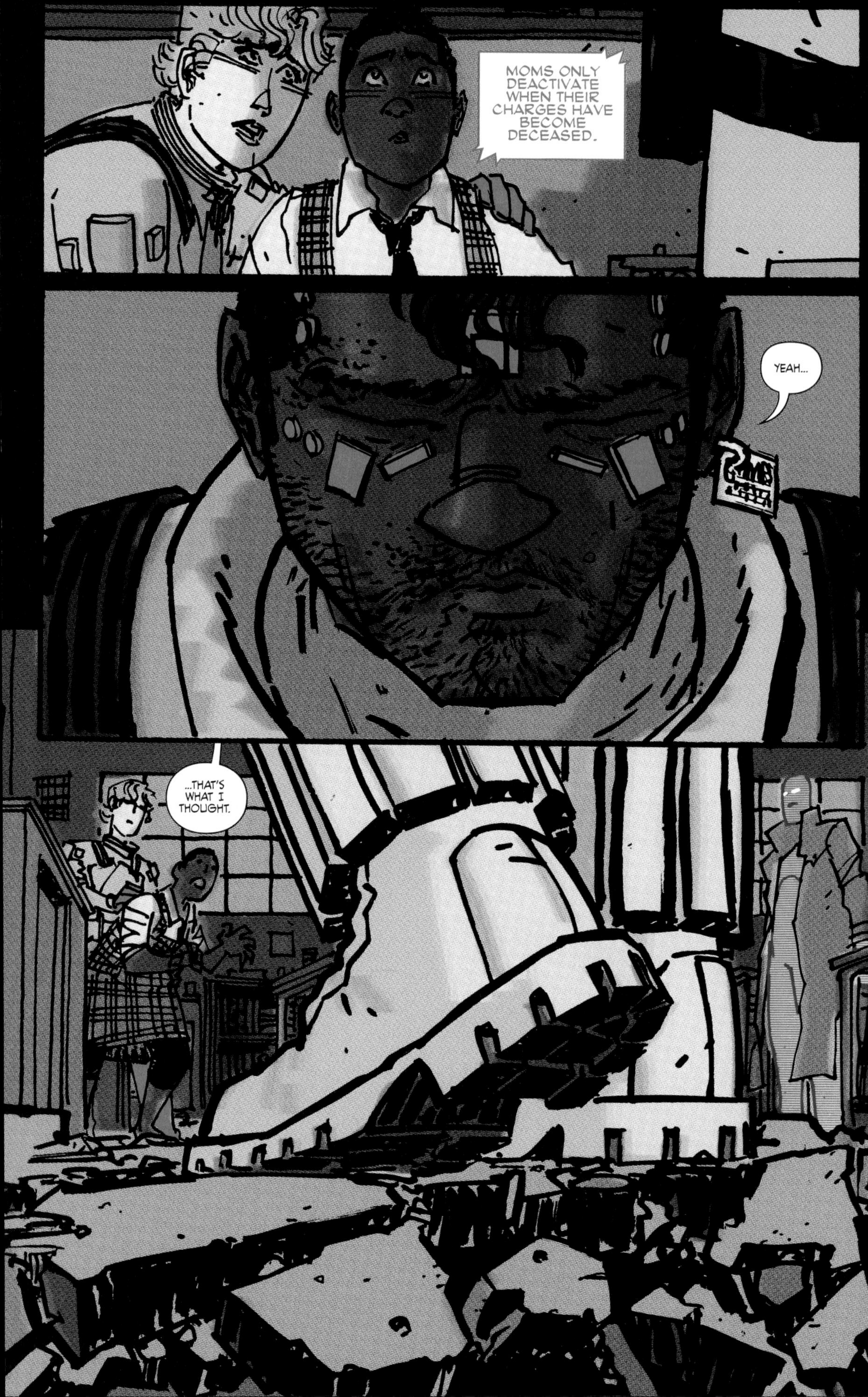
MOMS ONLY DEACTIVATE WHEN THEIR CHARGES HAVE BECOME DECEASED.
YEAH...
...THAT'S WHAT I THOUGHT.

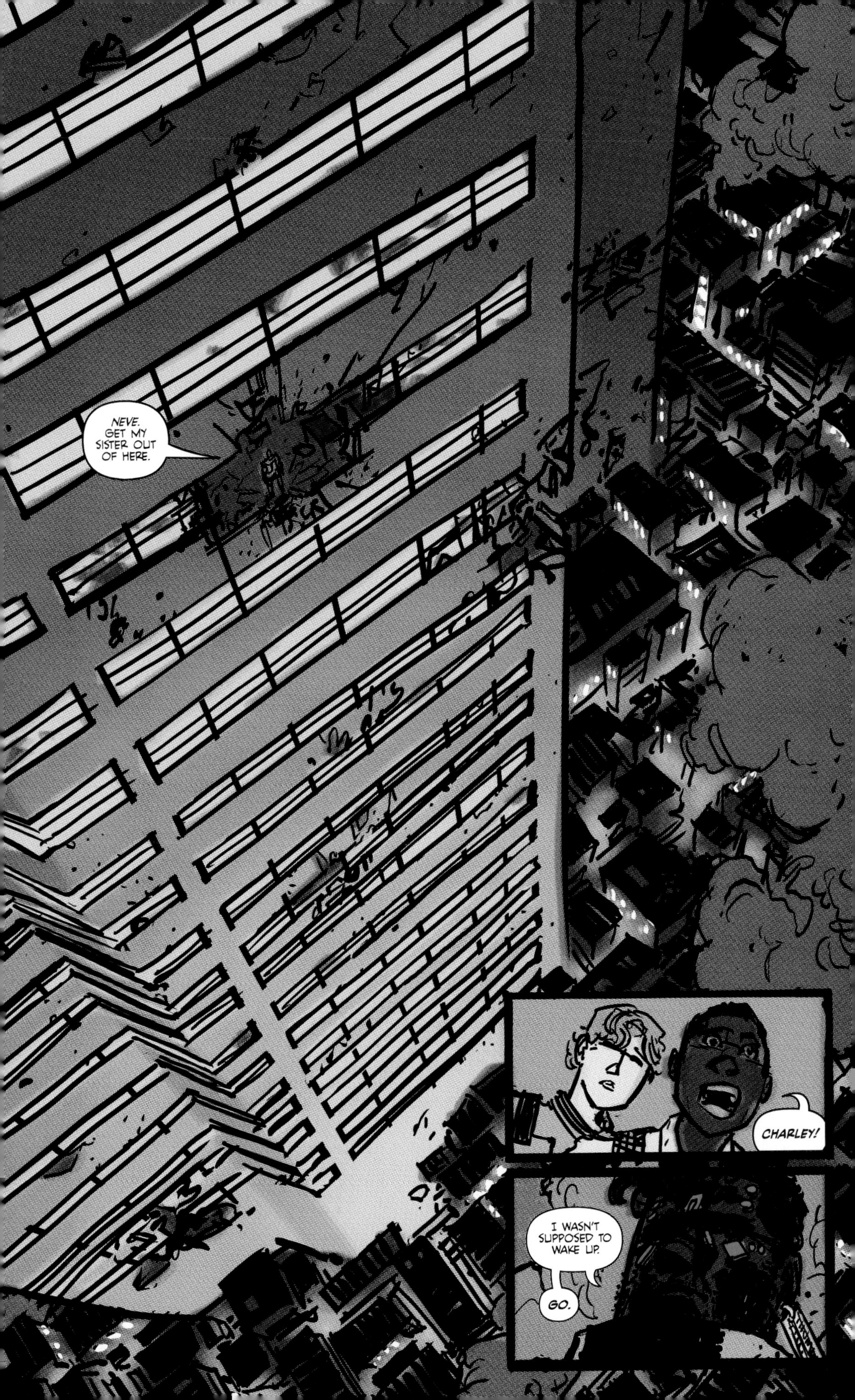
NEVE. GET MY SISTER OUT OF HERE.
CHARLEY!
I WASN'T SUPPOSED TO WAKE UP.
GO.

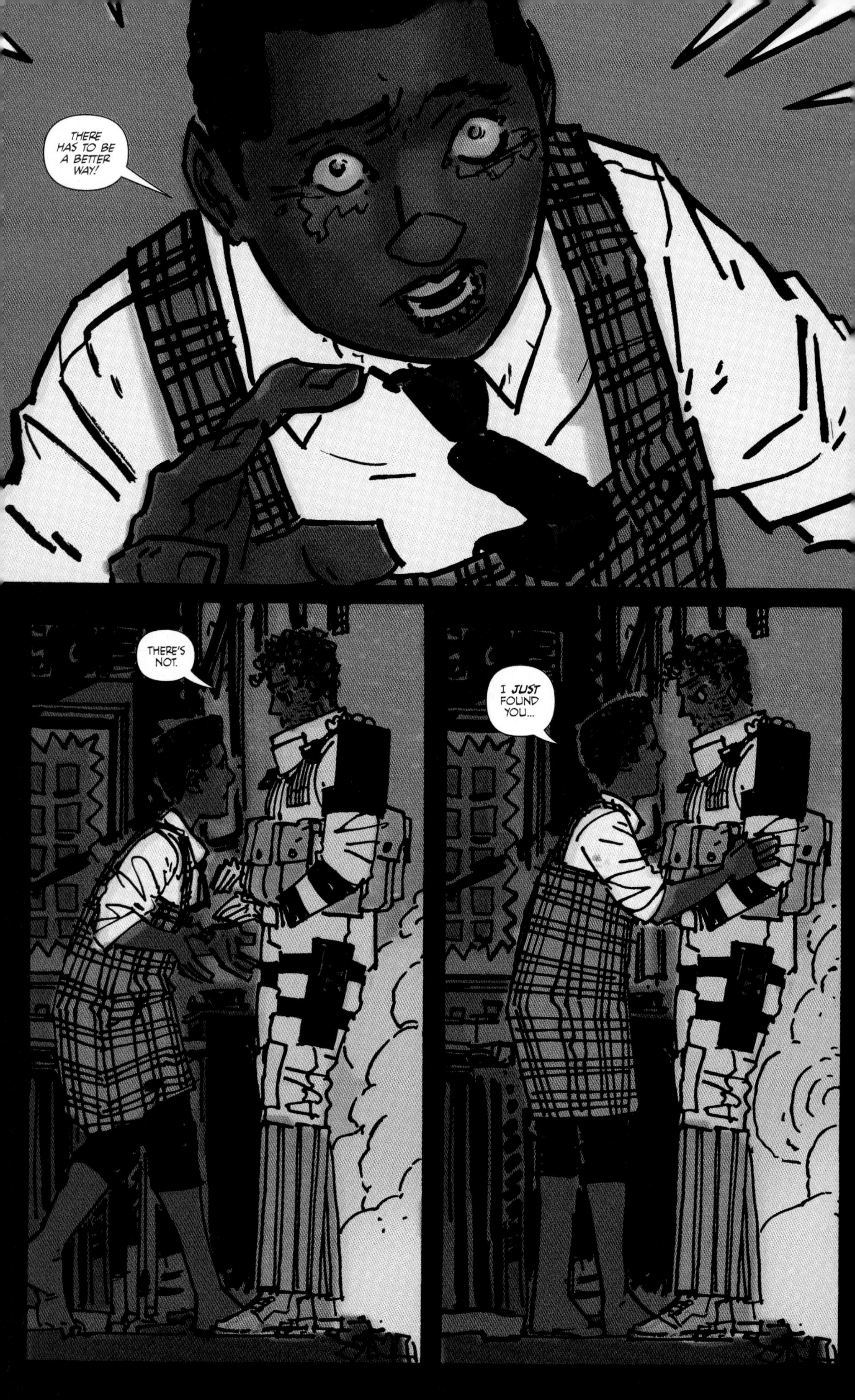
THERE HAS TO BE A BETTER WAY!
THERE'S NOT.
I JUST FOUND YOU...

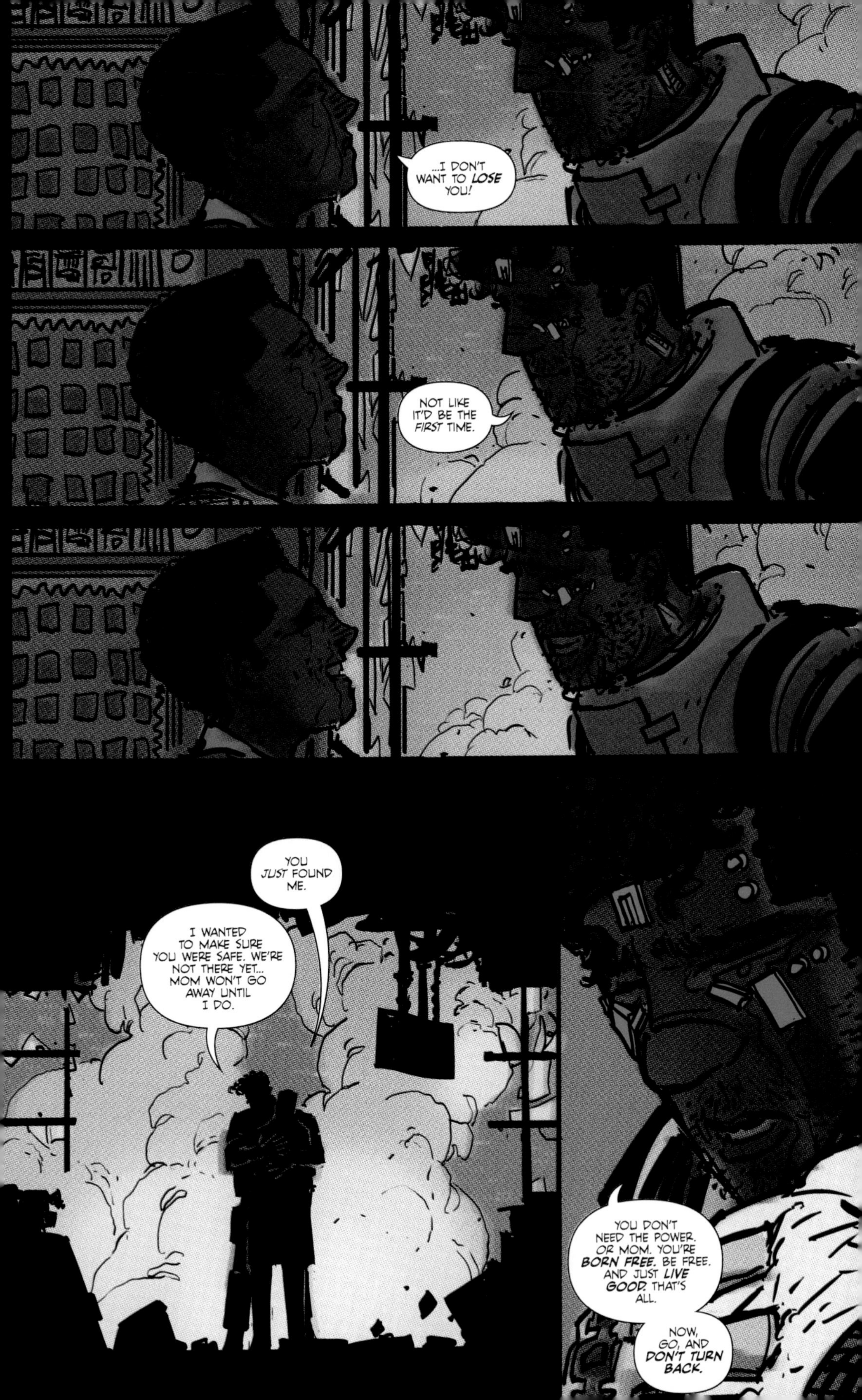
...I DON'T WANT TO LOSE YOU!
NOT LIKE IT'D BE THE FIRST TIME.
YOU JUST FOUND ME.
I WANTED TO MAKE SURE YOU WERE SAFE. WE'RE NOT THERE YET... MOM WON'T GO AWAY UNTIL I DO.
YOU DON'T NEED THE POWER. OR MOM. YOU'RE BORN FREE. BE FREE. AND JUST LIVE GOOD. THAT'S ALL.
NOW, GO, AND DON'T TURN BACK.

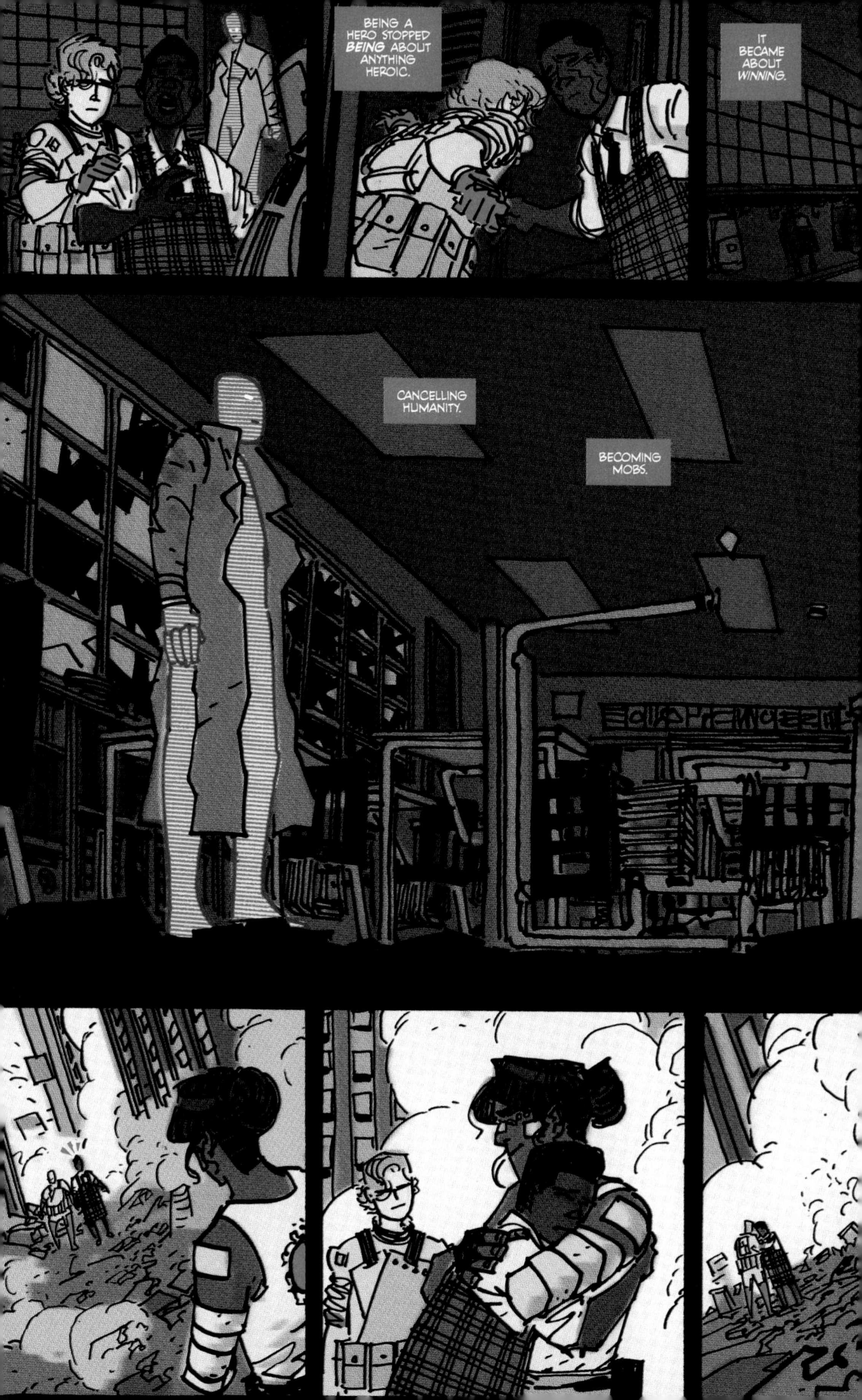
BEING A HERO STOPPED *BEING* ABOUT ANYTHING HEROIC.
IT BECAME ABOUT *WINNING*.
CANCELLING HUMANITY.
BECOMING MOBS.

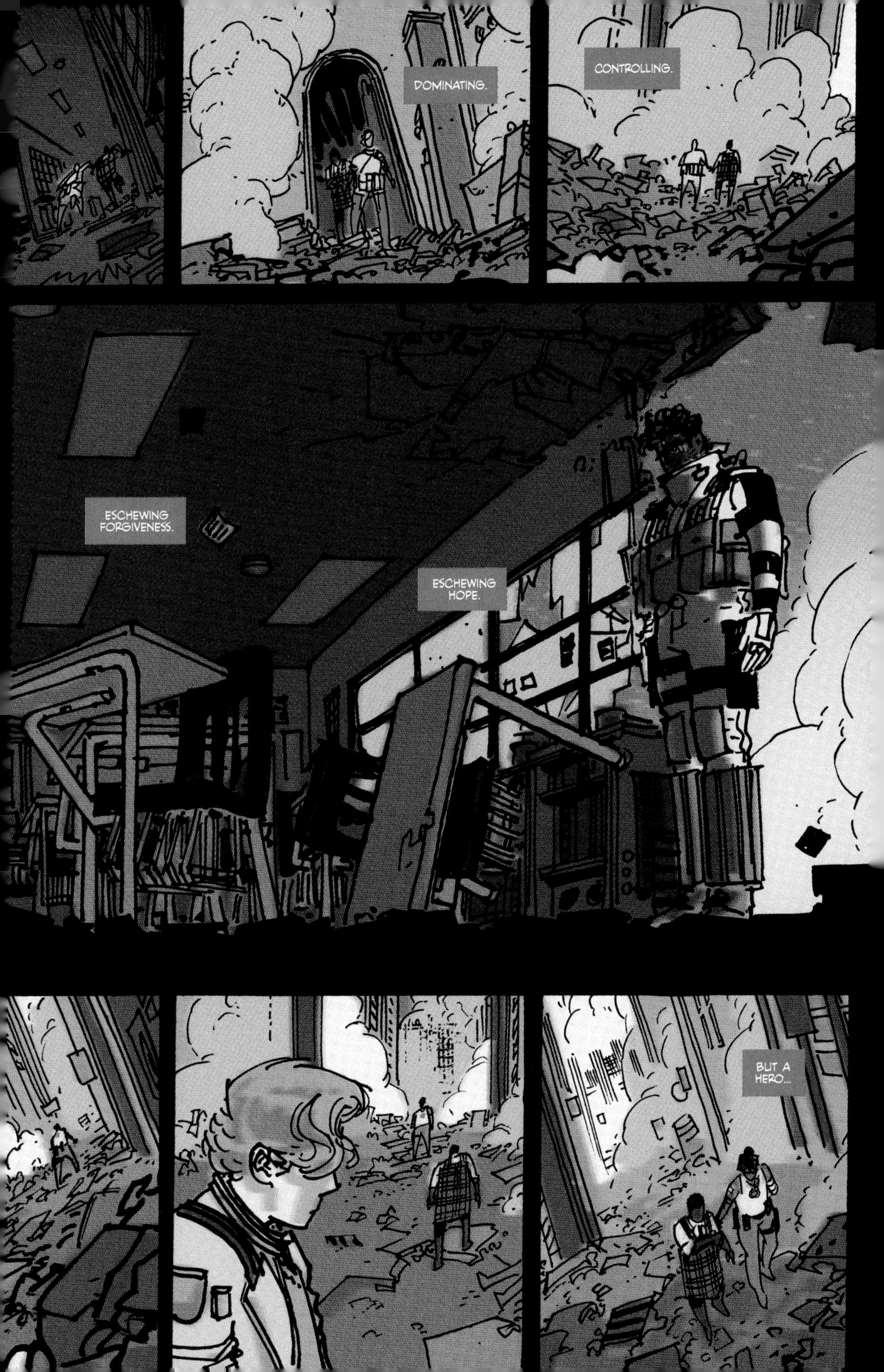
DOMINATING.
CONTROLLING.
ESCHEWING FORGIVENESS.
ESCHEWING HOPE.
BUT A HERO...

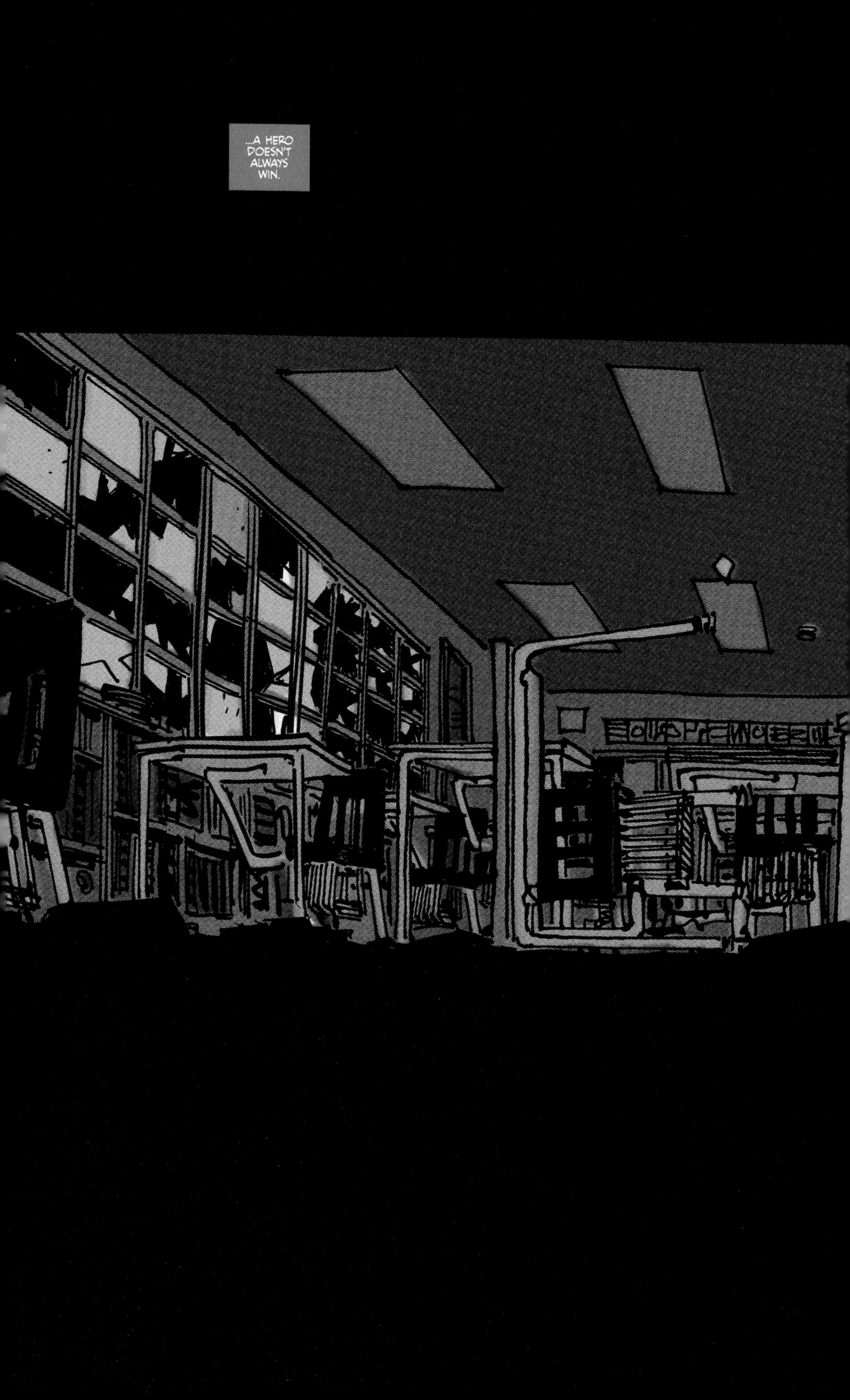
...A HERO DOESN'T ALWAYS WIN.

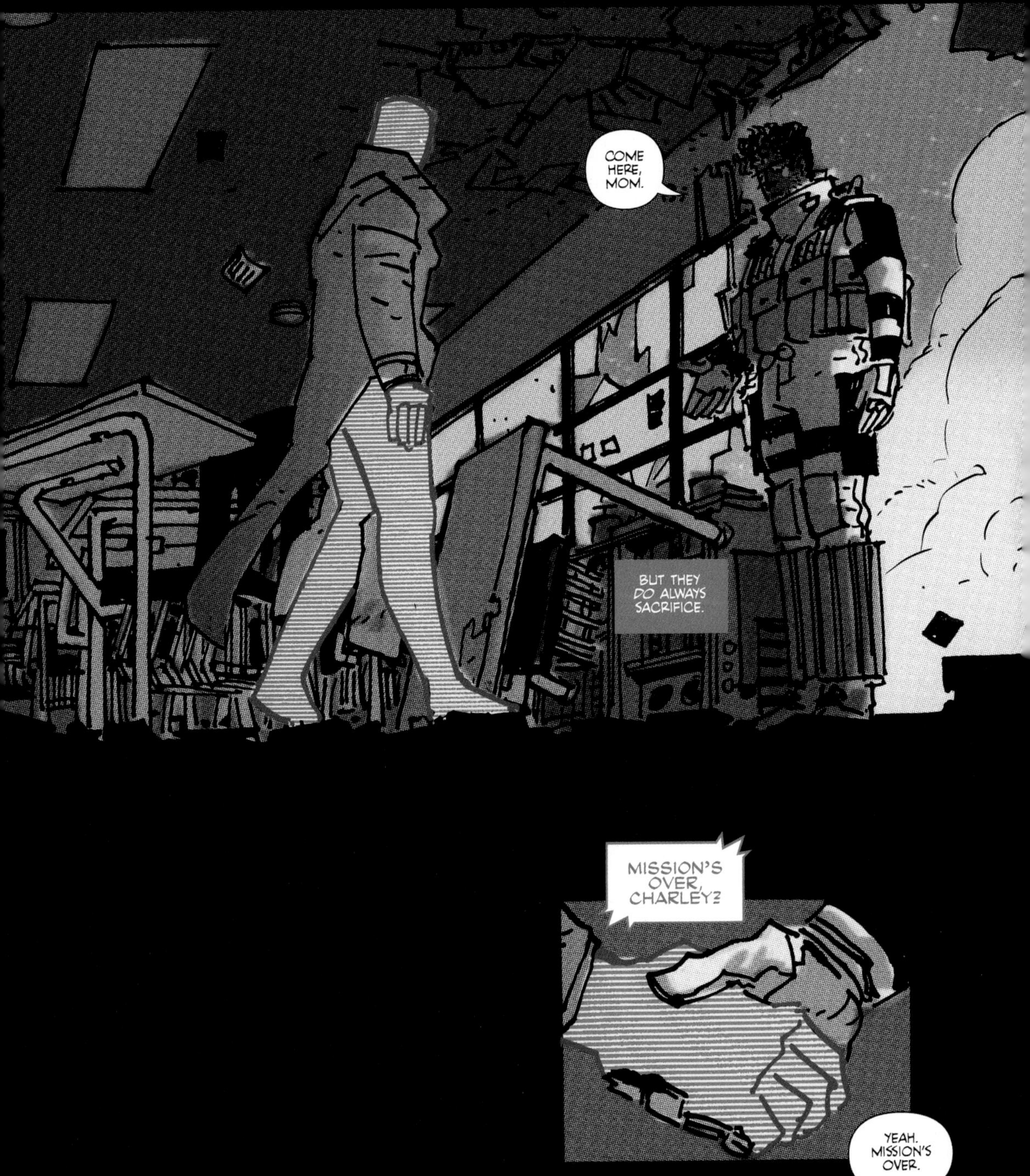
COME HERE, MOM.
BUT THEY *DO* ALWAYS SACRIFICE.
MISSION'S OVER, CHARLEY?
YEAH. MISSION'S OVER.

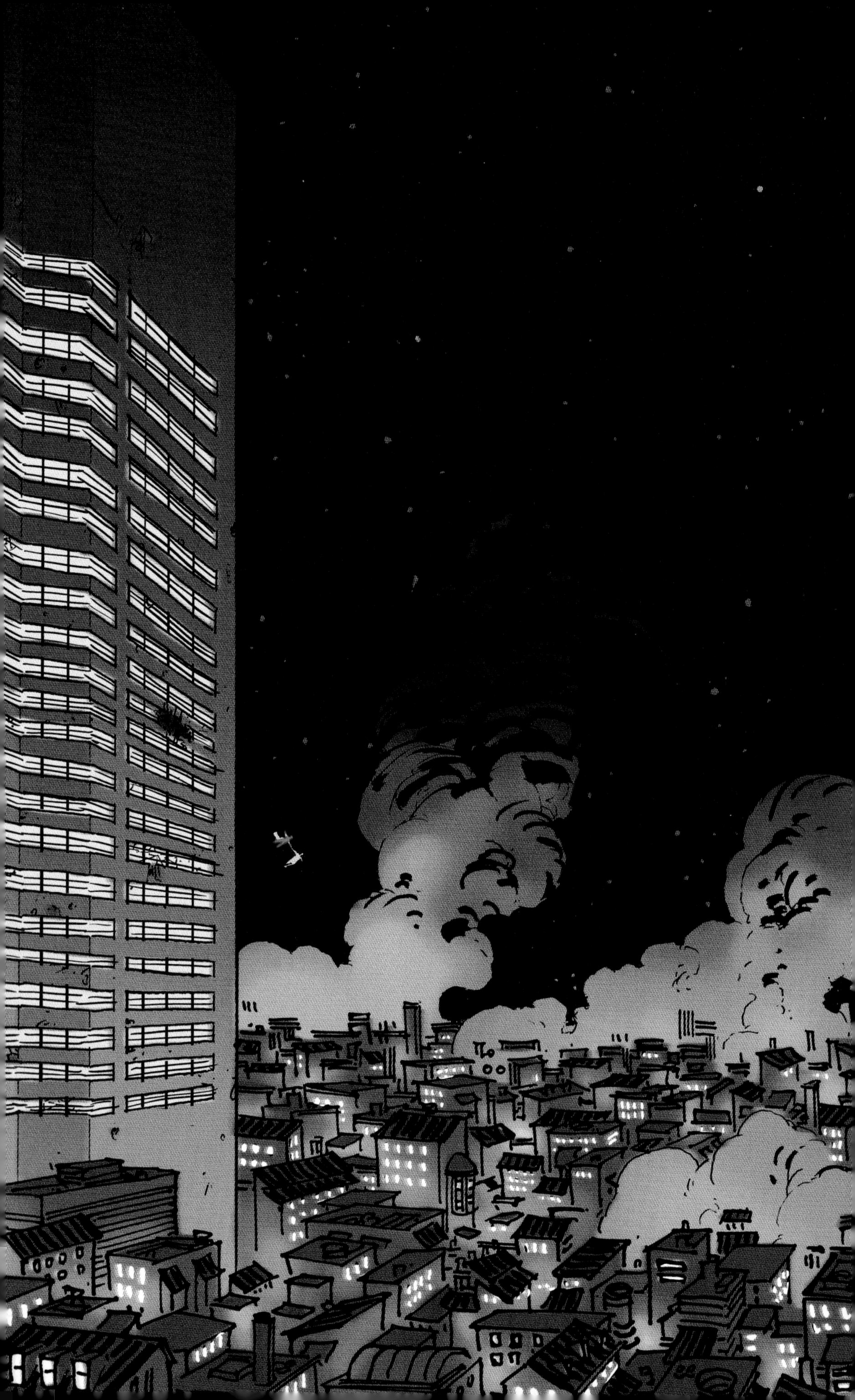

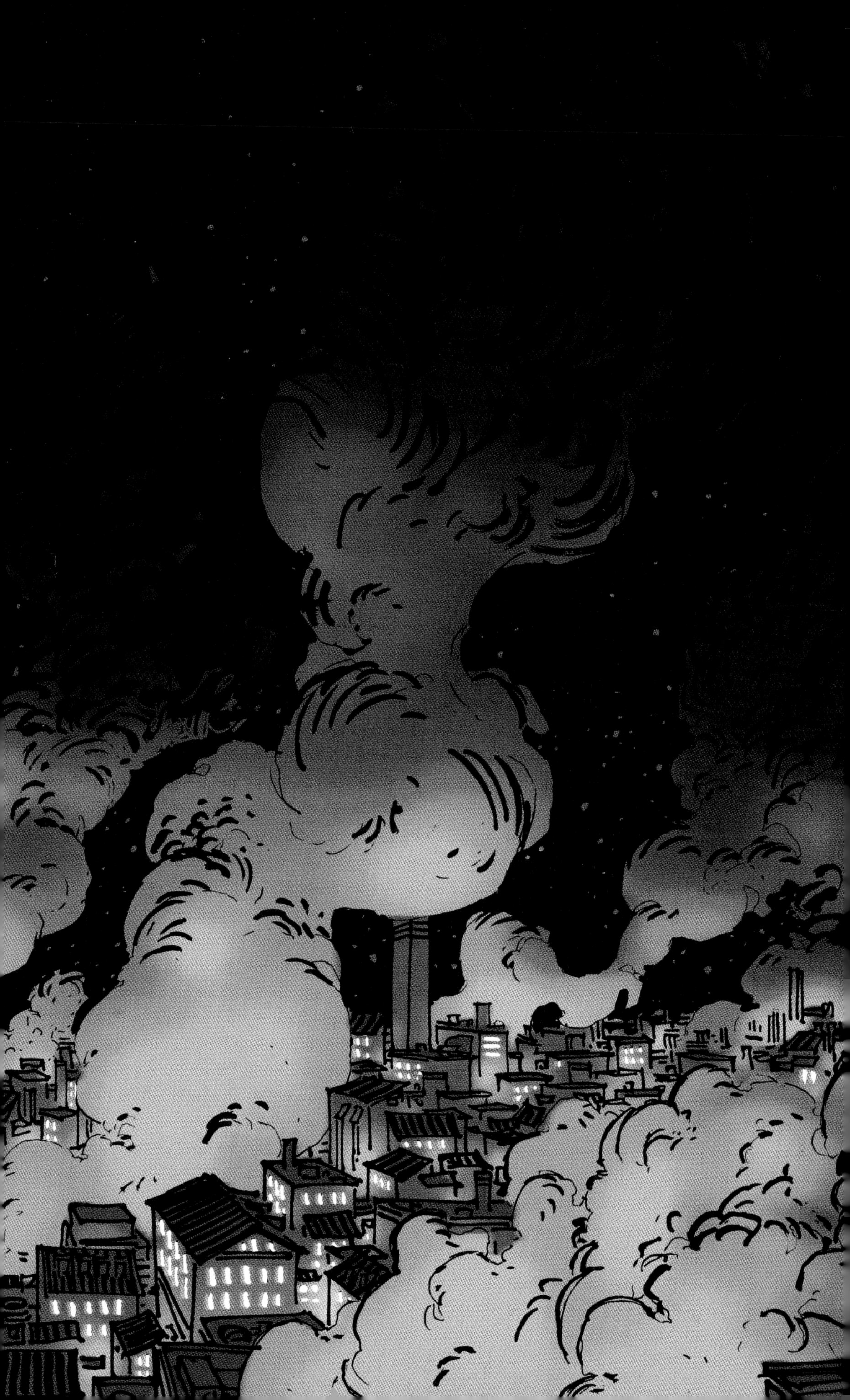

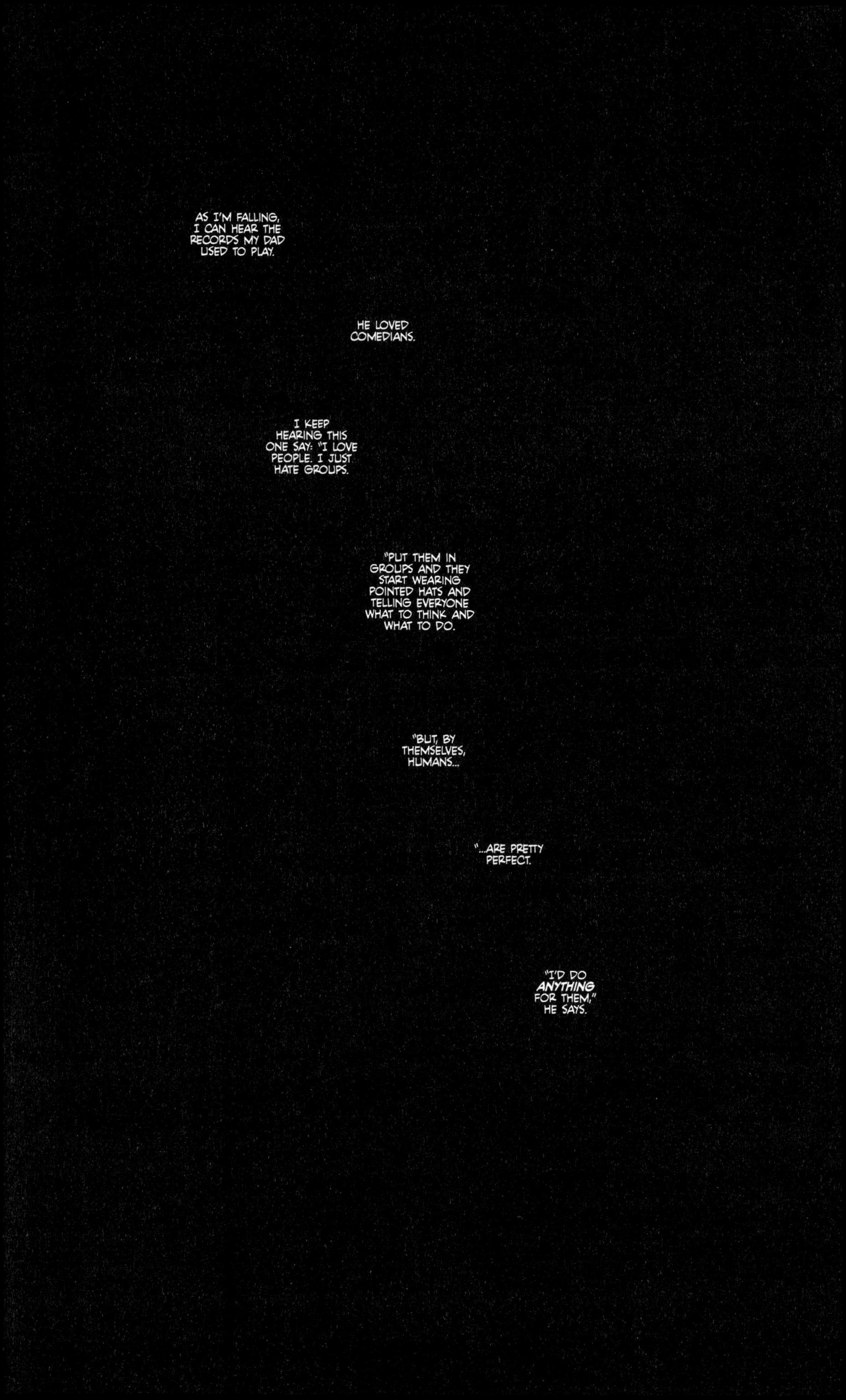
AS I'M FALLING, I CAN HEAR THE RECORDS MY DAD USED TO PLAY.
HE LOVED COMEDIANS.
I KEEP HEARING THIS ONE SAY: "I LOVE PEOPLE. I JUST HATE GROUPS.
"PUT THEM IN GROUPS AND THEY START WEARING POINTED HATS AND TELLING EVERYONE WHAT TO THINK AND WHAT TO DO.
"BUT, BY THEMSELVES, HUMANS...
"...ARE PRETTY PERFECT.
"I'D DO *ANYTHING* FOR THEM," HE SAYS.

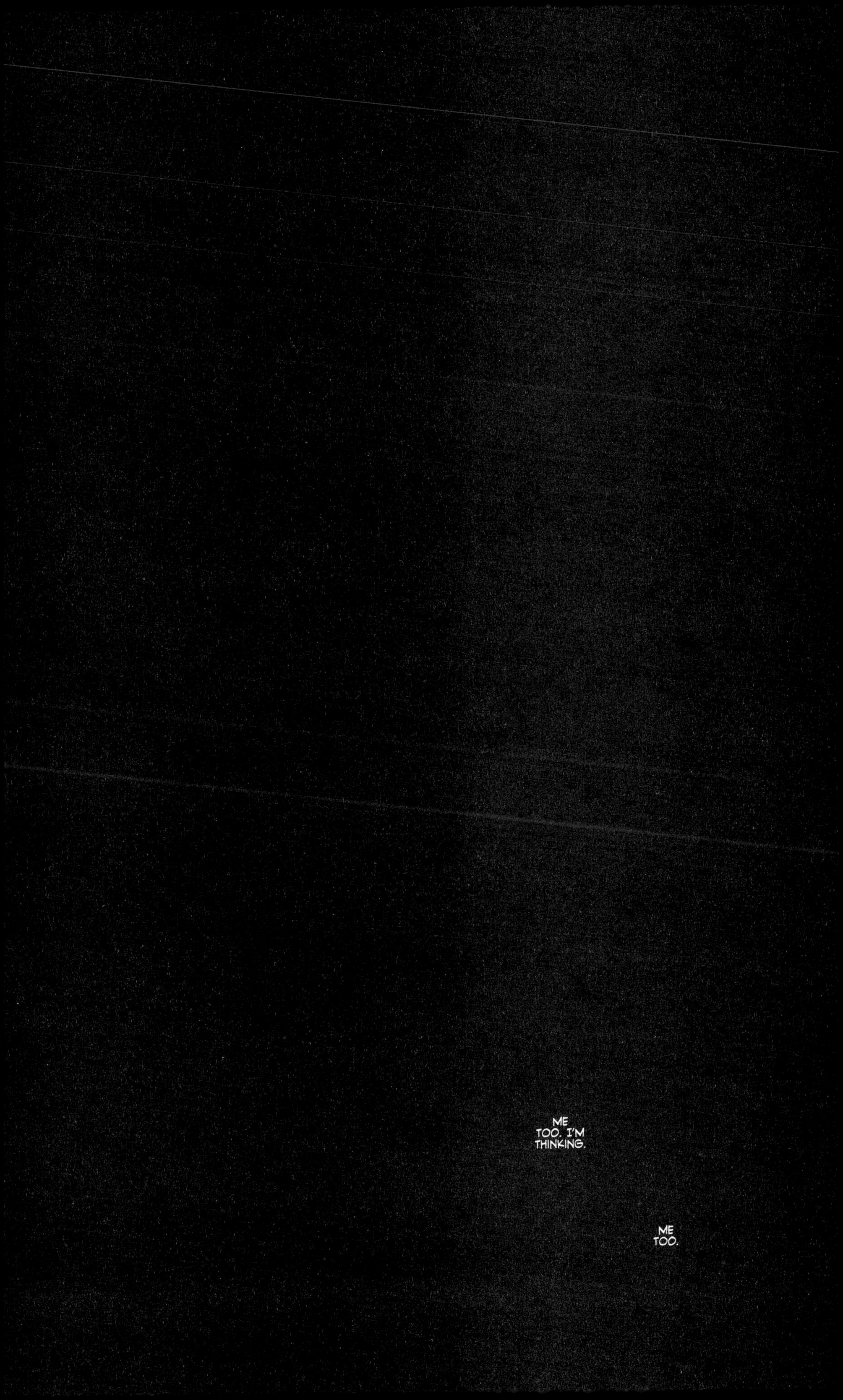
ME TOO. I'M THINKING.
ME TOO.

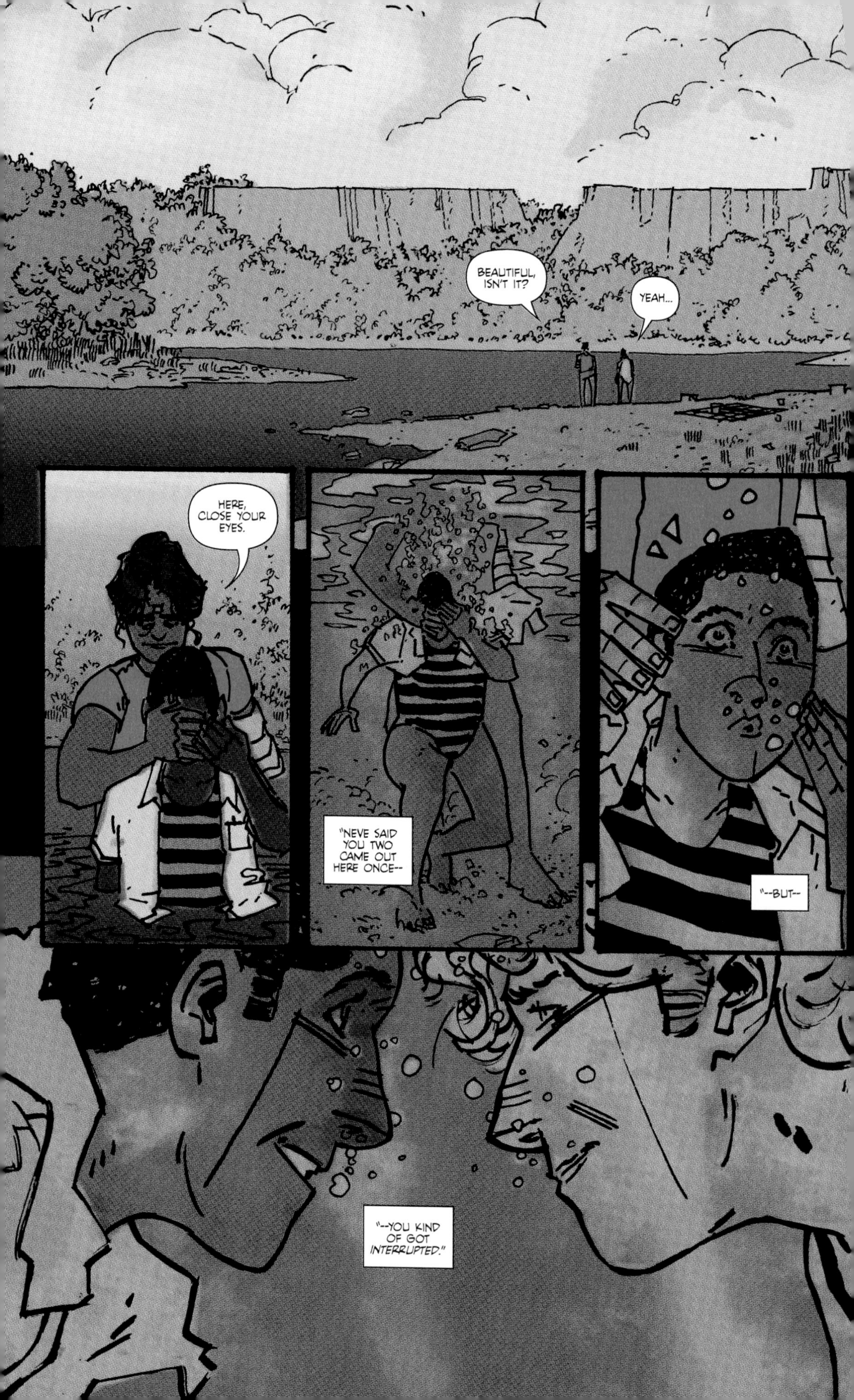
BEAUTIFUL, ISN'T IT?
YEAH...
HERE, CLOSE YOUR EYES.
"NEVE SAID YOU TWO CAME OUT HERE ONCE--
"--BUT--
"--YOU KIND OF GOT *INTERRUPTED.*"

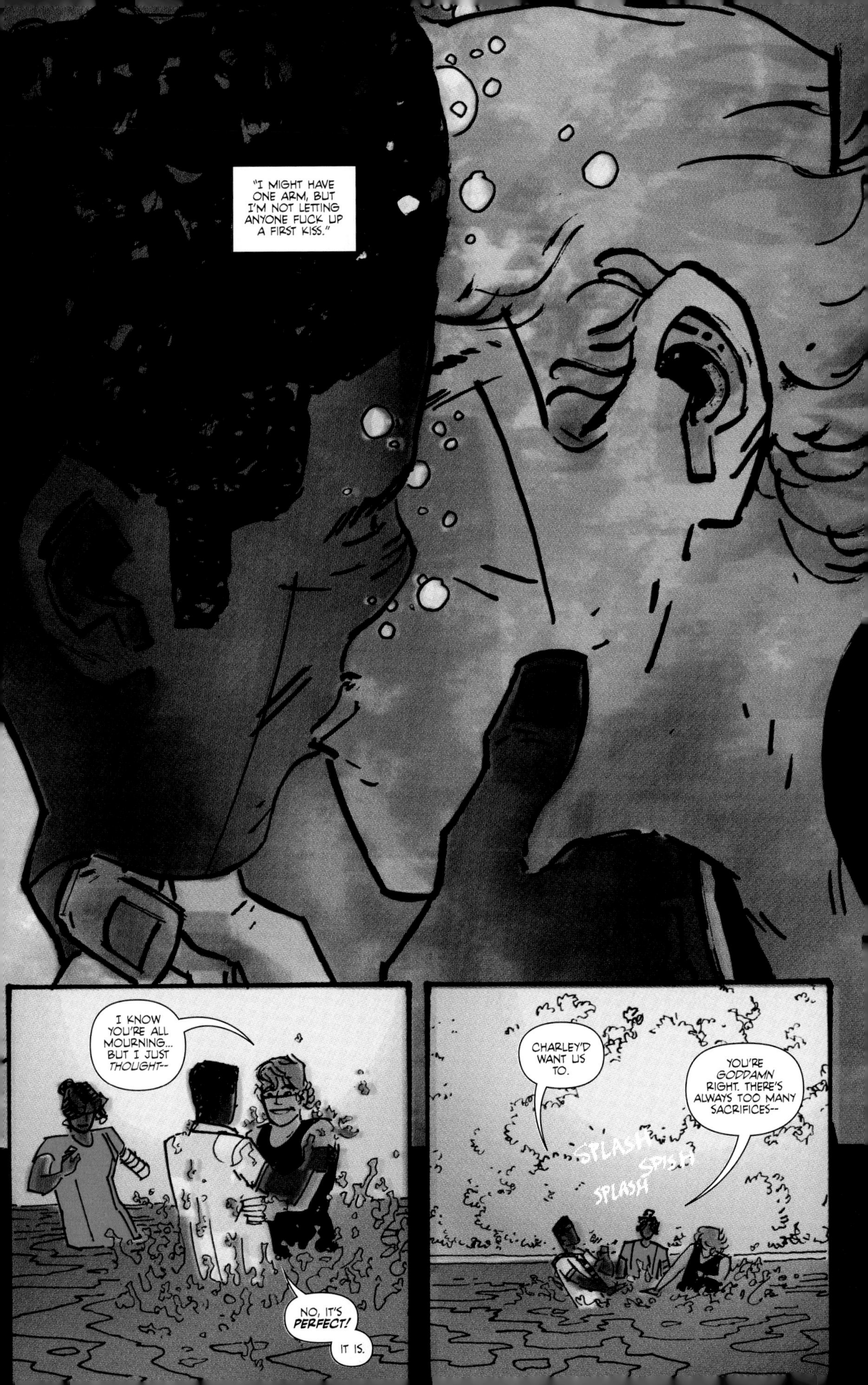
"I MIGHT HAVE ONE ARM, BUT I'M NOT LETTING ANYONE FUCK UP A FIRST KISS."
I KNOW YOU'RE ALL MOURNING... BUT I JUST *THOUGHT*--
NO, IT'S ***PERFECT!***
IT IS.
CHARLEY'D WANT US TO.
YOU'RE *GODDAMN* RIGHT. THERE'S ALWAYS TOO MANY SACRIFICES--
SPLASH
SPISH
SPLASH

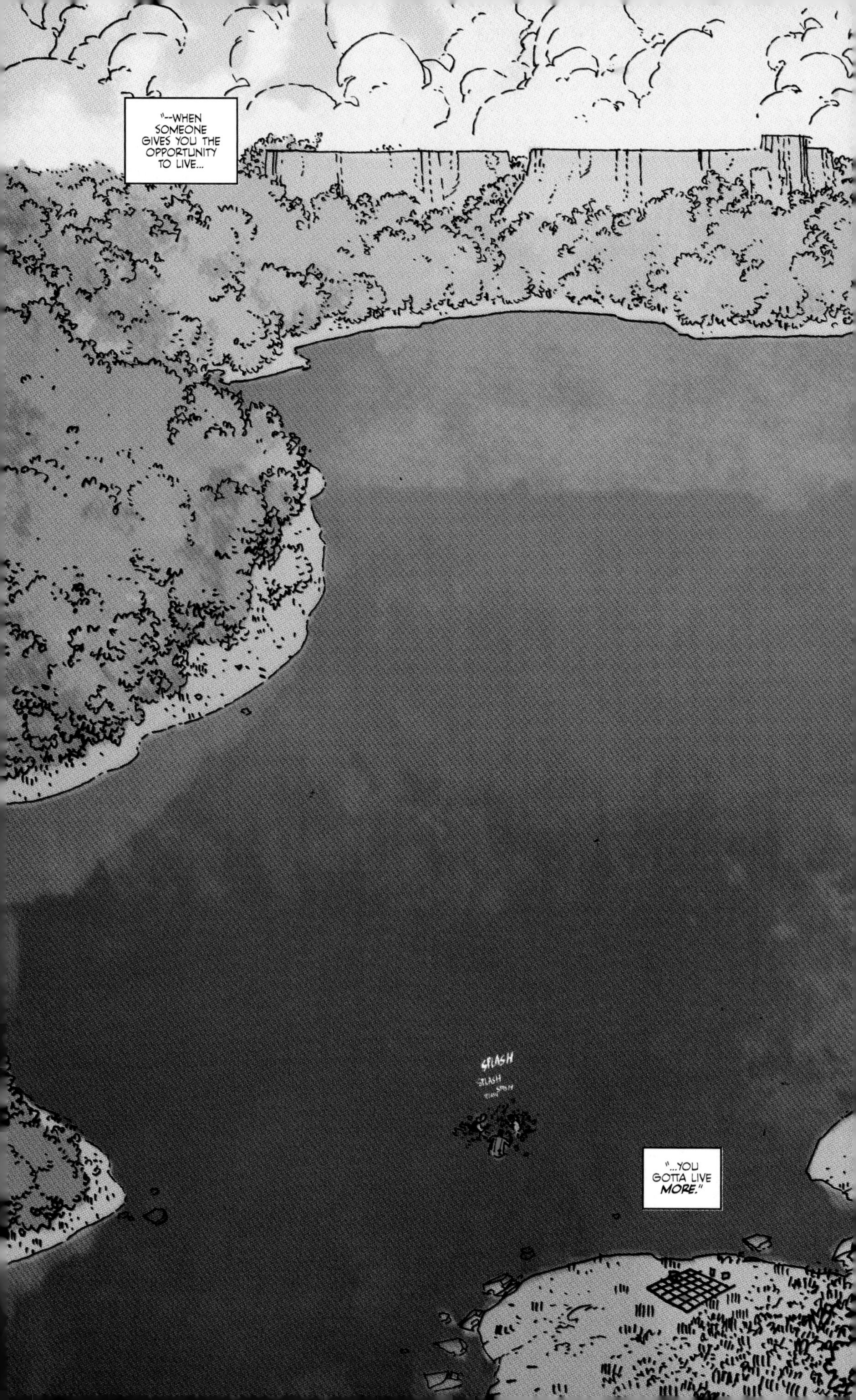
"--WHEN SOMEONE GIVES YOU THE OPPORTUNITY TO LIVE...
SPLASH
SPLASH
"...YOU GOTTA LIVE ***MORE.***"

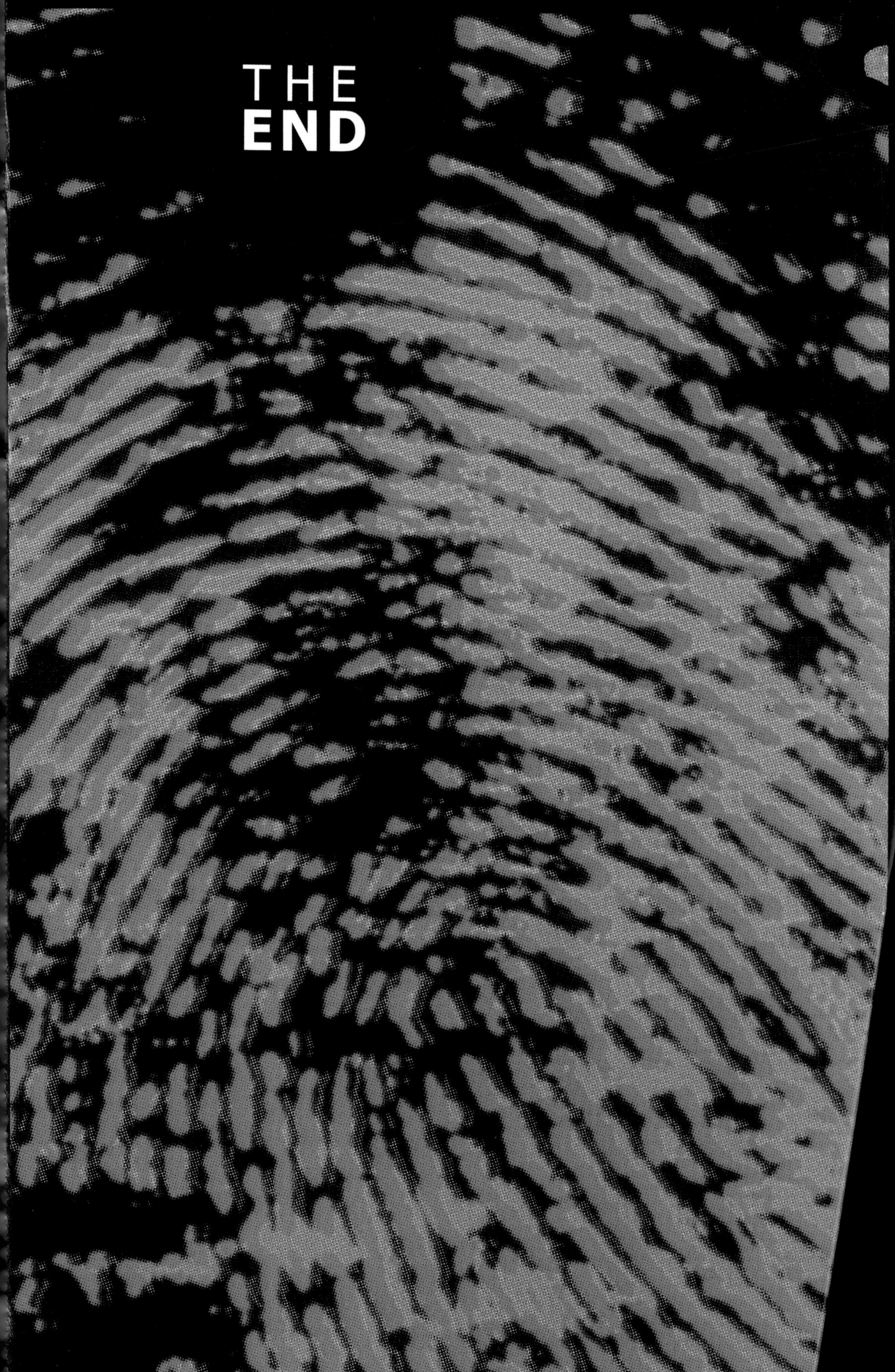
THE
END

Hayden's sketchbook

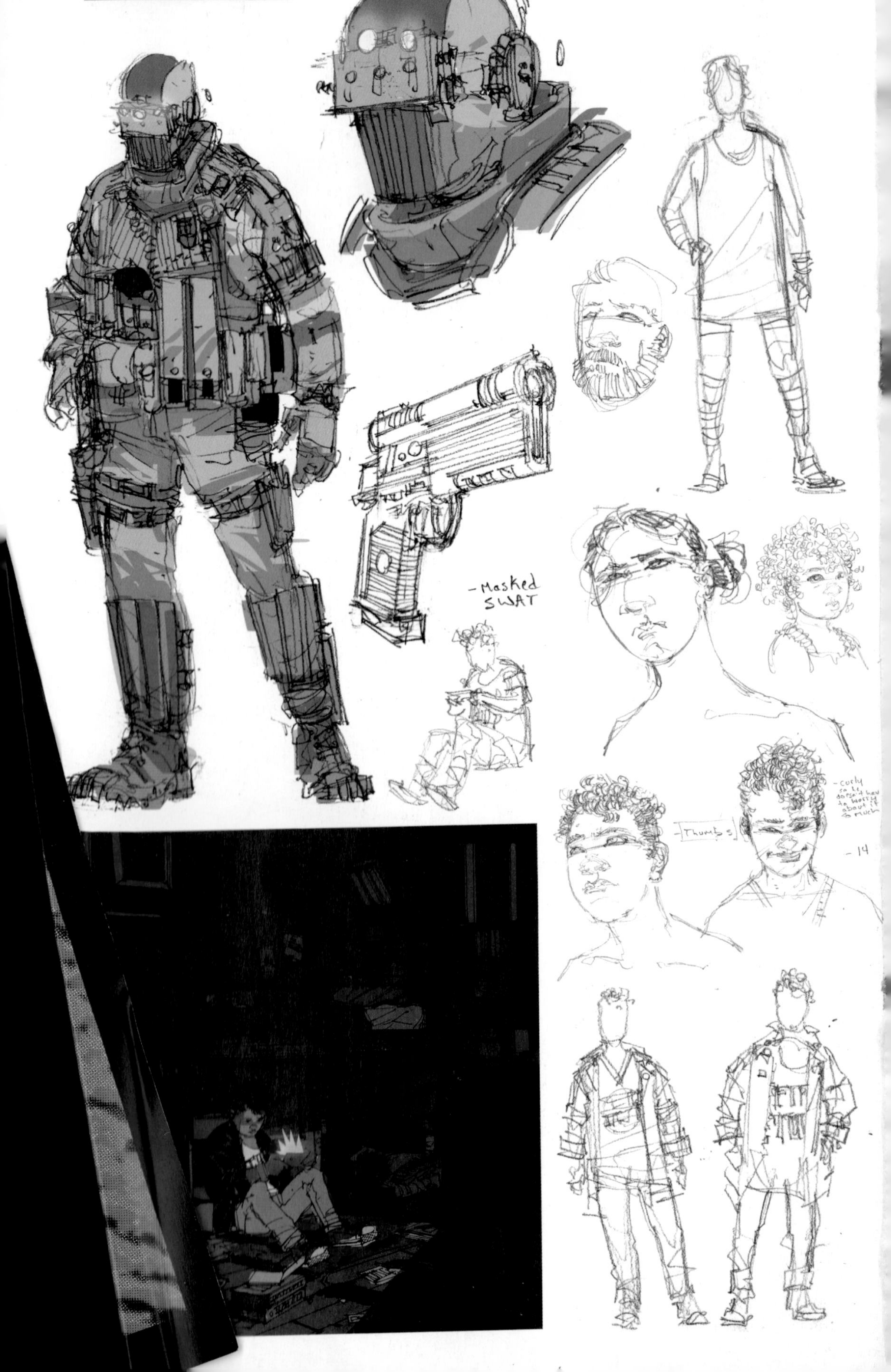
-Masked SWAT
Thumbs
-curly so he doesn't hav to worry about it so much
-14